FIRST
FOUR
BY
SHANNON

FIRST FOUR BY SHANNON

- *Case Pending*
- *The Ace of Spades*
- *Extra Kill*
- *Knave of Hearts*

by Dell Shannon

WITH A FOREWORD BY THE AUTHOR

Nelson Doubleday, Inc.
Garden City, New York

CONTENTS

FOREWORD
by Dell Shannon

There are certain earnest and intense would-be writers of fiction who like to explain to captive audiences that All Is Inspiration—"The characters simply take over and write the story." Now, as any professional writer knows, if we waited for Inspiration to prod us to produce, nothing would ever get written; perhaps even more than any other job, the writing of fiction requires a lot of hard slogging labor, physical as well as mental. But the odd thing is—again as any professional writer will testify—that on occasion a character will "take over"; the impersonal little black marks on the page, representing letters which evoke sounds and words in our reading minds—a kind of shorthand to convey the gamut of human experience and emotion—suddenly resolve themselves into a three-dimensional person.

This is not Inspiration, if indeed there is such a thing. I can only call it interference, and a wildly unimaginable kind of interference it is. For it occurs not on the part of an inanimate object, but something far more ephemeral—a ghost—nothing more than a conceived plan for a character intended to appear and further the plot action, either significantly at length or briefly in one scene. I suppose the firmly agnostic philosophers would nod intelligently and murmur something wise about *déjà vu,* that curious condition in which (the philosophers have decided) one area of the brain jumps a few beats ahead of the rest.

At any rate, you are writing staidly along, aware that this known and planned character is about to enter the scene, when suddenly it becomes apparent that it is somebody else, somebody new, a different character entirely: and the whole scene shimmers, changes, and evolves into something unplanned.

On occasion this can be gratifying, if the character concerned is of brief importance to the plot. The result is often a satisfying little vignette, a sharpened, rounded few lines of prose and dialogue conveying a much more convincing sense of individual personality than your earlier conscious intention.

But if the character is to be of major importance to the plot as a whole, this kind of impertinence—this impossible action on the part of what is nothing more than the insubstantial shadow of a ghost—can be extremely awkward indeed for the writer.

For there, quite suddenly, this character *is*. There is nothing to be done about it. An individual, three-dimensional, full-blown personality has appeared on the scene; it must be coped with somehow, whatever devastation and change it must wreak on all your original plot ideas and plans.

You may have intended the story to take off in a northeasterly direction, but now that this character has appeared, a character of entirely different stuff than you had planned, it is obvious that the plot is headed southwesterly, and that is that: nothing to be done about it. Of course you are still responsible for the actual writing, for refashioning scenes and people and emotions and actions consistent with the new direction; but the center of things has shifted and it is a different story than you had thought it was.

This is what happened to me early in the writing of *Case Pending;* and the sudden unexpected emergence of Lieutenant Luis Rodolfo Vicente Mendoza onto the page had profound and far-reaching consequences. I had intended that book as a tour-de-force suspense novel, a one-time thing, based on a slightly offbeat plot. Instead, I found myself at the end of it still insistently possessed of an egotistical, sharply defined, inescapable Character, who was clamoring insistently to occupy another book; and this shook me somewhat. I was accustomed, in producing books, to the careful and tedious research which had gone into my period novels, and to building characters in deliberate and leisurely development; Mendoza was something new in my experience. However, there he *was:* he existed, and he refused to be ignored; he insisted on appearing on more printed pages, and more . . . The immediate consequence of that was *The Ace of Spades.* By the end of that one I had discovered that it was a good deal more fun, and a good deal easier, to write such books than long-winded tomes of historical novels;

and I had settled down with Mendoza in a kind of temporary truce. With scarcely a pause I proceeded on to *Extra Kill*. But it was with *Knave of Hearts* that it dawned on me that I had, willy-nilly, entered into an involuntary partnership, probably for life; I was stuck with Mendoza and his emerging cohorts, and there was nothing in this world I could do about it.

At this point my long ingrained habit of doing careful research to produce authentic backgrounds came again to the fore; if I was fated to produce novels about police officers, police cases, the police job, it behooved me to find out all about the job, and the L.A.P.D. and other police forces. I found this extremely interesting research: the background of general knowledge that detectives must possess, the content of police examinations, techniques of investigation and interrogation, legal aspects of the job, the fascinating world of forensic laboratory investigation in police work, and the vast but tightly organized and superbly structured network of that top police force in the world, the Los Angeles Police Department.

Perhaps my experience as a historical novelist, accustomed to the meticulous research of details, made it second nature to me, in constructing police-procedural novels, to create as authentic a background as possible. But that is simply necessary spadework. Whatever kind of novel a writer is producing, the major yeasty ingredient is always people: people is what fiction is all about, and perhaps no other professional job in the modern world brings its practitioners more varied experience with all sorts of people than police work. In a sense it is not a well-rounded job: police officers see very little of the good, the true, and the beautiful; they are in too many cases dealing with the mud at the bottom of things, the sordid, the stupid, the random violence. But in another sense it is a job more sharply defined than any other of this century; there are no fuzzy edges around that job, no gray areas, no vaguenesses. And I believe this is the one basic reason why so many people enjoy reading about it—not only the novels of police procedure, but the other novels so vaguely and generally categorized as "mysteries." For this century seems to have forgotten or abandoned the absolutes: the eternal simple standards fencing apart right and wrong, good and evil. And there is an instinctive understanding, however deeply buried, in human people that the fence exists. The glib modern philosophers tell them convincingly that it doesn't, but they know better by their deepest gut feelings; and they turn with relief from the vague plottings of the fictioneers endlessly mouthing the modern shibboleths of amoral sociology, to a fictional world where there is solid ground underfoot. A world where right and wrong, good and evil, are starkly defined: though it is so much oftener goodness and stupidity—a world without fuzzy edges around the perimeter. For like it or not, that is the real world we all inhabit; and in a very special sense, the detective novel is the morality play of the twentieth century.

Of course, if I had deliberately set out to create a series of detective novels about a certain set of characters, I would have ended up with something quite different than the people who occupy these books. Mostly they all, like Topsy, just grew. Mendoza arrived on the scene entirely evolved, unchangeable, his own man: nothing of mine. It is entirely implausible, and in my saner moments I disapprove, that he should be wealthy; but there it is, a fact of life. There is nothing more detestable than a man of such compulsive neatness and persnicketiness; but there he is. It is not so strange, perhaps, that he should be a card shark; for some reason a good many of my protagonists have been, although personally my feeling about card playing parallels what Robert Benchley once wrote in reviewing a certain play, that it's a good way of killing time for those who prefer it dead. Most of Mendoza's cohorts are far more plausible types of police officers; and of course over the years they have evolved, here and there, into three-dimensional characters, so that the whole crew is now, we might say, a cohesive cast frozen in time between books, taking up renewed life with each new one. The two senior sergeants Hackett and Higgins, ingenuous-looking Landers, earnestly religious Piggott, simple-minded Grace, the plodder Glasser, handsome Palliser, Schenke, Conway, and Galeano, and all their concerns and individualities gradually grow and emerge in one book or another over the years. And over the years they have experienced some interesting occasions together, aside from the monotonous run-of-the-mill cases turning up day by day in any big-city police bureau: they have shared changes and troubles, laughs and surprises—the grim chase of all the thieves and killers and lunatics and fools which makes up the working day of the professional police officer. At the same time, they are only human, with human problems and foibles even as the rest of us.

And over the years, that one-time lone wolf Mendoza has acquired a surprisingly varied household retinue, quite aside from the cats: starting with the twins and proceeding to an adopted grandmother, the dog Cedric, a third offspring, and at last hearing (as of June 1979) a small flock of sheep on a newly refurbished country estate. I have the distinct premonition that those sheep are going to cause trouble; but that Mendoza will find out later on . . . all of which may stimulate interest in new readers to catch up on the entire series.

But the four novels contained in this volume constitute the beginnings: they mark the time when the cast was only tentatively being assembled, shaking down together, a cast later to be widened and further developed. As with the advent of Mendoza, much of it came as a little surprise to me as events and people unfolded on the page; though what emerges as a surprise to the writer is probably the result of a great deal of hard labor in the unconscious mind (or is it?).

In spite of all the labor, I have enjoyed following Mendoza and his retinue over the years, in finding out more about them all and passing it on to interested readers. I hope all Mendoza's old fans will welcome this omnibus volume if for no other reason than nostalgia, and that new readers may find their interest aroused to look for the later books and find out What Happened Next.

FIRST
FOUR
BY
SHANNON

CASE PENDING

ONE

When Gunn came down the hall to his office at half-past eight, he found Curtis waiting. Curtis was holding up the wall beside the door; he opened his eyes at Gunn's step. He looked tired and rather dirty.

"And a good, *good* morning to you too, chief," he said. Gunn didn't like to be called chief.

"What'd you draw?" Gunn unlocked the door.

"Just what we expected. I won't come in—I'm going home to bed—I can give it to you in ten words. Williams showed up about eight, you'll get that on Henry's report. Went in, about twenty minutes later came out with our Ma Williams, and they went down to the Redbird bar on Third. Ten-forty, shifted to the Palace. Henry called me from there and I took over at midnight. They drifted home about half an hour later and stayed. His car's still outside."

"Well, now," said Gunn, pleased. "Fancy that."

"And for your further information," said Curtis, "I damn near froze to death sitting it out in my car. Next time I'll take along another blanket and a portable radio."

Gunn grinned benignly and told him to go home. He went on through the stenos' room to the center of three partitioned-off rooms at the rear, hung up his hat and coat, and sat at the desk. Henry's report was neatly centered, waiting for him there; Henry never missed getting in a written report immediately, however late his duty. *Williams in 7:57,* it announced laconically, and the rest of what Curtis had said. Very nice, thought Gunn.

So now they knew that Mr. John Williams hadn't deserted his wife and four children. The county had been passing over sixty-three dollars and fifty cents per month to Mrs. John Williams for four months, on her claim of desertion and failure to provide. The kids had to be fed, had to be sheltered and clothed—after a fashion—by somebody. It appeared that once again the county had been rooked. Williams was a skilled carpenter, probably making good money on an out-of-town job. Gunn made a notation on the report, *Morgan to see,* and sighed. Naughty, naughty, Mr. and Mrs. Williams, collusion to defraud the state—and maybe next time they'd think up something slicker.

He got out his file of current investigations, wrote a brief summary of the conclusions in the Williams case, and set the file page aside for refiling among cases completed. He flicked over the rest. He heard the girl stenos begin to drift into the outer office.

Rossiter. Brankin. Peabody. Prinn. Fraty. Kling. A new one, Lindstrom. There were follow-up reports to be typed in on six or seven of them; he took those out to the stenos. "Morning, girls." Morgan and Stack came in together.

"I want to see you about that Mrs. Gold," said Stack.

"What about her?"

Stack followed him back into his office. "I told you I finally caught up to the guy—the Reno D.A.'s office found him, he's working in some joint there as a waiter. I had it all set up to crack down on him, see. Reno says he ought to be good for seventy-five a month, and I went round to give the glad news to the missus. And then the rabbi puts the kibosh on it."

"What rabbi?"

"Mrs. Gold's rabbi. He was there. He says please will we just drop the whole thing and leave it to him—I guess he figures it'll be less of a disgrace or something if he can handle it—"

"Oh," said Gunn. "Well, he might have something there. If he can get it without any fuss, so much the better. Man'd feel better about it if he's persuaded instead of forced, the money'll come easier—less chance we'd have more trouble. It works out with ministers sometimes, but we can't let 'em stall forever. You tell him we'll give him a couple of weeks to try it his way before we crack down." Gunn went out with Stack and looked into the room next his own; Morgan was sitting there at one of four desks, looking at some papers. "Oh, Dick."

Morgan looked up. "Yes, sir?" he responded dully.

"Little job. Henry and Curtis have tied up the Williams case. Another collusion, way you figured. Williams is weekending—they were at a bar until midnight and it's a good chance you'll catch him still in bed with her if you make it snappy. Here's the report."

Morgan got up. "All right. Williams—yes."

Gunn looked at him more closely. "You look a bit off-color."

"I'm all right," said Morgan. He did not look it. As he took his top-coat from the peg behind the door, Gunn saw his hand shaking. He was the thin, sandy type that doesn't change much between boyhood and old age, doesn't look much different sick or well. But there were lines around his mouth now that Gunn hadn't seen before, and his eyes looked tired, as if he hadn't slept. He had a little trouble folding the paper Gunn handed him, putting it away in his pocket.

"How's Sue?" asked Gunn casually. "And Jan?"

"Fine," said Morgan, buttoning his coat carefully. "Just fine, thanks."

"Must get together again soon, Christy was saying just last night—she'd like to kidnap that Janny of yours, kind of lonesome with our three grown and off."

"Oh—yes, sure. I guess so. We'll do that, thanks."

Gunn stood in the door of his office, absently jingling the coins in his pocket, and watched the other man out to the corridor. What was wrong with Morgan? He felt some responsibility for Morgan, unreasonably, for it had been his doing that Morgan got this job. Dick Morgan was the son of an old friend of Gunn's, and he'd known the boy most of his life. Boy, well, Dick was thirty-eight, but it depended where you sat: Kenneth Gunn was sixty-two. And good as he'd ever been too, once he'd got out of the hospital after that business last year; but the doctors wouldn't pass him for active duty again. Nearly forty years' service, and then a home-made bullet out of a punk's zip-gun retired him. And Bill Andrews got the promotion to head of Homicide instead. Way the cards fell, and Bill was a good man; but Gunn hadn't known what to do with himself that six months. He'd jumped at this minor post in the D.A.'s office; and he could say now, a year later, he'd given Kelleher something to talk about at the next election, by God.

It was a new department, this little corps of investigators—the husband-chasers, inevitably they were called; and if Gunn couldn't claim their job was as important as the one he'd done for forty years in and out of uniform, at least the Scot in him took pride in reckoning how much they saved the taxpayers. He's set up the organization himself, and it served as a model for those some other counties were building, here and in other states. He and his crew had tracked down over two thousand runaway husbands so far, to pry minimum child-support funds out of them anyway. Authorities in other states had co-operated, of course, but it came out even: they'd picked up deserters for other D.A.'s offices from Maine to Oregon, too. Gunn had the exact figure whenever Kelleher wanted it; to date it was upward of half a million dollars this office had saved the county in support of deserted wives and children. There'd been a time a man could walk out and it was nobody's job to locate him, make him provide for a deserted family. These days, no. He couldn't go across the Arizona or Nevada line and thumb his nose at the California taxpayers.

Gunn himself hadn't had any idea what a staggering sum casual desertions cost the state, until he saw the figures last year. And he could have doubled the amount saved by now if he could have another dozen men, another dozen office clerks. This was the hell of a big town, and it attracted the hell of a lot of indigents and transients, as well as the usual shiftless ones any city had.

But he wasn't thinking about that as he looked after Dick Morgan. He stood there passing a hand over his jaw in a habitual gesture, a big hefty man with a round, amiable face and thinning hair, and for a minute he worried about Morgan. Dick had had some rough breaks: just out of college when the war came along, and he was married and had a child by the time it was over so he never did go back to finish his law course, but like so many others went into a big-company job. Then they lost the child, one of those unnecessary accidents, a drunk in a car, turning down their street just at random. That had nearly finished Sue, because she couldn't have another. . . . Sure, they put the drunk in jail for manslaughter, but what good did that do a six-year-old girl, or Sue and Dick?

Dick's father had been alive then and living with them, and Gunn used to drop in there. Hadn't done old Rob Morgan any good either, losing his only grandchild like that. After a while they'd put their names down with a couple of adoption agencies, but those places were so damn finicky; they'd waited almost five years before they got Janny —but Janny was worth it. And just about then had come one of those squeeze-plays, a company merger, a few new hatchet men from the front office, and Dick was out—at thirty-seven, with nowhere to go, a mortgaged house, and less than a thousand in the bank.

Gunn wouldn't have blamed him for feeling bitter. At the same time, being Gunn, he wouldn't have had Dick Morgan on his staff—old Rob, sympathy, or no—if he hadn't known Dick could handle the job the right way. It wasn't a job that paid anything like what Dick had been earning before, but it was a job and Dick had seemed grateful and certainly competent and reasonably contented with it.

To anyone who didn't know him, Dick's manner just now might suggest a touch of indigestion, or a spat with his wife at breakfast, or an unlucky bet on the ponies. But Gunn knew Morgan for a man of abnormally equable temper, and that little nervousness and bad color meant a lot more than it would with another man. Besides, Dick and Sue never had spats; Sue wasn't that sort. And Dick didn't bet—or drink, either. Not since eight years ago.

Gunn hoped the boy wasn't in for another piece of rough luck somehow. Janny, maybe—some illness? Some people walked all their lives with bad luck at their shoulders.

No good worrying about it now.

His phone rang and he stepped back into his office to answer it. The voice at the other end was the heavy bass of Captain Bill Andrews. "Say, Ken, among your little brood of wives you wouldn't have one Sylvia Dalton, would you?"

"Don't think so. Why?" Gunn riffled through the current file before him.

"Well, it was just a thought. Maybe you noticed by the papers that New York sort of misplaced Ray Dalton the other day. He was up on a three-to-five and got himself paroled, but he never did report in to his officer. New York thinks now—the usual information received—he lit out west, specifically to these parts, and'll be obliged if we can return the goods undamaged. Thing is, the party that said he headed west also said it was to see his wife. I came up with the bright thought that wives of crooks don't usually like to work very regular, and maybe this one was accepting our hospitality."

"Not unless she's doing it under another name. It's a thought, all right."

"Yeah. You might just check for initials. I can give you a make on her."

"I've got nothing else to do but your work," said Gunn. "I don't know every one of our customers personally, you know. Sure somebody sees 'em all, but I've got eleven men on duty. Yes, sure, I'll check with them. Send over the make. Don't I remember Dalton? It rings a bell—"

"It ought to. The Carney job, five-six years back. Cameron and Healey were on it—liquor store knocked over and two men shot, proprietor and a clerk. We couldn't tie Dalton to it tight enough, but he was in on it. I guess at that we made him nervous enough to run back east, and New York put the arm on him for another job."

"I remember," said Gunn. He leaned back in his chair and regarded the ceiling. For a minute, with the familiar shoptalk, he almost had the illusion he was back at headquarters in a real job, not this makeweight piddling business, and under Kelleher too . . . but, damn, a job worth doing. "It's worth a try," he said. "Any kids?"

"One, a boy about twelve-thirteen."

"O.K.," said Gunn. "I'll have a look, might come up with something."

Morgan drove slowly down Main Street, not cursing at the traffic; he handled the car automatically, stopping for pedestrians, for red lights.

Mrs. Williams lived on a run-down street among those that twisted and came to dreary dead ends the other side of Main. He would surprise Mr. and Mrs. Williams together and deliver a little lecture on the dangers of conspiracy to defraud. Maybe it wasn't so stupid of them to pull the shabby little trick, the commonest one in the list, with scarcely any attempt at secrecy; until the formation of this new department, God knew how many people had got away with it for years.

The problem created, Morgan thought as he had before, went beyond the Williamses or any individual—or the amount of public money. In essence, a social problem, and not a new one. If it wasn't money from this county office, it'd be money from another: people like the Williamses didn't give a damn. Williams, letting himself be branded a wife- and child-deserter, getting a job and a cheap room somewhere out of town, sneaking back for week-ends with his family, all to cheat sixty-three-fifty a month out of the county—on top of the three hundred or more he could earn as a skilled workman.

At a bar last night with his wife until midnight. Last thing they'd worry about was leaving the kids alone: four kids, the oldest eleven. It was a shabby, cheap neighborhood, almost a slum, though there were worse streets. People like the Williamses didn't care where or how they lived: often they had more money than others who lived better, but their money went on ephemeral things—on flashy cars and clothes and liquor.

Morgan was driving a six-year-old Ford. He wouldn't be surprised to find that Williams' car was a new model, and something more expensive.

But all that was on the surface of his mind; he couldn't, for once, be less concerned. Deeper inside a voice was screaming at him sound-lessly, What the hell are you going to do? *Ten thousand bucks. Ten thousand.* . . . All right, so he knew what he ought to do: Richard Alden Morgan, law-abiding citizen, who'd always accepted respon-sibilities and stood on his own two feet, and where had it got him? So it was just the breaks: everybody had bad luck. But, God damn it, so *much* bad . . . And a damn funny thing to think maybe, but if he could blame himself (or anybody), some concrete way, reason he'd just brought it on himself, he wouldn't feel so bitter. Nothing like that with Dick Morgan, he thought in savage sarcasm: respectable, righteous Morgan who paid his bills and lived within his income, Morgan the faithful, considerate husband and father—how did the old song go, *everything he should do and nothing that he oughtn't-t-O*—and got kicked in the teeth all the same. You could say "the breaks," but it damn well wasn't fair that Sue should be dragged under with him—Sue hadn't done anything, neither of them had done anything to deserve—

Janny hadn't done anything. Except get born.

He coasted gently to the curb two doors from the apartment house where the Williamses lived, and sat for a minute, getting out the watchers' report, rereading it but not really taking it in. Parked smack in front of the apartment was a year-old Buick, a two-tone hardtop. That'd be Williams, sure; Henry had taken down the license.

All right, so he knew what he ought to do. Go to the police, tell the story. Honest citizen. Sure. The police would take care of the man with the pock-marked face and dirty nails and cold gray eyes and the rasp-ing voice that said *Ten thousand bucks, see.* And would that be the end of it? Like hell it would. The juvenile court would have something to say then, miles of red tape to unwind, and in the end they'd lose Janny anyway—he knew how those things went, how judges figured, how the cumbersome, impersonal law read. It was all the fault of the damned pompous law to start with: the silly God-damned inhumanly logical rules of the accredited agencies.

Suddenly his control broke one moment and he pounded his fist on the steering wheel in blind, impotent fury. Not *fair,* after everything else —the panic in Sue's eyes, the panic he heard in his own voice telling her—*ten thousand*—what the *hell* could he do? The police. The money. No choice for him even here, it had to be the police; he couldn't raise money like that.

You had to be logical about it. Juvenile hall, a state foster home, an orphanage, still better than anywhere with that pock-marked hood, the kind of woman he'd—

Ten thousand. The car wouldn't bring five hundred. They still owed four thousand on the house, a second mortgage wouldn't—Sue's engagement ring, the little odds and ends of jewelry they had, maybe another five hundred if they were lucky.

He'd sat still to be kicked in the teeth for the last time. If he could get from under this by forgetting every righteous standard he had— But it wasn't so easy, it never was. So, go and rob a bank, hold up a liquor store, sure, get the ten thousand. It wouldn't cancel out: the threat would be just as potent, and in a month, six months, a year, there'd be another demand.

He straightened up after a while and took a couple of long breaths. It wasn't any good agonizing round and round in the same circle, they'd gone over all this a hundred times last night. He'd just have to play it by ear. Meanwhile he had a day's work to do—conscientious, methodical Morgan, he thought tiredly.

He got out of the car, slipping the ignition key in his pocket. See the Williamses and try to put the fear of God into them. The county wouldn't prosecute this time, on a first offense involving a relatively small amount: the courts were working overtime as it was. Morgan looked up Commerce Street to the corner of Humboldt, where something seemed to be going on—he could see the tail end of a black-and-white police car, its roof light flashing, and the fat Italian grocer had come out of his corner shop with a few early customers. Whatever it was, a drunk or a fight or an accident, it was round the corner on Humboldt.

He started up the worn steps of the apartment. After he'd dealt with the Williamses he might as well drop in on Mrs. Kling, and that new one was somewhere around here too, if he remembered the address—he got out his case-notebook to look. Yes, Mrs. Marion Lindstrom, 273 Graham Court.

TWO

There were worse streets than Commerce, but it wasn't a neighborhood where anyone would choose to live, except those who didn't think or care much about their surroundings, or those who couldn't afford anything better. Ironically, only a few blocks away rose the clean modern forest of civic buildings, shining with glass and newness and surrounded by neat squares of asphalt-paved parking lots. Like many cities, this one sprouted its civic and business center in its oldest section, inevitably bordered with slums. It might look easy to change matters with the power of condemnation, the expenditure of public money, but it wouldn't work out that way if the city fathers tried it. There'd grow up other such streets elsewhere if not here; there were always the people who did not care, the landlords who wouldn't spend on repairs. Every city always has its Commerce Streets.

Commerce started ten or twelve blocks up, at the big freight yards, and dead-ended two blocks down from Humboldt. It was a dreary length of ancient macadam lined mostly with single houses—narrow, one-storey, ramshackle clapboard houses as old as the century or older, and never lovingly cared for: here and there was one with a fresh coat of paint, or a greener strip of grass in front, or cleaner-looking curtains showing, but most were a uniform dun color with old paint cracked, brown devil grass high around the front steps. About halfway down its length, the street grew some bigger houses of two storeys, square frame houses not much younger and no neater: most of those were rooming houses by the signs over their porches. Interspersed with these were a few dingy apartment buildings, a gas station or two, neighborhood stores—a delicatessen, a family grocery; and in windows along nearly every block were little signs—SEWING DONE CHEAP, CANARIES FOR SALE, FIX-IT SHOP, HAND-TAILORING.

Agnes Browne lived behind one of the signs, that said primly, SEAM-STRESS, in the ground-floor right window of the house at the corner of Commerce and Wade, two blocks up from Humboldt. She worked as a waitress at a dime-store lunch counter; the sewing added to her wages some, and anyway she liked to sew and figured she might as well get paid for it. She didn't care much for going out and around; it still made her kind of nervous. She couldn't help but be afraid people were look-ing at her and thinking, Huh, kind of dark even for Spanish, wonder if— When the landlady said Browne didn't sound very Spanish, Agnes had told her it was her married name and she was a widow. But she was kind of sorry she'd ever started it now; it was like what the minister said for sure, about the guilty fleeing where no man pursueth. It hadn't been the money, she could earn as much anyway, maybe even more, at a dozen jobs colored girls got hired for; but there were other things be-sides money. Only she felt guilty at making friends under false pre-tenses, and as for Joe, well, she just couldn't. Joe was a nice boy, he had a good job at a garage, he was ambitious; he'd asked her for a date half a dozen times, but it wouldn't be right she should take up with him. Not without telling him. A lot of girls would have, but Agnes didn't figure it'd be fair. All the same, she liked Joe and it was hard.

She was thinking about it this morning as she started for work; seemed like she couldn't think of anything else these days. She was a little late, it was ten past eight already, and she hurried; she could walk to work, it was only two blocks down to Main and four more to the store.

As usual she cut across the empty lot at the corner of Humboldt. There'd been a house on the lot once, but it had been so badly dam-aged by fire a few years back that what was left of it was pulled down. Now there was just the outline of the foundation left, all overgrown with weeds—devil grass and wild mustard. Agnes had tripped over the hidden ledge of the concrete foundation before, and skirted it automat-ically now; but in the middle of the lot she tripped over something else.

When she saw what it was she clapped a hand to her mouth and backed away without picking up the purse she'd dropped. Then she ran across to Mr. Fratelli's store where there was a telephone. Agnes knew her duty as a citizen, but that didn't say she liked the idea of getting mixed up in *such* a thing.

Huddling her coat around her, listening to Mr. Fratelli's excited Ital-ian incoherence, she wondered miserably if the cops would ask many questions about herself. Probably so, and go on asking, and find out everything—maybe it served her right for being deceitful, the Bible said *that* never did anybody no good in the long run, and wasn't it the truth. . . .

"I figured you'd like to take a look before they move it," said Hackett on the phone. "The boys just got here. If you want I'll put a hold on the stiff until you've seen it."

"Do that." Lieutenant Mendoza put down the phone and rose from his desk. Hackett was the one man under him who fully respected his feeling in such matters, though it was to be feared that Hackett put it down to conscientiousness. The truth was less flattering: Mendoza always found it hard to delegate authority, never felt a job well done unless he saw to it himself—which of course was simply egotism, he acknowledged it. He could not do everything. But Hackett, who knew him so well, had a feeling for the nuances; if Hackett thought he should see this, he was probably right.

When he parked behind the patrol car twenty minutes later and picked his way across the weed-grown corner toward the little knot of men, one of the patrol officers there remarked *sotto voce,* "That your Mex lieutenant? He don't like to get his nice new shoes all dusty, does he?"

Detective-Sergeant Arthur Hackett said, "That's enough about Mexes, boy. For my money he's the best we got." He watched Mendoza stepping delicately as a cat through the tall growth: a slim, dark man, inevitably impeccable in silver gray, his topcoat just a shade darker than his suit, his Homburg the exact charcoal of the coat and with the new narrow brim, tilted at the correct angle and no more. Mendoza's tie this morning was a subtle foulard harmony of charcoal and silver with the discreetest of scarlet flecks, and the shoes he was carefully guarding from scratches were probably the custom-made gray pigskin pair.

"My God, he looks like a gigolo," commented the patrolman, who was only a month out of training and meeting plainclothes men for the first time on the job. "What brand of cologne does he use, I wonder. Better get ready to hold him up when he takes a look at the corpse." He hadn't enjoyed the corpse much himself.

"Don't strain yourself flexing those muscles," said Hackett dryly. "Like Luis'd say himself, *las apariencias engañan*—appearances are deceiving."

Mendoza came up to them and nodded to the patrolmen at Hackett's mention of their names. At close quarters, the young recruit saw, you

could guess him at only an inch or so under your own five-eleven, not
so small as he looked; but he had the slender Latin bone structure,
minimizing his size. Under the angled Homburg, thin, straight features:
a long chin, a precise narrow black line of mustache above a delicately
cut mouth, a long nose, black opaque eyes, sharp-arched heavy brows.
A damn Mex gigolo, thought the recruit.

"I thought you'd like to see it," Hackett was saying. "It's another
Carol Brooks."

Mendoza's long nose twitched once. "That is one I'd like to have inside. You think it's the same?" His voice was unexpectedly deep and
soft, with only an occasional hint of accent to say he had not spoken
English from birth.

"Your guess, my guess, who knows until we get him?—and maybe
not then." Hackett shrugged. "Take a look, Luis."

Mendoza walked on a dozen steps to where other men stood and
squatted. The ambulance had arrived; its attendants stood smoking and
waiting, watching the police surgeon, the men from headquarters with
their tape measures and cameras. Mendoza came up behind the kneeling surgeon and looked at the corpse; his expression stayed impassive,
thoughtful, and he did not trouble to remove his hat.

"When would you say?" he asked the surgeon.

"Oh—morning. Didn't hear you—you always move like a cat. It's a
messy one, Luis, see for yourself. Between ten and midnight, give or
take a little." The surgeon hoisted himself up, a stoutening, bald, middle-aged man, and brushed earth from his trouser legs. "I'll tell you
what she actually died of when I've had a better look—strangulation or
blows—my guess'd be the head blows. There was a sizable rock—"

"Yes," said Mendoza. He had already seen the rock, jagged, triangu-
lar. "She was cutting across from Commerce, so she knew these
streets." A faint track made by foot traffic, just out from the corner of
the house foundation, and the woman lay across the track.

"Daresay," grunted the surgeon. Hackett strolled up and the patrolmen followed, the recruit concealing reluctance. "No identification yet
but you probably will have if she's local. Either she wasn't carrying a
purse or he took it away with him."

"Never get prints off that rock," added Hackett to that. "You see
what I mean, Luis. First off, it looks like any mugging, for what she had
in her bag. I don't say it isn't. You take some of these punks, they get
excited—Doc'll remember the ten-dollar word for it." Hackett, who
looked rather like a professional wrestler, adopted the protective color-

ation of acting like one on occasion; possibly, thought Mendoza amusedly, in automatic deference to popular expectation. In fact he was —unlike Mendoza—a university graduate: Berkeley '50. It was a theory that Mendoza did not subscribe to: he had never found it help-ful—or congenial—to pretend to less intelligence than he had. "They're after the cash, but they get a kick out of the mugging too. Horseplay."

"Yes, I know," said Mendoza. "This doesn't look like horseplay."

"She wasn't raped," offered the surgeon.

"I can see that for myself. She's on her way home, at that time of night—maybe from late work, from a friend's house. There's a full moon, and she knows these streets—she doesn't think twice at cutting across here. But something is waiting." He sank to his heels over the body, careful to pull up his trouser knees first, and regarded it in si-lence for a long minute.

Before it had been a body it had been a young and pretty woman: in fact, a very young one, under make-up lavishly applied. The too-white powder, the heavily mascaraed lashes, the smeared dark-red lipstick, was a mask turned to the pitiless gray sky of this chill March day. The unfashionable shoulder-length hair, where it wasn't stiffened with clotted blood, was bleached white-gold, but along the temples and at the parting showed dark. "Coat pockets?" he murmured.

"Handkerchief and a wool scarf," said Hackett.

"To put over her hair in case it rained," nodded Mendoza. "Then she had a handbag too."

"So I figured. Dwyer and Higgins are looking around the neigh-borhood." A bag-snatcher, whether or not he was also a murderer, sel-dom kept the bag long; it would be tossed away on the run.

Her clothes were tasteless, flamboyant—tight Kelly-green sweater with a round white angora collar, black faille skirt full-cut and too short, sheer stockings, black patent-leather pumps with four-inch heels, over all a long black coat with dyed rabbit round the collar and hem. Mendoza felt the coat absently, expecting the harshness of shoddy ma-terial: cheap, ill-cut stuff.

Two very different corpses, he reflected, this tawdry pseudo blonde and Carol Brooks. Carol Brooks, six months ago, had been an eminently respectable and earnest young woman, not very good look-ing, and she had died in the soiled blue uniform-dress she wore for work. Otherwise, no, the corpses weren't so different.

"Yes," he murmured, and stood up. "He didn't intend murder, to start with—I don't think. He hadn't any weapon but his hands. And he didn't reach out to find one, blind, like that, and pick up the rock—it wasn't used that way, Art. He had her down, she was fighting him, trying to scream—he was strangling her, finding it not quick enough—and he slams her down on the ground, hard, just by chance on the rock. I can see it going like that. Unpremeditated violence, but once it unleashes itself"—he looked down at the body again—"insane violence."

"Here comes Bert," said Hackett, "with the handbag. Not that it'll maybe take us very far."

"That's a loaded question for the so-called expert," said the surgeon, looking interested over the flame of his lighter, "but I'll say this, at least —he must have gone berserk for some reason. Nobody can say sane or insane just on *that* evidence—unnecessary violence. *That* sort of thing is apt to be vicious personal hatred, or a couple of other quirks."

"You're so right," said Mendoza. "You'll make a report all embellished with the technical terms, but to go on with for the moment?"

"Her neck's broken. Excessive laceration of the throat. Half a dozen head wounds, all but one on the back of the skull—the one that killed her, I think, is this here, on the temple. Maybe she turned her head in struggling and— The left shoulder is dislocated. She was struck repeatedly in the face with a fist. You can see the cyanosed areas, there. Her right arm is broken just below the elbow. The whole torso has been damaged, kicked or maybe jumped on. Fractured ribs, I think, and internal injuries. It's on the cards some of that was done after death, but I don't know that it'll be provable—probably a very short time after, of course. There's some damage to the left eye, as if a finger or thumb had been—"

"Yes. It was Dr. Bainbridge who made the autopsy on Brooks," said Mendoza. "You wouldn't remember. That is the one thing of positive resemblance. Otherwise"—he flicked away the burnt match and drew deep on his cigarette, shrugging—"any mugger after a woman's bag, who used a little too much violence."

"So?" said the surgeon. "Ever catch that one?" Mendoza shook his head.

"Well, here we are," announced Hackett, who had gone to meet Dwyer. "In plain sight in the gutter a couple of blocks away." It was the bag one would have predicted she would carry: a big square patent-leather affair with a coquettish white bow cluttering the snap-fastener. *"Ya lo creo,* as we might put it, huh?"

Mendoza lifted his upper lip at it. "Before you get promotion and cease to be my junior in rank, Arturo, you will have perfected your vile accent. It may take years."

Very delicately Hackett delved with two fingers into the bag's interior and came up with a woman's wallet, bright pink plastic, ornamented all around the border with imitation pearls. Mendoza regarded it with satisfied horror: the very object this girl would have admired. "Lot of other stuff here—doesn't look as if he took a damn thing. Funny he put the wallet back after grabbing the cash, if— He might've figured the wallet alone'd be spotted quicker and picked up, but then again muggers don't think so far ahead usually, and this one, I don't see him in a state to think at all, after *that*. If—"

"*¡Basta!* One thing at a time."

"Her name was Elena Ramirez. No drivers' license. Dime-store snapshot of herself and, I presume, current boy friend. Social Security card. Membership card in some club. I.D. card—address and phone—little change in the coin purse—that figures, of course, he'd take the bills—"

Dwyer said, "Prints are going to love you for putting your fat paws all over that celophane."

"All right," Mendoza cut off Hackett's retort abruptly. "Give me that address, Art. I'll see the woman who found her and then the family—if there is one. Dwyer, you and Higgins can begin knocking on doors— did anyone hear a disturbance, screams perhaps? When we know more of the background, maybe I'll have other jobs for you. They can take her away now."

Hackett drifted over to Fratelli's grocery behind Mendoza. In two hours, tomorrow, Hackett would be the man nominally in charge of working this case; a lieutenant of detectives could not devote all his time to a relatively minor case like this. The fact annoyed Mendoza, partly because he had an orderly mind, liked to take one thing at a time, thoroughly. Even more did it irritate him now because it was intuitively clear to him that this girl and Carol Brooks had met death at the same hands, and he wanted very much to get that one inside, caught in a satisfactory net of evidence and booked and committed for trial.

If one murder was more or less important than another, neither of these was important: the kind of casual homicide that happens every week in any big city. This girl did not look as if she would be much missed, as if she had been a human being with much to offer the world, but one never knew. Carol Brooks, now, that had perhaps been a loss —yes. He remembered again the warm gold of the recorded voice a trifle rough as yet, a trifle uncertain, but the essential quality there. However, his cold regret at missing her murderer had nothing of sentiment in it. The reason was the reason, in a wider sense, why Luis Mendoza was a lieutenant of detectives, and—most of the time—regarded fondly by his superiors.

There are people who enjoy solving puzzles: he was not one of them. But—probably, he told himself, because he was a great egotist, and his vanity was outraged to be confronted with something he did not know —once a puzzle was presented to him he could not rest until he had ferreted out the last teasing secret. It was not often that he was faced with a complex mystery; the world would grow a great deal older before police detectives in everyday routine met with such bizarre and glamorous situations as those in fiction. *Por desgracia,* indeed: unfortunate: for complex problems inevitably had fewer possible solutions.

This thing now, this was the sort of puzzle (a much more difficult sort) that Mendoza, and all police detectives, met again and again: the shapeless crime that might have been done by anyone in the city— mostly impersonal crime, this sort, with destiny alone choosing the victim. The shopkeeper killed in the course of a robbery, the woman dead at the end of attack for robbery or rape, the casual mugging in an alley —nothing there of orderliness, the conveniently limited list of suspects, the tricky alibis, the complicated personal relationships to unravel: criminal and victim might never have met before. Or perhaps it might be an intimate business, a personal matter, and only arranged to look otherwise—and if it were, so much the easier to find the truth, for one had then only a few places to look.

But so often it was the casual, shapeless thing. And there are always, in any efficient city police force, the policemen like Luis Mendoza, single-mindedly, even passionately concerned to bring some order and reason, some ultimate shape, to the chaos. Not necessarily from any social conscientiousness—Mendoza cared little for humanity *en masse,* and was a complete cynic regarding the individual. Nor from any abstract love of truth or, certainly, of justice—for all too often the criminals he took for the law evaded punishment, this way or that way; and Mendoza sometimes swore and sometimes shrugged, but he did not lose any sleep over that. Being a realist, he said, *Lo que no se puede remediar, se ha de aguantar*—what can't be cured must be endured. Nor from ambition, to gain in rank and wages through zeal—Mendoza desired no authority over men, as he resented authority over himself, and his salary would not begin to maintain his wardrobe, or a few other personal interests. Nor even solely from earnest attention to doing one's job well.

The only reason for such men, the end goal, is the contemplation of the solved puzzle: the beautiful completeness of the last answer found. It is so with all these men, whatever kind of men they may be otherwise. Having the orderly mind, they must know where every last odd-shaped small piece belongs in the puzzle, no matter if the picture comes out landscape or portrait or still life, so to speak.

Mendoza, in fact, forced to file away an unanswered question—as he had six months ago in the Brooks case—felt very much the way an overnice housewife would feel, forced to leave dinner dishes in the sink overnight. It worried him; it irritated him; and in every free moment his mind slid back to the thing left undone.

He said now absently to Hackett, *"Eso se sobreentiende,* it's not so good that he's been loose for six months—one like that." With only a few people he didn't watch his tongue, or even let it drift into the Spanish deliberately; and that (as Hackett was fully aware) was a mark of affection and trust.

"Oh, I don't know, Luis. One dame every six months, pretty damn moderate, come to think." Hackett glanced at him sideways. "So you think it's the same joker too."

"That eye. It's a little psychological point, maybe—" Mendoza tossed away his cigarette and paused with his hand on the shopdoor. "Or am I being too subtle? In a fight with another man, anything goes —one of you may have an eye gouged out. But to do that to a woman, and a woman you have already made helpless— Well, what do we call insane? You and I have seen it, there are men lust turns sadistic, and they're not legally insane. But I don't think this is one of those, Art. I didn't think so with Carol Brooks. Because of that eye business. And Bainbridge says to me, *de paso,* just what Dr. Victor says now—probably much of the damage is made after death. Only just after, but— *Dije para mí,* it's a wild one, never mind the doubletalk of the psychiatrists. A real, hundred-percent, guaranteed genuine wild one—*mucho loco."*

"Hell, I said the same thing. And you know what that means, *chico* —work or brains don't count in catching him. He's got no sane reason for picking this girl or that. It'll be luck, that's all, if we do. My God, he might not know himself what he's done, and a hundred to one the only way we'll ever put a name to him is if he happens to have a brain storm in front of witnesses next time. Probably he's living quiet as you please, an ordinary guy nobody'd look at twice, maybe going to work every day, comin' home prompt at six to kiss his wife and look at the sports page before dinner—goes to church every Sunday—never done a thing anybody'd think queer. It'll just be the way the cards fall, if and when and how soon we get him."

"It isn't always," said Mendoza, "the hand dealt to you, so much as the way you play it."

"You should know. How much do you average a year in poker winnings, anyway?"

"Sometimes enough to buy my shirts."

"That ain't hay for you, at what, twelve bucks a throw. . . . You know something else? When we do catch up with him, he's going to be some guy who's got the reputation of being the kindest, mildest, sweetest-tempered *hombre* God ever put on earth. Everybody who knows him'll say, Oh, John couldn't be the one, he'd never do such a thing, officer! Want to bet?"

Mendoza laughed, abrupt and mirthless. "Don't I know it! I only hope he doesn't have another brain storm before we catch up to him. No one's ever accused me of being a sentimental man, *¡no, por Dios!*— but I don't care for his notions of how to treat women." He swept the Homburg off, passed a hand over the thick, Indian-straight black hair that grew to a widow's peak, and opened the door.

THREE

The girl who had found the body was nervous, too nervous. Not a nice experience, but it had been over an hour ago, and if she had nothing to do with it, why was she trembling and stammering and eying the policemen as if she expected the third degree? Mendoza was mildly curious.

She was a rather pretty girl, about twenty-seven, neat rounded figure, modest and dowdy in a clean cotton housedress. Fine olive-tan complexion, big brown eyes, minimum of make-up: a respectable girl.

"Her name was Elena Ramirez. I realize you wouldn't be likely to recognize anyone you knew under the circumstances—so, did you know Miss Ramirez?"

"Oh, no, sir, I never heard of her." She twisted her hands together and her eyes shifted away. "I'll be awful late for work, sir, I don't know nothing—"

Mendoza let her go. "Sergeant Hackett will drive you to your job and explain why you're late"; and to Hackett, "Conversation—find out what you can about her, and then see what you can pick up where she lives. I don't think she's got anything to do with it, but one never knows. I'll see the family. That takes us to an early lunch, maybe—Federico's at twelve-thirty, O.K.?—we'll compare notes."

"Está bien," said Hackett, and joined Agnes Browne outside. The Italian grocer, hovering to get Mendoza's attention, asked excitedly if he had said Ramirez—the family Ramirez over on Liggitt Street, would that be? Sacred name of God, what a terrible thing—ah, yes, he knew them, only to nod to, the *signor* comprehended—sometimes the wife came in to buy, not often—God pity them, to lose a daughter so—no, no, the girl he did not know at all—she was assaulted, assassinated by some madman, then?

"So I think," said Mendoza. The men from headquarters had dispersed; the ambulance was gone, the patrol car was gone. Across the street he saw Dwyer leave the first house next to the corner lot and head for the neighboring one. Mendoza crossed to his car and stopped to light a cigarette; he looked at the car thoughtfully, getting out his keys. He believed in buying the very best piece of merchandise obtainable of what one set out to buy, giving it loving care and using it until it fell to pieces. A thing like a car, that by this scheme was with you for years, you got acclimated to one another, it had personal individuality for you, it was more than a mere machine of transportation. The austerely elegant black Ferrari club-saloon was only thirteen years old, just into middle age for a Ferrari, and it would be mad, extravagant, to give it up: he had no intention of doing so: but there was no denying that with the increase of traffic and parking problems, its size was a disadvantage, not to say a nuisance. The trouble was, if he did buy a new car, it would be one with less than twelve cylinders—unless he should buy one of the new, smaller Ferraris, which was piling madness on madness.

He muttered, *"Es difícil,"* got in and started the engine. ("Now look, Mr. Mendoza," the mechanic had said patiently, "the number o' cylinders isn't anythin' to do with how good the car is! If you knew *anythin'* about engines atall—! I know it sounds to you like you're gettin' more for your money—facta the matter is, about all it means is it costs more to run, see? Sure, this is the hell of a great car, but you'd be just as well off, get just as much power and speed, with say something like that Mercedes six—I mean if you got to have a foreigner—or one of them slick hardtop Jaguars—")

Liggitt Street, a block the other side of Main and one down, was a bare cut above Commerce. Not so many signs in windows, and the houses, most as old and poor, better cared for. The Ramirez house was one of the two-storey ones; as he came up the walk, he saw that the curtains at the narrow front windows were clean and starched, a few flowers planted against the low porch.

He did not mind breaking bad news to strangers, and often it was of help to notice reactions: little things might tell if this was as impersonal fate as it looked, or had reasons closer to home. But he fully expected that a good deal of time would be wasted, from his point of view, while they assimilated the news, before he could decently ask questions.

He was not wrong there. The family consisted of Papa, Mama, assorted children between three and sixteen, an older daughter perhaps twenty-one, and a stocky middle-aged man who bore enough resemblance to Papa that his designation as Tío Tomás was superfluous. Mendoza waited through Mama's hysterics, the dispatching of a message to the parish priest, the settling of Mama on the sofa with a blanket, cologne-soaked handkerchief, glass of wine, and her remaining brood nested about her comfortably. He found a cracked pink saucer in obvious use as an ash tray and smoked placidly in the midst of the uproar, eyes and ears busy.

Not native Mexican-Americans, these, not a couple of generations across the border. The kids, they had the marks of smart American kids, and their English was unhesitating, sparked with slang; but Mama, fat and decent in ankle-length black cotton, and Papa, collarless neck scrawny above an old flannel bathrobe, were Old Country. It was no different, Mexican, German, Lithuanian, whatever—always there was bound to be a little friction, the kids naturally taking on freer modern ways, the old ones disapproving, worried, and arguments about it. So? The man called Tío Tomás sat in a straight chair behind the sofa and said nothing, smoking tiny black Mexican cigarillos.

"You know I must ask you questions," said Mendoza at last, putting a hand on Manuel Ramirez' arm. "I'm sorry to intrude on your grief, but to help us in hunting whoever has killed your daughter—"

"*Sí*, yes, it is understood," whispered Ramirez. "I—I tell you whatever you want to know. *María Santísima*, my brain is not working for this terrible thing, but—excuse, mister, I don't speak so good in English—"

"Then we speak Spanish."

"Ah, you have the tongue, that's good. I thank you—pardon, mister, the name I did not—"

"Lieutenant Mendoza."

"Mendoza." He gave it the hard Mexican pronunciation that was ultimately Aztec, instead of the more elegant Spanish sibilance. "You are —an agent of police?"

"I am. I'll ask you first—"

"The gentleman's good to wait and be polite." It was the oldest girl, coming up quietly, looking at him with open curiosity; she was pale, but had not been weeping. She was not as pretty as her sister had been, but not bad-looking, in a buxom way. "Of course we know you got to ask questions, but look, Papa, no sense disturbing Mama with it—I guess you and me can tell him whatever he wants. Let's go in the kitchen, if that's all right, mister?"

"It is Lieutenant, Teresa," said Ramirez distractedly; he let her urge him through a shabby dining room. Mendoza strolled after: she threw him a glance over her shoulder of mixed interest, anxiety, and a kind of mechanical female blandishment. The kitchen was big, cold, reasonably clean. "Please to sit down, sir—if you would accept my hospitality, a glass of wine—it's only cheap stuff—" Ramirez was trying to pull himself together; the conventional courtesy was automatic.

"No, no, thanks. Tell me first, I believe your daughter lived here with you?—then you must have been worried that she didn't come home last night? Do you know where she was?"

The girl answered from where she had perched uneasily on the kitchen table. "Sure, we were worried. But she might've gone to stay overnight with a girl friend, or—well, you know how it is, we sort of talked back 'n' forth and kept waiting for her maybe to call one of the neighbors with a message—Mrs. Gomez next door lets us—"

"Where had she gone and when did she leave?"

"She was—she was just out on a date. I don't know where they were going. Ricky, he was here for Elena about seven, I guess, and they went right after." In answer to the query only begun, she added hurriedly, "Ricky Wade, he's a boy Elena's—Elena had been going with a lot. A nice boy he is, you needn't go thinking anything about him, see. I don't

know where they were going, but they did go to the Palace rink a lot—
that roller-skating place, you know. Silly, I say, but Elena's—Elena was
just a kid, she liked it."

"She would have had nineteen years only the next month," murmured Ramirez. "It was wrong, Teresa, I said so! We should have gone
to the police at once, at once! Elena was a good girl in her heart, she
was properly brought up, never would she have done such a thing—all
the talk around and around, I should have let you and Mama talk and
gone to the police myself—"

"What would she not have done, Miss Ramirez?" asked Mendoza.

"Oh, well, I s'pose we got to say or you'll think it's funny we didn't
seem more worried." Her mouth tightened. "We were going to do
something about it this morning, don't know what, but— We *were*
awful worried, you can see that, way Papa and I both stayed home
from work—it wasn't as if Elena ever did nothing like that before, stay
away all night and not call or nothing. But—well, we got to thinking
maybe her and Ricky'd eloped—you know, over to Las Vegas or somewhere, to get married in a hurry—"

"It is not true!" exclaimed Ramirez excitedly, jumping up. The
bathrobe fell open to reveal his spindly legs and unexpectedly gay pink
cotton underpants. "It is a wicked lie, that Elena is got in trouble with
this fellow and has to run away and marry quick! She is a respectable
girl, never would she—oh, she does this and that Mama and I don't
like, sure, but she's young, it's different times and ways now, I know
that—she's impatient, she wants the moon like all youngsters, but never
would she—"

"I never said she did, I never! But after they made up and he came
back, she sure meant to keep him, she was set on marrying him some
day, you know good as I do. All I *said* was, if he all of a sudden
wanted to elope, she wouldn't take the risk of losing him, she'd say yes
quick!"

"Did you disapprove of this Mr. Wade, then?" asked Mendoza of
Ramirez casually.

"Disapprove—" He moved his thin shoulders wearily. "He is not of
the faith. I don't know, if Elena wanted so bad, I— You don't have
nothing to say about it any more, anyway, fathers. The kids, they go
their own way. She wouldn't have been happy in such a marriage, that I
thought. But it wasn't really serious, they were just youngsters—"

"Elena was serious, all right!" said Teresa. She turned to Mendoza.
"Look, you might's well know how it was, an' weasel round like I

s'pose you got to, to be sure Ricky didn't have nothing to do with—with killing her. That's silly, he wouldn't. Elena met him in school three years back, see—that's Sloan Heights High, where I went too. Only I had the sense to finish, and she didn't—wanted a job so's she could buy a lot of splashy clothes 'n' all—soon as she turned sixteen, she got a work permit an' a job uptown in a Hartners' store, putting stuff on the models in the windows, unpacking in the stock room, like that—"

Ramirez moved restlessly. "All this foolishness," he muttered, "keeping girls in school so long—history and algebra, it don't teach them any better to keep house and bring up the kids. And Elena always give Mama her five dollars a week, regular, like she should."

"I'm not saying nothing against her, Papa, only she should've finished like I did, learned typing and all, so's to get a better job. Sure she gave Mama money, and bought things for the kids too, she wasn't stingy. All I—"

"Mr. Wade," murmured Mendoza.

"That's what I'm *getting* to. She saw I was right in the end, see? Because the Wades, they reckon they're a lot too good for the likes of us, they didn't like Ricky taking up with Elena. Mr. Wade, he works for the city, they own their house and all that—you know. Elena, she liked Ricky a lot, sure, he's a nice boy like I said, but at the same time she saw it'd be kind of a step up the ladder for her, marry into a family like that. She didn't want to stay on Liggitt Street all her life, well, who does? But the time she had a little fight with Ricky, 'n' don't go thinking it was anything serious, just a little spat like, she started thinking how silly it'd be to really lose him—I know all this because she talked it over with me, see, nights—we got the same room. I mean, she thought, he's used to different sorts of ways and she got worried she wouldn't know how to act right about things like that if they got married."

"It was foolishness," said Ramirez. "That school place for teaching the fascination. But it's Elena's money, if she wanted—"

"Fascination?" Momentarily the subtle color of near-synonyms in the Spanish misled Mendoza.

"No, it wasn't," said Teresa. "It's—it was worth the money, Papa, and that Miss Weir's real nice, you know I seen her once, when I met Elena uptown to shop. It's a charm school"—turning back to Mendoza—"you know, they teach you what's right to wear and so on. Me, I say it was O.K. for Elena to try to improve herself, sure. Even if she had to quit her job like she did, it's a six-week course an' every day—she could get another easy enough after. What *was* silly about it, those Wades aren't all so much that she had to feel nervous about them! Mother of God, you'd think they were millionaires with a butler maybe like in the movies, way she talked. He's just a bookkeeper in some office, but—you know—they're the kind put their noses in the air at *us,* dirty low-class Mexes, they say to each other, *an'* Catholic which they don't like so much either. Me, I don't let people like that bother me, not one little bit. Maybe we do rent a house instead of owning one, an' maybe our street isn't so high-class, an' we don't have no car or telephone or electric washing machine—maybe Papa does just drive a delivery truck—what's that got to do with anything? We're respectable folks, Papa's worked for Mr. Reyes all the time since he come over, and that's nearly twenty years, and we don't owe nobody no money like I'll bet the Wades do. I got a good job typing for *El Gente Méjico,* 'n' I've saved nearly three hundred dollars toward furniture an' so on for when Carlos and me get married this summer—which I'll bet is more than Mrs. Wade can say she did!" Teresa gestured contemptuously. "People like them, let them talk! But it bothered Elena, see."

"You have much common sense," said Mendoza with a smile. "I think Carlos is lucky. So nothing was said last night about where your sister and Mr. Wade were going?" She shook her head. "But you would certainly have expected that he'd see her home?"

"Oh, sure. I can't figure out how she come to be alone—she must've been, for whoever—did it—to sneak up on her. You said—the corner at Commerce an' Humboldt? She must've been on her way home then, and from that Palace rink too, coming that way."

"We'll find out. Mr. Ramirez, you'll have to identify the body formally, and there'll be an inquest, of course. I'll send someone to take you down to the morgue."

"Identify—that mean you're not sure it *is* Elena?" asked the girl sharply.

"No, that we know. It's only a formality of the law."

"Yes, I understand," said Ramirez. "You're kind, we thank you."

Mendoza took the girl's arm and led her out to the dining room. She looked up at him alertly, half-suspicious. "Well, what now?"

"No need to upset your father more," he said easily. "Will you give me the address of this school your sister attended, please—how long had she been going there?"

"A—about three weeks it was, yes, just three because today's Saturday an' she began two weeks ago last Monday. I don't know that it was doing her much good at that, she couldn't seem—"

"Miss Ramirez, you're a smart girl. You can look at things straight, and I don't think you'll lie to me just to defend your sister's memory. Tell me, do you think she'd have let a stranger pick her up, as they say?"

Teresa put a hand to her cheek. "That's a hard one to answer, mister. Right off I'd say no, an' not to, like you said, make out Elena was better than she was. When I said we're respectable folks, that wasn't no lie either—us girls've been raised proper, know what's right 'n' wrong, even if maybe we don't know everything like about which forks an' spoons. No, sir, Elena wouldn't ever have gone with a strange fellow, way you mean, somebody whistled at her on the street or offered her a ride. But it might be she *would* think it was O.K. if it was somebody she'd seen around, if you know what I mean, and he acted all right. This rink place, f'r instance, she went there a lot, belonged to some crazy club they got for regular customers, and if some fellow there got talking to her and maybe offered her a ride home, if she was alone, or said he'd walk with her, she might've thought it was O.K., if he seemed polite and all. She—she couldn't size people up very good. I know—I told her time an' again—she made herself look cheap, bleaching her hair and all that make-up, but she wasn't like that really. She was—" her face twisted suddenly—"she was just a kid. Rollerskating . . ."

"I see, thank you. Someone will come for your father—you'll see he's ready? I'll cease to intrude for the moment then, but as this and that comes up, one of us will be back to ask more questions."

"I s'pose you got to."

"Were you very fond of your sister, Miss Ramirez?" he asked, soft and offhand.

She was silent, and then looked up to meet his eyes. "She was my sister. That don't say I couldn't see her faults—nobody's all good or bad. It don't seem fair—she should die like that before she was even nineteen, hadn't had nothing much. But it's a thing that happens, people dying, age don't seem to have an awful lot to do with it sometimes. Little babies, like a couple of Mama's. You got to figure God must know what He's doing. And think about them that's still alive."

There was in her round brown eyes all the sad, inborn, fatalistic wisdom of the primitive tribe living close with the basic realities of life and death.

At the door, Mendoza met the priest just arriving: round-faced, rich-voiced, middle-aged Irishman, the self-introduction as Father Mon-aghan unnecessary to guess his ancestry. "You are—? Oh, yes—but what an incredible, tragic thing, I can hardly believe— Before I go in, then, Lieutenant, perhaps you would tell me in more detail—" And when he had heard, steady blue eyes fixed on Mendoza, he said quietly, "God grant you find this poor wicked man soon. If there is any way I can be of help— I know this district well, and most of those living here, you know—"

"Yes, thank you, we'll keep it in mind."

"You said, Lieutenant—Mendoza? At least it must be some comfort to them that one of their own people should be investigating, one of their own faith who—"

"Not for some while of that or any, Father."

"Ah," said the priest, "but not forever, my son, will you say that to God. One day you will return the full circle."

Mendoza smiled, stood back to let him pass, and went out to the porch. Adjusting his hat, he said to himself, *"¡Muy improbable, venga lo que venga—nada de eso!"*

The man called Tío Tomás was leaning on the porch railing. He showed yellow snags of teeth in a brief grin. "Nothing doing—that's what I say to them kind too. All they're after is money. For a cop maybe you got a little brains." The grin did not change his wary cold eyes. His skin was bad, showing relics of the smallpox.

"You will be a brother to Manuel Ramirez, I think."

"Sure, that's right, but I don't live here, I'm just visiting. Too bad about Elena, she was a nice kid."

Mendoza looked him over thoughtfully. "I'll hear your permanent address."

"I live in Calexico, I got a business there, I didn't have nothing to do with—"

"Indeed?" said Mendoza; small satisfaction warmed him for some-thing, however irrelevant and minor, to take hold of. The most respect-able families had black sheep, and this was one of them, that he could see with half an eye. "You're a Mexican national, not a citizen? I'll see your entry permit." The man brought it out promptly; it was in order. "Exporter. What do you export?"

"I got a silversmithy," said Ramirez. "Nothing big, you know, just a man and four girls—jewelry. You know how the tourists go for native stuff, and here too. I make a better profit on it up here even with the duty, you can mark it up higher. I'm just up on a little business trip."

"With success?" asked Mendoza genially.

"Oh—sure, sure. Got to get back, though, the business don't run itself." His eyes shifted. "Say, I won't have to stay, just account this thing about Elena? I didn't have nothing to do with— I mean, it was some crazy fellow killed her, wasn't it—"

"It would be as well if you stay for the inquest," said Mendoza, gave him a last smiling inspection and went unhurriedly down the walk to his car; he felt the man's eyes on him. He drove back to Commerce and caught Higgins and Dwyer comparing notes before leaving for headquarters. No one in the block had heard anything unusual last night.

He had not expected much from that. He sent Dwyer with the headquarters car over to Liggitt Street, to keep an eye on Tomás Ramirez. "Maybe a waste of time. Maybe something for us, but not connected with the murder. He's been in trouble, I think he's been inside, anyway he doesn't like cops—not too close. Exporter, his papers say. He might be just that, indeed."

Dwyer said, "Marijuana—or the big H. Sure, he might. And how about this, Lieutenant—the girl finds it out and either says she'll turn him in or wants a cut, so he—"

"Whatever he is or isn't, he's small time. I don't think so, but of course it's a possibility we'll have to check. Stay on him, I'll send a man to relieve you." He took Higgins back to headquarters to pick up another car and ferry the father down to the morgue.

Himself, instead of returning to his office where he should be attending to other matters, he set off to see the Wades. There should be just time before lunch. It was a very routine errand, something for Hackett or even one of Hackett's underlings, and not until he was halfway there did Mendoza realize clearly why he felt it important to see to it himself, why he had gone to the Ramirez house. The sooner all this personal matter was cleared out of the way, proved to be extraneous, the better. And he must satisfy himself doubly that it was irrelevant, because it was always dangerous to proceed on a preconceived idea. He had been seized by the conviction, looking at the body, that this girl had been killed by the killer of Carol Brooks—but it was little more than a hunch, an irrationality backed by very slender evidence.

Carol Brooks, three miles away over in East L.A.—maybe a bigger loss than this girl had been. A young, earnest, ambitious girl, who had earned her living as a hotel chambermaid and spent her money not on clothes but voice lessons—with an expensive trainer of high repute, too, who thought a good deal of her, was giving her a cut price. He had said she needed constant encouragement, because she didn't believe a black girl could get very far, unless she was really the very best, and she'd never be *that* good. Maybe she would have been; no one would ever know, now.

Nothing very much to support his conviction, on the surface evidence. And he must guard against holding it blind, if other evidence pointed another way. As it would—as it did. Nobody lived long without giving at least a few people reasons for dislike, sometimes reasons for murder. They might turn up several here. And that was the easy way to look for a murderer, among only a few, the immediate surroundings and routines of the girl who'd been killed.

If he was right, they'd need to spread a wider net. For someone quite outside, someone without logical motive. Someone, somewhere among the five million people in this teeming metropolitan place sprawling in all directions—someone who was dangerous a hundred times over because the danger from him was secret, unsuspected.

This time Mendoza would like to get that one. Because he had missed him six months ago, another girl was in a cold-storage tray at the city morgue now.

FOUR

They met for a not-too-leisured lunch at Federico's, out on North Broadway. Hackett left him to mull over what meager information they had; his own next stop was obviously the skating rink. The waiter whisked away the relics of the meal, apologetically; they never hurried you at Federico's, you could sit as long as you pleased. "More coffee, sir?"

"Please." Mendoza brooded over his refilled cup; he should go back to his office and occupy himself at being a lieutenant; there were other cases on hand than this.

The girl who had found the body, nothing there immediately: nothing known against her, but little emerged of her background either. It was a very long chance that she had anything to do with it, but of course she had to be investigated. As did every aspect of the Ramirez girl's life. And after that, where to look?

He drank black coffee and dwelt for a moment on Mrs. Elvira Wade. In her appallingly cluttered, tasteless, middle-class-and-proud-of-it living room: a God-fearing upright citizen, Mrs. Wade, who had spread a little too much in the waist and hips, not at all in the mind.

"Of *course* we didn't like it, to say the least—a Mexican girl—and *such* a girl, all that cheap-looking bleached hair and perfectly dreadful clothes, but of course they're always so fond of garish colors, you know. And then of course there was the *religious* question. Really, boys have no sense, but it's *beyond* me how a son of mine could be so taken in, after all you'd think he'd have some finer instincts, the way I've tried to bring him up. Not that I'm not sorry for the poor thing, the girl I mean, and one shouldn't speak ill of the dead. I try to take a Christian view I'm sure and after all people can't help being born what they are, but when it comes to accepting them into one's *family*—"

It was something, however, to have embarrassed such a woman even momentarily: her belated furtive glance at his card, her ugly pink flush, almost ludicrous. "And of *course*," she had added hurriedly, "there's all the difference in the *world* between people like that and the real high-class old Spanish families, everyone knows *that,* I understand the peasant class is actually mostly Indian and the real Spaniards wouldn't have anything to do with *them.* But I'm sure you can see how we, my husband and I, felt—"

Mendoza sighed into the dregs of his coffee. It did not, apparently, cross Mrs. Wade's mind that she had perhaps, in a sense, contributed to the girl's death. The boy had been strictly forbidden to see Elena again ("really such strong measures were *necessary,* though he is nineteen and ordinarily I don't believe in *iron* discipline"), and when it was discovered, through a garrulous acquaintance of Ricky's, that he had *not* borrowed the family car to go to the movies last night but to take Elena to that awful skating place—"Well, I said to Mr. Wade, when it comes to lying to his own parents, *something drastic* must be done! You can see how she corrupted him, he'd never done such a thing before—I said to Mr. Wade, you'll go right down there and—" So Mr. Wade (could one conjecture, breathing fire, or were the men married to such women capable of it?—at least he seemed to have acted effectively) had, by bus, sought out the Palace rink, publicly reprimanded the erring Ricky, and fetched him ignominiously away. After this soul-searing experience, nineteen-year-old Ricky had probably been in no state to consider how Elena would get home, and if it had occurred to the Wades, presumably they had thought a girl like that would be used to going about alone at night.

As, Mendoza conceded, she had been: she had probably got home alone before. He pushed his coffee cup round in a little circle, aimlessly; and of course the girl would also have been angry, humiliated—quite possibly she might have let a stranger pick her up, a thing she wouldn't ordinarily do. Someone at the rink?

He wondered what Hackett would find out there. He paid the bill, redeemed the Ferrari from the lot attendant, and instead of turning back downtown for headquarters, negotiated his way through the bottleneck round the Union Station and turned up Sunset Boulevard. It had begun to rain steadily, after long threat.

The address Teresa had given him was close into town, along the less glamorous stretches of that street. It proved to be the upper half of a small office building, not new. A narrow door and a steep stair brought him to a landing and a sign: THE SUNSET SCHOOL OF CHARM. A mousy girl with a flat figure and harlequin glasses was scrabbling among papers at the receptionist's desk.

"Miss Weir?"

"Oh, dear me, no." She moved the glasses up to focus on him better. "No classes on Saturday, sir, and we don't enroll gentlemen anyway."

"Which is not what I am here for," said Mendoza, annoyed at the implication. "I want to see Miss Weir on private business."

"Not here on Saturdays. . . . Of course I have her home address, but I don't know—oh, well, I suppose it's all right."

New directions took him, tediously, several miles into Hollywood, to a street of solidly middle-aged apartment buildings, a little shabby, thirty years away from being fashionable addresses, but neatly kept up. The row of locked mailboxes in the foyer of the Blanchard Arms informed him that Miss Alison Weir lived on the fourth floor. A hand-lettered placard further informed him that the elevator was out of order. Mendoza said mildly, "Damn," toiled up three flights of dark, dusty-carpeted stairs, pressed the bell of 406 and, regaining his breath, hoped his quarry was in.

When the door opened to him, he was gratified for more reasons than one. Miss Alison Weir was worth the drive through traffic, worth a wasted afternoon. A middling tall young woman, with an admirably rounded yet slender figure, less conventionally pretty than charmingly provocative—rather square chin, a nose too small, a mouth too large, alert gray-green-hazel eyes under feathery brows, a magnificent matt-white complexion, and crisply cut and curled hair somewhere between copper and auburn, which was moreover nature's own choice for her. Her tailored dress was exactly the color of her hair, there were discreet gleams of topaz costume jewelry, her lipstick and nail polish were of the same burnt-orange shade. Twenty-nine, thirty, he said to himself: recovered, thank God, from the arch uncertainty of girlhood, and miraculously not bent on maintaining it: one might even suspect that great rarity in a woman, a sense of humor.

"Yes?" And her voice matched the rest of her, a warm contralto.

As he produced his credentials, explained, he swore mentally at the destiny which involved the woman in a case. It was not a good idea to mix personal matters with the job, and he was scrupulous about it. Until this woman was proved definitely to be clear of any connection with the case—he would be extremely surprised if she had, but it had to be checked, of course—strictly business, Luis, he said to himself regretfully.

"Good lord!" she exclaimed. "Well, come in, Lieutenant—you're lucky to catch me, I've just got in myself."

"Then you're excellent advertisement for your business. Any woman who can come in out of a rainstorm looking so charming—" It was the usual apartment of this vintage, but the personal touches were firmly individual: a good many books in cheap low cases against the wall, a row of framed pen sketches above them, a coffee table with Chinese teak underpinning topped with a large Benares brass tray, in serene indifference to incongruity with the rest of the furniture, and an enormous aerial photograph of a suspension bridge over the simulated hearth. He sat down facing that, at her gesture, on the sofa, and disposed his hat and coat beside him.

"I shouldn't give myself away," she smiled, "but I came in looking like a drowned rat, I'm afraid. I'd be in a hot bath now if Marge hadn't called to warn me that a mysterious sinister-looking stranger—"

"That one's not such a good advertisement," he grinned.

"But I can't keep books. What's all this about the Ramirez girl? Cigarettes in that box, by the way—and don't you usually hunt in couples?"

"I've got no business hunting at all," said Mendoza, lighting her cigarette, then his. "I ought to be in my office doing this and that about a dozen other cases. As it is, I'm tying up loose ends"—he gestured—"you might say, on the perimeter of this business. I don't think it was a personal business, you see—I think it was more or less chance that the Ramirez girl was the one killed—but we have to be sure. I don't know what I expect from you, but you've been seeing the girl five days a week for the last couple of weeks, and anything she said to you—any little problem she mentioned, maybe—?"

"I see." Alison studied her cigarette. "You're always reading about these things in the papers—never think of its happening to anyone you know. The poor kid . . . I don't know that I can tell you anything."

"I'm hoping you can't," he said frankly. "We've already run across a couple of things in her personal life that might—just might—have led to murder. They have to be looked into. If you tell me something else, that's got to be investigated too. And I don't believe anything personal is behind it, I don't want to waste time on that."

"I see," she said again. "One of these psychos, blowing off steam every so often, on anyone convenient at the moment."

"They exist. Something like that, anyway. And I don't think this is his first, either. I'd like to find him before he, shall we say, has the impulse again."

"Amen to that," she said seriously. "But how on earth do you even start to look for a man like that? It might be anybody."

"I could give you a superior smile and say, We have our methods." He shrugged. "There are places to start looking. The records of any recently discharged mental patients—our own records of similar assaults—sex offenders who might have graduated to something more serious. We went through all that on the first case."

"And didn't come up with anything? So then what do you do?"

"Then," said Mendoza rather savagely, "you file all the records neatly away marked Case Pending, and you wait for it to happen again. Of course ideas occur to you about other places to look—but to put them into effect, I'd need about three times the number of men I've got." He sighed and put out his cigarette. "Of course, if one like that kills a dozen people a week, and obligingly leaves evidence to show it's all his own unaided work, the upper echelons get excited—and I get the men. But nobody, not even a lunatic killer, reaches the top of his career all at once—there's a build-up."

"Everyone has to start small?" She smiled briefly. "I see what you mean. Well, I don't think I can add anything to what you've probably got from her family and so on, but fire away—what do you want to know?"

"Did you have much to do with the girl personally? You teach classes, or whatever they're called, yourself?"

"Oh, lord, yes, I'm all there is. It may sound like a racket, Lieutenant, and maybe it is in some cases, but I think I offer them something, you know." She leaned to the table to put out her cigarette; her smile was wryly humorous. "The ones like this girl—and some others who might surprise you. Natural good taste and so on isn't standard equipment with the so-called upper classes. I've known girls from the same sort of background as Elena Ramirez who knew how to dress and had better instincts, as we say, than girls from wealthy homes. Mostly I get girls who are serious about improving themselves, but what they want to know, all I try to get over to them, is pretty simple. The very basic things about clothes and make-up and manners. You wouldn't believe what some of them look like when they come—"

"But I would," said Mendoza sadly. "I've seen them in the street, for my sins. Generally in those things mistakenly called toreador pants."

She threw back her head and laughed, and he admired the clean white line of her throat. "Oh, my lord, I know!"

"I have no moral objection whatever, you understand—in fact it's enough to turn a man celibate for life—it's the aesthetic view I object to."

"And how right you are, with most of them. Well, as you might say yourself, ¿A qué viene eso? What—"

"You speak Spanish, Miss Weir?"

"By accident. I was born in Durango—my father was a structural engineer and worked in Mexico a good deal. That"—she nodded at the big photograph—"is his last piece of work. Funny sort of décor for a living room, I suppose I'm sentimental about it—he was very proud of it." She lit another cigarette. "In a sort of roundabout way, that's how I got into this business. You see, I'm a painter—or shall we say I hope I am—and that doesn't bring in much of a living unless you're really good—or at least known. Dad didn't leave me much, and I have to earn a living some way. What with moving around the way we did for his work, I got a rather sketchy education, and then like a fool I quit high school to get married—which turned out a mistake in more ways than one—and, well, I thought I'd try this, and it's worked out surprisingly well. Leaves me a fair amount of time for my own work, and at the same time I really enjoy it, you know. Not to bore you—"

"But how could you indeed?"

"And this isn't getting to what you want to know, anyway. It's a fairly small group, I never take more than twenty-five in a class and it's usually around twenty girls. I try to keep it on a more or less personal basis, you see. The course is six weeks, five days a week, but some of that time is spent on group reading and some on—private counseling, to give it a fancy name. Generally, I'll see each girl privately, oh, say a total of two hours or so a week. So you see, while I knew the girl, you can't say I knew her intimately."

"But you're no fool at sizing up people," he said placidly, leaning back, arms folded behind his head. "And the girl poured out her problems into your sympathetic ear?"

"That she did. You probably know about that—the superior boy friend and his family's objections. She was rather a pathetic little thing, really—awfully earnest, but—" She paused for a word.

"The first one comes to your mind about her," he prompted softly.

"Stupid," said Alison unhesitatingly. "She was stupid. She had no imagination, subtleties of any sort just didn't penetrate—you know the type. Oddly enough, her older sister is quite intelligent—I met them in town one day—"

"Yes, that girl has brains."

"Elena was honest, and—though she didn't look it—quite a respectable girl, in the old-fashioned sense. Immature for her age. But stupid."

"Immature and honest," he murmured. A little something there. The man Tomás, if there was anything in that, this girl would probably have been too stupid to discover it. If anyone in that household had seen something suspicious about the visiting uncle, it would not have been Elena, but the sharp-eyed Teresa. "That's no surprise," he said, half to himself. "Even dead, she was—unsubtle. I haven't met the boy yet—judging by Mrs. Wade, I'd say that his persistence was less attraction to Elena than rebellion against his mother."

"Like that?" She looked amused, and then sobered. "But that's another thing that happens, Lieutenant—the old, old story. I've never laid eyes on him either, don't know what kind of a boy he is, but—"

"Oh, yes, that's the first thing one thinks of here—if it was a private killing, so to speak. If she was pregnant, if she could make trouble for him, if he lost his head— It's happened. It'll happen again. We'll find out if it happened here."

"And how easy," she said, "to talk about it like a—crossword puzzle. After all, she's dead. Nineteen . . . She had a private session with me yesterday. She said she'd decided to stop bleaching her hair—" Alison stopped abruptly and looked up at him. "I *have* thought of something, but it doesn't sound like much—"

"I'll tell you whether it does when I've heard it, Miss Weir—or is it Mrs.?"

"I got my own name back after the divorce," she said absently. "It was only a year. And aren't you the autocratic male. Well, for what it's worth, Elena asked me yesterday what to do about 'a guy annoys you'—that's how she put it—she said he 'sort of' followed her and stared at her."

"*¡No me diga!*" He sat up. "Don't tell me! That might be it, you know. Tell me every last little word she said about it!"

"But there wasn't anything, really! I'm afraid I didn't take it as very important. You mean it might have been—?"

"It might have been. There aren't any rules for lunatics—or part-time lunatics—but even lunatics don't often kill utter strangers without some reason. Nor what you or I'd call a logical reason, but a reason. I'm not even at the point of guessing about that here, but it's probable that at least he'd seen the girl before—consequently she may have noticed him. Let's have it—all of it!"

Alison looked stricken. "You'll want to murder *me,* Lieutenant—I didn't give her a chance to say much about it. In fact, I used it as an excuse to give her a neat little lecture on Making Oneself Conspicuous. She said—let me think!—'Miss Weir, what should you do about a guy annoys you?' and I asked, Annoys you how? That was when she said he 'sort of followed' her and stared at her. And as I say, I seized the opportunity to point out that sometimes a girl seems to invite such attentions by making herself look cheap—and so on and so on—" Her voice died; she shut her eyes and pressed both hands to her cheeks, trying to remember. "There *wasn't* anything else—she said she understood about that, and that was when she told me she'd decided to stop bleaching—we talked about different things, you know, one thing leading to another—"

"That you needn't tell me! Women, they never keep to the subject!"

"But there *was* something else, I know it. Yes—" She straightened. "Just as she got up to leave, she said, 'But it's not exactly like that, Miss Weir, like he was trying pick me up or nothing like that. It's just —funny. Awful funny.' And I said something like, Well, just be sure you're not encouraging him, and that was that—she left, her consultation time was up."

"God favor me with patience!" said Mendoza violently. "And they say women are curious and fond of gossip! This girl tells you some strange man is annoying her, and you talk about hair dye and never ask one question? She says there's something 'funny' about him, and you—"

"How should I know it was anything important? If I'd—no, but listen, Lieutenant—*she* didn't say it as if *she* thought it was important, anything to be worried about! You see? If there'd really been anything *very* queer about him, to frighten her—" Her voice dropped.

"Yes, you've remembered that she was a stupid girl," he said sardonically. "And how did she mean that 'funny'?"

"*Extraño,* like that—she said, 'It's just funny' or 'He's just funny,' and then she said it in Spanish, as if the English word didn't quite express what she meant. *Es un muchacho extraño.*"

"I will be damned," said Mendoza. "Something at last, maybe. 'A queer boy.'" He looked at her in cold exasperation. "And you didn't ask so much as where and when she saw him, what he looked like?"

"There's a saying about hindsight," retorted Alison, but meekly. "Would you have?"

"No, but then I'm not a woman. My God, I'd have thought you'd be a *little* curious! Well, it can't be helped." He got up. "I'll ask you to make a formal statement about this, if you will."

"Yes, of course." She went to the door with him. "Where do I go and when?"

"Tomorrow will do." Abruptly in better humor again, he smiled down at her. "I'll take you down to headquarters myself, not to expose any of my sergeants to temptation. I make it a rule not to mix business with pleasure, but if you turn out to be irrelevant to business, I'll be back—*con su permiso.*"

"Permission be damned, you mean! I do like your nerve," said Alison pleasantly, leaning on the open door. "When you're quite satisfied that I didn't murder the girl—maybe because she was so stupid —or egg your lunatic onto her, you'll condescend to find me good enough to be seen with. *Un hombre muy arbitrario,* in fact! And doesn't it occur to you that I might have a possessive six-foot admirer hanging about to raise objections?"

"What, to compete with *me?* I don't let those worry me any day."

"As if I needed telling. What time tomorrow?"

"In a hurry to be rid of me? One o'clock?"

"But *naturally,*" she said, widening her eyes at him. "I'm panting for you to get to work and absolve me of guilt, what else, with such a reward offered? One o'clock—I'll be ready." The small amusement faded from her eyes then and she added, "I hope I *have* helped. Good luck with it."

"That I've had my share of for today. Until then." Scarcely a wasted afternoon, no—however you looked at it. He reflected pleasurably and with anticipation on Alison Weir—a sophisticated, shrewd, sensible woman (deliver him from romanticizing and possessive young girls!) and a very lovely one—until he slid behind the wheel and started the engine. He then removed his mind from her firmly and thought about what she had told him.

Hackett was waiting for him in his office; Hackett had been busy, and there was quite a list of miscellaneous bits and pieces to think about. Of greatest importance was the Ricky Wade business. That had to be looked into: it was so obvious. Hackett agreed with that: he would call there this evening, to catch both the boy and the father at home: a phone call assured that they would be, Mrs. Wade sounding surprised and uneasy (but what have *we* to do with this sordid matter, her tone implied).

The proprietor of the rink had been out, but some useful information had been obtained from his two employees, and Hackett was to see him at four. Two of Hackett's men were now out chasing down the patrons definitely stated to have been in the place last night. That was a place to be very thorough, the rink and everybody connected with it, for the girl had almost certainly been on her way home from there.

When Hackett left, Mendoza shoved aside everything to do with this case, conscientiously went over all the other pending matters under his authority. The still-unidentified corpse found in the frieght yards; Sergeant Clock hadn't come up with anything new. The liquor-store holdup, a clerk shot; Sergeant Brice was on a faint track there, from the usual anonymous Information Received. The woman who'd shot her husband before witnesses: nothing to investigate but much tiresome routine, collecting statements for the District Attorney's office, in that sort of thing. Sergeant Galeano thought he had it about tied up now. A new memo from the captain's office, more routine: particulars of a man New York wanted for parole violation, one Ray Dalton, five-ten, one-eighty, age 42, Caucasian—

Mendoza swore to himself and reached for Hackett's notes again.

The two men at the rink, Hayes and Murphy, described themselves as attendants. They kept the place cleaned up (Hackett's comment: "This is news to anyone who's seen it"), one of them was on the floor at all times during open hours, to hand out skates and generally keep an eye on the patrons, and on occasion they spelled Ehrlich, the owner-proprietor, at the ticket desk. Not often, because Ehrlich didn't trust nobody much but himself with money. Ehrlich's wasn't getting rich, but business was so-so: most nights and Saturday afternoons they had maybe thirty, forty people in. All kids, sure: teenagers; some of those were crazy about it, maybe the ones had been too poor ever to have skates. They were good enough kids, not punks: the kind of kids carried switchknives, roamed round in gangs, all that, got in trouble with the cops—to them kind roller skating was for the birds. Sure, the kids got noisy and rambunctious sometimes like kids do, but there wasn't never anything real bad, knives pulled or an honest-to-God fight. No, neither of them ever remembered an adult coming in—not to *skate*. There'd been a kind of fad for it once, like that miniature golf and ping-pong, that was when Ehrlich had opened this place, but nowadays anybody grown-up, they'd feel like a damn fool roller skating. Well, the chairs round the sides were for people to sit and watch, sure, but this wasn't like an Ice Palace where there was a show to see, for God's sake —just a bunch of kids skating—nobody came just for that, the chairs were mostly used by the kids themselves, resting and talking.

As for the club thing, it wasn't really a club but a kind of season-ticket deal, see. You got a cut rate if you joined as a "regular patron": there weren't no meetings or nothing, all a card meant was they'd paid three or six months in advance. All the kids with cards didn't neces-sarily know each other: sometimes yes, sometimes no. A card was an automatic pass good for three nights a week up to the date on it. What with kids sixteen and seventeen getting maybe forty a week at some job, a lot of them had more money than was good for them, to throw away.

Both men knew the Ramirez girl and confirmed that she had been in last night. What with the row, they could hardly miss her. Ehrlich had been damned mad about it too, the guy saying the rink was a low dive and all: Ehrlich was death on liquor in the place. This fellow barged right in, about twenty minutes to ten it was, and pulled the kid off the floor—one that was with this girl. Gave him hell, way the kids both looked: but not shouting, private-like at the side of the rink, see, where it was kind of dark, account the overhead lights were just in the middle, to light the skating floor. The fellow took the boy out finally, maybe five minutes later—practically dragged him, hardly give him time to take his skates off and turn them in. Yes, off the premises—Ehrlich probably saw them go out to the street or wherever, he was arguing at the guy and followed them. The girl was mad too, naturally. And she didn't stay long after; a couple other kids come up and talked to her, but she probably didn't feel much like staying to skate alone, thought it made her look silly, have her boy friend dragged away from her like that. She took off her skates when the other kids left her, and turned them in to Hayes who was on duty then, and left the floor. Murphy, who was having a cigarette in the little foyer, had noticed her come out; she'd gone into the rest room—those were opposite sides of the foyer, with the ticket desk in the center. Ehrlich was sitting there again by then, he would have seen her too. She was in the rest room maybe five minutes, and come out, and left. That was maybe ten or five after.

It sure was awful, what had happened to her—to think of a guy who'd do that walking around loose. No, neither of them could say offhand if anybody left right after her—the kids came and went all the time, there was a Coke machine in the foyer. And what the hell were the cops getting at with that?—somebody from here the one killed her? If Ehrlich heard that he'd hit the ceiling—besides, they were all *kids* in here last night, like every night, and no kid had done *that*.

Dwyer had called in at one-thirty to report that Tomás Ramirez had left Liggitt Street and was sitting alone in a bar—and that it might be a good idea if the relief man sent to join Dwyer understood Spanish. Sergeant Lake's prim script appended *Sent Smith,* so that had been taken care of.

Mendoza got up restlessly and stood at the window, not really focusing on the panoramic view of the city spread out before him. He wished the Ramirez house had a phone; there was, he had thought, no such great urgency about the matter that it could not wait a couple of hours —he would stop on his way home, or Hackett could see them tomorrow. Now suddenly he felt that it *was* urgent.

It was four o'clock. He told himself he was a single-minded fool, and on his way out told Sergeant Lake he'd be back in half an hour. He drove the few blocks to Liggitt Street, and as he pulled up at the curb before the house Teresa Ramirez came out. Scarf over her hair for the rain, shabby brown coat, folded string shopping bag—on her way to market, probably for tonight's dinner. ("You got to think about them that's still alive.") He lowered the window and beckoned her.

She ducked in beside him for shelter from the rain, held the door shut but not latched. "You found out anything yet?"

"A little. Something else I want to ask you about."

"Well, O.K., only I got the shopping to do—but it don't matter, I guess, if it'll help you catch this fellow."

"I'll drive you wherever you're going. Did your sister—"

"That's real nice of you, but I don't want to put you out. But maybe you get gas allowance on the job?—excuse me, I don't mean to sound nosy, but I guess you don't get paid much, driving such an old car, and I wouldn't want you should go out of your way for me—"

"No trouble at all," said Mendoza without a smile. "Tell me—and take your time to think about it—did your sister say anything to you recently about being annoyed by a man who followed her and stared at her?"

"They did, sometimes," she said, nodding. "I told her it was account of her looking so—you know—and that Miss Weir at that school said so too. But—you mean special, just lately? I can't remember she mentioned anything like that. . . . Wait a minute though, she did! Only it wasn't a man like that, like you mean, somebody whistling at her or making smart cracks. Way she said it, it was more as if there was something sort of *funny* about it. She didn't say much—just about some guy who stared at her, got on her nerves, you know. She said she was going try find out who he was, and get him to stop."

Mendoza almost dropped his cigarette, suppressing an exclamation. "She said that? It sounds as if he were someone local then, someone who lives or works around here?"

"I don't know anything about that, I don't think she mentioned any particular place she'd seen him—except—she *did* say, and I guess that must've been what she meant, she thought she knew somebody who knew this guy. A kid over on Commerce Street, she said. . . . No, I don't know if this kid lived on Commerce or she'd maybe just seen him there, see. She just said, next time she saw him she was going to ask him who this other guy was, and tell him tell the guy stop bothering her."

"She had seen this boy with him?"

"Maybe. I don't know. She must've, or how would she know the boy knew him? All Elena said she knew about him, was his name's Danny. . . . I didn't pay much notice to it, she didn't sound like it was anything important, just—like it made her kind of mad because it was so silly."

Do we start moving at last? Mendoza asked himself. A little something, a nuance, no more—maybe nothing at all—but a starting place. He was pleased. He asked her where she wanted to go.

"Main an' First, it's nice of you. . . . You mean you think this guy might be the *one?* But it wasn't anything at all, or I'd sure have remembered and told you before! She didn't sound like she was *scared* of him or anything. You might ask that Miss Weir about it, though, if you think it's real important, because Elena did say she was going to tell her all about it—maybe she told her more than she did me."

FIVE

Martin Lindstrom put on the blue corduroy jacket that was getting too small for him, and buttoned it up slowly. He didn't feel very good.

"Where you going?" she asked sharply.

"Just out awhile." He still had fifteen cents left but that wasn't enough to get into a movie, except the one over on Main that had Mexican pictures, and those were never any good even if you could talk Mexican, nothing interesting in them.

"You be back for supper, mind! I don't want you gallivanting all over the streets alla time like these kids their mothers don't care what they're up to. Why you got to go out, Marty? It's raining something fierce, you better stay home."

"I—I—got to see a guy, 's all," he said. "One o' the guys at school, Ma, I said I'd help him with his homework, see."

"Oh." Her tight mouth relaxed a little; she was proud of his good marks at school.

It was a lie; and he didn't want to go out in the rain, but he didn't want to stay here either; he felt bad, but he wasn't sure about what exactly, just everything. He'd been feeling that way a long while, all wrong but not knowing how or where, seemed like. Of course he knew when everything had sort of started to get on top of him like this, it was after Dad went. He wondered where Dad was now. The funny thing was, and it was part of the bad feeling now, he ought to be feeling better about everything because of what that guy this morning said about finding Dad.

"Ma," he said. "Ma, you think that guy *will*—you know—find him, and—" He looked back at her from the door; right then, he dimly knew himself, he was begging her for the reassurance, Things will get like they used to be.

"I don't care if they do or not," she said, and besides the crossness in her voice there was the quivering fear he sensed from her almost all the time now. "It's not right," she whispered to herself, "asking a person all them questions. Just because you get where you got to ask relief, they think they can go nosing into ever'thing. Not as if I *like* to take charity —didn't ask till I *had* to. Nobody in our family ever been on charity before—comes hard to a respectable woman allus held her head up an' took nothing from nobody. Way they act, you'd think I was doing something wrong, ask for enough keep a roof over our heads 'n' food in our mouths. Forty dollars a month!" She sat hunched in the rocker, thin arms hugging her flat body. "County's got millions. Come poking around with their *questions* before they let me have forty dollars!"

"He only ast four-five things, Ma—"

"He ast four-five things too much! What business is it of *theirs?* No, acourse, they won't find your dad, they'll *never* find him." She said that with fear, with hope, with insistence. "If your dad was minded go off like that, he'd be real careful make it so's nobody'd ever find him, an'— an' it's seven-eight months back he went, too."

The boy was silent. He knew all sorts of things in the dumb, vague way thirteen does know—hardly aware that he knew. She made out she didn't mind Dad going off, except for the money, but she did. She was afraid and making out she wasn't. He knew there were things in her mind that for years she'd shut away somewhere, and now they'd got out, they were shapeless unseen monsters, crowding in on her and him both.

"Don't you stay out later than six," she said. "Six is supper like allus."

Then, all of a sudden, he knew why he felt bad—why he'd been feeling like this all the time since. In awful clarity it came to him that things never stayed the same, or even got back to what they'd been before. However bad things were, you were safe, knowing what a day would be like, tomorrow and next week; but it would change so you didn't ever know, and you couldn't stop it any way. *She* wanted to, and she thought she had, and now she'd found nobody ever could. One of the invisible monsters right here with them now was the threat and promise of change to come.

It was knowledge too big for thirteen, and he turned blindly and ran out, and down the dark rickety stair into the rain.

The rain was cold coming down but like mostly in California when it rained it wasn't really cold, not cold like back in Minnesota with the snow and all. The snow was kind of nice, though—Dad said—Dad didn't like California much—maybe he'd gone back east, and—

He stopped, breathless, and leaned on the window of the drugstore on the corner there, as if he was looking at the picture of the pretty girl saying Instant Protection, but he didn't see anything in the window. *Oh, Dad!* he cried in silent agony.

He'd lost Dad too, just then, and forever. It wouldn't matter if Dad came back, things would never be like they were, ever again.

"Hi, kid," said Danny behind him.

Marty turned, eager for companionship, for anybody to talk to. "Hi, Danny, wh-what's new?" It came out kind of squeaky-sounding, like a real little kid, and embarrassed him all the more because of Danny being—well, Danny.

"Nothin' much. Say, Marty—"

Mr. Cummings had already turned on the lights in the drugstore, the rain made it so dark—it was getting dark anyway, fast—and Marty could see their blurred reflections in the glass of the window. They looked funny together, him and Danny Smith, but maybe only to anybody knew them. Because he was so big beside Danny, he'd grown so fast just this last year—Dad said their family always did start to grow awful young—last month when all the kids got measured for gym in school, he'd been sixty-eight inches and some over, and that was only four inches shorter than Dad. In the glass there, sideways, he saw himself looking man-size, looming alongside of Danny—but it was the other way round inside them. Danny was like a grown-up somehow, things he knew and said and did, not having to be in any special time, and always having money, and sometimes he smoked cigarettes. It wasn't just Marty, he guessed most of the guys around here felt the same about Danny, and Danny sort of bossed them around, and they let him.

The figures in the window glass weren't sharp, just shapes like, but just the way the smaller one moved you'd know it was Danny, didn't have to really see his sharp straight nose and the way his forehead went up flat, not bulgy, into black hair that was wavy like a girl's with a permanent, or his eyes that moved a lot and were bluer than most blue eyes.

"Say, Marty, why'd you run off las' night?" Danny was asking. "At the show, alla sudden—we hadden seen it right through yet either. You scareda your ole lady, hafta get home when she says?"

"I didn't so sudden," he said quickly. Danny and a lot of the guys around here, they thought that was funny—both kinds of funny; they sort of needled you if your mother said a certain time and you did what she said. "I just decided to," he said. "It wasn't a very good pitcher anyway."

"You kiddin'? It was—"

"I seen it before," said Marty, desperately.

Danny just looked at him. Then he said, "You been down t' see where the murder was?"

Something moved a little, dark and uneasy, at the very bottom of Marty's mind. "What murder?"

"Jeez, don't you know *anything* happens? Right down at Commerce an' Humboldt, you know where that house burn' down across from the wop store. It was some girl, an' boy, was she a mess, blood all over an' one of her eyes punched right out—whoever did it sure musta been mad at her—I dint get there till after they took her away, but you could still see some o' the blood, oney the rain—"

Marty's stomach gave a little jump. He put his right hand over that place on the left sleeve of the blue corduroy coat, where the mark was. It wasn't a very big spot, but it showed dark against the light blue and it was stiff. It hadn't been there this time last night when he put the jacket on; he'd noticed it this morning.

I got it in the theayter last night, he told himself. Of course it wasn't blood. Something on the seat in there, it was.

Empty lot where a house had burned down. All of a sudden he remembered how it had been, in the dark last night: something tripping him, hard squarish cement something when he felt of it, like what was left when a house was burned. A lot of grass around it.

No, it wasn't, he said in his mind frantically, *it wasn't like that, I must remember wrong.* His mind said back at him, *Like you remembered wrong before?*

Danny was going on talking but he couldn't listen. *Please, oh, please, it can't have happened again.* It never did happen, nothing happened before, you just remembered wrong is all. You can't ever be sure in the dark, and it was night then too, of course it had to be, it was always night when—

—When things happened. A light green shirt that time because it was hot, it was summer, and the mark didn't come out when she washed it, you could still see where it'd been. That wasn't blood either, acourse it wasn't, how could it be?

He said louder than he meant to, "I—I got to go home, I better not be late for supper," and walked away fast as he could. He didn't want to hear any more about it, *or he might remember too much*. There wasn't anything *to* remember, he was just making up stories in his head to try and scare her, because he—

There were long times when he never thought about it, but when he did, it was all right there sharp and clear, more like *it* pounced at him instead of him remembering. That other night. *The first time*. Wet red mark on the green shirt and her scolding—because it was late. The big doll with the pink dress and goldy hair. And next day people talking about—what had happened—to that colored girl.

He was almost running now, trying to run away from the voice in his mind, and he blundered into a man walking the other way. The man said something and put out a hand to steady him on his feet, but Marty pulled away and dodged round the corner into Graham Court. He leaned on the broken-down picket fence of the corner house and he hit it with his fist, the breath sobbing in his throat, tears squeezing out from tight-shut eyes.

"I *tole* her," he said low in his throat. "I *tried* tell her!" It was all he could do, wasn't it? What else could thirteen years old do?

But there wasn't much to tell, that time or this time—he really remembered, knew his own self. She said so. He didn't know, he must've remembered wrong, or he was a wicked boy just trying to scare her. Making up stories that couldn't be so.

And she washed the green shirt but the mark still showed after.

After a while Marty straightened and went on, slowly, down the little cul-de-sac. He didn't want to go home; just two things pulled him that way, drearily, as they had before. Habit, and Dad's voice that time a while back, slow and easy like always, Dad saying, "You want to be nice t' your ma, Marty, an' help her all you can, an' don't do nothing to worry her. I know it ain't easy, times, but things ain't easy for her neither. You got to remember she come of folks had a lot more than the Lindstroms, back home—her pa Ole Larsen was a rich man, eleven hundert acres he had all good land too, an' his girls never wanted for nothing. Maybe them Larsens did give theirselves airs, but maybe they had reason too, an' anyways your ma never had cause to makeshift an' scrimp on nothing, till she married me—an' it ain't exactly been a easy row to hoe for her, not noways. I know she gets cross-tongued once in a while, but you got to remember things is hard for her too."

That had been before—anything happened. If it had.

Marty went up the stairs of the apartment building slow, hanging onto the shaky railing. He felt another thing he'd got to feeling almost all the time lately, and that was as if there were two of him: one was a little kid whose ma was right whatever she said or did, just naturally because she was Ma—and the other was, well, nearest he could come was Marty-separate-from-Ma, who knew Ma might be wrong about some things. He tried to push that Marty away, because he didn't want to *really* know that, but seemed like that Marty was getting stronger and stronger in him. At the same time there were two other Martys, the one that was just a wicked little boy making up stories—and the one that knew different.

That one was scared, deep and cold inside. Because it was all his fault, must be, even if he'd never meant, never known, if he'd just sort of forgot for a while—

And the bad feeling had begun maybe when Dad went away, but what had made it *so* bad ever since was—that first time, back there on Tappan Street on a breathless night in late September.

He'd *had* to tell her. Things happened that were too big for you, frightening and confusing, that you couldn't do anything about yourself —you told your ma or dad, and they knew what to do. Only Dad hadn't been there.

And there was a third place the real bad feeling started, after she wouldn't believe, wouldn't listen—when she did something she'd never done before, ever: when she went out and bought a newspaper, and read about—It. And said like to herself in a funny kind of whisper, "Only some nigger girl, anyways. Prob'ly trash—just trash."

And the next day she'd gone and found this place for them to move, account it was cheaper, she said.

He got to the dark top of the stairs, and he thought frantically, I *got* to tell her. I got to try. Because—

He was sick and shaking with fear, with guilt, with the weight of a thing thirteen couldn't bear alone. The door was locked like always and he knocked and she said sharp, "Who is it?"

"It's me, Ma, let me in." And there wasn't any other way to say it than he did, then: "Ma, it's happened again! Ma—please listen—I didn't *mean* to—I never meant nothing to happen—but it must've, because—"

She just stood and stared at him.

"—Because it *was* blood on my coat, 's morning." He gulped and went on through the lump in his throat, "And—and the place they found—it—it was right where I—"

The fear pulled her face all tight and cross-looking for a minute, but then it changed to being mad at him, and she said quick, "I don't listen to a boy tells lies!"

He looked at her dumbly. He knew what else she'd say, like she had before; but this time he knew something else—that what she said wasn't just at him, it was at that place *she* had way inside her where she knew it was so—it was to shut the door to that place and forget it was there at all. And now she was asking him to help her, seemed like, not mad any more but *asking*.

"You get washed an' eat your supper while it's hot, an' then you set right down to that schoolwork you shoulda done last night—I'm allus tellin' you, don't want to end up like your dad, not enough schoolin' for a decent job—you're a real smart boy, Marty, you take after my folks, an' last thing I do I see you get educated good, maybe even college. But you got to remember you don't know ever'thing yet, see, an'—an' kids get mixed up in their minds, like, that's all—"

He whispered, "I'm not awful hungry, Ma."

And all the while the secret was there in the room with them, neither of them daring to look at it open: that she wouldn't see for what it really was, that he was getting more and more afraid of—that they had to live with somehow.

Danny stood there by the drugstore awhile after Marty left. On top of his mind he thought, That big lummox of a Lindstrom kid, sure a dumb one. But most of him was occupied with the job he was on, and he felt kind of tensed-up because it was the first time his dad had taken much notice of him, acted like he was a person with any sense, and he wanted to do this right.

It had been a big surprise to him to feel the way he did. Asked him last week, he'd have said it wasn't nothing to him, whatever his dad did or said—been three and a half years since he'd laid eyes on him, anyways—and that went other way round too, they'd always just sort of stayed out of each other's way. Same as with his mother, but she was just a nothing, like a handful of water, and there was at least something *to* his dad. And he'd felt a new, funny feeling when his dad said that: *Kind of a sharp kid, you can maybe be some use to me.*

Besides, this was different from hooking little stuff off store counters or stripping cars at night. This was a big job.

When the man came, he spotted him right off from what his dad had said he looked like; but he waited awhile, just went on looking in the drugstore window. The guy stopped and stood there too, waiting, under the store canopy. Nobody came past after him, and when Danny walked down the block there weren't any cops watching from alleys, nobody at all. It was all going just like his dad had planned, but of course you had to play it smart. Danny walked back to the drugstore; he didn't stop by the guy waiting there, just slowed down, and he said, "He's changed his mind, mister, he says meet him at the Paradise Bar on Second, right now."

The man said, "What?" sort of dumb and surprised, and then he made as if to grab for him, but Danny slid away in the dark, into the alley round the corner, and waited. After a minute the man started to walk up toward Second Street, not very fast; he looked back a couple of times, but once away from the corner lights it was dark and Danny stayed close up against the buildings.

On Second Street there were more lights, but people on the sidewalk, too, to hide him; he stayed farther behind, but he could still see the guy when he turned in under the pink neon sign that said PARADISE. So that was O.K. And no cops.

Danny turned and sauntered back to the corner; another man stood there, looking in the window of the liquor store. "O.K.," said Danny. "He's in, and no cops."

"You sure?"

"You think I can't smell a cop?"

The man relaxed a little, grinned. "Maybe you ain't so smart as you think, but I guess you're not so dumb neither. Chip off the ole block like they say, huh? O.K., you go along. Now I just let the guy stew awhile an' get real worried." He went back to looking in the window.

Inside the bar a jukebox was pounding, and the blood-hammer in Morgan's head began to keep time with it. He went all the way in to the last of the little booths opposite the bar, and sat down; the waiter who came up gave him a sour look for taking a booth instead of going to the bar, but he didn't say anything and he'd come over promptly because Morgan was a lot better dressed than the usual customer in here and might be drinking something besides beer or wine.

Morgan asked for whiskey, but when it came he just left it there on the table; he'd never been much of a drinker and not at all the last eight years, since— Which was a useless gesture, maybe: morbid.

He sat there and waited. The place wasn't crowded on a rainy night, only ten or a dozen men at the bar. It was stuffy, too hot after the street, and he realized he still had his coat on, slid out of the booth to take it off, fold it beside him. The clock on one side of the bar said half-past six, but Morgan knew he'd better keep his eye off the clock— the man wanted him to sweat, and might not show up for hours. In his mind he knew that, while all the rest of him was tense and agonizing to get *to* it, have it done, the ultimate doom arranged.

He lit a cigarette and set himself to wait, and wait, and wait some more; and his intellect told him further (methodical, plodding Morgan) that if he let himself go over and over this thing emotionally, he'd be in just the softened-up state the bastard wanted, at the end. So he made himself think about anything, everything else than Sue and Janny.

The first thing he seized on to think about was that boy. Using a youngster, for this. That was a conventional thought out of the small neat circle of life he'd always lived in up to now: correction, up to being on the job he held now, for that (even before his own private nightmare) should certainly have taught him about lives lived elsewhere and otherwise, where children weren't automatically screened from the uglier realities because they were children.

It didn't occur to him that the boy was just relaying a message, didn't know what he was mixed into: he'd seen his expression. And there were two things about that, that turned this into something like a real nightmare where ordinary sights and sounds made no sense or a new monstrous kind of sense. That boy hadn't realized, maybe, that there on the rain-swept empty corner, as he swaggered past Morgan, the lights from the store fell unshadowed on him. Oh, yes, the boy had known just what he was doing.

Morgan looked down at his hands on the wet, scarred table, and as he looked they began to shake violently, so he put them in his lap.

Quite a handsome boy. Even in that deceiving light, he had seen the regular features, fair skin with the black hair and blue eyes all the more emphasized for it, the thick brows going up in little wings at the end. He knew that curve by heart, the very angle, *Janny's brows winging up at the corners of Janny's blue eyes—*

Not to think about Janny, or Sue. Janny, just about now, being tucked into bed with that ridiculous stuffed tiger Mrs. Gunn had got her, that she was so crazy about. Warm and powdery from her bath, buttoned into the woolly blue pajamas.

That boy had just had on jeans and a leather jacket. That boy who was, who must be—

For God's sake! said his mind to him savagely.

He glanced sideways at the clock. It was twenty-five minutes to seven.

He remembered a while ago, couldn't remember where, reading an article on juvenile delinquents that had interested him. It was funny, there was a clear picture in his mind of himself saying to Sue, "The man's got something there, you know," but he couldn't recall now who the author was, some official or a senator or whatever. Anyway. Often the most intelligent children, it said, those with imagination and ability, the nonconforming minds any society needs—but for this and that reason turned in the wrong direction.

All right, yes; up to a point; some of them, the leaders. Most, well—

Hell, maybe the man was right.

The boy—*led to Janny and he mustn't think about Janny*. Quick, something else.

Another boy. Barging into him in the street there, dodging past. Didn't know it was a boy—big as a man, as tall as Morgan himself— until he heard the sobbing light breath, had a glimpse of him close in the reflected street light. That was the Lindstrom boy, that one; they lived around here, of course. Clumsy big ox of a kid, one of those got all his growth at once, early, and wouldn't quite learn how to handle his size for a while; and still so baby-faced, any roundish, smooth, freckle-nosed thirteen-year-old face, that you expected to see half a foot below where this one was. Lindstrom was what, Danish, they grew big men mostly.

Generalizing again, he thought; you couldn't, of course. The archetype Scandinavian wasn't a wife-deserter, but this one was. That report wasn't made up yet either, and he had to have it ready Monday morning for Gunn. . . . Something queer there about the Lindstroms, something that smelled wrong, hard to say what. It could be another case of collusion to get money out of the county, but Morgan didn't think so; he didn't think that, whatever was behind the indefinable tension he'd sensed in that place, it came from dishonesty. Anything so—uncomplicated—as dishonesty. The woman was a type he knew: transplanted countrywoman, sometimes ignorant, frequently stubborn at clinging to obsolete ways and beliefs, always with a curious rigid pride. That type might be dishonest about anything else, but not about money.

Invariably the first thing that kind said to him was, "I've never asked nor took charity before." Marion Lindstrom had said that. She hadn't told him much else.

But the report had to be made out, and the hunt started for Eric John Lindstrom.

It was a quarter to seven. Morgan kept himself from watching the door; his mind scrabbled about desperately for something else irrelevant to occupy it. He heard the door open, couldn't stop himself looking up to see: outside he was still uncomfortably warm, but there was an ice-cold weight in his stomach, and it moved a little when he saw the man who'd come in—a stranger, not the one.

And right there something odd happened to him. Suddenly he knew what was behind the queerness he'd sensed in that Lindstrom woman, this morning. The few minutes he'd been there, talked to the woman and the boy. It was fear: secret fear. He knew it now because it was his own feeling: the sure recognition was emotional.

He thought without much interest, I wonder what *they're* afraid of.

At seven o'clock, because of the looks he was getting from the barman, he drank the whiskey and ordered another. It was cheap bar whiskey, raw. At a quarter past seven he ordered a third; he decided the whiskey was just what he'd needed, because his mind had started to work again to some purpose, and suddenly too he was no longer afraid. That was a hell of a note, come to think, getting in a cold sweat the way he had without ever even considering whether there were ways and means to deal with this, come out safe. What had got into him, anyway? There must be a way, and what he'd told himself this morning still went: to hell with any moral standards. If—

When at half-past seven someone slid into the booth opposite him, he'd almost finished a fourth whiskey. He looked up almost casually to meet the eyes of the man across the table, and he wondered with self-contempt that didn't show on his face why he'd ever been afraid of this man.

"You been doin' some thinkin', Morgan?" The man grinned at him insolently. "Ready to talk business?"

"Yes," said Morgan, cold and even. "I've been doing some thinking, but not about the money. I told you before, I haven't got that kind of money."

The man who called himself Smith laughed, as the barman came up, and he said, "You'll buy me a drink anyways. Whiskey."

The barman looked at Morgan, who shook his head; he'd had just the right amount now to balance him where he was. "Don't give me that," said Smith when the man was gone. "You're doin' all right. You got money to throw away once, you got it to throw away twice."

Money to throw away . . . But that was perfectly logical reasoning, thought Morgan, if you happened to look at things that way. He looked at Smith there, a couple of feet across the table, and he thought that in any dimension that mattered they were so far away from each other that communication was impossible. He found, surprisingly, that he was intellectually interested in Smith, in what made him tick. He wondered what Smith's real name was: he did not think the name the woman had used two years ago, Robertson, was the real name any more than Smith. Smith's eyes were gray: though his skin was scarred with the marks of old acne and darkened from lack of soap and water, it was more fair than dark. And his eyebrows curved up in little wings toward the temples. Morgan stared at them, fascinated: Smith had worn a hat pulled low when he'd seen him before, and the eyebrows had been hidden. The eyebrows were, of course, more confirmation of Smith's identity. With detached interest Morgan thought, Might be Irish, that coloring.

"You know," he said, "you might not be in such a strong position as you think. Your story wouldn't sound so good to a judge—not along with mine."

"Then what're you doin' here?" asked Smith softly.

And that of course was the point. Because it was a no man's land in law, this particular thing. Anyone might look at Smith, listen to what that upright citizen Richard Morgan had to say, and find it incredible that any intelligent human agency could hesitate at making a choice between. But it wasn't a matter of men—it was the way the law read. And in curious juxtaposition to the impersonal letter of the law, there was also the imbecilic sentimentality, the mindless lip service to convention —the convention that there was in the physical facts of parturition some magic to supersede individual human qualities. He could not take the chance, gamble Janny's whole future, Sue's sanity maybe, on the hope that some unknown judge might possess a little common sense. Because there was also the fact that, as the law took a dim view of buying and selling human beings, it didn't confine the guilt to just one end of the transaction.

Smith knew that, without understanding it or needing to understand it; but the one really vital fact Smith knew was that there had never been a legal adoption. They had hesitated, procrastinated, fearing the inevitable questions . . .

"—A business proposition, that's all," Smith was saying. "Strickly legal." His tone developed a little resentment, he was saying he had a legitimate grievance. "You made a Goddamn sharp deal with my wife, a hundred lousy bucks, an' you got away with it, she didn't have no choice, on account she was up against it with me away like I was, flat on my back in the hospital I was, an' the bills runnin' up alla time— you took advantage of her not knowin' much about business, all right! I figure it same way like a bank would, Morgan—innerest, they call it, see?"

There was an appalling mixture of naïve satisfaction and greed in his eyes; Morgan looked away. (Interest, just how did you figure that kind of interest? Twenty-six months of a squirming warm armful that weighed fourteen pounds, eighteen, twenty-two, and a triumphant twenty-nine-and-a-half?—he forgot what the latest figure was, only remembered Sue's warm chuckle, reporting it. Twenty-six months of sticky curious baby-fat fingers poking into yours, into the paper you were trying to read, into what was almost a dimple at the corner of Sue's mouth: of the funny solemn look in the blue eyes: of ten pink toes splashing in a sudsy tub. That would be quite a thing to figure in percentages.)

"You can raise the dough if you got to," said Smith.

"Not ten thousand," said Morgan flatly. "I might manage five." And that was a deliberate lie; he couldn't raise five hundred.

"I don't go for no time-payments, Morgan." The gray eyes were bleak. "You heard me the first time. I give you a couple days think about it, but don't give me no more stall now. Put up or shut up."

Poker, thought Morgan. Bluff?—that he'd bring it open, go to law? You couldn't take the chance; and in this last five minutes it had come to him that he didn't have to. There was only one way to deal with Smith, and Morgan knew how it could be done, now: he saw the way. He could take care of Smith once for all time, and then they would be safe: if necessary later, he could handle the woman easier, he remembered her as an indecisive nonentity. There was, when you came to think of it, something to be said for being an upright citizen with a clean record. And it would not trouble his conscience at all. In the days he'd worn Uncle's uniform, he had probably killed better men, and for less reason.

There was hard suspicion now in the gray eyes; Morgan looked away, down to his empty glass, quickly. He'd been acting too calm, too controlled; he must make Smith believe in his capitulation. He made his tone angry and afraid when he said, low, "All right, all right—I heard you the first time! I—I guess if I cash in those bonds—I might—but I'll get something for my money! You'll sign a legal agreement before you touch—"

"O.K., I don't mind that."

"You've got to give me time, I can't raise it over Sunday—"

"Monday night."

"No, that's not long enough—"

"Monday," said Smith. "That's the time you got—use it. Make it that same corner, seven o'clock, with the cash—an' I don't take nothing bigger than fives, see?" He slid out of the booth, stood up.

"Yes, damn you," said Morgan wearily. Without another word Smith turned and walked toward the door.

Morgan took out his wallet below the level of the table, got out the one five in it, held it ready. When Smith looked back, going out, Morgan was still sitting there motionless; but the second Smith turned out of sight to the left, Morgan was up, quick and quiet. He laid the five on the table and got into his coat between there and the door; outside, he turned sharp left and hugged the building, spotting the back he wanted half a block ahead.

Because Kenneth Gunn, who had been a police officer for forty years and sure to God ought to know, had once said to him, "They're a stupid bunch. Once in a long while you get a really smart one, but they're few and far between. The majority are just plain stupid—they can't or won't think far enough ahead."

Maybe this was Smith's first venture into crookedness, but it should qualify him for inclusion in that; Morgan hoped so. There was a chance that the boy was posted to watch, of course; but he had to risk that. The precautions about the meeting place, beforehand, were to assure Smith that Morgan came alone: and satisfied of that, Smith's mind might have gone no further.

Smith had made another mistake too, one frequently made by men like him. They always underestimated the honest men.

It had stopped raining and turned very cold. This was the slack hour when not many people were out, and it was easy to keep Smith spotted, from pool to pool of reflected neon lights on the sidewalk. If he had looked back, he'd have found it as easy to spot Morgan; but he didn't look back. He walked fast, shoulders hunched against the cold, round the next corner to a dark side street.

When the trail ended twenty minutes later Morgan told himself, almost incredulously, that his luck had turned; he was due for a few breaks. . . . He'd had a job to keep Smith in sight and still stay far enough back, down these dark streets, and he'd lost all sense of direction after they got off Second. But at that last corner, stopping in shadow, watching Smith cross the narrow street ahead, Morgan realized suddenly where they were. He was at the junction of Humboldt and Foster, a block down from Commerce; it looked as if Humboldt ended here, where Foster ran straight across it like the top bar on a T, but it only took a jog, started again half a block to the left. What made the jog necessary was Graham Court, a dreary little cul-de-sac whose mouth gaped narrowly at him directly opposite. He'd been here before, just this morning. And Smith was going into Graham Court.

Morgan jaywalked across Foster Street and under the lamppost whose bulb had been smashed by kids, and into Graham Court. It was only wide enough for foot traffic: there were three dark, dank, big frame houses on each side, cheap rooming places, and right across the end of the court, a four-story apartment building of dirty yellow stucco. A dim light from one of the ground-floor windows there showed Smith as he climbed the steps and went in.

"I will be damned," said Morgan half-aloud. Luck turning his way? —with a vengeance! The building where the Lindstrom woman lived: where on his legitimate comings and goings Richard Morgan, that upright and law-abiding citizen, had every reason to be, a real solid beautiful excuse, good as gold.

And that was just fine, better than he could have hoped for: he saw clear and confident how it would go, now.

SIX

Mendoza realized they'd have to let the Danny go: it might not be impossible to find the Danny Elena Ramirez had known, if it would be difficult; but more to the point, there was no way of identifying the right Danny. What was interesting about this matter was that by implication it narrowed the locale.

He had formed some very nebulous ideas—mere ghosts of hypotheses—overnight, out of the evidence a second murder inevitably added to the evidence from a first one; and he thought that a restricted locale was natural, if you looked at it a certain way. At least, it was a fifty-fifty chance, depending on just what kind of lunatic they were hunting. If he was the kind (disregarding the psychiatrists' hairsplitting solemn terms) whose impulse to kill was triggered suddenly and at random, the odds were that his victim would be someone in the area where he lived or worked: and considering the hour, probably the former. If he was the kind capable of planning ahead, then the place of the crime meant nothing, or very little, for he might have cunning enough to choose a place unconnected with him. But to balance that there was the fact that madmen capable of sustained cunning generally chose victims by some private logic: they were the ones appointed by God to rid the world of prostitutes, or Russian spies, or masquerading Martians. Like that. And to do so, they had to be aware of the victims as individuals.

So there was a chance that this one, whatever kind he was, lived somewhere fairly near the place he had killed. And that might be of enormous help, for it suggested that he had lived (or worked) somewhere near the place Carol Brooks had been killed last September. If he was the man who had killed her, and Mendoza thought he was.

Sunday was only another day to Mendoza; he lay in bed awhile thinking about all this, and also about Alison Weir, until the sleek brown Abyssinian personage who condescended to share the apartment with him, the green-eyed Bast, leapt onto his stomach and began to knead the blanket, fixing him with an accusing stare. He apologized to her for inattention; he got up and laid before her the morning tribute of fresh liver; he made coffee. Eight o'clock found him, shaven and spruce, poring over a small-scale map of the city in his office.

When Hackett came in at nine o'clock, he listened in silence to Alison Weir's contribution of the *muchacho extraño* who stared, and grunted over the neat penciled circles on the map. In the center of one was the twenty-two-hundred block of Tappan Street, and in the center of the other the junction of Commerce and Humboldt. Each covered approximately a mile in diameter, to the map scale: call it a hundred and fifty square blocks.

"Now isn't that pretty!" said Hackett. "And where would you get the army to check all that territory—and for what? The idea, that I go along with, and if your pretty circles happened to have prettier centers, say like Los Feliz and Western, I'd say we might come up with something, just on a check to see who'd moved where recently. But you know what you got here!" He stabbed a blunt forefinger at the first circle. "About half of this area is colored, and none of it, white or black, is very fancy. Which also goes with bells on for the other area. Out on the Strip, or along Wilshire, a lot of places, you've got people in settled lives, and they leave records behind. City directory, phone book, gas company, rent receipts, forwarding addresses. Here—" he shrugged.

"You needn't tell me," said Mendoza ruefully. "This is just a little exercise in academic theory." In these networks of streets, some of the most thickly populated in the city, drifted the anonymous ones: people who wandered from one casual job to another, who for various reasons (not always venal) were sometimes known by different names to different people, and who owned no property. Landlords were not always concerned with keeping records, and most rent was paid in cash. There were also, of course, settled, householders, responsible people. For economic reasons or racial reasons, or both, they lived cheek-by-jowl, crowded thick; they came and went, and because they were of little concern to anyone as individuals, their comings and goings went largely unnoticed.

"If we had a name—but we'd get nothing for half a year's hunt, not knowing what to look for. *¡Qué se le ha de hacer!*—it can't be helped! But if the general theory's right, there's a link somewhere."

"I'll go along with you," said Hackett, "but I'll tell you, I think we'll get it as corroborative evidence after we've caught up with him by another route. Somebody'll see a newspaper cut, and come in to tell us that our John Smith is also Henry Brown who used to live on Tappan Street. We can't get at it from this end, there's damn-all to go on."

"I agree with you—though there's such a thing as luck. However!" Mendoza shoved the map aside. "What did you get out of the Wades?"

"Something to please you." Circumstantially, the Wades were counted out. Ehrlich and his two attendants at the rink had seen father and son leave, and agreed on the time as "around ten to ten." The girl had been a good ten or twelve minutes after them. By the narrowest reckoning it was a twenty-minute drive to the Wades' home, probably nearer thirty, and a neighbor had happened to be present in the house on their arrival, an outside witness who was positive of the time as ten twenty-five. There hadn't been time, even if you granted they'd done it together, which was absurd. . . . The Wades, *pater* and *mater familias,* might be snobs, with the usual false and confused values of snobs (though much of their social objection to the Ramirez girl was under-standable: Mendoza, supposing he were ever sufficiently rash or un-wary to acquire a wife and family, would probably feel much the same himself). But it could not be seriously conjectured that a respectable middle-aged bookkeeper had done murder (and such a murder) to avoid acquiring a daughter-in-law addicted to double negatives and peroxide. And if he had, it would hardly be in collusion with the boy.

"The boy," said Hackett, "hasn't got the blood in him to kill a mouse in a trap anyway—all you got to do is look at him."

"I'll take your word for it," said Mendoza absently. He wasn't inter-ested in the boy, never had been much; the Wades were irrelevant, but he was just as pleased that by chance there was evidence to show that. And the Wades ought to be very damned thankful for it too: they'd probably never realize it, but without that evidence the boy could have found himself in bad trouble. From Mendoza's viewpoint that would have been regrettable chiefly because it would have diverted the investi-gation into a blind alley. They had wasted enough official time as it was.

He looked again at his map, and sighed. The lunatic—of this or that sort—was his own postulation, and he could be wrong: that had some-times happened. Ideally an investigator should be above personal bias, which—admitted or unconscious—inevitably slanted the interpretation of evidence. And yet evidence almost always had to be interpreted—full circle back to personal opinion. There was always the human ele-ment, and also what Dr. Rhine might call the X factor, which Men-doza, essentially a fatalist as well as a gambler, thought of as a kind of cosmic card-stacking. Much of the time plodding routine and teamwork led you somewhere eventually; but it was surprising how often the sudden hunch, the inspired guess, the random coincidence, took you round by a shorter way. And sometimes the extra aces in the deck fell to the opponent's hand, and there was nothing you could do about that. The law of averages had nothing to do with it.

"I dropped in to see if the autopsy report's come through . . . oh, well, suppose we couldn't expect it over Sunday. Nothing much in it anyway. Back to the treadmill—" Hackett got up. "I've still got some of the kids to see, ones at the rink that night."

"The rink," said Mendoza, still staring at his map. "Yes. We'll probably get the autopsy report by tonight—the inquest's been set for Tuesday. Yes—*Vaya . . . todo es posible*. Yes, you get on with the routine, as becomes your rank—me, I'm taking the day off from everything else, to shuffle through this deck again, *por decirlo así*—maybe there's a marked card to spot."

He brooded over the map another minute when Hackett had gone, and penciled in a line connecting the two circles. He shrugged and said to himself, Maybe, maybe—folded the map away, got his hat and coat and went out.

Downstairs, as he paused to adjust the gray Homburg, a couple of reporters cornered him; they asked a few desultory questions about the Ramirez girl, but their real interest was in Sergeant Galeano's husband-killer, who was of a socially prominent clan. The more sensational of the evening papers had put Elena Ramirez on the front page, but it wasn't a good carry-over story—they couldn't make much out of a Hartners' stock-room girl, and the boy friend wasn't very colorful either. The conservative papers had played it down, an ordinary back-street mugging, and by tomorrow the others would relegate it to the middle pages. They had the socialite, and the freight yard corpse, besides a couple of visiting dignitaries and the Russians; and a two-bit mugging in the Commerce Street area, that just happened to turn into a murder, was nothing very new or remarkable.

Maneuvering the Ferrari out into Main Street, Mendoza thought that was a point of view, all right: almost any way you looked at it, it was an unimportant, uninteresting kill. No glamor, no complexity, nothing to attract either the sensationalists or the detective-fiction fans. In fact, the kind of murder that happened most frequently. . . . The press had made no connection between Elena Ramirez and Carol Brooks. No, they weren't interested; but if the cosmic powers had stacked the deck this time, and that one stayed free to kill again, and again, eventually some day he would achieve the scare headlines, and then—*de veras, es lo de siempre,* Mendoza reflected sardonically, the mixture as before: our stupid, blundering police!

Once off the main streets here, away from the blinding gleam of the used-car lots, the screamer ads plastered along store-fronts, these were quiet residential streets, middle-class, unremarkable. Most of the houses neatly maintained, if shabby: most with carefully kept flower plots in front. Along the quiet Sunday sidewalks, dressed-up children on the way to Sunday school, others not so dressed up running and shouting at play—householders working in front gardens this clear morning after the rain. This was all Oriental along here, largely Japanese. When he stopped at an intersection a pair of high-school-age girls crossed in front of him—"But honestly it isn't fair, ten whole pages of English Lit, even if it is on the week end! She's a real fiend for homework—" One had a ponytail, one an Italian cut; their basic uniform of flat shell pumps, billowy cotton skirts and cardigans, differed only in color.

At the next corner he turned into Tappan Street; this wasn't the start of it, but the relevant length for him, this side of Washington Boulevard. He drove slow and idle, as if he'd all the time in the world to waste, wasn't exactly sure where he was heading: and of course he wasn't, essentially. It was a long street and it took him through a variety of backgrounds.

Past rows of frame and stucco houses, lower-middle-class-respectable houses, where the people on the street were Oriental, and then brown and black; there, late-model cars sat in most driveways and the people were mostly dressed up for Sunday. Past bigger, older, shabbier houses with Board-and-Room signs, rank brown grass in patches, and broken sidewalks: dreary courts of semi-detached single-story rental units, stucco boxes scabrous for need of paint: black and brown kids in shabbier, even ragged clothes, more raucous in street play. A lot of all that, block after block. Past an intersection where a main street crossed and a Catholic church, a liquor store, a chiropractor's office and a gas station shared the corners. Past the same kind of old, shoddy houses and courts, for many more blocks, but here the people on the street white. Then a corner which marked some long-ago termination of the street: where it continued, across, there were no longer tall old camphorwoods lining it; the parking was bare. The houses were a little newer, a little cleaner: they gave way to solid blocks of smallish apartment buildings, and all this again was settled middle-class, and again the faces in the street black and brown.

At the next intersection, he caught the light and sat waiting for it, staring absently at the wooden bench beside the bus-stop sign on the near left corner. Its back bore a faded admonition to Rely on J. Atwood and Son, Morticians, for a Dignified Funeral. There, that night, Carol Brooks had got off the bus on her way home from work, and some time later started down Tappan Street. She had had only three blocks to walk, but she had met—something—on the way, and so she hadn't got home. . . . The car behind honked at him angrily; the light had changed.

Across the intersection, he idled along another block and a half, slid gently into the curb and took his time over lighting a cigarette. Three single-family houses from the corner, there sat two duplexes, frame bungalows just alike, one white and one yellow. They were, or had been, owned by the widowed Mrs. Shadwell who lived in one side of the yellow one. On that September night the left-hand side of the white one had been empty of tenants, the tenants in the other side had been out at a wedding reception, the tenants in the left side of the yellow duplex had been giving a barbecue supper in their back yard, and Mrs. Shadwell, who was deaf, had taken off her hearing aid. So just what had happened along here, as Carol Brooks came by, wasn't very clear; if she'd been accosted, exchanged any talk or argument with her killer, had warning of attack and called for help, there'd been no one to hear. She'd been found just about halfway between the walks leading to the two front doors of the white duplex, at twenty minutes past nine, by a dog-walker from the next block: she had then been dead for between thirty minutes and an hour.

It occurred to Mendoza that he was simply wasting time in the vague superstitious hope that the cosmic powers would tap his shoulder and drop that extra ace into his lap. He tossed his cigarette out the window, which was now by law a misdemeanor carrying a fifty-dollar fine, and drove on a block and a half: glanced at the neat white frame bungalow where Carol Brooks had lived, and turned left at the next corner. This was a secondary business street, and it marked one of the boundaries: that side Negro, this side white. The streets deteriorated sharply on the white side, he knew, lined with old apartment buildings only just not describable as tenements. He turned left again and wandered back parallel to Tappan, turned again and then again and came to the corner where the bus stopped, past the two duplexes, and drew into the curb in front of the bungalow numbered 2214.

A woman came up the sidewalk from the opposite direction, turned in at the white house, hesitated and glanced at the car, and turned back toward it. Mendoza got out and took off his hat. "Mrs. Demarest. I wondered if you still lived here."

"Why, where else would I be?" She was a tall, slim, straight-backed woman, and had once perhaps been beautiful: the bones of beauty were still there, in her smooth high forehead, delicate regular features, small mouth. Her skin was the color of well-creamed coffee. She was neat, even almost smart, in tailored navy-blue dress and coat, small gold earrings. She might be seventy, she might be older, but age had touched her lightly; her voice was firm, her eyes intelligent. "It's Mr. Mendoza," she said. "Or I should say 'Lieutenant.' You know, if I was a superstitious woman, Lieutenant, I'd say there's more in it than meets the eye, you turning up. Did you want to see me about something?"

"I don't know. There's been another," he said abruptly. "I think the same one."

"Another colored girl?" she asked calmly.

"No. And miles away, over on Commerce Street."

"That one," she said, nodding. "I think you'd best come in, and I'll tell you. It's nothing much, though it's queer—but it's something you didn't hear about before, you see. At first I thought I might write you a letter about it, and then I said to myself"—they were halfway up the walk to the house, and he'd taken the brown-paper bag of groceries from her—"I thought, it's not important, I'd best not trouble you. But as you're here, you might as well hear about it." She had been away from Bermuda half her life, but her tongue still carried the flavor, the broad A's, the interchange of V's and W's, the clipped British vowels. She unlocked the front door and they went into the living-room he remembered, furniture old but originally good and well cared for. "If you'll just fetch that right back to the kitchen, Lieutenant—you'll have a cup of coffee with me, we might as well be comfortable and it's always hot on the back of the stove. Sit down, I'll just tend to the Duke here and then be with you."

The cat surveying him with cold curiosity from the hallway door was a large black neutered tom; he established himself on the kitchen chair opposite Mendoza and continued to stare. "I didn't remember he was the Duke," said Mendoza.

"The Duke of Wellington really, because he always thought so almighty high of himself, you know. We got him Carol's second year in high, and she was doing history about it then. Cats, they're like olives, seem like—either you're crazy about them or you just can't abide them. I remembered you like them. It's why I was out, after his evaporated milk. Fresh he won't look at, and the evaporated he lets set just so long till it's thick the way he fancies it. You see now, he knows I've just poured it, he won't go near. You take milk or sugar?—well, I always take it black too, you get the flavor."

She set the filled cups on the table and sat in the chair across from him. "You'll have missed your granddaughter," he said. It was another absurd superstitious feeling, that if he asked, brought her to the point, it would indeed be nothing at all.

"Well, I do, of course. Sometimes it doesn't seem right that there the Duke should be sitting alive, and her gone. It'd be something to believe in some kind of religion, think there was a God Who'd some reason, some plan. I never came to it somehow, but maybe there is. I've had two husbands and raised six children, and luckier than most in all of them—and you could say I've worked hard. It was a grief to lose my youngest son, that was Carol's dad, but I had to figure I'd five left, and the other grandchildren too. Take it all in all, there's been more good than bad—and what you can't change, you'd best learn to live with content. I enjoy life still, and I don't want to die while I've still my health and my mind, but you know, Lieutenant, I won't be too sorry in a way when the time comes, because I must say I *am* that curious about the afterward part."

"It's a point of view," he agreed amusedly. "So am I now and then, but I'd rather be curious than dead."

She laughed, with a fine gleam of even white teeth. "Ah, you're lucky, you're half my age! But I said I'd something to tell you. It's just a queer sort of thing, maybe doesn't mean much." She sipped and put down her cup. "Maybe you'll remember that that night when Carol was killed, I told you I hadn't been too worried about her being late home, because she'd said something about shopping along Hawke Street, that'd be when she got off the bus. It was a Monday night, and all the stores along there, they stay open till nine Mondays and Fridays. There's a few nice little stores, and it's handy—not so crowded as downtown, and most everything you'd want, drugstore and Woolworth's, besides a Hartners', and a shoe store and a couple of nice independent dress shops, and Mr. Grant at the stationery-and-card place even keeps a little circulating library—and then there's Mrs. Breen's."

He remembered the name vaguely; after a moment he said, "The woman who had a stroke."

"That's right. She's had that little shop a long while, and sometimes you find things there that're, you know, unusual, different from the big stores. You mightn't remember, no reason you should, but on the one side she's got giftware as they call it—china figures and fancy ash trays and vases and such—and on the other she's got babies' and children's things. Real nice things, with handwork on them, the clothes, and reasonable too. You'll remember that your men asked around in all the shops if Carol had been in that night, to get some idea of the time and all. And that was the very night Mrs. Breen had a stroke, so you couldn't ask her if Carol'd been in there, and it didn't seem important because you found out that she'd been in the drugstore and a couple of other places."

"Yes—nothing unusual anywhere, no one speaking to her, and she didn't mention anything out of the way to the clerks who waited on her."

"That's so. It didn't seem as if Mrs. Breen could've told any more. She was alone in her place, you know, and all right as could be when her daughter come at nine or a bit before, to help her close up and drive her home. It was while they were locking up she had her stroke, poor thing, and they took her off to hospital and she's been a long while getting back on her feet. Well, Lieutenant—let me hot up your coffee— what I'm getting to is this. It went out of my mind at the time, and when I thought of it, I hadn't the heart to bother about it, didn't seem important somehow—and Mrs. Breen was still in the hospital and her daughter'd closed up the shop. It'd have meant asking her, Mrs. Robbins I mean, to go all through the accounts and so on, and with her so worried and living clear the other side of town too, I just let it go."

"You thought Carol had been in and bought something there?"

"It was for Linda Sue," she said, and the troubled look in her eyes faded momentarily. "My first great-grandchild, see, my granddaughter May—that's Carol's cousin, May White—Linda Sue's her little girl. May and Carol were much of an age, and chummed together, and Carol was just crazy about Linda Sue. It was along in June, I remember, Carol saw this in Mrs. Breen's, and she wanted to get it for Linda Sue's birthday in October. She told me about it then, and if I thought it was foolish, that much money, I kept still on it—she wanted to get it, and it was her money. Twenty dollars it was, and she asked Mrs. Breen if she could pay a bit on it every week or so. Mrs. Breen's obliging like that, and she said it was all right, but she left it in the window for people to see, case anybody wanted one like it she could order another."

The Duke, who had been drowsing between them, suddenly woke up and began to wash himself vigorously. Mrs. Demarest finished her coffee and sighed. "It was a doll, Lieutenant—and while that seems like an awful price for a doll, I must say it was a special one. It'd be nearly as big as Linda Sue herself, and it was made of some stuff, you know, that looked like real flesh—and it had real hair, gold hair it was, that you could curl different ways, and it had on a pink silk dress with hand smocking, and silk underwear with lace, and there was a little velvet cape and velvet slippers, rose color. Well, Carol was buying it like that. I wasn't sure to a penny how much she still owed on it, up to that night. And of course Monday wasn't a payday for her, I didn't think it was likely she'd stopped in at Mrs. Breen's that night, because she'd do that the day she got paid, you see. It was just that she *had* paid on it, but as I say, way things were, I didn't bother about going ahead with it. There was time to sort it out, Mrs. Breen and Mrs. Robbins are both honest. I got other things for Linda Sue's birthday, and once in a while I just said to myself, some day I'd best ask about it, straighten it out with Mrs. Breen.

"Well, just last week Mrs. Breen came into her shop again. She was sick quite a while, and then up-and-down like at her daughter's, and now she's better, but not to be alone any more, and she's selling off what stock she has and going out of business. So I went round, last Thursday it was, to ask about Carol's doll.

"And Mrs. Breen says that Carol came in that night and paid all the rest she owed, and took the doll away with her. She remembers it clear —the stroke didn't affect her mind, she's a bit slower but all *there*. She didn't hear about Carol for quite awhile, naturally, being sick and all, and of course when she did, she naturally thought everyone knew about the doll. Because you remember—"

"Yes," he said. He remembered: in the glare of the spotlights, the stiffening disfigured corpse and the several small parcels scattered on the sidewalk. A card of bobby pins, two spools of thread from the dime store: a magazine, a bottle of aspirin, a candy bar from the drugstore: an anniversary card from the stationery store. He looked at Mrs. Demarest blankly. "That's very odd," he said. "She *had* it—the woman's sure?"

She nodded vigorously. "She showed me the accounts book, Lieutenant. There's the date, and while there's no time put down, it's the next-to-last entry that night, and she says the last customer came in was a woman she knows, a Mrs. Ratchett, and it was just before nine. She thinks Carol came in about eight-thirty, a few minutes before maybe. Probably it was the last place Carol stopped, you see—nobody else remembers her with a big parcel. She paid Mrs. Breen seven dollars and forty-six cents, all she still owed, and she didn't have the doll gift-wrapped because she wanted to show it to May and me first. And she took it with her." Mrs. Demarest held out her hands, measuring. "Like that it'd have been—a big stout cardboard box, white, a good yard or more long, and maybe eighteen inches wide and a foot deep. Heavy, too. And inside, along with the doll, three yards of pink silk ribbon and the tissue paper for wrapping it, and a birthday card. The whole thing was wrapped up in white paper and string, and Mrs. Breen made a little loop on top for her to carry it by."

They looked at each other. "But that's *very* damned odd indeed," he said softly. "Not much time there, you know. She was dead by nine, at the latest. It's possible that someone else came by and found her first, didn't want to get involved, but picked up the biggest parcel, maybe the only one he noticed in the dark, on the chance that it was worth something. But you think, in that case, he—or she, of course—might have taken time to snatch up the handbag too, after cash . . . and that hadn't been touched, the strap was still on her arm."

"I guess you'd better hear how she came to get the money, not that it matters. One of the girls worked at the hotel with her came to see me, two-three days afterward—a nice girl she was, Nella Foss—to say how sorry they all were, and give me a little collection the hotel people'd taken up. They thought maybe I'd rather have the money, you know, instead of flowers for the funeral—it was real thoughtful of them. Well, Nella said that very afternoon there'd been a lady just checked out of the hotel came back after a valuable ring she'd left, and Carol'd already found it, doing out the room you know, and turned it in. And the lady gave her five dollars as a present. I expect Carol decided right off she'd finish paying for the doll with it. At the time, I thought of course what was in her purse, three-eighty-four it was, was what she'd had left out of the five."

"Yes . . . but so little time! Do we say it was the murderer took it away? Just that?—not a finger on her handbag after cash? And why?"

"Now, that I couldn't say," said Mrs. Demarest, placidly. "It's queer, certainly. I'd say the same as you—well, I guess detecting things is just a matter of using common sense and reasoning things out. I suppose somebody might think there was something valuable in a big parcel like that, and steal it just on the chance—but a thief who'd do that, it's just not logical he wouldn't take the handbag too, at least rummage through it." She cocked her head at him, and her brown eyes were bright as a sparrow's. "Lieutenant, would you think I'm a woolgathering silly old woman—you're too polite ever *say* it, if you did—if I said, Maybe whoever took it knew right well what was in that parcel?"

"You'd say whoever killed her? For a doll—"

"I don't know that. Maybe somebody else, first—or afterward. But I can tell you something else. I've studied about it, and I went back to ask Mrs. Breen a couple other things. I said she'd left the doll in the window, didn't I? Well, I go past there three-four times a week, up to the market, and I do think I'd've noticed if that doll had been gone out of the window right *after* Carol was killed, and put two and two together, and asked then. But Mrs. Breen took it out of the window about a week before, so I didn't expect it there, if you see what I mean. And she says now, reason she did is that she had notice from the factory or whatever that made them, that they weren't making this particular doll any more—so she didn't want to show it, and have to disappoint anybody wanted one. And, this is what I'm getting at, the morning of that day Carol was killed, there was a woman came into the store and wanted to buy that doll. She wanted it real bad, Mrs. Breen said she was almost crying that she couldn't have that one or get Mrs. Breen to order another, and she stayed a long while trying to argue Mrs. Breen into selling her the one Carol was buying."

An extra ace to pad his hand, Mendoza had hoped: but could it be? Such a small thing—such a meaningless thing! "Did she know this woman?"

"She'd seen her before. It was a white woman, Lieutenant, from over across Hunter Avenue. She couldn't call the name to mind, but she thinks she's got it written down somewhere because the woman made her copy down her name and address and promise to find out couldn't she get a doll like that *somewhere*. You'd best see Mrs. Breen and ask, if you think it means anything at all. . . . She thinks she remembers it was a middling-long sort of name, and started with an L."

SEVEN

Mendoza felt rather irritated at the cosmic powers; if they intended to direct a little luck his way, they might have been more explicit. Still, one never knew: it might lead to something.

The gift shop was closed, of course; he would come back tomorrow. And it was possible that this Breen woman had simply told a lie to avoid having to pay back twelve or thirteen dollars; but such a relatively small amount—and Mrs. Demarest was emphatic on assurance of her honesty. Judge for himself . . .

He drove tedious miles across the city, cursing the Sunday traffic, to Alison Weir's apartment, and was late by some minutes. She opened the door promptly and told him so, taking up her bag, joining him in the hall. She was in green and tan today, plain dark-green wool dress, high-necked: coat, shoes, bag all warm beige, and copper earrings, a big copper brooch.

He settled her in the car and sliding under the wheel said, "Unsubtle, that dress. Every woman with red hair automatically fills her wardrobe with green."

"It's only fair to tell you," said Alison amiably, "that like practically all women I *detest* men who know anything about women's clothes."

"As intelligent people we should always try to overcome these illogical prejudices." He had not moved to start the engine; he smiled at her. "You know, it would be regrettable if you were lying to me, Miss Weir."

The little amusement died from her green-hazel eyes meeting his. "Do you think I've lied to you? Why? I—"

"No, I don't think so. But Teresa Ramirez says her sister meant to tell you about this 'queer boy,' and yet you don't know quite as much as she told Teresa."

"I told you about that. She probably did mean to tell me a lot more, but I took up her consultation time with lecturing her. You can't regret it any more than I do, Lieutenant! If I'd listened to her—"

"Yes," said Mendoza. He'd turned sideways to look at her, his right arm along the seat-back; he laughed abruptly and slid his hand down to brush her shoulder gently, reaching to the ignition. "I'll tell you why I'm not just a hundred percent sure—I mustn't be. Because I'm working this on a preconceived idea, and that's dangerous. I find something that doesn't fit, I'm tempted to think, let it go, it's not important—because I don't want to prove my beautiful theory wrong. Just now and then I *am* wrong, and it's not an experience I enjoy."

"I see. I also dislike egotistical men."

"Mi gatita roja, what you mean is that you dislike the ones honest enough to admit to vanity—nobody walking on two legs isn't an egotist. And you should have more common sense than to talk so rudely to a rich man."

"Are you?"

"I am. None of my doing—in case you were thinking of bribes from gangsters—my grandfather was shrewd enough to buy up quite a lot of land which turned out to be just where the city was expanding—office buildings, you know, and hotels, and department stores—all crazy for land to build on. And fortunately I was his only grandson. It was a great shock to everybody, there he was for years in a thirty-dollar-a-month apartment, saying we couldn't afford this and that, damning the gas company as robbers if the bill was over two dollars, and buying secondhand clothes—my God, he once got a hundred dollars out of me on the grounds of family duty, to pay a hospital bill—and me still in the rookie training school and in debt for my uniforms! And then when he died it all came out. My grandmother hasn't recovered from the shock yet—she's still furious at him, and that was nearly fifteen years ago."

"Oh. Why?"

"For fifty-eight years she'd been nagging at him to stop his gambling —she'd been telling him for fifty-eight years that gamblers are all wastrels, stealing the food out of their families' mouths to throw away, and they always die without a penny to bless themselves. And that's where he got his capital—his winnings. And to add insult to injury—because if she'd known about it, she'd have found some way to save face and also, being a woman, something else to nag him about—he managed to get the last word by dying before she found it out. Frankly, I think myself it wasn't all luck, the old boy wasn't above keeping a few high cards up his sleeve, but you know the one about the gift horse. And unfortunately," added Mendoza, sliding neatly ahead of an indignant bus to get in the right-turn lane, "by then I'd got into the habit of earning an honest living, and I've never cured myself."

"Well, it's an *original* approach to a girl," said Alison thoughtfully. "Such a fascinating subject too—I've always been so interested in money, if only I'd had the chance to study it oftener I might have developed real talent for it. But I must say, I should think you'd bolster up your ego more by doing the King Cophetua business, instead of practically offering a bribe. Not at *all* subtle."

"I'm always loved for myself alone. And why? *Es claro*—a woman of high principle like you, she's afraid to be taken for a gold digger, so she starts out being very standoffish. She's so busy convincing me she's not interested in my money, *vaya,* she's never on guard against my charm."

"Ah, the double play. I keep forgetting you're an egotist. But what about the stupid ones?—the ones like Elena, all bleached curls and giggles and gold ankle chains? The ones those tired middle-aged businessmen—"

"*¡Vaya por Dios!* I never go near such females, except in the way of work. There's no credit to the marksman in an easy target."

"Or to the wolf who catches the smallest lamb? I see what you mean."

"So I'll let you have the last word. You'll do me a favor tomorrow—"

"What?" She regarded him warily.

Mendoza grinned at her. "Don't sound so suspicious, I don't operate so crude and sudden as that! Look, I want you to ask all your girls if Elena said anything at all to them about this staring man. Don't tell them much, don't lead them—a couple of them might make up this or that to be important—but you'll be more apt to get something helpful out of them if anything's there to be got. Official questioning might encourage them to romanticize."

"Oh, well, certainly I'll do that, I meant to anyway. Yes, I think you're right about that."

At headquarters he piloted her upstairs to his office. She looked around curiously. "What exactly is the procedure? I've never done this before."

"I've made a rough draft, here, of the substance of what you told me. Just look it over and see if you want to change or add anything, and then we'll get it typed for you to sign. And what do *you* want?" he added as Hackett wandered in after them. "I thought you were safely occupied for the afternoon."

"Una espectativa vana," said Hackett, spreading his hands. "Kids! It's the damnedest thing, they'll be budding Einsteins at twelve, but the minute they hit their teens I swear to God they all turn into morons. You'd think they were blind and deaf." His eyes were busy on Alison.

"It's a phenomenon known as puberty," said Mendoza. "Nothing?"

"Nada. You goin' to remember your manners, or do I count as the hired help around here?"

"Miss Weir—the cross I am given to bear, Sergeant Hackett."

"The brawn," said Alison wisely, nodding at him. "I knew you must have somebody to do the real work."

"And she has brains too," said Hackett admiringly. "You got a visitor, Luis, before I forget. That Ramirez girl." He jerked a thumb.

"Oh?" Mendoza got up. "You'll excuse me, Miss Weir—if this caveman type gets obstreperous, you've only to scream."

Standing there by the clerk's empty desk in the anteroom, before she spoke, she wasn't this century at all. Black cotton dress too long, the shabby brown coat over her arm, and a black woolen shawl held around her, both hands clasping it at her breast. No make-up: she'd come straight from church, from late mass, probably. This large official place had somewhat subdued her.

"You wanted to see me, Miss Ramirez? Sit down here, won't you?"

"Oh, thanks, but it won't take long, what I come for. I wasn't sure you'd be here, Sunday an' all, I thought I'd ask could I leave a note for you—" She took a breath. "There was some of your guys come with a warrant, to look all through Elena's things—Mama, she just had a fit, she don't understand about these things so good—"

"I'm sorry it troubled her. We have to do that, you know."

"Sure, I know, it don't matter, we haven't nothing to hide."

He wondered: the visiting uncle? The faint defiance over the honesty in her round brown eyes looked convincing. He thought, whether they caught the shifty Tío Tomás at anything or not, that was a wrong one; but he also thought the Ramirez family hadn't an inkling of that. He waited; she had something else to say. She fidgeted with the shawl, burst out a little nervously, "I—I thought of something else, Lieutenant, that's why I come."

"Yes?"

"I don't want to sound like I'm telling you your own business, see, but—well, you *are* sort of looking into that Palace skating place, aren't you? I mean—"

"We are. Why?"

"I don't know nothing about it," she said. "I never been there myself, and anyway I guess this don't have anything to do with it, I mean who- ever runs it, you know. But I got to thinking, after you asked me yester- day about any guy bothering Elena, I tried to remember just what she did say, if there was anything I hadn't told you. And I remembered one more thing she said. It was when she was talking about this fellow watching her, she said, 'He gets on my nerves, honest, I nearly fell down a couple times.'"

"Now that's very interesting," said Mendoza.

"See, she must've meant it was at the rink she saw him. Once, any- ways. Because where else would being nervous make her almost fall down? I—"

"Yes, of course." And there were a number of possibilities there; a little imagination would produce a dozen different ideas. He thought about some of them (Ehrlich, the attendants, the other kids) as he thanked the girl for coming in. Alison came out of his office with Hackett and was sympathetic, friendly with Teresa, asking conven- tionally about the funeral. The girl was a little stiff, responding, using more care with her manners and grammar.

"Well, I—I guess that's all I wanted tell you, Lieutenant, I better get home—"

Alison sent Mendoza a glance he missed and another at Hackett which connected; he said he was going that way, be glad to drive her home, and gave Alison a mock-reproachful backward look, shepherd- ing Teresa off.

"Your draft's quite all right. Hey, wake up, I said—"

"Yes," said Mendoza. "Is it? Good." He summoned one of the stenos on duty, took Alison back to his office to wait, gave her a chair and cig- arette but no conversation. She sat quietly, watching him with a slight smile, looking round the room; when the typed pages were brought in she signed obediently where she was told and announced meekly that she *could* get home by herself.

Mendoza said, "Don't be foolish." But he was mostly silent on the drive across town. When he drew into the curb at the apartment build- ing, he cut the motor, didn't move immediately. "Tell me something. Did you like dolls when you were a little girl?"

"Against my better judgment you do intrigue me. Most little girls do."

He grunted. "Ever know any little boys who did?"

"When they're very young, otherwise not. Though I believe there are some, but they can't be very normal little boys. The psychiatrists—"

"I beg you, *not* the doubletalk about Id and Ego and Superego. Especially not about infantile sexuality and the traumatic formation of the homosexual personality. *Esto queda entre los dos.* Just between the two of us, I find a most suggestive resemblance between the Freudians and those puritanical old maids who put the worst interpretation on everything—and with such damned smug-satisfaction into the bargain."

She laughed. "Oh, I'm with you every time! But what's all this about dolls?"

He got out a cigarette, looked at it without flicking his lighter. "Suppose you're taking one of those word-association tests, what do you say to that?—*doll.*"

"Why, I guess—*little girls.* Why?"

"And me too," he said. "Which is what makes it difficult. Well, never mind—inquisition over for today." He lit the cigarette and turned to her with a smile. "You'll have dinner with me tomorrow night, tell me what you get out of your girls, if anything."

Alison cocked her auburn head at him. "I seem to remember you said you didn't mix business and pleasure. Do I infer I'm absolved already?"

"I'm always making these impossible resolutions." He got out, went round and opened the door for her. "Black," he said, gesturing, "something elegant, and *decolleté.* Maybe pearls. Seven o'clock."

She got out of the car, leisurely and graceful, and tucked her bag under her arm; she said, "Charm isn't the word. But I have heard—speaking of the Freudians—that there are some women who really enjoy being dominated. Seven o'clock it is, and I'll wear what I damned well please, Lieutenant Luis Mendoza!"

"*Mi gatita roja,*" he said, smiling.

"And," said Alison, "I am *not* your little red kitten, you—you—*¡tu macho insolente!*"

"What language for a lady. Until tomorrow." He grinned at her straight back; there was—he was aware—a certain promise in being called an insolent male animal, by a female like Alison.

It sat on the corner of Matson and San Rafael, a block up and a block over from Commerce and Humboldt. Not really much of a walk home for Elena, a quarter of an hour by daylight: down San Rafael to Commerce, to Humboldt, across the empty lot and down a block to Foster where Humboldt made a jog to bypass a gloomy little cul-de-sac misleadingly called a court: another block to Main, another to Liggitt and half a block more to home. Little more than half a mile, but that could be a long way at night. Main was neon lights and crowds up to midnight anyway, but these other streets were dark and lonely.

It was a big barn of a building. Matson Street wasn't residential, but strung with small warehouses, small business that must permanently balance on the edge of insolvency—rug cleaning, said the faded signs, tools sharpened, speedy shoe repair, cleaning & dyeing—and in between, the secretive warehouses unlabeled or reticent with WHOLESALE PARTS, INC.—MASTERSON BROS.—ASSOCIATED INDUSTRIES. At Matson and San Rafael, there was a graveyard for old cars on one corner, with a high iron fence around it (SECONDHAND PARTS CHEAP), and warehouses on two other corners, and on the fourth the Palace Roller Rink. The building wasn't flush to the sidewalk like the warehouses, but set back fifteen or twenty feet, to provide off-street parking on two sides.

Mendoza parked there, among six or eight other cars: mostly old family sedans, a couple of worked-over hot-rods. It was ten past four, a good time for the experiment he had in mind. He fished up a handful of change from his pocket, picked out a quarter, a dime, and a nickel, and walked up to the entrance.

There were big double doors fastened back, but at this time of year, the place facing north, not much light fell into the foyer. That was perhaps ten feet wide, three times as long up to the restroom doors at either end. There was a Coke-dispensing freezer and a big trash basket under a wall dispenser for paper cups. In the middle of the foyer was a three-sided plywood enclosure with a narrow counter bearing an ancient cash register; and inside, on a high stool with a back, sat Ehrlich the proprietor, a grossly fat man in the late sixties, bald bullet-shaped head descending to several rolls of fat front and rear, pudgy hands clasped over a remarkable paunch: wrinkled khaki shirt and pants, no tie. Ehrlich, peacefully drowsing—still, very likely, digesting a solid noon dinner which had ended with several glasses of beer. Mendoza surveyed him with satisfaction, walked quietly up and laid the silver on the counter. The fat man roused with a little grunt, scooped it up and punched the register, and produced from a box under the counter a sleazy paper ticket, slid it across. Mendoza picked it up and passed by.

At the narrower door into the main part of the building, he glanced back: Ehrlich's head was again bowed over his clasped hands. So there we are, thought Mendoza. The man had raised his eyes just far enough to check the money: if the exact change was laid out, a gorilla in pink tights could walk by him without notice.

The second door led Mendoza into more than semidarkness. It was a rectangle within a rectangle: a fifteen-foot-wide strip of dark around all four sides of the skating floor. That was a good hundred and fifty feet long, a little more than half as wide, of well-laid hardwood like a dance floor. There was an iron pipe railing enclosing it, with two or three gaps in each side for access to the occasional hard wooden benches, scattered groups of folding wooden chairs, along the four dark borders. A big square skylight, several unshaded electric bulbs around it, poured light directly down on the skating floor, but not enough to reach beyond: anywhere off the edge of that floor it was dark. The effect was that of a theater, about that quality of light, looking from the borders to the big floor.

Straight ahead from the single entrance, at the gap in the rail there, sat one of the attendants, sidewise in a chair to catch the light on his magazine. Beside him was a card table, a cardboard carton on it and another on the floor; those would hold the skates. Not just the skates, Mendoza remembered from the statements taken: flat shoes with skates already fastened on—something to do with the insurance, because as Hayes (or was it Murphy) had put it, otherwise some of these dumb girls would come in with four-inch heels on. As Elena had, he remembered.

It was shoddy, it was dirty, a place of garish light and dense shadow, of drafts and queer echoes from its very size. No attempt was evident to make it attractive or comfortable: the sole amenities, if you could so call them, appeared to be the Coke machine and, at the opposite side of the floor, an old nickel jukebox which was presently emitting a tired rendition of "The Beautiful Blue Danube." And yet the fifteen or twenty teenagers on the floor seemed to be enjoying themselves, mostly skating in couples round and round—one pair in the center showing off, with complicated breakaways and dance steps—half a dozen in single file daring the hazards lined down the far side, a little artificial hill, a low bar-jump. Those girls shrieked simulated terror, speeding down the sharp drop; the boys jeered, affected nonchalance. It was all very innocent and juvenile—depressingly so, Mendoza reflected sadly from the vantage point of his nearly forty years.

But he hadn't come here to philosophize on the vagaries of adolescence. . . . If you went straight down to the attendant, to give up your ticket and acquire your skates, you would be noticed; otherwise, he could easily miss seeing you. Mendoza had wandered a little way to the side from the door, and stood with his back to the wall; he was in deep shadow and he'd made no noise. He stood there until his eyes had adjusted to the darkness, to avoid colliding with anything, and moved on slowly. He knew now that it was possible to come in here without being noticed, but could anyone count on it five times out of five? There would be times Ehrlich was wider awake, for one thing.

He sat down in a chair midway from the railing, twenty feet from the attendant. In five minutes neither the man nor any of the skaters took the slightest notice of him. He got up, drifted back to the wall, and began a tour of the borders.

When he got round to the opposite side of the floor, he made an interesting discovery. In the corner there a small square closet was partitioned off, with a door fitted to it. He tried the door and it gave to his hand with a little squeak. He risked a brief beam from his pencil-flash: rude shelving, cleaning materials, an ancient can of floor wax, mops and pails. Hackett was quite right; nobody had disturbed the dust in here for a long time. He shut the door gently and went on down the rear width of the building.

The jukebox was never silent long; it seemed to have a repertoire only of waltzes, and now for the third time was rendering, in all senses of the word, "Let Me Call You Sweetheart."

He came to the far corner and with mild gratification found another closet and another door. "At a guess, the fuse boxes," he murmured, and eased the door open. A quick look with the flash interested him so much that he stepped inside, pulled the door shut after him, and swept the flash around for a good look.

Fuse boxes, yes: also, of course, the meter: and a narrow outside door. For the meter reader, obviously: very convenient. He tried it and found himself looking out to a narrow unpaved alley between this building and the warehouse next to it.

And does it mean anything at all? he wondered to himself. He retreated, and now he did not care if he was seen or not; he kept the flash on, the beam pointed downward. . . . How very right Hackett had been: this place had not been so much as swept for years. But full of eddying drafts as it was, you couldn't expect footprints to stay in the dust, however thick. He worked back and forth between the rail and the wall, dodging the chairs. He had no idea at all what he was looking for, and also was aware that anything he might find would either be completely irrelevant or impossible to prove relevant to the case.

Now, of course, he had been noticed; he heard the attendant's chair scrape back, and a few of the skaters had drifted over to the rail this side, curious. He didn't look up from the little spotlight of the flash: he followed it absorbedly back and forth.

"Hey, what the hell you up to, anyway?" The attendant came heavy-footed, shoving chairs out of his path. "Who—"

"Stop where you are, for God's sake!" exclaimed Mendoza suddenly. "I'm police—you'll have my credentials in a minute, but don't come any closer."

"Police—oh, well—"

And Mendoza said aloud to himself, "So here it is. But I don't believe it, it's impossible." And to that he added a rueful, "And what in the name of all the devils in hell does it mean?"

In the steady beam of the flash, it lay there mute and perhaps meaningless: a scrap of a thing, three inches long, a quarter-inch wide: a little strip of dainty pink lace, so fine that it might once have been the trimming on the lingerie of a very special doll.

Ehrlich went on saying doggedly, "My place didn't have nothing to do with it." That door, well, sure, the inside one oughta be kept locked, it usually was—but neither he nor the attendants would swear to having checked it for months, all three maintaining it was the other fellow's responsibility. Mendoza found them tiresome. Hackett and Dwyer, summoned by phone, if they didn't altogether agree with Ehrlich were less than enthusiastic over Mendoza's find; Hackett said frankly it didn't mean a damned thing. He listened to the story of Carol Brooks' doll and said it still didn't mean a damned thing.

"I don't want to disillusion you, but I've heard rumors that real live dolls sometimes wear underwear with pink lace on—and just like you say, it *is* nice and dark along here. Not havin' such a pure mind as you, I can think of a couple of dandy reasons—"

"And such elegant amenities for it!" said Mendoza sarcastically. "A wooden bench a foot wide, or a pair of folding chairs! I may be overfastidious, but I ask you!"

"There's a classic tag line you oughta remember: It's wonderful anywhere."

"So maybe it doesn't mean anything. Nevertheless, we'll hang onto it, and I want a sketch of this place, showing that door and the exact spot this was found."

"O.K., will do." There was always a lot of labor expended on such jobs, in a thing like this, that turned out to have been unnecessary; but it couldn't be helped. And in case something turned out to be relevant, they had to keep the D.A.'s office in mind, document the evidence.

"And what happened to you?" added Mendoza, turning on Dwyer, who was sporting a patch bandage taped across one eye.

Dwyer said aggrievedly he ought to've run the guy in for obstructing an officer. All he'd been doing was try to find out more about that Browne girl who'd found the body—as per orders. First he'd got the rough side of her landlady's tongue—the girl wasn't home—for asking a few ordinary little questions, like did the girl ever bring men home, or get behind in the rent, and so on—you'd have thought she was the girl's ma, the way she jumped on him—if the police didn't have anything better to do than come round insulting decent women—! She's still yakking at him about that when this guy shows up, who turns out to be some friend of the girl's, and before Dwyer can show his badge, the guy damns him up and down for a snooper and hauls off and—"Me, Lieutenant! It was a fluke punch, he caught me off balance—"

"That's your story," said Hackett.

"I swear to— Me, walking into one off a guy I could give four inches and thirty pounds—and his name turns out to be Joe Carpaccio at that!"

"So now you've provided the comic relief, what did you get?"

"Not a damn thing but the shiner. Except she's only lived there three months or so. But how could she be anything to do with it, Lieutenant?"

"I don't think she is, but no harm getting her last address."

"Well, that was why—"

"Let me give him all the news," said Hackett. "You take the car and go on back, send Clawson over to do a sketch. And then go home and nurse that eye, you've had enough excitement for one day." Dwyer said gratefully he'd do that, he had the hell of a headache and he must be getting old, let anything like that happen. Hackett said, "Let's sit down. I've got a couple of little things for you. First, Browne. I was bright enough to ask for her last address when we took her formal statement —let her think it was a regulation of some kind—thought it might be useful. And you might say it was. She gave one, but it turned out to be nonexistent. Which is why I sent Bert to sniff around some more."

"That's a queer one," said Mendoza. "You think it's anything for us?"

Hackett considered. "It doesn't smell that way to me, no. She struck me as an honest girl, and sensible too, which means it's not likely she's mixed into anything illegal. But they say everybody's got something to hide. We might trace her back, sure, but I think all we'd find would be the kind of thing innocent people get all hot and bothered about hiding —an illegitimate baby or a relative in the nut house, or maybe she's run away from an alcoholic husband. I think it'd be a waste of time myself, but you're the boss."

"It might be just as well to find out," said Mendoza slowly. "In a thing like this, any loose end sticking out of the tangle, take hold and pull—maybe it isn't connected to the main knot, or maybe it is—you can't know until you follow it in."

"O.K., I got more for you." The brief flare of the match as he lit a new cigarette brought some looks his way again. The kids on the floor were more interested in them than skating, now—gathering in little groups, slow-moving, to whisper excitedly about it; some of them would have known Elena.

Mendoza stared out at them absently, listening to Hackett. It was now just about thirty-three hours since the body had been found; a lot of routine spadework had kept a lot of men busy in that time. A dozen formal statements had been taken, from the Ramirez family, from three or four of the kids present here on Friday night, from Ehrlich and the two attendants, from the Wades and their visiting neighbor. A great many other people had been questioned, and of course written reports had been turned in on most of this and a new case-file started by the office staff. Again, as six months before, routine enquiry was being made into all recently released or escaped mental patients, and the present whereabouts of persons with records of similar violent assaults. The official machinery had ground elsewhere, arranging for the coroner's inquest. . . . As inevitably happened, crime had touched the lives of many innocent people, had grouped together an incongruous assortment of individuals whose private lives had in some part been invaded, you could say—if incidentally and with benevolent motive.

And—he finally stopped fingering the cigarette he'd got out five minutes ago, and lit it—he would offer odds that if, as, and when they caught up with this one, it would turn out to be one of the many homicides any police officer had seen, which need never have happened if someone had used a little common sense, or more self-control, or hadn't been a little too greedy or vain or possessive or impatient.

Like Mrs. Demarest, he sometimes felt it would be nice to believe there was a master plan, that some reason for all this existed. He disapproved on principle of anything so disorderly as blind fate.

"After telling you you're chasin' rainbows," Hackett was saying, "I'll give you a little more confirmation. I saw the Wade boy again, and he says maybe there was such a guy, Elena mentioned it to him. Twice. He thinks the first time was about a week ago, but they were out together two nights running and he won't swear which it was—they came here both nights. Anyway, she asked him did he see the guy sitting there at the side staring at her all the time—"

"Here," said Mendoza, sitting up. "Right here? So—"

"Don't run to get a warrant. The boy says he looked, and there was somebody sitting where she said, but he couldn't see what he looked like in the dark, just that there was somebody there. He didn't pay much attention, because he thought it was just one of the other kids, and Elena was imagining things—'like girls do,' he said—when she said it was the same guy she'd seen in here before, and that he never took his eyes off her. You'll be happy to know that Ricky also came to this conclusion because he didn't see how she could recognize a face that far off, in this light—he couldn't. He wears glasses for driving and movies, and he didn't have them on, never wears them in here on account of the danger of breakage."

"*¡Fuegos del infierno!*" exclaimed Mendoza violently. "Of course, of course!"

"Go on listening, it gets better. He says Elena told him she'd seen the guy here five or six times, always in about the same spot, but Ricky thought then she'd maybe seen a couple of different kids, different times, and imagined the rest. O.K. On Friday night, when they first got here, she looked, and he wasn't there. But later on, all of a sudden she spotted him, and made Ricky look, and there he was—or there somebody was. Now, mind you, just like her sister, Ricky didn't think she was afraid of this fellow, that there was anything like that to it. If he had, if she'd acted that way, all the people she mentioned it to would've thought of it right off, and I read it myself that she started out being kind of flattered and annoyed at once, which would be natural, and then just annoyed. Because there was something 'funny' about him. So, when she spotted him again Friday night, she acted so worried about it that Ricky decided to get a closer look, to watch for the guy again, if you follow me. Elena said he'd showed up so sudden it was like magic, one time she looked and no guy, and about three seconds later she happened to look again and there he was—"

"Yes, of course. So?"

"So then, finish. Before Ricky gets over to take a close look, Papa comes in breathing righteous wrath and yanks him out."

This time Mendoza didn't swear, merely shut his eyes.

"And if you're still interested, Smith has tagged the Ramirez uncle visiting what is probably a cat-house on Third—at least the address rang a bell, and I checked with Prince in Vice—he pricked up his ears and said we'd closed it twice, and he was glad to know somebody had opened up again, they'll look into it. After that Ramirez took a bus way across town to treat himself to a couple of drinks at a place called the Maison du Chat, on Wilshire. Which Smith thought was sort of funny because it's a very fancy layout where you get nicked a dollar and a half for a Scotch highball, and six dollars for a steak because it's in French on the menu."

"I don't give one damn about Ramirez' taste in women, let Prince look into that. The other, yes, we'll follow it up—find out what you can about it, it may be a drop for a wholesaler. If anything definite shows up, throw it at Narcotics then and let them take over."

"I'm ahead of you. I got Higgins and Farnsworth on it. All they got so far is the owner's name, which is Nicholas Dimitrios." Hackett dropped his cigarette and put a careful heel on it. "Just what's your idea about all this, anyway?—dolls, yet! I don't see you've got much to get hold of."

"¡Me lo cuenta a mí!—you're telling me! But I'll tell you how I see it happening. Somewhere around here is our lunatic—and don't ask me what kind he is—nor I won't even guess why he finds a back way into this hellhole and gets a kick out of watching these kids on skates. It makes a better story if you say he was following Elena. Anyway, here he is, and nobody else seems to have noticed him particularly. Neither of the attendants has much occasion to come down to this end of the floor, and if any of the kids noticed him, they took him for one of themselves. And about that, de paso, I think we can deduce that he's a fairly young man. Elena called him a boy, and the odds are an older man would have been noticed by others in here, would have stood out —as it is, I think he was seen, casually, by some of the kids, and accepted as one of them. On the other hand, he seems to have taken some care not to be noticed much, sitting back against the wall—" Mendoza shrugged. "It's pretty even, maybe, but I think the balance goes to show he's fairly young. All right. She had seen him at least once elsewhere, with another boy or several others, one of whom is named Danny—"

"All of which is very secondhand evidence."

"Don't push me. He was here on Friday night, he saw her leave alone. Evidently he hadn't made any attempt before to approach her, speak to her, and I think he did then because he saw her boy friend taken out and thought this was his chance. He followed her, using his private door, so Ehrlich and the attendants didn't notice him leave. So he had to walk round the building, which put him just far enough behind her that he didn't catch up for a block or so. Finish. And I don't know why he killed her, if that was in his mind from the start or a sudden impulse. I'm inclined to say impulse, because you couldn't find two girls more different than Brooks and this one—so he doesn't pick victims by any apparent system, though there's holes in that reasoning, I grant you—he may have some peculiar logic of his own, of course."

"I'll buy all that, but there's no evidence at all, a lot of hearsay and a lot of ifs. And how do you tie in Brooks and the doll?"

"Oh, damn the doll," said Mendoza. "I can't figure the odds on that, if it ties in or not—it's just as possible that somebody stumbled on Brooks after the killer left her, and stole the thing—or that she was robbed of it before she ran into the killer. And I can say—*claro está!*— it's a lunatic, and the same lunatic—and when we find him, we'll find that last September he had some reason to frequent Tappan Street. There's even less evidence on all that." He stood and took up his hat from the bench, flicked dust off it automatically. "Here's Clawson. I'm going home."

"I might've expected that—walk off and leave me enough work so I can't try to beat your time with that redhead."

"That," said Mendoza, "to quote another classic tag line, would be sending a boy to do a man's work. But you have my permission to try, Arturo—I never worry about competition."

EIGHT

All the same, that doll intrigued him; it was such an incongruous thing.

When he unlocked the door of his apartment, automatically reaching to the light switch as he came in, the first thing that met his eyes was the elegant length of the Abyssinian cat draped along the top of the traverse-rod housing across the front windows, a foot below the ceiling.

Which meant that Bertha was here. Bast intensely resented Bertha and her vigorous maneuvers with mop, dustcloths, and vacuum cleaner, and took steps to keep out of her way. He was unsurprised to find her there on a late Sunday afternoon; the seven or eight people who shared Bertha's excellent services were used to her ways. If she felt like doing a thorough job on the Carters' Venetian blinds when she ought to be at the Elgins', or got behind because she'd decided to turn out all the Brysons' kitchen cupboards, she was apt to turn up almost anywhere at any time, and no one ever complained because, miraculously, Bertha really did the work she was paid for, and had even been known to dust the backs of pictures and the tops of doors.

She appeared now from the kitchen, jamming an ancient felt hat over her tight sausage curls. "I was just leavin'. There you go, switchin' on lights allovera place—your bill must be somethin' sinful! You found out yet who that dead man in the yards was?"

He admitted they had not; and yes, the forces of law were so unreasonable as to have arraigned the society beauty for murder, even after hearing all the excellent reasons she had for shooting her husband. He looked at Bertha thoughtfully (the average mind?) and said, "Do me a favor, and pretend you're taking one of those word-association tests, you know, I throw a word at you and you say the first thing that comes into your head—"

"I know, it's psychological." She looked interested.

"So, I say *doll* to you—what do you think of?"

"Witches," said Bertha. "I just saw a movie about it last night. The witch takes and makes this doll and names it and all, and sticks this big pin right through—"

"I get the general idea," said Mendoza sadly. "Thanks very much, that'll do." Witches: that was all they needed! When Bertha had slammed the door cheerfully after herself, he took off his coat, brought in the kitchen step-stool, and spent five minutes persuading Bast that it was safe to trust her descent to him. That was one puzzle he would never, probably, solve: she had no trouble getting up there, but hadn't yet found out how to get down. As usual, she emitted terrified yells as he backed down the steps, and, released, instantly assumed the haughty *sang-froid* of the never-out-of-countenance sophisticate. She turned her back on him and studied one black paw admiringly before beginning to wash it.

There were times Mendoza thought he liked cats because, like himself, they were all great egotists.

"Witches," he said again to himself, and laughed.

"And you put that coat away tidy where it belongs! On a hanger, not just anyhow. Clothes cost money, how many times I got to tell you, take care of what we got, no tellin' when we can get new."

"All right," said Marty. He got out of bed and picked up the corduroy jacket. He couldn't take down a hanger and put the jacket on it and hang it over the rod, all with his eyes shut, but he did it fast and he tried not to look down at the floor. She was fussing round the room behind him.

But he couldn't help seeing it, even if he didn't look right *at* it, and anyway, he thought miserably, even if he never opened the closet door, never had to see it, it didn't change anything—the thing was still there, he'd still know about it.

So did she, and for another reason he only half-understood himself. That was partly why he got the door shut again quick. She might know, all right, but she was different—if she didn't see it, she could keep from thinking about it. He felt like he was in two separate parts, about that, the way he felt about a lot of things lately—twin Martys, like looking in a mirror. He didn't see how she could, but in a funny kind of way he didn't want to make her *have* to see it—long as she could do like that.

He got back in bed and pulled the covers up. It was just like something was pulling him right in half, like two big black monster-shapes were using him for tug of war. And he had to just lie there, he couldn't do anything, because *she* wouldn't. And even if she was wrong, she was his Ma, and—and—

She said from the door, "You be real good now, no horsing round, you go right to sleep." She sounded just like always.

A funny idea slid into his mind then, the first minute of lying there in the dark—alone with the secret. He wondered if she'd forgot all about it, if maybe now she could look right *at* it and never really see it at all. Like it was invisible—because she wanted it to be.

But even in the dark with the door shut, he could still see it.

The box had gone a long while ago, got stepped on, and the big piece of thin white fancy paper and the pink shiny ribbon had got all crumpled and spoiled pretty soon, from handling. . . . The doll wasn't new any more either. It sat in there on the closet floor, leaning up against the wall, even when he shut his eyes tight he could see it.

It had been awful pretty when it was new, even if it was just a silly girl's thing. It wasn't pretty any more. The spangly pink dress was all stained and torn, and most of the lace was torn off the underwear, and one of the arms was pulled loose. The gold curls had got all tangled and some pulled right off, and one of the blue eyes with real lashes had been poked right in so there was just a black hole there and you could hear the eye sort of rattle around inside when you— The other eye still shut when the doll was laid down.

Marty always had a funny hollow feeling when he heard that eye rattling round inside. You'd think sometime it'd fall out, but it never did.

He'd been lying here, felt like hours, still as he could, in the dark. This was the worst time of all, and lately it had been getting harder and harder to let go, and pretty soon be asleep. Because in the dark, it seemed like the secret was somehow as big as the whole room, so he couldn't breathe, so he felt he had to get *out* and run and run and tell everybody—yell it as loud as he could.

He lay flat, very still, but he could hear his heart going *thud-thud-thud*, very fast. You were supposed to say a prayer when you went to bed, she'd made him learn it when he was just a little kid and when they lived over on Tappan and he'd gone to the Methodist Sunday school, it'd been up on the wall there in the Sunday-school room, the words sewed onto cloth some fancy old-fashioned way and flowers around them, in a gold frame. He could see that now sort of in his mind, red and blue flowers and the words in four lines. It was the only real prayer he knew by heart and he was afraid to say it any more, because if you said any of it you had to say it all and it might be worse than bad luck to say the end of it. *If I should die before I—*

Most of the time, like at school, anyway in daylight, he could stand it. But this was the bad time, alone with it. A lot of feelings were churning around inside him, and they didn't exactly go away other times, they were still there but outside things helped to push them deeper inside, sort of—school and baseball practice and being with other kids and all. But like this in the dark, they got on top of him—a lot of bad feelings, but the biggest and worst of all was being just plain scared.

There were times, like yesterday, when he thought she was too; and then again, seemed like, she made up her mind so hard that nothing so awful like that could be so, for her it just wasn't. Maybe grownups could do that. He sure wished he could. Like looking right at that doll and never remembering, never thinking—

Marty felt shameful tears pricking behind his eyes, but the fear receded a little in him for the upsurge of resentment at her unfairness. . . . She'd told a lie, a lie, he knew it was a lie, he wasn't crazy, was he?—if Dad had been there she'd never have dared say he was the one telling lies, but—what could you do when a grown-up, your own Ma—

"I *bought* it," she'd said, and he thought he remembered it was one of the times she sounded afraid too. . . . "I did so buy it, Marty, you're just pretendin' not to remember!—you got to remember, all that money —I saved it up, and I bought it *yesterday*—" About the money wasn't a lie; she had, but the rest wasn't so, he remembered—

What he remembered made terrible pictures in his mind, now he put it all together.

The fear that was never very far away now, even at school—outside —came creeping over him again like a cold hand feeling.

The doll. It had been awful pretty—then.

He wished he could forget that picture, all it said under it, in the newspaper. She hadn't got it this time, she wouldn't talk or listen about anything to do with it now—seemed like something just made him get that paper, and it had cost ten cents too. Elena. It was a pretty name. But he wished he could stop seeing the picture because it was the same girl, he'd known it would be but it was worse knowing for real sure—the picture—and the very worst about it was something silly, but somehow terrible too. *The picture that looked like that doll when it'd been new.* Before the eye had—

He thought he heard a noise over by the closet door. It wasn't really, he told himself. It wasn't.

In California they didn't hang people for murder, they had a gas chamber instead. It sounded even worse, a thing maybe like a big iron safe and with pipes that—

But other people, they shouldn't get killed like that—even if he didn't know, didn't mean—even if Ma— It wasn't right. Dad would say so too, whatever it meant, even something awful like the gas.

Somebody'd ought to know, and right off too, before it ever happened again. But Ma—

And that was a noise by the closet door.

Primitive physical fear took him in what seemed like one leap across the room and out to where it was light, in the parlor.

She had an old shirt in her lap she'd been mending, the needle still stuck in it, but she was just sitting there not doing anything. "What's the matter with you now?" she asked dully.

He tried to stop shaking, stop his teeth chattering. "P-please, Ma, can I—can I sleep out here on the sofa, I—I—I don't like the dark, it—"

She looked at him awhile and then said, "You're a big boy, be scared of the dark."

"Please, Ma—"

"I guess, if you want," she said in almost a whisper. She went in and got the blanket off his bed.

He lay on the sofa, the blanket tucked around him and face turned to the arm but still thankfully aware of the comforting light. And after a while a kind of idea started to come to him—about a way he might do . . .

Because somebody ought to—and she'd never let—she'd made him promise on the Bible, something awful would happen if you broke that kind of promise, but if he didn't *say* anything, just—

It was a frightening, tempting, awful idea. He didn't see how he could, he didn't know if he'd dare. And *where?*—it had to be a place where—

Danny said cops were all dumb. But Marty didn't think that could be right, because his dad must know more than Danny, and Dad had always said, Policemen, they're your friends, you go to them for help, you're ever in trouble.

Trouble . . . he felt the slow hot tears sliding down into the sofa cushion, fumbled blind and furtive for the handkerchief in his pajama pocket. The gas chamber. *I never meant nothing bad—*

But you had to do what was right, no matter what. Dad always said, and anyway it was a thing you just knew inside.

Morgan had got used to the oddly schizophrenic sensation—that was the word for it, wouldn't it be, for feeling split in halves?—more or less. He wondered if everybody who'd ever planned or done something criminal had the feeling: probably not. The visible Morgan, acting much as usual (at least he hoped so), going about his job—and the inside one, the one with the secret.

That one was still, in a detached way, feeling slightly surprised at this Morgan who was showing such unexpected capacity for cool planning. (The Morgan who'd been kicked around just once too often and this time was fighting back.)The original Morgan was still uneasy about the whole thing, but quite frankly, he realized, not from any moral view-point: just about Morgan's personal safety, the danger of being found out.

He wrote down the address as the man read it out to him. "How's that spelled?—it's a new one to me."

"T-A-P-P-A-N. Over past Washington some'eres, I think."

"Well, thanks very much," said Morgan, putting his notebook away.

"I still can't hardly belive it," said the clerk worriedly. "Lindstrom, doing a thing like that! Last man in the world, I'd've said—why, he thought the world of his wife and the boy. Never missed a lodge meeting, you know, and I don't ever remember talkin' with him he didn't brag on what good grades his boy got at school, all like that. One of the *steady* kind, that was Lindstrom—no world-beater, but, you know, *steady*."

"That so?" said Morgan. He lit a cigarette. He felt a kind of remote interest in this Lindstrom thing, no more, but it constituted his main lifeline, and it must appear that he'd been working hard on it, been thinking of nothing else all today.

"Never any complaints on him, he always did an honest day's work, I heard that from a dozen fellows been on the job with him. He was working for Staines Contracting, like I said. He was a member here for three years, always paid his dues regular. We did figure it was sort of funny, way he quit his job and quit coming to meetings all of a sudden. When his dues didn't come in, we sent a letter, but it come back. But things come up in a hurry sometimes, sickness or something. You know. Last thing in the world I'd've expected a guy like Lindstrom to do—walk out on his family." He shook his head.

"You haven't heard anything from him since, no inquiries from other lodges of your union?"

"No, not since last August when he stopped showing up."

"Well, thanks." The man was still shaking his head sadly when Morgan came out to his car.

It it hadn't been for this other thing, he'd have been interested in the Lindstroms more than he was. Funny setup: something behind it, but hard to figure what. Had the hell of a time getting a definite answer out of the woman about where they'd been living when the husband walked out. Sometimes they let out something to one of the neighbors, a local bartender: it was a place to start. Then, when he did, she gave what turned out to be a false address. He hadn't tackled her about that yet; it wasn't the first time such a thing had happened, and there were other ways to check. He'd found Lindstrom, got this last address for him, through his affiliation with the Carpenters' Union.

The thing was, concentrate on Lindstrom today, keep the nose to the grindstone. Forget about tonight, what was going to happen tonight. It would all work out fine, just as the inside, secret Morgan had planned it.

There was only one thing both Morgans were really worried about, and that was, *whether* and *when,* about telling Sue. Not, of course, before; she mustn't guess, or she'd be too nervous with the police. Not easy to put over the story on her, Sue knew him too well, but he thought he'd got away with it—that he was still stalling Smith, trying to bring him to compromise. It was going to be very tricky, too, afterward, when he had given the police one story and had to meet Sue before them. There was also the woman and the boy, but you had to take a chance somewhere. It was very likely that the woman (if indeed she was still living with Smith at all, and knew about this) would be too afraid of getting in trouble herself to speak up. And Sue was very far from being a fool; Sue he could count on.

It would go all right, always provided that the man was *there.* Otherwise it could be awkward, but Morgan figured that as Smith was renting a three-room flat instead of just a room, the chances were that his wife, or some woman, was with him, and he'd be home sometime around the dinner hour. So that was the first way it might go: the upright citizen Morgan, visiting one of his cases on his lawful occasions—if it was after hours, well, it was a case he'd got interested in, there was no law against zeal at one's job. The Lindstroms' flat was on the second floor; Smith's was on the third, so the mail slots told him. Those landings would be damn dark at night, not lighted anyway. Wait for him to come down on his way to collect—*the ransom,* only word—wait on the second-floor landing. And get up close, to be sure—but no talk. The first story, then: this man put the gun on me at the top of the stairs, before I got to the Lindstroms' door—I never saw him before, no, sir—he was after my wallet, when he reached for it I tackled him, tried to get the gun—we struggled, and it went off—

Remember (and not much time to see to it, after the shot) to get his prints on the gun. They were so very damned careful and clever these days, about details.

And if he missed Smith there, it would have to be in the street. If he was at that corner: or, if again he redirected Morgan to a bar, stall him off in there, and follow. A chance again, that the bartender would be honest, would remember them together: but in most of these places down here, hole-in-the-wall joints, the chance probably on Morgan's side. The second story: I was on my way back to my car, when this man tried to hold me up—

They would never trace the gun, never prove it didn't belong to Smith. Nobody could. Morgan had taken it off a dead German in 1944, the sort of ghoulish souvenir young soldiers brought home, and he'd nearly forgotten he had it; he had, being a careful man, taken the remaining three cartridges out of the clip, but they'd been put with the Luger in the old cash box his father had kept for odds and ends, locked away in a trunk in the basement. Morgan had gone down there at three this morning, when he was sure Sue was asleep, and got the gun and the cartridges. It was an unaccustomed weight in his breast pocket right now.

He ought to be somewhere around where this street came in; he began to watch the signs. The third was Tappan. He turned into it and began to look for street numbers.

At that precise moment, Mendoza was having an odd and irritating experience. He was discovering the first thing remotely resembling a link between these two cases (if you discounted that gouged-out eye) and it offered him no help whatsoever. If it wasn't merely his vivid and erratic imagination.

"I'm real glad I clean forgot to th'ow that ol' thing out," said Mrs. Breen, soft and southern, "if it's any help to you findin' that bad man, suh. Ev'body knew Carol thought the world an' all of her, nice a gal as ever was. Terrible thing, jus' terrible."

Mendoza went on looking at the thing, fascinated. It was a good sharp commercial cut, three by five inches or so, one of a dozen in this dog-eared brochure, three years old, from a local toy factory. Mrs. Breen, maddeningly slow, determinedly helpful, had insisted on hunting it up for him, and as he hadn't yet penetrated her constant trickle of inconsequential talk to ask any questions, he'd been forced to let her find it first.

"You can see 'twas a real extra-special doll. Tell the truth, I was two minds about puttin' it in stock, not many folks'd spend that much money."

Was it imagination? That this thing had looked—a little—like Elena Ramirez? After all, he told himself, the conventional doll would. The gold curls, the eyelashes, the neatly rouged cheeks, the rosebud pout, the magenta fingernails. The irrational thought occurred to him that even the costume was exactly the kind of thing Elena would have admired.

He said to himself, I'm seeing ghosts—or catching at straws. What the hell, if the thing did look like her, or the other way around? *Dolls.* The whole thing was a mare's nest. Overnight he had begun to suspect uneasily that he was wrong, dead wrong about this thing; he hadn't taken a good long look at all the dissimilarities—he'd wanted to think this was the Brooks killer again, without any real solid evidence for it. Wasting time. Look at the rest of the facts!

Brooks: the handbag not touched. Ramirez: bag found several blocks away. True, apparently nothing taken, for Teresa said she wouldn't have been carrying more than a little silver, to the rink where she'd leave her bag and coat on a chair at the side.

Brooks: colored, not pretty, not noticeable. Ramirez: very much the opposite.

Brooks: attacked on a fairly well-frequented street, in a fairly good neighborhood—just luck that there hadn't been a number of people within earshot. Ramirez: attacked in that lot away from houses and in a street and neighborhood where a scream wouldn't necessarily bring help.

The chances were, just on the facts, that there were two different killers: say irrational ones, all right, because there didn't seem to be any good logical reason for anyone in either of the private lives wanting those girls dead. But two: and the first could be in Timbuctoo by now.

He was annoyed at himself. He said, "May I have this? Thank you." Let Hackett laugh at him for an imaginative fool! "Now, about this woman, the one who came in and wanted to buy the doll—"

"Shorely, Lieutenant, I had a good rummage firs' thing this mornin' when Mis' Demarest call me 'bout it, and I found that bitty piece o' paper with the name and address—"

NINE

Because afterward, thought Morgan (both Morgans), there would be a time when Sue would look at him, that steady look of hers, and want the truth. And he had better know what he was going to say.

He wondered if he could tell her half the truth convincingly (my God, no, I never *meant*—but when he got mad and pulled a gun, I—and afterward, I knew I couldn't tell the police the whole story, you know—) and go on forever after keeping the rest a secret. He'd never been very good at keeping secrets from Sue. But a big thing like this—and there was also the consideration, wouldn't it be kinder, fairer, not to put this on her conscience as it would be on his? Let her go on thinking it was—accident. Because he guessed it would be on his conscience to some extent. You couldn't be brought up and live half your life by certain basic ethics and forget about them overnight.

All the while he was thinking round and about that, at the back of his mind, he was talking to this woman, this Mrs. Cotter, quite normally—must have been, or she'd have been eying him oddly by this time. He saw that he had also been taking notes in his casebook of a few things she'd told him, and his writing looked quite normal too.

As usual now, he was having some trouble getting away: people liked to talk about these things. You had to be polite and sometimes they remembered something useful. He managed it at last, backing down the steps while he thanked her for the third time.

His car was around the corner, the only parking space there'd been half an hour ago; now, of course, there were two or three empty spaces almost in front of the building. As he came by, a long low black car was sliding quiet and neat into the curb there. The car registered dimly with him, because you didn't see many like it, but he was past when the driver got out. It was the car, a vague memory of it, pulled Morgan's head round six steps farther on. The driver was standing at the curb lighting a cigarette, in profile to him.

Morgan stopped. Absurdly, his mouth went dry and his heart missed a few beats, hurried to catch up. *You damn fool,* he said to himself. *They're not mind readers, for God's sake!*

But, he thought confusedly, but— An omen? Today of all days, just run into one—like this. Casual.

That was a man from Homicide, a headquarters man from Kenneth Gunn's old department. Lieutenant Luis Mendoza of Homicide. Morgan had met him, twice—three times—at the Gunns', and again when their jobs had coincided, that Hurst business, when one of the deserted wives had shot herself and two kids.

Luis Mendoza. Besides the childish panic, resentment he had felt before rose hot in Morgan's throat: unreasonable resentment at the blind fate which handed one man rewards he hadn't earned, didn't particularly deserve—and also more personal resentment for the man.

Mendoza, with all that money, and not a soul in the world but himself to spend it on: no responsibilities, no obligations! Gunn had talked about Mendoza: ordinary back-street family, probably not much different from some of these in neighborhoods like this—nothing of what you'd call background . . . and the wily grandfather, and all the money. What the hell right had he to pretend such to-the-manner-born —if indefinable—insolence? Just the money; all that money. Do anything, have anything he damned pleased, or almost. And by all accounts, didn't he! Clothes—and it wasn't that Morgan wanted to look like a damned fop, the way Mendoza did, but once in a while it would be nice to get a new suit more than once in five years, and not off the rack at a cheap store when there was a sale on. That silver-gray herringbone Mendoza was wearing hadn't cost a dime less than two hundred dollars. An apartment somewhere, not in one of the new smart buildings out west where you paid three hundred a month for the street name and three closet-sized rooms, but the real thing—a big quiet place, spacious, and all for himself, everything just so, custom furniture probably, air-conditioning in summer, maid service, the works. It was the kind of ostentation that was like an iceberg, most of it invisible: that was Mendoza, everything about him. Nothing remotely flashy, all underplayed, the ultraconservative clothes, that damned custom-built car you had to look at twice to know it for what it was, even the manner, the man himself—that precise hairline mustache, the way he lit a cigarette, the—

A womanizer, too: he would be. And easy to think they were only after the money: not, for some reason, altogether true. God knew what women found so fascinating in such men. But he remembered Gunn saying that, a little rueful as became a solid family man, a little indulgent because he liked Mendoza, a little envious the way any man would be—*Poker and women, after hours, that's Luis, his two hobbies you might say, and I understand he's damn good at both.* . . . A lot of women would be fools for such a man, not that he was so handsome, but he—knew the script, like an actor playing a polished scene. And all for casual amusement, all for Mendoza, and when he was bored, the equally polished exit, and forget it.

Gunn had said other things about Mendoza. That he was a brilliant man—that he never let go once he had his teeth into something.

All that, while the lighter-flame touched the cigarette, and was flicked out, the lighter thrust back into the pocket. Mendoza raised his head, took the cigarette out of his mouth, and saw Morgan there looking at him. And so Morgan had to smile, say his name, the conventional things you did say, meeting an acquaintance.

"How's Gunn these days? He's missed downtown, you know—a good man. I understand that's quite an organization he's set up."

Morgan agreed; he said you ran into some interesting cases sometimes, he had one now, but one thing for sure, you certainly had a chance to see how the other half lived—but that'd be an old story to Mendoza.

"That you do," said the man from Homicide, and smoke trickled thin through his nostrils; if he took in the *double-entendre* he gave no sign of it.

"Well, nice to run into you—I'll give Gunn your regards." Morgan seemed to be under a compulsion to sound hearty, make inane little jokes: "I hope, by the way, we're not concerned with the same clients again, like that Hurst business—nasty."

"I want 2416."

It was the building Morgan had just left; he said, "That's it. Be careful of the third step—it's loose. I nearly broke my neck."

"Thanks very much." And more conventionalities of leave-taking, and he was free. He started again for his car. The gun was suddenly very heavy there against his chest. When he got out his keys, he saw his hand shaking a little. *Damn fool,* he thought angrily.

It's going to be all *right.* Just the way I want it to go. No matter who, no matter what. And, by God, if it isn't, if the very worst happens—whatever that might be—this was one time anyway he wouldn't stand still to be knocked out of the ring. He'd have tried, anyway.

Mrs. Irene Cotter was rather thrilled and wildly curious. *Two* men, *detectives* of all things, calling in one morning, and both about those

Lindstroms. If you'd asked her, she'd have said—in fact, she was saying it now to Mendoza—that most any other tenants she'd ever had while she was manageress here, and that'd been eleven years, were more likely to bring *detectives* around. That blonde hussy in 307, for instance, or Mr. Jessup who was, not to beat round the bush, just a nasty old man—and there'd been that couple in 419 that got drunk most nights and threw things.

She told him about them all, at some length and, when she remembered, taking pains with her grammar, because this one was a lot more interesting-looking, and seemed more interested in her, than the first one. She always thought there was *something* about a man with mustache. This one looked a little bit like that fellow in the movies, the one that was usually the villain but personally she thought about a lot of the movies she'd seen with him in that the girl was an awful fool to prefer some sheep-eyed collar-ad instead, but there was no accounting for tastes. And a real gentleman too, beautiful manners; of course that was one thing about these Mexes, people said things about them, but of course there was classes of them just like anywhere, only when they were highclass like this one, you said Spanish.

"—And I tell you, when he up and left, and everybody knew it, nobody couldn't hardly believe it! You'd never have thought they was that kind at all, fly-by-nights I mean that don't go on steady, you know what I mean, all their lives. But I tell you, lieutenant, I like to sort of study people, and G— goodness knows I get the chance in my job, and I said to myself at the time, There's something behind it."

"There usually is. The man left in August, you said, early."

"I couldn't swear to the date, but it was after the rent was due—*and* paid. They was never a day late. Good tenants. Maybe the first week."

"And how long did the woman and boy stay on?"

"Oh, I can tell you that to the day. It was the twenty-second of September they left, she told me in the morning, late, round noon maybe, and they went that night. I remember because she was paid to the end of the month, but they went before, and I *did* think that was funny, because it must've meant she'd paid extra wherever they were moving, you know, to move in before the first. And already bein' paid up to the first here, you'd think— Of course, all *I* know, *she* didn't say, they might've been going back east or somewheres. I did ask, account of mail, not that they ever had much of that, mostly ads—but she never said, just looked at me as if I was being nosy. And I'll tell you something else, Lieutenant, you can believe it or not, but that was just ex-

actly the fourth time I'd spoke to Mis' Lindstrom, all two years they'd
been here. That was the kind they was—her, anyways. Why, they'd
moved in a week or more before I ever laid eyes on *her*—it was *him*
rented the place, and paid, and like people mostly do they moved in at
night, after work, you know—not that they had much to bring, a few
sticks o' furniture. But I was telling you about when *he* went. It was
Mis' Spinner in 319 told me, right next to them, they had 320, you can
see that I wouldn't notice right off, especially with them, sometimes I'd
see him going off in the morning or coming home, but not every day.
And Mis' Spinner thought I ought to know he'd left, at least hadn't
been there she didn't *think* four-five days, time she told me. Well, they
was paid up to the end of August, I didn't go asking questions till then,
none o' my business, but when September first come round, it was *her*
come down to pay the rent and then I did figure, better know where
we stood, if you see what I mean. Without wanting to be *nosy*," added
Mrs. Cotter virtuously. "She wouldn't admit he'd gone and left her,
froze right up and said I needn't worry about the rent, and some rigmarole about he was called back east sudden. But alla same, it wasn't a
week before she had to get herself a job, so I knew all right. And if
you ask me—"

"Where did she work, do you know?"

"Sure, it was a night job cleaning offices downtown—the Curtis
Building. And that's what I was goin' to say, Lieutenant—that kind of
job, it shows you what she was *like*, and you ask me, it all ties in, it was
prob'ly all her fault, whole thing. She was one of them old maids married like they say, for *sure*. Went around with a sour look alla time,
never a smile or a friendly word in passing—and as for looks! Well, I
don't s'pose she was more than forty, and I tell you, she looked like her
own gran'mother! Hair screwed up in a little bun behind, and skin like
a piece o' sandpaper, you could tell she never took any care of herself,
prob'ly used laundry soap and that's that—never a scrap of make-up,
and cheap old cotton house dresses was all I ever seen her in. You
know's well as me there's no call for a woman to let herself *go* like that,
these days! And if she acted to *him* the way she did to everybody else,
even the youngster, well, between you 'n' me 'n' the gatepost, I don't
blame him for walkin' out. A man can take just so much. She'd've been
the kind wouldn't let him sleep with her either, a regular prunes-an'-
prison old maid like they say, if you know what I mean. Why, if she'd
taken a little trouble, fix herself up and act nice, she coulda got a better
job, waiting in a store or something, you know, daytimes. There's just
no *call* for a woman to look like that, if she's got any self-respect! But

she wasn't one you could talk to friendly, you know, give any advice, like—she was downright rude to everybody tried to make friends, so after a while nobody tried no more, just left them be. And I do think *he*'d have been different. Times he came by to pay the rent, or if you met him goin' out or like that, he always acted friendly and polite. I figure he just got good and fed up with the whole way she was—it musta been like livin' with a set bear trap."

The detective grinned at that and she permitted herself a ladylike titter, smoothing her defiantly brown pompadour. "I gather you didn't exchange much casual talk with the woman at any time."

"Nobody did, she wouldn't let 'em. . . . Ever hear her mention goin' to buy a *doll?* That I did not. It wasn't a girl she had, it was a boy, I thought I said. Marty, his name was. He favored his dad, I must say he was a nice-raised boy. Always took off his cap to you, and he was real quiet—for a boy, you know. He'd be about eleven or a bit past when they come, and that last year they was here, he all of a sudden'd started to shoot up, early like some do—going to be as big as his dad, you could see. A real nice boy, he was, not like his Ma at all. . . . Well, I'm sure I don't know why she'd be buying a *doll,* unless it was for some of their fambly back east, might be she had a niece or something. But *for goodness' sake,* Lieutenant, won't you tell me what this is all about—what's she *done?*—or is it *him?* I mean—"

"I don't know that either of them's done anything. It's a matter of getting evidence, that's all, not very important." He was standing up.

"Oh. I must say, I can't help being *curious*—two of you coming, same day, ask about *them!* You can't blame me for that, couldn't you just—"

"So Mr. Morgan was asking about the Lindstroms too?" He looked thoughtful, and then smiled and began to thank her. She saw she wouldn't get any more out of him, but that didn't stop her from speculating. The Lindstroms, of all people!

Mrs. Cotter watched him down the walk to his car, heaved an excited sigh after him, and hurried upstairs to tell Mrs. Spinner all about it.

The clock over the row of phone booths, in the first drugstore he came to, said ten past twelve. Mendoza spent an annoying five minutes looking up the number in a tattered book, finally got the office, and just caught Gunn on his way out to lunch.

"Oh, Luis—how's the boy?—good to hear from you. Say, I'm afraid Andrews' idea didn't pay off, you know, about that hood New York wants for jumping parole. It was a long chance, find him through the wife, and of course it may be she's collecting from some other county agency. If he wants— What's that? Sure thing, anything I can tell you . . . Morgan, well, he's probably having lunch somewhere right now."

"It's one of his cases, that's all. And all I want from you is the present address. The name is Mrs. Marion Lindstrom. Apparently she's only recently applied for relief."

"If we're working on it, that's so, within a few months anyway—it'll be right here in the current file, hang on and I'll look."

Mendoza opened the door for air while he waited. He was rapidly developing a guilty conscience: wasting time over this meaningless thing. He didn't get paid—or shouldn't—for listening to inconsequential gossip. A dozen things he should have been doing this morning besides—

"—Graham Court," said Gunn's voice in his ear.

"Oh? Any idea approximately where that is?"

"Somewhere down the wrong side of Main, that area—below First or Second. We've got—"

"*¡No puede ser!*" said Mendoza very softly to himself. "It can't be, not so easy, I don't believe it. . . . When Morgan comes in, tell him to wait, I want to see him. Call me at my office *immediatamente*—or even quicker! I want everything you've got on these people. Let me have that address again."

It was Gunn, of course, and not Hackett, who said all the things Hackett might say later; before outsiders, like this, Hackett paid lip service to rank. Gunn had once been Mendoza's superior; he spoke up. By the same token, of course, Mendoza wouldn't have talked so freely if Gunn hadn't been a retired Homicide man.

"You've got your wires crossed, Luis. What you've got here is just damn-all, it doesn't mean a thing. First off, how many people d'you suppose moved out of that section of town last September? There's no narrowing it down to a couple of blocks, you have to take in at least a square mile—call it even half a mile—at a guess, seven-eight thousand families, because you're taking in apartments, not just single houses. In that kind of neighborhood people aren't settled, they move around more. And—"

"I know, I know," said Mendoza. "And that's the least of all the arguments against this meaning anything at all. But say it—it's not even very significant that the move should be from the twenty-four-hundred block on Tappan to within two blocks of Commerce and Humboldt, because those are the same sort of neighborhoods, same rent levels, same class and color of people. All right. Evidence—!" He hunched his shoulders angrily, turning from staring at the view out Gunn's office window. "Say it. Even if it *is* the same killer, no guarantee he lived anywhere near either of the girls. So all this is *cuentos de hadas,* just fairy tales."

Hackett made a small doleful sound at his cigarette. "I guess you're saying it for yourself, Lieutenant."

"You've got no evidence," Gunn said flatly. "You'd just like to think so, which isn't like you, Luis. What the hell *have* you got? I—"

"I've got two dead girls," said Mendoza, abrupt and harsh. "And they don't matter one damn, you know. The kind of murders that happen in any big town, this week, next week, next year. No glamour, no excitement, no big names. Nothing to go in the books, the clever whimsy on Classic Cases or the clever fiction, ten wisecracks guaranteed to the page, a surprise ending to every chapter, where fifteen people had fifteen motives for the murder and fifteen faked alibis for the crucial minute, conveniently fixed by a prearranged long-distance phone call. They weren't very important or interesting females, these two, and anybody at all might have killed them. *You* know," he swung on Gunn, "this kind of thing, it doesn't go like the books, the clues laid out neat like a paper trail in a game! You start where you can and you take a look everywhere, at everything—¿Qué más?—and then you start all over again."

"*I* know," said Gunn heavily. "What I'm saying is, you've got nothing at all to link these two cases. The doll, that's really out of bounds, boy, that one I don't figure any way. The odds are that somebody found the girl, didn't report it, but picked up the package—"

"You're so right," said Mendoza. "It was dark, and her handbag was half under her, almost hidden."

"Well, there you are. They were killed the same general way, but it's not a very unusual method—brute violence."

"That eye," said Hackett to his cigarette.

Gunn looked at him, back to Mendoza. "If it's a real hunch, Luis, all I've got to say is, keep throwing cold water at it—if it just naturally drowns, let it go."

"What else am I doing?" For they both knew that it wasn't ever all pure cold logic, all on the facts: nothing that had to do with people ever could be wholly like that. You had a feeling, you had a hunch, and you couldn't drop every other line to follow it up, but a real fourteen-karat hunch turned out to be worth something—sometimes. Say it was subconscious reasoning, out of experience and knowledge; it wasn't, always. Just a feeling.

"All right," said Hackett amiably, "cold water. I don't like the doll much myself. I said I'd buy all that about the guy at the skating rink, but there's nothing there to show it's the same one. In fact, the little we *have* got on that one, it suggests he admired the girl, wanted to pick her up—like that, whether for murder or sex."

"So it does," said Mendoza. "And no hint of anything like that for Carol Brooks."

Gunn opened his mouth, shut it, looked at Hackett's bland expression, and said, "You saw both bodies, of course—you're a better judge of what the similarity there is worth."

"Oh, let's be psychological," said Mendoza. "Not even that. Art says to me before I looked at Ramirez, 'It's another Brooks'—maybe he put it in my mind."

"Sure, lay it on me."

There was a short silence, and then Mendoza said as if continuing argument, "Nobody's interested in this kind of killing, no, except those of us who're paid to be interested. But it's the kind everybody ought to take passionate interest in—the most dangerous kind there is—just because it's without motive. Or having the motive only of sudden, impulsive violence. The lunatic kill. So it might happen to anybody. *Claro que sí,* let one like that kill a dozen, twenty, leave his mark to show it's the same killer, then he's one for the books—the Classic Case. And don't tell me I've got no evidence these were lunatic kills. It's negative evidence, I grant you, but there it is—we looked, you know. Nobody above ground had any reason to murder the Brooks girl, and she wasn't killed for what cash she had on her. The couple of little things we've got on Ramirez, nothing to lead to murder—and she wasn't robbed either. Not to that murder. I don't have to tell you that brute violence of that sort, it's either very personal hate or lunacy."

Morgan cleared his throat; he'd been waiting in silence, a little apart, his case book out ready, if and when they remembered him. "I don't want to butt in, you know more about all this, but I can't help feeling you're on the wrong track here, just for that reason. These people— well, after all—I don't suppose you're thinking the woman did it, and a thirteen-year-old kid—"

Again a short silence. Hackett leaned back in his chair and said conversationally, "I picked up a thirteen-year-old kid a couple of months ago who'd shot his mother in the back while she was watching T.V. She'd told him he couldn't go to the movies that night. You remember that Breckfield business last year?—three kids, the oldest one thirteen, tied up two little girls and set fire to them. One died, the other's still in the hospital. I could take you places in this town where a lot of thirteen-year-old kids carry switch-knives and pull off organized gang raids on each other—and the neighborhood stores. And some of 'em aren't little innocents any other way, either. Juvenile had a couple in last week—and not the first—with secondary stage V.D., and both on heroin."

Morgan said helplessly, "But—this kid—he's not like that! He's just a *kid*, like any kid that age. You can tell, you know."

"Something was said," cut in Mendoza, "about his size, that he'd started to get his growth early. How big is he?—how strong?"

"Almost as tall as I am—five-eight-and-a-half, around there. Still—childish-looking, in the face. But he's going to be a big man, he's built that way—big bone structure."

"Weight?"

"Hell, I can't guess about all this," said Morgan angrily. "As far as I can see you've got no reason at all to suspect the Lindstroms of anything. I don't know what's in your mind about this boy—you talk about lunatics and juvenile hoods, so O.K., which is he? You can't have it both ways. The whole thing's crazy."

Mendoza came a few steps toward him, stood there hands in pockets looking down at him, a little cold, a little annoyed. "I've got nothing in my mind about him right now. I don't know. This is the hell of a low card, but I've got the hell of a bad hand and it's the best play I've got at the moment. Carol Brooks was killed on September twenty-first, and these people left that neighborhood—unexpectedly, and in a hurry—within twenty-four hours. The woman was working at night, so the boy was free to come and go as he pleased. Shortly before Brooks was killed, the woman showed interest in an article Brooks was buying on time, and it now appears that the girl had this with her before she was killed and it subsequently disappeared. I'm no psychiatrist and I don't know how much what any psychiatrist'd say might be worth, here—the boy just into adolescence, probably suffering some shock when his father abandoned them. Let that go. But he's big enough and strong enough to have done—the damage that was done. If. And I may take a jaundiced view of the psychological doubletalk, the fact remains that sex can play some funny tricks with young adolescents sometimes. All right. These people are now living in the neighborhood where Elena Ramirez was killed. I don't say they had anything to do with either death, or even the theft. I'd just like to know a little more about them."

Morgan shrugged and flipped open his notebook. "You're welcome to what I've got. Mrs. Lindstrom applied for county relief six weeks ago, and was interviewed by a case worker from that agency. She says her husband deserted her and the boy last August, she has no idea where he is now, hasn't heard from him since. She took a job between then and a week or so before she applied, says she can't go on working on account of her health. She was referred to a clinic, and there's a medical report here—various troubles adding up to slight malnutrition and a general run-down condition. Approved for county relief, and the case shoved on to us to see if we can find Lindstrom, make him contribute support. He's a carpenter, good record, age forty-four, description—and so on and so on—they both came from a place called Fayetteville in Minnesota, so she said," and he glanced at Gunn.

"Yes," said Gunn thoughtfully, "and what does that mean, either? Sometimes these husbands head for home and mother, we usually query the home town first—and I have here a reply from the vital records office in Fayetteville saying that no such family has ever resided there."

"You don't tell me," said Mendoza.

"This I'll tell you," said Morgan, "because we run into it a lot. Some of these women are ashamed to have the folks at home know about it, and they don't realize we're going to check on it—the same with former addresses here, and she gave me a false one on that too, sure. It doesn't necessarily mean—"

"No. But it's another little something. What have you got on the boy?"

"Nothing, why should I have? He exists, that's all we have to know. He's normal, thirteen years old, name Martin Eric Lindstrom, attends seventh grade at John C. Calhoun Junior High." Morgan shut the book.

"That's all? I'd like to know more about the boy. We'll have a look round. No trace of the father yet?"

"It's early, we've only been on this a few days. Routine enquiries out to every place in the area hiring carpenters—to vital records and so on in other counties—and so on."

"Yes. Will you let me have a copy of all that you've got, please—to my office. We'll keep an eye on them, see what shows up, if anything. Thanks very much."

When the two men from Homicide had gone, Gunn said, "Get one of the girls to type up that report, send it over by hand."

"O.K.," said Morgan. "I suppose—" He was half-turned to the door, not looking at Gunn. "I suppose that means he'll have men watching that apartment."

"It's one of the basic moves. What's the matter, Dick?"

"Nothing," said Morgan violently. "Nothing at all. Oh, hell, it's just that— I guess Mendoza always rubs me the wrong way, that's all. Always so damned sure of himself—and I think he's way off the beam here."

"It doesn't look like much of anything," agreed Gunn. "But on the other hand, well, you never can be sure until you check."

TEN

"I have the feeling," said Mendoza—discreetly in Spanish, for the waiter who had seated them was still within earshot—"that I'd better apologize for the meal we're about to have."

"But why? Everything looks horribly impressive. Including the prices. In fact, after that automatic glance at the right-hand column," said Alison, putting down the immense menu card, "*I* have the feeling I've been in the wrong business all my life."

"I never can remember quite how it goes, about fooling some of the people, etcetera." Mendoza glanced thoughtfully around the main dining room of the Maison du Chat, which was mostly magenta, underlighted, and decorated with would-be funny murals of lascivious felines. "It's curious how many people are ready to believe that the highest prices guarantee the best value." The waiter came back and insinuated under their noses liquor lists only slightly smaller than the menus. "What would you like to drink?"

"Sherry," said Alison faintly, her eyes wandering down the right column.

"And straight rye," he said to the waiter, who looked shaken and took back the cards with a disappointed murmur.

"*Not* in character. I'd expected to find you something of a gourmet."

"My God, I thought I'd made a better impression. The less one thinks about one's stomach, the less trouble it's apt to cause. And I know just enough about wine to call your attention to those anonymous offerings you just looked at—port, muscatel, tokay, and so on. At three dollars the half-bottle, and they'll be the domestic product available at the nearest supermarket for what?—about one-eighty-nine the gallon."

"They're not losing money on the imported ones either."

"About a one hundred percent markup." He looked around again casually, focused on something past her shoulder, and began to smile slowly to himself. "Now isn't that interesting . . ."

"I couldn't agree more—I said I've always found the subject fascinating. You're pleased about something, and it can't be the prices."

"I just noticed an old friend. And what's more, he noticed me. He isn't nearly so pleased about it." The waiter, doing his best with pseudo-Gallic murmurs and deft gestures with paper mats to invest these plebeian potions with glamour, served them. Mendoza picked up his rye and sniffed it cautiously. "*¡Salud y pesetas!* And if this costs them more than a dollar a fifth wholesale, they're being cheated, which I doubt."

"Why did we come here? I gather it's new to you too."

"We came because I'm interested in this place, not as a restaurant—professionally. Of course I also wanted to impress you."

"You have."

"And I'm gratified to find you see through these spurious trappings of the merely expensive. Next time I'll take you to a hamburger stand."

"You will not. I like an excuse to get really dressed up occasionally." She had, after all, compromised with his dictation: pearls, and a very modest *décolleté,* but for the rest an oyster-silk sheath.

"I complimented you once, don't fish for more so early," said Mendoza placidly. "And what I expected to get by coming—besides rooked out of a little money—I don't know. Mr. Torres-Domingo is an unexpected bonus. You see, the uncle of your late pupil went out of his way to visit this place last night, which seemed a little odd."

"Oh! I should think so. Who is the other gentleman you mentioned?"

"I wouldn't say gentleman. He just barely avoided an indictment for homicide about eighteen months ago—he was then the proprietor of a bar on Third Avenue. Another gentleman who later turned out to have been a small-time wholesaler of heroin got himself shot full of holes by a third gentleman who subsequently said that Mr.—the first gentleman

—had offered him a substantial sum of money to do the job. We didn't doubt his word—after what showed up—but unfortunately there just wasn't enough evidence. The first gentleman retired modestly across the Mexican border, though he is an American citizen, and it's interesting to know he's back home. I don't want him for anything myself, but Lieutenant Patrick Callaghan will be very interested to hear that he's now the headwaiter at a fashionable restaurant."

"I deduce that the lieutenant is on the narcotics team, or whatever you call it."

"And as you and I are not the only people in the world who speak Spanish, we will now cease to talk shop. . . . What are we offered? All the standard Parisian concoctions. Women living alone subsist mostly on casseroles anyway, no treat to you—I suggest the one concession to Americanism, a steak."

"Medium well," she agreed meekly. And when the waiter had gone, "May I ask just one question? People make a lot of money in that—er —business you mentioned. Wholesaling you-know-what. Why should they go to all the trouble of holding down regular jobs too? I always thought of them as—as coming out at night, slinking furtively down alleys, you know—like that—not punching time clocks."

"Oh, God!" he said. "Now you've taken my appetite away. Well, there's a den of crafty bloodsucking robbers in Washington—you'll have heard of them—"

"Which ones?"

"It says Bureau of Internal Revenue on the door. Now, the L.A.P.D. couldn't get one useful piece of evidence against the gentleman I mentioned—as we can't always against a lot of others in a lot of businesses, and I do mean big businesses, on the wrong side of the law. But we can't poke our noses into some things those fellows can. A hundred-thousand-dollar apartment house—a new Cadillac—a mink coat for the girl friend—you *are* doing well, Mr. Smith, how come you never told your uncle about it? And if Mr. Smith can't explain just where it all came from, he's got a lot more grief than a mere city cop could ever hand him."

"Oh, I *see*. I do indeed. Cover."

"And then," added Mendoza, not altogether humorously, "when uncle has stowed Mr. Smith away in jail for tax evasion, the indignant public points an accusing finger at us and says, Corrupt cops!—they must have known about him! Stupid cops!—if they didn't find out! Why wasn't he arrested for his *real* crimes? You try to tell them, just try, that it's because we have to operate within laws about evidence designed to protect the public. . . . I wonder whether I ought to call in and tell Pat's office about this." Mr. Torres-Domingo, who had made a precipitate exit on first catching sight of him, reappeared round the screen at the service doors, polishing his bald head with a handkerchief. He shot one furtive glance in Mendoza's direction, pasted on a professional happy smile, and began to circulate among the tables, pausing for a bow, a word here and there with a favored patron. "Oh, well, there's no hurry—he won't run away, and for all I know he's reformed and hasn't any reason to anyway."

The steaks could have been less tough; the service might with advantage have been less ostentatious. Mendoza asked her presently whether she'd got anything useful from any of the girls.

"I wondered when you'd ask. Nothing at all, I'm sorry to say—she hadn't said anything to any of them about that. But she didn't know any of them well, after all."

"No. I didn't expect much of that. I've got a queer sort of—can I call it a lead?—from another angle, but I don't know that that means much either. . . . What do you think of the murals? I've never asked you what kind of thing you paint."

Alison said the murals constituted a libel on the feline race and that she was herself unfashionably pre-Impressionistic. "This and that—I'm not wedded to any one particular type of subject. Now and then I actually sell something." They talked about painting; they talked about cats. "—But when you're away all day, you can't keep pets, it's not fair."

"Nobody keeps a cat. They condescend to live with you is all. And as for the rest of it, *I* moved. It's miles farther for me to drive, and the rent's higher, but it's on the ground floor and they let me put in one of those little swinging doors in the back door, out to the yard. You've seen the ads—*let your pet come and go freely*. Yes, a fine idea, but she won't use it—she knows how it works, but she doesn't like the way it slaps her behind, and she got her tail pinched once. Fortunately all the other seven apartments are inhabited by cat people. Four of them have keys to mine and run in and out all day waiting on her, which of course is what she schemes for. I believe Mrs. Carter and Mrs. Bryson," he added, looking around for the waiter, "alternate their shopping tours and visits to the beauty salon—coffee, please—"

"And pairhaps some of our special brandy, sair?"

"That I need," said Alison, "after listening to this barefaced confession. Battening on the charity of your neighbors like that—"

"One of the reasons I picked the apartment. The Elgins keep her supplied with catnip mice, they buy them in wholesale lots, having three Siamese of their own. Of course there *is* a man two doors down who has a spaniel, but one must expect some undesirables in these unrestricted neighborhoods." The waiter came back with the coffee, the brandy, and the bill on a salver, contriving to slide that in front of Mendoza by a kind of legerdemain suggesting that it appeared out of thin air, not through any offices of this obsequious and excellent servant. Mendoza looked at it, laid two tens on the salver and said now he needed the brandy too.

"I have no sympathy for you," said Alison.

When they came out into the foyer, Mendoza hesitated, glancing at the discreet row of phone booths in an alcove. "I wonder if I *had*—" There had appeared no bowing, smiling headwaiter as they left the dining room, to make the last honors to new patrons, urge a return. "Oh, well," and he put a hand automatically to his pocket for more largesse as one of the several liveried lackeys approached with Alison's coat.

"So 'appy to 'ave 'ad you wiz us, sair and madame—I 'ope you enjoyed your dinnair? You mus' come back soon—*Holy Mother o' God,* what the hell was that?" Between them they dropped the coat; the lackey took one look over Alison's shoulder, said, "Jesus, let me out of here!" and dived blindly for the door, staggering Mendoza aside. The second volley of shots was a medley of several calibers, including what sounded like a couple of regulation .38's. From the dark end of the corridor off the foyer plunged a large, shapeless man waving a revolver, and close after him the tuxedo-clad rotundity of Mr. Torres-Domingo, similarly equipped. The checkroom attendant prudently dropped flat behind his counter as the large man paused to fire twice more behind him and charged into the foyer.

"Wait for me, Neddy!" Mr. Torres-Domingo sent one wild shot behind him and another inadvertently into the nearest phone booth as he continued flight.

The first man swept the gun in an arc round the foyer. "Don't nobody move—I'm comin' through—"

Mendoza recovered his balance, shoved Alison hard to sprawl full length on the floor, and in one leap covered the ten feet to the gun as it swung back in his direction. He got a good left-handed grip on the gunhand as they collided, his momentum lending force to the considerable impact, and as they went down landed one right that connected satisfactorily. Neddy went over backward and Mendoza went with him; the gun emptied itself into the ceiling as they hit the floor with Mendoza's knee in the paunch under him; Neddy uttered a strangled *whoof* and lost all interest in the proceedings.

Mr. Torres-Domingo yelped, fired once more and hit the plate-glass door, turned and ran into the embrace of an enormous red-haired man in the vanguard of the pursuit, which had just erupted down the corridor. The red-haired man adjusted him to a convenient position and hit him once in the jaw, and he flew backward six feet and collapsed on top of Mendoza, who was just sitting up. One of the three men behind the red-haired man dropped his gun and sank onto the divan beside the checkroom, clutching his shoulder.

There was a very short silence before several women in the crowd collecting at the dining-room door went off like air-raid sirens. Mendoza heaved off Mr. Torres-Domingo, sat up and began to swear in Spanish. The red-haired man bellowed the crowd to quiet, and turned to the man nearest him: "Find a phone and call the wagon and an ambulance—and"—flinging round to the man on the divan—"just what in the name of Jesus, Mary, and Joseph did you think *you* were doing, you almighty bastard? You—"

"*¡Hijo de perra!*—take your hands off that man, you son of a Dublin whore!" Mendoza shoved him away and bent over Higgins, who was fumbling a handkerchief under his coat. "Easy, boy—"

"It's not bad, Lieutenant—I just—"

"Before God!—Luis Mendoza!—does *this* belong to you? Just what the holy hell are *you* doing in this?—you tellin' me *you* put this blundering bastard out back there—to bitch up two months' work and the first chance I've had to lay hands on—I ought to bust you right in the —I ought to—"

Mendoza twitched the handkerchief from the red-haired man's breast pocket, wadded it up with his own, shoved Higgins flat on the divan and pulled aside the coat to slap on the temporary bandage. "Temper, Patrick, temper! We're in public—you'll be giving people the idea there's no loyalty, no unity in the police force. And listen, you red bastard, next time you have to knock a man out to arrest him, for the love of God don't aim him at me—you've damn near fractured my spine! There's the squad car. For God's sake, let's clear this crowd back— who's this?"

The little round man who had popped out like a cork from the dining-room crowd was sounding off in falsetto. "I am the manager—I am the owner—what do you do here in my place, shooting and yelling? I

call the police!—what is all this about?—shootings—gangsters—I will
not have gangsters in my nice quiet place—"

"Then you shouldn't hire one as a headwaiter," said Mendoza. "And
you should also change your butcher, your steaks are tough." He
pushed past him and went over to Alison, who was just somewhat shak-
ily regaining her feet. "I don't usually knock them down the *first* date,
mi vida—apologies! Are you all right? Here, sit down."

"*I'm* all right," said Alison, "but you owe me a pair of stockings."

Morgan had read somewhere that marijuana did this to you, played
tricks with time, so first it seemed to slow down, almost grind to a full
stop, and then sent everything past you at the speed of light. His watch
told him he'd been standing here on this corner just an hour and twelve
minutes, no more and no less; for a while it had felt like half eternity,
and then, a while after that, time began to go too fast. Where he'd been
tense with impatience, wound up tight for action—*God, God, make
him come*—suddenly, now, he could have prayed for time to stop. Not
now, he said to Smith frantically in his mind, you can't come now, until
I've thought about this, figured it out, got hold of another plan.

Oh, Christ damn Luis Mendoza and his little slum-street mugging!—
what the hell did that matter, some damn-fool chippy knocked off,
probably she'd asked for it, and that crazy idea about those Lindstroms
who couldn't by any fantastic stretch of the imagination have had anything to do . . . Because, yes, this upright citizen Morgan had a good
innocent reason to visit that apartment house, he wouldn't care if the
whole L.A. police force stood by in squads to watch him go in—but
after he was clocked in by men watching, he couldn't lie in wait maybe
an hour, and do what he'd come to do, and then say *Just as I got to the
top of the stairs*— Nor could he call at the Lindstroms' first, thinking to
say, *Just as I was leaving*— That woman might not be very smart but
she could tell time, and suppose he'd left her half an hour before, as
might well happen? Also, of course, there was no telling about the
cops: where and how and how many. It might be a desultory thing, one
man outside up to midnight, something like that; it might be a couple of
men round the clock; it could be a couple of men inside somewhere.

So he hadn't dared go near Graham Court at all. It had had to be the
street corner; and on his way here, and up to a while ago, he'd been
telling himself that after all the street was safer. Once you were off
Main, off Second, along here, the streets were underlighted and there
weren't many people; in all this while he'd stood and strolled up and

down outside the corner drugstore here, only four people had come by, at long intervals. Safer, and also more plausible that Smith would try a holdup on a darkish side street, instead of in the very building where he lived.

Morgan had been feeling pretty good then: ready for it, coldly wound up (the way it had been before action, when you knew action was coming) but—in control. He'd known just how it would go, Smith coming along (he'd been wary before, sent the boy to check that Morgan had come alone, but this time he wouldn't bother, he thought he had Morgan and—*the ransom*—tied up); and Morgan pretending nervousness, saying he had the money locked in the glove compartment, his car was just round the corner. Round the corner, an even narrower, darker street. Sure to God Smith would walk a dozen steps with him . . .

Safe and easy. Sure. Before a while ago, when the scraggly bald old fellow had peered out the drugstore door at him.

Morgan knew this window by heart now. Everything in it a little dusty, a little second-hand-looking: out-of-date ad placards, the platinum blonde with a toothy smile, INSTANT PROTECTION, the giant tube of shaving cream, the giant bottle of antiseptic, the cigarette ad, GET SATISFACTION, the face-cream ad, YOU CAN LOOK YOUNGER. In a vague way he'd known the drugstore was open, but the door was shut on this coolish evening, he hadn't glanced inside. When people came by, he'd strolled away the opposite direction: nobody had seemed to take much notice of him—why should they? And then that old fellow came to the door, peered out: Morgan met his glance through the dirty glass panel, by chance, and that was when time began to race.

God, don't let Smith come now, not until I've had time to think.

The druggist, alone there, pottering around his store in the hopeful expectation of a few customers before nine o'clock, or maybe just because he hadn't anything to go home to. Time on his hands. Looking out the window, the door, every so often, for customers at first—and then to see, only out of idle curiosity, if that fellow was still there on the corner, waiting. . . . All that clutter in the window, Morgan hadn't noticed him; not much light, no, but enough—and without thought, when he was standing still he'd hugged the building for shelter from the chill wind. Most of the time he'd have been in the perimeter of light from the window, from the door. God alone knew how often the old man had looked out, spotted him.

The expression in the rheumy eyes meeting his briefly through the dirty pane—focused, curious, a little defensive—told Morgan the man had marked him individually.

And hell, hell, it didn't matter whether the druggist thought he'd been stood up by a date, or was planning to hold up the drugstore, or was just lonely or worried or crazy, hanging around this corner an hour and twelve minutes. The druggist would remember him. . . . That was a basic principle, and only common sense, in planning anything underhand and secret—from robbing Junior's piggy bank to murder: *Keep it simple.* Don't have too many lies to remember, don't dream up the complicated routine, the fancy alibi. The way he'd designed it was like that—short, straight, and sweet. Now, if he went on with it that way, there'd be the plausible lie to figure out and remember and stick to: just why the hell had Morgan been hanging around here, obviously a man waiting for someone?

Half-formed ideas, wild, ridiculous, skittered along the top of his mind. You know how it is, officer, I met this blonde, didn't mean any harm but a fellow likes a night out once in a while; sure I felt guilty, sure I love my wife, but, well, the blonde said she'd meet me— I tell you how it was, I'd lent this guy a five-spot, felt sorry for him you know, guess I was a sucker, anyway he said he'd meet me and pay— Well, I met this fellow who said he'd give me an inside tip on a horse, only he wouldn't know for sure until tonight, if I'd meet him—

All right, he thought furiously, all *right;* of all the damn-fool ideas . . . So, produce the blonde, the debtor, the tipster! It couldn't be done that way.

He stood now right at the building corner, close, out of the druggist's view. Think: if, when Smith comes, what are you going to do now? What can you do?

The little panic passed and he saw the only possible answer: it wasn't a very good one, it put more complication into this than was really safe, but that couldn't be helped. Obviously, get Smith away from this place. The farther away the better. In the car. Stall him and get him into the car, and Christ, the possibilities, the dangers *that* opened up—couldn't drive far, maybe not at all, without getting him suspicious. Sure, knock him out with a wrench or something as soon as they got in, fine, and have it show up at the autopsy later on. Great, shoot him in the car under cover of the revving motor, and get blood all over the seat covers. All right: think.

Yes. It could be managed, it had to be: the only way. In the car, then, right away, and in the body, so the clothes would get the blood.

Have to take a chance. Then quick around to Humboldt or Foster, only a few blocks, both dark streets too, thank God; park the car, get him out to the sidewalk, get his prints on the gun, make a little disturbance, fire another shot, and yell for the cops. *I was on my way to visit this case I'm on, when*— And the druggist no danger then, no reason to connect a holdup there with his corner.

Not as safe, but it could work: maybe, with luck, it would work fine.

Now let Smith come. Morgan was ready for him, as ready as he'd ever be.

He looked at his watch. It was seventeen minutes past eight.

And suddenly he began to get in a sweat about something else. Smith had made him wait on Saturday night, deliberately, to soften him up: but why the hell should Smith delay coming to collect the ransom he thought was waiting?

Cops, thought Morgan—cold, resentful, sullen, helpless—*cops!* Maybe so obvious there outside, inside, that Smith spotted them—and thought, of course, Morgan had roped them in? God, the whole thing blown open—

ELEVEN

Cops, Marty thought. Cops, he'd said. Funny, the words meant the same, but seemed like people who didn't like them, maybe were afraid of them, said "cops," and other people said "policemen."

He sat up in bed in the dark; it was the bad time again, the time alone with the secret. And a lot of what made it bad was, usually, not having outside things to keep him from thinking about it, remembering; but right now he had, and that somehow made it worse.

He sat up straight against the headboard; he tried to sit still as still, but couldn't help shivering even in his flannel pajamas, with the top of him outside the blanket. If he laid right down like usual he was afraid he'd go to sleep after a while, even the long while it'd got to taking him lately; and he mustn't, if he was going to do what he planned safe. He had to stay awake until everybody else was asleep, maybe two, three o'clock in the morning, and then be awful quiet and careful. . . . Like a lesson he was memorizing, he said it all over again to himself in his mind, all he'd got to remember about: don't make any noise, get up when it's time and put on his pants and jacket over his pajamas and get—it—and remember about the key to the door, take it with him so's he could get back in. He knew where the place was, where he was going; it was only three blocks over there, on Main Street. Wouldn't take long, if nobody saw—or if—

This was the only way to do it if he was going to, and the worst of that was it didn't seem like such a good idea now, a kind of silly idea really but he couldn't think of anything else at all, without breaking the promise, doing the one unforgivable thing. He'd tried this morning, he'd waited until she was busy in the kitchen, thought he could pick—it —up and call out good-by and go off quick, before—

But it'd gone wrong, he wasn't quick enough; and she'd come in, looked awful queer at him—funny, a bit frightened—and said sharp, "What you up to, still fooling round here?—you'll be late for school, you go 'long now," and he'd had to go, with her watching. So now he was waiting until there'd be nobody awake to see.

And maybe it was silly, it wouldn't make anything happen. Cops, he thought confusedly: but he did remember Dad saying, all new scientific things and like that, they were a lot smarter and some real high-educated now, from college. It might—

Cops. He didn't like loud voices and people getting so mad they hit each other. It made him feel hollow and bad inside—in the movies you knew it was just put on, and when you were interested in the story you didn't mind so much, but even there sometimes it made you feel kind of upset. That was the first time, tonight, he'd seen Danny's dad—since he'd come with them. Danny didn't seem to be ashamed at all, tell his dad had been in jail back east, said it like it was something to brag about, but that was how Danny was. Marty sure didn't think he could be much of a dad to brag on, jail or no jail.

He shut his eyes and just like a movie saw it over again—himself going up the stairs to Danny's apartment, as if he wanted go to the movies with him, Ma'd given him thirty cents, said he could go—and the loud voice swearing inside, "*Cops!* You think I can't smell a cop?— yeah, yeah, you say that to me before, so you walk right past a couple the bastards outside an' never see 'em more'n if they was—listen, what the hell you been up to, bringin' *cops* down on the place—"

And Danny, shrill, "I never done nothing, I—"

"Don't talk back t' me, you little bastard—I ain't fool enough to think, *him*—I got him too damn scared! If I hadn't spotted them damned—might've walked right into— What the hell else could they be after, watching the house? Couldn't've traced *me* here—you been up to some o' your piddling kid stuff, heisting hubcaps or somethin', an' they—"

"I never— Listen, I—"

And the noise of fists hitting, Danny yelling, and something falling hard against the door—Danny, he guessed, because then it opened and Danny sort of fell out and banged it after him and kicked it. It was dark in the hall, Marty had backed off a ways, and Danny didn't see him. Danny leaned on the wall a minute there, one hand up to the side of his face, maybe where his dad had hit him—it looked like his nose was bleeding too—and Marty thought he was crying, only Danny never did, he wasn't that kind. And then the door opened again and Mr. Smith came out.

A tough-looking man he was like crooks in the movies, and there in the room behind that was just like the living room in the place Marty lived a floor down, was Danny's ma, he'd seen her before, of course, a little soft-looking lady with a lot of black hair, and she looked scared and kept saying, "Oh, please, Ray, it's not his fault, please don't, Ray."

"Oh, for God's sake, I ain't goin' do nothing! So all right, kid, maybe I got my wires crossed an' it's somethin' else—hope to God it is—but listen, come here, you gotta go and do that phone call for me, see, I can't—"

Danny yelled at him, "Be damned if I will, bastard yourself!" and kicked at his shins and bolted for the stairs as the man snarled at him. Marty had crept back even farther toward the dark end of the hall; Mr. Smith didn't see him either. He made as if to go after Danny, stopped, said, "Oh, hell!" and went back into the apartment.

And Marty slid past the shut door and downstairs, but he didn't see Danny anywhere on the block. He wondered if Danny was hurt bad, his dad looked pretty strong. And if he'd ever hit Danny like that before—probably so, if he got mad that way a lot. For a minute, thinking about it, Marty felt some better himself, because maybe his own dad had gone away and left them, but he'd sure never, ever, hit him or said bad things to him—or anybody. Marty's dad, he always said it beat all how some fellows were all the time getting mad, you always sure as fate did something dumb or wrong when you was mad because you couldn't think straight. There was only a couple of times Marty could remember his whole life when Dad had got real mad, and then he didn't swear or yell, why, he'd never heard Dad say a *damn,* he was right strict about swearing. He didn't talk an awful lot any time, but when he was mad he didn't say anything at *all.*

He'd been awful mad, that last time—that night before he went away. Just didn't come home.

And on that thought, everything it made him remember, Marty stopped feeling better, and stopped wondering why Mr. Smith was so mad at Danny, what he'd been talking about.

He hadn't gone to the movies after all. It was a kind of crook picture and he didn't much want to see it really, though if he'd been with some other fellows he'd've had to pretend he did because it was the kind of thing everybody was supposed to like.

And now he was sitting here in the dark, alone with the secret, waiting for it to be time. And remembering, now, what Mr. Smith had said about cops. Cops outside, watching the house. Something funny happened inside Marty's stomach, like he'd gone hollow, and his heart gave an extra thud. Were they?—was it, was it because—

You had to do what was right, no matter what. Even if it meant you'd die, like in the gas thing they had in California. He knew, and he didn't see how his Ma *could* think a different way, it wasn't right people should get killed—like that—even if he hadn't ever meant, ever known even— Somebody ought to know, and stop it happening again. That was why he was sitting here cold and scared, waiting. Somebody. He hadn't exactly thought, *the cops*—but of course that was what he'd meant. And all of a sudden now, thinking about them maybe outside, *cops* meant something different, terrible, to be more scared of than anything—anything he knew more about. . . .

Sometimes in the movies yelling at guys and hitting them and a thing called the third degree—the gas chamber in California—but once Dad had said, about one of those movies Marty'd told about, that was bad to show, it was wrong because policemen weren't like that at all any more, that was other times. A bright light they had shining right in your eyes and they— But Dad said—

Marty shut his eyes tight and tried to get back to that place, couldn't remember how long ago or if it was Tappan Street or Macy Avenue, where there'd been Dad just like always, sitting at the kitchen table, digging out his pipe with his knife and looking over the top of his glasses and saying—and saying—something about policemen being your friends, to help you.

He couldn't get there, to Dad that time. Where he got to instead was that night before Dad—didn't come home. He was right there again, he saw Dad plain, awful mad he'd been for sure, his face all stiff and white and a look in his eyes said how hard he was holding himself in. Dad saying slow and terrible quiet, "I can't stand no more, Marion—I just can't stand no more."

And Marty knew right this minute just how Dad had felt when he said that. Because he felt the same way, not all of a sudden but like as if he'd only this minute come to know how he felt, plain.

I just can't stand no more.

He relaxed, limp, against the headboard, and a queer vague peace filled him. Like coming to the end of a long, long walk, like getting there—some place—at last, and he could stop trying any more.

It didn't matter what place, or what happened there. It was finished. *I just can't stand no more.*

The gas, and the cops whatever kind and whatever they did or didn't do, and even—more immediate and terrible—his Ma, and what would happen afterward, when she found out. Anything, everything, nothing, it wasn't anyways important any more.

Something had to happen, and what did it matter what or how? Maybe there were those cops down there, even two or three o'clock in the morning, and they'd see him when he came out with—it—and take him to the police station. Maybe not; some other way, the way he'd thought or—maybe they already *knew,* he couldn't see how but they might. And in the end maybe they'd make him break the promise. It didn't matter how it came: he knew it would come, and it was time, he didn't care.

Time for the secret to be shown open, the terrible secret.

When Morgan finally moved, he was stiff with cold and the sense of failure, a resignation too apathetic now to rouse anger in him. He had known half an hour ago that Smith wasn't coming. Why he'd gone on standing here he didn't know.

He turned and went into the drugstore; hot stuffiness struck him in the face after the cold outside. The druggist was rearranging bottles on a shelf along the wall; he turned quickly, to watch Morgan—didn't come up to ask what he wanted. Maybe he thought he was going to get held up. Morgan scraped up all the change in his pocket, picked out a quarter, went up to the man.

"May I have change for the phone, please?"

"Oh, sure thing." The cash register gave brisk tongue; a kind of apologetic relief was in the druggist's eyes as he handed over two dimes and a nickel.

As soon as he was inside the phone booth, Morgan began to sweat, in his heavy coat in that airless, fetid box. He sat on the inadequate little stool and dialed carefully. After two rings the receiver was lifted at the other end.

"Sue—"

"Dick!"—their voices cutting in on each other, hers on a little gasp. "I thought you'd call—been waiting—"

"Has he called?" asked Morgan tautly. "He didn't show, he won't now, and I'm afraid—darling, I'm afraid he's spotted those damn cops and thinks—"

"I don't think so." Her voice steadied. *"She* called, Dick. About ten minutes to eight. She said to tell you he'd got 'hung up' and couldn't make it, it'd have to be tomorrow night—and you'd get a phone call some time tomorrow, to tell you where and when."

Morgan leaned his forehead on the phone box for a second; a wave of tingling heat passed over him and he felt weak. *"He* got—delayed? He didn't—that's damn funny, I don't— Sue, you sure it was the woman, the same—?"

"I'm sure, darling. You remember what a soft, ladylike little voice she had, and she spoke quite well too, not glaringly bad grammar— she's had some education—but awfully timid and meek, as if she was *cowed.* I recognized it right away—and she sounded like a child reciting a lesson, as if she was reading the message off—"

"The woman," he said, "the woman. So she's still with him. Yes, we didn't think she was lying then, about being married. Yes, a cut above him all right, probably one of those natural doormats—husband's just being the superior male when he knocks her around. *He*—God, I was afraid—so it's just another breathing space, until tomorrow night. I wonder why."

"I don't *like* it—can't stall with him forever, Dick—and in the end we can't pay, he'll— What can you *say* to him any more, to make him—"

"Listen," said Morgan, trying to sound authoritative, confident (don't let her suspect how you're planning to deal with it, convince her), "it's the money he wants, he's not in any rush to get this thing open in court, that's the *last* thing he wants. It's his only hold on us, he's not so anxious to let go of it."

"I—suppose not. But—Dick, I—I've got to where I just want it *over* and *decided,* whichever way. This hanging on—"

"I know, darling, I know. Maybe tomorrow. I'll be right home—half an hour."

Lieutenant Callaghan was a good deal less than mollified to be presented with such small fry as Tomás Ramirez; he had been lying hopefully in ambush for a certain big-time eastern wholesaler, and had —as he informed Mendoza bitterly—had a leash on Mr. Torres-Domingo and assorted friends for some time. What the hell good did it do to pick up a minnow like this Ramirez, who just ferried the stuff across the border in small lots? If Mendoza was interested, they had known about the Maison du Chat for quite a while, and a usually reliable source of information had led them to expect the wholesaler on the premises tonight, to set up a deal with Neddy, Mr. Torres-Domingo being the middleman. At nine o'clock they'd expected him, and so it was very probable that he'd been, maybe, a hundred feet away from the kitchen door when Mendoza's bright boy had got a little too close to the game and flushed it early. And so their chances of getting him now, or even another line on him, were just about nil.

And if Mendoza could remember back seventeen years to when, God help us and if this good-looking redhead here would believe it, he and Mendoza had been in the rookie school together, Mendoza just might recall that one of the first things they'd been told was that there were different divisions within any big-city police force. And that one division was sort of expected to play ball with the others, seeing that they weren't exactly in competition with each other.

"Well," said Mendoza mildly to that, "I suppose I could have checked with you first, certainly if anything definite had showed up— but Ramirez was only one of those vague hunches, you know."

"Sure, sure, we all know Mendoza's hunches! Second sight he's got, maybe a crystal ball, I wouldn't know, our little genius Luis Rodolfo Vicente Mendoza! One look, and he says, that naughty fellow's got a stack of H. in his back pocket, and won't my good old friend Pat jump for joy to have a little of his work all done for him! Oh, he's a star, our Luis! Hey presto, and I've ended up with a couple of hired-salesmen punks I could've taken two months ago, instead of the real big boy— and our Luis thinks he does me a favor to give me this Ramirez!"

"Now when did I say so? It's the way the cards fall," said Mendoza philosophically. "These things happen. My crystal ball doesn't always show me the right picture—"

"That you can say twice," said Callaghan. "Got you in trouble before —got you a bullet in the leg in that Brawley business, and right now, by God, I'm sorry it wasn't in the head! And I'll never know how you hypnotize these respectable, high-class, good-looking women to go round with you." He looked at Alison there in the drafty corridor outside his office at headquarters. "You look like a decent God-fearing Irish girl."

"Only on my mother's side—she was a McCann," said Alison solemnly. "And I think it's sheer surprise, Lieutenant—for any man these days who thinks he can still order us around, the dominant male, you know. By the time we've recovered enough to begin to talk back—"

"It's too late, I know." Callaghan shook his head at her. "You watch yourself. I've got another piece of advice for you, lady—whatever else you do with him's your own business, but don't ever get into a hand of poker with him. And seeing you've done about all the damage you can do tonight, Luis—on headquarters business, that is—I guess you can get out of my sight and take her home."

Mendoza rubbed his nose and said he wouldn't presume to teach Lieutenant Callaghan his job, but he did think that Ramirez—

"Oh, get out, scat!" said Callaghan. "He's on his way here now, I sent two men after him while you were phoning your bright little boy's wife. I can't hold him on anything, unless one of these two involve him or we find the stuff in his possession—both of which are likely to happen. Not that I give a damn about him, but thank you *so* much for pointing him out, and now good night to you."

Mendoza grinned at him, said, "*¡Uno no puede complacer a todo el mundo*—one can't please everybody! Be good, Pat—*hasta más ver,*" and took Alison's arm down the hall to the elevator. "And now," he added, "*la familia* Ramirez is due for another shock."

"Yes, poor people. I must see them, to return half the tuition she'd paid, you know. I didn't like to blunder in the very day after, but I thought at the inquest I might have a chance to—"

"You haven't been subpoenaed, you notice. A very routine affair. Maybe twenty minutes—adjourned awaiting further evidence—that's how it'll go. Come if you like, but it'll be very dull, I won't be there."

"I'd like to think that was a *non sequitur,*" said Alison, "but I'm afraid you didn't mean it that way. I suppose that ex-football-star sergeant will represent you. I think I *will* go. I've never been to an inquest and it's an excuse to take the morning off. Besides, I do want to see the family, only decent."

Mendoza looked at her and shook his head, getting out his car keys. "Occasionally I agree with Pat—astonishing how I seem to acquire these high-principled women."

"That," said Alison sedately, "is a very premature verb." And twenty minutes later, at her apartment door: "Don't forget those stockings. Size—"

"Nine and a half, thirty-three inches, I'd guess it."

"Mmh, yes," said Alison, "and entirely too good a guess it is."

"Women, we never satisfy them—they don't like us too callow and they don't like us too experienced!" He laid a caressing hand round her throat. "I'd said to myself, very gentlemanly this time, maybe next time I'll kiss her good night, but I told you I'm always breaking resolutions . . . and sometimes even twice—or three times—if it seems like a good idea."

"Once was *quite* enough," said Alison rather breathlessly, pushing him away, "for three days' acquaintance!"

"So we figure it like compound interest, *chica*—I'll add up how much it comes to per week."

"Good night, *mi villano optimista*," said Alison firmly.

He smiled at the closing door; he never liked them too easy.

At about the same time that Alison Weir was struggling with the zipper of the oyster-silk sheath and reflecting that Lieutenant Callaghan's advice about watching herself was an excellent idea, Agnes Browne was standing in the cold dim rooming-house hall, shivering in just her slip and the cotton robe she'd tied round her when Mrs. Anderson called her to the phone.

"You *shouldn't've*," she kept saying, almost crying. "Hitting a policeman like that, Joe, it's terrible, they might've arrested you—you shouldn't go losing your temper like that."

"Well, they got a nerve, snooping around you just on account you found a body! What the hell they after, anyway? You didn't have anything to do— Listen, Agnes, I don't get it, Rita says there was a guy came up to her after work, another cop, asking about you—I guess she told you—I just got in, had to work late, and when she—"

"Oh, dear," whispered Agnes to herself. "I—I know, she called me . . ." Rita was Joe's sister who worked the same counter as Agnes, it seemed funny to think if she'd got that job at Kress's instead she'd never've met Rita or Joe, and it'd been just chance really—and she couldn't wish she *hadn't,* but—"Oh, dear." Asking questions about how long had she known Agnes, Rita said, and like that. They must *suspect.* "I—I don't know what they're after, Joe, but no call for you to get in trouble account of me, it's my own—"

"You got nobody to talk up for you, I guess your friends got a right to—"

"You *mustn't,*" said Agnes in agony. "It's awful good of you, Joe, but you don't *know*—you—you better just not b-bother about me any more, because—" But she couldn't come out with it like that, over the phone, hear what he'd say, know what he'd think—she just hung up quick and went back to her room, shut herself in.

It'd been bad enough feeling guilty all the while, worrying, but when it came to getting your friends in trouble— Agnes dried her eyes and blew her nose and thought forlornly, Well, that's that. And serve her right too. Tomorrow morning, go to *them* and tell the truth—shame the devil, like her grandma used to say—and have it done with, that was all. Whatever they'd do to her for it. And afterward Joe and Rita and the others that'd been nice, that she'd like having for friends, they wouldn't want any more to do with her when they knew, but you couldn't expect different, she'd just have to take her medicine was all. Better go to the store first, tell Mr. Snyder she was quitting, she'd have to anyway—and it'd mean finding another room too, because Mrs. Anderson wouldn't—

And it was silly, go on crying like this, when it was all her own fault. . . .

TWELVE

The rookie who'd been riding the squad car that answered the call to Elena Ramirez' body was on night shift this week, and came into the precinct station on Main to check out at five past eight that morning, with his partner. They found the desk sergeant and a couple of the day men who'd just reported in guffawing over something on the sergeant's desk.

"We got a present from an anonymous admirer, boys—ain't she purty? I guess somebody figures we're not getting enough feminine companionship."

The rookie went up to look, and it was a doll—an old, dilapidated half-broken-apart doll lying there. A big one, good three feet long. "Where the hell did that come from?" asked his partner.

"Vic found it propped up against the door when he came on just now."

"Like somebody'd sat it up there on purpose," said Vic. "The damnedest thing. Kids, I guess."

"Aughh," said the desk sergeant, "what some o' these punks think is smart! Here, Vic, stick it out back in the trash, will you? I—"

"Just a minute, Sergeant," said the rookie. He had a funny feeling looking at the thing; it was crazy, but— "Hey, Pete," he said to his partner, "does it kind of remind you of something? Look at the way it's got that one eye—I mean—it's the damnedest thing, but that dead girl over on Commerce, Saturday—you know. I mean—"

They all looked at it again and Pete said what about it, and the rookie said weakly, well, he'd just wondered if there could be any connection. "I mean, it's crazy, but maybe the boys downtown'd be interested—"

"In *this?*" said the sergeant. "Now that'd be something. I can just see myself calling headquarters, ask if anybody down there wants to play dolls."

"No, but—" The longer he looked at it, the funnier the feeling got. They had a little more backchat, the rest of them kidding him because that had been his first corpse and he hadn't acted as hard-boiled as maybe he should have; and the sergeant finally said, if he wanted to play detective so bad he could do it with his own dime and be sure and tell whoever he talked to it was strictly his own idea, none of the precinct's responsibility. They didn't think he'd have the nerve to do anything like that, but by then he was feeling stubborn about it, and he said all right, by God, he'd do just that, and got Vic to change a quarter for him and called downtown.

He got hold of Hackett after a little argument with Sergeant Lake, and in the middle of talking with him Hackett broke off to relay the news to Mendoza who'd just come in. The rookie hung on, listening to the lieutenant's exclamation in the background, and then jumped as

Mendoza's voice came crackling over the wire: "Tell your sergeant I'm coming right around—leave it as it is, and stay there yourself!"

"Yes, *sir!*" said the rookie, but the wire was already dead. Ten minutes later Mendoza walked in and took a look at the doll before he remembered to throw a good-morning at the sergeant.

"*¡Vaya una donación!*" he murmured very softly to himself, and his very mustache seemed to quiver with excitement. "Now what does this mean? But by God, whatever it means, it's the one—no odds offered!" He swung on the sergeant. "Let's hear all about it!"

There wasn't much to hear, when they got down to definite details. It had been sitting up against the left side of the double doors, in a position where it wouldn't either interfere with that door's opening or necessarily be noticed, in the dark; this was an old precinct station, and the doors were set at the back of a recessed open lobby at the top of the front steps, which was temporarily unlighted due to defective wiring. Consequently there was no *terminus a quo;* the thing might have been there since midnight and gone unnoticed by the various patrolmen going in and out during the night; or it might have been put there ten minutes before Vic found it, though it was likelier to have been before daylight.

And of course every man there had handled the thing, but it was no good swearing about that now. Mendoza demanded a sheet of wrapping paper and swathed the doll in it carefully; Prints would have to isolate any strangers from the precinct men, that was all.

"So I've you to thank for this," and he turned to the rookie, who was nearly as surprised as the sergeant. "What's your name?" The rookie told him. "I'll remember that, you showed intelligence. What struck *you* about it?"

"Well, I—it's crazy, Lieutenant, but the way it looked lying there, it reminded me of that dead girl—the eye and all—it was just a sort of feeling—"

"Yes. You're a good man. Any time you want to get out of uniform, when you're qualified, I'll be glad to put in a word for you."

The rookie, who had heard a little more about Mendoza by this time, stammered incredulous gratitude; the sergeant was struck dumb; and Mendoza walked out with the doll cradled tenderly in his arms.

He could not resist showing it to Hackett before he delivered it to Prints; they looked at it lying there on his desk, mute, ugly, and enigmatic, and Hackett said, "I laid myself open—say it—I told you so."

"I'm magnanimous this morning. But that's the only thing I *could* say about it, boy—I'm just one big question mark about it otherwise. What the *hell* has it got to do with this?"

"Don't look a gift horse in the mouth. *Ya veremos*—I hope."

"Waiting for time to tell is just what we can't do, damn it. Take it down, will you?" While Hackett was gone he called Gunn's office.

"Morgan? He just got in—"

"*Bueno*," said Mendoza happily. "I want him. Now. Immediately. Sooner. Apologies to take him away from his job, but I need him."

Gunn said resignedly all good citizens had a duty to aid the police when requested and he'd shoot him right over. Mendoza looked up another number and called it. "Mrs. Demarest? Lieutenant Mendoza. I want to see you some time today. I think we've got the doll, and I want your identification—if it is. Also Mrs. Breen's. . . . I don't know one thing about it except that I've got it—it just came out of the blue. Look, I won't ask you to come all the way down here, suppose you see if you can get hold of Mrs. Breen for some time this afternoon, and I'll bring it to your house. I probably won't get it back from Prints until noon, anyway. . . . Right, then, you'll call me back."

Waiting for Morgan, he called Callaghan in idle curiosity about Ramirez. They had found an ounce and a half of uncut heroin in a plastic bag taped to the underside of the bureau in his room at the Ramirez house, he had been taken into custody, and yes, Callaghan agreed that the rest of the family looked innocent enough but of course a check had to be made. And was what he heard in the background evidence of how they usually examined witnesses in Homicide because if so it ought to be reported to the Chief.

"I'm just about to find out," said Mendoza, and hung up. Somebody out in the anteroom was shouting angrily; he could hear Hackett saying, "Now take it easy," and a woman saying something else. He opened the door in time to see a little dark fellow take a swing at Hackett which almost connected. Hackett, looking as surprised as a Great Dane attacked by a belligerent Peke, held the fellow off with a hand on the chest and went on saying, "Take it easy now—"

The woman was Agnes Browne, and she was saying, "*Joe!* Oh, you mustn't—please, Joe—"

"What's all this about?" Mendoza plucked Joe off Hackett and swung him around. "Now calm down, all of you, come into my office and let's hear about it—Miss Browne, or it's Mrs. Browne, isn't it—"

"No, it's n-not!" said Agnes desperately. "That's just what I came to tell you, sir—only I went to tell Mr. Snyder I was quitting first, and

Rita *would* go and call Joe, and he has to come after and start all this ruction—he doesn't mean any harm, sir, please—"

"The hell I don't! I'd like to know what the hell you guys are up to, persecuting an innocent citizen what it amounts to and by God I'll see it carried to the Supreme Court if—you got no reason—just because she happened—"

"Oh, *Joe!* They *have.* I—I couldn't tell you, but now I got to—I came to confess and have it all done with, I know I've done awful wrong, sir, but please, Joe didn't know—"

Hackett said to nobody in particular, "I better apologize to Dwyer, I see how he came to walk into it." Joe stared at Agnes in astonishment and subsided, and Mendoza told them all to sit down.

"You want to confess what?" he asked Agnes.

She collapsed into a chair and began to cry. "I'm *black!*"

They all looked at her. Hackett said, "Well, I'll be damned. You see, Luis, I told you—it was that sort of thing, nothing at all. Now we know . . . You don't look very black to me, Miss Browne."

"I *am*—it's the *law*—I—I know I don't *look* so—my mother was half white, sir, and my dad more'n half, they didn't either, I'm about an eighth I guess or something like that, and everybody always said I could pass, and I thought I'd—but I've felt just awful about it, I've never done anything against the law before, sir, I swear I haven't! I—I don't know if that counts, makes any difference to how long I'd maybe have to go to jail—"

"Nobody's goin' to put you in jail!" said Joe.

"It's the *law!*" sobbed Agnes. "*They* know it's the law! And I gave a wrong address and all, I s'pose they found out and then of course they'd suspect something funny—"

"Well, now, I grant you we got some damn funny laws on the books," said Hackett, "but that's a new one to me, Miss Browne."

"It *is* the law, most states and I guess here too. I know it was wrong, sir." She emerged from her handkerchief to blow her nose. "It says anybody with any black at *all* who pretends—"

"Oh, *that* one," said Hackett. "I forget now, does it say it's a misdemeanor or a felony?" He looked at Mendoza.

"I seem to remember it says misdemeanor," said Mendoza, "but offhand I wouldn't know whether the mandatory sentence is thirty or sixty days. A judge—"

"Now *listen,*" said Joe.

"A judge might have a little trouble finding the latest precedent, somewhere around 1900 I should think."

"They leave all that stuff in to make life hard for law students," said Hackett. "There're some a lot funnier than that."

"Don't ridicule the law," said Mendoza severely. "If you ask me some of those ought to be looked up and enforced. There's another one that says it's a misdemeanor for a female to wear male clothing in public, and if you've ever walked down Broadway and seen all the fat women in pants—"

Agnes stared at them a little wildly and asked weren't they going to arrest her? "Agnes *honey*," said Joe, as if the sense of it had just penetrated, "you mean *that's* why you'd never go out with me, always acted so— Well, I'll be damned!" He leaned on Mendoza's desk and laughed. "You want to know something, I—I been in kind of a sweat about it because I figured it was on account I'm Catholic and you wouldn't have nothing to do—"

"Why, Joe! However could you think such a thing of me, I'd never— why, that's *un-American,* go judging people by what church—"

"Yes, I think there's a law about that too," agreed Hackett thoughtfully.

"Honey, one-eighth isn't so awful black, you know. Matter o' fact, you're a lot lighter-complected than me, and far as I know I got nothing but Italian both sides back to Adam. Though I guess at that a lot of us'd get some surprises if we knew everything *was* in our family trees like they say. You stop crying now, Agnes, it's all right, you see it's all right—"

"But—you mean you don't *care*—and they aren't going to arrest—"

"Well, I tell you, Miss Browne," said Mendoza, "the court calendars are pretty full, and we don't want to overburden the judges. I think we'll just forget it, but maybe Mr. Carpaccio here—it *is* Mr. Carpaccio? —would care to take the—er—probationary responsibility for your future good conduct, in which case—"

"That's a damn good idea," said Joe. "Come on now, Agnes, stop crying and come with me, you see they're not going to do nothing to you, it's nobody's business but yours. . . . Don't I care? Listen, honey, you're the nicest girl I ever knew and the prettiest one too, and I couldn't care less if you're all colors of the rainbow. And no, Rita won't care either, I'd like to see her try— Besides, I read some place about a thing called Mendelian law, it says—"

"Take her away and explain that one thoroughly," advised Mendoza, shooing them out to the anteroom. "Yes, yes, Miss Browne, you're very welcome, thank you for coming in. . . . Morgan, good morning, what kept you? Come in here, I've got a job for you."

Morgan wasn't enthusiastic about the job, took it on somewhat grudgingly, while taking Mendoza's point of view. "I've got no real reason to ask questions about this boy, and the school people would undoubtedly raise an uproar, want to know all about it, if a Homicide man walked in wanting to know all about one of their seventh-graders. There may be nothing in it anyway, and in any case not much to find out at the school, but it's obviously the first place to go for information about him. They may be a little surprised at your office wanting to know, but they won't be alarmed about it, and everybody's so used these days to being asked irrelevant questions by busybody government agencies, ten to one they won't think twice about it. Try to see his teacher—or all his teachers, if there are more than one—and his school records. I've jotted down some questions you might ask."

"All right." Morgan took the memo ungraciously. "I'll get what I can for you, but I do have a job of my own, you know—and things I've got to do today."

"I realize that." Mendoza also realized that some of the reluctance was due to the fact that Morgan didn't like him much personally; that was just one of those things. Morgan being a reasonably intelligent man, Mendoza didn't put it down to any irrational prejudice, though he wasn't much concerned with the reason if there was one. Probably not, just a matter of personal chemistries; and he never wasted time trying to ingratiate himself with people who felt that way. He'd had the same reasonless reaction himself often enough to know that it *was* a waste of time. He merely thanked Morgan politely, saw him out, and deciding he could not decently call down to Prints, to see if they'd found anything interesting, before eleven, sat down to look over the latest reports on his other current cases.

Before he had read the first three lines of what Sergeant Brice had to tell him, another disturbance commenced outside his door. He said resignedly to himself, *"¡Me doy por vencido!"* and went to investigate. As he might have expected, it was a delegation representing the family Ramirez, consisting of Papa, Teresa, and Father Monaghan. Ramirez was being impassioned in Spanish, and Hackett was patting his shoulder and repeating, *"No se sofoque Usted, amigo—es O.K., comprende?"*

"Lieutenant—" Teresa clutched at his arm. "Please, you got to believe none of us knew what my uncle was up to—"

"Never, never, never!" Ramirez whirled to state his case to higher authority. "This villain, this bandit, to bring such disgrace on the family — I swear before God to you, never would I have him in my house if I knew what he is guilty of! And now you're thinking bad things for all of us, that we're all criminals—I swear to you—"

"Calm yourself, my son, I've told you the police will judge fairly, you must not worry. Lieutenant, I do hope there'll be no misunderstanding, I'm quite certain these people had nothing to do—"

"Yes, yes, yes," said Mendoza. "Ramirez—quiet! You've been in this country long enough to know that we're not ogres! Listen now. Your brother has broken the law and he will go to prison, but his crime isn't in my jurisdiction, understand? He was arrested by my friend Lieutenant Callaghan, and I have spoken with the lieutenant, who agrees with me that you people very likely knew nothing of the crime, although naturally he must investigate that. You understand that there must be investigation when a crime is committed. But if you've done nothing wrong, you have nothing to fear from the police."

"You see, Papa, I kept telling you it was all right, they'll find out we didn't have nothing to do with it, and Uncle will say too, he's not that bad, try to pull us into it! Thanks, Lieutenant, that was real nice of you, say that to this other cop—now don't take on so, Papa—"

They got Ramirez calmed down a little. Mendoza, suddenly struck with a not very hopeful idea, but you never knew and no harm to try, took Teresa down to Prints to look at the doll.

"No, I never seen nothing like that before. . . . Why? Is it something to do with—? But how could it be?"

"Now there you've asked me something," he sighed. "Yes, it is something to do with it—that I can tell you now, at least I'm ninety-eight percent sure. But what, that's another question."

"It's— I don't like it," said Teresa, shuddering. "All pulled apart like that."

"Yes . . . I suppose you haven't got anything for me yet," he said to Carter.

"We've got a lot of dandy prints, Lieutenant—whether they'll tell us anything—" and Carter shrugged. "Let's see, you gave us the names of five of our own men handled it, well, I've got a couple of the boys checking records now, to eliminate those. At a guess, we've got two or three different people besides—I think. Tell you more when I know which to eliminate. We'll see if the strangers match anything in the other records, and have a look at the psychos on file first, way you suggested. You can have her back any time, by the way—we've finished with her."

"Thanks very much." Mendoza folded the paper round the doll and carried it back upstairs with him. He spent another five minutes on additional reassurances to Ramirez and the priest, got rid of them, unwrapped the doll on his desk, and said, "Now we'll just see if we can match up that little clue you were so superior about."

"What? Oh, that," as Mendoza tenderly slid the dainty strip of pink lace from its envelope. "Today's great thought, I'd forgotten—my *God*," said Hackett suddenly, "look at the time, I'll be late for that damned inquest, and it's old Curly too, he'll give me hell—have fun, *amigo*," and he snatched up his hat and ran.

The two women looked at it in silence for a minute and came out with twin reactions.

"Well!" said Mrs. Demarest. "What kind of a mother would go and let a child treat an expensive doll that way! Breaking things up just out of mischief, it's a thing I always saw *my* children got a good spanking for—just leads to trouble later on."

"A sinful waste—wicked," agreed Mrs. Breen, looking horrified. "A downright destructive youngster, must be, whoever's had it. I never saw anythin' like—"

"I've begun to think that might be an understatement—about who's had it," said Mendoza. "But is it the doll Carol bought?"

"Yes, *suh*, it is," said Mrs. Breen promptly, "or one just like it, because if I got to *swear*, well, of course I couldn't do no such thing. I just had the one in stock, not figurin' I could sell more'n that, you know, an' I couldn't guess how many of 'em the factory might of made, an' they'd be all just alike, except some was dressed in blue and some in pink like this here. But it's just exactly *like* the one Carol bought—or 'twas when it was new."

"Would there be some kind of a serial number on it, I wonder?" suggested Mrs. Demarest. "The factory maybe could tell what store they'd sold it to. Little cheap things, there wouldn't be, but a thing that was going to sell for twenty dollars—"

"Yes, it's possible. I haven't looked, the thing's in such a state I don't want to handle it more than necessary, and if there is a number the factory'll know where to look for it. That we'll find out. Now look at this."

He brought out the three-inch strip of lace. "I'll swear to you this came off some part of the clothes, but it's not possible to fit it on anywhere."

They bent over it, over the doll, looking. "It's just like the lace on the underwear," agreed Mrs. Breen. "Same exact color. I reckon the factory could tell you for sure, 'bout that—but there's not an awful lot o' the lace left on, an' if it got torn off different times, well, there wouldn't be no fitting this piece where it was."

"I can't get over the way it's been—" Mrs. Demarest raised troubled eyes to him. "Can you tell us about it, Lieutenant, how you came to find it?"

Mendoza leaned back and lit a cigarette. "I'll tell you what I know— you tell *me* what it means! Carol bought this thing the night she was killed. That morning, a Mrs. Marion Lindstrom tried to persuade you," stabbing the cigarette at Mrs. Breen, "to sell it to her, and, when you refused, was insistent that you find out whether you could get her one like it, and left her name and address—"

"Real uppity she was," nodded Mrs. Breen, "as if I *could,* if I wanted."

"So. Carol was killed and the doll stolen. No evidence either way, as to whether the killer or someone else took it. Now, Mrs. Lindstrom lived just two blocks up from here, across Hunter Avenue—and the next day, though it lacked a week to the end of the month and her rent was paid to then, she moved—unexpectedly and hurriedly. We can conjecture it was pure chance she ended up where she did, in a place called Graham Court, down the wrong side of Main. She'd have to take what was available right that day, if she was anxious to move at once— and what was available, of course, within the limits of what she could pay. All right. Time goes on, and last Friday night another girl is killed, within two blocks of this Graham Court. Killed the same way, and as was the case with Carol, there is absolutely nothing in her private life which gave anyone reason to kill her. She wasn't as bright a girl as Carol, she had very bad taste and not too much education, but she was an honest girl and well enough liked—and I don't suppose she wanted to die, you know."

"Ah, poor thing," said Mrs. Demarest.

"She was on her way home from a roller-skating rink, alone because her boy friend's father, who disapproved of her, had come and hauled the boy home with him. Fortunately they're out of it on evidence. This time the handbag was taken, found a couple of blocks away, but as far as we can tell nothing was stolen. Now, take a look at *me,*" said Mendoza, sitting up. "I'm visited by a hunch—it's the same killer—and I've got no evidence whatever, that means anything, to back me up. Not until you told me about this doll. Then I've got Mrs. Lindstrom's name, and then I find out she's living in the same neighborhood this time too, and where that does get me? If I checked back on all the people living around there, I might find half a dozen others who'd moved there from *this* general neighborhood in the last six months. One of those things. . . . *But,* where d'you think I found this little piece of lace? On the floor of that skating rink. There's some vague evidence about a boy or a young man who's been in the habit of sneaking into the rink by an unused door, and who—so the dead girl complained to several people —stared at her in a 'funny way.' I think he's the one, but that's mostly another hunch and I know nothing else about him, I've got no line on him at all. Except that *maybe* he dropped this little strip there one time —and that doesn't say it came from the doll. I say to myself, I'm wool-gathering, all this doesn't mean one damned thing. And then this morning somebody leaves that doll carefully propped against the door of the precinct station down there—three blocks away from Graham Court."

"Well, that *is* queer," said Mrs. Demarest interestedly. "But this Mrs. Lindstrom, she wouldn't be the one—"

"There's not much to go on there either—yet. Her husband deserted her about a month before Carol was killed. There's a thirteen-year-old boy. All I know about him right now is that he's a big, strong boy— shot up early—big as a man, and probably strong enough to have done —what was done. I don't know if he did, or why he might have. I'm getting what I can about him, but"—he shrugged—"you can see I've got no real evidence to warrant a full-scale investigation."

"I don't know 'bout your rules for that kind o' thing," said Mrs. Breen, "but it shorely is queer, all that. Don't seem hardly possible, though, that a boy thirteen—and why'd she want a doll so bad, her with only a boy?"

Mendoza sighed and stood up. "I haven't even got an excuse to go and ask her that—and she'd only tell me it was for her favorite niece back east, anyway. I'm hoping the factory can identify this definitely, and in that case I'll want you both to make formal statements about it. . . . Thanks very much, I'll let you know as soon as I can."

THIRTEEN

The phone call had come through, Sue said when she eventually got Morgan at the office after lunch, about eleven o'clock. It was the woman again, again sounding as if she were reading the message, refusing to answer questions, say anything else.

"I tried to— I thought if I could appeal to her, remind her of what she said before, what we—but she just gave a little gasp and said, 'Oh, I couldn't, Mis' Morgan,' and hung up. Dick—"

"Yes," he said, making meaningless scribbles on the note pad in front of him. Henry was there at his desk across the room, Stack right alongside under the other window; Morgan couldn't say much directly. "Go on."

And what it came to was—right back to Graham Court. Seven o'clock, Smith's message said, at Graham Court, the address and apartment number carefully read out. Morgan might as well come to him, ran the message (insolently phrased, sounding the opposite in the woman's soft voice), and he needn't think account of things going haywire last night he'd stopped meaning anything he'd said. He'd be waiting alone for Morgan at seven, and this had better be the pay-off, or else.

"All right," said Morgan steadily, "I've got that. Seven, that's early. I'd better not try to make it home first. Mean?—just more bluster, is all —don't worry, hon. You'd better expect me when you see me, O.K.?"

He put down the phone and went back to his open case book there on the desk, pretending to check notes, add a word here and there, but not really seeing anything on the page.

Two things said themselves over in his mind. *The apartment*. And, *Alone*. (Smith, of course, unknowing that he had any prior knowledge of the apartment, any other reason to be there.) It added up—for Morgan, and also to a couple of things that were no concern of Morgan's but interesting: that *alone* suggested that Smith had seen to it that neither the woman nor the boy had any idea how much money he was expecting, and that and the revealing of his home address suggested that very likely he was planning to decamp with the money, maybe at once.

What it added up to for Morgan the murderer was safety—maybe. Depending on where Mendoza's men were. He thought he might get some information on that point when he saw Mendoza an hour from now, with this stuff from the school.

From the time on Saturday night when the cold fact had penetrated his mind that the only real lasting safety was Smith dead, circumstances had been forcing on Morgan certain changes of his original plan he didn't much like. He looked at this one from all the angles; it was better than the street holdup in a way, and it would, of course, have to do.

You were always seeing something like that in the paper. A man shot himself, hanged himself, slashed his wrists in the bathtub: no known reason, no prior threat.

The tricky factor was the timing. If Mendoza's men were inside, it couldn't be done at all: they'd be too close, and not unlikely in a position to know at which floor Morgan stopped. But if they were outside, then—which way, before or after the Lindstroms? Before, he thought. Quick and quiet up to the third floor, and no backchat with Smith: as soon as the door was shut behind him in Smith's place, and Smith away from it. And no fooling around with any attempt to muffle the shot, a suicide wouldn't bother and there wouldn't be time. Gun in his hand: prints. Thirty seconds? There had to be a good chance he'd have time to be outside the door again, at least, before anyone else got there. There was a narrower chance that he could get halfway down the stairs before that. People exclaimed, talked a little, wondered, before they went to see. The ideal thing would be Morgan standing in the second-floor hall, just ready to knock on the Lindstroms' door, when doors opened and people came out saying, "Was that a shot?"

But Morgan halfway down (which was also halfway up) would do. *I'd just got to the Lindstroms' door when— I knew it was a shot up here, I started up to see—*

That was all he needed to say; none of his business, nothing to link him to an unexplained suicide.

Sue, of course no question here of passing it off as accident. It couldn't be helped. He'd got past worrying about the side effects; he was feeling now the way she'd said, Let's for God's sake get it done and over, any way at all.

Because, if he'd be honest with himself, he wasn't sure he could do it —that all this would come to any action in the end.

He had to do it, the only possible solution. He'd seen that clear on Saturday night.

Which of course was the point. If you got yourself wound up to a place where you were ready to do murder, you ought to do it right then while, so to speak, the spring was tight. He hadn't; he'd had three nights and nearly three days to think about it, and now he didn't know if, when the chips were down, he could really bring himself—

He touched the gun under his coat; he'd been carrying it because he was afraid Sue would find it if he left it around the house. He thought angrily, uneasily, Ethics be damned: what loss is that hood? He'd decided this, he was just being a damned coward, to think—

You got a little cowardly when you were thirty-eight, with a wife and child and a mortgage on the house and debts and a job that paid just forty-two hundred a year.

And once he'd thought, if he could feel he was to blame for getting into this mess— But of course he was, they both were, they'd known at the time it was a silly and dangerous thing to do.

Which brought him back to the woman, because he supposed—if you looked at it from all sides—and remarkable as it might seem, she wouldn't want to lose her husband, whatever kind he was.

People, thought Morgan tiredly: people.

The agencies' bright brisk assurances: we like to find *just* the right child for the individual parents: patience! The endless forms. The investigators: questions, questions. Time going by, and both of them afraid, *never,* and Sue—

And then, that woman. Just by chance sitting next to Sue in the lounge of a department-store rest room. "Such a lovely baby, Dick, I couldn't help saying—only a month old, and darling, she hasn't even named her, wasn't that interested—she—" Later they both thought, less lack of interest in the baby than preoccupation with the husband. Oh, obviously that curious mixture of obsession (that couldn't really be called love), dependence, and fear . . .

He was awful mad when he heard about the baby, he didn't want another kid, they take a lot of time and all, you know. And I can't go out to work now, with it to look out for. He's—my husband, he's back east, he's—well, he's sick, see, awful sick, in the hospital, and can't work. I'd just as soon—anyways, I guess it'd be better off with folks like you. . . .

Yes, silly: dangerous. All that you forgot, confronted with the warm round armful that would be Janet Ann Morgan. A little sense you tried to use, you got the woman to sign a statement saying she was relinquishing the child voluntarily, and you told Dr. Fordyce that Sue was nervous, didn't trust the agency's medical tests, wanted his report too. And Dr. Fordyce, very probably, could make a pretty shrewd guess at the truth, but he was an old friend and he figured, maybe, that it wasn't up to him to be an officious busybody. And all the tests saying just what Janny had been telling everybody since—*such a lovely baby*.

And now, Smith. Robertson, the woman said: Smith, Brown, Green, what the hell if it was O'Kelly or Bernstein or Gonzales. . . . There he was, and he was the danger: it would all come to nothing if he were out of it, the woman was a nonentity with no force in her. So that left it right up to Morgan, and this was the only way he could see open to him.

When he came round to that point again, he got up and shut the case book. On his way over to Police Headquarters, he told himself that from another angle, it was safer really—if you came to murder—to do it cold, thinking. If you had to, if you could, if you could face the issue and take the only decision . . .

The waiter at Federico's saw Mendoza come in, and when he presented the menu also brought the two fingers of rye that was usually Mendoza's one drink of the day, and, five minutes later, the black coffee. They never hurried you at Federico's, and they knew their regular patrons.

Mendoza brooded over the coffee; he had something else to think about now, which was probably quite irrelevant, and that was Morgan.

Morgan, so much friendlier than he had been this morning, expanding on what information he'd got at the school, and then asking questions. Had Mendoza got anywhere on the Lindstroms, anything suggestive from the men watching the apartment, and just how did they go about that anyway, he'd think it was an awkward job, that they'd be spotted . . . oh, from a car, and tailing the woman when she—and only up to midnight, that was interesting. . . .

Morgan, being affable in order to ask questions? And just why? Morgan—now Mendoza looked at him with more attention—strung-up, a little tense, putting on an act of being just as usual. So all right, he was worried about something, he'd had a fight with his wife, he was coming down with a cold or—quite likely—he'd felt a trifle ashamed of his barely courteous manner this morning and was trying to make up for it.

There were more interesting things to think about than Morgan. Over his dinner Mendoza thought about them.

The school, somewhat bewildered at being asked but polite to an accredited civic agency, said in effect that young Martin Lindstrom was one of its more satisfactory pupils. A good student, not brilliant but intelligent, co-operative, well-mannered and reliable. He had a good record of attendance and punctuality. He was somewhat immature for his age, not physically or academically but socially: not a particularly good mixer with other children, shy, a little withdrawn but not to any abnormal degree. Mrs. Lindstrom had never attended any P.-T.A. meetings, none of the teachers had ever met her, but that was not too unusual.

The tailers. Mendoza had debated about taking them off: a waste of time? Not likely to come up with anything, and there was no real reason to single these people out. . . . In twenty-four hours she had left the place only once, between seven and eight last evening, the boy then being home; she had walked three blocks to a grocery store on Main and home again with a modest bag of supplies.

On Thursday she had an appointment at the county clinic. He toyed with the idea of putting a policewoman in there, to inveigle her into casual conversation, but what could he hope to get, after all? No lead, no line . . . He'd like to talk with her himself, judge for himself what kind of woman— See the boy, get some idea— Remembering Mrs. Cotter's graphic description, he reflected that Mrs. Lindstrom wouldn't be an easy woman to talk with, sound out.

The doll, his only excuse for approach, and not a very good one. He knew now definitely that it was the same doll: the factory had identified it by a serial number as the one sold to Mrs. Breen, and that was something: it might be a lot. Definite facts he liked: this was one of the few he had to contemplate in this business. But—as he'd said to Mrs. Breen and Mrs. Demarest—make it an excuse to see the Lindstrom woman: forget Elena Ramirez and go back to Brooks, say, you were inordinately interested in this piece of merchandise—and all the rest of it. She would only tell him some plausible tale of a niece or godchild, and that was that—no further excuse to pry at her.

He got out the little strip of lace and booded over that a while. He muttered to it, *Eso no vale un comino*—not worth a hang!" Both ends of this thing had come to a dead stop: blind alleys. There was nowhere new to go, on either Brooks or Ramirez. And yet at the same time he felt even more certain now that the cases were essentially the same case, that the Lindstroms were the link (or one of them), and that just a couple of steps beyond this dead end lay something—someone—some one more definite fact—that would lead him to the ultimate truth, and to a murderer.

He had also, for no reason, a feeling of urgency—a feeling that time was running out.

When he left Federico's he went back to his office. And that was for no reason either. He stood there, hat and coat still on, looking down at that doll on his desk.

He thought, It might mean this and it might mean that, but the one thing it meant, sure as death, was that somebody was trying to tell him something with it. And what he would like to think somebody was telling him was that the Lindstroms were definitely involved.

Suddenly he swore aloud, folded the wrapping paper round the thing and thrust it under his arm. There were times you had to sit down and think, and other times you had to act, even if you weren't sure what action to take—there was a chance you'd pick up a new lead somehow, somewhere, if you went out and about just at random.

Take the excuse: go and see the woman, talk with her—about anything; something might show up, he might get the smell of a new line.

It was just before seven when he nosed the Ferrari into the curb outside Graham Court. Already dark, but the city truck had been around, finally, to replace the bulb in the street lamp a little way down from the entrance to the cul-de-sac, and he recognized the man just turning in there, walking fast.

Morgan. Small and rather dubious satisfaction slid through Mendoza's mind for a possible answer to this one little irrelevant puzzle: Morgan, perhaps, infected with boyish detective fever, using his own excuse to get at the Lindstroms?

If so, and if they were involved in this thing, the blundering amateur effort might warn them—or it could be useful, frightening them into some revealing action.

Mendoza got out of the car and stood there a minute at the curb with the doll under his arm, debating his own next move now—whether to join Morgan or wait until he came out.

Marty hadn't gone home after school, and he wasn't lying to himself about why: he couldn't. He was just plain scared, more than he'd ever been before his whole life. It had been bad enough this morning, he'd got out just as quick as he could, long before usual, and of course she couldn't come after to drag him back, make him answer questions. This morning had been pretty bad.

He'd had some idea what was going to happen right off, but he just hadn't cared—then. The thing was, maybe like a silly little kid believing in fairies and like that, when he thought about the afterward part (vague and eager) he'd thought, if it was going to tell Them anything at all, it'd be right away, and maybe even by this morning—some time today—everything would—

Not like that. Maybe not even *some time today*. Maybe never. And what might happen now, when he went home, he just couldn't imagine how bad it'd be, or even *what* it might be. She knew he had something to do with its being gone, with the door always locked inside and all.

And besides Ma, what she'd do and say and ask—

This had been about the longest and awfullest day of his whole life. He'd got up early, before it was light even: he hadn't really got to sleep after he was back in from—doing that—just laid there miserable and scared and wondering what would happen now. And then getting out soon as ever he could, after it started to happen. He hadn't really had breakfast, she'd been too upset and he thought some scared too, to fix much, and he hadn't wanted that; and she hadn't fixed his lunch to carry either, so he didn't have any.

Times today he'd felt sort of empty, but not like being hungry. An awful day, other ways: all the ways it could be. He'd been dumb in history class and Mr. Protheroe had scolded him, and then in English class he'd felt so sleepy, couldn't lift his head up hardly, take in what Miss Skinner was saying, and she'd been mad. He was glad, sort of, when it was three thirty and school was out, but another way he wasn't, because it was at least somewhere to *be*.

He didn't go home. He had the thirty cents Ma'd given him, hadn't bought anything in the school cafeteria at lunchtime, because he wasn't hungry then, but now he was and he bought a ten-cent chocolate bar and ate it while he just walked along going nowhere. Staying away from home.

He walked for a while, just anywhere, and sat on the curb sometimes to rest; he started to feel like he couldn't breathe, from being so scared and not knowing what to do.

Because he had to go home *some* time. There wasn't anything else to do, anywhere else to go. It'd get dark, and he couldn't go on walking, sitting on curbs, all night.

Somewhere along one street, down near Main, he met Danny's ma. It was just starting to get dark then. She saw him, and she made him stop, and said, "Oh, you're the boy lives downstairs, aren't you? You know Danny, Danny S-Smith, don't you?"

"Yes, ma'am," said Marty, and he took off his cap like Ma and Dad both always said you ought to talking to a lady or when you came inside, to be polite.

"Oh, have you seen him anywheres? Was he to school today?"

"No, ma'am, I guess he wasn't, I haven't seen—"

"Oh, dear," she said in her funny soft little voice. "I guess he's for sure run off. I don't know what I better do about it. You see, his dad was kind of nice to him awhile, just lately, an' then he got mad at him, and I guess it sort of *turned* Danny—d'you suppose? Boys, they're funny anyways—never know what they're up to." It was like she was talking to herself. "I better ask Ray what to do. Only he said not to come home till eight anyways. Oh, well—" and she smiled sort of absent-minded at Marty and went past and he saw her stop and look at the ads outside the movie house there and go in.

He couldn't be bothered, think much about her or Danny.

It got darker, and then it was really dark and getting cold too, and his head began to feel funny, light, and he wasn't sure he could keep on walking, like, even if he sat down somewhere he might fall over.

There wasn't anything left to do but go home. And it'd be worse now, after a whole day. . . . And worse too with Ma, because he'd stayed away so long.

It took a long time to get there, and he thought for a while he'd never get to the top of the stairs. And now he wasn't feeling so awful scared any longer—like he'd got past that—part of him was just feeling sick and so tired and wanting to get home because that was the place to go when you felt that way, and another part just wanted to have it all over with, whatever *was* going to happen.

He leaned on the door when he knocked and waited for her to come, and so when the door opened he almost fell down, and she grabbed at him. She hadn't called out sharp, way she always did, who was there, first before unlocking—but he hardly noticed.

"Marty!" she said, and there wasn't so much crossness in her voice as he'd expected, she sounded—almost like the way he'd been feeling— plain scared. "Marty, where you *been?*—I been nearly crazy all day— you got to say what you did, where you—go an' get it back! Marty—"

And that was the first time he ever remembered she didn't right away lock the door—but he didn't notice that much either, right then.

Gunn was starting a cold, and left the office early. As usual, he denied the vague stuffy sensation in the head, the little soreness in the throat, the general feeling of lassitude; he said he wouldn't dare have a cold after the way she'd been stuffing him with Vitamin C all winter. Christy, having been married to him for thirty-nine years next June, ignored that, stood over him to see he finished the glass of hot lemonade and honey, and said he'd better have something light for dinner instead of the hamburger, and why didn't he get into his robe and slippers and be comfortable, so far as she knew nobody was coming in.

Gunn said defiantly he felt perfectly all right, never better. "Of course," said Christy briskly, "but no law against making yourself *comfortable.*"

"I suppose you'll give me no peace until I do," said Gunn, relieved at being argued into it. And then the phone rang, and she said vexedly, There, if that was the MacDonalds wanting to play bridge tonight they could go on wanting—not, of course, because Gunn wasn't feeling well but because she didn't feel like it herself.

He had his tie off, in the bedroom, listening to her murmuring protests at the phone, when she came to the door and said crossly it was somebody who insisted on speaking with him, wouldn't take no for an answer. So he went out and picked up the phone.

"Mr. Gunn?" said a male voice, confident, courteous, used to doing business over the phone. "I've got a little deal for you, sorry to disturb you at home, but I'm glad I've finally got hold of you—your office let me have your number. You don't know me, I'm Earl King, King Contracting out on Western—but your office sent a memo to me, and I guess a lot of other places, about a fellow named Lindstrom, wanting to know if he'd applied for work or been hired, under that name or any other—"

"Yes?" Gunn sat down beside the telephone table.

"Well, I've got him for you. It was quite a little surprise to me, I tell you, because of the kind of thing it is—deserting his family—if you'd asked me, I'd have said he was the last man. He's been working for me nearly six months, one of my steadiest men, and under his own name too. When—"

"Well, that's fine," said Gunn. "We're glad to know where he is, and in the morning—"

"Wait a minute, this is just the start. When I got your form letter asking about him, well, there wasn't any doubt it *was* him, name and description and all. But I tell you, it staggered me. I couldn't help feeling there must be something on his side, you know, because of the kind of guy he is. And I didn't want to go and haul him off the job in front of the other men, make a big thing of it. What I did, I met him at the job half an hour ago when he'd be through for the day, and tackled him about it. No trouble at all, he broke right down, said he was glad it'd come out and he'd thought it would before this, and anyway he'd been feeling so bad about it he couldn't have gone on much longer—"

"That's fine," said Gunn, yawning. "Glad to hear it. He's decided to go back to his family? So that's that." Surreptitiously he swallowed, testing that soreness at the back of his throat.

"Well, not quite," said King. "Now the dam's broken, he's been telling me a lot of things, but more to the point he insists on seeing you— you're the one's after him, so to speak, and he's in such a state—well, he's one of those terribly honest fellows, you know, can't sleep if they forget to pay for a cup of coffee at a drugstore counter—you know what I mean. He's got to get it all off his chest right away, to you."

"In the *morning,*" said Gunn, remembering that Mendoza would also be interested and want to see Lindstrom, "if he'll come—"

"I can't talk him into that, Mr. Gunn. He's in *such* a state—not wild, you know, don't mean that, but— Look, I can't help feeling so damned sorry for the guy, he's sort of desperate—keeps saying he can't rest till he explains how he came to—you see how it is. Look, if you'll agree to see him tonight, I've said I'll drive him over there. I know it's an imposition, but—there's one thing about it, too, I don't know but what it'd be just as well for— Well, I think you'll be interested, and if—"

"Oh, hell," said Gunn. But this was, in a way, a funny sort of job, and you ran into these things sometimes. Strictly speaking it was Morgan's case and he ought to be the one to handle this, but let it go. At least it didn't mean going out again, and an hour should take care of it. "All right, bring him here if it's like that. Have you got the address?"

"Just a minute, I'll take it down. . . . That's quite a little drive, don't expect us much before seven, O.K.? Thanks very much, Mr. Gunn, I hope this isn't interfering with any plans—I appreciate it. He's really a nice fellow, I can't help feeling he— Well, we'll see you about seven then, thanks again."

Gunn hung up and said "Hell!" again. Christy wasn't very pleased either, said she thought he'd given up being on twenty-four-hour call when he retired. But she got dinner a little early, and they'd eaten and Gunn was sitting in the front room in his robe and slippers when the doorbell sounded, while she cleaned up in the kitchen. He'd left the porch light on; he went and let them in, brought them into the living room.

King, fortyish, nice-looking, responsible-looking fellow. And Lindstrom, a big man, tall and also broad, still in his work clothes, and yes, the very look of him making you think, The last man. A steady type, you'd say—mild blue eyes behind steel-framed glasses, square honest-looking face, big blunt workman's hands twisting his white work cap.

"Come in, sit down, won't you?"

Lindstrom burst out, nervous apologetic, "It's awful good of you, see me this way, and Mr. King too, drive all this far over—I got to thank you—I just got to tell, explain to you, sir, I—I don't mind whatever you got to do to me for it, it was a terrible wrong thing, I knew that all the while, I felt so bad after—but I—"

"No one's going to do anything to you, Mr. Lindstrom. It's just that when a family is deserted, you understand, the county has to support them, and we try to find the husband to save ourselves a little money." Gunn smiled, to put the man more at ease. "It costs the county quite a bit, you know. Even in a case like your wife's, where there's only one child—"

Lindstrom looked down at his cap; for a minute it seemed as if his big hands would tear it apart, straining and twisting. "That's what I—you don't *understand*—I—" He raised desperate, suddenly tear-filled eyes to Gunn. "I—we—got two boys," he said. "Two. The—the other one, Eddy, our oldest one, he's—not right. Not noways. She wouldn't ever hear to—even when that doctor said— But she allus kep' him hid away from ever'body too, account of being—shamed. Secret, like."

FOURTEEN

Morgan stepped inside the dark, smelly front hallway of the apartment building and shut the door after him. This was it, here and now. And it was the damnedest thing, he'd expected it to feel like going into action, but instead—a little ludicrously—he felt exactly the way he had when he'd been in that senior play in high school. Walking out on the stage, all the lights, painfully conscious of every breath he drew, every slightest gesture, and yet somehow divorced from himself so that he moved with a stranger's body, spoke with a stranger's voice.

This was it, this was it. Start now. Remember—and as he went up the first half-dozen steps, sudden sharp panic stabbing at the back of his mind (the way it had been that time on the high-school auditorium stage, oh, God, suppose I forget—) that he'd forget just the one detail of his plan that would bring the whole thing down like a house of cards on top of him.

Think about what you're doing. You'll be all right, you're getting keyed up to it now, you know what you've got to do, you've *decided,* and now time's run out, you're on—move!

Quick, because you've been watched in, every second counts now, the timing is the important factor here. You'll be all right, you can do it.

He went fast up the stairs. There were sixteen steps, and a tiny square landing, uncarpeted, and then you turned up six more steps to the left, to the second-floor hall. The door to the Lindstroms' apartment was just across there, and the next flight right around from the top of those stairs, left again. He got to the landing, and his breath was coming too short— God, he'd never do it, out of condition, another flight and he wouldn't have strength to aim the damn gun— But he had to hurry, he had to—

A woman screamed ten feet away in the dark hall. And screamed. And the third scream shut off sharp and final, cut off as with a knife.

After that it was mostly reflex action for Morgan. The only conscious complete thought he remembered having was, Not destiny I should kill Smith: every time something happens to stop it. That in his mind while the screaming sounded, and then he was across the landing and plunging up the six additional steps, and in the hallway—behind that door there, no noise now, no screams, and then other sounds, and a boy's frantic voice, *"No, don't, Eddy, don't, please—"*

He expected the door to be locked, he pounded on it to let them know someone was here, coming. Afterward he remembered it wasn't until then he realized it was the Lindstroms' door—and now, no voices inside but a queer grunting, thrashing-around noise that raised the hair on his neck, and he put his shoulder to the door, shouting warning.

It was not locked, it swung in under him, almost threw him head foremost. Feet on the stairs below: a voice calling something.

He didn't see the woman, not then. Only one lamp on in the dingy room, a body on the floor, a big dark figure crouched over it, with hands reaching—

"What's going on here, what—" He was halfway across the room; he stopped, seeing the woman then, twisted limp figure sprawled across the threshold of the bedroom; he looked away from her, dry-throated, saw the big figure had straightened to come at him, lumbering. In the full light then, coming with guttural mouthings, and Morgan saw what it was, saw—

Blind, instinctive, he clawed for the gun in his pocket. The butt caught in the pocket lining; hands took hold of him and slammed him back against the wall and he thought all the breath was knocked out of him, he couldn't— Animal gruntings, a fetid breath hot on his face. He tugged desperately at the gun and it came free, the pocket tearing loose, as he went down full length on his back, and hands lifting, holding, smashed his head down against a chair leg.

Dark exploded inside his head, he was blind, he was done, but the gun in his hand, and he jammed it into what was on top of him, just at random, and pulled the trigger.

Johnny Branahan had been riding patrol cars for nearly twenty years; he was growing a spare tire around his diaphragm and he wasn't quite as quick on his feet as he'd been when he was a rookie. He wasn't a particularly ambitious man, or the brainiest man in uniform, but he was a good cop, within certain limits: he did the job he was supposed to do the way it was supposed to be done, and he wasn't one of those did just as little as he could get away with, either. He was conscientious about studying the lists of hot cars and wanted men.

The call came over at six minutes past seven, and they were quite a way off, so even with the siren going they were the fourth car to get there. An assault, it was, by the code number, and must be a three-star business, some sort, with four cars called in. The ambulance was already there, and quite a crowd—honest to God, you'd think they grew up out of the ground, let anything happen—

Wilkinson and Petty, Slaney and Gomez, handling the crowd: he spotted them as he braked the car, and Gomez caught his eye and called to him as he and his partner got out. "Upstairs, Johnny—second floor, the lieutenant's up there."

"Right," said Branahan. He was puffing a little when he got to the top of the stairs; it was the apartment right there, door open, and he could see the white-coated interns inside, just lifting a stretcher.

"This one's a D.O.A. too," said one of them. "We'll come back for those— O.K., boy, let's get the show on the road." Goldstein and Costello were handling the smaller crowd up here, tenants, trying to get in to see the blood, see the corpses, honest to God you wondered what got into people—

"All right, folks, let the doctors through, now—"

As the interns came out with the first stretcher, the crowd parting reluctantly, he caught a glimpse of another man in there, one of the downtown men, Lieutenant Mendoza from Homicide. Quick work, he thought, and moved back himself to give room to the interns at the top of the stairs.

That put him at the foot of the stairs to the next floor, and out of the corner of his eye he saw a man crouched halfway down those stairs, and got a flicker of movement as the man retreated a little way, farther into the dark up there.

It wasn't brains made Branahan go up after him, any conscious process of reasoning. It was just that as an experienced cop he knew there must be something funny about anybody who didn't come rushing up to join the crowd when anything like this was going on.

He started up the stairs, and above him heard sudden movement, and then the fellow began to run—light and fast—up toward the next floor; so then of course Branahan ran too, and caught up with him at a door the man was fumbling at, and swung him around. It was damn dark up there, and he had his flash out ready; he shot it in the man's face and said, "Hold it, brother, let's see what you look like."

The man swore and swung on him, so Branahan belted him one on the side of the head with the flash, and the man staggered back against the wall. Branahan took a second look and was pleased; he'd had reason to remember this name and face on the wanted lists again, because he'd picked this hood up once before, five-six years back.

"Well, if it isn't Ray Dalton," he said. "Up on your feet, boy. Hey, Andy, up here! I got a deal for us! It's just a damn shame, Ray, you so homesick for California you couldn't wait to head west—but New York's kind of mad at you on account you spurned their hospitality. You oughta learn better manners, Ray— No, you don't, me bucko, just hold it now," and the bracelets clicked home as Andy came pounding up the stairs.

By nine o'clock the excitement was about all over; they were tying up loose ends there at the General Hospital. If you could say anything like this really ended, or ended satisfactorily, maybe this had. The woman was dead, and the murderer was dead; the boy wasn't badly hurt; Morgan had a slight concussion and could go home tomorrow, they said.

The reporters had come and gone, after the usual backchat with the nurses about flash-shots and noise. This would make the front page tomorrow morning, just once, and not as a lead story; people would talk of it a little and then soon forget it.

"Also," said Mendoza to Hackett, lighting a fresh cigarette, "we can't claim to have done much about winding this up, can we? Just the way the deal ran—sometimes you get a hand you can't do a damn thing with."

"That's the way it goes sometimes. But I don't know, Luis—you'd linked this up, in the process of time—"

"I think so, yes. It only needed somebody with official excuse to get into that apartment for any length of time, you know—sooner or later such an outsider would have heard or seen something to rouse suspicion, and then the lid would have blown—with what we had already."

"One hell of a thing, who'd have— And damn lucky in a way it ended like this, nothing worse. I've got no sympathy for that woman, that I'll say—she got what she asked for. But when you think what it must have been like for that kid, for the husband, all these years—" Seven years, the husband said, since they'd come west away from home where everybody knew.

"Mother love," said Mendoza, and laughed. They had quite a lot from the husband about that, by now: incoherent, poured out in sporadic bursts jumbled together with self-apology. *I knew it was awful wrong of me, but I got to a place where I just couldn't stand no more. An' I thought, if I wasn't there, it'd be bound to come out—they'd make her put him away somewheres—account it was getting where she couldn't handle him herself, all I could do to manage him, times, he was so big, you know.* They were silent awhile, thinking about it.

Mother love, maybe: also pride, shame, ignorant conviction of guilt. An obsession: if he was to be put away, questions, forms, people knowing; and also habit, also familiarity, saying the doctor back home was wrong, no danger, poor Eddy just like a little kid, he'd never— A little kid twenty years old, six-feet-four and stronger than most men.

Ashamed of him, but refusing to send him away. And quite possibly aggravating the whole mental state by the unnatural secret life she forced on him in consequence—on all of them. Moving in or out of places by night, watching, waiting, so that none would see. Keeping him in by day, close-watched: if she had to go out, the husband home from work, the boy home from school, to keep watch. Taking him out like a dog for exercise after dark, keeping to unlighted side streets. Training him like a dog, no noise inside the apartment. Building three lives around the one unproductive life, everything else subordinate to looking after Eddy and keeping Eddy a secret from everyone else.

I figured she'd have to give it up, if I wasn't there. He got into, well, like rages they was, times—any little thing'd set him off, wanted to smash things, you know, an' she couldn't handle—Same time, he knew lots o' things you wouldn't expect, an' it was like that doctor said, when he got to be fourteen, fifteen, you know, getting to be a man, like, he—It got harder, he kept wanting get out, away, by himself, an' then when you'd bring him back, say no, he got just terrible mad, couldn't see why—

Of course Lindstrom had argued with her. Not the kind of man to be very articulate. Not the kind of woman to listen, reason, understand clearly what she was doing and why.

And I never did think he'd ever turn on any of us—on his own Ma! Didn't seem possible, if I'd thought that I'd never in this world gone off like I did. I knew it was awful bad for Marty, sleeping same room and all, 'twasn't fair—but she wouldn't never listen. I just got to a place where—

Mendoza dug his cigarette into the tub of sand in the corridor there and repeated, "Mother love."

"People," contributed Hackett rather savagely. The pretty blonde nurse came out and said they could see the boy for just ten minutes, if they wouldn't let him get too excited, he'd been in shock after all and needed rest and quiet.

The boy had tight hold on his father's hand, sitting up in bed looking at them a little uncertain, a little scared still. "We don't bite," said Mendoza, smiling down at him. "There's just a few little questions we want to ask and then we'll let you go to sleep."

"Yes, sir. I—I *want* to tell you—how it was, it was my fault, I know that—let him get away, when I knew how he was, he'd maybe get in trouble. But I—but I— That first time, it was all account of that doll, it was awfully silly but he wanted it so bad, he saw it in the store window, there was a light left on even when it was shut, you know, and times I took him out, nights, we went past a couple times and I couldn't hardly get him away from it, he—"

"He took funny notions like that," said Lindstrom. "Don't you get excited, Marty, I'm right here to watch out for you now, and all they want to know, I guess, is about—about today." He looked still a little dazed and shaken, but his voice was reassuringly stolid.

"But I *want* to tell—about everything, have it over . . . Ma, she'll be awful mad—I made things happen like they did." He hadn't been told about his mother yet; there was time. "I—I was scared to tell her, first, that time—over on Tappan—and then I had to, account of knowing what he'd done. Ma said—she told him she'd buy it for him, see— the doll. She'd saved up the money—"

"Waste, waste," muttered Lindstrom. "Foolish, but she'd do such, whatever he—"

"And then I guess she couldn't, somebody else— And that night, I was out with him, he ran off and I couldn't catch up—I looked everywhere, I went to that store but they'd taken the doll out of the window a while before, he wasn't— And when I f-found him, he *had* it, a great big box and inside— I thought he'd stole it, I *shouldn't't've* let him get away like that—"

"You take it easy now," said Hackett, soothing; he glanced at Mendoza. They could both reconstruct that one, Brooks, now. Eddy peering in the shop window, seeing Carol come out with the doll. *His* doll, that he'd been promised, that she had no right to. Following, working up to anger at her thievery.

"I—when I heard—about that girl, and I remembered there was a little spot on his shirt, like blood—I *had* to tell Ma, but she wouldn't listen, she wouldn't believe he'd— She said I'd just forgot, she had so bought the doll, and I was making up bad stories—"

Mendoza sighed to himself; he had heard that animal mothers too always gave more attention to the runt of a litter, the sickly one . . . "I'd like to hear something about the skating rink, Marty. This girl, this time."

"Yes, sir. That was even more my fault, 'cause I knew how bad he could do, then. I *shouldn't've*—but Ma'd got kind of sick, she was doctoring at the clinic and couldn't go out with him any more nights, I had to every night. And sometimes it was kind of hard, things I wanted to do with other fellows, like movies sometimes—you know—I—he got away a couple times more, and once when I found him he was at that place, he'd found a sort of little back door that was open and he was getting in, and I had to go after, I had an awful time getting him to come away—he liked the music, and he liked to watch them going round and round. And— Dad, *you* know how when he liked anything he'd be good and quiet, just sit there still as could be, hours sometimes — I thought it was all right! I—I went with him a couple of times, and he never moved, just sat there watching and listening, see. So I thought, he'd do like that long as that place was open at night, never bother nobody, nobody knew we was there at all. And, Dad, it wasn't like cheating to sneak in without paying like that, because we wasn't *using* it, I mean didn't go to skate. I thought I could just, sort of, leave him there and it'd be all right, he'd just sit and never do nothing. And I did, a lot of times, I went off and to a movie or somewheres, not to see it all through but mostly, you know—and came back to get him, and he was fine, right where I'd left him."

"And at the rink," said Mendoza softly, "he saw a girl, a pretty girl who looked like his beautiful doll. . . . How'd I know that? Why, I'm a detective, Marty."

"He was—funny—about the doll," said the boy with a little gasp. "I mean, I guess he sort of—loved it—but same time, he did things to it— bad things. Yes, sir, it was like that—at that place, he saw this girl, he got terrible excited about it, kept talking about her— I mean, what— what he meant for talk, he couldn't ever talk real plain, you know. It was really that, sort of, that'd tell you what he was like, because just to look at him, he—"

Yes; not until you looked twice, saw the eyes, the lumbering walk, or heard the guttural attempts at speech, would you know. Otherwise, to the casual look, just a big young man, maybe a little stupid.

"Once down on Commerce, when I was with him, I saw her too—he —tried to go up and talk to her, I got him away then. And I guess she was a little scared, remembered me anyways, I mean what I looked like, even if it was dark—because a couple days after, in the daytime, I saw her in the street again, and she made like to say something to me, but she never—Danny was with me, he—"

"You're doing fine, but don't try to tell everything, just take it easy."

"He wanted—to skate with her, round and round, to the music," said the boy faintly. "I shouldn't never have left him there that night. I got sort of scared about it in the movies, I thought I'd better—and he was gone! I looked everywheres, but it was so dark and I didn't dare call at him very loud, people— And when I did find him, it was right *there,* that lot where— I didn't know then, I didn't, I never saw *her!* He had a lady's handbag, I didn't see that until we was down the street a ways, and I thought he'd stole it. I just dropped it, like, didn't know what else —he didn't mind when I took it, he—"

So that built up Ramirez for them. He saw the boy she was with taken out, and the girl left alone. So now was his chance to go skating round and round with his pretty doll who'd come alive for him—and that was all, probably, he'd followed her for: to tell her that, ask her. And the girl, confronted there in the dark, alone, in the empty lot, with the animal mouthings, the eager pawings, losing her head, struggling to get away— And that was all it had needed.

Mendoza said, "All right, Marty, that's all for right now. You just try to stop thinking about it. Go to sleep and don't worry any more."

"He was just wild, find the doll was gone, 's morning." The boy lay back tiredly on the pillows, his eyes closing. "I think even Ma was real scared then—so was I—and tonight, well, she'd been telling him all the while I'd—get it back for him—and when I said I couldn't, he—"

"Yes, we understand all that. Don't worry about it now—everything's over."

As they turned to the door Lindstrom said rather desperately, "Please, sir, I got to ask you—will they—will they do anything to—to my boy or me for being to blame about this? I mean, I want to do what's right, I ain't trying to get out of anything, but—"

Mendoza turned back to him. "There's no legal responsibility involved here really, now the boy's dead, Mr. Lindstrom. I couldn't say, it's an academic question, under other circumstances very likely the D.A. and the grand jury might have decided to call it criminal negligence. As it is, I scarcely think so. Certainly not the boy, a minor couldn't be assumed responsible. . . . I might add, however, that at any time these seven years *you* could have taken action, if and when it seemed—indicated. A word to any of a number of agencies—police, county health, doctor, hospital—"

"She made us *promise!*" burst out the boy. "She made us promise on the *Bible!*"

Mendoza looked at them a minute more, smiled, said good night, and followed Hackett out to the corridor. "Any comment?" he asked, very soft and amused.

"*Nada,*" said Hackett heavily. "Just—*people*. Leave it there. Are we wound up here?"

"I want to see Morgan."

FIFTEEN

"The gun," said Mendoza.

"Damn lucky—I had it on me," repeated Morgan. He was all there, himself, sitting up smoking a borrowed cigarette, not much of a bandage to frighten his wife when she came; but he'd had just enough sedation to slow his mind somewhat, at the same time loosen his tongue.

"I don't deny it. You've saved everybody quite a bit of trouble—including the expense of a trial. It's only a small point, Mr. Morgan, and maybe you'll think I'm being unnecessarily careful. But as of the moment, California law says you don't need a license for firearms unless you're carrying them on the person or— I needn't quote the whole thing, that's the relevant part. License, Mr. Morgan?—and not that it's any of my business, but how did you come to be carrying a loaded gun on a visit to one of your cases?"

"It's all shot to hell now," muttered Morgan, "all for nothing—and you know, I don't think—I don't think I could've done it anyway." He looked at Gunn, at the other side of the bed—Gunn, who'd had to get dressed and come out after all. "I'll tell you," he said, "I'll tell you—didn't go there to see Mrs. Lindstrom, Mendoza. I went to kill a man. A man named Smith."

They heard about Smith in disjointed phrases. Gunn's round, amiable face got longer and more worried by the second. "Oh, you damn fool, Dick—can't have been thinking straight—should've come to me, gone to the police, he couldn't—"

"Oh, couldn't he! Can't he! I remember enough law— Extortion? The law doesn't take your unsupported word, does it?"—turning on Mendoza, who shook his head. "What could I do, what else could I—? Well, there it is—wasn't intended, I guess—and now we're right back where we were. God, I don't know—"

"Smith," said Mendoza. "Description?" And when he'd pried that out of Morgan, "Yes, well, he won't be troubling you for a while. His real name's Dalton, he's a small-time hood on the run from parole in New York, and we picked him up tonight in the middle of the other excitement. He's got two years coming back east."

"Oh, God, you don't mean it—he's—all this for—"

"Take it easy, Dick," said Gunn, sitting down, looking almost sick with relief. "That doesn't mean you're out of the woods, but it makes it the hell of a lot easier. If the woman's so—tractable, the way you say, there shouldn't be any trouble. Put it through nice and quiet, get her to see a lawyer with you, there shouldn't be any contest, just a routine thing. Dalton wasn't after Janny, only the money, he wouldn't—"

"You think—no hitch, do it like that? If we—oh, God, I hope so, we've both been about crazy—" Morgan sat up and clutched Gunn's arm. "You said Sue's coming?—want to tell her—tell her it's all right, or almost—"

"Sue's coming, you lie down. I called Christy, she's gone over to stay with Janny, and Sue'll be taking a cab down, on her way right now, probably."

Mendoza stood up. "There'll be an inquest, of course, but purely formal. You needn't worry about it. Self-defense, justifiable homicide. Which is a very damned lucky outcome for you, Morgan. You don't know how lucky. If you want the Luger back, you'll have to apply for a license."

"Oh, well, keep it, I don't want it. I—I feel *fine,*" said Morgan, and laughed. "Wish Sue'd get here. You can have the damn gun. Glad now —didn't use it—or the way I planned, anyway—"

"Just as well." Mendoza looked down at him, smiling very faintly. "I'd advise you, Morgan, not to get in a situation again where you start thinking about murder. In the first place, it never solves any problems, you know—only creates more. And in the second place, from what you told me of your plans for this one, it wouldn't take a full-fledged lieutenant of detectives to spot you for X about half an hour after the corpse began to cool. However, as it is we're all very happy you happened to be in the right place at the right time—and congratulations on the rest of this working out for you." He nodded to Gunn, still looking amused, and went out.

After a minute Morgan said, "Damn him—that's—when I thought I was being so clever, too . . . but I suppose he's right, at that. Just—something about him—puts my back up, is all."

Gunn sneezed, said, "Oh, hell it *is* a cold," and took out another cigarette. "Well, you know—Luis," he added soberly, "maybe he's just what they call overcompensating, for a time he was only another dirty little Mex kid in a slum street. You know? Tell you one thing, Dick, he's a damned good cop—if a little erratic now and then," and he grinned. He found a packet of matches, looked at it without lighting the cigarette. "He's also a very lonely man. Which maybe he'll find out some day."

Morgan moved restlessly. "Give me another one of those, will you? I wish Sue'd come . . ."

"Philosophizing?" Mendoza came up behind Hackett in the lobby.

"Yeah, I guess you could say I was," said Hackett, who'd been standing stock-still, staring vacantly at the wall. "I guess so. You know, this whole thing—it just struck me—what for? What's it mean?"

Mendoza laughed and shrugged. "*¿Quién sabe?—¡Sabe Dios!* Nice to think it means anything."

"No, but it makes you wonder. You look at it and you can work up a fine righteous wrath against that damn fool woman, against the ignorance and false pride and plain damned muddle-headedness that's killed three people—four, if you count him—and all unnecessarily. But was it? The way things dovetail, sometimes—Morgan just happening to be there, and with a gun on him—because if he hadn't had, you know, I don't think he could have handled that one alone, I don't think any two men— Without the gun, maybe Morgan dead too. And maybe it was all *for* something, Luis—that we don't know about, never will. To save the boy—maybe he's got something to do here, part of some plan. You know? Maybe," and Hackett laughed, "so Agnes Browne could get all straightened out with her Joe. Maybe so the Wades can keep their nice high-class superior-white-Protestant bloodline pure."

"Comforting to think," repeated Mendoza cynically. "That's why I'm a lieutenant and you're a sergeant, Arturo—every time I formulate a theory, I want evidence to say it's so, or I don't keep the theory. *¿Comprende?* On that, there's no evidence. If you want to theorize, *chico,* maybe it all happened so I could meet this pretty redhead! Change, please, if you've got it—*¿Date prisa, por favor!*"

Hackett took the quarter and gave him three nickels and a dime. "You watch yourself with that one, boy—I got a hunch you don't get something for nothing there."

"All these years and you don't know me yet. Wait and see. *Hasta luego*—eight o'clock sharp, we've a lot of routine to clear up." Mendoza went over to the row of public phone booths.

When Alison answered the second ring he said, "Luis. Would you like to hear a story of human foibles and follies? . . . Yes, we've got him, it's all over. But for the routine. I'll be with you in twenty minutes, you'll be interested to hear all about it."

"Well, yes, but it *is* rather late—"

"Night's still young, *chica.* Twenty minutes," he repeated firmly, and hung up on her reluctant laugh.

Hackett was gone. Mendoza stood on the steps, lighting a cigarette, and the dead man in the freight yards wandered through his mind. The next thing, now. Tomorrow. A couple of rather suggestive little things, there: might yield the ghost of a line to look into. . . . When he came out to the street, somebody in a brash new Buick had sewed him up tight in the parking space; it would take some maneuvering to get the Ferrari out. He swore, getting out his keys; no denying at all that a smaller car— He might just look into it, no harm in looking. Maybe that Mercedes . . .

He slid under the wheel and started the engine. Meanwhile, Alison. He smiled to himself; he expected to enjoy Alison. . . .

THE
ACE
OF
SPADES

ONE

"Oh, damn," said Alison Weir. *"Was* it the next block? I could have sworn—"

"You left the car right here," said Patricia Moore firmly. "I remember noticing that particular bed of begonias. Especially fine ones." Pat's British raising, as it affected gardens and the King's English at least, was incorrigibly untranslated to citizenship.

"I'm not sure. All these little streets look so much alike. Damn. I don't know why I wore these shoes, my feet are killing me. *¡Qué incomodidad!—¡es el colmo! I thought* it was along here—"

"I notice you revert to Spanish a bit oftener these days," remarked Pat, sitting down placidly on the low brick wall flanking the sidewalk and fanning herself with the program of the exhibit they'd been looking at. "The car's been stolen, obviously."

"Don't be ridiculous," said Alison crossly. "Who on earth would want it?" She sat down beside Pat and lit a cigarette. "It's Luis' fault," she added. "After Dad died and I came back north, I didn't have much reason to use Spanish, you know, except for an occasional girl coming in to school— But there *is* one thing about it, it does give vent to one's feelings better than English sometimes. . . . It must have been the next block."

"You and your policeman. It was here. I remember distinctly. It's been stolen. Did you leave the keys in it?"

"If you think," said Alison, "that I have attained the age of thirty without acquiring a little sense—of course I didn't. And really I must say I should think I could visit a respectable place like the County Museum in broad daylight without having my car stolen. If we'd been in a bar down on Skid Row it'd be different."

"Wickedness flourishes everywhere," said Miss Moore philosophically.

"And I can't say the exhibition was worth it. Personally I think Renoir was overrated."

"That's your photographic eye. You're inclined to be over-realistic yourself. Too much detail. And such *strong* color—of course I suppose it's only to be expected from a red-haired Scots-Irishwoman."

"I refuse," said Alison, "to discuss painting techniques sitting on bricks with the thermometer at a hundred. It's ridiculous. I want to go home and take off my clothes and have a large cold drink. *Can* it have been stolen?"

"It happens every day," said Miss Moore. "You'd better call the police. You've got an in with them, they'll probably produce it for you in no time."

"Luis isn't Traffic, he's Homicide. I suppose I had. Oh, damn!" said Alison. "And I don't suppose there's a public phone nearer than the central building. No rest for the wicked. And I cannot imagine why anybody should take the thing—of course they might not have got far, that's one comfort, if you don't know just how to manipulate that hand-choke, it dies on you every fifty feet . . . I wonder if I'd look *very* odd if I took off my shoes? You see teen-agers going barefoot—"

"Really, Alison!" Miss Moore, who was dumpy, dowdy, and without an iota of personal vanity, but with strong notions of respectability, regarded her severely. "I'll walk back with you, and you shouldn't delay reporting it."

"I suppose not." Alison got up with a grimace, and they started back to the building they'd just left. The one public phone, of course, was at the very end of a long marble hall, and when they got there neither of them had a dime. Under Pat's disapproving eye, Alison accosted a passer-by and got change, and eventually was put through to Traffic.

"Yes, ma'am," said an efficient, reassuring voice there. "The exact location, please. . . . If you'll just remain on the spot, there'll be an officer there directly to take particulars."

Alison thanked the voice gloomily. "And now we have to walk all the way back there again, and after they've taken down all the details they'll drive away in their nice new patrol car, and we'll have to come back here to call a cab."

"A *cab?*" said Miss Moore. "Sheer extravagance! There's a bus goes right down Exposition Boulevard—"

"Yes, I know, you can take it if you like," said Alison. They went back and sat on the wall. In about five minutes a black and white patrol car came along and a uniformed officer got out of it and projected courteous efficiency at them. Description of car, please—when was it parked here, when was the loss discovered?

"It was about two-thirty, wasn't it, when we got here? And if you can tell me why anybody should deliberately— I remember there was a brand-new Buick right ahead. It's a Ford, almost thirteen years old, light gray, a two-door sedan. I've got the license number on a thing on my key chain."

"Oh, that's very helpful, ma'am. You didn't leave the keys in it, then?"

"Certainly not, I don't know why you always automatically assume women drivers are all fools—"

"Now don't take it out on the officer," said Pat. "Don't they have ways of starting it going somehow without a key?—I've read—"

"That's so," said the patrolman, who'd taken another look at Alison and doubled his gallantry. "And some of these kids, you know, the hot-rodders, they *want* old stuff like that, to strip down and rebuild."

"That makes me believe the stories about the younger generation having no sense," said Alison.

He laughed, handing back her key ring. "Chances are we'll pick it up within a few days, Miss Weir. You'll be notified, of course. Damn inconvenient, but there it is—it happens every day to a lot of people. Don't worry, it'll go on the hot list right away."

"Thanks very much. . . . And now back to the phone to call a cab, what did I tell you? I've heard there *are* some people in L.A. who don't own cars. How do you suppose they exist?"

"The lesser breeds without the law. We manage to get about on the two feet Providence provided," said Miss Moore. "Much healthier. Also better for the figure, although—" She compared her dumpiness to Alison's excellent distribution of poundage, and laughed.

The Los Angeles Police Department is a large one, and not all the men in it are acquainted with one another. In the ordinary way, Sergeant Edward Rhodes of Traffic would not have had any contact with the Homicide division, but as it happened one of his personal friends was Sergeant Landers of that office. Through Landers, Rhodes had heard this and that about Landers' superior, Lieutenant Luis Rodolfo Vicente Mendoza, and over a period of time he had caught some of Landers' hero worship for this personage. Both of them were young unmarried men, and over their coffee breaks and shared dinners in cheap restaurants, they talked shop.

Rhodes, in fact, cherished a secret ambition toward some day getting into Homicide himself, and Mendoza had not only a professional reputation any man might envy, but other kinds. Mendoza was, by all accounts, quite the hell of a fellow in three ways—at his job, at a poker table, and with the girls—and thereby hung a number of tales, which Landers had passed on at length.

So Rhodes, from a distance as it were, had set Mendoza up as a model. Not that he could ever hope to attain some of Mendoza's attributes: for one thing, there was all the money. Mendoza had come into a sizable fortune from a miserly grandfather and didn't stint himself enjoying it. Landers guessed that he didn't pay a dime less than two hundred bucks for any of his suits; he dressed to the nines, dapper and elegant, never a hair out of place, the precise line of black moustache always trimmed even and neat, the long narrow hands manicured—but nothing flashy, everything quiet, good taste. And he'd just taken delivery of a new car, which both of them had admired in the lot—it had cost the equivalent of Rhodes' salary for three years. It was a long, low, custom-built gunmetal-colored Facel-Vega, a two-door hardtop sports coupé, and Landers reported with awe that it was said to be capable of acceleration from a stand to a hundred m.p.h. in eighteen seconds, only Lieutenant Mendoza never drove that way, he was real careful with a car and had never got a moving-violation ticket at all, ever.

It wasn't to be supposed either that Sergeant Rhodes could ever attain the talent—as per Mendoza's reputation—for uncanny hunches and brilliant deductions. But he could admire—from a distance—and that he did.

As it further happened, Landers had casually heard from Sergeant Lake, who was desk man in Mendoza's office and now and then had to track him down out of hours, the name of Mendoza's current girlfriend, or at least one of them. Landers had even met her once, when he was relaying some urgent information to Mendoza, and reported her to be evidence of Mendoza's excellent taste—a real redhead, and quite something, he said. Funny sort of name for a girl, Alison: but for that reason it had stayed in Rhodes' mind.

Which was why he noticed it on the list of hot cars, and read the meager information with interest. A thirteen-year-old Ford: he thought instantly, respectfully, a nice girl, not a gold-digger, taking Mendoza for his money. Of course, *that* kind Mendoza wouldn't be such a fool to take up with in the first place. Landers said she ran one of these charm schools, and painted pictures on the side—kind of an artist. Couldn't have much money, driving a car like this. . . . His chivalrous instincts were aroused, and also he had a vague vision of Mendoza dropping into Traffic—say some time when Captain Edgely was around to hear—and thanking him for such an efficient, excellent performance of his job in the matter.

He exerted himself, therefore, with dispatch, to find Alison Weir's car for her; he sent out a special bulletin about it, and each morning eagerly scanned the list of stolen cars located.

But it wasn't until Thursday—it had been stolen on Sunday afternoon—that it turned up, on a routine check of overparked cars. Out in a rather lonely section of Compton, left along a new residential street.

It was brought in and Rhodes looked it over. Awful old piece of junk, he thought. These kids!—no discipline, no principles at all these days. Anything sitting around loose, if they wanted it for half an hour—

That was about half past four on Thursday afternoon, and he succumbed to temptation, called Miss Weir, reported the finding of the car, and said it wasn't any trouble at all, he'd deliver it himself, bring her the formal papers to sign acknowledging its recovery.

Not exactly according to Hoyle, but he went down to the garage and got one of the boys to start the Ford for him and trail him in a patrol car to bring him back, and drove up to Hollywood to Miss Weir's apartment.

"We'll have to ask you to look it over, Miss Weir—you know, say what damage's been done, if any." Landers had been quite right: nothing cheap, a plain sort of tan summer dress, not too much jewelry, but a looker, in a ladylike way: you didn't often see real red hair that wasn't carroty, and she had the complexion to go with it, milk-white, and hazel-green eyes.

"Oh, certainly," said Alison, "but I don't suppose there's much they could have done to it. It's seen quite a lot of life already." She came downstairs with him obligingly. "It's never really got used to the good roads up here—you see, it was the last car my father bought, he was a construction engineer and worked a good deal in Mexico, it passed its adolescence mostly down in Coahuila, negotiating burro trails, and I really think it's suspicious of anything else. . . . Well, I can't see that it looks any different." She opened the door and peered in. "The seat covers have had that rip for months, and that dent in the dashboard, that was Ferdinando Gomez the time he got the D.T.'s and Dad drove him down to the missionary hospital. No, it's all just the way it was. Nothing missing from the glove compartment as far as I can tell—heavens, what a lot of junk one does accumulate."

"You want to be sure, Miss Weir, before you sign the receipt—on account of the insurance, you know. If you put in a claim—"

"Oh, lord, I'm just thankful to have it back, and still running—I don't see any need to do that. There doesn't seem to be anything wrong mechanically?"

"Well—er—" said Rhodes.

"I mean, it *is* running?"

"Oh, it *runs,* sure, I just drove it up, of course."

"Well, then, that's all right. I still can't imagine why they took it. Where'd you find it?"

He told her, handing over the receipt and a pen. "Just kids, probably, out for a joy ride. It'd been sitting there quite a while, they didn't keep it long."

"Well, thank you *very* much," said Alison with a nice smile, handing back the receipt and pen. "I *am* glad to have it back."

"No trouble at all," said Rhodes gallantly. Possibly, he thought, she'd say something to Mendoza: such a nice efficient officer who brought it back; but in any case he'd been interested in meeting her. Of course, he reflected further on the ride back to headquarters, she'd actually have been better off if they'd wrecked that piece of junk and she could put in the full insurance claim.

The car had come back on Thursday, and Alison drove it to her school next morning and back again that afternoon, and found it just the same as usual. On Saturday she drove it down to the beach, up past Malibu, where she spent most of the day working on what turned out to be a rather unsatisfactory seascape. Unloading her painting gear when she got home, she reflected that the poor thing was badly in need of a bath—a job she loathed—but it was later than she'd thought, and she had barely an hour to get dressed before Luis came to take her out to dinner. Tomorrow, she'd clean the car. The better the day the better the deed.

So late Sunday afternoon found her in the cramped apartment garage, equipped with a stiff brush, several rags, and a pail of water. She started by brushing out the inside—seats and floor. The front seat had accumulated quite a surprising amount of sand from her jaunt to the

beach, and she brushed vigorously, getting well down into the crack between the back and the seat, kneeling on the seat to press it down.

Sand, dust, anonymous fluff, and dirt—and of all things, a long dried
twig with a couple of mummified leaves clinging to it, probably blew in
the window and got crushed down—she ran two fingers down the crack
to be sure of getting it all out, and suddenly felt something else there,
and delved farther. Damn, when she pulled the opening wider the thing
just slipped down—but eventually, at the expense of a torn nail and
several muttered curses, she persuaded it out, and looked at it.

"*¿Y qué es esto?*" she said to herself absently, turning the thing over
in her palm. "What on earth is it and where did it come from? How
very odd . . ."

TWO

The body turned up that Monday morning, halfway down a narrow
alley opening on Carson Street not far from Main. Unlike a lot of alleys
down there, this one wasn't used for anything much, and as the corpse
was beyond the entrance, it hadn't been discovered at once; some kids
had finally stumbled over it, running through. Sergeant Arthur Hackett
went down with a crew of men to look at it, and was not enlightened.
Or, if the truth were told, much interested.

It wasn't that he expected the kind of corpses and mysteries found in
the paperback novels at drugstores, every time he got a call to a new
case; that sort of thing just didn't happen; at least in his nine years' experience of being a cop he'd never run across it. But some corpses were
just naturally more interesting than others, and this one was, in a word,
routine.

"Just another piece of flotsam," he said to Mendoza when he came
back. "On the big H and finally took too much of a jolt and didn't
come out of it. God knows who he was—probably nobody cares any
more."

"Really," said Mendoza. "Nothing on him to say?"

"*Nada*. Maybe he'll get identified by somebody while he's on file, but maybe not, too. You know how they drift. Not very important either way, I'd say." Hackett brought out a manila envelope. "Here's all he had on him. Damnedest thing how they set out to commit suicide—what it amounts to. He was a good-looker, and I'd say not over thirty."

"A lot of answers on that one," said Mendoza, "and maybe as many answers as there are users." Business had been a little slack lately, and he was unoccupied for the moment; idly he up-ended the envelope on his desk and looked at what it disgorged.

A clean folded handkerchief, plain white, cheap cotton, dime store variety. A flat longish box bearing the name of a chain drugstore and containing a much-used and dirty hypodermic syringe and several needles. A cheap pocketknife. Forty-eight cents in change. A crumpled package of cigarettes with three left in it. A scrap of paper, irregularly torn across one edge, about four inches wide at the broadest part and narrowing down to a point. Torn off a corner of something.

"What's this?"

"Piece torn off a letter or something, I suppose. I wouldn't have seen it at all, but the staple bit my finger when I was going through his pockets. You can see the holes—there were a couple of pages, or more, stapled together. I just stuck it in, thought there might be something on it to say who he was, but—"

"Yes," said Mendoza, "and an odd sort of letter it seems to have been. Nymphs and dolphins. *¡Comó, oyé!* I'd heard that heroin gives some people hallucinations, but what superior hallucinations!"

"What? Let's see, I didn't—"

Mendoza passed it over. Automatically he began to tidy the desk, setting the deceased's possessions in a neat little pile at one side, brushing off tobacco crumbs, lining up the ashtray with the blotter and desk-box. That was Mendoza: the orderly mind, place-for-everything-everything-in-its-place. Probably one of the reasons he had acquired a little reputation as an investigative officer: ragged edges worried him, the thing left all untidy, patternless. He might be and often was irritable at the frustration of continually being presented with another box of jigsaw pieces to put together, but he was constitutionally unable to leave them alone until every last little piece had been fitted in where it belonged.

He glanced up at Hackett, and got out a cigarette: a slim dark man, the black hairline moustache, the sharp arch of heavy brows, the widow's peak, punctuation marks to a long nose and a long jaw: impassive, an unremarkable if regular-featured face, but it could flash into sudden charm when a smile touched the dark eyes. "Nymphs," he said. "*¡Caray, qué hombre!*"

Hackett looked at the two lines of typing on the scrap of paper. It had been torn off the right-hand top edge of the page, and the typing was double-spaced; there was such a wide margin, however, that only four words were included on the scrap. The top line said, *verse, nymph* and the end of the line below it said, *small dolphin.* "That *is* a damn funny one," he agreed.

"A *small* dolphin," said Mendoza, leaning back with closed eyes, smoking lazily. "Somehow that makes it sound so much more—mmh—individual, doesn't it? Only a small dolphin. I wonder what it was all about. *Nothing* else on him? Well, well. You know, that dolphin—to say nothing of the nymph—intrigues me. I think I'll go down and take a look at him."

"As you please," said Hackett, "but it's just another dope case, obviously. Or are you going to have one of your hunches about it and say he's the heir to a Bulgarian millionaire assassinated by the Communists?"

"Once in a while," said Mendoza, getting up and going to get his hat, "I read a detective novel—and once in a while I wish I was in one. Everything made so easy for those boys, such complicated problems that inevitably there are only a couple of possible answers. I don't think there are any Bulgarian millionaires left. But I haven't much else to do at the moment, for once, and I may as well take a look."

He went down to the morgue and looked at the dead man. There were aspects of the dead man which mildly interested him further. Hackett had said, good-looking—that was an understatement. Even several days dead, it was a handsome face: a purity of line like a cameo profile. A young man, twenty-eight to thirty, and his indulgence in heroin hadn't left any apparent marks of dissipation on him. A tallish, well-set-up young man, he'd have been.

Mendoza went back to his office and sent down word that he'd like the autopsy report expedited. Not that there'd be much in it, but on the other hand—a *nymph* and a *dolphin*—it might be something a little more interesting than it looked at first glance.

The dolphin, in fact, stayed so persistently in his mind that he was somewhat absent-minded with Alison that evening, and when she complained he apologized by telling her about it.

"A dolphin," said Alison, intrigued despite herself. "It sounds exactly like the start of a detective story, doesn't it? That *is* odd."

"A *small* one," said Mendoza almost plaintively. He was relaxed on the end of his spine in her largest armchair, minus jacket and tie; the temperature still stood at ninety.

"It reminds me of something—what? . . . Did you have any English literature in high school?"

"That's a long time back," said Mendoza. "Probably some was inflicted on me. . . . *Por Dios,* twenty-two years ago, and the school's been torn down—that old Macy Street school—when they built the new Union Station. I had to cross through Chinatown to get there." He laughed. "Then we moved, because Johnny Li-Chong taught me to shoot Chinese craps, and my grandmother was horrified. Gambling's still one of the major sins to her. I was supposed to be selling papers after school, and I never told her when I quit—I found I could earn twice as much running a Spanish Monte bank in the back room of Johnny's father's restaurant over on Main. *Caray,* she was pleased, the old lady, when I started to bring her five dollars on Saturdays instead of two—I'm a good smart boy to get a raise in salary so quick! You know something, I never did tell her. She'd have raised the roof—another good-for-nothing going the same way as the old man, gamble his last copper—or hers. That five dollars on Saturdays, it came in useful. And the old man sitting on nearly three million bucks then, in a dozen banks, and swearing about a four-dollar gas bill. Damn it, you encourage me to maunder . . ."

"Earn twice as much?" Alison took him up. "I don't know but what your grandmother's right—"

"I said Spanish Monte, *chica,* not three-card. Perfectly legitimate deal. I was never as crazy a gambler as the old man—"

*"¡A otro perro con ese hueso!—*give that bone to another dog!" Alison laughed. "You'd gamble the gold in your teeth if you had any."

"Well, not," said Mendoza, "without asking about the odds. And very young I found out what a lot of gamblers never seem to—the odds always run in favor of the bank. It's simple mathematics. Even at seventeen, I never just sat in at Monte—that way, as somebody's said, madness lies. I saved my money, industrious young fellow that I was, and set up as a banker. But what was it you asked me? There was a poor devil of an English teacher, Mr.—Mr.—Mr. Keyes. The only thing I remember about high school English is that Mr. Keyes had a passion for Chaucer, and it wasn't until he made me read some of *The*

Canterbury Tales and I came across the Miller's Tale that it dawned on me there might be something interesting—pornographically speaking—in these musty old classics."

"Really. Maybe I missed something, not finishing high school."

"Women don't get a kick out of pornography, or so the psychiatrists say."

"Psychiatrists, hah. Since when do they know what they're talking about? What I was going to say—your small dolphin somehow reminds me of something in—*can* it be Dickens, or was it Trollope?—there was a housemaid who had an illegitimate baby, and when they criticized her she said, Please, ma'am, it was only a little one."

He laughed. "And very logical too. Damn it, what *could* it mean? Unless it's some new pro slang I haven't caught up with yet. *Nymph* would be easy enough in that connection—if a little fancy—but the dolphin eludes me."

"Which reminds me further," said Alison, "I have a mystery for you too." She got up and opened the top desk drawer. "I told you some idiot had borrowed my car. Well, when it came back I got round to cleaning it, and I found this in the crack down between the seat and the back."

Mendoza took the thing and looked at it. "Foreign coin of some kind."

"Holmes, this is wonderful—how do you do it? That I can see. But no engraving or whatever it's called, to say what country or anything."

"No. I'll tell you something else, it's old—maybe damned old. Not milled, and not a true circle." It was not very big; and it was a silver coin, or had some silver in its alloy, though darkened. On one side of it was a design vaguely resembling that on some early U.S. coins, an eagle with outspread wings, but head down; it seemed to be holding something in its talons. The other side bore a design he couldn't puzzle out: a thing which might be a stylized flame growing out of a vase, or a bell with curlicues on the top of it, or two roundish triangles point to point. "Somebody's pocket-piece," he suggested. "A man's, probably, because owing to the curious fact that tailors still put side pockets in our trousers at an acute angle, things do tend to fall out when we're sitting down. Of course, it might also have got pulled out of a woman's purse when she reached in for a handkerchief or something. Are you sure the thing wasn't in the car when it was stolen?"

"No, of course not. Which is exactly what that sergeant said. It occurred to me that it might be some sort of clue to whoever'd taken the car, and I thought I ought to tell them about it, you know—so I called, and got hold of the man who brought it back. A very nice obliging young man named Rhodes. And he asked, was I sure one of my own friends hadn't lost it in the car beforehand—which I'm not. Anyway, he said, it probably wouldn't be much of a clue, and I might as well keep it or throw it away. I do want to ask around, see if someone who's ridden with me might have lost it. I suppose it might have been someone's lucky talisman, something like that—but you'd think whoever'd lost it would have said something, in that case—asked me if I'd found it—if it was someone I know."

"*De veras*," agreed Mendoza absently, still looking at it. "It feels old, somehow. I wonder if it's valuable at all. Curious. You might take it to an expert and ask."

"Well, surely nobody'd have lost anything worth much and not tried to follow it up, everywhere they might have—though if it *was* whoever took the car— Oh, well, I'll keep it awhile and ask everyone, just in case." She dropped it back in the drawer.

Presently Mendoza put on his tie and jacket and went home, and as he cut up fresh liver for the dignified Abyssinian feline who lived with him, the sleek brown green-eyed Bast, and let her out and let her in, and undressed and had a bath and went to bed—and eventually to sleep, after Bast had walked her seven mystic times around a circle and chosen exactly the proper place to curl up beside him—he did not ruminate at all on Alison's little find, but on his own puzzling small dolphin.

The autopsy report was waiting for him on his desk next morning, and he read it with interest. The deceased, said Dr. Bainbridge, had died of a massive injection of heroin. Probably not long prior to death he had received a blow on the head, a blow severe enough to have rendered him unconscious—a blow to the parietal area on the left side. He had been dead between five and seven days—impossible to pin it down further; say between last Monday and last Wednesday. He had been six feet one inch tall, around a hundred and seventy pounds, and between twenty-six and thirty years of age. He had a medium-fair complexion, black hair, and brown eyes; not much dental work, an excellent set of teeth—no scars or birthmarks—blood type O. His fingerprints were being checked in their own records and in Washington, to try to identify him.

But all that was the least interesting of what Bainbridge had to say.

"The body," so the report went on, "bore at least two dozen puncture marks in the areas which a drug addict most commonly uses for injections—both arms and thighs. However, when I came to examine these areas in detail, it was evident that none of these had in fact penetrated an artery, or much below the first layers of the epidermis."

"Well, well," said Mendoza. He called Hackett in and got Dr. Bainbridge on the inside phone. "This corpse. The one with the puncture marks. What did you think about that?"

"Did you haul me away from work just to ask that? I should've thought even a lieutenant of detectives could reason from here to there. The obvious deduction is that he was not an addict. Maybe somebody wanted to make it look as if he was, or maybe it was him, I wouldn't know—people do damned funny things. Maybe he committed suicide and those marks are relics of where he kept trying to get up his nerve. You get that kind of thing, of course."

"Yes, but heroin's not a very usual method. And why and where would he get hold of any if he wasn't an addict? And why and where did he get that knock on the head?"

"That's your business," said Bainbridge.

"Well, you examined the body pretty thoroughly—"

"I did. I'll tell you this, Luis. In the ordinary way, an autopsy wouldn't have uncovered that about those puncture marks. No reason to—er—go into such detail. But I happened to notice that not one seemed to have left any cyanosis—he was very well preserved, of course the clothes had helped, and he was on his back, so all the natural death-cyanosis had settled there—and you'd ordinarily expect to find local cyanosis, black-and-blue spots to you, around the most recent of the punctures. And a few others which had faded some, being older. You know, what always shows up on any user. A real mainliner, he's giving himself a jolt two or three times a day, and pretty damn clumsily too—even if he uses a hypo instead of the teaspoon method, he leaves bruise marks. Well, I noticed that, and I investigated, and I think all those marks were made about the same time, and after he was dead, or just before."

"Now isn't that interesting!" said Mendoza. "I presume the body's still in the morgue—"

"Did you think I'd take it out to Forest Lawn and bury it myself?"

"What I meant was," said Mendoza patiently, "you're done with it, you're not doing any further research? It's on file, ready to be looked at by anybody who might know it?"

"Complete with replaced organs and roughly sewn together, yes. Don't tell me you want a complete analysis of everything."

"But I do, I do, *amigo*. Please. If possible, what he had for his last meal, any chronic diseases, any foreign bodies or inflammations, any suspicious differences from other bodies, etcetera. Look at everything."

Bainbridge uttered a howl of protest. "But, my God, there's no *reason!* We know he died of heroin, and after all this time there won't be much else—"

"You go and look. What kind of injection was it, by the way? Could it have been a normal dose?"

"You know as well as I do how that varies—it *could* have been. A pretty big one to be called that, but the kind of jolt a lot of users take."

"Mmh. Well, you go and look." Mendoza put down the phone and grinned at Hackett. "I knew that dolphin had something to say to us, Art. This corpse is a bit more mysterious than you thought."

"So it seems," said Hackett, still reading the autopsy report. "I'll be damned. But it can still be an ordinary business, Luis. His first shot maybe, and he overdoes it or has an idiosyncrasy for it—like they say." Hackett found the role of the big dumb cop useful, and sometimes forgot to lay it aside in private; as he also looked the part, it came as a little surprise to most people that he was, in fact, a university graduate. "And he was nervous about the shot and made a lot of tries at it."

"Could be," conceded Mendoza. "Could still be. . . . Cigarettes but no matches. Handkerchief but no billfold—where most of us carry some identification."

"You've done time down on Skid Row like most of us—you know how they live, hand to mouth. I've picked 'em up, dead, drunk, and sober, without so much as a handkerchief on 'em."

"Sure," said Mendoza, "and once in a while with a few hundred-dollar bills in a back pocket." He picked up the inside phone again and called the crime lab, and got Dr. Erwin himself. "Over at the morgue is a body, and I presume they still have its clothes. The body of a handsome young man who died of a shot of heroin. I'd like the clothes gone over thoroughly, if you'll be so good." He added the last as a sop to Dr. Erwin's reputation; you didn't give arbitrary orders to a criminological scientist who had several times been consulted by Scotland Yard's C.I.D.

"What for?"

"Anything. If I knew specifically I'd have told you."

"Really, Luis," said Dr. Erwin, annoyed, "must you be so difficult? We do like to have some idea, you know."

"Me, I'm not a chemist," said Mendoza. "I read in the papers that criminological scientists make miracles these days—peer at the microscope and tell the cop on the case just who and what to look for. Science, it's wonderful, ¿no es verdad? You just take a general look and see what turns up."

"Really," said Erwin. "Oh, well, we'll do our best."

"I wonder—" Hackett was beginning, when Sergeant Lake looked in the door and said Lieutenant Carey would like to see whoever had that Carson Street homicide. Carey of Missing Persons.

"Ah," said Mendoza happily, "the next installment of this thrilling mystery, maybe. Bring him in, Jimmy."

THREE

Carey was a big stocky man with a pugnacious jaw. He'd been a lieutenant only a few months; neither Hackett nor Mendoza knew him well. He came in on the sergeant's heels and nodded at them. "I had a memo from Sergeant Hackett—about this latest unidentified corpse you've got. It might be somebody we're looking for."

"Sit down and let's hear the details. Have you looked at the corpse yet?"

"Just got back from the morgue. I didn't have a photo, but I think it's him all right. Stevan Domokous, working as a clerk. Greek but had his first papers."

"My God," said Hackett, "I must have caught it from you, Luis—hunches—that's close enough to Bulgaria, isn't it? Was he a millionaire's son, Carey?"

"I don't know," said Carey, looking a little surprised. "But he's been missing about the right time, and the description matches. Fellow came in to report it last Wednesday—head of a local import and export firm, an Andreas Skyros—I'd lay a bet on that one being a millionaire, all right. Dressed to the nines, diamond ring, gold tooth, custom-made suit, the works. He's a citizen, but came from the old country—you can cut his accent with a knife."

"I take it this Domokous hadn't any family here, if it was this fellow came in. Friend, or *is* he a relative?"

"Employer. Domokous was working for him. Skyros said he felt kind of responsible, the guy was lonely, didn't speak English so well yet, you know. Which was how come, when Domokous didn't show up for work last Tuesday, he went round to see him, see if he was sick—or maybe sent one of the other fellows, I don't know. Domokous had a cheap room in a hotel on Second Street, we went over it. Not much there, a few odds and ends of clothes—no cash—album of family pictures from the old country—stuff like that. He paid by the week and it was almost up, they wanted the room—they'd seen him last on Monday—so seeing there wasn't much and it looked as if he hadn't taken off voluntarily—I mean, Skyros said probably he wouldn't have had much else but what was there—we impounded it, cleared out the room. Skyros says, and of course he's got something, that a stranger here, he's apt to get in trouble easy—wander into the wrong part of town, run into a mugger, something like that—"

"Which happens to a lot of people who've lived here all their lives," said Hackett ruefully.

"And Skyros said too that he maybe felt a little worried sooner than he would have about anyone else because the guy wasn't the kind to take up with any cheap skirt all of a sudden, or go off on a bender. Anyway, when Domokous didn't show up on Wednesday, he comes in."

"So we'd better have Mr. Skyros take a look at the corpse," said Mendoza. "But even if it is Domokous—very nice to know, but it doesn't explain much besides. Where do we find Skyros?"

"Oh, this is very sad," said Mr. Andreas Skyros. He sat down on the bench along the corridor and brought out a handkerchief to polish his bald head and his glasses. "I don't pretend, gentlemen, I had any great —you know?—emotion about the young man, this way, that way—" he shrugged massively. "He was such a one to feel sorry for, you know what I mean? But a very good, honest, hard-working young man." As Carey had said, Mr. Skyros had a thick accent, but he also had a good command of English; for the rest, he was large, round, genial, and obviously prosperous. "Tell me, how does he die?"

"He had an overdose of heroin," said Mendoza. He stood in front of Skyros, hands in pockets, watching him.

"Oh, God help us, so? I was sorry he has no family here, but perhaps it is better, none to know this sad thing. You know? I— Gentlemen, perhaps we go somewhere else to talk? I don't like dead people all around."

"Certainly," said Mendoza cheerfully, "we can go back to my office, if you like."

"I would be so pleased to buy you gentlemen a drink," said Skyros wistfully.

"Now, now, you mustn't corrupt our morals, Mr. Skyros! Not at all necessary."

"Oh, my, no, you mustn't think such a thing," protested Skyros. In Mendoza's office he polished his pink skull again. "But such weather, a foretaste of hell, isn't it? I go out in it as little as possible—my office nice and air-conditioned, like this." He glanced around approvingly. "I didn't know they're so kind to you policemen now. Since the new building is up, isn't it, I suppose?"

"That's right. The laborer worthy of his hire, you know," said Mendoza, beaming at him. "So you do positively identify the body as that of Stevan Domokous. We're very glad to know who he is. Have you any more information about him we ought to know?"

"I am afraid I have, gentlemen. A terrible thing. I know the law says those who take drugs, dope you say, are guilty of offense too, but so many of them,"—he spread fat hands—"only victims of those who sell! Domokous, as I have said to Mr.—Lieutenant?—Carey, he's been in this country only less than a year. I don't think any family back home, all dead in the wars maybe, you know?—and he's lonely. Me, I know him only, let's see, three months—it was the last June he comes to work for me. He's been in New York, but somebody tells him—he says to me—that California, it's like Greece a little, down south, the climate you know, and vineyards—olive trees, isn't it? He thinks he likes it better. But he's a very shy, what's a good word, diffident young man—he doesn't make friends easy—and for the girls, oh, God help us!—a pretty girl looks at him, he runs!" Skyros rumbled a laugh.

"You surprise me," said Mendoza. "A handsome young fellow like that?"

"Oh, well, people, queer. Another one without his looks, the girls crazy for him because he's got the charm. Domokous, maybe he never knew he was good-looking, isn't it, and it don't mean so much without the, as we say, personality."

"How true," said Mendoza. "That's very well put. He was lonely. No hobbies, not many acquaintances."

"Like I say. Of course, I don't know him except as one of the fellows works for me—he helps unpack things sometimes, keeps the record books in the stockroom—but you gentlemen know, you make a success in business, you got to keep a personal eye on it, isn't it? So I'm out there in back, coming and going, I see the fellows there, talk to them, try to be a little friendly—you know. So I know Domokous like that. And yes, he's lonely. Don't know what to do with himself out of working hours, he tells me. And I must tell you, gentlemen, I've been suspicious maybe he's been up to something like this, the last month it is. At first I think he's maybe drinking a little too much, he's not so quick at his work and so on, a couple times I'm there I see him—you know—stumble against things, like he's as we say tight. But now it seems it was this dope. Now I know, I say to Lieutenant Carey, he's not the kind go off getting drunk somewhere, that's why I wonder when he goes off sudden, like this, say nothing about quitting. But a little difference, you see—way he's been, that I see, it's not that he's bad drunk, to fall down—just unsteady, you know?—like he's drinking a little all the time. I've read in the papers, isn't it, how these men selling this dope, they act friendly, talk you into trying it once only, to make more customers? Gentlemen, I see it could happen so with Domokous—anybody acted friendly with him—you know? He'd want to keep new friends."

"I see," said Mendoza interestedly. "Yes, that's very plausible. Tell me, Mr. Skyros, did you ever—mmh—remonstrate with him, over not doing his work properly—ask him about the reason? Did he ever say anything to you about such a hypothetical new friend?"

"That's what I come to," said Skyros, leaning forward earnestly. "And I don't know does it help you at all, gentlemen. But these terrible men, this terrible business—and so many unhappy young people they get, I read, like Domokous—anything we can do to help, we must. Yes, I have spoken to Domokous, I ask if he's maybe taking a little too much wine, and he says—now I see, he knew better than to confess the truth—he says maybe so, he's got acquainted with a couple of nice jolly fellows who like to drink more than he's used, and just to be friendly, you know, he goes along. But he says he knows it isn't good, and don't mean to go on. He says, like to himself, you know, 'I just tell Bratty, I can't afford it no ways!'"

"Bratty," said Mendoza. "When was this, Mr. Skyros?"

"I got to think. It'd be about three weeks back."

"Ah. Now, of course, when there's no family to claim the body, the city'll take care of the burial—but perhaps you'd like to arrange for a little something extra? The morgue authorities—"

"I been thinking," said Skyros, nodding. "It's a sad thing. And a long while since I come from the old country, but he came from there too—young man, try to do better for himself—ambitious. Sad to end so. If it's O.K. with the law, gentlemen, I claim the body and see there's a little kind of service, nice and respectful, you know."

"That's very good of you, sir," said Lieutenant Carey.

"Well, we got to be charitable sometimes. Thank you very much, gentlemen, and I hope I help you a little."

Carey got up on Skyros' departure. "Well, I guess that's that. My part of the job cleared up anyway, and I suppose you'll be turning this over to Callaghan in Narcotics."

Mendoza leaned back and shut his eyes, and Hackett looked at him in wary exasperation as Carey went out. "Whenever you're that genial and polished, I suspect you. If that amiable Greek knew you better he'd suspect you too, like hell. What didn't you like about him?"

"*Un cuestión insensato*. He tells us Domokous had been wearing a monkey on his shoulder for some time. We know—or are pretty sure—he hadn't."

"We don't know he hadn't been drinking. The kind that ends up on foolish powder is the kind ripe for other sorts of what the head-doctors call escape methods too. Liquor as well as other dope. Nine times out of ten they've tried 'em all before they get to the bottom."

"*Es verdad*. Granted."

"Well? What's in your mind?"

"I wonder," said Mendoza dreamily, "how much Mr. Skyros will report on his income tax that this charitable funeral cost him—and how much he'll actually lay out. . . . Go and brief somebody to pick him up, will you—home or office—we'll run a tail on him awhile."

"And why, for God's sake?"

"*¡Yo he hablado*—I have spoken!"

"O.K., O.K.," said Hackett, and went to dispatch the tail.

When he came back Mendoza said, "You've forgotten the nymph and the dolphin. Sure, look at it once, it might be just the run-of-the-mill thing. Domokous inveigled into trying a jolt just for kicks, he gives himself too big a one—after being so nervous about it he makes a couple of dozen tries at getting the needle in—and passes out. The dirty hypo, obviously used—maybe the pusher sold that to him too. But look at it twice. How does that kind of thing usually go? You don't need to be told, the pusher either superintends the first jolt, to see the mark gets just the right kick to make him want another, or he hands out precise instructions. Even if it was his first shot, Domokous ought to have known better than to give himself such a dose. And he had a room. He must have known a little something about the effect to expect—that he'd probably be incapable for a while—and he wouldn't want to get picked up on the street full of heroin. Why go down that alley, like any vagrant drifter, instead of home? A mainliner, sure—you get that— when they've just bought a deck, they can't wait for a pick-up, they'll hit the nearest semi-private spot. But apparently it *was* his first experiment. Much more natural for him to have secluded himself in his hotel room."

"Why do you suppose he didn't?"

"I don't know, but it could be because he never intended to experiment with heroin at all. And because even a cheap hotel on Second Street is an awkward place to smuggle a body into." Mendoza took up the phone again and asked for Lieutenant Callaghan in Narcotics. . . . "Patrick, *mi amigo bueno,* does the name Bratty ring any bells in your head?"

"Bratti," said Callaghan. "Mr. Giuseppi Bratti. It does indeed. Like a whole cathedral full of bells, all playing tunes. And I'm committing slander to say it, because we've got no evidence at all. You know how that goes—damn legal red tape—you got to have a bookful of witnessed statements to make a charge, and how the hell d'you get a user to tell all when he knows damn well it means a charge on him too? —or another kind of witness when he knows some loyal friend in the pusher's gang'll see he gets beaten up but good some night? Bratti runs a stable of pushers. Probably about a dozen. One of six or seven fairly big-time boys—local, that is—operating wholesale hereabouts. He'll do his own wholesale buying from some syndicate agent, but who and which I couldn't say. Eventually we hope to be able to. Probably the same agent who supplies other local runners. Naturally we have an eye on Bratti, but nothing yet to take to court."

"Difficult, I know. And an eye on all the others?"

"Those we think we've spotted. Kind of like batting at mosquitoes, of course—you get one, there's another one right there to carry on."

"Would you know whether Bratti has offended anybody lately?"

"It's very damn likely," said Callaghan. "He offends me every time I think about him. But I wouldn't know, specifically. . . . Oh, quite the respectable merchant on the surface—he owns three restaurants—lives in an apartment over by Silver Lake. And now, why?"

"I couldn't say, right now. It's this new corpse, the one full of heroin—"

"I noticed it, Hackett sent me a memo as maybe an interested party. Bratti cropped up behind it, I hope?"

"Away out in left field. I'll let you know if anything more definite comes up, *un millón de gracias* . . ." Mendoza relayed that to Hackett. "Now. Just file this in our minds, and let's get back to the corpse. I want to see all his possessions, but I don't suppose there's much interesting there—"

"If you're not just making up fairy tales," agreed Hackett, "it'd be a lot easier to ransack a hotel room than bring a body back to it."

"—In fact, I think the only thing of real interest we've got is this little scrap of paper. I think it may have been the one thing they missed, down in the bottom of his pocket—such a little thing. Just take another look at it. Torn off the right top corner of the page—doesn't that say a little something to us? Stapled: you find people who work in offices, businesslike people, writing personal letters on the typewriter and stapling the sheets together—but at the *left* top corner. Since his was stapled at the right, I'm inclined to think it was also stapled at the left, and who does that to a letter—and a letter, or anything, of only a few sheets? I don't think that scrap came from a letter. I think it came from a list of some kind, a list containing a good many pages stapled like that across the top. A *nymph* and a *dolphin,* it says. So, I'm reaching for it maybe, but Skyros—who employed the corpse—is an import-export dealer. And among the various items imported from abroad these days are, as usual, a lot of bric-a-brac—ornaments for the gracious home—porcelain and alabaster and bronze figurines, vases, and so on. The kind of thing you might reasonably expect to find decorated with nymphs and dolphins."

"Yes, I see what you're driving at. It's a nebulous sort of connection, but could be. How do you read it, maybe he found out something funny about Skyros' business and got taken off to prevent his talking? But how and why heroin?"

"I'm not reading it any way yet," said Mendoza. "I want to know a lot more about everything first. About Skyros, most of all. Business, private life, the works."

"And as usual I'm the office boy to do all the finding out," said Hackett. "O.K., I'll get busy and we'll see what turns up.

FOUR

Alison got home as usual about half past four that afternoon; classes at her school were over at four, and she hadn't any errands to do. She was feeling irritable and out of sorts—principally the weather, she reflected, stripping off her clothes and heading for the shower—why on earth she'd ever settled in this climate! Scarcely from ignorance, either, after having been mostly brought up in Mexico, which could be even worse. Doubtless from an unconscious love of martyrdom, she told herself savagely, emerging from the shower shuddering: and not only the climate. So, if she hadn't settled down in L.A. and opened this damned charm school, she wouldn't be saddled with these little morons who paid her to tell them to take a bath occasionally and not pluck out all their eyebrows or wear lace to a picnic. Also, of course, she wouldn't have met Lieutenant Luis Mendoza, which might have been another good thing.

She sat at her dressing table and was annoyed at its clutter, result of a series of mornings of hasty dressing: she tidied it automatically, and of course that reminded her of him all over again—Luis rearranging things all neat on the coffee table, the desk, anywhere in reach of him, and apologizing—"My grandmother says I'd get up off my deathbed to straighten a picture on the wall." Way he was built: one of those tidy-minded people. Luis. Just as well she was somewhat the same way, because, if—

She bent forward, brushing her hair vigorously, angrily. And that was woolgathering with a vengeance, all right! Anybody as smart as Alison Weir—or as smart as Alison Weir *ought* to be, at least—with one abortive short-lived marriage behind her and thirty years of varied living, should know Luis Mendoza for what he was at one look. Luis—like one of his beloved cats, fastidious, independent, aloof. Not for any one woman, maybe ever.

Luis . . . She laid down the hairbrush; and the phone rang. "Oh, hello, Pat," she said, putting false cheerfulness in her tone.

"I just called to say that Cheryl Bradley dropped in this morning, and I asked her about that thing you found—you'd said she'd ridden home with you from that dreary party at the Mawsons'. It's not hers, she says."

"Oh, well, thanks. That really about covers everybody I know who might've lost it in the car. I think it *must* have been whoever took it. You know, the more I look at it the more I feel it is awfully old and might be valuable. Luis said so. . . . D'you suppose I ought to advertise it? I mean, if anyone showed up to claim it I could tell that Sergeant Rhodes—"

"Nobody would dare," said Miss Moore.

"But if I said something like, found in the Exposition Park area? They might not realize it'd dropped out in the car—"

"Finders keepers," said Miss Moore. "*I* don't suppose it's anything but a worthless so-called lucky piece, but just to be on the safe side, I'd advise you to take it to an expert and see if it *is* worth anything. And in the unlikely event that it is, take the profit and return thanks to Providence."

"Yes," said Alison, "but— Oh, well, I suppose it is the sensible thing to do. Thanks anyway. Are you going to the Vesperian exhibition on Friday? Then I'll pick you up, about one o'clock? O.K., thanks, Pat." As she put the phone down and went back to the bedroom to finish applying lipstick, the door-buzzer sounded, and she said to herself, "Damn," snatched up her dressing gown and struggled into it on the way to the door.

The woman standing in the hall didn't look quite like the ordinary house-to-house salesperson: nor did she act like one. She surveyed Alison head to foot and said, "But I did not expect such a one! You look to be, how is it said, a cut above!"

"I beg your pardon," said Alison. The woman was dark, elegant, exquisitely dressed: middle height, slim but rounded, waxen-white complexion, dark eyes cleverly elongated, polished dark hair in the latest fashionable cut, cameo-pure features. Over thirty, but not much, and not looking it. And dressed in what Alison instantly recognized as not only the latest fashion and exactly the right thing for her, but the latest original fashion, for which a very respectable sum of money must have been paid out. That subtly-cut powder-blue silk-faille afternoon gown, the elbow-length gloves to match, the small bit of blue frivolity with a veil meant for a hat, the sapphire (-colored?) earrings and bracelets, the big diamond on the ungloved hand, the cobweb stockings, the spikeheeled black patent pumps, the black faille bag with a big rhinestone initial—an ornate L—all of them, probably, would have cost as much as Alison earned in six months. And the cloud of musky, heavy scent wafting out from her, as much again per application, very likely.

"It is not you with cause to beg the pardon," said this apparition, "but *him!* Is he here?" Her gaze swept over Alison's printed rayon dressing gown. "You are in the center of dressing—undressing? If he is here—I come in, I wish to speak with him!"

"You *don't* come in," said Alison, angry and bewildered. "What is it you want? You must have mistaken the apartment—"

"No, no, I memorize the address! Miss Alison Weir, it is? You have very nice hair, my dear, if one does not mind the color. I come in!" And she brushed by Alison regally, to the middle of the living room. "But what a pity to live in such a little squalid flat! Can you do no better?"

"Look *here!*" said Alison, furiously conscious that the dressing gown had only cost nine dollars new and that she was in her bare feet and hadn't any lipstick on, "this is *my* apartment and I don't know you—if you don't leave at once—"

"Naturally you do not know me. You have a temper—so indeed have I. Is he here?" She swept into the bedroom, into the bath, back across the living room to look into the kitchenette. "Ah! He is *not* here! But you expect him, perhaps?"

"Are you implying," said Alison, drawing herself up to her full sixty-four inches, "that I—"

"Imply, what is this? You need not put on the good face for me, miss! I beg you, be calm, I have no quarrel with you at this moment! It is that women, we should be sisters together, not so, and help one another? That is why I have come. I reason, here it is probable I find him alone—except for you, of course—and it is much better to make the direct talk. I promise myself, I will restrain my temper, I will be dignified —however difficult, considering the dishonor he uses with me! But I see he is not here."

"I must ask you to leave," said Alison in her iciest tone.

"I will go, because he is not here and it is of no use to stay. A pity, for I had in my mind all the things I wish to say to him, and you know how, when one loses one's temper, the words go out of the head and one can only stutter! But you will tell him, miss, I am not so stupid and innocent as he think! You will tell him, he does not give Lydia the—the *stall,* the *run-about,* forever!—you see I know even your American slang, I am not what he would say the easy mark! You tell him this—that I deal direct with him, one chance more I give him to be honorable with me—in two days, he take it or he leave it—and he will be very wise to take it! He knows where I am to be found." She gave Alison a significant, queenly nod and sailed out the door.

For thirty seconds Alison was too possessed by rage to move. Then she whirled for the phone at the desk, had to look up the number, dialed it wrong twice, finally got police headquarters and demanded the Homicide office, got Sergeant Lake. "I want to speak to the lieutenant. . . . Oh, yes, I'll hang on! With pleasure! . . . This is the lieutenant speaking? Lieutenant Luis Rodolfo Vicente Mendoza, the well-known great lover? *Well,* Lieutenant, I have several things to say to you —" and she took a deep breath and commenced to say them, beginning with the announcement that if he thought it amusing to hand out her name and address to his other girl-friends, she did not, and in any case she didn't feel at all flattered to be one of a company which included this Lydia—

"What, who? What have I done?" protested Mendoza. "It's a lie! *¿Come dice? Tómelo con calma, chica—*"

"—Lydia," said Alison distinctly. "If you search your memory, or maybe you keep a neat little list of them all, you'l remember her, I'm sure! A black-eyed hussy in spike heels and a Jacques Fath original— with a phoney-sounding accent—and about half a pint of Chypre. *Surely* you haven't forgotten Lydia? You really should keep a list! Yes, *¡villano, tú canalla, tú calamidad!*—I *am* annoyed, *¡estoy muy molesto!—¡no lo niego!*—looking at me as if I was a peasant or something, and smelling like a high-class brothel—very nice if one likes the color, she says, this—this—*¡perra negra!—¡nunca abbía visto tamaño descaro,* such impudence! *¡Es demasiado,* too much!"

"Wait a minute, *chica,* calm down, what the hell is this all about? *¡Eso no es cierto*—I'm absolutely innocent, I don't know any Lydia! I never—"

"Oh, you liar—*¡tú mentiroso!—¡no tengamos la de siempre,* the same old story! And, damn it, I hadn't even any lipstick on—looking at me as if I was—and—"

"*¡Vaya despacio, no hay tal!* I swear to you—what the devil is all this? I'm innocent as day, *querida*. . . . All right, all right, hold everything, I'm coming round, I want to hear about this! *¡Por Dios!*—ruining my reputation, calling here through the switchboard—*¡no metan tanta bulla,* not so much noise!"

"I couldn't care less, and besides they must all know what you're like by now—I wouldn't doubt having a good laugh over it— Men! A—a—a poor man's Gabor, looking down her nose at me—"

"I'm coming, I'm coming!—*¡ni qué niño muerto!*—nonsense!" The phone clicked firmly in her ear.

Alison went on talking to herself, kicking the hassock in passing and groping after some of her father's favorite swearwords, for about five minutes. Then she went to the kitchen and got down the bottle of rye, and eyeing it began to laugh. So all right, how senseless could you get? She didn't like rye, but he never drank anything else.

"Is it safe to come in?" asked Mendoza when she opened the door. *"Querida mia,* what have I done to deserve this? One female at a time enough to keep any man occupied!"

"Have you placed Lydia?" asked Alison grimly.

"I have not. I never knew one. I don't know one now. I don't want to know one. *Mi novia, mi hermosa,* why would I want a Lydia—"

"Now you just keep your distance!" said Alison. "Oh, yes, try to pass it off and make me forget it! Walking in cool as you please, this *hussy,* and calling it a squalid little flat!—it's a wonder I didn't kill her—"

"No, really now, no joke—no little games, *chica!*" He pulled her down beside him on the couch. "What happened?" She told him, more or less coherent by then. "I will be damned," said Mendoza. *"Honestamente,* I don't know her—don't know anything about it. What the hell could have brought her here? She knew your name, you said? Me, for better or worse I was raised halfway a gentleman—you don't bandy females' names around! I'm surprised at you, thinking such a thing of me."

"Well!" said Alison, relaxing slightly. "I was mad. *With* reason. And she said—"

"Yes, let's hear it all, as clear as you remember. . . . That's a very funny little story. Where could she have got your name? And a couple of things she said—all that about dealing direct—it doesn't exactly sound like any romantic affair, does it? More !ike a business deal of some kind, maybe? . . . And who is 'he'? I wonder . . . *¡un momento!* —the car! Now I do wonder—whoever took the car—maybe she'd had a ride in it, and noticed the registration slip, and thought you were the girl-friend of the thief. It could be."

"I suppose so," said Alison doubtfully. "It seems sort of far-fetched. . . . Luis? You're not just making it into a mystery to take my mind off, are you?"

He laughed and kissed her. "You're too suspicious. I don't know one thing about it—it's just a funny little story. Go and get dressed—that amber thing—and I'll take you to dinner. *Más primero, acérquese*— come nearer. . . . O.K., *querida?*"

"Well, O.K.," said Alison with a sigh. She drew away and looked at him, head cocked. "Of course, I might feel a little more satisfied if I didn't happen to know you're an awfully good poker-player. . . . D'you want a drink while I'm getting dressed?"

It was after midnight when Mendoza got home, to the rather old-fashioned apartment building on a quiet dead-end street, and put the car away in the garage, let himself into his apartment. The sleek brown Bast greeted him with pleased soft cries. Various visitors had left five notes in a row propped on the mantel; he read them from the left to right as he took off his coat and tie. That autocratic old lady Señora Teresa Maria Sancia Mendoza, who at eighty-six was enjoying life far more than she had in her youth, living in a Wilshire Boulevard apart-ment and telling everyone grandiloquent lies about her impeccable Castilian ancestry, informed him in a black scrawl that he should be more careful about what persons he gave access to his quarters; she would not put it beyond this Carter woman to pry into one's drawers, having found her on the premises when she called. And it was nearly two weeks since he had come to see her, and she trusted he would not forget her birthday next week. When he acquired a wife, which was devoutly to be hoped for, as he was not getting any younger, these affairs would be better arranged for him—always supposing he had the sense, which she frequently doubted, to choose a sensible and satis-factory wife. She much desired that he should make time to visit her soon, as there were some pleasant new neighbors she would like him to meet.

Mendoza grinned at the scrawl: the old lady had been trying for fifteen years to get him married to a comfortable, modest, practical wife —of her own choice—preferably one who could coax him back to the priests. Probably had a new candidate to trot out.

Mrs. Carter from across the hall informed him that Bast had had her wheat germ in fresh liver at four o'clock and he was *not* to give her any more until Thursday.

Mrs. Bryson from upstairs, front, informed him that she had let Bast out for a little run at nine o'clock.

Bertha, the eminently satisfactory maid-of-all-work who managed the domestic lives of the whole apartment population, informed him that he was out of half-and-half and that there was a sale on that coffee he liked this week at a local market.

Mr. Elgin from upstairs, rear, expressed himself as uneasy concerning Bast and that smart-aleck young Siamese tom of his; it was, he thought, quite possible that he and Mendoza might find themselves joint owners of some crossbred kittens presently.

Mendoza looked at Bast. "What, have you grown up finally and discovered sex? Misbehaving yourself, *gatita*—he's a good year younger than you! Well, time will tell," and he wandered into the bedroom unbuttoning his shirt.

But he sat up another half hour, ruminating not only on his latest corpse, but now on Alison's visitor—and a few other things.

FIVE

When Hackett got to the office on Wednesday morning, early for once, there was someone waiting to see Mendoza—Sergeant Lake passed over the business card noncommittally under the visitor's eye. *Charles Driscoll*, and the name of a national insurance firm.

Hackett looked Driscoll over. About forty, tallish and broadish, sandy, and by the coolly insolent stare he gave in return, a brash one. Flashy pencil-striped suit off the rack, a garish tie. "Yes, Mr. Driscoll, if you'd like to come into the office?"

"You wouldn't be Lieutenant Mendoza," said Driscoll, standing up, "don't tell me."

"Sergeant Hackett. Just come in, the lieutenant'll be here soon." Hackett exchanged a look with Lake, left the office door open, saw Driscoll settled in the armchair beside the desk facing the door, and offered him a cigarette.

"Thanks very much. Quite a setup you've got here—compared to most police H.Q.'s." Driscoll ignored Hackett's proffered lighter, produced an ornate black-and-gold one of his own.

"We find it satisfactory," said Hackett.

"But kind of stultifying all the same, you know—" Driscoll gestured with his cigarette. "I always feel sorry for you guys—having to stay inside so many rules and regulations. Must be damn annoying. Bein' in the private-eye line myself, I know all the ropes, if you get me. Though *I* get the hell of a lot more interesting cases than you poor bastards, acourse. . . . That your lieutenant?" He dropped his tone only a little, looking out to the anteroom where Mendoza had stopped to have a word with Sergeant Lake. "My, my, what the best-dressed man will wear—quite the gigolo, isn't he? Protégé of the Chief's, to be sittin' at a lieutenant's desk? Doesn't look much like a cop."

Mendoza came in and said good morning to Driscoll. "Some odds and ends on Domokous, Art—go out and see Dwyer, will you, he's just checked in. . . . Now, what was it you wanted to see me about, Mr. Driscoll?"

Hackett went out regretfully. He wasn't equipped by nature to reach the Driscolls with any kind of back talk that really got to them: they just made him mad, and that only pleased them, naturally. About thirty seconds from now, when Mendoza had sized him up, Driscoll was due to be snubbed more subtly than he'd ever been in his life, and it would have been gratifying to see. Mendoza was so good at that kind of thing when he wanted to be—the polished aristocrat condescending to the bumptious peasant. He could get more insult into one polite phrase than any other man Hackett knew, and all smooth as silk on the surface.

What Dwyer had to say was that Domokous' wallet had turned up. Empty of cash, whether or not it had held any, but everything else probably intact, and not much: I.D. card laboriously filled out in English, Social Security card, L.A. Public Library card, and that was all, except for a snapshot of a girl, a rather fuzzy close-up of a not-very-pretty dark girl smiling into the camera. The wallet had been turned in to a Main Street precinct station by a housewife who'd found it near the corner of San Rafael and Main; she said it had contained no cash when she picked it up.

And that tied in to a run-of-the-mill business, sure. Somebody coming across Domokous in that alley, either dead or unconscious, and taking the only thing of value on him—a few bucks, maybe, in the billfold —taking the cash, dropping the billfold on the street. Kind of thing that happened every day, this way or that way.

Hackett thought himself that Luis was building this thing up into more complexity than the facts indicated: so, all right, say that scrap of paper was part of a list of some kind, to do with Skyros' business. Domokous had been a clerk there, no reason he shouldn't have it in his pocket, was there? You wanted to be intricate about it, say it'd got torn off accidentally and he'd felt guilty, stuck the torn piece in his pocket instead of throwing it away.

Domokous still looked quite straightforward to Hackett. He didn't like Mr. Skyros much, any more than Mendoza did—a very canny customer and out for profit for Mr. Skyros every time, but what was that? A lot of people like that. Most people. Domokous was just another victim of a pusher, probably one of those employed by this Bratti.

But, run-of-the-mill or not, there was still routine to be done on it. Hackett went down to Carey's office, signed the necessary forms, and received the contents of Domokous' hotel room. Not much: he went through it desultorily. A suit, probably his Sunday one, fairly new if cheap: a few shirts, socks, a little underwear, a modest pile of dime store handkerchiefs: odds and ends of personal possessions otherwise —an ancient cardboard-covered album of family snapshots, all obviously dating from years back in the old country—a little box containing an old-fashioned tie pin with a red glass stone in it, a tarnished silver ring, an old pocket watch—a couple of letters in some language Hackett took to be Greek, funny-looking sort of stuff, both recently postmarked *Athens*.

He'd gone through collections like that often enough before, the relics left of a life: they always secretly saddened him a little. All there was to show—whatever sort of life it had been, good, bad, or indifferent; and so immediately losing any importance, what had had value in someone's mind. . . . *No pockets in a shroud,* he thought vaguely, putting the album back in the cardboard carton where Carey had stashed the smaller articles.

Dwyer, Higgins, and Reade were on Skyros; Dwyer had reported in, and so far as Hackett could see there wasn't much there either. All looked on the level, perfectly ordinary. Andreas Skyros, Inc., had been operating for seventeen years, dealt mostly in European imports from a number of countries; Skyros had never been in trouble with the law, privately or businesswise. He was married, but had no family: owned a house in a good residential district of west Hollywood, and ran an almost new Buick; his wife had a new Chevvy convertible. He was doing all right, especially in the last six or seven years, but all aboveboard. So? Skyros was exactly what he looked like. The whole thing was a mare's nest.

He left Domokous' possessions with Sergeant Lake for Mendoza, and drove down to Skyros' offices on Figueroa. Skyros wasn't in, which was just as well; Hackett introduced himself to the clerk in the front office, and interviewed all the personnel who'd worked with the dead man— four other stockroom clerks and the bookkeeper, a pretty brunette. He didn't get much more than they already had, or anything to contradict Skyros except a nuance or two.

Sure, Domokous had been kind of lonely, they all said: couldn't seem to settle down, like. Quiet sort, and not talking English so good he couldn't join in, if the sergeant saw what they meant—didn't get jokes and so on. They'd all liked him well enough, but what with his being quiet anyway and not talking the language much, he was hard to get to know, and he hadn't been here long. He liked to read, used to go to the public library and get books in his own lingo. But he had a girl, all right—he'd said a little something about her, and he had her picture in his wallet. The girl bookkeeper spoke up then, pertly, and said maybe he had but if she was any judge and she figured she was, he wouldn't have let that hamper him—way he eyed her every time she came out back. Awfully good-looking he'd been, and it was terrible, have anything like that happen—she'd never have thought he was the kind to go for dope. Which the others confirmed: reserved, you might say, but not nuts, or queer any way.

None of them remembered Domokous ever mentioning anyone named Bratti. And none of them could say what his girl's name was or where she lived. And it didn't matter much, because probably the news story would bring her in—unless, of course, she'd been mixed up in his death somehow, which didn't seem likely.

The news story about Domokous' identification had, in fact, already brought her in; she was sitting on the edge of a chair in Mendoza's office, looking less grieved than sullen. She was about twenty-five, dark and thin, no striking beauty but not ugly either. She sat with head bent over her clasped hands, and looked at Mendoza through a tangle of black hair fallen across her cheek.

The other woman said nervously, "He was a good young man, sir.

Never would he do such a thing as that you say. He save his money to marry Katya, like we tell, in the spring they are to marry, all is arranged." She was in black like the girl, a spare old woman, patience and tragedy in her big dark eyes. The grandmother. Slav, from this place or that, and definitely Old Country; but the girl born here, probably—little accent. "Someone tells lies about him, fixes up a lie, to make you think this. Stevan, not even much wine he drinks—he's careful with money."

"It's that man, where he worked!" burst out the girl.

"And what makes you say that, Miss Roslev?" asked Mendoza.

"When he did not come, on the Thursday, for Katya's birthday, we knew something bad happen—the man at the hotel, he knows nothing, and we did not like to go to his place of work—Katya said— And all the time, lying out so, dead, none to care for him, pray for him— Oh, it is bad to think! And he is so of hopes, the long journey here and the better chance to make success—"

"Always you're so scared!" said the girl contemptuously. "Think this looks bad, that don't look right—had my way, I'd have gone and asked, all right! I knew there was something funny going on—Stevan, he was worried—"

"Katya, you talk too much, you get us in trouble," whispered the old woman. "We don't know nothing at all, it's only in your head—only we know Stevan was a good boy—"

"He was too good!" said the girl. "*I* said—oh, well, never mind that. . . . You scared even come to the police, they don't eat you, here."

"Katya, so rude to the officer, please take care."

"But Miss Roslev's quite right, we don't bite," smiled Mendoza at her. "Why do you think his death is connected with Mr. Skyros?"

"I'll tell you why, what I came to say, see? Stevan, he told me about it—told *us*—last time he was there, it was. He'd found out something about this Mr. Skyros—something bad, he thought— See, he'd had to work late one night, there was a big shipment some kind come in—and he went up to Mr. Skyros' office, ask him something, and heard him and somebody else talking—and he said it sounded like it was about something bad, crooked you know—he said. I wouldn't put it past Mr. Skyros, be mixed up in something like that, only—"

"Something crooked. What kind of something, what did he overhear exactly?"

"I don't know," she said, sullen again. "Just, it was about a lot of money, he said. Worth an awful lot. He didn't say exact—but I thought —maybe since, he found out more, and they killed him so's he couldn't tell, see? Because he said then—police ought to know about crooks, if they was—"

"Katya, you shouldn't say, we don't know for sure— Mr. Skyros, a lot of money he'll have, he see you get in jail, to say—"

"I guess not! I'm not afraid o' him, nor the cops neither! You go and ask *him* what he knows, see?"

"But you haven't given me anything very definite to go on, Miss Roslev. If you could remember a more specific phrase, a word?"

She was silent awhile, looking at him; and then she said, "I s'pose you got to have more, like you say. Can't do nothing if you don't know. . . . Well, I told you anyhow. I guess—all I could tell you, mister—and maybe—"

"Katya—" The old woman was still nervous of Mendoza, of Authority; and the girl let herself be urged out. . . . Mendoza was still ruminating on them when Hackett came in, and they exchanged news.

"It's nothing at all, of course. No, I wouldn't be surprised if Skyros sails a little close to the wind in business, but so what? Even if Domokous had somehow got hold of proof, I don't see Skyros doing murder over it, do you? More likely to buy him off. And that kind of murder—a very pro business. . . . Of course, there's such a thing as cover. And maybe he's running more businesses than one. Like Mr. Bratti. Yes, a couple of little points in what these other clerks said. I have an idea that Mr. Skyros, shrewd a businessman as he may be, underrates us just a little, you know. He didn't think we'd check up far on what he said about Domokous—and evidently he didn't know about Katya Roslev and her grandmother. But nothing much to get hold of in all that."

Hackett agreed. "By the way, what did that obnoxious insurance fellow want? I was sorry to miss the snubbing you'd hand him."

Mendoza grinned. "Why, Art, you know we're trained these days to be as polite as can be to civilians. I never said a cross word to him."

"I'll bet," said Hackett. "I gathered he's an insurance investigator."

Mendoza regarded his lighter meditatively. "If the head-doctors are right in some of their theories—which I frequently doubt—our Mr. Driscoll must have a king-size inferiority complex. Overcompensating, as they say, like mad. He's read all the paperback mysteries about the smart-as-paint private eyes—quite a fad lately for making them insurance detectives, you know—and he knows just how he ought to act. I'll bet you fifty to one he religiously wears a shoulder holster and drinks five Martinis before dinner whether he likes them or not, or could hit the side of a barn with a shotgun. And addresses every female under forty as Beautiful—and, *Dios,* how he'd like to have everyone think they all fall for him in rows and he's never slept alone for the last twenty-five years, since he was a precocious teen-ager."

Hackett laughed. "I read him the first look too. What was he after?"

Mendoza snapped the lighter and lit his cigarette. "I'm damned if I know. And also damned curious. What he wanted to know was why Skyros had been here yesterday. And when I told him and asked why he was interested, he came out with a couple of smart-aleck unfunny wisecracks, said it was private firm business and I wouldn't be interested anyway, and swaggered out. Private eyes, you know, they always act that way with these stolid stupid regular cops."

"You don't say—interested in Skyros? So maybe it's an insurance racket—this piece of crookedness that's going to be worth a lot of money? I wonder if Skyros ever had a warehouse burn down or something like that, and the insurance company's a little leery of him, looking into his private life?"

"Which bright thought crossed my mind too. I've got Landers looking into it. I also attached a tail to our Mr. Driscoll. After all, he asked for it. . . . No, nothing in Domokous' stuff, I didn't think there would be. Maybe there never was, or maybe somebody got there first. One thing, I want those two letters translated *pronto*. And—" Mendoza sat up and called Sergeant Lake. "Has Higgins called in on Skyros? Where is he now?"

"Just a little big ago. From the Beverly-Hilton—looks like Skyros is fixing to have lunch there with some dame."

"Well, well. Could this also be the same dreary old tale, tired middle-aged businessman cheating on his wife? I think I'll go and take a look —you can hold down the regular table at Federico's, Art."

Higgins was propping the wall just outside the main dining room of the hotel, looking a little seedy in comparison with most of the guests and visitors in this haunt of sophisticates. When he saw Mendoza he stepped out to meet him."

"It's O.K., Lieutenant, he can't see us from where they're sitting, and there's only one entrance—I looked. The dame kept him waiting quite a while, and I grabbed a sandwich at the bar where I could keep an eye on him. Six bits for a cheese sandwich!"

"Well, it goes on your expense account," said Mendoza.

"It's the principle of the thing. Highway robbery. This looks kind of N.G. to me—he's just been ordinary places, home and work—and if he's stepping out on his wife, it's not exactly illegal, you can't arrest him for that. Me, I never can figure out why they bother. Go to all that trouble, thinking up lies to tell the wife and so on. I don't say there isn't any female worth it, but I do say they'd be the hell of a lot smarter to get rid of one before they take on another."

"But then you're a very moral fellow," said Mendoza.

"It's not my morals, it's my blood pressure," said Higgins. "I like a quiet life myself. You quitting the tail on him?"

"No, you carry on." Mendoza went into the dining room, glanced around casually for Skyros, was trapped by an obsequious headwaiter, just as he spotted him, and ensconced at a small table where all he could see of Skyros' companion was her hat. It was a large hat, with a transparent stiff brim of black lace, and sat nearly on the back of her head, effectively screening her profile when she turned, and a good deal of Skyros across the table. Visible below it were round white shoulders only partially covered by a black-and-white printed gown, low-cut back and (probably) front, and one round white arm bearing a wide gold bracelet, a scarlet-nailed hand extravagant in gesture.

"Something to drink before lunch, sir?"

"No, thanks," said Mendoza, whose vices did not include alcohol as one of life's necessities. He ordered at random, an unobtrusive eye on Skyros. He would not be displeased if Skyros happened to notice him: this whole thing was up in the air, nothing to get hold of, and if Skyros was mixed up in it in any way, it could be useful to give him the idea that they knew a bit more than they did. Frequently that prompted a suspect to do something silly and revealing.

Skyros, however, wasn't doing much looking around; he seemed entirely occupied with the girl-friend. At the same time, he didn't look quite like a man entertaining the extracurricular sex interest. He wiped a perspiring brow frequently in spite of the air-conditioning; he fidgeted with the cutlery, and his expression was now unhappy, now falsely genial. The girl-friend was doing most of the talking; he tried to interrupt several times and shrugged at failure.

Mendoza ate an anonymous lunch absently, watching and thinking. They had almost finished when he came in; they sat over drinks of some kind—brandy, by the glasses—and as the waiter whisked Mendoza's plate away, offered more coffee, Skyros got up. The woman was

more leisurely, sliding gracefully out of her chair, smoothing her skirt
—revealing a pair of eye-catching legs ending in slim spike heels.
Skyros put a gallant hand on her elbow as they turned for the door.

And she was something to be gallant about, all right: a very handsome piece of goods indeed, in exotic style. Black hair in a smooth
fashionable coiffure, dead-white complexion, sharply arched brows,
dark red lipstick, flashing stones at her ears and throat.

They had to pass within a few feet of his table to reach the door, and
Mendoza watched them steadily, willing Skyros to look and see him:
but Skyros was oblivious, wiping his brow again, looking agitated. And
she was scarcely, by her expression, bent on exuding glamour; she
looked very angry. They came past, the woman still talking in an undertone over her shoulder, and he caught a phrase or two—not English:
Greek, Russian? He also caught a waft of powerful musky scent. And
then they were out the door and gone—transferred to Higgins.

"Will that be all, sir? A little cognac perhaps?"

"No, that's all. . . . ¡qué disparate!" said Mendoza to himself,
reaching for his wallet. "¡Bastante! This is making up fairy tales with a
vengeance." Alison's black-eyed hussy in spike heels, smelling like a
high-class brothel. . . . "Impossible. Ridiculous. This is *not* one of Mr.
Driscoll's paperback thrillers!"

SIX

"But you must be sensible, dear madame!" said Mr. Skyros. "These
wild ideas—" He wiped his brow agitatedly.

"I am surprised," said Madame Bouvardier, "that a businessman
should be so impractical. But two thoughts I have about this also, and
n'importe the second one. I find you irritating in the extreme, Mr.
Skyros."

"My dear lady, there is a saying, one cannot have one's cake and also
eat it. This insurance money, it is obviously impossible to claim it
when—"

"It is not impossible at all, and I see nothing whatever criminal in doing so! I will most certainly not do as you suggest, to give it back to them and tell this elaborate lie of how I recover the collection! The company, it has insured the Lexourion collection, has it not? The, what is the word, premium, it is paid—all is good faith both sides—very well —the collection is stolen, it is gone, so the company must pay. Why do they not pay me? That is their business. Anything else to do with the collection, it is my business. It belonged to my father, I am his only child, naturally it now belongs to me. There is nothing difficult to grasp here."

"But, my dear lady—you do not suppose the insurance firm will pay, or allow you to keep the money, without investigating—when they find you again have the collection—"

"Naturally they investigate. There is a man comes to see me only yesterday, a very unpleasant ill-bred man named Driscoll, who does not know how to behave with a lady. But then he is of course an American. I must say, I find it uncouth of these insurance people that they should at once suspect there is wrongdoing—but I am very gracious to him, I tell him he is welcome to search, he can see I have not got it, they know from the police it is truly stolen, and it has not been sold to anyone by the thieves—the police watch, I daresay, the insurance men also, and it is still vanished. Very well, then they must pay. I am not a fool, Mr. Skyros, and I do *not* let it be at all obvious that I have got the collection back! In Europe, there are men of honor who will pay me privately to have the privilege to house it. But also, I do not allow myself to be held up by gangsters! This—this Irishman, this Donovan, he is not an honorable man and he is also much too greedy. In the nature of things, a thief sells his plunder in secret, he is lucky to receive a fifth of its value—this is well known. The bargain you say you made with Donovan, for ten thousand of your dollars. And now he tries to withdraw, he says it is not enough, he will have twenty. I think I was a fool to trust you to make the bargain."

"Dear madame, you surely don't suspect that I would be dishonest with you? I protest—it's only a favor on my part, I'm earning no profit—"

"Me, I am Greek too," she reminded him darkly, "if I do live in France most of my life—we know each other! Better to deal with this gangster directly. I am not afraid of gangsters, I have seen them on the films. They are like little children playing with wooden guns, behaving very *tough* as you say, but stupid men without cunning. Well, there is another saying, two can play at one game. He will keep the bargain he has made or he will be sorry."

"I assure you, *not* children," said Skyros. "I would not dream of allowing you to deal with such men—they can be very dangerous—you know how they have already killed this poor clerk of mine, because he overheard some talk—"

"Yes, but they would not offer harm to *me,* for in that case they get no money at all! I will see that he keeps the bargain, and after the insurance money is paid, all is accomplished, and I take the collection home."

"All is *not* accomplished. You can't have it both ways, we shall all be in trouble if you persist. It will be known you have the collection again, the insurance people will call you a thief—"

"That is very stupid and bad faith, they are liable to pay when it is stolen, anything afterward is my own affair. And besides—"

"But you can never smuggle it out of the country—"

"Oh, that is easiest of all! But there is no need to discuss that at the moment." Suddenly she produced a gracious smile, reached to pat his hand. "You have done your best, Mr. Skyros, to help me in this matter, and be sure I appreciate it. It is only, perhaps, that I am one of those people, I never feel a thing is properly done unless I do it myself! Do not worry about me, my friend—I know my own business."

"But I do beg you to take care," he said earnestly. "Do not be foolhardy, dear lady."

"That I never am, Mr. Skyros."

Women! thought Mr. Skyros exasperatedly. Especially these strong-minded ones. The deal had been set up—in a bit of a hurry, admittedly, but a perfectly straightforward deal—before he had met the woman, and he had never expected her to be so difficult. And worst of all, he had a vague feeling that she no longer trusted him as the innocent middleman.

He drove back to town, shut himself into his office, and called Donovan. "She is obstinate, very obstinate. She refuses to pay more, and my friend, I think we'd better leave it there, isn't it? The profit's not so bad—and she has some crazy ideas in her head, you know, get us all in trouble—"

"Listen, I'm not born yesterday, I know what it's worth now and when I know it's insured for two hundred thousand smackers, listen, Skyros, I don't go along with no piddling deal like ten G's! Particular when I got to cut it with you. You set it up with my kid brother, so O.K., but I'm handling both our affairs now just like it allus was, and you're dealin' with me now. She's got no choice—she wants the stuff, she pays."

"But, my friend, she is the only customer!"

"That don't necessarily mean she can set the price. She takes it or leaves it. You say she wants it damn bad. O.K., then she pays." The phone slammed down at the other end.

Mr. Skyros cast his eyes to heaven and swore several oaths in two languages. He was a fool ever to have got mixed up in this business. And it had looked so easy, so casual, to start with—money dropping from heaven! All, you might say, for a few kind words spoken. Nothing to it at all. This crazy female—this crazy idea about the insurance. A thousand devils, she'd get them all in jail with her if she tried that! And try to talk to her! Sure, sure, the ordinary thing, the diamond necklace, the bearer bonds, it's just another little deal, you keep the insurance easy—company can't prove anything. But a deal like this, just not good sense. The customs— Two hundred thousand—

For that matter, try to talk to Donovan, who was just as crazy. These low-class robbers, no understanding of finesse, not the most rudimentary cunning. It was a simple matter of supply and demand, couldn't he see that? Here was a thing almost impossible for a fence to dispose of in the underworld market: no fence would take it off his hands, much less give him ten thousand for it. And here was a buyer willing to pay that. One could not be too greedy: it never paid in the end. One had to sell goods for what one could get. And now, because Donovan got this crazy idea in his head—

Mr. Skyros swore again. He had the dreadful feeling that this thing, which had looked so little, so easy, was putting him in personal danger. He had always been so careful (like Bratti, and one thousand curses on him too) to keep clear of the business on the surface, stay looking respectable. If any of this came out at all . . . And Domokous had come very close to connecting him. Inevitable that he'd had to appear in that business, and it had been a brilliant inspiration, to try for two birds with one stone, involve Bratti in the death—but had it come off? He hadn't dared say more. He was confident in any case that Domokous was written off safely.

But he felt as if he was walking a tightrope between Donovan and this crazy woman. Just because both of them were so greedy. The love of money, reflected Mr. Skyros unhappily, is the root of all evil. Indeed.

And about that time his bookkeeper came in to tell him that the police had been there asking questions about Domokous, and gave him something else to worry about.

"Listen, I don't like it, Jackie," said Denny Donovan anxiously to his brother. "Ask me, the quicker we're out from under this one the better. Why, hell, it's all gravy anyways—only luck I got the stuff first place—"

"I ain't no flat wheel," said Jackie Donovan obstinately. "Who was it had sense enough find out how much it *is* worth, 'stead o' taking this Skyros' word for it? Anybody crazy, pay two hundred G's for *that,* but that's what the guy said, I told you. So O.K., we don't let go for less 'n twenty."

" 'S bad luck," said a dreamy voice from the other side of the room. "Allus bad luck, anythin' to do with an ace o' spades—bad luck. Don't want mess with it, Jackie. Get shut o' the hot stuff, an' shut o' the ace o' spades."

"What the *hell!*" said Jackie. "So what if she's an ace o' spades? I ain't so damn superstitious. You guys lost any sense you had since I got sent across, ain't been here keep an eye out, fix deals for you. Angelo never did have much, but look at him now—out on a sleigh ride half the time—"

"I quit any time I want, Jackie," said Angelo in the same dreamy voice, "any time. Don't matter. Smarter'n some guys, before *or* after a fix, me—never got inside on a taxi, I didn't."

"You just shut up! And you just as bad, Denny—lost your nerve, gone to pieces! Don't tell me ain't all your fault the kid brother got it— if you'd held things together like, kept it steady 'n quiet like I allus did, Frank wouldn't never've got onto *that* lay, my God—sure there's money in it, but you got to draw a line somewheres! So Angie thinks it's bad luck get mixed up with an ace o' spades, so O.K., me, I think it's bad luck get mixed up with pushers! But here's the deal thrown into our laps, and only sense to get what the traffic'll stand!"

"I tell you, Jack, you kinda lost track o' things while you been in." Denny was nervous, criticizing. "It just ain't so easy no more, make a living. Don't pay near so good, account o' the cops are different, sort of, even worse 'n just fifteen years back. You can't blame Frank—just the breaks, it was—besides, Jack, like I said I don't figure it was awful damn safe, go out to that museum place like you did—I mean, hell, *they* ain't got nothing to lose, they mighta called the cops right off—"

"My God, you ain't seen no sign of it, have you? So O.K., they didn't bite on buyin' the stuff under the counter like I maybe thought, it was just a try, anybody's crooked give 'em the chance not get caught, even professors or— So it didn't come off, but that guy told me what it's really worth, didn't he? Insured for two hundred G's, he said— Oh, the hell with it! You just gone soft in the head, Denny. Listen, you remember just how it used to be, see, just let ol' Jackie do the brainwork for you, boyo. Don't worry about nothing, just do how I say, and everything'll be O.K., see?" Jackie Donovan banged him on the shoulder and made for the door.

"Where you going?"

"None o' your business where—you hear what I just say? Way it used to be, Denny—ol' Jack's the brains o' the outfit, you just leave it to him and don't ask no questions, see?"

Denny watched him out uneasily. "I still don't like it," he said half to himself. "Ask me, something fishy about the whole deal, anybody pay so much as a sawbuck for that stuff. Lot o' dirty old stuff you couldn't even—"

"Ask no questions, you get tol' no lies," said Angelo. He rolled over on the sagging old couch in the corner of the shabby room and smiled sleepily at Denny. "Jackie, he get some older inside, don't he? Maybe forget a li'l bit, how things go. Maybe not the same ol' Jackie, fifteen years back, you guess?"

"I—well, kinda, I guess," said Denny unwillingly. He fidgeted around the room. "Sure, I guess—only natural, for a little while—you know, Angie, away *that* long—only natural. He get back on an even keel, O.K., couple of months maybe."

"Sure. Maybe. Look a lot older, Jackie."

"Well—fifteen years," said Denny. "I—you know something crazy, what really bothers me—that damn car! Crazy fool thing. This perfeckly good almost brand new Caddy I get for him, a *present,* an' he says he can't handle it—goes off like that an' stalls her, an' that place too—comes back with this piece of old junk, my God, pickin' up a thing like—stickin' me with a hot short to get rid of! Says he can't get the hang o' these new models, dashboard like a airplane or something —Jackie! Don't make sense. Well, fifteen years . . . So O.K., maybe he's got something, get all we *can,* but I don't like the setup. That Greek—well, I got no grudge on him for bein' Frank's boss, he acted real sorry, he allus treated Frank O.K., I guess, but—"

"Not Skyros watch out for. The ace o' spades. Bad luck."

"Oh, damn it to hell!" said Denny. "I wish to God I'd never picked that damn place to knock over!"

"He quotes proverbs at me," said Madame Bouvardier, "so I too remember one, Berthe. When in Rome one behaves like a Roman."

"Yes, madame," said the maid stolidly.

"So—so!" Madame Bouvardier could not think in silence; indeed, she seldom did anything in silence; and she kept her excellent Berthe, though she was not *chic* or very intelligent, because Berthe was utterly loyal and it did not matter what one said before her. "Since I have no longer a husband to arrange these affairs, I am pleased enough that this Skyros offers himself, as a compatriot and a sympathizer, to help me come in touch with these robbers. But no, I am not a fool, and I have now thought twice. Since when should a Skyros be so obliging for no profit? I think perhaps he gets a little piece of that money, and when I agree at once to the price, they think I am so anxious I will pay anything! Well, they must think again. Berthe, I will have another glass of wine."

"Yes, madame."

"It is true I am anxious to have it—in his dotage, my father was, heaven rest him—to think of selling it in America! Sacrilege! These precious relics of our nation's past—of course it is also true that for the moment it would perhaps be unsafe that the collection remain in Athens, so close to these never-enough-to-be-cursed Russians, who knows what enormity they conceive next? But it should *not* be in America, for these uncouth strangers to own! We shall see that it is taken out safely, Berthe. I say *we,* for you are the seamstress, and I have thought of an excellent way to carry it. It shall all be sewn in the hems of my clothes—piece by piece—*well* wrapped, of course, and only a few in each, lest the weight make the customs officers suspicious. But this is for the future. Before, there is this Donovan." She sipped wine reflectively. "Skyros need not think I am so ignorant. I have seen on the films how it is here, with the gangsters. Quite like the war, Berthe. This little gang and that little gang, and bitter rivalries between. And the police are not at all like the police in Paris, intelligent and honorable men—they are quite as bad as the gangsters, everyone knows that. They would not interfere if they were paid—but only if it is necessary, I do not want to pauperize myself in this affair. We shall see, about that. For the rest, well! This red-haired woman of Donovan's— this Alison Weir—has told him my message by now, he has one more day to take the offered price. If he does not—" She got up and paced back and forth to the window, to the little wine-table, sipping again. "Ah, let him try to give me the *stall*—I know a trick for that too! These gangsters, one may hire them. One goes to them and says, such a one I wish shot, and the bargain is made. *Voilà!* And I even know one, or at least the name, I remember one small thing Skyros says—it is as if to himself, but I hear the name. Italian—all gangsters are Italians. Except a few like this Donovan who are Irishmen. I have not made up my mind whether I have him shoot Donovan or this red-haired woman— Answer the door, Berthe."

When the maid came clumping back into the suite she bore a card. "It's the man who was here before, madame. Monsieur Driscoll."

"Ah, how annoying! But I must be very polite to them, until they have paid me the money. Very well, let him come in."

SEVEN

Jackie Donovan sat on a bench in Pershing Square, watching the pigeons, and smoked cigarettes nervously. Pigeons! he thought, savage at himself. Him, Donovan, two weeks out and he sat watching pigeons in the park. The hell of a lot of things he'd kept thinking about, wanting, promising himself for when he got out, and what the hell was wrong with him, he couldn't just go and—

All *different,* somehow. He felt he couldn't get a hold on anything.

Like the car. Damn good of Denny, have it all ready and waiting like that. Handling cars since he was a kid, God, the first job he'd got dropped on for was hopping shorts—but it was *different*. Kept reaching for the clutch, just habit; my God, he'd driven a couple those first automatics that come out, couple years before he was sent across this time, he ought to catch on quicker. And tell the truth, these freeways, they scared the bejesus out of him. They had different kinds of signals too, those little green arrows, first off he couldn't figure them out. Oh, hell, give him a little time, things bound to be kind of strange at first. That was the longest stretch he'd done, after all. Fifteen years.

The women looked different too. Wearing skirts short again, well, *that* was O.K., but most of them, it looked like, with these funny short haircuts too—crazy—straight, like a man's, left just anyhow, not curled.

But things like that he'd kind of expected. Bound to be changes. Have to get used to things outside again.

What he hadn't expected, what made him feel funny inside, was this —this not being *sure*. Him, Donovan! Always the brains—ask Jackie, Jackie'll know just how—and God, he didn't, no more. Things in the business changed too, all kinds of the business, names he didn't know, all the old fences gone, new fellows all over. He felt kind of still out of everything.

And some things he'd pulled—Jesus, a ten-year-old kid swiping stuff off dime store counters'd know better— Him, Donovan. Been on the list of Ten Most Wanted, once, he had. A big-timer.

He kept thinking about that short—goddamned crazy thing, it didn't *matter*. He'd felt nervous with the Caddy, and when she stalled out there, that day, it'd been kind of like an excuse he was waiting for. That short he'd picked up—you could've fixed her up a little, a real nice piece to handle—you knew where you *were* with her. Always liked a hand choke, and these new things, you never— She didn't ride so good maybe, but—

He'd like to've kept her.

The damn hot short—

It was a hot feeling in his chest, the little panic. Hadn't told Denny, hadn't told anybody how he'd lost that little bit. God, like a kid couldn't be trusted out with a dime— Him!

It must've been in the car. All he could figure: he hadn't had a hole in his pocket, and he'd looked good. Damn fool to carry it loose. Must've come out in that car, somehow.

Well, all right, so it could be fixed up. O.K. No call to get in a sweat about it. It was just damn lucky he knew how to find the car, on account—damn it, the kind of short he was *used* to—he'd had a kind of crazy idea of keeping it, all on the up-and-up, so's not to mess around with new plates. Denny said you'd pay the hell of a lot for safe plates now. Thought about making up some story, about seeing it parked, wanting it just for transportation like they said—after the guy had it back, go and offer him a hundred bucks for it. So he'd remembered the name on the registration. Funny name for a guy.

Just a little piddling job. Ten to one the thing down in the seat somewhere, nobody knowing it was there. Just had to look up the address, that he didn't remember, find the garage, get in easy—tonight—and go over the car. Why the hell all this sweat about it? Nothing to it. And nobody'd ever know he'd done such a damn fool thing.

All *right,* he thought vaguely, angrily.

Go look up the address, public phone someplace, now. And maybe have a little drink on the way. O.K.

They nicked you six bits for Scotch mostly now. Hell of a thing. Except joints where it was baptized stuff, or made under the counter and like to send you to the General.

And that was another thing. This deal better go through pretty damn quick. Nice of Denny to have a little stake for him, coming out—pull off that job special, celebrate his getting out—but it hadn't been so much as he'd figured, Denny said, account half of it turning out to be this crazy stuff no fence'd look at.

All the more reason, get as much as they could.

He walked out of the park slowly and started down Sixth Street toward Main. He felt more at home down on Main. As much as he did anywhere.

If just things—ordinary things—didn't look so *different.*

He was forty-three years old this year, and he'd spent almost twenty-two of them behind bars.

What the hell, thought Driscoll, and drank out of the bottle, shuddered. He had never consciously admitted to himself that he didn't really like the taste of whiskey. It was just one of the things you did, any kind of a fellow at all.

The whiskey settled sickly in his stomach and he groaned involuntarily, slumped down on the hotel bed. Damn hot weather. Damn miserly company wouldn't allow enough expenses for a decent hotel, air-conditioned. Damn Howard, supercilious—suspicious— *Not quite up to par lately, Driscoll, and—er—complaints about your offensive manner—I'm afraid—*

Hell with Howard. With his record, let Howard fire him—always find another job. Damn old-fashioned company was all, obsolete ideas about things. You had to keep up a front, play it smart. People took you at face value. So all right, maybe he had been pouring it down kind of heavy, my God, *everybody* did—any fellow who *was* any kind of fellow— Set your brain working better, gave you bright ideas sometimes—and besides—

Damn cops. That Mex, sneering at him—so damn polite, looking down his nose— Looked like a damn gigolo. That suit, Italian silk: and the cuff links the real thing too—money—a cop: sure, sure, so they said, rare exception these days find a crooked cop!—higher standards, higher quality of men— Probably just as many as there always were, anybody could be bought—

Dirty Mex cop, looking down his nose. Damned if he'd tell him anything. Sure, hell of a lot easier, ask for help on it—their records— fellow who handled the case—way you were supposed to do it. But he could handle it alone, and make Howard sit up and take notice— Say to Howard, damn regular cops no help at all, didn't bother with 'em—

Something going on, all right. Something fishy. That foreign skirt, snotty bitch the way she looked at him, she owned the stuff, or would when the estate was transferred, she had an interest—a racket, sure, shouldn't be hard to get evidence on it, *that* stuff.

Crack it but good, and say to Howard (act real tough, people took you for what you looked like), say, There, boy, who's not doing so hot these days, who's slipping, hah?

He sat up unsteadily and reached for the bottle again. Say to Howard—

"Ekaterina Nikolayevna Rosleva," said the old woman softly, "speak the truth to me now."

The girl knew she was in earnest, by the formal address—the old-country form. Anything to do with the old ways and ideas she hated, reminder of how people looked down on her for the foreign name— she'd been born here, she was a citizen, wasn't she?—it wasn't fair. She hated living with the old woman, her slow old-fashioned ways, her endless stories about old days and people all dead now: she resented having to share the money she earned, for this hole-in-the-corner place and food and all it took to live, two people. If it wasn't for the old woman, she could escape.

"Ekaterina—"

"All right, all right, I heard you!" she said, ladling out soup carelessly into the bowls on the table. "What you think I haven't told you?"

"There is something in your mind, I know."

"So there's something in my mind. Usually is. Work I got to do tomorrow, clothes I got to mend, bills I got to pay." She sat down opposite and picked up her spoon.

"You forget, we ask the blessing first."

Escape—how she'd planned it! She resented the old woman, but one did not leave relatives to public charity, it was a duty. Secretly and often she thought of the old woman dying—then she would be free. She'd go right away from this place, didn't matter where so long as it was a long way off; she'd just leave everything, and start to be some-body else. Somebody new. Not Katya Roslev, but Katharine Ross, good American name, and a better job too, in a high-class shop where ladies came, to watch and listen to for how they acted. All her money her own.

"Somehow I do not feel it is a good thing in your mind," said the old woman. "You should be thinking of Stevan. Praying for his soul."

"I am thinking of Stevan," said Katya submissively. It was no lie: she was. For perhaps the first time with any real feeling—gratitude.

Catch her marrying a Stevan Domokous! He had been the old woman's idea: *old-fashioned*. These days!—fixing it up all like they did in the old country a hundred years back, *thousand* years back—the bishop and all—a good steady hard-working young man of good fam-ily, if all alone in this country. Bah! And to him that's how it had been too—way a man took a wife—picked for her dowry and family and character—not interested in *her,* he'd been, in herself. And a slow one, anyway: a plodder. Honest: too honest.

She'd have found some way out of *that* before spring, that was sure. Katharine Ross, secure in another life, was going to marry somebody with another nice American name and a better job than a clerk's, and that was for sure too. It was a pity Stevan had to die, but at least it did get her rid of him; she was sorry for him, but there it was, it had hap-pened. And maybe it was good luck for her another way, an exciting way too. Escape.

Money, always money, there had to be. Oh, he had been a slow one! That night, when he'd said about Mr. Skyros talking: she'd said to him, after, when they were on the way to the movies, maybe if he let Mr. Skyros think he heard more, knew all about it, he'd get some pay to promise not to tell. He'd been shocked—or scared, she thought con-temptuously—he said, not honest: anything bad the police ought to know!

Well, she wasn't one to split hairs like that. If there was some easy money to be had, she'd take any chance at it. And she'd take care to be smarter than Stevan too—protect herself. She could say she'd written it all out, what he'd told her—about the money—and the writing was—it was in the bank, in one of those boxes rich people kept, where nobody could get at it but her—they'd never dare harm her then.

She'd been a fool to come out with it to that policeman, but she hadn't thought about it clear then—seen the chance it offered.

Money. It might be a lot of money. Could she ask for a thousand dollars? Even five thousand? Escape: because that would be the duty money, to leave behind for the old woman—the old woman off her mind then—she could manage on the little she'd saved from her salary —go away with a clear conscience then, the old woman provided for— and start her new life, a long way off.

"You are very silent, Katya," said the old woman.

"I am thinking of Stevan, as you say I should," said the girl, and held back a smile.

EIGHT

The two letters from Athens proved to be from casual friends, apparently; there was nothing in them of any significance—references to other friends, to politics, to a church festival of some kind, the weather, questions about Domokous' new life in America.

Nothing else interesting turned up from the more complete examination of the body, or from Dr. Erwin's patient scrutiny of the clothes.

"I suppose I'm a fool to say it," said Hackett, "because a lot of times when I say you're barking up a tree with no cat in it, all of a sudden something shows up to prove your crystal ball gave you the right message. And don't complain about mixed metaphors, I'm just a plain cop. But I think it's a dead end. Everything doesn't always dovetail so nice and neat as a detective story, you know."

"Unfortunately, no," said Mendoza. "Ragged edges. No hunch, Arturo—or not much of one. Just—" he swiveled around and looked thoughtfully out the window of his office, "just the little funny feeling you get, on discard and draw—better hold onto this worthless-looking low card, next time round it might be worth something. . . . Damn. I wish I had four times as many men as I had, to keep an eye on everybody. What it comes down to, I don't know much of anything about it at all, I just have the definite conviction there's something *to* know. I'm not really justified in keeping so many men on it, but— Damn." He got up abruptly. "I'll be up in Callaghan's office if anybody wants me."

And that was on Thursday morning; he missed Alison's call by five minutes.

He found Callaghan in a temper. Having gone to some trouble to secure enough evidence to charge a certain pusher, Callaghan had wasted yesterday in court only to hear the bench dismiss it as inadmissible by the letter of the law. "So, my God in heaven, there's got to be law—but what the hell do they expect of us when they tie one hand behind our backs and give us a toy cap pistol and say, Now, boys, you go out and protect the public from the big bad men! Jesus and Mary, next thing they'll be saying to us, Boys, it isn't legal evidence unless you collect it on the northeast corner of a one-way street during an eclipse of the moon! They——"

"Very annoying," agreed Mendoza, sitting down in the desk chair to be out of Callaghan's way as he paced. Callaghan was even bigger than Hackett, which was saying something, and it was not a large office.

"You can talk!" said Callaghan bitterly. "All you got to think about is dead people! Who was there, who wanted them dead? Clear as day— evidence all according to the book! Nobody says to you—"

"Oh, we run into it too, occasionally. Now calm down and talk to me about Bratti."

"I don't want even to think about Bratti," said Callaghan. "I'm goin' to quit the force and take up some nice peaceful occupation like farming. Why should I knock myself out protecting the public? They don't give a damn about me. They call *me* an officious cop, persecutin' innocent bystanders—"

"You'll wear out the carpet, Patrick."

"And I'll tell you something else! One thing like this—and the good God knows it's not the first or the last—and every single pro in this town, he has a good laugh at the cops, and he gets twice as cocky as he was before, because he knows damn well we can beat our brains out and never get him inside—"

"You'll give yourself ulcers. Bratti."

"Get out of my chair," said Callaghan, and flung himself into it and drove a hand through his carrot-red hair. "What about Bratti?"

"He'll be in competition with some others in business on his level. Middlemen, who run strings of pushers."

"Oh, all very businesslike these days. Sure. Same position, almost exactly, as the fellow who owns a lot of slum tenements. Fellow who says, hell, you always get some people who like to live like that, why should I go to the expense of cleaning up the place, make it a little fancier for 'em? In six months it's just as bad. I don't cut my profits for any such damn foolishness. But he doesn't live there himself, oh, no, he's got a nice clean new house out in Bel-Air. He hires an agent to collect the rent so he needn't mingle with the *hoi polloi* and listen to complaints. *If you get me.* Gimme a cigarette, I'm out. . . . There's Bratti. And in this burg, call it about a dozen like him. Sure, 'way up at the top there's a hook-up with the syndicate—with the real big boys, and we know where *they* are these days. Sitting happy as clams in some country where they can't be extradited—even if, God help us, we had any admissible evidence to charge 'em with—"

"Pray a moment's silence," said Mendoza sardonically, "while we return thanks to the Bureau of Internal Revenue for small mercies."

"Very damn small," said Callaghan gloomily. "Sure, sure, about the only legal charge on some of those boys. Only some of them. I'm not worrying about 'em— I can't, who can?—like worrying about the bomb. I don't know the answer to the syndicates, except it's a little bit like killing fleas on a dog—you've got to get after the little ones so they can't grow up to be big ones—and you can't stop a minute because they breed like, well, fleas. The ones here and now I got to worry about are the syndicate agents and the boys like Bratti and the boys they hire. The port authorities can worry about the stuff coming in, and isn't it God's truth, they could do with ten times more men like all of us. It gets in. This way, that way. And it gets to the agents. And they get it to the Brattis. And the Brattis—wearin' kid gloves and takin' great care of their respectable surfaces—they see it gets to the pushers. Everybody making the hell of a profit every time it changes hands—strictly cash basis, no credit—because it gets cut so much on the way. A little deck of H worth a hundred bucks raw, coming in, by the time it gets to Bratti to distribute, it's twenty times bigger and worth a thousand times the cash."

"This isn't news to me, friend. I've been on the force just as long as you. All about Bratti, *por favor.*"

"I could write a book," said Callaghan, "and what good would it do me? I don't know what kind of background he came from, but I'd guess he's had a fair education, he uses pretty good English. Let that go. I don't know where he got his capital. For the legitimate business, that is

—about *that* I know, it's out in the open for anybody to see—ambitious young man makes good: starts with one small hole-in-the-wall joint and builds it up. Once in a while it does make you think—he's doing all right on the right side of the law, you know. A lot of people saying the pros, it's because they get branded—nobody'll give 'em a job, nobody'll teach 'em a useful trade, so they stay pros—that's not the answer, as any cop could tell them. They've just got a kink somewhere. I don't know how long Bratti's been in the other business. That kind, they spring up overnight like toadstools. And when he drops dead of a heart attack—*or* when we get the goods on him—and the position's open, somebody else'll be right there to take over. Just as he took over —or maybe built up *that* business for himself. No, my God, that's not the syndicate thing—why should the big boys worry about organizing that low?—it's standard business procedure. And how do I know about Bratti? I'll tell you, though God help me if I ever said it to a judge! About eighteen months ago we picked up a pusher by the name of Fred Ring—we thought we had some nice solid evidence on him—but at the last minute the witness reneged and jumped bail on us, and he had a record so the judge looked down his nose and said the mere signed statement wasn't worth a whoop in hell, and threw it out. But while we had Ring, we ran a tape on some of his interviews with visitors, all underhand as hell—and of course since that Supreme Court decision *that's* inadmissible evidence too—but it gave us Bratti's name. We gathered Bratti was paying the lawyer. Which put Ring, ten to one, as the head pusher. Bratti and the boys like him, they don't want too many of these irresponsible underlings knowing their names and faces and addresses. For one thing, it's not very unusual for a pusher—the man on the street—to sample his own goods. There's a big turnover in pushers: the personnel, as a business report'd say, fluctuates. Some of 'em get to be customers, on the other side of the fence, and that kind— or any of 'em—could be dangerous to the next highest man on the totem pole. O.K. There'll be one, usually, heading the string, taking delivery of supplies and handing 'em out, the one who knows the middleman. We think Ring was it at the time. We kept a very close eye on him, but didn't get anything. We have also been keeping an eye on Bratti, with the same result. Ring didn't last long after that—"

"Fished out of the bay one foggy morning?"

"Why, you bloodthirsty Latin," said Callaghan, "you ought to know as well as me we're twenty, thirty years away from that kind of thing. Of course not—he got to liking his own wares too much and finally passed out in the General. They aren't gangsters any more, they're just syndicate men, and employees of syndicate men, and customers of the syndicates. Like the big corporations of other kinds, the syndicates deal with subsidiaries—and it's all very quiet and business-like. They know it doesn't pay, it's not only dangerous to their continued operation but cuts into net profits, if they go roaring around like I've heard tell they used to, pumping lead into anybody gets in their way. That just doesn't happen any more. The big boys are awful leery of the law these days, and the hell of a lot smarter—they've found out, for one thing, a smart shyster is less expensive in the long run than the old-fashioned can-nister man you just gave orders to go out and bump off So-and-So, and don't waste cartridges. Look at Bratti. Thirty years ago Bratti would have been a barely literate lout—standard type as per the Hollywood version—anybody'd know him for a gangster minute they laid eyes on him. Today, you can't tell him from any other man in the crowd, except maybe he's a little better dressed. He knows how to behave in polite so-ciety, he's married and has a couple of kids, he pays his bills on time, he's a respectable householder. Far as I know, never even got a traffic ticket. Most of 'em are like that these days, the boys with any authority —even the junior executives. One thing, they've got to have cover for the tax boys in Washington, and most of 'em are running legal businesses on the side. They've found out it's a lot nicer, quieter life havin' a permanent home and all, not being on the run half the time. Sure, human nature doesn't change, and there are still the feuds be-tween gangs of this sort and that, the jealousy *and* the fear and the loose-mouths who'll tell what they know to anybody pays 'em, and the men who'll do the same thing to pay off a grudge. But why should Bratti or anybody else keep a hot cannon man at his elbow? Almost im-possible to tattle to the cops on one man, you know—a threat on one is a threat on all, and all of 'em know that."

"You're lecturing," complained Mendoza. "Now listen to me for a minute. I've got a very simple little problem, nothing so vast as yours by a long way. Here's a dead man, full of heroin. I don't *know* whether it was his first shot or whether he gave it to himself, on the evidence, but in my own mind I'm pretty sure it was, and he didn't. It looks, and it could be so, as if he went down an alley to take his little jolt, took too big a one and died there. A lot of holes in him where users stick their needles—arms and thighs—but all put in him, the surgeon *thinks,* after death. Can't swear positively it wasn't just before death, that it wasn't him, getting up nerve. If it was, that doesn't, of course, look like a habitual user. But it could have been his first, voluntary jolt. O.K. His employer was one Andreas Skyros, importer, prosperous, looks very much according to Hoyle on the surface, ¿comprende? He's very shocked and sad over this unfortunate misguided young fellow led into bad ways by new acquaintances. And he says when he reprimanded the young man for being slow at his work, the young man mentioned the name Bratti as—by implication—one of the said acquaintances."

"You don't say," said Callaghan. "Not much there. Bratti wouldn't be working the street himself, making up to potential customers, all pals together, Try a little of this for what ails you."

"Exactly. I have the feeling that—as so often happens—we're being underrated. Nobody else who knew the corpse remembers him mentioning the name. So I just got to wondering about Mr. Skyros."

"Never heard of him."

"But there was heroin in the corpse—that's how it got to be a corpse. And—"

"Down on Carson Street," nodded Callaghan. "I got the memo somewhere. Whereabouts?"

"In an alley just down from Carson and Main."

"You *don't* say," said Callaghan. "Bratti's first joint is on that corner —he still owns it. He branched out later in classier directions—has a place out on Ventura and another on La Cienega now."

"*Vaya, vaya,*" said Mendoza, "does he indeed? That makes me wonder even harder. Have you ever sat in a game, Pat, with a pro sharp?— where the cold deck was rung in, and cards forced on you?"

"Yes," said Callaghan, "or I got a strong suspicion I have, anyway. I've sat in some hands of draw with you, before you got to be a millionaire and can't be bothered to shuffle a pack for less than five hundred in the kitty. Mind you, I could never prove it, you're too damn smooth, but a couple of times I had the distinct feeling that you had another deck up your sleeve."

"Slander," grinned Mendoza. "It's just that I have more courage and skill as a gambler—you've got no finesse, and you let the thought of the rent and the car payment intrude and back out too soon. Fatal. What I started to say was, I just had a feeling that that casual throwing off of Bratti's name was—mmh—something like the dealer handing me a royal flush first time round, out of a deck of readers. And me, it's maybe evidence of a suspicious and ungrateful nature, but a long while

ago I learned you don't get something for nothing. I wouldn't be sur
prised about the royal flush if that particular dealer owed me a little
favor—¿como no?—but as it was, why should Mr. Skyros hand it to
me on a silver platter?"

"You think he did?" Callaghan cocked his head at him. "I don't deny
it, you get feelings about these things, I know. Our Luis, crystal ball in
his back pocket."

"I think he did," said Mendoza. "I think he knew what card he was
dealing me. And so I wondered, you know, if maybe Mr. Skyros had
some little grudge on Mr. Bratti. And if so, why."

Callaghan got up and paced down the office. "It's a piddling little
thing. . . . And I might feel the hell of a lot more inclined to take you
at face value if *I* didn't have a suspicious nature—knowing you—and
get the unworthy idea maybe you just haven't got the men to spare to
keep an eye on this Skyros."

"You wrong me. I'm being scrupulous—keeping you briefed on what
might be your business."

"Andreas Skyros. Where?"

Mendoza told him home and office address. Callaghan wrote them
down. "You think *I've* got any more men to send out?" he asked. "And
on a homicide! That's your business. For a change, *I've* got a hunch.
End of this thing'll be a homicide charge, nothing for me at all, and
you'll be the one to get your name in the papers—arresting officer. Talk
about cold decks. O.K., O.K., I'll have a look into it."

"Muchas gracias," said Mendoza meekly.

He came back to his office and among other things found the message about Alison's call. Quite a few other matters, besides this nebulous business of Stevan Domokous, under his jurisdiction; and in any
case he was scrupulous about mixing business with outside concerns.
Ten-forty: she'd probably be lecturing her current class on the proper
use of mascara or something similar. He went over a few reports on
other present cases, from Sergeants Galeano, Clock, and Schanke;
cleared up some accumulated routine. It was eleven forty-five when he
called her, at her office.

"I wouldn't have bothered you," said Alison, "it's none of your
business—scarcely so melodramatic as homicide—but really it is mad-
dening, how even these days so many men seem to have it firmly fixed
in their minds that all females are scatterbrained and prone to hysterics

I grant you, some of it's our own fault—these women who make a fetish of being career girls, twice as efficient as any mere male. I mean, a lot of it's automatic self-defense on the part of the implied mere males, and I can't say I blame them. Shakespeare—you know—protesting too much. Better or worse, famales *are* apt to be less objective about things, it's the way we're made. Which I suppose is my excuse, automatic seeking for sensible male advice."

"Yes," said Mendoza, "I agree with you every time, what you mean is women jump to conclusions and call it intuition. What—"

"And there's the pot calling the kettle black," said Alison. "What else is one of your famous hunches? Well, never mind. The thing is, somebody broke into my garage last night and apparently went over the car. As if they were looking for something, anyway that's what it looked like to me. When I came to get it this morning, the front seat was all pulled out—teetering on the supports. So far as I can see nothing was taken, but—"

"I'll be damned," said Mendoza. "Look, meet me at Federico's for lunch, I want to hear about this."

"Well, all right, but I can't take much time—it's a little drive. Half an hour?"

"Half an hour."

He was waiting for her when she arrived. "I've already ordered, save time. Now, go on from where you left off. What about the garage door? I don't know that I've ever noticed the garages—usual arrangement, couple of rows of them, single garage for each apartment?"

"That's right. And to anticipate, none of them have windows, and five other garages had their padlocks forced. Mr. Corder happened to come out just after me, and found his broken, and we looked, and found the others. I hadn't thought much about mine, you see. It's an old one, the padlock, and rusted, and it does stick sometimes—I'll think it's closed and then find it's just stuck halfway. I suppose it's careless of me, but quite a few times I've put the car away after dark and next morning found the padlock wasn't closed properly. So I hadn't thought twice about finding it that way this morning. Not until I saw the car, with the driver's door open and the seat pulled out. Everything intact as far as I can see—there wasn't anything there to take, of course, except some maps and cleaning rags in the glove compartment."

"The seat," said Mendoza. "That thing you found—"

"Yes, I thought of it right away. It doesn't seem to belong to anyone

I know. And we have it dinned into us so much about co-operating with the police—I was just trying to be a dutiful citizen. I called that sergeant again and told him about it, but he obviously thought I was imagining things—just a nervous female. Well, I thought *somebody* ought to know—"

"He didn't send anyone up to look?"

"Oh, yes. At least *he* didn't, but he said to call the local precinct. Which Mr. Corder already had. And a couple of men came up and looked at everything. It was a nuisance, of course, made us both awfully late—but we left everything just as it was for them. And they looked in the other garages, and said it was probably kids."

"Any other car touched?"

"No. And that was just it. It was only mine. So I told those men all about it, because it seemed rather open-and-shut to me. There being no windows, I mean—he didn't know which garage, and he had to try several garages before he found the right car. And they looked at me pityingly—these imaginative females!—and said all over again it was probably kids, just messing around."

"Yes. You can't really blame them, on the face of it it sounds too vague and—apologies—the sort of thing a nervous female might dream up. But it *is* suggestive, isn't it? It might be—it could be—whoever dropped that thing. And on the other hand—all that trouble, hunting up the car and so on, just for— Has there been any vandalism of that sort, kids roaming around at night and getting into mischief, in the neighborhood?"

"Not that I know of."

"And nothing to get hold of on it, any more than on my little business. . . . And I might have known," added Mendoza as Hackett drifted up to the table, "that I couldn't have lunch in peace, not opposite a pretty female anyway, without you barging in."

"It's not the redhead," said Hackett, "—hello, Miss Weir, and apologies to tell the truth—it's the chance of sticking you with the check, Luis."

"Neither of you'll be sitting opposite long," said Alison. "I've got to get back. I wondered if I ought to advertise it, you know—d'you think it'd do any good?"

"I do not. If he, she, or it knows for pretty certain it must have been lost in the car, they'd recognize an ad as a trap."

"Oh!—of course, I didn't see that. But it's such a little thing—"

"Yes. One piece of advice I'll give you, knowing your casual habits, *chica*. Put the chain up on your door and keep those two windows near the fire escape locked."

"My lord, you don't really think—? But I'd suffocate, those are the north windows where the only air comes in— You can't think, just for a little thing like that—?"

"Somebody went to a little trouble to look in the car. If it wasn't just kids' random mischief, and you're not imagining things. *No se sabe nunca*—one never knows. . . . You remember what I say now, *¿comprende? Y hasta muy pronto,*" as she rose to leave.

"Well, all right, I can't stop to argue now," said Alison, and fled back to her class.

"And what was all that about, if it's any of my business?" asked Hackett.

"It's not, but they say two heads are better than one." Mendoza told him.

"That's a funny one, all right. Maybe one of these superstitious nuts, it's his best lucky talisman or something?"

"Could be. I don't know. I don't know anything about anything," said Mendoza, regarding his coffee gloomily. "And there's another funny little thing tied up to it that— Maybe I'm getting old, Art. Losing my grip."

"All come out in the wash," said Hackett. "The trouble with you is, you've got what they call a tortuous mind. You build up little picayune things to worry about, that don't mean a damn. Like this Domokous thing. It's *un callejón sin salida,* boy—a dead-end street. Higgins checked in on Skyros just after you left. If he's playing games with the exotic brunette, they haven't even got to Post Office yet. He goes from home to office and vice versa, and that's all. The brunette—I borrowed one of Galeano's men to check on her—is staying at the Beverly-Hilton. She's one Madame Rafael Bouvardier, of Paris, and she's apparently loaded. Has her own maid with her, and a suite. No expense spared."

"That was the picture," agreed Mendoza. "What's her first name and what's she doing here?"

"How should I know? She hasn't confided in the hotel people. Just a pleasure trip, probably. Though why pick L.A. in this season, God knows. She's been here about three weeks. Don't tell me you want her tailed too. We just haven't got a man free."

"But I can think of unpleasanter jobs," said Mendoza. "I might even take it on myself—keep my hand in, so to speak."

"*¡No hay más,* that's all, brother!" said Hackett. "Since when do you need practice chasing skirts? Just an excuse to take the afternoon off!"

NINE

Mendoza had said, no hunch; and he didn't have that unreasonably sure conviction that this or that was so. It was more on the order of that uneasy doubt as to whether one had left the gas turned on or the faucet running.

He had the further guilty feeling that he was wasting time, but he drove out to the Beverly-Hilton, and was waiting his turn at the desk clerk to frame some discreet questions about Madame Bouvardier, when he saw her descending the nearest stair into the lobby. No expense spared, that you could say again, he reflected: very Parisian, very exotic—again the wide lace-brimmed hat, another black-and-white printed silk gown, what at least looked like diamonds, long gloves, fragile high heels.

And well met: so, wasting time, but might as well be hanged for a sheep as a lamb. He abandoned the line at the desk and strolled after her, with a vague idea of picking her up somehow, all very gentlemanly and polite, and getting confidential over a drink—as confidential as she could be persuaded, and at that he flattered himself he was far more accomplished than any of his sergeants.

But she didn't establish herself conveniently in the lobby, the adjacent lounge, or the bar; she walked purposefully out the main door, and Mendoza drifted up in time to hear her ask the doorman for Madame Bouvardier's car.

"Yes, madame, the chauffeur's just gone out, he'll be here directly, madame."

Hell, thought Mendoza, and turned back for the side door and sprinted for the Facel-Vega in the middle of the lot. Hired car and driver, the chauffeur calling from the lobby to announce arrival—he wouldn't be sixty seconds picking her up. He thrust coins at the attendant and switched on the engine almost in one motion.

But he was just in time, taking the wide curve out to Wilshire, to catch a glimpse of the lace hat through the rear window of a stately black middle-aged Chrysler. He was held up a couple of cars behind, but the Chrysler wasn't hard to keep in view along here; it went straight up Wilshire at a steady pace, heading back for Hollywood. Before they got into town, Mendoza managed to pass the cars ahead and fall in directly behind it.

A couple of blocks this side of La Brea, the Chrysler turned left and went round the block, and Mendoza dropped back a little, guessing at a stop. Middle of the block, and the chauffeur'd gone round to drop her on the right side; he hopped out smartly, illegally double-parked, and opened the door, and out she came, said a few words. Probably as to where and when to pick her up. Mendoza was legitimately caught in this lane by the halted Chrysler, an excuse for watching. The chauffeur touched his cap, grinned apology over his shoulder at Mendoza, and ran around to the driver's door again. And Madame Bouvardier vanished through the door of an elegant black-glass-and-marble-fronted shop labeled in discreet gold script, *Shanrahan and MacReady*.

"Well, well," said Mendoza sadly to himself. "A mare's nest. With a clutch of wild goose eggs in it." But he turned the next corner, miraculously found a parking space, and strolled back to keep an eye on the black glass door.

In twenty minutes it opened and she came out and turned in his direction. He stayed where he was, propping the wall of the bank on the corner, and his flagging interest was slightly aroused by her expression as she passed him: she was biting her lower lip, looking thoughtful and annoyed. She carried no parcel, and her bag was too small to conceal even a little one.

She walked on half a block, stopping a few times to look in windows, and disappeared into the plush elegance of Chez Frédéric, Coiffures.

"Oh, hell," said Mendoza to himself. She hadn't stopped at the counter in there, but with a white-robed attendant at her elbow passed on into the rear premises. Be there for hours, very likely.

What did he think he was doing, anyway? You couldn't expect a tailing job to turn up something interesting in the first hour. If he wanted to know more about the female, put a man on her, and preserve patience.

And no reason she shouldn't have gone where she did. A place any woman might go. But, as long as he was here—

He turned around and walked back to *Shanrahan and MacReady.*

Mr. Brian Shanrahan welcomed him into the chaste quietude of the shop with subdued cries of delight, or what passed for that with a dignified middle-aged professional man of repute.

"And what may I have the pleasure of showing you today? Perhaps at last something in a wedding set? I have—"

"You and my grandmother," said Mendoza.

"And how is the charming señora? Such an interesting old lady—"

"You find her interesting," said Mendoza, "because she's the cautious type who likes to put money into portable value she can look at instead of six percent common stock, and is one of your best customers. It's not for want of telling she hasn't grasped that you figure a two hundred percent mark-up."

"Now that's slander, Mendoza," said Shanrahan aggrievedly. "Seldom more than a hundred and fifty. And if it's something for her birthday, she was in and briefed me thoroughly. There's this bracelet she has her eye on, very fine stones, if you'd like to look—"

"No," said Mendoza. "It's ridiculous, and I refuse to be a party to it. I'd like to inherit something from her eventually besides stock for a secondhand jewelry shop. I didn't come in to buy anything, I want some information."

Mr. Shanrahan sighed and asked what about.

"A few minutes ago a woman came in here—a very exotic, expensive-looking young woman—black and white ensemble, lace-brimmed hat, gloves—"

"And diamonds in some very old-fashioned mountings," nodded the jeweler intelligently. "Friend of yours?"

"Heaven forbid, not my type—"

"Didn't know you had one."

"What did she want? Who waited on her?"

"As a matter of fact I did."

"Of course, you took one look and she spelled Money, so you wouldn't trust her to an underling."

"Or I tried to. She looked at a couple of things, but she wasn't really interested. If she hadn't—um—as you say, looked quite so expensive, I might have put her down as an amateur novelist looking for information. The first thing she came out with was, what enormous value all these beautiful things must represent, we must have to be very careful about thieves. Did we have a burglar alarm? Did we have a night watchman? Had we ever suffered a robbery? All in machine-gun style, and a *very* thick accent."

"¡*Vaya por Dios!*" said Mendoza. "I refuse to believe that she came in to, as the pros say, case the joint! Now what the devil—"

"Good God," said Mr. Shanrahan. "You don't think—"

"No, I don't, it's ridiculous, I just said so. A suite at the Beverly-Hilton, her own maid—and those clothes— Impossible."

"Good *God,*" said Mr. Shanrahan again. "Burglary. Don't even suggest it. Another one. We average three a year, and this is really too soon after the last—only three weeks. My heart won't take this sort of thing much longer—not to speak of the insurance company. Really, Mendoza!"

"Don't look at me, I'm not the mastermind plotting it—if there is a plot. Lose much in that one?"

"Oh, well, it could have been *worse,*" said Mr. Shanrahan discreetly. Mr. Shanrahan would always be discreet, even with an old customer who was by way of being a friend. He glanced sidewise at Mendoza, opened his mouth for further speech, decided against it, and whisked out his handkerchief to clean his glasses instead. "It's the principle of the thing. And, as I say, the insurance."

"Yes. Did this woman say anything else?"

"One has to be polite. I was—um—noncommittal, you know, and then she got onto insurance. We must have to carry a terrible amount of insurance, all these valuable things, and also, it was to be supposed, sometimes things which do not belong to us. Was it not a great financial burden? My God, Mendoza, you *don't* suppose—?"

"No, I don't. I don't know what she was after. *Insurance. ¡Media vuelta!*—right about face! I don't know anything, damn it. *¡Mil rayos!* So far as I know, she's simply a rich visiting foreigner, eminently respectable, and she didn't mean anything sinister at all—just talking off the top of her mind. And I am wasting the afternoon. I shall now cease to do so and go back to legitimate work."

"I hope to God you're right," said Mr. Shanrahan nervously. "Now just a moment, Mendoza, as long as you're here you might as well take a look at this bracelet—no *harm*—won't take a minute, just let me fetch it out for you—"

Mendoza looked at it, heard the price, said it was outrageous, and named another twenty percent below. Shanrahan told him coldly that

this was not a streetbooth in a village market, where haggling was expected; there were prices set and that was that, take it or leave it.
"Don't give me that," said Mendoza. "What with taxes and inflation
luxury business isn't living so high it can pick and choose customers.
How long have you had this in stock without a bite on it?" Shanrahan
looked offended and after much persuasion named a price five percent
under the original. They insulted each other for another five minutes
and came to a deadlock on the Federal tax, Mendoza refusing to be responsible for it. Shanrahan offered to split it with him.

"I'll think about it," said Mendoza, picking up his hat.

Shanrahan looked at him wistfully. "I live for the day when you get
hooked by some predatory empty-headed blonde."

"And you'll still be hoping when they nail down your coffin," said
Mendoza.

He went back to his office and ruminated. First causes, he thought,
so, what about Domokous? Look at the facts available, build it up from
there.

Hackett had collected a number of little facts by now. The Second
Street hotel was largely tenanted by residents, not transients; there was
supposed to be a desk clerk on duty most of the time, but actually it
was a desultory job. The clerk remembered Domokous going out that
Monday night about seven o'clock, but couldn't say whether he'd come
in again; didn't recall seeing him go out on the Tuesday morning, but
he might have—the clerk didn't always see residents in or out. And
friends of residents, if they knew the room number, would walk right
up; the clerk couldn't keep track of everybody.

It looked as if that Monday night might be the crucial time, because
Domokous hadn't come to work on Tuesday.

The clerk said he'd certainly never seen Domokous the worse for
drink; ditto, the other clerks and the pretty bookkeeper at Skyros, Inc.
The artistic little tale Mr. Skyros had told looked fishier in consequence.

But there could be—considering the nymph and the dolphin—a relatively innocent explanation. If Skyros was sailing a bit near the wind in
his business, say over some matter of customs duty, something like that
—it needn't have one thing to do with Domokous' death—Skyros might
easily be nervous, want the death passed off as smoothly as possible
without investigation too close to home. So he'd just bolstered up the

truth with enough imaginary detail to satisfy authority, get the cops off his neck.

Driscoll . . . Yes, quite outside Domokous' death, the insurance firm with an eye on Skyros? And Domokous just what he looked like, victim of a pusher. Those puncture marks in him— But it could be. People, as Bainbridge sententiously said, did some damned funny things. That knock on the head: all right, heroin didn't kill instantaneously, and he might have got it when he fell in that alley, when the heroin got to him.

A couple of funny little points that Mendoza didn't much like, the business about Bratti, for instance. Was there any connection between Skyros and Bratti? But even that could be innocent. Skyros might have heard the name from Domokous, some time when no one else was around. It just could be.

He had got that far thinking about first causes when Sergeant Lake came in and said, "There's the longest beard I've ever seen just came in —you can see there's some sort of fellow behind it, but not much of him—and says he wants to see you. Claims he's a priest of some kind."

"I've just gone out," said Mendoza, in instant reaction to the word. And then he said, "Wait a minute—a beard? A priest—a Greek? Possibly a Greek bearing gifts? Shoot him in, Jimmy!"

It was in truth a magnificent beard—pepper-and-salt, and curly; it cascaded from high on its owner's cheekbones to somewhere well below where his waist would have been if he'd had one. Mendoza eyed it with respect and ambiguous feelings. Having the tiresome sort himself which called for a second shave if he was to appear in public in the evening, he'd often thought how convenient it would have been to live in an era when beards were *de rigueur;* on the other hand, in this kind of weather it must be rather like carrying around a portable electric blanket. He stood up and took the proffered hand; above the beard a pair of gentle gray eyes blinked at him shortsightedly through old-fashioned round rimless glasses.

"I hope I don't disturb you inconveniently, Lieutenant. Er—Nikolas Papoulos, if I may introduce——"

"And you are a parish priest of a local Orthodox church. I think perhaps—sit down, won't you—you've come to tell me that you knew Stevan Domokous?"

"Dear me, you really are a detective, then." The eyes twinkled at him briefly. "We hear these days how efficient our police force is—just yesterday my wife called my attention to a most interesting article in the *Times*—but I digress—however, this convinces me. Efficient indeed."

The eyes lost their twinkle. "But it's a sad errand I come on, yes. And I should apologize not to have come before. But I've been ill, and also I hesitated—it really seemed a minor— It was only yesterday I learned of this dreadful thing. Er—Mr. Skyros, whom I do not know—he approached me about the service for poor Stevan. I understand the city morgue had only just released the body. I was much shocked, Lieutenant—and I may say grieved, for though I had not known Stevan long, he was a faithful attendant at church and seemed an eminently good young man. I could hardly believe it, in fact, I *can* hardly believe it."

Mendoza said conventionally that of course it was always a little shock to friends and relatives. It was charitable of Domokous' employer to assume the cost of the funeral.

"Er—I daresay," said the priest. He unwound the thin wire bows of his glasses from around his ears slowly and began to polish the lenses with his handkerchief. "I daresay. But—perhaps it's uncharitable of me," he said earnestly, and his myopic naked eyes swam blindly in Mendoza's general direction, "but much experience with human nature leads me to wonder about it."

"The Greek, in fact, bearing gifts?"

"Dear me, yes, very appropriate, Lieutenant. Indeed. I—dear me, it *is* difficult—I debated long with myself about coming. You know, one doesn't like to encourage *slander,* and yet, perhaps, it would be just as well for you to hear about it. I can only trust"—he began to wind the wires back around his ears, and his eyes swam into focus again, looking anxious—"that you will not place more importance on it than is actually warranted."

"Well, we're used to evaluating statements. What is it?"

The priest sighed. "It may mean nothing at all, you see. It seems that Stevan's death was only an unfortunate accident, that he was the victim of one of these drug peddlers—by what appeared in the newspapers, at least. I'd have said that it was quite incredible that he would be persuaded into such a thing, but I know these dreadful things happen. And it seems even more incredible that what he told me could have led to— to a *deliberate* accomplishing of his death—no, no, I cannot accept that. However, the more I thought about it—especially after Mr. Skyros called me—that is, one doesn't like to feel suspicious of the motives for charity, does one, but all the same— Well, I thought perhaps the police should hear. Just in the event that it *is* important. And I trust I am not spreading slander to tell you! Here is the matter, Lieutenant. Stevan came to me—now let me get the date right, I must be accurate—yes, a week ago last Sunday it was, the Sunday evening. He wanted advice. Perhaps you've heard that he was not quite as familiar with English as he might have been. Well, now, it seems that on the previous evening he had worked later than usual, and had had occasion to ask his employer some question, and so gone to his office. He said it was not usual for Mr. Skyros to be there after hours, but perhaps it was something to do with this shipment of goods just arrived; at any rate, there he was. And there was someone with Mr. Skyros—another man. Stevan heard them speaking together before he knocked on the door—you must not think he eavesdropped deliberately, but he hesitated to intrude, you see, when he heard that Mr. Skyros had a visitor, and possibly there was a transom open or something like that, I could not say. He was most disturbed over what he had overheard. He said it sounded to be something to do with a crime, and yet he wasn't sure—you see they were speaking English. And he asked me what I thought he should do. He was such a very honest young man." The priest sighed again.

"I'll tell you," said Mendoza slowly, "this isn't the first I've heard of that. His fiancée and her grandmother—the Roslevs—have been in. He mentioned it to them too."

"Ah, yes—I see—of course. Poor girl, poor girl. Not that I will say I feel quite the sympathy for Katya that I do for the old woman. . . . But then you know—"

"They couldn't tell me much. Possibly he told you more in any case. Did he tell you exactly what he overheard?"

"Well, frankly, Lieutenant, I must admit that I couldn't make much of it myself. He did try to repeat it to me. He heard Mr. Skyros say, 'It will be necessary to make up some story for the insurance people, madness to keep that money of course, they'll be keeping an eye on her afterward and there's all the trouble of taking the stuff out of the country—but that's for later, her business, and nothing to do with you, I'll fix up something.' And the other man, who sounded, Stevan said, very uneducated, uncouth, he said it was—er—'a hell of a lot of dough for *that* stuff.' And Mr. Skyros said something about it being all how you looked at it, and money made money, so the proverb said. He seemed, Stevan said, to be—how shall I put it—falsely genial with this other. And the other man said then, if that was so, how did he know it wasn't worth more than Skyros said; and Skyros replied that a thing one had to sell under the counter was worth only what a buyer was

224   FIRST FOUR BY SHANNON

willing to pay, and ten thousand was a good profit. And then the second man said something about the County Museum."

"The *County Museum?*"

"Well, the actual words Stevan quoted to me were, I think, 'that museum place out Exposition,' which I took to be—"

"Yes. Odd."

"It was, you see, the phrase 'under the counter' which worried
Stevan. He asked me what he ought to do, he said Mr. Skyros had been
kind to him, giving him a job when he was still slow at writing the English and so on, and he did not like to seem ungrateful, but that on the
other hand he wanted to become a good citizen, and anything bad, perhaps criminal, the police should know. I advised him—rightly or
wrongly—to do nothing unless he was sure of some wrongdoing. I said
he had really nothing to take to the police."

"Quite right," said Mendoza. "Nothing there at all, actually. That's
all he heard? . . . Yes. Well, I'm glad to hear a little more about it
than the Roslevs could tell me, but—"

"It doesn't seem to mean much? I am relieved to hear you say so,
Lieutenant. I only wondered—as I say, uncharitable of me. But I
thought it my duty to come and tell you, in case it should mean more to
you than to myself."

"Yes, very good of you to come in," said Mendoza absently.

"Er—businessmen—doubtless merely a little something to do with
his business—and Stevan misunderstood—I feel I may have been leap-
ing to melodramatic conclusions—"

"Well, one never knows." And was there any reason to ask for a formal statement? Hearsay evidence. Not yet: perhaps never. He thanked
the priest again, listened to a few more mild ramblings about Domokous, and saw him out politely.

Nada absolutamente, damn it. He refused to believe that Skyros or
anybody else had committed murder—and a fairly elaborate murder, at
that—to prevent that amiable, honest young man from repeating that
vague little story. It didn't mean enough. The obvious conclusion, if
you were determined to make it murder, was that if Domokous had
been killed over that business, he'd found out more about it, enough to
be dangerous. The priest had told him, do nothing unless you are sure
of wrongdoing. Had Domokous, perhaps, gone looking for something
more to say yes or no? And, to his misfortune, found it?"

TEN

Mendoza let all that simmer gently in his mind overnight—not much else he could do. It looked very much as if this was going to be one of those cases where there'd never be the evidence to bring anyone to book, even if he found the answer to the problem. The kind of thing where you were pretty sure there'd been funny business of some sort, but couldn't prove it. Of course, there was some gain: *if* Domokous had died because he was a little too honest, he had managed to call attention to Skyros and (if she had anything to do with it at all) Madame Bouvardier, and Callaghan at least would be taking a look at Skyros.

Once in a while you got something like that—the kind of thing Pat ran into more—no legal evidence available. And sometimes, a while later something else happened and you could say, Ah, so that's what was behind it—but ten to one no evidence forthcoming then—just the satisfaction of knowing for sure.

Insurance, he reflected. Mixed up in it somehow?—by the bits and pieces he had. A *nymph* and a *dolphin*—*¡oye, qué va!*—some precious shipment of imports? And what had the County Museum to do with it?

However, something useful might be got out of that fellow Driscoll. Citizens' duty to aid the police when requested.

He had no chance the next morning to do anything about that; he'd only get to his office when his inside phone rang.

"Returning favors," said Callaghan. "Fair exchange."

"What, have you got something already?"

"A kind of interesting little bit that might be more for you than me. My man took over Skyros from yours about four o'clock yesterday. De La Torres—very good man, nose like a bloodhound. Well, Skyros stayed late at his office, and along about seven o'clock he had a visitor. At the back door, and as it happened De La Torres was halfway down the delivery-entrance alley and it wasn't dark yet, daylight saving still being with us, and he had a look at him as the fellow went in. Door left unlocked for him, all very hospitable. And De La Torres recognized him, so he slipped up to the corner drugstore—taking a chance on losin' 'em both, but sometimes you've got to take chances—and put in a call for somebody to take on the guy when he left, if possible."

"And who was he and why did De La Torres know him?"

"Believe it or not his name's Prettyman. He isn't, very. We picked him up about three years ago for unlawful possession, that was before they put in the stiffer sentences, and he only got sixty days. No other record on him. But as it happened, De La Torres was the man picked him up, you see. And to anticipate you, there's no more evidence on him now, for all I know he's reformed and maybe Skyros is an innocent personal friend he's met since and he goes to see him privately at his office to chat about chess problems or the weather. Off the record, thanks very much for Skyros—I really think you got something there. We'll continue to look into it. Well, the office sent out Farr to join De La Torres, and when Prettyman came out—which was about half an hour later—Farr took him on. He drove down to Main and went into a bar there—Anselmo's—not a very hot reputation, been closed down a couple of times for serving juveniles and and getting caught with unlicensed stuff. In Farr goes after him, having his teeth in it by then, and Prettyman had teamed up with another fellow at a table. They stayed there awhile, and Prettyman was calling the other guy Denny. Farr got as close as he could, but there was a lot of noise in the place, as usual, and he just got snatches of what they said. Until in about half an hour they started out together. Neither of 'em was drunk, he says, just high, at the backslapping all-buddies-together stage."

"Has this story got a tag-line?"

"Wait for it, I'm getting there. Farr ambles out after 'em, and when they get to Prettyman's car round the corner—darker side street—he gets close enough to listen. And they're talking about Keats—"

"Now look," said Mendoza, "I've got no time to listen to interminable accounts of the funny dream you had last night. Tell your wife, she has to put up with being bored."

"Will you *wait* for it, damn it! I don't mean Keats who wrote poetry, I mean—or I think *they* meant—one Walter William Keats who's a burglar. At least, most of the time he is, he did a three-to-five stretch for it awhile ago, but he's also been picked up for armed robbery and assault. This I got from Burglary and Theft, I'd never heard of him myself, but what they call the context kind of led both Farr and me to guess what his lay is. Prettyman and Denny, whoever *he* is, were talking about Keats' bad luck, getting in bad with the best fence in town, and—

I'm coming to it now, you can start listening—Denny said, maybe he oughta try Frank's old boss, the Greek, *he* was kinda getting into that business himself. And Prettyman said, *Yeah,* was *that* so? And then—"

"The Greek. Same one Prettyman had just been visiting?"

"For what it's worth, Farr—who didn't know any of this background —said he sort of got the impression Prettyman was surprised and wanted to ask questions, but this Denny started in talking about something else and he didn't have a chance then."

"Mmh. Every time I acquire a little more suggestive information about this thing," said Mendoza, "it just makes it more complicated. Do I unravel this hearsay evidence right, that Denny was implying the Greek was turning fence? *Skyros?*"

"Maybe. And I haven't finished. Then Denny—who was a little higher than Prettyman—said, let's go see Amy, nice girl, Amy, and maybe take a bottle along. And Prettyman said Amy didn't go much for guys in his line of work, and Denny said, sure, she wouldn't mind, look at Angie, she liked *him* all right, didn't she? It was just, *you* know, Frank had been in it when he got his and it kinda reminded her, but Amy was O.K."

"Wait a minute, let me get this down. . . . Yes?"

"You've almost got it. Finally they spotted Farr and he had to go on past to his own car. In a minute they both climbed into Prettyman's, and went on down Main to Daggett Street. Ended up at 341. Farr put all this down in his notes while he sat outside. After awhile Prettyman came out alone and took himself down to a joint called the Elite at Daggett and San Pedro. I may add that this joint we're looking at lately, because a user we picked up last week let out that he'd been told you could get a fix there. And a while after that Prettyman went home, which is a cheap room in a Main Street hotel."

"Well, well," said Mendoza. "This is a little something to think about, isn't it? But what a funny combination—burglary and dope— and what lay do you suppose this Denny's on, fraud or something? Unless it's one of those masterminded crime rings, as per the detective stories of thirty years back, all this rigmarole doesn't make any sense at all."

"I can't help that, I'm just giving it to you as it came in. On account of your corpse. You said maybe the corpse knew something about Skyros, and likelier something about some crooked work in his regular business than any outside deal—but this seems to indicate that there might *be* some kind of outside business. Something funny, anyway. If he is the Greek."

"I don't deny it. What about 341 Daggett—pro house?"

"If it is, Vice doesn't know it. Aside from that I know nothing about Amy. How much do you want? I only had this thrown at me half an hour ago."

"I appreciate your good intentions," said Mendoza. "All you've succeeded in doing is arousing my curiosity to fever pitch. I really think I'll have to look into this myself—I couldn't explain to anybody just what to investigate. Thanks very much, I'll let you know if anything comes of it."

"Always happy to co-operate," said Callaghan.

Mendoza looked at his scribbled notes while he finished his cigarette, and then got up and reached for his hat. He had, he supposed, no business wasting time over such vague clues, on such a nebulous affair; but if he'd admit it to himself, he always hated to delegate authority. Now and then it made a little change, a little interest, to get out on the street again, at the core of a case, doing the work a sergeant or his underlings usually did, while the lieutenant waited to have all the loose ends handed him for tying up into neat knots. He might just begin the cast here, anyway.

Daggett Street, he thought. Twenty-three years ago he had lived on Daggett Street, down there the wrong side of Main. . . .

Hackett came in late because yesterday had been his sister's birthday; he'd had to go out there for dinner and it was quite a little drive back and forth, clear out to Arcadia; he hadn't got in until after midnight, and had overslept.

Sergeant Lake told him Mendoza had been in and gone out again, leaving a note for him. The note said, *"Inmediatamente,* contact Driscoll and find out what his interest is in Skyros." Hackett felt unreasonably exasperated; that was Luis for you, go on worrying at some insignificant little thing like this, like a dog with a meatless bone. There wasn't anything *in* this Domokous business.

But he dutifully called Driscoll's hotel, which he knew from the tail on him. Driscoll was out. Hackett left a request for him to call when he came in, and looked over the tail's report on him in desultory interest.

Mendoza had sized Driscoll up all right: the saga of his wanderings in the last thirty-six hours sounded remarkably like one of those pieces of fiction in which the emphasis was on pace rather than plausibility.

He had visited the local office of his company on Wednesday morning, when his tail was first attached; had, as the tail reported laconically, drunk lunch at a nearby bar, and then driven out to the County Museum in Exposition Park. He hadn't stayed there long, but gone on out Wilshire to the Beverly-Hilton. Stayed there about half an hour, come out, driven back to Hollywood and gone to another bar, where he made a phone call which, the tail deduced by the fact that he'd got a ten-dollar bill changed into quarters first, was a long-distance one. He had then had dinner and taken himself to what the tail reported was a damned stale burlesque show down on Main. Came out about nine-thirty ("thank God," the tail appended, "enough to put a man off women for life") and sought out another bar. Subsequently the tail had had to load him into a taxi—perfectly safe, as he had already passed out—and send him back to his hotel. On Thursday, not unexpectedly, he had stayed in all morning: emerged about one o'clock, looking about as you'd expect, and had again driven out to the County Museum. This time he stayed a couple of hours, and from there went to the Times-Mirror Building and stayed another couple of hours. The tail had been unable to track close enough to find out where he'd gone inside. He came out about six o'clock and had a sandwich and several drinks at still another bar. And then he went back to Hollywood to a much-vaunted live-revue theater.

Bound to enjoy himself if it kills him, deduced Hackett. The night tail reported in just as he finished reading, and said Driscoll hadn't shown before the day man came on, but he'd been middling high when he came in last night and maybe was nursing another little hangover.

Yesterday afternoon Mendoza had decided to put a tail on the exotic brunette, and since Callaghan had taken over Skyros, Hackett had transferred Dwyer, Reade, and Higgins to her. Higgins' report, up to midnight, was here. Madame Bouvardier had dined at her hotel, and had then been driven up to Hollywood by her hired chauffeur to an address near Silver Lake. She hadn't stayed there long, only half an hour or so, then returned to the hotel.

And what was there in all that? Exactly nothing. If Driscoll's movements said anything, they said he didn't seem inordinately interested in Mr. Skyros. And as for the woman—well! Jewelers, hairdressers, the hotel dining room, and probably some acquaintance in a good residential district—kind of thing you'd expect.

Nymphs and dolphins, thought Hackett. Once in a while one of Mendoza's hunches paid off, but a lot of them were duds too, and this looked like one of those all right.

About then Dwyer came in to report, on his way home; he said Hackett might have given him a break, and let him see something of this dame, on day duty—it wasn't, after all, often that a respectable married man had the chance to follow a skirt like that all over town on his legitimate job. As it was, she'd already been in her suite when he took over from Higgins, and he'd only had a brief look at her this morning before Reade showed up.

"Still in the hotel?"

"Was when I left. I kind of wandered in after the place woke up a little, you know, and around on that floor. About nine o'clock, just when I was expecting Reade, the door opened and out came the maid. It's the damndest thing," said Dwyer, yawning, "I don't figure they teach you right—I don't know—I took two years of French in high school, but they might as well have been talking Chinese, for all I could get of it. Except 'cabriolet'—maybe she was telling the maid to take a taxi, I don't know. Seemed to be sending her on some errand, anyway, by all the gestures—and you shoulda seen the bathrobe, Sergeant, or I guess that wouldn't hardly be the name for it—"

"Negligée," suggested Hackett.

"Or even something fancier. Pink, and a lot of lace. I guess the maid didn't like the idea of going, nervous about a strange town and all, they seemed to be having quite a little argument and the dame said an address over three-four times, finally wrote it down for her."

"All this was with the door open, or were you hiding in the bathroom?"

"Around the corner in the hall, sure, the door was open—like I say I didn't get any of the talk but it looked to me maybe the maid got cold feet at the last minute, you know, tried to back out. Anyway, finally she went off, and by that time Reade was there, he heard some of it too." Dwyer yawned again and produced a slip of paper. "I wrote down the address the dame said."

"O.K.," said Hackett, and Dwyer went off. The address didn't say anything to Hackett: just an address, in Hollywood somewhere, he thought. But as long as Mendoza was so set on looking at every little whipstitch . . . He called Driscoll's hotel again; Driscoll was still out. Probably wandering around the County Museum again, thought Hackett: or no, it wasn't open in the morning; he was probably at a bar. Oh, well.

He looked at a map, went downstairs and got his car, and drove up to Hollywood. It wasn't a classy street, and it wasn't by any means a slum street: just an ordinary run-of-the-mill district, and mostly lined— along this block—with middle-aged apartment buildings. The name of the one he wanted, as near as Dwyer had been able to transcribe it, was the Blon-shair Arms. There wasn't one by that name, but there was, in the middle of the block, a Blanchard Arms, and he deduced that was it. Apartment 406. He went around the block hunting a parking space, finally found one, walked back, went into the lobby and examined the rows of locked mailboxes with their little hand-written name slots.

And then he said aloud, "I *will* be damned! I will be *damned!*" What the hell was this?

The name on the box marked 406 was *Miss Alison Weir.*

Hackett straightened and stared at the blank wall opposite, feeling as confused as he'd ever felt in his life. Alison Weir?—what did she have to do with the elegant, expensive visiting Parisian at the Beverly-Hilton? Who also knew Mr. Andreas Skyros, employer of Stevan Domokous? It didn't make any sense. But there it was: Madame Bouvardier had known her address. Why?

Hackett debated looking up the address of her school and going to ask her; but on second thought reflected that it might really be said to be Mendoza's job.

He drove back downtown, and fidgeted around the office waiting for Mendoza to come in. No, Sergeant Lake said, he hadn't said where he was going. Nor when he might be expected back. He wouldn't be in the building because he'd taken his hat.

Where the hell had he gone? Hackett had a feeling he ought to know about this right away: and yet, what could it mean? He couldn't settle to any routine work; every time the phone rang he jumped at it.

But it was nearly noon before Mendoza called in. Hackett, belatedly wondering how he'd take it, relayed the extraordinary news. There was a moment's silence at the other end of the wire, and then Mendoza said, "*¡Qué demonio!—¡aguarda un momento!*—I wonder! By God, I wonder! Listen, Art—you there?"

"I'm still here."

"*Por Dios,* it'd be an incredible coincidence—or would it?—coincidences do happen, after all, and surprisingly often too. Listen, call down to Traffic and get hold of a Sergeant Rhodes. I want to ask him some questions. What time is it? . . . Look, bring him to lunch with us. I haven't got the car, come and pick me up, will you?—I'm at the corner of Daggett and San Pedro, the drugstore. O.K.?"

"Well, O.K.," said Hackett, and started to ask what he was doing down there, but Mendoza had rung off.

So he called down to Traffic and got hold of Rhodes. It had been some time since he'd had anything to do with Traffic, and for a few minutes he thought they must be scraping the bottom of the barrel all right these days, because Rhodes couldn't seem to take in what he was saying. "L-lunch? L-Lieutenant Mendoza?" he kept stuttering, and then apparently pulled himself together and said, "Oh, yes, sir, *yes,* sir, of course, I'll meet you at the front door in five minutes, sir—" And was off the phone before Hackett could remind him he was just talking to another sergeant.

ELEVEN

Mendoza had rather enjoyed himself that morning. In all the places he'd be going, the Facel-Vega would earn him too much attention, and he'd walked from headquarters down Main, out of the Civic Center. It wasn't often he had occasion to be on foot down here. Wasting time with a vengeance in a way, he thought as he turned into Daggett Street; but he didn't feel guilty at all.

Daggett Street hadn't changed much in twenty-three years, he'd noticed recently driving down it. Walking, he thought the cracks in the sidewalk might be the same. Different faces, that was all. He enjoyed the walk. Along here, you turned to look at anyone speaking English; these couple of blocks were all business, and the store-front signs said *Comestibles abarrotes, Ropas de Mujeres, Zapatos, Vino y licores,* and also, *¡Gangas! Venga Ud. y mire!—¡Venta por quiebra!* Always *bargains,* always *bankrupt sales.* . . . And the old and the new cheek by jowl: the old ones in rusty black, sometimes ankle-length: the young ones in the same bright this-year's fashions in the shops uptown.

In the middle of the third block he looked across at the sagging old frame apartment, wondered if Mrs. Gonzales still owned it; such very good *torrijas* she had made, and always one to spare for a hungry boy:

she'd had a son in medical college. . . . *"Los años, se pasan rapida-mente,"* he muttered ruefully to himself.

Then it changed, the street: signs in English, and presently an even frowsier look, something about the houses, the business blocks, not only shabby, but furtive and stagnant. Rooming houses, cheap hotels, bars, pool halls. And here was 341. Once a single-family house, with the third storey for servants: now bearing a sign, *Rooms Cheap,* but the fancy fretwork round every inch of eaves and porch was good as new.

He didn't think this place would be too particular, either about strange males calling on the female residents or about names; he smiled persuasively at the dispirited-looking woman who opened the door and asked simply, "Which room'll I find Amy?"

He was right; she never asked a question, but said, "Second floor, left front," and went clumping away down the hall without a back look.

So he climbed up to the second floor, knocked, and was rewarded with the sight of Amy in negligée—an affair of pink chiffon, not too clean, showing glimpses of a dancer's blue-mottled legs. The remains of last night's make-up were also visible as well as a dark parting in the silver-flax hair, and the burgundy-colored nail polish was chipped and ragged. She leaned on the doorpost and said coldly, "Yeah?"

Mendoza gave her a hopeful leer and said, "I'm looking for a couple of guys, and I been told they're friends of yours. Angie and Denny. You know where I could find either of 'em?"

Her expression didn't change. "Sorry, mister, never heard of 'em."

"Oh, yes, you did," said Mendoza. "Look, I got a favor to do this Angie, see. You do him a good turn, tell me where I can contact him."

"Is that so?" said Amy. "Well, that's just too bad, because I still don't know. And I don't like your looks much, mister." She stepped back inside the room and slammed the door.

Mendoza sighed and went back downstairs to the street. Nothing there, except the implied fact that the woman knew what kind of business those two were in—whatever it was and whoever they were—and that it was on the wrong side of the fence, whether she was personally mixed up in it or not. And, now he came to think, he should have stopped at that Anselmo's bar first; it was on the way here and now he'd have to go back.

He walked back to Main and found Anselmo's. A hole in the wall, dirty, ancient, and cheap. He wondered if the liquor was safe, but went in and ordered rye. It was raw, but well-diluted—what pro slang called baptized. The bartender, sole occupant of the place at this hour, was a hairy young fellow running to paunch already and with a pair of shifty eyes. Nice if generalizations were all true, thought Mendoza: most crooks had exceptionally honest faces, and most bartenders, honest or not, developed the shifty eyes from continual watching of customers.

"I'm looking," he said, "for a fellow named Angie. Know him? I got the word he comes in here sometimes."

"That so?" said the bartender. "Couldn't say. What you want him for?"

Yes; Angie definitely a wrong one, if his friends and/or acquaintances were so chary of admitting they knew his whereabouts. But did this fellow know him, or was he just cagy by nature? "Well, I might have a little job for him," said Mendoza at random. "Kind of a better deal than he's got now."

"Is that so?" said the bartender without batting an eye. "Well, you don't know his last name, can't help you, mister—couple of Angies come in here, now 'n' then. Couldn't say at all."

Mendoza left the rest of his drink and came out. The hell with it, he said to himself; anything you got on a wild hunt like this, you got with infinite patience. A man, several men, watching and waiting around corners sometimes for weeks before the one little word was dropped that told you something. It was time to turn this over to one of Hackett's men and get back to his office where he belonged.

Instead, he walked back up Daggett to San Pedro and found the Elite, which added to its name the misnomer of Club.

Inside, it was a small square place with a minute platform at one end for a band, now holding only a battered upright piano. Someone, a long time ago, had decorated it ambitiously with black lacquered tables and chairs, a home-carpentered banquette along one wall, and dime store decals on the wainscoting, an Oriental motif. Opposite the banquette was the bar: at the bar the bartender, two men standing; five others sat at one table over a hand of poker, monosyllabic.

Mendoza went up and leaned on the bar, leaving his hat on in deference to local custom. "Straight rye." It was surprisingly good quality; he told the bartender so. This was a bald middle-aged fat man who nodded shortly at the compliment without a word. Mendoza looked the other customers over casually.

Next to him at the bar, a big bruiser in a green nylon shirt and black slacks; just missed being handsome, in a saturnine rugged way: about forty. A smaller, older man, dark, needed a shave, lank black hair falling over one eye. At the table, the dealer was cadaverous, bushy-haired, young; the edge, a flashily dressed, very clean and pleasant-looking twenty-year-old; two of the others nondescript men in their thirties, who looked disconcertingly like respectable citizens—one in brown slacks, one in gray. And the fifth man was a pale brown Negro with the regular, handsome features of the West Indian, a soft British accent.

Mendoza half turned back to the bartender. "By the way, I'm looking for Angie. Where's he hanging out these days?"

Green Shirt glanced sideways at him; Bushy Hair hesitated the fraction of a second in picking up a card. The bartender might have been carved out of wood for all the expression he showed. "Sorry, mister, never heard of him." He turned away to answer the phone.

Mendoza finished his rye and came out. A wasted morning. But maybe some discreet looking around this place, and Anselmo's, and at Amy, might turn up something interesting eventually. Piggott, he decided. It was surprising how like a small-time pro Piggott could look and act, for a pillar of the Free Methodist Church and a cop with a spotless record. Let him mix with the crowd in here, and at Anselmo's, for a few nights.

He was tired and hot, and he'd begun to want his lunch. He went into the drugstore next to the Elite and called his office; and what Hackett had to tell him effectively took his mind off food. . . . Now what the hell was the connection here? That woman—*Lydia?* That Bouvardier female out at the Beverly-Hilton? Could it be, it must be, the theft of the car: it had to be, the only possible thing. Find out what there was to find out about the car, obviously. He told Hackett to get hold of Rhodes.

Leaving the phone, he realized what a scorcher of a day it was: must be up around a hundred and ten. And these squalid streets, these old buildings, airless and fetid. There was a fan turning above the door, but it only stirred the stale air. However, hotter out on the corner in the sun. He was out of cigarettes, and bought a pack from the rat-faced druggist, opened it and lit one, drifted over to join a couple of women looking at the magazines. But he didn't see them very clearly; his mind was working furiously at this new, curious feature of what he wasn't too sure he could call a case. . . . He looked up automatically when the door opened, though it was too soon to expect Hackett—

Green Shirt and Bushy Hair came in together, spotted him and looked pleased. Gray Slacks and Brown Slacks, behind them, collected the two women and trundled them out to the street. "This store's closed, ladies, come back some other time."

"Hey," said the druggist weakly, "I ain't either closed—"

"You are now," said Green Shirt, and slammed the door, locked it, and pulled down the shade. "Get in the back room, buster, and you didn't see or hear nothin' or nobody."

The druggist looked at him, licked his lips and backed away. "That's right, I didn't," he said. "I sure as hell didn't." He vanished into the rear of the store.

"Castro must be feelin' his oats, friend," said Bushy Hair to Mendoza, "send his errand boys round in broad daylight. Anyways, he sure looks like one o' Castro's boys, don't he?—cute li'l moustache an' all. This ain't healthy territory for you, friend. Castro oughta know that. Castro ain't took over from Pretty yet, or leastways he hadn't when we all went to bed las' night, an' I don't guess it'd happen without us knowing, hah, boys? He oughta send a bodyguard along with you anyways, if he wants you back any shape to do business for a while. Maybe he wants t' get ride of you, though, sendin' you out alone over here, askin' for Pretty's best boy to offer him another job? Kinda a shame, you so innocent 'n' all—nice li'l gennelman like you—and *ain't* he a fancy-dressed one, boys?"

"Real sharp," said Green Shirt, grinning.

"Pore fella," said Bushy Hair, poking a bony finger into Mendoza's chest.

Mendoza had the depressing suspicion that this was one of the occasions when he would wish he habitually carried a gun. *Entre la espada y la pared,* he thought in exasperation, between the sword and the wall! —haul out his I.D. card, fine—they didn't like cops any better than who they thought he was, but more important, he had no intention of letting it be known that a cop was asking around for Angie—whoever Angie was. ("Pretty's best boy"—well, well.) In that case, Piggott and every one of the rest of Mendoza's men could go on looking from now till Christmas: no Angie.

He smiled at Green Shirt and said, "Castro? Afraid I don't know him, you must have me mixed up with someody else." There was, of course, Hackett—and Rhodes—on the way, and not very far to come, a matter of blocks.

"Oh, boy, he's a fancy talker too," said Gray Slacks admiringly.

"He sure don't belong in this crummy neighborhood," agreed Brown Slacks.

"But we don't want to send him back to his boss," said Green Shirt, "without a little something to show what we think of him—do we, boys?" He produced a short weighted sap from an inside pocket and tested it thoughtfully on his palm.

"Oh, we sure as hell wouldn't want to do that," said Bushy Hair, and by legerdemain there was a flat black thing in his hand: a little click, and the switchblade shot out long and wicked.

Mendoza was alarmed by the thought that he must be getting old, to slip up on a thing like this. That phone call at the Elite bar had been the hairy fellow at Anselmo's, of course—or just possibly Amy. He'd been thinking too hard about Angie and Denny, and all the rest of this thing—too damned single-minded, that was always his trouble. He also remembered bitterly that he was wearing a new suit. But these things happened. He dropped his cigarette, gave Green Shirt a very nervous smile, and backed away; he said, "Now listen, mister, I haven't done anything—"

They were pleased, as this kind always was, to find the victim timid and fearful. They began to close in on him and he backed another few steps, brought up against a counter, and with his hands behind him felt around cautiously: cards of something, combs, and—ah—a large bottle. "You got me all wrong," he said.

"We got him all wrong, boys," said Brown Slacks. "Ain't that a shame!" He reached out, clicking open another blade, and took hold of Mendoza's tie. "I seem to remember I forgot to sharpen this, and me, I'm fussy about that, I don't like no dull knives—let's just see," and he sliced off a clean strip of the tie halfway up.

Brown Slacks didn't know it, but the tie was a Paris import and had cost twelve dollars two months ago. Mendoza was considerably annoyed: so annoyed that he forgot all about using delaying tactics until he should see Hackett's black sedan slide past the window, or Hackett's shadow on the shade, trying the door.

He said gently to Brown Slacks, "Now *that* you shouldn't have done, you bastard," and just on the chance, before beginning operations, he fired the bottle in his hand accurately at the big front window. It went through with a satisfactorily loud crash, but by then he was too busy to notice.

Brown Slacks, closest to him, was taken sufficiently by surprise to leave himself open, and Mendoza made a little room by a solid right to his mouth, staggering him back into a glass case. Bushy Hair came up in a hurry, knife straight out and low, but he came at such a convenient angle—possibly he had a higher-class background than Daggett Street and didn't expect it—that he walked smack into a nicely-timed kick in the groin, and went down flat on his back and dropped the knife. Mendoza dived after it and was helped on his way by Green Shirt falling on him from behind; he twisted away from the sap, heard it thud on the floor, missed the knife, rolled over and took the second blow of the sap glancingly on the temple. He heaved off Green Shirt desperately, staggered up on his feet again, and dodged as Gray Slacks swung at him.

He had no illusions about taking all four; all he wanted was to clear them out of the way to the door. There was a saying very apropos— *Más vale qué digan, Aquí corrió, y no, aquí murió*— Better they say, he ran here, and not, he died here.

He took a nasty slash on the arm from Gray Slacks' knife; Brown Slacks was picking himself up from the shattered case, swearing, and Mendoza kicked him down again, simultaneously dodging Green Shirt's vicious swing of the sap. Bushy Hair, groaning steadily and clutching his stomach, sat up obligingly just in time to trip Green Shirt, who fell into Mendoza's left hard enough to make him think something was broken, and sprawled flat—but he was up again, and coming back for more. Mendoza heard the door rattle and Hackett's voice outside—the Marines had landed. He shouted, "In, Art!" and saw Gray Slacks' knife slashing up for his stomach with a practised wrist-motion. He lunged for the wrist and got the blade first; it sliced deep across the ball of his thumb and palm, but a second later he had the arm in both hands, brought his knee up for leverage, leaned on it and heard the arm-bone snap.

As the man yelled, the door-panel smashed open and Hackett came in like a big bull, head down. He took in the situation as he came, and fell on top of Green Shirt, who was coming up behind Mendoza, and put him out of commission with the butt of his gun. Rhodes followed in time to collide with a blind swing from Brown Slacks, just up again; he let out a bellow of surprise and knocked Brown Slacks into the third glass case and unconsciousness.

Mendoza sat down on the end fountain-stool and wrapped his handkerchief round his left hand. "Very nice timing, Art," he said rather breathlessly.

Hackett put his gun away, looked at the havoc, and asked, "Is that an artery?"

"No, but it might as well be, the damage it's— I couldn't get to it right away. *¡Válgame Dios!* look at this suit! Three hundred bucks a month ago!"

"What the hell goes on here?" asked Rhodes, bewildered. "What—

suit? Lieutenant—" But training held; he didn't wait for an answer, went back to the door to stand off the crowd collecting, while Hackett found the phone and put in a call for a patrol car and an ambulance.

While they waited, he came and added his handkerchief to Mendoza's. "One of these days, my latter-day *conquistador,* you're goin' to do this just once too often—tackle a gang armed with switchblades and knuckle-dusters without so much as a cap pistol on you. And why I should do any worrying about it, the good God above knows, because it's probably the only way I'll ever get to be a lieutenant."

"*¡Quiá, imbécil!* You don't think this was my idea, do you? You think I took on four at once so everybody can say, That Mendoza, *¡qué hombre!*—a lion-eater! All I wanted was out, boy, but they were between me and the door, so it was *por malas o por buenas*—no choice." He struggled out of his jacket and cursed, feeling the slash in the sleeve. Most of that sleeve and a good deal of the front panel was generously bloodstained, and the other sleeve half out of the shoulder seam. "Three hundred bucks," he said bitterly, "and twelve for the tie!"

"My God in heaven," said Hackett, and went to meet the precinct men arriving.

TWELVE

The druggist sidled out of the back room and gazed mournfully at the wreckage, and Mendoza, who'd followed Hackett to the door, said in an urgent undertone, "Arrest me, Art—take me out all official-looking, nobody here must know who I am."

"Games, yet," said Hackett, grabbed him by one arm, and shoved him out. Mendoza sat in the ambulance while the interns bandaged him temporarily, refusing to go along to the General for stitches in his hand immediately; he'd have it seen to sometime today. He was publicly pushed into the back of Hackett's car.

"Tell the precinct sergeant somebody'll be down to give him details on this. Don't be a fool, I'm not much damaged, I'll see a doctor after lunch, and lunch I've earned." He looked at Rhodes, peering at him from the front seat still wearing a faintly astonished expression, and added, "And we've things to talk over. Let's be on our way, Arturo. Though how the hell I can go into a—oh, well, they know me at Federico's, and it's a hot day."

The head waiter, however, looked very surprised to see him with no jacket, no necktie, collar unbuttoned; and still more surprised when Mendoza demanded a drink before lunch. "I'm going to wash, I'm filthy—don't sit down, Art, go and call Pat Callaghan and brief him on this. Those four, I think, are more his business than mine, and he'll want to see them. He's the one sent me down there in the first place."

"That I want to hear about. I thought Callaghan was a friend of yours."

"He didn't know I'm getting senile," said Mendoza, "to walk into a thing like that—like a fool I had my mind on something else. And probably nothing to show for it but the wear and tear. —And get me an aspirin somewhere, that sap connected once and I've got a headache."

"What were you doing down there without a gun, Lieutenant?" asked Rhodes. "I mean, I'd think—"

"Oh, his tailor won't let him pack a gun," explained Hackett. "It spoils that nice shoulder-line, you know."

"That little joke I'm tired of. *¡Zape!* Go and call Pat!"

"I'm going, I'm going."

"You mean you never—why, that's asking for trouble, Lieutenant," said Rhodes earnestly. "Why, anyway?"

"Oh, I don't like loud bangs, they make me nervous," said Mendoza irritably, and vanished to seek soap and water.

Hackett joined Rhodes at a table before Mendoza reappeared. Rhodes, who was a big fair farmery-looking young man, still wore a bewildered expression. "I never heard that one," he said to Hackett. "About his not packing a gun. I mean, Landers—"

"You know Landers?"

"Yes, sure, and he—you know, talks about Lieutenant Mendoza sometimes, but he never mentioned that. Why doesn't he, anyway?"

"I'll tell you," said Hackett, and broke off to demand coffee and offer Rhodes a cigarette, "he's got this crazy idea, police exist to prevent violence and we ought to set an example. He says sure, out on patrol, anywhere you're apt to be in danger unarmed, O.K., but anything you got handy you're going to use when maybe it isn't strictly necessary. And a lot of perfectly good honest cops are still a little too quick on the trigger, if they've got it there six inches from their hand. He liked Wes

Rich, thought he was a smart boy, but he got him broke from sergeant last year after Rich shot that Prince kid—remember the one killed his uncle because the uncle used to get drunk and beat up his wife and the kid? Prince tried to run on the way to the station, and Rich shot him. Sure, he didn't aim to kill, but it isn't exactly like target-shooting for a score, is it? Luis said he needed another little spell as an errand boy to think it over."

"Well, my God," said Rhodes, "but it's not common sense to walk into the tiger cage without a whip and a kitchen chair."

"How right you are," said Hackett. "That Luis doesn't say. Just that it's a good idea to try other methods first, and if you never move a step without the whip, you never have to think of any other way of doing it."

"I see," said Rhodes thoughtfully.

Mendoza came up, looking slightly more presentable, looked at the rye the waiter had left for him and said, "I shouldn't have that, I've had two drinks already this morning—unprecedented, and you know what it does to me."

"I guess you've had enough of a workout already you won't be spoiling for another fight in the next half hour," said Hackett. "Live dangerously for once, drink it."

Mendoza did, said, "Ah, coffee, that's better. Did you get me some aspirin?"

Hackett gave him one and said Callaghan extended sympathy but was pleased to hear some of those boys from the Elite could be arrested for something, even common assault. He'd go right down to look them over, *and* their places of residence, and it might just be they could eventually be charged with something more, which would be very useful.

"They won't be charged with assaulting me, not by name anyway," said Mendoza. "I'm not appearing in this round. If there *is* any connection with this Domokous thing I don't want them to know I know it. Not that I know much, and God knows that."

"I want to hear about this little adventure. What took you down there?"

"Take too long to tell—it's very complicated: briefly, I got some names from Pat, I went to do some sniffing around myself, and while I had my mind on the names I inadvertently gave these boys the impression I was doing something else they didn't like . . . yes, suggestive in a way, and I want to hear what Pat thinks. But meantime—" He told the waiter to bring him anything edible and more coffee *inmediatamente*. "Rhodes—this *is* Sergeant Rhodes? What with one thing and another we don't seem to have been introduced—"

"Yes, sir, I'm Rhodes."

"I must be losing my grip, come to think—you couldn't answer questions without your records, I don't suppose you remember much about it offhand. Car theft. Miss Alison Weir, a week ago last Sunday, and you found the car and returned it a week ago yesterday."

"Miss Weir—oh, yes, sir, I do remember. I mean, I'd better explain, I know Landers in your office, you see, and he—that is—Miss Weir's a friend of yours, isn't she, and I happened to notice the name—"

"I see," said Mendoza. "And they say women are the gossips. Well, I want to hear everything you know about that business. Pretend I don't know anything about it—I don't, much—and give me all you remember, we can check your records later."

"Well," said Rhodes blankly. "Well, it was kind of an ordinary thing, Lieutenant. Probably kids—you know how much of that sort of thing we get. The car was pinched from Exposition Park that Sunday afternoon, I heard later Miss Weir and a friend of hers'd been to some art show at the County Museum—"

"*¡Quiá!* Now that I'd forgotten, if I ever heard it. The County Museum—what the hell has it got to do with this? A dignified, dreary spot like that—"

"Oh, I don't know, I kind of like museums," said Hackett. "But don't look at me for the answer. This much I'll contribute—Driscoll has gone there twice in the last two days. I don't know why, the tail was too far behind and lost him inside."

Mendoza laid down his fork and put a hand to his temple. "I'm in no condition to be given shocks, Arturo. And I'll never, by God, make any more jokes about implausibly complicated detective fiction. I wonder what kind of exhibitions they've got on at the moment. Anything in the nature of nymphs and dolphins?"

"You've let nymphs and dolphins seduce you away from any solid facts in this thing—the few we've got," said Hackett. "I don't think they've got a damn thing to do with it."

"I won't argue, I'm out of ammunition. Go on, Rhodes. What time and where from, exactly?"

Rhodes, who had stopped eating to follow this exchange with a furrowed brow, said, "What? Oh, the car—why, it was early afternoon when Miss Weir left it, I seem to remember—and I think the call to the

precinct went through about five o'clock. You know those little narrow
winding streets all round the park buildings—it was somewhere along
the one goes in front of the main museum building, a block or so down.
I figured it afterward, Sunday, you know, a public park with no admission fee—it was probably some teen-agers, just decided to take a joy
ride. You get an awful lot of that. I don't know what you think, sir, but
I put it down to people not being at home with their kids more, and
maybe some of this progressive education. Because a lot of 'em we pick
up, they're not what you'd call delinquents—it's just, my God, they
don't seem to know any better, don't see any reason at all why they
shouldn't take anything sitting around loose, if they've got a yen for it
at the moment. You know? And what with the big areas public schools
take in, there's bound to be a few real delinquents in a lot of them, and
quite a few kids from ordinary respectable homes pick up little tricks,
like how to do without an ignition key."

"Yes, all that I grant you. But most kids, this sort or that, go for
something new and classy."

"Well, not always," said Rhodes. "Some of 'em who go in for drag-
racing— But most of what we get from kids is just picking up anything
handy to ride around in a few hours. Another thing that comes into it is
taking a dare. My God, these kids!—it makes you wonder. I mean, one
of 'em says, Bet you haven't got the nerve to swipe a car, and the other
one's ashamed to chicken out. And mind you, both of 'em might be
from respectable homes, raised to know better."

"Also true," said Mendoza patiently, "but evidently whoever took
Miss Weir's car kept it longer than a couple of hours. Where and when
did it turn up?"

"I don't remember the exact address, sir, but it's in the records. It
was that Thursday, about noon, around there—a fellow called the local
precinct to report this car'd been sitting out in front of his house almost
two days. So the boys went and checked, and of course it was on the
hot list so they brought it into the headquarters garage. It was a new
tract street somewhere out in Compton, I think, and the fellow said
he'd first noticed it when he left for work on Wednesday morning,
early."

"Mmh. Abandoned there late Tuesday night. Did your boys go over
it?"

"Well, sure," said Rhodes. "The way we usually do, you know—I
mean, we didn't tear it apart looking, it's run-of-the-mill, stuff like that.
We looked for prints on the wheel and so on, in case we could match

them up to somebody in Records. I seem to remember that everything a driver'd touch had been wiped clean."

"Which does not," said Mendoza, "look like a bunch of kids out for a joy ride."

"Well, I guess not," admitted Rhodes. "But a pro—I mean, there isn't anything *in* hopping shorts unless you keep them, fake up new plates and so on, and sell them. We get a certain amount of that, of course. But a thing like this—car used a little while and then abandoned—it's practically always kids."

"Unless it's a getaway of some kind," said Mendoza. "Somebody on the run in a hurry, maybe his own car stalled or—"

"Somehow," said Hackett, "I got the feeling that if there'd been a job pulled at the County Museum—one of their Rembrandts missing, or an Egyptian mummy maybe, or the dinosaur skeleton—there'd have been a line or two about it in the papers. They might even have called in the police."

"All right, all right," said Mendoza. "I can do without the sarcasm. You didn't find anything in the car, nothing to point to who'd taken it. What about the mileage? Any way to check?"

"Well, it didn't seem very important, Lieutenant—I mean, why should we? I suppose there'd have been a check of some approximate kind, if there's a garage record on the doorpost as usual, for oil changes, and if Miss Weir could say what it was when the car was taken—"

"Which is very doubtful. Yes. And it's past praying for now, anyway. Damn. And what could it have told us? Nothing."

"Sir," Rhodes had been looking uneasy. "I don't know what this is all about, but if there's something more to that business than just—I mean, something important—maybe you ought to—or maybe you know—"

"That little thing she found, yes," nodded Mendoza. "I know. I don't know how it ties in, or what it means, but it seems to mean something, because somebody seems to be anxious to have it back. And to be pretty sure it was lost in the car."

Rhodes looked uneasier than ever. "My God, do *you* think it was something to do with that? Miss Weir called in—twice—and I thought —I told her—"

"Yes, and you were quite justified," Mendoza soothed him. "Don't look so worried. Exactly the kind of thing a nervous, scatterbrained female might think up. Persecution—or wishful thinking, I suppose the

head-doctors would say—big bad man pursuing her. But there are females and females, and as it happens Miss Weir is quite a level-headed
one ordinarily, and not given to seeing ghosts."

"Well, my God, I'm sorry, sir, I never—"

"No, not your fault, don't apologize, you couldn't know that, and I
don't say it's an absolutely sure thing even now. *I* may be seeing ghosts.
Maybe it was just kids broke into the garage, random mischief. But,
damn it, unless the car had something to do with it, how has Alison got
into this thing? That mysterious female out at the Beverly-Hilton—and
what has *she* got to do with Skyros? . . . . Wait a minute. Have I had
an inspiration? I wonder . . . Well, one thing I must do first is see her
—Alison, I mean—and get the key to her mailbox. Because it's fifty to
one that French maid left a note in it."

"Now that never occurred to me," admitted Hackett. "But it's not the
first thing you're going to do, *chico,* you're going to visit a doctor and
get some stitches in that thing."

"Who's the lieutenant here? Listen, Rhodes, you copy down all your
records about that business and send them up to my office, O.K.?
Thanks very much. And Art, you keep after Driscoll—that boy I want
to have a talk with, and some straight answers from! And I'll check up
on the note. And all right, Auntie dear, I'll go and get stitched up first."
Mendoza grimaced as he got up. "Damn it, I kept telling myself I
should have sent you or one of the boys instead, on that little jaunt this
morning. I'm out of condition for that sort of thing."

"So the exercise was probably good for you," said Hackett. "Maybe I
shouldn't have ambitions to be a lieutenant, it's a sedentary job. Come
on, grandpa, you can lean on me."

Mendoza saw a doctor and had eleven stitches taken in his hand, went
home and took a bath and changed into a whole suit and a clean shirt.
He then discovered that it was impossible to knot his tie with one hand
and the tips of two fingers on the other, did some cursing, investigated
that floor of the apartment to see who else was home, and met Mrs.
Bryson just going out. She laid down her purse and gloves on the bottom step, exclaimed over the bandage, and made a firm nautical square
knot for him, explaining ingenuously that she had a nephew in the
Navy, as he knew. Getting back into the car, Mendoza felt it uneasily
and hoped he wouldn't have to get her to untie it for him when he came
home.

He stopped at Alison's school on Sunset on his way downtown, and was surprised to find it closed. No class, no sign on the door—nobody there, and the door locked. He felt ridiculously uneasy over *that,* and sought the nearest public phone to call her apartment. He let the phone ring a dozen times, but got no answer. The school closed on a Friday, a weekday, and if she was ill she'd be home. Unreasonably he felt annoyed with Alison: where was she, just when he wanted her?

Well, it couldn't be helped; he'd check back later. He went on downtown, and straight up to Callaghan's office at headquarters. Callaghan wasn't there, and he fumed about that; hung around for ten minutes or so, and was just about to go down to his own office when Callaghan came in. He regarded Mendoza fondly, shepherded him into the inner office and installed him in the one comfortable chair.

"Once in awhile you really earn your keep around here, Luis. You've been real helpful today—you've got no idea how helpful. I think those four thugs you ran into are all pushers, it gave us an excuse to get a warrant to go through that Elite joint, and we came across quite a little cache of stuff—including about a thousand made-up reefers—in a back room. *And* a few decks on Prettyman and one of the others."

"Oh, Prettyman was one of them, was he? We weren't formally introduced."

"The big fellow in the green shirt was Prettyman. I understand you're acting coy, don't want to show in the business by being named victim of assault. Well, that's O.K., we got these two, Prettyman and Flores, charged with unlawful possession, and we can run through the assault on the others with a John Doe if the judge co-operates. Everybody else at the Elite had been warned by the time we got there, of course—not a soul in the place, more's the pity. . . . And now I'd like to hear a blow-by-blow account of how you got into the hassle in the first place."

"And there are some suggestive points in it," said Mendoza, and obliged. . . . "Castro—they thought I was working for him. As a pusher? If Prettyman and these others are on that lay, it rather looks like it, doesn't it? Can we build it up that Prettyman is a head pusher for somebody?—let's not say Skyros until we've got more evidence, but maybe. And he's supplying these others, his boys as they put it. And if they leaped to the conclusion that this Castro was trespassing on Prettyman's territory, and resented it so much, where does that put Castro? You know about Bratti, of course."

Callaghan blew smoke at the ceiling and said thoughtfully, "One thing this job's taught me is a lot of respect for the capitalistic system. You'd be surprised how much these little trade wars help us sometimes.

If there wasn't the opportunity for competition, we wouldn't get to know about half these bastards—whether we can get evidence on 'em or not, it's nice to know their names. And when a couple of minor territory-bosses get into a little war—maybe one of 'em trying to encroach, you know, hire a boy away to his string, or sometimes something right outside the business, jealousy over a woman or something like that—it makes a grudge, and that gives us an in. None of 'em are very smart on that level, you know, they can't think far ahead. I've known 'em get into street fights, yet, one little gang against the other, and all get hauled in—ruin a ten-thousand-a-week business for some damn-fool little personal grudge. And afterward, under questioning, you'll get the same thing sometimes—with luck, and if they're fools enough. Tell you anything they know about the other gang, to take them along on the skids too."

"Have you got anything like that from these?"

"It's early. I hope we will. I've seen all of 'em once. They're all still damn cocky, especially Prettyman. I'd better warn you, he's saying it was a trumped-up job, you were planted to give us an excuse to drag 'em in. But I don't think that'll do him any good with the bench, because he did have the stuff on him. I don't think we'll get much useful out of him, he's a little too smart. But I've got him well separated from the other three, he can't brief them, and they're still convinced, probably, that you were this Castro's boy. By what they said to you, sure, there's one of these little trade wars going on between Prettyman and Castro, and that does indeed put Castro as another head pusher—Prettyman's opposite number. For which middleman, I wonder?"

"Bratti," said Mendoza. "You want to bet? Skyros' opposite number."

"No bets with you. I got a wife and family to support."

"Yes, and also—look—that might say something to us about why Skyros tried to steer us onto Bratti. Heads or tails—either he didn't know Castro was Bratti's head man, and couldn't name him to us, or he thinks we're so dumb we wouldn't know Bratti wouldn't be out working the street himself. As I—mmh—divined at the time, he just wanted to get Bratti in trouble."

"Could be. Yes, it's kind of tempting to think, isn't it? And if so, naturally Prettyman's middleman supplier—let's commit slander and say Skyros—wouldn't have much use for Bratti. The grudge might even have come from there originally, personal fight between middlemen passed down to the lower level. Cutthroat competition. I hope by the time these three have stewed awhile, we may get some revealing remarks out of them. . . . Oh, sure, Prettyman yelled for a lawyer right away, and there'll be bail—but that gives us a little time to hang onto them, they won't come up until Monday probably, and meanwhile we may get to hear some more about Castro."

"And Angie," said Mendoza. "Who is Pretty's best boy. And who knows Denny, who from somewhere got the information that the Greek is turning fence. I didn't acquire these bandages in a spirit of altruism, you know—I was looking for something on my end of the business."

"Oh, granted," said Callaghan. "I'll keep my ears open, and issue instructions to the jailers ditto. I think maybe about tomorrow it might be helpful to move two of them in together and hear what they have to say to each other. Inadmissible evidence—self-condemnation—but very interesting sometimes, and points to other places to look for legal evidence. I'll keep your corpse in mind. And I'm also going to do a little looking at Amy."

"Who is, or was, this Frank that Prettyman and Denny mentioned?"

"No idea, I'll have a look at Records and see if we can turn him up."

"Well, I wish you luck." Mendoza stood up. "I hope you realize I've wasted most of the day doing your job. So far I've got nothing out of all this at all."

"Patience, maybe you will. I'll keep you posted."

THIRTEEN

Mendoza returned to his own office and called Alison's apartment again. No answer. Now where the hell was she? Off on a painting jaunt somewhere? Not on a weekday: she wouldn't close the school just for that.

He tried to remember the names of friends he'd heard her mention, and came up with only one whole one, Patricia Moore—hadn't he met her once?—dowdy Englishwoman, a commercial artist of some kind. He looked her up in the phone book and called there, but again drew blank.

It was four o'clock. His head was still aching, and he kept hitting that damned hand on everything in reach—the left one, praise heaven for small mercies. Hackett called in and said Driscoll had disappeared somewhere with his tail. "Hell and damnation!" said Mendoza, and sent Sergeant Lake out for coffee for both of them.

At four-thirty he tried the apartment and the school again. No luck. The night tail for Driscoll came in and asked whether the day man had called in to say where to pick him up. He hadn't. They waited around awhile for that, and nothing happened.

At five o'clock Mendoza said he was going home, he'd had a full day. He was to be called at once, *pronto,* when Driscoll was located or if anything else interesting broke. On the way home he stopped at Alison's school and apartment, and found both empty and silent.

Maddeningly, through the slots in her mailbox he could see several envelopes.

He couldn't say he was exactly worried about her—Alison could take care of herself quite well—but he didn't like it. He went home, to the haven of air-conditioning and an affectionate welcome from Bast; he managed to untie Mrs. Bryson's knot, made some coffee, and lay down to ruminate in peace, or in as much peace possible with Bast curled up on his stomach.

He woke up at a quarter of eight, decided it was too much trouble to get dressed and go out for a meal, and made himself an omelette. He fed Bast. He called his office: hadn't Driscoll been located yet? Yes, the day man had called in, the night man gone to relieve him, and Sergeant Hackett had been briefed when he came in after dinner, but by the time Hackett got there—to a restaurant on Fairfax—they'd both gone.

"*¡Fuera!*" said Mendoza. "Keep me informed, as soon as the tail calls in."

He had another cup of coffee. Bast lay purring steadily on his lap, and the clock-hands moved slowly around to nine-thirty. When the phone rang he jumped for it, and then had to stop to apologize to Bast, so rudely discarded. "Yes?"

"Myers just called in, sir. Driscoll's gone back to his hotel and looks like staying in."

"Ah," said Mendoza. "Thanks very much." He flung off his robe, dressed hastily, and this time carried his tie upstairs to Mr. Elgin. "By the way," he said as Mr. Elgin pulled the knot tight, "do you really think that precocious tom of yours—?"

"Well, I must say it looked that way to me," said Mr. Elgin, and elaborated.

"You can have first choice of the litter," said Mendoza generously, and Mr. Elgin looked alarmed.

"Oh, well—er—we *have* four already—"

"I might have known you'd disclaim responsibility. It's legal enticement, if you ask me. Why you had to bring home a tom—this oversexed delinquent with rape in his eye—"

"Now really, Mendoza—she's acting pretty coy with him, too—enticement on the other side, if you ask *me*. And he's not just *any* tom. It might be worse. Abyssinians are sort of first cousins to Siamese, they ought to turn out quite interesting kittens."

Mendoza said Elgin was a traitor and a coward, but he hadn't time to argue about it now. The night had begun to cool off a little, thank God. He drove down to Driscoll's hotel and found Myers in the lobby. "Is he sober?"

"Depends what you mean by sober, Lieutenant. Say, I heard you got banged up a little today, that looks pretty nasty. . . . Well, he was feeling pretty good when I picked him up, but dinner settled him down a little. He went out to see that dame at the Beverly, and Dwyer and I strolled up and down the hall outside—you know—and we gathered there was some sort of hassle going on. . . . Oh, the usual thing, you might say—not that I got any more of the French than Bert did, but it wasn't hard to figure. You can recognize swearing—even, er, ladylike swearing—in any language. She did most of the talking, and most of it after she had the door open and started ordering him out. By the gestures." Myers looked gravely amused. "Not very polite gestures. We figured he'd been trying to make her, maybe with not much finesse if you get me, and she said No nineteen different ways—at the top of her voice—and ended up by slapping his face. Good and hard—sounded like a shot."

"*¡No me diga!*" Mendoza laughed. "That I'd like to have seen. How'd he take it?"

"Oh, mad as hell. Insult to his vanity, like they say. He went straight down to the bar, but after a couple of drinks it probably dawned on him what kind of mark-up he was paying for the atmosphere, and he came back to town and found a cheaper place. When he left and came back here, he was high, but not quite passing-out high."

"And that might be just the way I want him," said Mendoza. "What's his room number? Come up with me."

He knocked on the door, waited, knocked again. A stir inside; Driscoll asked without opening, "Wha' the hell you want?"

"Open the door, Mr. Driscoll. This is Lieutenant Mendoza from headquarters, and I've got some questions to ask you."

"You go to hell," said Driscoll.

"Open the door or I'll get the manager to open it for me."

A long pause; then Driscoll fumbled at the lock inside and the door opened slowly, halfway. "Listen, why the hell you got to come round at this time of night? What d'you want with *me? Cops!* I'm a law-abiding citizen, you can't—"

"That's fine," said Mendoza. "Let us in, and we'll discuss this in private." He pushed Driscoll aside, went in with Myers and shut the door. The room was strewn with discarded clothes, careless: the bed a tangle of sheet and blanket. "You seem to be interested in a business way in a couple of people we're interested in too, and I'd like to ask your co-operation in the matter. Just what *is* your interest—or your company's interest—in Madame Bouvardier and Mr. Andreas Skyros?"

Driscoll looked at him blearily. "I don't have to tell you one thing. It's private comp'ny business. Nothing to do with cops—"

"But we think it has, Mr. Driscoll, and you should know that you're bound, both as a private citizen and an investigator, to co-operate with us when you're asked, give us any information you may have."

"You can go to hell!" said Driscoll, uneasily belligerent. "Smart boy cop—sure, take all the credit if I— By God, clean it up m'self, no *co-operation* from you smart boys—tell Howard so too— Go ahead, beat me up, why don't you—two of you, tha's jus' the way you boys like it, isn't it, two t' one!" His eyes focused momentarily; he laughed. "You been in a li'l ruckus already, Lieutenant?—wha' happen, you run up against somebody a li'l tougher, like maybe a five-year-old kid? Go on, jus' try—dirty Mex bastard—"

"That one I've heard from tougher ones than you, Mr. Driscoll," said Mendoza. "Just a little tougher. And we really don't operate that way, you know—it's not such a good idea to give the public reason to confuse us with the thugs. Do I understand you're refusing to give us any information you have?"

"You got it in one—bingo!" said Driscoll, and attempted another laugh.

Mendoza looked at him a moment more and said, "O.K., if that's the way you want to play it." He turned and came out, Myers behind, and Driscoll slammed the door after them.

"A real tough baby," said Myers. "Oh, my."

Mendoza grinned. "Suppose you hang around this floor while I go down and phone in for a warrant. Just in case he gets any ideas." He went down to the lobby, called his office and requested a warrant—material witness—as soon as possible. "I'll wait here for it."

It didn't take long. One of the night-duty sergeants brought it up, and Mendoza took him back up to where Myers was holding the fort. They had to make a little noise, banging on the door and threatening to get the manager, and an interested crowd had collected by the time Driscoll finally opened to them. Mendoza charged him formally and added, "You've got five minutes to dress, make it snappy."

"You can't do this to me—"

"Famous last words," said the sergeant. "In, buddy, and get your pants on. You're going for a joy ride. . . . I'll bet they turned him down for the Army, Lieutenant, he'd've learned a lot fancier cussing than that in the service."

The telephone brought Mendoza out of deep sleep, shrill and imperative. Mechanically he reached out to the bedside table, only half awake, and hit his hand on the edge; swore, coming further out of sleep, and turned over to reach the phone with his right hand. Bast, who was curled in a ball alongside him, uttered faint protests at being so rudely wakened.

"Mendoza speaking."

"This Lieutenant Mendoza of headquarters?"

"Yes." He was fully awake now. "Who is this?"

"Sergeant Polaski speaking, sir Kenneth Street precinct, Hollywood. We just had a call to a break-in and assault up here, and the neighbors seemed to think you ought to be informed—say the young lady's a friend of yours. A Miss Alison Weir, it's the Blanchard Arms on—"

"I know the address, what's happened?"

"Just got here ourselves, sir—somebody broke in and attacked her—"

"All right, I'm coming, you carry on!" He swore steadily at his hand as he flung on some clothes: a damned nuisance. It was five minutes before he left, leaving the light on behind him. Bast looked at it plaintively, uttered a philosophic sigh, curled up with her back to it and her tail across her eyes, and went to sleep again.

On the way across town Mendoza was absently interested to notice that the Facel-Vega was apparently capable of what the manufacturers claimed for it. A good many automatic signals were off for the night at this hour, and he ignored the ones that weren't. The force was shorthanded, but he'd have a word to drop to Fletcher in Traffic: despite the comparative emptiness of the streets after midnight, it wasn't until he was within a mile of his destination that a patrol car picked him up. He didn't stop, and it was a minute behind him when he pulled up at the curb. He got to the elevator before a patrolman caught him up, breathing wrath, to be calmed down and presented with identification.

There'd been another patrol car ahead of where he parked, and on the fourth floor there was quite a crowd. People in dressing gowns standing in their doorways, interested and excited; a very young patrolman taking notes as a pretty gray-haired woman gabbled at him; another on his knees earnestly studying the open door of Alison's apartment; a sergeant looking at something on the floor inside.

Mendoza snapped out his name and pushed past the kneeling man. "Sergeant—"

"Lieutenant Mendoza? Good evening, sir, I mean good morning, isn't it? I'm Sergeant Polaski." What he was looking at was a weighted short sap lying there near the door. "The—Miss Weir, she got a nasty crack on the head—doctor's with her now, he didn't think it was necessary to take her into hospital, but— The guy evidently got scared off in a hurry, before he could do much real damage. Woman across the hall, Mrs. Corder—by what we've got so far—she and her husband were just coming home, heard Miss Weir call out, and when the guy heard *them* coming, he ran, knocked the woman halfway down the stairs to get by, and of course the husband was so busy helping her up he can't give a description—and the stair light was out of commission anyway."

"Vaya, vaya," said Mendoza, and sat down in the nearest chair and took off his hat. "Out of commission. Or put that way. All right, Sergeant, that's good, you can carry on here just as you ordinarily would, but whatever you get I want sent downtown to headquarters to my office, O.K.?"

"Yes, sir."

"And I'll have some of my men up now to look around too." He went to the phone and called downtown, asked for a man from Prints and one of his own night staff. He discovered he'd come away without cigarettes, and emptied the box on the coffee table into his pocket, lit one. He dialed Hackett's number and was rewarded by an outraged voice.

"Don't you ever sleep? I'd think after the day you had—"

"I'm one of those people when I can't sleep I like to wake up everybody else. Now listen." He told him briefly what had happened. *"Pronto, inmediatamente,* go and find out where they were—call the tails—"

"Who?"

"¡Pedazo de alcornoque, imbécil! This is the Domokous business—I think—it could be. And damn it, would either of those we know about do it themselves?—hired men—nevertheless, we'll look. The Bouvardier woman and Skyros. Were they at home thirty minutes ago, and if not, where? We'll check where we can, at least."

"You mean I'll check," said Hackett bitterly. "All right, I'm on it. How's Miss Weir?"

"She has survived, I can hear her talking. You don't kill a woman until you kill her tongue. I'm about to hear what she has to say. Get busy, and call me here," he named the number, "when you've got anything." He hung up and went into the bedroom. The doctor, a thin sandy young man, was bending over Alison on the bed; he looked up sharply.

"Who are you? Here, young woman, you lie still, better not sit up just yet."

"Why, Luis," said Alison in a faint voice, sounding pleased, "you came out without a tie."

Mendoza said, "It's this damned bandage, I can't manage a knot." He sat down on the foot of the bed.

"Both been in the wars, have we? What happened to you?" She propped herself up to look at him.

"A little cut, nothing. I want to hear all about this, now. What—"

"You can't question her much now, Officer," said the doctor. "She's had a severe blow on the head, there's no concussion but she must have sedation and rest, and take things easy for a day or so. I understand you must know a few details, but five minutes is really *all* I can allow—"

"Qué va, qué va! Don't be stupid, she's a big strong healthy girl and not much hurt!" said Mendoza robustly.

Alison sat up straight and glared at him. "Of all the insulting things to —you—you—*¡Monstruo diabólico!* I might have been *killed*—"

Mendoza grinned at the doctor. "You see? She's half Irish, she can't resist a fight. You ever want to insult a woman, call her healthy."

"I'm *not* all right, I have a horrible headache—"

"Those tablets should take effect soon, Miss Weir, *if* you are allowed to rest."

"You haven't been in practice long, have you?" asked Mendoza. "You or me, yes, but she's female—do her much more good to talk about it. A nice hot cup of coffee and a cigarette—"

"*No* caffeine or tobacco!" said the doctor, looking as if he had suggested cyanide. "If people would only realize, the most dangerous drugs easily available to—I cannot recommend—"

"Coffee sounds fine," said Alison. "If those pills *do* take effect. You go and make some, Luis. I refuse to answer questions before I comb my hair and get into something decent." Her silk dressing gown had been ripped down the front, one sleeve torn away; she got off the bed unsteadily, clutching the torn edges together.

"Really, I *cannot* recommend—"

Mendoza took his arm and led him out. "Thank you very much for your services, Doctor." Spluttering, the doctor went away. Mendoza started water heating for coffee, thoughtfully making enough for everybody, and cast around in the refrigerator for something to make a sandwich of; he was hungry. The men from downtown arrived and he set one to printing the door, the other looking around generally here and downstairs.

Twenty minutes later he installed Alison in the biggest armchair with a cup of coffee, passed cups and a plate of sandwiches round to the sergeant, the very young patrolman who was ready with his notebook and pencil, and his own man Williams, who was yawning steadily, and sat down opposite Alison. "Very cozy, *¿no es verdad?* Do you want a cigarette now, *querida?*"

"Yes, please. Doctors!" said Alison. "If you were going to ask, I feel better, thank you. Though there's an awfully tender soft spot—" She fingered the back of her head and winced. She had combed her hair, powdered her nose, and put on lipstick, another house-robe, and looked reasonably herself.

"I should say there is a soft spot! I told you to put the chain up and keep the windows locked, damn it!"

"Well, but, Luis, it just didn't seem possible— Oh, all *right*, I know it was careless, but I was tired, and after everything *else*— Coming in to find that note I couldn't make head or tail of, and *then* that the apartment had been searched—"

"*¡Por el amor de Dios!* The apartment—and *that* didn't tell you to take extra care— ¿*Para qué,* what's the use? Females! And where in hell have you been all day? I—"

"And where were *you* when I tried to get you *then?* I called— Well, I wasn't sure, Luis, nobody could be, it was just little things, you know—"

"I don't know, but I'm going to hear every last little thing about it right now—come on, come on, tell!"

The young patrolman looked uneasily astonished at this peremptory manner of examining a witness, so contrary to the regulations in the police mannual, but set down his cup and poised his pencil. "Aren't you feeling tactful tonight!" said Alison. "The cave-man technique."

"Don't be obtuse, I had the hell scared out of me and this is reaction, the way a mother spanks her lost tot she thought was kidnaped. Real redheads, they're not picked up on every street-corner, it might be all of a couple of months before I found another. Let's take this in order, now. Where have you been and what time did you get home?"

"I went to the Vesperian exhibition. It was only on today, he's really quite an impossible autocrat, you know, does things just as he pleases and if it's inconvenient for other people that's just too bad. I had to close the school for the afternoon, I wanted to see it, he had all sorts of things never on view before. . . . The museum? Certainly not, I'm talking about Vesperian the dealer—gallery out on Santa Monica Boulevard. I picked up Pat about one o'clock and of course we met various other people there, and afterward—about five-thirty it'd have been— some of us went on to the Bradleys', and then just as it was breaking up Tony Lawlor came in wanting to talk about it all over again—really some very interesting things—and the upshot was we all went out to dinner in a crowd, to that Swedish place—"

"Yes, yes, this Bohemian riffraff you associate with, I know the kind of thing. What time—"

"That's a very old-fashioned view," said Alison kindly. "Bohemians are a good thirty years out of date. And we went back to the Mawsons' because Sally wanted us to look at a new thing Andy'd just finished. It was about ten-thirty when Pat and I left, and I dropped her and came straight home. There was some mail, and I brought it up with me and looked at it, and this note—left by hand—I couldn't make out *what* on earth it was—"

"Yes, and you've left your prints all over it, I suppose, and maybe some of the sergeant's men have too—where is it?—the bedroom—" Mendoza went to get it, brought it back delicately balanced on his palm, and laid it on the desk. "We'll have to isolate the extra prints, if possible, that's all. *¿Qué mono,* isn't this pretty? Ladylike fancy stationery, a *very* fine-pointed pen, and a mysterious message. *You will tell your Irishman gangster that since he does not come in touch with me to conclude the bargain, all is cancelled, for his dishonorable greed—I do not buy, I pay him nothing! Let him come and ask now for his original price, perhaps I think about it, but if not by tomorrow, I seek the police and tell them his name.*"

"Exactly like Agatha Christie," said Alison. "Isn't it? And of course, I thought of that Lydia right away—"

"So do I. *Caray,* yes, and so we know who Lydia is—and, *de paso,* I'm vindicated. A lot of names I've been called by a lot of people, but nobody ever accused me of being an Irishman. Yes, well, I want this gone over for prints—oh, hell, Hellenthal's gone with the rest of what he picked up—have you got any wrapping paper?" He went and got it, and covered the note carefully in an improvised folder with its envelope. "All right, go on."

"Well, I couldn't make head or tail of it, but I thought you'd better hear about it, so I called you at home, and you weren't there. So I thought I'd wait until morning, and then I noticed that the top drawer in my dressing table wasn't closed. And that's a sort of complex with me, you know, drawers left open—I never do—I may stuff things away all untidy, to keep it neat on the surface, but I don't like clutter, and I always shut drawers properly. Even if I'd been in a particular hurry when I left—and I wasn't, today. I—Luis, you *devil,* is this that special Roquefort I had in the—? It was for a *party,* I'm having some people in on Sunday—"

"You can get some more, it's good. Yes, go on."

"At a dollar and a quarter—"

"I'll buy it, I'll buy it! Go on!"

"Well! I felt a little uneasy about it, and I looked around—and there were two drawers in the desk not quite shut, and I thought I'd left the closet door closed—I usually do. But I couldn't swear to any of it, it just made me wonder a little. There isn't anything missing, not that there'd be much of real value to take, but the only good pieces of jewelry I have, my grandmother's topaz ring and a few odds and ends like that, weren't touched. I wasn't sure, I just felt—you know—a little queer about it. And you needn't remind me I was warned, I couldn't leave the chain up when I went out, could I? And I couldn't see that the door had been forced, and those windows onto the fire escape *were* locked."

"With plenty of time, he could try this and that master key or even take an impression and get a key made. It wasn't forced, no, but it might have been manipulated in some way. We'll take it off and have a look, and you'll have a new one installed anyway. What about that thing, that little coin? Where was it?"

"As a matter of fact I had it with me. I wanted to show it to Vesperian, he knows a little about a lot of things and I thought he might be able to say what it was. But I didn't get a chance to talk to him, as it happened. It's still in with the change in my coin purse, in my bag."

Mendoza went to find it. "This I'll take charge of. Yes, he came when you'd be gone and he could expect enough time to search thoroughly, for such a little thing. All he was after. And he did search, and didn't find it. So he figured you must be carrying it, and he came back to get it after you were home. . . . What the hell is its importance? But fifty to one, that's the answer."

"Yes, I thought of it, of course. But I wasn't sure, as I say, and it seemed incredible—even after the garage business—and I didn't see any reason to call the local precinct, there wasn't anything missing and I'd feel a fool—you know how they looked at me before! And I was awfully tired, all the talk and confusion in a crowd like that, you know —I thought I'd just call you about it in the morning, there wasn't anything to do at that hour. So I went to bed. That was about midnight. All right, so I was a fool not to think of the chain—but after all, he'd *been* there, how did I know he was going to come back? I've no idea what time it was when I woke up—"

"The call came through at one-forty, miss," contributed Sergeant Polaski.

"Then I suppose it'd have been ten or fifteen minutes before. I don't know what woke me—some little noise he made, maybe—but all of a sudden, I was awake, and I *knew* there was somebody in the apartment. I lay there for a minute, telling myself not to be a nervous idiot, you know how one does, and then I did hear something for certain, just a little slurred sort of sound in here—footstep on the carpet, I think. I got up as quiet as I could, and put on my robe—I had some vague idea of waiting until he came into the bedroom, if he did, and then slipping out to reach the phone and yell 'Police!' at least. I was terrified, it's a wonder he didn't hear my heart pounding. I waited for what seemed like ages, and then he *did* come in—I was over by the window, I just saw a big dark shadow move through the door. He had a pencil-flash—he was awfully quiet—and he just stood there inside the door, as if he was waiting for something. I thought—"

"That sounds," said the sergeant thoughtfully, "like an experienced man. He wanted to be sure you were sleeping sound. He could tell by your breathing."

"At the moment, I sounded to myself like a steam engine. I see. I suppose that was what gave me away—he heard me from the wrong place, not the bed—and maybe I made some noise moving. Anyway, all of a sudden he switched on the flash and swept it around, and saw me—I was almost to the door—and made a lunge for me. I was too frightened to scream, I didn't think I could make a sound to save my life, but I did try—I called 'Help!' or something, that was what the Corders heard—and I managed to pull away from him and ran in here —I thought if I could get to the phone, just to knock the receiver off and yell—and of course he came after me, and he must have knocked me out the first blow, because that's all I remember. When I came to, the Corders were dithering around and the police just getting here."

"He didn't even have time to snatch your bag afterward—he heard the Corders coming, and was afraid he'd be trapped—maybe he lost his head a little, dropping the sap he'd used. Yes, I see."

"Corder," said the sergeant, "he said something about there having been some other trouble lately—garage broken into—and he seemed to think Miss Weir'd want you called, sir—"

"Yes, I told him all about it that morning, you remember," said Alison.

"Well, sir, if this is mixed up with some case you're working, as I gather it is, it's out of our hands," said the sergeant, looking interested. "And if that's all the lady can tell us," he heaved himself up—"we'll be getting back to the station."

"You've been *very* kind," said Alison, smiling at him. "Thank you so much." The gracious effect was marred by a sudden wide yawn. "Oh, lord, I'm getting sleepy now, those pills—"

"Well, it's our job, miss, glad to oblige," said the sergeant gallantly. "If you'll be O.K. now, alone—"

"Oh, I'll be here," said Mendoza. "It's almost morning anyway—three o'clock—and I told my sergeant to call me here. She'll be O.K., and a new lock can be put on tomorrow."

The sergeant looked rather doubtful, but took himself and the patrolman out. Williams was nearly asleep in his chair; Mendoza shook him awake and sent him back to headquarters with the note to deliver to Prints. "And you are going to bed. With another of the doctor's pills." He steered her into the bedroom. "You'd better stay home and rest tomorrow."

"Yes, thank heaven it's Saturday," she said through another yawn. "Were you really worried, Luis?" she added sleepily, untying the sash of her robe.

"Oh, terrified—terrified. But then I scare easy." He kissed the corner of her mouth lightly. "Go to sleep."

She kissed him back drowsily. "Don't forget the Roquefort."

"*¡Qué joven,* what a woman! Good night, *gatita.*" As he came out to the living room the phone rang. It was Hackett, relaying the information that both Skyros and the Bouvardier woman had been, as far as was humanly ascertainable, virtuously in their own beds at the crucial time.

"Or at least, in their beds. Now can I go back to mine?"

"For what's left of the night. I could wish the bastard—whoever he was—had carried on this little caper tomorrow night, I've had a full day. However! Yes, I'll see you at ten o'clock, that gives you an extra two hours to get the rest a growing boy needs."

Hackett groaned and hung up. Mendoza carried all the dishes out to the kitchen and stacked them neatly, unable to wash them with one hand; struggled out of his jacket, took off his shoes and stretched out on the davenport, and thought some more through the last of Alison's cigarettes. Then he switched off the light, hitting his bandaged hand on the stiff parchment shade, and went to sleep.

FOURTEEN

Mr. Andreas Skyros had been a worried man even before he had those two phone calls. He would have said he could hardly have been more worried.

In the first place, there was the County Museum. He had seen Jackie

Donovan yesterday evening, and Donovan had let it out to him—in the most casual way, as if it was a bargaining point!—how he had found out about the insurance. These low-class crooks!—one would think that anyone with the intelligence God favored a dog would realize—! Donovan saying stupidly, "Well, hell, they wanted to buy it before, didn't they? If they'd bid higher'n she would—only sense to go an' ask!" Sense!

The County Museum . . . Mr. Skyros was not acquainted with its director, but he could vividly imagine what reception Donovan had had. And doubtless they had instantly called the police, or at least the insurance firm—God in heaven, yes, of course, that was how the insurance people had got onto it! For all he knew, they might have been quietly working away and found out everything—

No; stop; foolish to be so pessimistic. They could not—could they? —really have discovered anything. The insurance fellow had come to see Lydia Bouvardier, but unless she was lying, the insurance people had not seemed to know that she had actually been approached as yet. A crazy female, but not so crazy as to give that away, or Mr. Skyros' name, or Donovan's. Naturally not. And no one else *knew* anything about this, except Donovan's brother—

Mr. Skyros had a moment of quite violent regret. If only Jackie Donovan had not got out so soon! Another month in San Quentin, and the whole deal would have been over and done. Denny was another matter entirely than Jackie. An amiable, soft man, and stupid—even more stupid than Jackie—and very easy to handle. Denny, of course, had *needed* Mr. Skyros to advise him in the business—and it had again pointed the moral to Mr. Skyros of that proverb about casting one's bread on the waters. He was a man who liked to be pleasant and friendly whenever possible, and it had been only a thoughtless polite remark, that day after poor Frank's funeral, when Denny called to thank him for sending the money . . .

"I knowed it was from you, sir, I hope you don't mind, but I sort of felt like I ought to thank you— Frank thought you was a swell boss, he—"

At the time Mr. Skyros had been angry and alarmed; he was always so careful to keep his name and face right out of any provable contact, and here was someone entirely outside the business, someone with no interest in preserving secrecy—only because he had happened to be Frank's brother. Well, one could not prevent people from having relatives, of course. But this lout, Frank's brother, what line was *he* in?—

Mr. Skyros had heard, but could not recall now. But Denny sounded humble and anxious, and automatically Mr. Skyros had been paternally friendly, with an eye to winning his loyalty. And inevitably had said, "If there's ever any way I can help you, my friend—"

And had it not paid off! Not two months later, Denny coming to him with this—money for nothing, you could say. And agreeing to the price at once, so astonished that they might get such a price for it; *and* to the cut, fifty-fifty. It was, of course, a reasonable price—and a reasonable cut. After all, it was a rather delicate matter to handle, it required just the right touch, and Mr. Skyros was the man to handle it. He had, of course, no intentions of revealing himself as in touch with the original thief—he did not then know Lexourion's daughter; she might be an honest woman who would immediately go to the police at the mere suggestion.

He was quite pleased with the artistic little idea of the advertisement in the paper ostensibly to get in touch with the thieves. It had convinced her that he was only the helpful friend of her late father's, as he had represented himself; and of course it had been easy to persuade her to let him make the contact in that way—a lady could not be allowed to have such dealings with a criminal, when there was a gentleman willing to substitute. It had delayed matters, inevitably, there had to be plausible time allowed, to give it the appearance of—of verisimilitude.

But all so very easy and smooth. And then this one, this Jackie, must show up, just a little smarter—smart enough to see that Mr. Skyros had tied himself into it and must get his cut, but greedy for a higher price in consequence.

The County Museum, my God . . .

And this crazy woman, bent on defrauding the insurance company. Madness. Nothing out of Mr. Skyros' pocket, but could she not see that in a matter of this kind one must give a little in order to gain? True, two hundred thousand dollars was a respectable sum of money: Mr. Skyros could appreciate the temptation, to get it back twice. But it was *not* such a thing as cash, or nice bearer bonds, or a handful of diamonds—anonymous, unidentifiable. Wherever this thing showed up, it would be known; and it could not be sold piecemeal, its actual intrinsic value was as a whole: split it up, and it was worth nowhere near that amount. If she wanted anything out of it, the pedigree, so to speak, had to be clear. Men to buy in secret, she said: nonsense: anyone who laid out that kind of money wanted to boast of it.

So, this nice plausible little story for the police and the insurance men, one easy to believe, for they too would know it was nothing a thief could sell to a fence. Perhaps to make them think—it was an idea —that the thief had aimed for her all along, to hold it at ransom, as it were. A nice story about this telephone call, this meeting with a disguised fellow—no, not to be identified, so little she'd seen of him—the exchange of cash for the collection. And there she was with it in her legal possession, able to sell it openly.

Everybody made a profit that way. My God, she had no guarantee the old man would have left her anything at all: had he lived longer, the thing would have been sold, and heaven above knew she had plenty of money already; he might very well have left everything to some society or college, who knew? The ten thousand profit to Mr. Skyros (though she need not know he had a piece of it, of course) and the Donovans was the little price she paid for clear title to it, for being able to realize something from its sale.

He had thought anyone would see that, even a scatter-headed female. A thing like this, my God, the insurance people would be like starving tigers on a manhunt if they suspected—and of course they *would* suspect, not being fools. But she did *not* see, she was determined to keep that money: Mr. Skyros, sitting at his desk that Friday afternoon worrying, mopped his brow agitatedly. Bring them all down on her like— like the Assyrians in that poem, she would, and eventually on Mr. Skyros too. Because she would naturally not hesitate, come to the point, to name him, believing he was an innocent upright businessman with all his ways open to inspection.

And, oh, God, this Domokous business . . . He had thought the police were quite satisfied about Domokous, but were they? Were they still investigating? God only knew. Mr. Skyros had just returned from the funeral, where he had received another little shock—Domokous had been engaged, the girl was there. The girl—a sullen-looking young woman—now what might she want, asking if she could come to see him tomorrow afternoon? He would tell her, he decided, that Domokous' salary had been due, and he felt she should have it in lieu of any family. Yes. The picture of the kind, friendly employer he had presented at the funeral. Maybe she only wanted to ask him for a job or something.

Domokous . . . Really a chapter of accidents, *that* had not been necessary at all. These violent people—no finesse, no understanding! Domokous had known nothing; Mr. Skyros had seen at once that he was only too anxious to believe it a misunderstanding, and any halfway plausible little story would have sent him away satisfied. But *not* after he'd been knocked unconscious from behind. Or even before that, after the little argument with Donovan there—

Suddenly Mr. Skyros sat bolt upright in his chair and called upon God. He had remembered something. He saw Domokous with that list in his hand, picked up from the desk, and Donovan swearing, reaching for it—he heard the little snap of tearing paper. Part of it had torn away—had it? If so, what had become of it? Did it include anything which might be dangerous?

He must ask Donovan about it.

These terrible violent men. Killing, that *was* dangerous: a prudent man found other means, did not get into situations which might lead to such actions. But circumstances, as the saying went, alter cases. There Domokous *was,* knowing that something wrong was going on, and what to do with him? He was not the type to be bought off, *that* Mr. Skyros knew: a most tiresomely honest young man.

Two birds with one stone. Involve Bratti. One could hope, at least. But Mr. Skyros had not at all liked anything about that business; he had had as little to do with it as possible. . . .

He had been worried then, sitting there in his office thinking about it; but three minutes later his worries increased. The phone rang and he took it up to hear the voice of one Eugene Castro, whom he had once known well.

"Listen," said Castro, "the boss don't like fancy tricks played on him. . . . You know what I mean. Big joke, hah, telling your Frog lady-friend about how Bratti's a real old-fashioned gangster, hot cannon man at his elbow night 'n' day—hah?—so she tries to hire him to take off a guy she don't like. That's a dilly of a joke, Skyros—real belly laugh!"

"What? My friend, I don't know what you're talking about—"

"Skip the friend. It kind of annoyed the boss, an' I wouldn't say but what it's maybe give him ideas. You *can* still buy it, you know just where to go an' who to see, contact a dropper for rent. You pull another one like that, an' the boss just might go lookin', Skyros." The receiver thudded in his ear.

Mr. Skyros clutched his temples. Heaven above knew he was not sorry that Bratti was annoyed, but—! "Your Frog lady-friend"—what had this crazy woman been up to now?

And then the phone rang again, and it was Angelo, with the news that Prettyman and three of his boys were in jail, and the Elite raided and the entire month's supply confiscated.

Jackie Donovan was worried as hell, and the worst of it was, it wasn't the kind of worry he could share aloud with anybody. Not even Denny. God, Denny least of all—Denny always looking up to him as the boss, Jackie the one knew all the answers, called all the shots. Always *had* been. So, sure, it was just this first little while, kind of getting back on his feet after that long a stretch—but he didn't like this funny feeling, not being *sure*.

Doing things a ten-year-old kid—

Like a nervous kid on his first job.

That sap. Dropping it like that. And of course he'd had gloves on, but he'd handled it before without, and he didn't know whether the holding it with the gloves after would have maybe wiped out all the prints.

He sat in the park thinking about it, worrying about it, but worrying a lot harder about something else. About a feeling he'd been having since he remembered about the sap, a feeling he hadn't even dared admit to himself until just now.

That sap, maybe with a print. So they'd know. And they'd put him back inside.

And he didn't care—he wanted to be back inside.

No! Acourse that was a crazy damn-fool thing, just part of being first out after so long. He'd be feeling his old self, thinking like his old self, pretty soon now, and looking back to all this and laughing. Private-like, to himself.

Some guys did get that way. So they felt—lost—outside. Inside, you *knew* about everything. Just what was going to happen, when. You didn't have to think, and plan, and worry. Some guys got so they didn't like it outside; it was easier in.

Jackie Donovan, my God, wasn't one of those! Fifteen years or fifteen hundred, he'd never be one of those!

Better think about that little thing. How the hell to get it back. Not in the car, that he was sure of, and so he'd figured she'd must have found it. He'd been surprised it turned out to be a dame, the name such a funny one; but all the easier, in a way—he'd had plenty of time, go through the apartment careful, and he'd swear it wasn't there. So then he'd figured she had it on her—and *that* had gone all wrong . . .

Everything, God, going wrong. He thought vaguely maybe he oughtn't ever to've let Denny and Frank get to where they just waited for him to give the orders: if they'd had to think out things for themselves, maybe they wouldn't have got into such messes when he got sent across, wasn't there no more. Well, so O.K., they'd made out all right, in a sort of way, but just no sense about looking ahead. Getting tied up to pushers . . . That Angelo. Well, all right, Angie'd been a good guy once, lot of fun sometimes, a nice little guy, and dependable too: jobs he'd done with them, Angie'd maybe pulled them out of a spot, couple of times—good driver, then, he'd been. You could figure it was old times had held Denny to Angie, and that was fine, ordinarily: nobody liked a guy ran out on his pals. But the minute Angie had got onto *that* lay, and started taking sleighrides himself, Denny ought to've dropped him but quick. Instead, he let Angie take Frank into it, and—

Water under the bridge. You had to think about here and now. Damn fool Denny bunking down with Angie—just have somebody to talk to, after Frank was gone! Jackie hadn't got the straight of this business yesterday, if somebody had talked or the cops had just found out something on their own, and he didn't much care. It'd given him the excuse to pull Denny out, anyways. To say, maybe if somebody'd talked, the cops knew about all of them, about Angie too, and better they split up. Angie'd seen the sense in that. Didn't matter where Angie'd gone; let him go his own way from now on, forget him. Angie said, now this other guy was inside, and marked, probably he'd get his job—specially as he knew the middleman Skyros. Well, knew who he was. That kind, like Skyros, was usually leery of getting known much, but Angie happened to know him, account of Frank—way Denny'd got in with him too, on this other deal.

And what a deal. Of all the crazy things: Jackie'd got to feeling a little like how Denny did, better get shut of it any old way.

When you came down to it, anything they got off it was profit, like Denny said. Ten thousand for *that*. But it really griped him that Skyros had to get a fifty percent cut—sure, so he'd set it up with the dame, but what was there to that? My God, if he'd got out sooner himself, before Denny made the deal, he could have set it up with her just as good, and the ten thousand between him and Denny. Skyros, this chiseler . . .

So what about that little thing he'd lost? He was wondering now if maybe that other dame had ever had it at all. He'd thought of the car, first place, because things did slip out of your pockets sometimes, sitting down; but it could have happened other ways. When he came back to the Caddy, that day, he'd been feeling kind of mean—way that guy in there had looked down his nose at him—and you didn't notice things much, feeling like that. Maybe when he reached to get the keys, it had dropped out. Could be. Dropped onto the grass in the parking there, or in the gutter. Could've been laying there ever since—unless they cleaned up, a gardener with a rake or something—but a little thing like that . . . If it was in the gutter, other shorts'd gone over it, it might be covered up with leaves and muck— Not awful likely anybody would have found it.

But, God, how could he go and look? He thought he could remember just about where, but in a place like that, everybody noticing . . . He could say he'd dropped his keys or something—yes, and ten to one a gardener, or some kids, wanting to help look. Oh, the hell with it—if he did find it, no need let anybody see, stick it in his pocket and pretend to keep on looking for what he'd said he'd lost. Nobody would notice.

If he didn't get it back, *that* would be noticed all right.

That damned sap. If there was a print— Didn't want get Denny in trouble. Just as well Denny didn't know anything about it; he could say so, if—

Donovan got up and walked out of Pershing Square, down Sixth to Main, and down Carson to the cheap rooming house where they'd moved last night, him and Denny. There wasn't a garage; the Caddy was sitting on the street. The Caddy Denny'd gone and got back for him. He got out his keys slowly, got in and started her. He felt a little bit easier with her now.

He drove out Exposition to the park and into the grounds, found a place to put the Caddy, and walked up to where he'd parked that day, near as he remembered. There were parked cars almost solid here, damn it, couldn't go crawling under every one to see. But he did what looking he could, peering along the gutter between cars.

After awhile, just as he'd figured, a guy came along and stopped and asked what was wrong. "I dropped my keys somewheres," said Donovan, "somewheres right along here, I *think* it musta been—damn fool thing to do, but you know how these things happen."

"Oh," said the guy, "that so? Hope you find 'em, damn nuisance all right. You don't, you better go and ask at the Lost and Found desk in at the museum—maybe somebody's turned 'em in."

"Gee, yes, maybe so," agreed Donovan. The guy got into the car by the curb there and started the engine. Donovan realized maybe he'd been suspicious he was looking her over with an eye to hopping her. But it left a space free to look at. . . . He waited for the guy to jink her out into the street, and all of a sudden he noticed something and his heart dropped.

The car didn't have fender aprons, and as it pulled out he could see the treads of the back tires; and on the left one, there was an old bent metal slug of some kind half-buried in the rubber, sticking there. . . . This damn hundred-and-ten weather, the asphalt going all soft, your shoes'd stick to it sometimes, crossing the street—a little thing like that, sticky with asphalt, getting glued onto a tire easy, carried away God knew where. Or more likely, ground down into the asphalt when tires went over it.

For half a minute there he felt like he could cry, just sit down on the curb and bawl like a kid. He felt the sweat trickling down his back, in the merciless muggy heat; and he knew for sure that thing was gone for good, he'd never get it back. He thought of what trouble *that* would make.

He thought of Angie saying, anything to do with an ace of spades, bad luck. And maybe Angie was right.

And all of a sudden, again, he felt kind of homesick—for the place you didn't have to worry what was going to happen tomorrow . . .

Driscoll lay awake miserably on the hard cell cot and worried over his sins. What the hell Howard would say to *this*—well, all right, he knew what the hell Howard would say! And damn it, you could say all Howard's fault in the first place—*picking* at him, criticizing—so he wanted, by God, to show Howard just how good he was—

Damned cops. All bullies, taking any excuse to—

And unless he was the hell of a lot luckier than he'd been lately, this would mean his job.

All right, so he'd just have to do what he could on it, now. Tell the damned cops what they wanted to know, all pals together, apologized all over the place for how he'd acted—personal troubles, he'd say, he knew he'd been drinking too much—lay it to that—give a guy a break, I didn't mean to— So they wouldn't go sending any official complaint to the company. Howard needn't ever hear a word about it, with any luck. O.K.

His head was aching and his stomach felt queasy; he groaned, trying to get into a comfortable position. Ease up on the drink, sure, after this. Better try. But God, he'd like one now, get him through, help him—

He couldn't sleep, and it seemed morning would never come, so he could start to get this all straightened out—as straight as he could, anyway . . .

FIFTEEN

Lydia Bouvardier was feeling not so much worried as irritated. She was irritated at Mr. Skyros, at this Donovan, very much so at that insurance man, and at the situation in general. A good deal of her irritation was occasioned by the fact that nothing seemed to be as she had thought— as it *should* be.

She applied lipstick carefully and said, "Go, try to get this Skyros at the telephone again, Berthe. . . . More and more I have the feeling that he is not to be trusted! All these fine excuses why he cannot put me in touch with this Irishman—no business for a lady, he says. And in any case he does not know where Donovan is. Which is absurd, of course he knows. If I could but again meet Donovan face to face, ah, I see he makes the bargain quickly!"

She made a little exclamation of annoyance and snatched up a tissue to wipe away the minute ragged speck of lipstick on her excellent white teeth. . . . It was not only irritating, but puzzling. She had thought it a brilliant inspiration, about the jewelers. One gathered from the *romans de policiers* that that kind of thing was quite common here; it was well known that Americans would do anything for money. Very probably the owners of the place robbed had been in the affair with the robber, in order to defraud the insurance firm—the jewels taken they would then have back, and recut and remount to sell them. So, naturally, they would know the thief *and* where he was to be found. A delicate little matter, to speak frankly to them, explain that she had no care for that aspect, it was their own business, but if they would be so obliging to inform her where Donovan was staying. . . . Once they understood clearly that she knew the ins and outs of the affair, and were reassured of her tolerance in the matter—

One was aware that it was nothing out of the way here, all Americans were quite lawless. But it appeared that she had been wrong. The gentleman there in the shop, introducing himself—the same name as that on the door, one of the owners then: he had positively exuded respectable integrity. That she had recognized almost instantly: one might as well suspect the present Minister of Finance of robbing the national treasury.

In fact, when one came to the point, that was far more likely.

That red-haired woman . . . It had looked to be a respectable apartment, very poor of course, but— Not probable that Donovan was actually living there. And he had ignored her messages.

And when one thought twice, it would be foolish to have Donovan shot, or his mistress, for in the one case he could not conclude the bargain, and in the other he would only be more annoyed. But perhaps to let him see that she was *not* a fool, to threaten him convincingly— And so she had been very practical, remembering the name Skyros had said, a cheap gangster (which was just as well, she did not want to lay out too great a sum on this), and looking it up in the directory.

But, *zut!*—he was not a gangster at all. He did not wear a black shirt, or leave his cigarette in the mouth-corner like an *Apache,* he spoke quite grammatical English, and at first he had been very polite. Later he had been annoyed, which of course was understandable if he was not a gangster.

"They say Mr. Skyros is not in his office, madame, but he is expected there after lunch."

"Ah, how provoking!" exclaimed Madame Bouvardier. "All this, it leaves me exactly where I have started! Since this Irishman makes no reply to my messages, which he must have had by now, he is evidently determined to remain obstinate. Perhaps he and Skyros have made it up between them to be obstinate, yes. Well, this Skyros shall have some plain language from me today, that I can promise!"

Mr. Skyros did not sleep much on Friday night. He got up very early, pleading business to his wife, and arrived at his office before eight o'clock, before his employees. He locked himself in and went to the small safe he kept on the shelf of the filing cupboard; from this he took five twenty-dollar bills. Then he put on the gloves he had brought with him, sat down at the desk, and addressed an envelope to one Mr.

Chester Scott, attorney-at-law. He cut a strip of paper from a clean page and printed on it in carefully disguised letters, *In account with M. Prettyman,* and attached it to the bills with a paper clip. He put this small parcel into the envelope, sealed and stamped it, unlocked the door and left the office.

Outside, he sought his car and drove down to the main post office, and mailed the envelope at the curb box without leaving the car. Heading back for the office, he felt just a trifle more cheerful; there was one little matter off his mind, at least. But from the few details he had heard, no lawyer could get Prettyman off the hook, with the stuff found on him—a year at least. . . . Mr. Skyros was not much worried about the lawyer. He was not a very scrupulous lawyer, he was used to dealing with such clients as Prettyman, and he would not bat an eye at receiving this anonymous retainer. It was necessary to guarantee the Prettymans such services, of course, for otherwise they might feel a grievance and talk a bit too much while they were inside. No reasonable man could object to paying out a moderate sum for loyalty.

By the time he arrived back at his office the staff had come in, and the pretty bookkeeper gave him a cheerful good morning. "Gee, it's going to be hot again, Mr. Skyros—even this early you can tell."

"This time of year, one wishes maybe to live in Alaska, isn't it?" returned Mr. Skyros genially. "I bet all your friends, they envy you in a nice air-conditioned office. Maybe I ought to cut something off your salary for the advantage!" He passed on into his office, sat down and worried a little more, waiting for the phone call.

When it came, he had thought of a place. Sometimes it was inconvenient, going all round to get somewhere, but it was only sense to be careful. About the cops you never knew: they could be almost cunning sometimes, and if they did know about others besides those they'd taken, and were watching . . . "Come to the airport," he said. "Municipal Airport, isn't it? In the men's room, the main building."

Such a nice public place, and perhaps—if he was ever asked about it —he'd been thinking of a little holiday somewhere, inquiring about fares. Yes.

He told the bookkeeper he'd be back after lunch, and drove out to the airport. A terrible drive in traffic in this weather, but these things always came up at inconvenient times. He sought out the men's room and waited; whenever someone else came in he pretended to be washing his hands, straightening his tie. And presently he was joined by the man he waited for, but, my God, he had this stupid lout, this Denny, with him.

"We kinda figured I maybe oughta come along, Mr. Skyros, on account you never met Angie before and I could say he *is*."

"No names, for the love of heaven," implored Mr. Skyros. "All right, I am assured, this is he himself." And then they all fell silent, as a pair of men came in. Mr. Skyros washed his hands industriously, looking at Angelo Forti out of the corner of his eye. No, him he had not met before, but he knew a good deal about him from Prettyman. A useful man —for the time being—because he was, by what Prettyman said, such a very persuasive salesman. A specialist in the high school kids, looking a little like a kid himself, though not young—but a small, frail-looking man, a man nobody could ever be afraid of, a little not-unhandsome man with dreamy dark eyes. And of course, also the profit was higher on Angelo, since he was a user himself. But for that very reason Mr. Skyros much disliked having any dealings with him, and *that* was going to pose a little problem. . . .

"It was Castro," said Angelo, turning his soft dark eyes on Mr. Skyros as they were left alone. "Way I heard it. One of his boys come around askin' for me, probably an offer get me into that string, see, and Pretty and some o' the boys, they just figured rough him up a little. You know. No trouble. But it kinda went wrong—I don't know, seemed the guy was a little bit tougher than he looked—there was quite a ruckus, and somebody called the cops."

"Such a thing!" said Mr. Skyros crossly. "All over such a little business!" There were times he wished he had never had a disagreement with Bratti, and actually that had been unnecessary too, looked at calmly. A little matter of a thousand dollars or so, and it was quite possible that it had not been Bratti or Castro who had waylaid Hogg and taken the stuff from him. Hogg had not been able to say, he had been riding high himself at the time—madness to get on the stuff, these irresponsible people!—and Mr. Skyros had perhaps leaped to a conclusion. But that was past praying for now, the quarrel established.

"I figured," said Angie, "I take over for Pretty, and maybe so, you tell me now where to pick up the stuff and when? It'd be just fine, you got some stashed away maybe now, on account the cops got everything at the Elite."

Yes, and here was the problem. Mr. Skyros had no desire at all to put Angelo in Prettyman's shoes: you could not trust any man who was on the stuff himself. Angie might be worth his weight in gold as a pusher, but to take any responsibility—my God! To know dangerous information—one never knew what that kind would do.

He gave Angie a genial smile and said, "Well, now, you see, my friend, I haven't just made up my mind, I've thought maybe it's a good idea to lie quiet awhile. If the cops know some more than it looks like —dropping on the boys so—"

"Ah, that was just the breaks," said Angie. "They don't know nothin'. Just happened find the stuff on Pretty, after that ruckus. Everything's O.K. I can get you three-four new guys, no time at all, to take over. Find a new drop, the Elite closed up. No trouble."

"Well—" said Mr. Skyros. "I take a little time to think it over." It was awkward: very awkward. There would be all the nuisance of contacting someone else to take over. Someone reasonably trustworthy. And Angie would hear about it. And Angie knew—

"Time," said Angie, and he smiled very sweet and slow at Mr. Skyros. "Not too much time, because I'll be needing some more myself pretty much right away. And I done favors for you, big favor not so long back, didn't I, and I'm right here to take on where Pretty left off. No trouble. I don't want no trouble, you don't want no trouble, nobody wants trouble, Mr. Skyros."

Dear heaven, no, thought Mr. Skyros, turning away as another man came in. He straightened his tie at the mirror with a shaking hand; the genial smile seemed painted on his face. Angie knew— Speak of dangerous information! Angie knew too much entirely already. Really he had Mr. Skyros at bay . . .

"Big favor I done you. Acourse there's this deal o' Denny's—and Jackie's—kinda hangin' fire, ain't it, maybe you've been kinda worryin' over that. And can't say I blame you," said Angie thoughtfully. "This deal with the ace o' spades. Anything to do with an ace o' spades, bad luck."

Ace of spades—a widow, that was what they called a widow, these low-class crooks, remembered Mr. Skyros distractedly. All about that Angie knew, too. When things got a little out of hand, they very rapidly got a lot out of hand—it seemed to be a general rule. All just by chance, and in a way tracing back to poor Frank, all of it, because naturally—brothers, living together—and Angie—

Mr. Skyros did not at all like the look on Angelo's regular-featured, almost girlishly good-looking face—or indeed anything about Angelo. Mr. Skyros was not a man who thought very much about moral principles; he found money much more interesting; but all the same he thought now, uneasily, of the way in which Angelo earned his living—

and paid for his own stuff—and eyed the soft smile, and the spaniel-
like dark eyes, and he felt a little ill.

"Look, my friend," he said, "in my life I learn, how is it the proverb
says, better an ounce of prevention to a pound of cure. I stay in business so long because I'm careful. Two weeks, a month, we talk it over
again, and maybe if nothing happens meanwhile to say the cops know
this and that, then we make a little deal, isn't it?"

"That's a long while," said Angie. "I tell you, you want to leave it
that way, I don't fool around with it. I go over to Castro and get fixed
up there. I can't wait no two weeks."

And Mr. Skyros didn't like Angie, but what with Prettyman and
three of his boys inside, and not likely to come out— And Angie such a
valuable salesman, Prettyman said— All the nuisance and danger of
getting in touch with practically a whole new bunch of boys— Why did
everything have to happen at once?

Denny said stupidly, "Why, you ain't turning Angie down, are you,
Mr. Skyros? I mean, we all figured—I guess anybody'd figure—Angie—"

Angelo gave him an affectionate smile. "Mr. Skyros too smart a
fellow want to get rid of me," he said. "It's O.K., Denny, everything's
O.K. Ain't it, Mr. Skyros?"

Oh, God, the name repeated over and over, anybody to hear— Not
being a fool, Mr. Skyros knew why. But aside from everything else, it
would scarcely be pleasant to have dealings with one who was nominally an underling and actually held—you could say—the whip hand.
And all because of Domokous! If Mr. Skyros had dreamed of all the
trouble that young man would eventually cause—

Of course, there was another factor. Angie worth his weight in gold
right now, but these users, they sometimes went down fast. Who knew,
Angie might not last long. . . . The sweat broke out on Mr. Skyros'
forehead as he realized he had been actually thinking—hoping—planning—perhaps—

Good God above, had not Domokous been enough?

He patted Angelo's thin shoulder paternally. "Now you don't want to
go talking that way," he said. "Sure, sure, you're the one take over for
Pretty, soon as I get the supply, get started up again, isn't it? You don't
need worry, Angelo. I tell you, I know how it is with you, my friend, I
sympathize, and I'll make it a special point—a special favor—get in
touch, and get some stuff just for you. I don't know if I can manage it

tonight or tomorrow, but I'll try my best, my friend. You see, you got to remember, we all got schedules, like any business! My man, he won't be around a little while, he just fixed me up with this stuff they took out of the Elite. It's awkward, you see that, isn't it?"

"Well, that's your business, Mr. Skyros," said Angie, and his dreamy eyes moved past Mr. Skyros' shoulder to gaze vaguely out the ground-glass window. "I appreciate it, you do that. Sure. We don't none of us want no trouble. . . . I'm in a room over the Golden Club on San Pedro, you just ask for me there, you want see me. Or maybe I call you —tonight? About nine o'clock, I call and see if you got any. A couple decks for me, Mr. Skyros—and ten-twelve to sell, see, I like to have a little ready cash."

"Oh, now, I don't know about that much," said Mr. Skyros. "And you know, Angelo, Pretty, he always keeps it a strict cash basis, like they say—"

"Sure," said Angie. "Sure, Mr. Skyros. Fifty a throw, that the deal? Sure. I bring you the cash, say five hundred for ten decks. Never mind how much I cut it, how much I get," and he smiled his sleepy smile again. "Standard deal, Mr. Skyros. You go 'n' have a look round for it."

"I do my best," said Mr. Skyros earnestly, "just for you, my friend. This is awkward for everybody, isn't it, we all got to put up with inconvenience sometimes. But I do my best for you." He got out of there in a hurry, brushing past another man in the door, mopping his brow.

The expedient thing—yes, very true, one must make do as one could, in some situations. It could all be straightened out later. Not very much later, but when things had settled down a little. After this deal with the Bouvardier woman went through. An ace of spades. . . . He was not a superstitious man, but he felt perhaps there was a little something in that, indeed. He rather wished he had never got into the business, and still—scarcely to be resisted, a nice little profit with not much work involved, easy money . . .

Katya Roslev, who would be Katharine Ross so very soon now, rang up her first sale of the day and counted back the change. She did not notice that the customer seized her purchase and turned away without a smile or a word of thanks. Usually she marked the few who did thank you, you didn't get that kind much in a place like this: and she played a little game with herself, seeing how downright rude she could act to the others, before they'd take offense, threaten to call the manager. Funny how seldom they did: used to it, probably. The kind who came into a cheap store like this! Grab, snatch, I saw that first! and, Here, I'll take this, I was before *her,* you wait on me now or I don't bother with it, see! This kind of place . . .

She'd be through here, just no time at all—leave this kind of thing 'way behind. Off at noon, and she'd never come back. Never have to. Money—a lot of money, *enough.* She'd be smart about it, get him to give it to her in little bills so's nobody would suspect—maybe couldn't get it until Monday account of that, the banks— But that wasn't really long to wait. Not when she'd waited so long already.

No need say anything at all to the old woman. She had it all planned out, how she'd do. She'd say she didn't feel good on Sunday, couldn't go to church—there'd be a little argument, but she could be stubborn—and when the old woman had gone, quick pack the things she'd need to take, all but the dress she'd wear Monday, and take the bag down to that place in the station where you could put things in a locker over-night, for a dime. Then on Monday morning—or it might have to be Tuesday—get up and leave just the usual time, and last thing, put the money in an envelope under the old woman's purse there in the drawer. She wouldn't be going to get that for an hour or so after Katya had left, go do the daily shopping. No need leave a note with it, either—or maybe just something like, Don't worry about me, I'm going away to make a better life.

A better life. Escape. It wasn't as if she wanted *much.* She didn't mind working hard, not as if she figured to do anything *wrong* to live easy and soft—all she wanted was a *chance,* where she wasn't marked as what she was. To be Katharine Ross, and work in a nicer shop some-where, at a little more money so she could have prettier clothes, and learn ladies' manners and all like that, and get to know different people than up to now, not just the ones like her here, with foreign-sounding names, the ones went to the same church and— Different place, different job, different people, she'd be all different too. Prettier, she'd do her hair another way; smarter, and wear different kinds of clothes—she'd be Katharine Ross, just what that *sounded* like.

"You've give me the wrong change," said the customer sharply. "Think I can't count?"

Katya made up the amount in indifferent silence. She was listening to other voices, out of the future. Some of those vaguely-imagined new, different people. *Oh, Katharine's awfully nice, and pretty too, I like Katharine— Let's ask Katharine to go with us, she's always lots of fun —Katharine—*

Soon, very soon now . . .

SIXTEEN

Mendoza didn't wake until nearly nine-thirty. It was going to be another hot day; already the thermometer stood close to ninety. Alison was still sound asleep; he made fresh coffee and searched through all the desk drawers for more cigarettes before thinking of her handbag, and found a crumpled stray cigarette at its bottom, which tasted peculiarly of face powder. He left a note propped on the desk asking her to call him sometime today, and drove home.

After he'd got out fresh liver for Bast, he paused to look at her crouched daintily over her dish. Surely she *was* just a trifle fatter around the middle? He seemed to remember reading somewhere that Abyssinians had large litters, and suffered a dismaying vision of the apartment overrun with a dozen kittens. *"¿Y qué sigue despues?*—what then?" he asked her severely. "A lot of people are so peculiar that they don't like cats, it's not the easiest thing in the world to find good homes for kittens—and, damn it, you know very well if I have them around long, impossible to give them away! And I suppose now that you've finally grown up, if a little late, you'd go on producing kittens every six months or so. Yes, well, it's a pity to spoil your girlish figure—which all those kittens would do anyway—but I think when you've raised these we'll just have the vet fix it so there won't be any more. . . . I wonder if the Carters would take one. . . . And it's no good looking at me like that," as she wound affectionately around his ankles. *"Todo tiene sus limites*—a limit to everything, *¿comprende?* We will not keep more than one, and there'll be no more!"

He had a bath and shaved. He looked up the number and called Miss Champion, the receptionist-bookkeeper at Alison's school, and told her to go round to the apartment in an hour or so; explained. Miss Champion twittered: she'd put up a notice and go *right* round, what a terrible *thing*, and—what?—oh, yes, she'd take some cigarettes with her. Mendoza looked in the book again and called a locksmith, told him to go and install a new lock, but not before eleven o'clock. Then he folded his tie to take with him and drove downtown.

He found Hackett already there, reading a report. "You've got an excuse," said Hackett, taking the tie from him, "but I'll bet you've never checked in so late since you made rank. Hold your head up, I can't get at it with— No, I know it's not as pretty a job as you'd do, but I didn't join the force to learn how to be a valet. This is from Callaghan. I don't know how much it'll say to you—, it doesn't say much to me."

Mendoza sat down and took the page. It was a copy of an official card from Records, and it sketched in the person and salient points of career of one Francis Joseph Donovan. Five-ten, one-seventy, hair black, eyes gray, complexion medium, Caucasian, male. One short stretch in reformatory as a minor, for car theft: one three-year term seven years later for burglary: picked up several times for questioning on various occasions thereafter, but no more charges or sentences after he'd got out from serving that one eight years ago. Suspected rather recently of having turned pusher, considering known associates. Callaghan had appended some notes to the terse concluding sentence of the record. A little over three months ago, Frank Donovan had been pointed out to a traffic patrolman, by a high school boy, as the man who had approached him and made some pitch the boy thought was leading up to offering marijuana or some other dope. There'd been lectures at school about these guys, he said, and a movie—and this one acted kind of like that. So the patrolman had gone up to ask some questions, and not being satisfied with the answers had searched Donovan and come across a handful of reefers; whereupon Donovan had tried to run, the patrolman had gone after him, shouted warning, fired once over his head and once at his legs—but it was hard to take careful aim when you were running, and he'd got him through the spine. Donovan had died that night in the General.

"Mmh, yes," said Mendoza. "And I don't like that kind of careless business as a rule—it gets in the papers, the public talks about trigger-happy cops—but once in a while it saves everybody a lot of trouble. This kind, a year inside for unlawful possession, what is it? They can't be cured." He turned the page over and read a further notation in Callaghan's big scrawl. *I think this is the Frank those two meant. He*

*left a widow, Mrs. Amy Donovan, address you know on Daggett. She
works at a joint on Main, the Golden Club, singing with a cheap
combo. No record.* "Well, well. Don't tell me we're beginning to
straighten all this out. At least place some of the people, even the ones
on the outside edge of the business. Like the house that Jack built.
Prettyman who knows Skyros who knows Lydia."

"I don't know Lydia. Suppose you bring me up to date."

Mendoza obliged. "The only way I can figure it is that this part of it
goes back to the theft of Alison's car. Somebody dropped this thing in
it"—he brought it out, looked at it, passed it over—"and is anxious to
have it back. So anxious he's made several elaborate attempts for it.
Which reminds me," and he reached for the phone, called down to
Prints, and asked if they had anything on that sap or the letter he'd sent
in. Nothing but a confused mess on the sap; a variety of prints on the
letter. As was only to be expected, damn it. He called the lab and asked
if anything had turned up on that lock. Marks inside, little fresh
scratches, where the thin arms of the stiff-wire tools from any complete
burglar's kit had groped for the right combination of pressures. "There
you are. An experienced man. Not, of course, Lydia—somebody else.
Which fits in, in a way, you know, because Lydia apparently thought
Alison was—mmh—somebody else than she is. *Caray,* what a series of
little accidents! Yes, I *think* Lydia had a ride in that car while the thief
had it, and noticed the registration slip, and leaped to the conclusion
that the car belonged to the thief's girl-friend. I can see that happening,
can't you? And she also tells us that the thief is an Irishman. Donovan
is an Irish name."

"You aren't supposing," said Hackett, "that Frank Donovan got up
out of his grave, where he'd been peacefully decomposing for a couple
of months, and stole Miss Weir's car out of the park?"

"No hay tal. But the Irish are a prolific race," said Mendoza. "And
just what has that got to do with Stevan Domokous? So, we can say for
maybe ninety percent sure that Skyros is a middleman dope-runner, on
Bratti's level, and a rival of Bratti's—that Domokous somehow found
out about it, couldn't be bought off, and had to be killed. And on the
principle of killing two birds with one stone, Skyros told us a nice little
tale about Domokous mentioning Bratti, hoping to tie Bratti up to it.
That I see. But who and what is Lydia? I thought I'd had an inspiration
yesterday, I had a little vision of Skyros being more important than a
middleman, importing the stuff himself, cunningly stashed away in the
hollow insides of his foreign bric-a-brac—say inside this nymph and

that dolphin, you know. But on second thoughts, I realized that the customs boys surely must know about that old dodge, it'd never do."

Hackett agreed absently, still looking at the coin. "Funny-looking thing. Looks damned old, doesn't it? There's a fellow down in Records, O'Brien, I ran into him at lunch one day awhile back—he's an amateur what-you-call-it—numismatist. I wonder if he'd know anything about what kind of thing this is."

"No harm to go and ask. Take it if you like. . . . Yes, of course it looks like a straightforward pro business—whether it was murder or not, legally speaking. From the little we've got on it. And yet, Lydia—"

Hackett was still turning the little coin over in his fingers. "*I* think," he said suddenly, "you've got hold of a couple of different picture puzzles, and're trying to fit pieces from both into one picture. It could be that Domokous is just exactly what he looks like—and Skyros didn't know one thing about it, but took the little opportunity it offered to mention Bratti's name in connection, hoping it'd take root, so to speak. And whatever business this is about Miss Weir's car, and whoever took it, and about this thing, and this Bouvardier woman, it hasn't anything to do with the dope-peddling."

"*Eso es lo peor,*" said Mendoza, "that's the worst of it. I have a feeling that's so, it's something different entirely. But both Skyros and Lydia are tied up to both ends of it."

Hackett eyed him exasperatedly. "Sometimes I wonder why I don't put in for a transfer to some nice quiet routine place like Traffic or Records. Where I'd have a chance of getting a superior officer with just an ordinary-bright I.Q., who didn't go off at tangents after ghosts nobody else can see."

"So why don't you?"

"I'll tell you. Just one reason. It's always helpful toward promotion if you've got another language besides English, and I'm improvin' my Spanish quite a lot working under you. . . . Does that blank stare mean you've had another idea?"

"A brilliant one," said Mendoza truthfully. It had just occurred to him that by what Mr. Elgin said those kittens should be due about the middle of next month: which meant that they'd be ready to leave home and mother just around Christmas. Such an excellent excuse for the unsolicited gift. Of course one would want to be sure of choosing people who liked cats, would provide good homes—but so much easier to present the seasonal gift than chase all round first asking the hopeful question, Wouldn't you like—?

It was definitely an idea. "Well," and he stood up, "if I'm going to get anything done today at all—my God, look at the time, nearly noon, the whole morning wasted. I want to see Driscoll and find out where the insurance comes in, if he's chastened enough to tell me."

"I'll go hunt up O'Brien. I called Callaghan's office, by the way, just before you came in—he's over at the jail questioning your thugs. Maybe he'll get another little piece for you to fit in."

"I'm not," said Mendoza, "nearly so interested in the thugs as I am in Lydia—"

"*¡Naturalmente!*" said Hackett. "She's female!"

Mendoza met Callaghan just emerging from the inside block of the county jail. "Anything new?"

"This and that," said Callaghan. "Come and have lunch with me, I'll brief you. I've earned it, God knows, been hammering at these boys most of the morning."

"I haven't got time. Owing to various excitements I was up half the night and I've wasted half today already. I've got some hammering to do myself. Tell me here."

They sat down on the bench along the wall and lit cigarettes. "Prettyman isn't coming out with anything. He's a smart boy. Also there's probably a deal set up—usually is—about his boss getting a lawyer for him, and in return he keeps his mouth shut. The lawyer—we see a lot of him and a couple of others the same kind—knows what the setup is, but so long as he gets his fee he figures what the hell. Somebody's got to represent the Prettymans in court, and he might as well get a piece of what's going. From the other three I've got a little useful talk about this Castro, but they don't know who his immediate boss is, of course— they're just punks. I did also hear a few things about this Angie."

"Ah," said Mendoza.

"It seems to tie up in a sort of way, but I don't see what it ties up *to*. What they dropped about Angie—I had to put two and two together on it, because they're trying to be awful damn cagy, you know—I gather he's another pusher like we figured, in this same string—"

"Yes, Pretty's best boy."

"And he's been sharing quarters—maybe still is, but it's on the cards when we hauled these four in and went through the Elite, the rest of 'em'd scatter quick in case we had 'em spotted—with one Denny. That is, if it's the same Denny that Prettyman knows. Seems likely. And from a couple of little things, I don't think Denny's on this lay at all."

"That figures. Denny. For Dennis? Another Irish name."

"Well, we come all sorts like other people," said Callaghan. "Does that say anything to you?"

"I don't know. Maybe. That's about it? Well, I'll go and ask my questions and maybe this'll mean a little more." Mendoza went on in and requested admittance to Driscoll.

Driscoll was a sorry sight after his hours in a cell; he was disheveled, he needed a shave, his eyes were puffy and bloodshot, and he was probably suffering from a headache and a bad case of indigestion—he looked it. He almost fell on Mendoza, babbling eagerly at him the minute he came in sight.

"Lieutenant, say, I certainly owe you an apology, way I've been acting—don't know what got *into* me, I know better than to act that way —you've got to make allowances, I've been drinking kind of heavy, had some personal worries on my mind, you know how it is—"

The jailer banged the cell door shut and Mendoza surveyed Driscoll leisurely. "So you're ready to co-operate now, Mr. Driscoll? Yes, I rather expected you'd take it like this. You have been a nuisance, Mr. Driscoll—I might say a damned nuisance. Ordinarily men in your job are quite co-operative and polite, we find—especially those associated with as large and well-known a firm as yours. Despite popular fiction, it usually does pay an investigator—public or private—to remember his manners, you know. At least I've always found it so. There's an old saying that one catches more flies with honey than with vinegar."

"Listen, Lieutenant, my God, I know all that, I said I been worried, drinking a little heavy, and you know how it takes some—couple of drinks, they're spoiling for a fight, pick a fight with anybody looks at them—I'm kind of like that—"

"So am I," said Mendoza conversationally, leaning on the door, "so I don't drink much. It saves a lot of trouble."

"I want to apologize, I know I've made you mad, and no wonder. Don't know what got into me, I know better—listen, you'll give me a break, Lieutenant, you look like a regular guy, you won't complain to the company, will you?—swear I never acted like this before, and—"

"I am not so constituted," said Mendoza, "that I enjoy being fawned on, Mr. Driscoll. I don't give one damn for your relations with your company, but I should doubt that you keep your job much longer whether or not I issue an official reprimand. All I'm interested in right now is some straight answers you should have given me three days ago."

"Yes, sure, I *know,* Lieutenant, be glad to tell you whatever you want to know. . . . Skyros . . . Well, I'll tell you, maybe I better just let you have it from the start, see, tell you just how it was . . ." Driscoll went on talking for some time, going into elaborate details.

And that built-in sense of order somewhere inside Mendoza, that thing that was rendered so acutely wretched by the wrinkle in the rug, the picture hanging crooked, the untidy scattered pieces of the jigsaw puzzle—it began to settle down into peace and cease to nag at him. It was satisfied. So that's how it is, that's the pattern, or a large part of it; just the background to fill in. Oh, very nice—pieces dovetailing into each other neat and meaningful. Yes. He felt better than he had all week, since this had been on his mind. He even began to feel slightly benevolent toward Driscoll.

At the end of what Driscoll had to say, he saw to the necessary forms for his release and drove happily back to headquarters. His mind was busy filling in background details, and of course there were a few little things he still didn't know—

Such as who *had* killed Stevan Domokous—

But such a large part of it unraveled now, the rest ought to be untied easily. . . .

He stopped at First Aid and had his hand redressed, thinking that he'd probably be too busy the rest of the day to bother with it. And he was not wrong.

Sergeant Lake greeted him with relief. "I was hoping you'd be in pretty soon, knowing how it's on your mind sort of, Lieutenant. One of Callaghan's office men just called down, said they had orders to relay any news about this Skyros. The tail they've got on him had just called in, said there was the hell of a ruction of some sort going on in his office, and a call out to the precinct—"

"For God's sake, what about? All right, I'd better go and find out," and Mendoza snatched up his hat again and made back for the elevator.

SEVENTEEN

Mr. Skyros had had only one brief moment of alarm. Of all the little shocks and worries he had suffered lately, this was the easiest to handle, because he knew about Domokous. Earnest young Domokous saying, "A little it worried me, sir, I don't like to think bad things about you, and maybe I just misunderstood some meaning—"

Domokous had known nothing definite, so obviously the girl knew nothing.

Really a most unattractive girl: that long sallow face, tangled black hair—and she was staring at him with bright-eyed vindictive triumph, as if she actually thought she had said something meaningful.

"My dear young lady," he said, smiling, sure of himself, "first I say I'm very sorry to see Stevan's girl with such thoughts in her head—it's not a nice thing. And you're all wrong, you know, this is a very silly little business altogether, you have got this funny idea from Stevan, I know, yes, but it was just a little mistake."

"It wasn't no mistake!" she said. "He told me all about it—he'd found out just what you're up to—that's why you killed him, I know! I know about *everything,* Mr. Skyros—but you won't hurt me, you won't dare, see? I've got it all wrote down, just like I say, black 'n' white, an' I got it put away in a box at the bank, where nobody can't get at it but me. See? But you give me the five thousand dollars an' I won't tell— that's fair, isn't it? I'd promise never to tell—"

Mr. Skyros laughed. "Miss Roslev—really, I don't know what I should say to you, this silly little thing, this nothing! I don't want to call the police, tell them this bad thing, how you have such crazy ideas—"

"You wouldn't dare—I know!"

"But that's just what I tell you, young lady, you *don't* know, isn't it? You don't know anything at all. Come now, what is this bad thing I'm supposed to do, eh? I steal from somebody, I break in a house to rob, maybe? And you say, my good God, me, I murder Stevan? Now this isn't funny, I don't like it."

"I know what you done! And it's all wrote down—"

"Then you let me in on the secret, eh? What is it all about?"

"Stevan *told* me—he'd found out—"

"But nobody tells me," said Mr. Skyros. "Now you listen to me, young lady. Yes, sure, poor Stevan, maybe he tells you how he hears a little something one night, makes him think bad things about me. This I don't doubt he says to you, because he comes to me and tells me, he's worried for it—such a nice honest young man he was, isn't it?—and I have set his mind at rest. It was a little mistake was all, he don't know some of the words we use in a business way, you see. And I straighten it out in his mind, so he knows everything's O.K., I'm no big public enemy like the papers call it! That's all it was, a little mistake, you see? This you didn't know, that we'd talked it over—poor fellow, he's dead before he sees you again, I suppose. And I'm patient to explain, tell you how it was, because I'm sorry for you, such bad ideas in your head."

She stared at him stupidly, across the desk there. "That's not so, that's a lie! I *know*—about a lot of money—there, that tells you I know! An' I'll tell *everybody* if you don't give me—"

"Oh, my good God in heaven," exclaimed Mr. Skyros. "This is a comedy, like in the films—only maybe not so funny. Very good, young lady, you go to the police and say, this Andreas Skyros is a bad man, he's figuring to steal a lot of money—you tell everybody just how and where and when, isn't it? Only you can't tell, nothing you've got to tell, and this *I* know! Now be sensible, Miss Roslev, go away and put these crazy ideas out of your head."

"No!" she said, and she leaned forward, gripping the edge of the desk hard, fingers pressed bone-white. "It's all lies—I do too know—everything about it! And I'll tell—you got to give me five thousand dollars right now—then I won't—"

"Oh, go away, young woman!" said Mr. Skyros crossly. "I'm a very patient man, and I don't want to make a big fuss about this little nonsense, call in the police and tell them you put these silly little threats on me—poor Stevan's girl, it wouldn't look nice at all!—but I don't put up with it all day either. A lot of craziness in your head is all. You stop bothering me, go away, forget it."

"You just wouldn't *dare*—the cops—I do *too!* You *got* to. I'll tell—"

"Now look," said Mr. Skyros, and stood up. He knew it was scarcely a chance at all he was taking; the girl knew nothing in any case, she was only bluffing, and how she had thought to get away with it was beyond his understanding. But she would not go to the police, and it would not be necessary that he carry out a threat to do so. Of course he could not do that—it was only that she must be made to understand her ridiculous position. "Now look, young woman. I'm patient like I say, I explain to you how it happens, this little mistake. It's nothing, you know nothing, because there's nothing to know—and that's all to say about it. I don't like to do such a thing, but I can't be pestered like this, and you don't leave my office, then I call the police and tell them how you try to blackmail me—over nothing, just a silly idea—"

"—Wouldn't *dare*—"

"Now, who do they listen to, I ask you? Me, I'm a respectable businessman, an honest man, my own place, never in any kind of trouble, and no—no axe to grind I got, like they say—" He shrugged. "Why should I tell lies about this unimportant girl—some kind of cheap job, a cheap little couple of rooms somewhere, a girl nobody knows or cares about much, isn't it? Nobody pays any attention to you, Miss—"

"You old devil!" she screamed at him suddenly. "You *got* to give me that money, you *got* to—you—" She sprang to her feet, still gripping the desk, leaning across it. "You *got* to, you *know* you got to," she panted. "I *got* to have—"

Suddenly Mr. Skyros felt just a little nervous. It was absurd, of course, but her eyes were quite wild, she sounded— And nobody else in the building, so far as he knew: the office staff had all gone off, Saturday afternoon . . . "I don't got to do anything," he said. "You go away and calm down, or I call the police."

"You—you—*I got to have that money! I'll kill you—if you don't*—" Her hand darted out like a snake, snatched up the letter-knife from the desk. It was a miniature Indian dagger of brass—Mr. Skyros had a fancy for such things—with a curved blade, and while it was not quite as razor-sharp as a real dagger would be, it could probably inflict some damage—its point was sharp enough. Mr. Skyros stepped backward involuntarily, tripped over his desk chair, and half fell sideways, clutching at the desk.

"Now, young lady, don't you be foolish," he started to say.

"Kill you—I just *got* to—" And she was on him like a cat, rushing around that side of the desk. Mr. Skyros felt the knife-point bite deep into his upper chest and let out a shrill yelp, staggering backward toward the window with some idea of calling for help. She flew at him again, sobbing with fury, and then the door opened and a nondescript man ran in, got her from behind by the arms, said, "What the hell's going on here?" and blew a whistle out the window.

Mr. Skyros collapsed into his desk chair and squinted fearfully down at his chest. There was some blood; he tore his shirt open and was rather disappointed to find only a minute puncture in the pink soft flesh. "This—this fiend of a female," he gasped to the man, "she—"

Running footsteps pounding up the stairs, a uniformed patrolman. "Darcy, headquarters," said the other man. "Attack of some sort, you better call the wagon. Listen, sister, you just calm down and stop trying to fight me, you're goin' nowhere right now."

Mr. Skyros sank lower in his chair and moaned to himself. Police— having to hear all about it—and no telling what this terrible woman would say— These crazy females!

"That's right, sister, you take it easy for a change," said the man. The girl subsided suddenly into a straight chair, and crouched there bent forward, hair falling over her face, silent and sullen.

Mendoza got there in time to follow the patrol car in to the precinct station. He took Mr. Skyros along, volubly protesting. Mr. Skyros' little wound was given first aid, and he was asked if he wanted to charge the young woman formally with assault.

"Look," said Mr. Skyros earnestly, "let's not make the big thing out of this, isn't it? I'm sorry for the young lady, that's all. She's this poor Domokous' girl, going to marry him she was, and maybe she's a little lightheaded—a little crazy, you know—with the grieving for the poor boy. You see what I mean, gentlemen. She's got some crazy idea in her head—I don't know, don't ask *me* how females get ideas!—that it's, somehow, because he works for me he gets himself killed like that, you see? *I* don't know how she figures, gentlemen, she comes, says a lot of crazy things that don't make any sense at all, says it's all my fault poor Stevan dies—don't ask *me* why she thinks like that! It's a terrible thing all round, poor Stevan and now his girl acting like she's crazy—but I don't want any big trouble about it, bad for everybody, isn't it? I'm sorry for this poor girl, she don't know what she's saying, you know. She don't hurt me much," said Mr. Skyros bravely, "just a little scratch like, and I don't hold any grudge on the poor girl. You let her go home, get calmed down, maybe see a doctor—I don't charge her with anything, gentlemen."

But it wasn't quite as simple as that. Mendoza let Skyros go; he had a pretty good idea of what was behind this, and there wouldn't be anything more to be got out of Skyros. The last couple of remarks the girl had made in his office that day—he could add two and two and figure she'd had a second thought; maybe the little Domokous had told her that time might be material for blackmail. It could just be that Domokous had told her more, though it didn't seem likely when what he'd told the priest added up to nothing, really. And what was it worth if he had—hearsay evidence? Still . . . So he let Skyros go, and saw the girl there in the precinct sergeant's office.

"You went to Mr. Skyros' office to threaten him, Miss Roslev," he said. "What did you have to threaten him with? . . . You can tell me, you know, and I can see he's punished for it, if it's something very bad." Almost instinctively he spoke as one would to a child, for her blank stare. She had made no attempt to tidy herself, comb her hair, refasten her blouse where its buttons had pulled apart in the little struggle.

She just stared at him vaguely. After a moment she said, "Five thousand dollars. He's *got* to pay me. I *know*—I do so know."

"What do you know, Miss Roslev?"

"He's *got* to," she said. "Just *got* to. Or I'll tell. A lie, say I don't know nothing. I do too. An awful lot o' money—Stevan said—about an awful lot o' money. Five thousand dollars, I thought."

"Yes. What about it, Miss Roslev?"

She looked at him a long moment, and her eyes focused on him, and then she smiled a small, scornful smile and said, "That's not my name. I'm Katharine Ross. I'm *Katharine Ross,* I don't have nothing to do with these people, funny foreign-sounding names, nothing I got to do— my name's Katharine—Katharine—Katharine—I'm Katharine Ross and I—"

Mendoza went out and told the sergeant it might be a good idea to call in a doctor to look at her, also to notify the grandmother as next of kin. Maybe she was shamming, maybe she thought Skyros had charged her and she'd get out of it playing crazy, but he didn't much like her looks.

And it didn't matter a damn, it wouldn't be legal evidence anyway; but he hung around to hear what the doctor said. And of course that didn't mean a damn thing either: a lot of double talk! Thus the doctor —shock, perhaps temporary amnesia, perhaps an unstable personality; one could not really say definitely without intensive psychiatric examination, and naturally one was not equipped—oh, well, as to *competent,* one would not like to say—

Mendoza said a few things to himself about modern psychiatric theories, and went out to the charge room. The grandmother was there by then, and the priest had come with her. Any man in the force ran across both attitudes his first day in uniform, but Mendoza had never much liked meeting either one: the old woman saw Authority to be feared, always tyrannical; the priest, Authority to be ultimately relied on, always knowing all the answers.

Mendoza didn't know all the answers any more than another man. He told them what he knew. And because one day it might be legally important (though he didn't think so) whether Katya Roslev really knew something or didn't, he went with the old woman and the priest back to the room where she sat slouched in a chair, silent, under the doctor's eye.

"Katya, the gentleman, Mr. Skyros, he is kind and don't ask the police to shut you in jail,"—the old woman, timid—"you can come home with me now, I know you don't mean anything wrong, whatever it is you do. Katya—"

The girl looked at her blankly. "Go home?" she said. "Home—with you? I don't know you. My name's *Katharine Ross*. Good American name. I don't know you—funny old foreign woman, can't even talk English good—I don't know *anybody* like you, I never *did*—"

"Oh, Katya, you don't say such to me—me who raises you from a baby, tries to teach you all how to do right—how is it you say, you don't know me? It is your own great-mother speak to you, my dear—it's not to matter, what you've done, you know I don't stop loving you —it's all right, Katya—" She went off into her own tongue then, probably saying it all over.

"I don't know you or your damned foreign talk, you old bitch!" screamed the girl at her, harsh and sudden. "Go away—go away—go away!"

The priest exchanged a look with Mendoza and led the old woman out; she had fallen silent, looking stunned. "Perhaps it's foolish to ask what you think, Lieutenant? Such a distressing—"

"Not for me to say. They'll take her into hospital, of course—the General."

"But always I am kind with her," whispered the old woman. The priest shook his head and shepherded her away.

And it was, that, very much a side issue; Mendoza switched his mind back to the main problem, driving back to headquarters.

Hackett had wandered through Records looking for O'Brien in vain; he didn't know him well. Finally he asked, and was told that O'Brien wouldn't be in until afternoon, off on some special job. Hackett swore mildly and took himself out to lunch. Coming back, he just missed Mendoza, heard about the undefined excitement at Skyros' office and wondered about that. He looked over the tails' reports on the Bouvardier woman, which contained nothing of interest at all.

About two o'clock he went down to Records again and found O'Brien, who looked more like a school principal than a policeman, half-hidden behind a stack of file-size record cards. "Heard you were asking for me," said O'Brien.

"Nothing official." Hackett pulled up a chair. "It's this little thing. I remembered you saying your hobby is coins. It's cropped up in something of Luis Mendoza's, and we wondered if you could give us any idea what it might be. If anything. For all I know, it's just a souvenir medal from a midway shooting gallery or something like that."

"Let's have a look," said O'Brien. He took the thing in his palm, weighed it, whisked out his handkerchief to polish it and then stopped, looked at it again, made a little clicking sound with his tongue, and put the handkerchief away without using it. "He said, "But it can't possibly —it must be a replica—" He opened a drawer, brought out a magnifying lens, and bent over the coin laid flat on his desk; presently he turned it over very delicately and examined the other side.

"Well?" said Hackett.

"Where'd you get this?" asked O'Brien.

"Apparently somebody lost it in a hot car."

"Jesus H. Christ," said O'Brien in an awed small voice. "And you or Lieutenant Mendoza have been carrying it around loose in your pocket—"

"Why not? What is it, anyway? Is it worth anything?"

"Worth anything," said O'Brien. *"Worth*—well, I wouldn't like to guess what, offhand, I'm not a real expert—and besides, you wouldn't often find a thing like this in such good condition. Not *fine* condition, but technically very good, and of course you could hardly expect anything better. I'll be damned. I will be damned. Carrying it around loose—"

"What *is* it?" asked Hackett. "I thought it looked pretty well beaten up myself. I suppose you could polish it, if it's silver—"

O'Brien clutched the magnifying glass like a bludgeon and asked if any vandal up in Homicide had tried to polish it.

"No, of course not, and why the hell all the excitement about it?"

"I'm not an expert," said O'Brien, "as I say. But my own interest has always been mostly in the older foreign stuff, and I can tell you just a little something about this, Sergeant. Though I've never seen anything like it outside a museum, which is where it ought to be. This is a Greek coin, I wouldn't say from which city but most likely Athens or Elis or just possibly Syracuse, and I'd place it as dating from somewhere around 400 B.C."

"What? You don't mean—"

"That's what I said. It's a silver *stater,* the common currency of the Greek city-states. Probably one of the oldest Greek coins extant, and in wonderful condition. It can't have circulated much—those early coins wore down very rapidly, you know, not being milled—and not so much alloy, either. All made by hand—you can see it never was a true circle —and stamped with handmade dies. The eagle with the hare in its talons, here on the obverse, that's a device you find rather often on Greek pieces of the period—never seen one before, just photographs— really marvelous detail, considering—and this thing on the reverse is Zeus's thunderbolt, stylized of course, but beautiful—beautiful work. I can't imagine where this came from, such condition—just dropped in a *car?*—but—" Suddenly O'Brien fell silent, mouth open, bounced straighter in his chair, stared excitedly from the coin to Hackett, and finally said again, *"Jesus* H. Christ. Listen, Sergeant—I wonder—listen, there was a big collection of Greek coins stolen just about a month ago, the most important collection, and the biggest, in existence—the Lex- ourion collection—and one of the things makes it so valuable, all the pieces are—were—in wonderful condition, not *mint,* you couldn't ex- pect it, but very good. The County Museum was angling to buy it, I remember reading about it in the *Times.*"

"I'll be damned," said Hackett, and now he felt almost as excited as O'Brien looked, "I wonder—this could be a big piece of the story! Thanks, we'll check that—thanks very much, O'Brien," and he reached for the coin.

"No, you don't, you Goth," said O'Brien. "Wait just a minute, now." He rummaged in the drawer. "Whether this is part of the Lexourion collection or not, it's worth the hell of a lot of money and a lot more than that in historical importance—you're not going to ruin its condi- tion. Have the owner suing you for damages, you don't want that, do you? Here," and he stowed it away, carefully wrapped in Kleenex, in the little paper-clip box.

EIGHTEEN

When Hackett came into the office he found Mendoza there, standing at his desk, hat still on, which meant he was slightly excited about something, talking on the inside phone.

"*¡Válgame Dios!* What use are your files to me? I want to talk to the man who worked the case, I want Goldberg! . . . Where? *¡Fuegos del infierno!* What the hell is he doing in San Francisco? Isn't he working here any longer? . . . You send a full-fledged lieutenant to ride herd on a two-bit mugger? . . . Yes, Sergeant Gomez, I am annoyed. Doubtless Burglary knows its own business, but . . . Well, what time does the plane get in? Four-fifteen, *muy bien*. I'll be here to catch him —I presume he'll be bringing this desperate criminal to headquarters *pronto*—when he's delivered the goods. I might even buy him a drink if he can tell me some things I want to know. About four forty-five? . . . What? *¡Vaya por Dios!* All right, all right, if it's midnight I'll be here, I want to see him. *Gracias* very much for nothing." He put down the phone, swept off his hat, and flung himself into his chair. "Fates conspiring! They must send Goldberg off to escort this mugger home for indictment, just when I want him. And of course some special Air Force maneuvers or something have routed the San Francisco flights to land at Municipal instead of Burbank—another hour's drive in traffic, he won't be here until after six at a guess. . . . You've missed some excitement, by the way," and he told Hackett about Katya Roslev.

Hackett scarcely paid attention, full of his own news. "Listen, Luis, I've got something—it might be a lot—I got O'Brien to look at this coin, and he says—"

"I can guess," said Mendoza. "Maybe part of the famous Lexourion collection. I've heard about it from Driscoll. Why do you think I want to talk to Goldberg?"

"Oh, hell, and I thought I'd got ahead of you for once. So what did Driscoll part with?"

"A lot of the story." Mendoza lit a cigarette and shouted to Sergeant

Lake to bring in some coffee. "The Lexourion collection, it seems, is one of the largest and most valuable collections of ancient Greek coins in existence. It was amassed over a period of many years by one Alexander Lexourion, whom I somehow see as one of those amiable fuzzy-minded professors, but actually I believe he was a hard-headed businessman. About two months ago Lexourion came here, with his collection, to negotiate with the L.A. County Museum, which was thinking of buying it. And he'd no sooner got here than it was stolen, under funny circumstances too, which I trust Goldberg can tell me more about. And Lexourion gets such a shock hearing about it that he has a stroke and passes out. Now, the collection is insured for two hundred thousand bucks, and naturally the insurance company sits up and takes notice—"

"And wouldn't they," agreed Hackett. "But what in God's name could a burglar do with a thing like that? I mean, it'd be like stealing the Mona Lisa or—"

"And I hear even that's been done once. Yes, of course, that was the first thing in the insurance company's collective mind. Nobody could sell such a thing to a fence. There are, I understand, about seven hundred-odd coins altogether, and separately they'd be worth something but not nearly so much as in a collection. And also, a thing like that, there's what you might call a pedigree attached, you know—anybody who'd be interested in buying it would want to be assured that it *is* the Lexourion collection. Well, the same thing leaped into my mind as the insurance company thought of, both of us having some experience of human nature—"

"Fraud," said Hackett. "But Lexourion didn't know, if he died of the shock."

"Ransom," said Mendoza. "Steal it and sell it back to the original owner. And the owner just might try—being understandably annoyed at having to pay for his own property—to figure out a way to hang onto some of the insurance money. Sure, a little awkward, but I suppose even today you'd find a few private collectors who might buy the thing secretly, if they were assured of the pedigree, and very possibly—if it was smuggled out of the country—the insurance company'd find it hard to follow the transaction *or* do anything about it. Now!" He regarded with pleasure the coffee Sergeant Lake had just brought in, and drank some. "This may be years getting settled legally—not our business—probate and so on. Lexourion died intestate, and therefore his legal next of kin comes in for whatever he had to leave. And who, Mr. Bones, do you suppose is his legal next of kin? One Madame Lydia Bouvardier, his only child. Lydia Bouvardier. Such a romantic-sounding name, isn't it?"

"And isn't that nice to know," said Hackett. "But what's it got to do with Stevan Domokous dead of heroin in a Carson Street alley?"

"*Tengo paciencia, allá veremos*—with time all will be clear. I hope. A little something I've tied up, at least. Driscoll, damn him, delayed us on this thing nearly a week—longer—he should have come in and laid the facts on the line the minute he landed here, and I'd take a small bet Goldberg will want his hide nailed to the door of his office for keeping it secret. Though you can also say the director of the museum was lax —but I'd take another little bet that Driscoll let him think *he* was in touch with the police, so the director didn't do anything about it himself. These glory boys, out to play to the grandstand . . . About three weeks after the collection was stolen—in fact, Arturo, on the same Sunday afternoon that Alison attended that exhibition at the County Museum—the museum director had a very odd and mysterious visitor. About this I'd like to know more than Driscoll passed on secondhand, but I expect Lieutenant Goldberg will be even more passionately interested, and do the direct investigating. Now my curiosity's beginning to be satisfied, I'm rather liking this case, you know—it encroaches on other peoples' jobs, and they're doing so much of the work. . . . This visitor asked the director if he'd be interested in buying a collection of Greek coins, and even hinted at the Lexourion collection. The price mentioned was fifteen thousand dollars, which—not surprisingly— struck the director as a little suspicious, considering that if it *was* the Lexourion stuff, that was insured for two hundred thousand. By the sample the visitor produced to show him, he said, it might have been the Lexourion stuff. Naturally, since the museum had been interested, he was tolerably familiar with it. And from what he said to Driscoll, I gather that the visitor didn't seem exactly the type to go in for collecting ancient Greek coins, and the director instantly put two and two together and wondered if he was, so to speak, being offered hot goods."

"A *sample*," said Hackett. He got out the little box and looked at the silver *stater* O'Brien said was twenty-three hundred years old. The thunderbolt of Zeus . . . "Could be, just possibly, this little thing?"

"Could be, very possibly," said Mendoza in dreamy satisfaction. "I can't say why he might have hopped Alison's car. Ridiculous sort of thing to do—but there it is. I think he did. After he left the director. The director thought it over, and then he made a little mistake. Instead of calling us, he called the insurance company. I deduce he was thinking of avoiding publicity. Handle the thing nice and quiet, just in case he was wrong and the visitor was a *bona fide* collector. Anyway, the insurance people shot Driscoll out *pronto,* of course—because why? Because Lexourion's daughter had come over from Paris—legal business, I suppose there's miles of red tape to untangle about the estate even though he wasn't a citizen—and this looked as if the thief was maybe getting bids on the collection."

"Now wait a minute," said Hackett. "You're not telling me that anybody—even the dumbest pro in business—would think he could sell it under the counter to the County Museum?"

"Just look back over your career, *chico*. Only nine years you've been in, compared to my seventeen, but you've met them—you know them. One of the reasons the paperback detective thrillers are so damn fantastic, to anybody who's had a little contact with the real thing. How often have you said to yourself, Nobody can be *that* stupid! Nobody but a pro—never mind what lay he's on, never mind whether he's a juvenile just starting out hopping shorts, swiping little stuff off dime store counters, or a very much ex-con just out from a twenty-year stretch for armed robbery and assault. They don't come any dumber, when it comes to—mmh—both the ordinary sort of knowledge almost anybody in any crowd has, or what you might call the nuances of ordinary human give-and-take. One of the reasons they're pros, Art—you know as well as I do—they haven't got even the rudimentary empathy, the little imagination about other people, that most people have. . . . The simplest things, the smallest things, they just don't *know*."

"That's so, God knows. But you'd think anybody—still, of course, that *is* so."

"Most of the reason we're kept busy," said Mendoza. "Well, as I say, Driscoll's sent out but quick to look into this. It would be Driscoll, of course. Water under the bridge—let it go—we know now, anyway. Driscoll pokes around, asking questions of the director, of our Lydia, and he reads what the papers had to say at the time about the robbery —damn fool way to investigate, half the time they get details wrong or some officious editor cuts out the relevant facts—and he comes to some conclusions. Your guess is as good as mine as to whether the conclusions were born of whiskey or solid deduction. One of his methods seems to be trying to make any female involved in a case, possibly on the theory that women always speak the truth in bed—which, *de paso,* graphically illustrates his appalling lack of experience."

"And what conclusions did he come to?"

"He thinks that our Lydia is up to something. I agree. She is," said Mendoza, "a widow. A romantic, young, beautiful widow. Her late husband was upwards of sixty when she married him, and an extremely wealthy man—land-rich and munitions-rich—and she was a tender innocent young thing of seventeen. I don't think. A young lady with her head screwed on very tight—take the cash and let the romance go. Very sensible, ¿no es verdad?"

"Oh, *absolutamente,*" said Hackett with a grin.

"He also thinks—and again I agree—that Mr. Andreas Skyros is not merely a social acquaintance of our Lydia. He doesn't know whether or not she's been approached about buying back the collection, but he thinks she will be if she hasn't been, and that she would probably be willing to dicker about the—mmh—ransom. One thing that emerges, by the information he has from his company, is that our Lydia disapproved of the intention to sell the collection in the United States, would prefer to see it, say, in the Louvre or somewhere like that, if they'd be interested. At any rate, Driscoll says, and quite reasonably too, that if Mr. Skyros was a purely social acquaintance—maybe someone she had a letter of introduction to—she'd be going to his house, entertained by his wife, whereas it looks rather like a business relationship."

"So it does. Where do you figure Skyros comes in? And still all this doesn't say any one thing about Domokous."

"I don't know," said Mendoza. "It's easy to build up stories about it —as Mr. Skyros would say, isn't it? I'm hoping Goldberg can add a few details to pin down which of the stories might be the right one."

Lieutenant Saul Goldberg sneezed, groped blindly for more Kleenex in his breast pocket, and said thickly through it, "Id's the whiskey, I'b allergic to id."

"Then why drink it?"

"What, turn down a free drink?" Goldberg, his sinus passages temporarily clear, sat back in the booth and sipped cautiously. "I'm allergic to so damn many things," he said gloomily, "that I've just given up doing anything about it. Life's too short, and the allergy specialist too free with my money. Everything in the house non-allergenic, yet—I'm surprised they don't tell me to get rid of my wife and kids as well as feather pillows and all the rugs. Have all the more money to hand them. And I've still got the allergies, so I say the hell with it, I just buy Kleenex. And besides the cat found her way home, and we hadn't the heart to give her away again after that. You want a kitten, by the way,

Mendoza? She seems to've stopped somewhere on the way. Four cute little gray and white fellows, one black."

"Coals to Newcastle, I think I'm going to have some of my own. . . . So it doesn't show yet, very funny, now forget your sinuses and tell me what you know about that job at Shanrahan and Mac-Ready's, where that collection of Greek coins was part of the loot."

"Hey, you got something on that?" asked Goldberg, looking interested.

"Maybe. You tell me what you know first. . . . Damn it, Shanrahan mentioned it too, but how was I to know?"

"You're welcome to what I've got. Sometimes you got to sit on these things awhile—that's what I'm doing now. That was a damn funny job, in some ways—"

"Stop a minute. One little thing that struck me funny: what was a collection of Greek coins doing in the safe of a fashionable jeweler?"

Goldberg grinned. "That's one of the funny things. And ordinarily I've got no sympathy for pro burglars, but you know, I did kind of feel for the guy who pulled the job—it must've been quite a little shock, not to say disappointment, when he found out what he'd got away with. I'll tell you how it happened. This Greek, Lexourion, who owned the stuff—"

"Yes, I know about him."

"He'd just landed here. He'd never been here before, it was on account of the possible deal with the County Museum he came, but it like any of these hobbies—you know—there're specialty magazines, clubs, societies, and so on—and he did know somebody here: Mac-Ready. MacReady is an amateur numismatist too. It seems they'd been corresponding, all enthusiastic and friendly, for some time, and so MacReady was all set to entertain the old boy when he got here, and of course to see his famous collection. Well, Lexourion got in by plane one afternoon, MacReady met him, and they go straight up to Mac-Ready's house and spend a couple of hours looking at the collection. You know how these fanatic hobbyists are. And after awhile, when they're thinking about going out for dinner, all of a sudden Lexourion realizes it's too late to stash the stuff away in a bank vault as he'd meant to do, pending his interview at the County Museum. So Mac-Ready, naturally, says there's no trouble about that, they'll just put it away safe in the store vault for the night—good as a bank any time, burglar alarm and so on."

Mendoza sat back and laughed. "I see—I see. How very embarrassed Mr. MacReady must have been."

"That's an understatement," said Goldberg. "Especially when the poor old fellow dropped dead, hearing about it. Because of course that was the very night somebody picked to knock over Shanrahan and MacReady. It was a pro job, kind of routine. I wouldn't say it was a really slick job, but it was pro all right. And I'm pretty sure just one man. He came in through the skylight in the back room, and of course he had to be damn quick. These burglar alarm systems," and Goldberg looked rueful, "they're just dandy if you've got old-fashioned cops walking a beat, and in a place where the precinct station isn't ten miles away. He had about ten-twelve minutes after he tripped the alarm, and that he knew, and he used it. He set a charge of Dinah on the safe door and blew her, and he scooped up what was on top, probably all he could carry, and got clean away before the patrol car got there. Didn't leave any prints, of course. It was a neat enough little job. And when I think how he must have felt, when he got home with the loot and looked it over—" Goldberg laughed. "That's the reason I say one man; what was gone would just about make a one-man load, say in a ditty bag or something like that. This collection was on top of everything else in the safe, naturally, and I guess it must have looked impressive to him, way it was described to me. It was in an even dozen big square leather-covered boxes, each one about the size of a desk tray only thicker, because there are three tiers in each one, trays, you know. The trays are covered with velvet and have indented beds for each coin. And there was a manila folder in the lid of the top box with a complete list and description of every coin in the collection. You know, I'd love to've seen his face when he opened that first box and saw a lot of dirty old foreign coins instead of a handful of sparklers."

"Crime doesn't pay," agreed Mendoza amusedly. "Did he get much else?"

"About ten grand worth of the real stuff, but he wouldn't get much for it, you know. Matter of fact I think I know what he did get for it, a little over thirty-five hundred bucks." Goldberg finished his drink and got out a cigarette.

"Ah, now we get to it. You had a line on him?"

"I didn't," said Goldberg, "until I got hold of an excuse to search old Benny Hess's place. You might think we could've stopped worrying about Benny—he was over eighty and all crippled up with arthritis, *and* he had a nice little estate built up from the proceeds of a misspent life

—a lot of it cannily transferred into his daughter's name, too—but they don't change, do they? I—oh, hell," and he began to sneeze again, groped for the Kleenex. "Damn cigarettes. Doctor says I shouldn't smoke at all. The hell with him. Benny was a fence, and a big one. He got inside for it just once—he was a pretty smart boy. Kept a junk sec- ondhand store out on Pico Boulevard. Well, about ten days, two weeks ago, Benny's number came up and they hauled him off to the General, and seeing as he wasn't coming back to complain about the officious cops persecuting an innocent citizen who'd paid his debt to society, I got a warrant and went through his place but very thorough. There were a coupie of other little things we were looking for at the time, of course. And we found Benny had a very pretty setup, just like in the stories, you know: dugout room under his living quarters, with a safe in it yet, and being a businesslike old guy, he'd kept records too—there was a ledger. Very abbreviated entries, but I could read between the lines—some of 'em. In the safe was about half the Shanrahan and MacReady stuff—the real stuff—he hadn't got rid of yet. And in the ledger, among other things, I came across this entry of thirty-five hun- dred and some-odd bucks, listed under *Donovan,* and that added up awful easy in my mind."

"Donovan," said Mendoza fondly. *"¡Venga más!*—the thing is clear —*y más vale tarde que nunca,* better late than never! Oh, very pretty. You knew the name?"

"Sure I knew the name," said Goldberg, catching the waiter's eye and beckoning. "I owe you a drink—I'll be sorry for this, those damn sinuses, but what the hell—same again. Sure I did. And it kind of made a little sense too, because the Donovans always stuck pretty close together—"

"More than one?"

"Three. One down, two to go. There was—"

"Francis Joseph," said Mendoza, smiling at his new drink. "Poor fellow, executed without benefit of a trial, just because a high school kid paid attention to a lecture for once."

Goldberg looked at him. "And what's Homicide's interest now? You've gone into the Donovans?"

"He just showed on the edge of something. About the others I don't know. Tell me—tell me all, *amigo.*"

"Well—the Donovans," said Goldberg. "Pros from a pro family. The dad was a stick-up specialist. Died in San Quentin doing his third stretch, when the boys were in their teens, I'd guess—before my time.

There's Jackie, and Denny, and Frank. All of 'em did time in reformatory for hopping cars, petty theft, and so on. Typical record sheets."

"I've seen Frank's."

"Then you've seen Denny's, except for the last line. Jackie—this is some fancy deduction of my own, he was one of my first arrests when I was a tender young rookie—Jackie was always the boss. Jackie was the one with a little more on the ball, as much as that kind of pro ever has. There was a time Jackie Donovan was on the F.B.I. list of Most Wanted. Back there about twenty years, eighteen years ago, there was a little gang—reading between the lines, and by what a couple of desk men in Records and my own office tell me, men who were around then and remember. The three Donovan brothers, and a little Italian fellow named Angelo Forti. Stick-ups, a few, but mostly burglary. After they all got through being minors and getting slapped on the wrist for being naughty boys, we got Jackie twice—a one-to-three and a three-to-five— both times for burglary. Denny, a one-to-three—same first count as Jackie. On that one, the little Italian was the driver, and he was only just past eighteen and he said he didn't know what they were up to, didn't know nothing about nothing, and the judge listened to him and put him on probation. He's never done any time at all—I don't know where he is or what he is doing now. And—"

"Angelo," said Mendoza. "Angie? Oh, yes—very nice. Maybe I can give you a hint. Yes, go on."

"The third time Jackie was picked up, he was either alone or the others got clean away. Pay your money and take your choice. I made that pinch, my first job after I ranked sergeant it was. Damn, the time goes. . . . Third count for him, they gave him the book and he got a taxi, fifteen years. He did the whole stretch too, because the parole chief we've got in now is a tough one, *which* is all to the good and more power to him. . . . Reason I saw a little kind of logic in it, and hooked up the Shanrahan-MacReady job with that *Donovan* entry in Benny's ledger, it's because Jackie Donovan was just due to come out. About three weeks back, from that fifteen-year stretch."

"Oh, this I like to hear," purred Mendoza. "But not soon enough to have done that job?"

"Uh-uh. I figure that was Denny. The way I say, these Donovans always stuck pretty close. Family feeling, you know? When I saw that entry in Benny's ledger, under the date which'd have been just about the time whoever did the Shanrahan-MacReady job was disposing of the loot, I had a kind of sentimental little vision, you know. Here's

Jackie Donovan coming out after fifteen long years inside—and maybe his loving brother Denny figured on making a little celebration. I don't know what Denny's been doing since—God knows we get enough casual stick-ups and break-ins we never can get anybody for, it could be he's managed to support himself that way, just smart enough to take nothing but cash, you know. Anyway, I wondered. I've had a little bet with myself that the proceeds wrung out of Benny Hess went to arrange a celebration party for Jackie Donovan. *And* I might add," said Goldberg, "that I did a little private cussing that I didn't know about it until after Jackie *was* out, or I could've put a leash on him to lead me to Denny. If you see what I mean."

"As it is, you don't know where either of them is?"

"I wish to God I did. That entry is enough to let me haul Denny in for questioning, at least. But ninety percent of this is all in my mind— just like the head-doctors say—*and,*" added Goldberg bitterly, "some of the allergy specialists. . . . I haven't got anything to take to the D.A. And now I've bared my heart to you, what's your interest and have you got anything more useful to hand me?"

"Maybe you'd better have another drink," said Mendoza. "I'm going to tell you something that'll raise your blood pressure." He told Goldberg about Driscoll and the mysterious visitor to the County Museum, and Goldberg invoked the Almighty, burst into a paroxysm of sneezing, called down curses on all stupid civilians, and emerged from fresh Kleenex to finish his second drink.

"Damn specialists. Tell me to avoid nervous tension. All in your emotions. What the hell do they expect, that I'll give up all my seniority and go and grow roses somewhere quiet? I will be damned. My God, these private eyes . . . I'll tell you, Mendoza, I can't say at that it comes as a big surprise. Donovan I couldn't lay my hands on, but I'd have taken a little bet there was some negotiation going on about that collection. We're reasonably smart these days, you know, and I can add one and one as easy as the next man. It was obvious no fence'd take on that kind of thing, and so I thought about it—along the lines of that one about the lost horse and the idiot boy—and—do you know that Lexourion's daughter is here?"

"My God," said Mendoza, "don't tell me I've been keeping three men busy on eight-hour shifts all to do work you've been doing too?"

Goldberg sat back and laughed. "There you are, too many cooks. Dangers of a big organization. Sure I've had men on her. What else could Donovan—if it was Donovan—do with a thing like this collection? And at that, I've had moments of doubt. I mean, a dumb small-time pro like Denny Donovan—would he even read the papers next morning to know what he had? I had another little vision of him dumping all those boxes in a pawnshop for five bucks—only of course they haven't showed up."

"I don't know for sure about Donovan," said Mendoza, "but whoever it was, he knew. That visit to the museum director—"

"Sure, and I'm going to be awful damn interested in what that one looked like," said Goldberg. "And the only surprise to me about that is the direction it took. Because I thought a little harder, after I had the word that the daughter was in town, and I asked myself how I'd handle it, say I was a middling-smart pro like Jackie Donovan stuck with that stuff—because Jackie was out by then—and I thought one like that might think it was just worth a five-buck investment—just on the chance, you know. So I sent a man down to look through the classified ads the last three weeks—"

"¡Hijo mio!" said Mendoza affectionately. "A man after my own heart. Exactly what I'd have done. And did you come up with anything interesting?"

"I think so," said Goldberg. "In two ways, you might say. There was an ad run in the personals for five days—haven't got a copy on me, but I can supply you—an ad that said, quote, Concerning Greek money, party will negotiate. Box So-and-So, unquote. It makes you wonder sometimes, doesn't it? You'd think they'd realize after a while that even the run-of-the-mill rookie in uniform's got an I.Q. over seventy-five."

"Isn't it the truth! And of course you went down and asked who'd placed the ad."

"One Andrew Jackson placed it. I shouldn't think any connection of the late general. There were no answers to Box So-and-So at all."

"None?"

"None. Which makes you think about a few other things. I was kind of persistent, and finally got hold of the girl who had taken the ad in the first place, not that I had much hope of her remembering anything about Andrew Jackson. But she did. I don't think she could pass a standard Civil Service exam, she's the kind has to stop and think what comes after C in the alphabet, but she placed him because she's female. Sex, it's wonderful. She said he was an awful handsome young fella—just like a movie star—looked like that new fella in movies now, couldn't remember his name but he's Greek or Italian or something, just awful handsome. She—"

"*¡Arriba!*" said Mendoza. "Goldberg, I could kiss you! I think we do arrive somewhere. Yes, we'll show her the corpse's photograph—but it does look open-and-shut. Very satisfying."

Goldberg sneezed and said plaintively, "Elucidate."

"With pleasure," and Mendoza lit another cigarette and began to talk. . . .

NINETEEN

Time never meant much to Mendoza when he was working a case; he chased Goldberg back to his office to get the name of the classified-ad girl, called the *Times,* and bullied the editor of that department into giving him her home address. He had caught Hackett just on the point of leaving; he passed over the address. "Go down to the morgue, get their file shot of Domokous and see what she says about it."

"That one I don't see," said Hackett, who had had a brief account of their joint deductions and got out the silver *stater* again to show Goldberg. "If it was Domokous who placed that ad for Skyros, why didn't he say something to the priest or the girl when he was talking about—"

"I don't think he ever thought twice about the ad—connected it with anything else. There are several little excuses Skyros could have given him: it was an advertising stunt, say, or a business code of some kind, or a joke on somebody—can we even be sure Domokous read the thing? Skyros probably had it all typed out neatly, together with the false name and address as of the advertiser, all Domokous had to do was hand it over the counter and pay, and all the girl had to do was count the words. Just luck she happened to remember him, and in connection with the ad. Of course Goldberg"—Mendoza beamed on him—"did catch her immediately afterward while it was fresh in her mind. I can see Domokous doing that as just a little errand for the boss, maybe on his lunch hour, and forgetting it by the next day. And of course, damn it, he's not around to have his memory jogged and tell us it *was* Skyros' ad—but it's another little handle."

"It all ties up, all right. This Denny pulled the break-in and found he was stuck with the collection—but how can we figure Skyros got into it?"

"He knew Frank," said Mendoza. "It's got to be that—use a little imagination on it. Frank wasn't his head pusher, of course—that we can say almost for certain—but maybe he'd got confidential with Prettyman, maybe Prettyman talks a bit too much when he's tight or something—if that's so, pity we can't slip him a bottle in jail—anyway, Frank knew Skyros' name if nothing else. And Frank was probably sharing quarters with Denny at the time. There's Angie too. Angie in the same string of boys. Guess at it—it always pays the ones like Skyros to be nice and friendly to the boys, if anonymously. Maybe he contributed some money to pay for poor Frank's funeral, something like that, and Denny knew who he was from Frank before and called up to thank him. Anyway, they were acquainted—if only just acquainted—somehow. I can guess at this part of it. You know what restricted circles, so to speak, the pros like Denny move in. He might not have known anybody—or *of* anybody—except Skyros, who might be expected to know a bit more about that collection than he did, who might give him a little advice about how to realize something from it. And of course it'd look like easy money to Skyros. . . . Considering that ad, and the fact that he hasn't attempted to hide his acquaintanceship with Lydia Bouvardier, I don't think she's been allowed to realize that he's anything but an ordinary helpful middleman—of the innocent variety, that is. Maybe he represented himself as a sympathetic friend of Papa's. Because no one actually answered the ad. It was a blind—it was to satisfy Lydia that that's how he got in touch with the thief."

"That sounds reasonable," nodded Goldberg. "He's a canny one?—longheaded fraud artist?"

"Oh, very careful indeed of everything to do with Mr. Skyros. . . . Let's not fight about him, Goldberg. It may be, with luck, enough will emerge that Callaghan'll have something on him too, and unless he did the actual murder—which I very much doubt—that charge'd earn him a stiffer sentence—we may as well let Pat have him. . . . But for some reason the negotiations have been delayed. Mmh. That little visit Lydia paid to Alison—and the note—yes, I wonder. You said Jackie Donovan was the one with a few more brains, Goldberg." Mendoza laughed. "I wonder if maybe Jackie put a monkey wrench in the works, by wanting to change the price. If he came out to find the deal set up, and told Denny he was a fool to take the first price mentioned—especially when

they had to cut it with Skyros—and has been trying to hold up Lydia
for more."

"You're building bricks without straw there, *chico*," said Hackett.

"Yes, first things first. With luck, we'll hear the details later! You go
and see this girl, that much we'll get cleared up tonight. Goldberg is
going to rout out the museum director—"

"I want to hear first hand what that visitor looked like," said Goldberg. "If it was either of the Donovans, I think I'd recognize a description. And that gives us another little something. I'll say this: Denny
would probably talk. He wouldn't mean to get anybody in trouble, but
he just can't help talking, and any kind of complicated little lie, he'd get
all tangled up in it. If we get something to put out a Wanted on the
Donovans, and pick them up, I think Denny would eventually give us a
lot more of the story."

"Which is very nice and helpful to look forward to," said Mendoza.
"But it would be even more helpful if we can get somebody else to talk.
And you know, if it's handled just right—scarcely worth while to trump
up a charge on her, and it'd probably never stick anyway—she's got the
money to hire a smart lawyer—"

"You needn't tell me," said Hackett, "what you're going to do. Somehow, all in the most innocent way, Goldberg, he always ends up with
the good-looking females in a case—if any. If just to question. I know,
you're going out to the Beverly-Hilton."

"She's not my type," said Mendoza. "But yes, I'll take her on, because neither of you have anything like what's called the élan to appeal
to her, and I'll get more out of her. I hope enough to add up to a
charge of some kind on Skyros."

But he didn't get out there at once. Just as he was leaving the office
the outside phone rang, and it was the Greek priest, apologetic.

"The old lady, she doesn't understand much about the law, Lieutenant. She has this conviction in her mind that you will say Katya was the
one who killed Stevan, because you think she's a lunatic."

"About that, who knows?"

"Indeed. But if you would be so kind to come by, just a few moments, let her hear you say it's not true—she won't believe me, she says
I would not know what the police think. It would be a kindness—"

"What's the address?" asked Mendoza with a mental sigh.

It was a shabby old frame apartment on a side street off Main; the
priest was waiting for him in the entrance. "Very kind," he repeated.
"Such a distressing thing—sometimes it's hard to understand the ways

of God, Lieutenant. I have been thinking of that passage: *From him who hath not shall be taken even that which he hath*. I know something of the story, you see: when she came here there was no Russian church near, she came to ours, and has been a faithful attendant. Not an easy or happy life—her husband deserted her long ago, and there were three children—two sons and a daughter. She could do nothing but domestic work, but she managed to raise them alone—it was a struggle. The older son was a sailor, and killed in an explosion at sea—his wife had died at Katya's birth—and the younger son was killed in the war. The daughter,"—the priest sighed—"perhaps malnutrition, or a hereditary disposition—she is in a tuberculosis sanatorium. There is, of course, no money but what Katya earned. She will be in straits if the girl—"

They climbed rickety, dirty stairs. "Pass by on the other side," said Mendoza. "What else? You see a good deal of it—I see more. The innocent bystanders. I know."

"But that," said the priest, "is not the terrible thing, Lieutenant. In this country, no one need starve, there is always charity. We have a church fund— No, it is not the material. If this poor girl is—incompetent, either temporarily or otherwise, there'll be these pompous doctors, I daresay, to say it is all the fault of her childhood environment and such nonsense. Always a difficult, sullen girl . . . And never any appreciation or gratitude shown for the struggle and sacrifice—not that the old lady wanted that—only a little love. And none of that either."

"It's not a thing to be manufactured," said Mendoza. They went into a bare, shabby room where the old woman sat huddled in a chair. He told her no one was thinking that her granddaughter had killed Stevan, she was not in prison; she was in the hospital, because it might be she was ill and needed treatment.

The woman listened in silence, her dark tragic eyes fixed on his. "You would know this—you are of high rank in the police. Do you tell the truth to me? . . . Yes, she's sick—sick she must be, to say such things to me—she doesn't mean it, you know, she doesn't know at all what she says—" anxious, turning to the priest.

"No, she does not know, she wouldn't say such things to you from her heart."

"If they would let her come home, I make her well and strong soon. . . . But I should take her clothes? They would let me in to see her, if I go there?"

"I don't know," said Mendoza. "Perhaps not if she's very ill, but you could ask."

"I will go," she said on a little gasp; and he knew that she would be very frightened, seeking that place of impersonal Authority, but she would go bravely and ask, for the love she bore one incapable of loving. And again her glance on him was half fearful.

He got away from the priest as quickly as he could afterward, feeling depressed.

"I apologize for intruding so late," he said to Madame Bouvardier.

"It makes no matter." Her eyes were busy, trying to sum him up. "You come from Mr. Skyros? On your card you write his name—"

"Well, let's say about Mr. Skyros. May we sit down?" Mendoza offered her a cigarette, smiling, laying on conscious charm. "You know, madame, it's not kind of you to come here and get yourself mixed up with criminals. You get yourself into trouble, and then you go home and say some very nasty things about these low-class Americans, which we don't deserve at all."

"But what is this? Me, mixed up with criminals? Who are you? It's a joke, maybe—"

"No joke. Lieutenant Mendoza of the police, madame." He produced his credentials. "You've been making quite a little work for us lately, you know. Although if you forgive me, I will say that my men have found it much more entertaining than following some lout of a suspected thief."

"I? Followed? What—" She was deciding whether to be angry or frightened.

"I won't eat you," grinned Mendoza. "Sit down and we'll make a little bargain. I think"—and it was a lie, but the easiest way to handle it and the only way to get anything out of her—"you've been an innocent victim in this case. Of course, you don't know our laws, and obviously a beautiful young lady like you, she doesn't waste her time studying books—"

She smiled and relaxed a little, beside him on the couch. "No, indeed I don't know about things here—imagine, I'm told the police are all uncouth *canaille* and look like farmers! Obviously also this is a lie."

"You're too kind—I hope so, madame. And then too, you are still grieving for your late father and possibly—shall we say?—not in any state to judge clearly. But shall we also say, it wasn't very wise of you to accept the proposal to buy back your father's collection from the thief."

"And now what has given you this idea?" She widened her eyes at him, wary, playing for time.

Mendoza laughed, brought out the little box, let her see the coin. "You recognize it? Good. . . . No, we have not got the rest, only this, but we will have. . . . Now, it's late, and there's no point in playing games, trying to trick each other. Cards on the table, madame. We know almost the whole story. Mr. Skyros has been negotiating for you with the thief, hasn't he? Very unwise to trust him—he is a professional criminal himself, you know—"

"But I do not know! What is this—Skyros? A—a gangster?"

"Well, that could be one word for it—"

"I have not trusted him, but this I did not imagine," she said thoughtfully. "How extremely odd."

"He has it arranged with the thief, you see. We have evidence on him," said Mendoza, hoping he told the truth, "and on several others—including Donovan." He watched her on that one, and saw that she recognized the name; so Goldberg hadn't been woolgathering, and they'd been right about that. "It is, in other words, all off, madame: they're about to be arrested and charged, and I am afraid it will appear as if you conspired with them—you understand—unless, of course, you speak out and tell the truth. All the truth. How you met Mr. Skyros, and all about the negotiating, and so on. But whether you do or not, that deal is off. I should imagine, however, that you'll get the collection back in time, when it's recovered."

Madame Bouvardier heaved a long sigh. "Well, at least that is something," she said practically. "Although I do *not* understand why the insurance company is not liable to pay also. The insurance is against theft, among other things, it is not?—very well—it is stolen, so they should pay! That is only logical. Whatever should occur later, it is nothing at all to do with that."

"Very logical," agreed Mendoza gravely, "but the ways of law are like the ways of God, madame—mysterious."

"You will have a little glass of wine with me. Berthe! I see you are a gentleman, *très gentil*, you are sympathetic, and also I think most accomplished at persuading the ladies! I will tell you about it—I tell you everything—it is to be seen there is nothing else I can do in this situation, and one must be practical. You are *quite* right," said Madame Bouvardier emphatically, rolling her eyes at him over her glass, "that I am entirely innocent in this affair—that it is against the law to do such, this I never knew! I will tell you how it came about, and beg that you believe me—"

"But who could doubt the word of so charming a lady?"

"Ah, you are so *sympathique*— I think I am much relieved after all it should end so. I tell you how it began, this Skyros . . ."

It was past eleven when he got home. And it was about all wound up, all but the tiresome routine, the collating of evidence, the further questioning, the formal taking of statements. He knew almost all about it now—though he still didn't know who had killed Domokous, but doubtless that would emerge—and he ought to be feeling pretty good about it. A little teaser of a business—some fairly complex details built up out of not much to start with. Interesting. Instead, he was feeling rather depressed.

That old woman, still a little on his mind. Nothing you could do about that kind of thing: there it was. In his trade he saw a lot of it. The innocent bystanders, as he'd said to the priest.

He sat up in bed smoking; at a little past midnight, on impulse and suffering a slight guilty conscience, he called his grandmother. The old lady was a night owl, up at all hours, but she told him instantly that he was extremely thoughtless to call at such a time, though it was something of a relief to know he was yet alive, not coming near her in all this long while. "Peace, peace," he soothed her, "I'm a public servant, my time's not my own."

"And so have you yet got a birthday gift for me?"

"You're too old for birthday gifts, my little pigeon."

"Little pigeon indeed, you're disrespectful. And since I never had any whatever all my life to fifteen years ago, I am making up lost time."

"I'll buy you a box of handkerchiefs. . . . I can't promise when I'll come, I'm just winding up this case. Day after tomorrow, maybe. And I know very well in any case what cunning plans are in your head—new neighbors I must meet! With a fair-to-middling pretty daughter or niece or cousin, confess it!—and you trying to play go-between."

"Wicked one, it's past time you are decently married. Are you so foolish at your age to believe in this Anglo-Saxon notion, true love for a lifetime, to base a marriage upon?"

"I was never so young or so foolish. I do quite well as I am. Have you visited the doctor about the stiffness in your knees?"

"Why should I pay money to the doctor to tell me I am getting old?

That I know. There is nothing else wrong with me at all, I've never had a sick day in my life—"

"There is a great deal wrong with you, and you still running back and forth to the priests it's to be hoped you confess it now and then. You tell lies, for one thing—all these elegant forebears direct from a castle in Spain! I myself distinctly remember your telling me that your own mother was half-bred Indian from the backwoods and never wore a pair of shoes until—"

"*That* is the lie, you remember quite falsely, and you're very rude to an old woman. . . . Now what is wrong, Luis? You're troubled for something. . . . Yes, you are, and wouldn't I know, that raised you from the nuisance of an infant you were?"

"It's nothing, a little something in this case is all . . . now, you don't want to hear about such things . . . well, it's only . . ."

She listened, and sighed in sympathy, and said, "You lie awake with the sore heart for this poor, poor woman, it is understood."

"Don't talk nonsense, it's well known I have a heart of flint."

"Oh, yes, indeed, like feathers it is hard, I know that very well—you begging the table scraps to feed every mangy stray cat and dog in the neighborhood! The poor soul, and one of these Russian heretics too, with only a false God to give comfort. Life, it bears hard, so it does. But God sends the burden according to the shoulder, boy. That, by what you say, she knows already—and her troubles have strengthened her. She will be all right, Luis, with time gone by."

"Let us hope," he said. "That there is always plenty of." When he put down the phone he felt better; he would sleep; and tomorrow, things to do—see the case wound up, find out all the details.

He drew his good hand down Bast's spine and she turned over on her back, four black paws in the air, and shamelessly showed him the very distinctly rounding pale brown stomach that began to say *kittens*. "You know something, *chica,*" he said, "it's the old ones who are tough. They've had it before, they won't die of it over again." He switched off the light and slid down beside her, and went to sleep while she still purred in his ear.

TWENTY

Mr. Skyros did not often attend church, but his wife did; he saw her off that Sunday morning, and retired to his den to mull over these various little awkwardnesses which had arisen. It seemed to him that one very good way out of the difficulty about Prettyman and Angelo would be to patch up the quarrel with Bratti. Doubtless he would need to fawn a little, own the fault entirely his own, that kind of thing, but Bratti was a sensible fellow, he would understand the position. And while it might seem on the face of it that Bratti would be only too pleased to see Mr. Skyros forced out of business, actually that was not the case. It was like any other business—it cost the wholesaler a certain amount to import the stuff, and the more steady customers he had, the cheaper he could afford to sell and still see his profits rise. Volume—always a determining factor in business.

It also seemed that the little trick Mr. Skyros had sought to play, planting Domokous' death at Bratti's door, had fallen flat: the police had not been intelligent enough to take the hint. And that was just as well: as it was, that little matter Bratti had never known anything about. If he could patch up the quarrel with Bratti, throw himself on Bratti's mercy, rent a few boys from him temporarily until business was started up again . . .

Also, some time today he must see Donovan, see that tiresome woman, and once for all conclude that deal. It had turned out to be more trouble and worry than it was worth.

At that point the doorbell chimed, and he went to answer it, putting on his usual genial smile for some neighbor or a Sunday peddler. The smile faded as he opened the door. "You fool, to come *here*—all open —go away! You cannot—it's madness—" Oh, God, that he'd ever become known to such a one! Trouble, always trouble from this kind—

Angelo laid a hand on Mr. Skyros' chest, pushed him back gently, and walked in. He was smiling his soft smile. And behind him Denny Donovan babbled anxiously, coming in too.

"Now you take it easy, Angie—look, Mr. Skyros, I just had to bring him, state he's in an' all—come round sayin' such things to me, *me*— like he'll take a knife to me don't I drive him—why, Angie, boy, you know I allus do anythin' for you, but you got to take it easy, don't do nothing to make trouble—listen, I'm sorry, Mr. Skyros, but he—"

"You fools, you must both go away at once! I will not have—"

"No trouble," said Angie. He walked Mr. Skyros backward another couple of steps; his little smile was fixed. "Only you got to give me some stuff right now, Mr. Skyros. Say last night, very sorry, you couldn't get none, wait awhile, Angelo. That don't do, Mr. Skyros. Now I got to have it. Right now."

"I haven't *got* any," said Mr. Skyros irritably. "Next week I get some, my man's around again then, Angelo. You be sensible now, go away and—buy yourself a fix from somebody—"

"Retail prices," said Angelo, "why do I go 'n' do like that, Mr. Skyros? You're the supplier—you got the stuff, you always got the stuff, —I pay you for ten decks, right now, an' so that way I got some to sell an' buy more—next week, tomorrow, next month—only I buy it now, Mr. Skyros. Fifty a deck, Mr. Skyros. You go 'n' get it."

"I haven't *got* any, fool!"

"Now listen, Angie, you see it's no good, you better come away an' do like he says—you be sensible now, Angie—"

Angelo slid a hand into his breast pocket and took out a knife. An ordinary bone-handled bread knife it was, with a blade about nine inches long. Mr. Skyros stepped smartly backward. "I don't want no trouble," said Angie softly. "Who else do I come to, who else'd have it? You're the supplier. Go 'n' get it. I need it right now, Mr. Skyros."

"For God's sake," Mr. Skyros implored Denny, "do something, take the knife away from him—I can't, Angelo, I tell you there's none here, you understand plain English, isn't it?—you be good, sensible, now—"

"Yeah, it's no good, Angie—you—you let me take you back downtown," chattered Denny nervously, "find somebody fix you up O.K.—"

"No trouble," said Angie, and put the point of the knife against Mr. Skyros' stomach. Mr. Skyros uttered a small moan and took another step backward, and the doorbell chimed again. "Needn't pay no notice to that, Mr. Skyros. You just go 'n' get the stuff. Right now. Because it's right now I got to have it." His liquid dark eyes were fixed, staring, above the little soft smile.

Mr. Skyros took another step. If he could get into the den, the dining room, slam the door between— Suddenly and irrelevantly he realized the lost benefit of being an upright citizen, who could (if possible to do so) take up the telephone and call for the police. But Angie paced with him step by step, holding the knife steady. The doorbell chimed again.

"Now listen—" panted Mr. Skyros. He was across the threshold of the dining room now, and suddenly over Angie's shoulder he saw movement out there beyond the French window—someone on the porch—a man coming up to peer in. It was that Lieutenant Mendoza, that man from police headquarters: and Mr. Skyros had never imagined that he would feel so happy to lay eyes on a cop. He sidled toward the windows, drawing Angie with him, and so far as he was thinking at all he began to formulate a vague tale about this lunatic breaking in, threatening him—

"Not that way," said Angie gently. "In, Mr. Skyros. Wherever you keep it. Go—"

"*Help!*" yelled Mr. Skyros, and plunged sideways and took prudent cover under the dining table. The French windows crashed in, glass shattering, and Mendoza and Hackett were in by the shortest route. There was a little scuffle; Mr. Skyros peered out fearfully, saw Angie safe in the competent grasp of Hackett, and scrambled out on all fours.

"Oh, Lieutenant, so happy I am to see you—such a thing—this crazy man breaks in, threatens me—"

"Indeed?" said Mendoza, dexterously picking Hackett's pocket from behind of his police special and leveling it at Denny. "How very ungrateful of him, turning on his employer. I *think* this is Angie, Art. It's awkward—I've only got one hand—maybe it'd be expedient to tap him lightly once, just to keep him quiet while you call up reinforcements. Who this is I don't know, but we'll sort it out later. Andreas Skyros, I have a warrant for your arrest on a charge of conspiracy to defraud . . ."

Mr. Skyros sat down in one of the dining room chairs and mopped his pink bald skull. "Oh, dear me, it's some mistake, gentlemen," he said mechanically. But if the truth were told, at the moment he was less alarmed at future danger than relieved to be rid of Angie.

Denny, as Goldberg had prophesied, talked. He tangled himself up in protestations of knowing nothing about any of it, ran out of lies, and then when they brought Jackie in—picked up in a Main Street bar without much trouble—he fell all over himself again to absolve Jackie from any connection. He was useful, filling in details for them.

Especially as Mr. Skyros, once he knew how deep in Lydia Bouvardier and Denny had put him, very wisely shut his mouth and requested a lawyer.

Jackie Donovan was unexpectedly amenable. Indeed, it almost seemed, as Goldberg said, that he was eager to tie himself into it, even before the museum director identified him. He drew the line, however, at taking the responsibility for Domokous—all he'd done to Domokous, he said, was knock him out. And got called a fool for it by Skyros. Domokous, walking in on them in Skyros' office that Monday night, after Donovan's first and only meeting with this Bouvardier dame—

"In," said Mendoza, "a hot car you'd picked up out in Exposition Park."

Donovan shrugged and said sure, if he knew so much about it. . . . He hadn't had anything to do with taking off Domokous. Thought Domokous'd found out about the deal, what he'd said then to Skyros— wanted to be bought off. Skyros acting soft with him, starting to make up some tale, but Domokous had picked up that list off the desk, and well, my God, you could see—story'd been in all the papers, that stuff pinched, and if he didn't know he'd find out, seeing those papers— So Donovan had batted him one, that's all, and got the list away from him —and he'd sort of staggered back, and let go, and the second time Donovan belted him he passed out—

"A list," said Mendoza. "Of the collection?" That was stacked up neatly on his desk, twelve big boxes. He looked, and found the manila folder, and opened it and took out the list. A number of pages, a thick wad, once stapled at both top corners—now the right-hand staple missing, torn away with a sizable corner of the top page. "Always so satisfying to see deductions proved," he murmured, and took out of its envelope the little torn scrap of paper found in Domokous' pocket, and laid it on the top page, matching the corners delicately. "Oh very pretty." The edges blended exactly; and the first two top lines now read sensibly,

No. 1-A cl. F:
Messana, silver tetradrachm, approximately 400 B.C. Obverse, nymph driving cart drawn by pair of mules. Reverse, hare with small dolphin.

"Oh, yes, I see. How nice. You didn't notice that Domokous had torn this away when you grabbed the list from him, and put it in his pocket —probably quite automatically."

"I didn't have nothing else to do with him, I didn't— Skyros says, fool, he didn't know nothing, but—"

And Skyros, of course, wasn't talking; and Denny hadn't been there, nor had Lydia Bouvardier. However, Denny had heard about it later, and—anxious to get Jackie clear, almost crying at the necessity to involve his old pal Angie in order to do that—he told them all about it. Which was nothing but heresay evidence, but there were things to do about that too . . .

Because after a fix, Angelo felt just fine, and amiably answered all their questions. Sure, he'd done this little favor for Skyros, so long as Skyros gave him a rebate on the stuff he used. Skyros' idea it was, make it look like the guy was a user, just took too big a jolt one time, 's all . . . it happens, and nobody pays much attention. Jackie, he had the guy in this car he'd hopped—Skyros, no, sir, he wasn't there—left it to Jackie—no, sir, why'd they go through his pockets? Skyros hadn't said to—no need—Skyros, he wanted him found, as who he was, and pretty soon. Planted an old hypo on him, sure, stuck him up a little, make it look good—open and shut. . . .

"Terminar," said Mendoza. "And don't tell me that any middling smart lawyer is going to claim self-condemnation, the confession for the fix. That I know. We'll just have to hope the judge has a little common sense and realizes it's a time and place to forget about the letter of the law. And what's the odds? If he gets off on the long count, he won't get off all the way—they'll send him for a cure—waste of the taxpayers' money—and I'll give you odds, if he does get off clear after that, in six months he'll have killed himself the way he killed Domokous. What is it they say about the mills of the gods?"

And Callaghan said philosophically, "Well, you can have Skyros. He's out of my hair, and when you've got enough on him to make it accessory to homicide, that'll put him away longer than a dope charge could. If the judge has got any sense at all—which I sometimes doubt any of 'em have."

And Goldberg said, "Well, I guess you've got the Donovans, a heavier charge than I could make, but I'd lay a bet that Denny anyway won't get as much of the book thrown at him as Jackie, and some day he'll be loose to make a little more trouble for me. All in the day's work . . ."

And Alison said thoughtfully, "I really think I'll have to get a new car. The idea of them transporting that poor man's body in it— What a funny complicated business it's been."

"Until we found out about it," said Mendoza. "Then, very ordinary. Just the way it came to light that made it look unusual at first." He sighed. "Now and then I wish something a little different would come along—one of those really interesting, bizarre, complicated cases out of a detective novel. . . . But not in this weather. Say along in December or January. Which reminds me—"

Alison got up, tugged the curtains farther aside in the hope of slightly better air. "It *should* begin to cool off a little now the sun's down. Would you like a drink?"

"Not that kind—rather have some iced coffee."

"So would I, I'll get it." . . . He followed her out to the kitchen, and there was a slight delay in filling the glasses. "Here," said Alison at last, "the ice is melting, idiot, let me go. Very bad timing—between getting it out and putting in the glasses—if you'd just think a little about these things—"

Mendoza swore as he hit his hand on the drainboard. "Damn this thing. They're taking the stitches out tomorrow, did I tell you?"

"I don't know that I should leap for joy to hear it, you're bad enough with one hand." She was struggling with the ice cubes, which hadn't melted enough to slide out easily.

"Stop fussing with that a minute and listen, I've got something important to ask you, *chica*. . . . No, I can't talk to your back, damn it— turn around here—this is serious, now."

"Yes," said Alison. Her heart gave a little extra beat. She laid down the ice tray.

"I want you to think about it and be sure," he said.

"Yes." She turned around to face him. He *was* looking very serious and solemn. "What—what is it?"

"Would you like a half-Abyssinian kitten for Christmas?"

EXTRA KILL

Jaques: And then he drew a dial from his poke,
And, looking on it with lack-lustre eye,
Says very wisely, "It is ten o'clock.
Thus may we see," quoth he, "how the world wags.
'Tis but an hour ago since it was nine;
And after one hour more 'twill be eleven;
And so, from hour to hour, we ripe and ripe,
And then, from hour to hour, we rot and rot;
And thereby hangs a tale."

—*As You Like It*, Act II, sc. 7

ONE

That he was making history was an idea that didn't enter the head of the rookie cop Frank Walsh. He was riding a squad car alone for the first time, which made him more conscientious than usual. He saw this car first when they pulled up at a stop light alongside each other on Avalon Boulevard; he'd never seen one like it and was still looking for some identification when the light changed and it took off like a rocket. He was going the same way, and it was still in sight when they passed a twenty-five-mile zone sign; it didn't slow down, and Walsh happily opened up and started after it.

The bad old days of quotas for tickets, all that kind of thing, were long gone—and Frank Walsh was twenty-six, no starry-eyed adolescent; nevertheless, there was a kind of gratification, a kind of glamour, about the first piece of business one got alone on the job. In time to come, he would have kept an eye on that car for a while, clocked it as only a little over the legit allowance and obviously being handled by a competent driver, and let it go. As it was, a mile down Avalon he pulled alongside and motioned it into the curb.

It was quite some car, he thought as he got out and walked round the squad car: a long, low, gun-metal-colored job, a two-door hardtop. This close he made out the name, a strange one to him—Facel-Vega, what the hell was that? One of these twenty-thousand-buck foreigners, probably with a TV director or a movie actor or something like that driving it, just to be different and show he had the money. Walsh stopped at the driver's window. "May I see your operator's license, please?" he asked politely.

The driver was a slim dark fellow with a black hairline moustache, a sleek thick cap of black hair, a long straight nose, and a long jaw. He said just as politely, "Certainly, officer," and got out his wallet, correctly slid his license out of its plastic envelope himself, and passed it over.

There was a woman beside him, a good-looking redhead who seemed to be having a fit of giggles for some reason.

Walsh checked the license righteously, comparing it with the driver. A Mex, he was, and quite a mouthful of name like they mostly had: Luis Rodolfo Vicente Mendoza. The license had been renewed within six months and matched him all right: five-ten, a hundred and fifty-five, age thirty-nine, eyes brown, hair— Walsh said, "You know, Mr. Mendoza, you were exceeding the limit by about fifteen miles an hour." He said it courteously because that was part of your training, you were supposed to start out anyway being polite; but he felt a little indignant about these fellows who thought just because they had money and a hot-looking expensive car the laws weren't made for them.

The driver said, "You're perfectly right, I was." He didn't even point out that practically everybody exceeded the limit in these slow zones; he accepted the ticket Walsh wrote out and put his license back in its slot, and Walsh, getting back in the squad car, was the least bit disappointed that he hadn't made the expected fuss.

It wasn't until his tour was over and he reported back to his precinct station that he found out what he'd done. It was the car that had stayed in his mind, and he was describing it to Sergeant Simon when Lieutenant Slaney came in.

". . . something called a Facel-Vega, ever hear of it?"

The sergeant said it sounded like one of those Italians, and the lieutenant said no, it was a French job, and what brought it up? When he heard about the ticket, a strangely eager expression came over his face. "The only Facel-Vega I know of around here—what was the driver like, Walsh?"

"He was a Mex, sir—why? I mean, his license was all in order, and the plate number wasn't on the hot list. Shouldn't I—?"

"And his name," asked Slaney in something like awe, "was maybe Luis Mendoza?"

"Why, yes, sir, how—"

"Oh, God," said Slaney rapturously, "oh, *brother,* this really makes my day! Walsh, if I could christen you a captain right now I would! You gave Luis Mendoza a ticket for speeding? You don't know it, but you just made history, my boy—that's the first moving-violation ticket he's ever had, to my knowledge."

"You *know* him, Lieutenant?"

"Do I know him," said Slaney. "Do I—? I suppose he had a woman with him?"

"Why, yes, there was a redhead—a pretty one—"

"I needn't have asked," said Slaney. "There always is—a woman, that is, he's not particular about whether it's a blonde or what. He looks at them and they fall, God Almighty knows why. Do I *know* him, says you. For my sins I went through the training course with him, eighteen years back, and we worked out of the same precinct together as rookies. And before we both got transferred, the bastard got a hundred and sixty-three dollars of my hard-earned money at poker, and two girls away from me besides. That's how well I—"

"He's a *cop?*" said Walsh, aghast. He had a horrid vision of riding squad cars the rest of his life, all applications for promotion tabled from above. "My *God,* I never—but, Lieutenant, that car—"

"He's headquarters—Homicide lieutenant. The car—well, he came into the hell of a lot of money a couple of years after he joined the force—his grandfather turned out to've been one of those misers with millions tucked away, you know? Oh, boy, am I goin' to rub his nose in this!" chortled Slaney. "His first ticket, and from one of *my* rookies!"

"But, Lieutenant, if I'd known—"

"If you'd known he was the Chief you'd still have given him the ticket, I hope," said Slaney. "Nobody's got privileges, you know that."

Which theoretically speaking was true, but in practice things weren't always so righteous, as Walsh knew. He went on having gloomy visions for several days of a career stopped before it started, until he came off duty one afternoon to be called into Slaney's office and introduced to Mendoza, who'd dropped by on some headquarters business. Slaney was facetious, and Walsh tried to balance that with nervous apology. Lieutenant Mendoza grinned at him.

"Cut that out, Walsh, no need. Always a first time for everything. The only thing I'm surprised at is that it was one of Bill Slaney's boys —I wouldn't expect such zealous attention to duty out of this precinct."

"Why, you bastard," said Slaney. "Half your reputation you got on the work of your two senior sergeants, and I trained both of 'em for you as you damn well know."

"Yes, Art Hackett's often told me how glad he was to be transferred out from under you," said Mendoza amiably.

All in all, Walsh was enormously relieved; despite his rank and his money Mendoza seemed to be a regular guy.

That happened in January; a month later, the memory of this little encounter emboldened Walsh to go over Lieutenant Slaney's head and lay a problem before the headquarters man.

"I've got no business to be here, Lieutenant," said Walsh uneasily. "Lieutenant Slaney says I'm a damn fool to waste anybody's time about this." He sat beside Mendoza's desk stiffly upright, and fingered his cap nervously. He'd called to ask if he could see Mendoza after he came off duty, and was still in uniform; he was on days, since last week, and it was six o'clock, the day men just going off, the night staff coming into the big headquarters building downtown with its long echoing corridors.

"Well, let's hear what it's about," said Mendoza. "Does Slaney know you're here?"

"No, sir. I've got no *business* doing such a thing, I know. I asked him about it, sir, and he said he wouldn't ask you to waste your time. But the more I got to thinking about it . . . It's about Joe Bartlett, sir, the inquest verdict yesterday—"

"Oh?" said Mendoza. He got up and opened the door. "Is Art back yet?" he asked the sergeant in the anteroom.

"Just came in, want him?" The sergeant looked into the big communal office that opened on the other side of his cubbyhole, called for Art, and a big broad sandy fellow came in: the sergeant Walsh remembered from last Friday night and yesterday at the inquest. He wasn't a man to look at twice, only a lot bigger than most—until you noticed the unexpectedly shrewd blue eyes.

"I thought you'd left, *now* what d'you want? I just brought that statement in—"

"Not that. Sit down. You'll remember this young fellow, he's got something to say about the Bartlett inquest. You handled that, you'd better hear it too."

"Bartlett," said Sergeant Hackett, and sat down looking grim. Nobody liked random killings, but the random killing of a cop, cops liked even less.

"I don't think that inquest verdict was right," blurted Walsh. "I don't think it was those kids shot Joe. Lieutenant Slaney says I'm talking through the top of my head, but—I tried to speak up at the inquest yesterday—maybe you'll remember, Sergeant, I was on the stand just before you were—but they wouldn't let me volunteer anything, just answer what they asked."

"What was it you wanted to say? Didn't you tell your own sergeant about it?"

"Well, naturally, sir—and the lieutenant—and they both think I'm nuts, see? Sure, it looks open and shut on the face of it, I admit that. Those kids'd just held up that market, they were all a little high, and they weren't sure they'd lost that first squad car that was after them— maybe they thought we were the same one, or maybe they didn't care, just saw a couple of cops and loosed off at us. We were parked the opposite direction, but they might've figured, the way the coroner said, that that first car had got ahead and gone round to lay for them."

Which had been the official verdict, of course: that those juveniles, burning up the road on the run from the market job, had mistaken the parked squad car for the one that had been chasing them and fired at it as they passed, one of the bullets killing Bartlett. They'd already shot a cashier at the market, who had a fifty-fifty chance to live.

"They say, of course, that they never were on San Dominguez at all, never fired a shot after leaving the market," said Hackett.

"Yes, sir, and I think maybe they didn't. I—"

"Giving testimony," said Mendoza, "isn't exactly like talking to somebody. Before we hear what brought you here, Walsh, suppose you give me the gist, in your own words, of just what did happen. I know Sergeant Hackett's heard it already, and I've read your statement, but I'd like to hear it straight."

"Yes, sir. We were parked on the shoulder, just up from Cameron on San Dominguez. That's almost the county line, and one end of our cruise, see. We'd just stopped a car for speeding and I'd written out the ticket. Joe was driving then and I was just getting back in, and in a second we'd have been moving off, when this car came past the opposite way and somebody fired at us from it. Four shots. It must've been either the first or second got Joe, the doctor said, by the angle—and it was just damned bad luck any of them connected, or damned good target shooting, that's all I can figure. The car was going about thirty. The shots came all together, just about as it came even with us and passed, and the way things were I hardly got a look at all. Joe never moved or spoke, sir, we know now the shot got him straight through the head . . ." Walsh stopped, drew the back of his hand across his mouth. He'd liked Joe Bartlett, who'd been a good man for a rookie to work with, easy and tactful on giving little pointers. Ten years to go to retirement, Bartlett, with a growing comfortable paunch and not much hair left and always talking about his kids, the boy in college, the girl still in high school. Also, that had been Walsh's first personal contact with violence, and while he'd kept his head it hadn't been a pleasant five minutes. "He slumped down over the wheel, I couldn't get at the controls until I'd moved him, it was—awkward, you can see that. I think I knew he was dead, nothing to be done for him—I just thought, got to spot that car. . . . I shoved him over best I could to get at the wheel, but by the time I got the hand brake off and got her turned, my God, it wasn't any use, that car was long gone. I was quick as I could be, sir—"

"It was just one of those things," agreed Hackett.

"I got the siren on, and I went after it, but no use, like I said. I saw that, and I pulled into the side and reported in what had happened. They told me to go straight to Vineyard and Brook, there was an ambulance on its way there already, so I did. That's where they'd finally picked up the kids, you know, just then. Price and Hopper, I mean, and Gonzales and Farber in the first car that'd been after them were called in too—they were there when I got there. Price had to fire at the car to get it to stop, and one of the kids was hit, not bad—you know all that, sir."

Mendoza nodded. "That's all clear enough. What's in your mind about it now? Your own sergeant and Sergeant Hackett had your story then, and you said, if I recall rightly, that it must have been those juveniles. Something changed your mind?"

"It looked," said Walsh, "like it must've been, sure, because what *else* could it have been? I mean, it's not as if there were a dozen cars around that area that night with somebody taking pot shots at squad cars out of them. When we came to sort it out, the times looked tight, but it could have happened like that, and how *else* could it have?"

"We went into it as thoroughly as possible," said Hackett.

"Yes, sir, I know. And I don't want to make out that I was mistaken in anything I told you, it's not that. It's just that when I came to think about the whole thing afterward—as a whole, if you see what I mean— well, it's nothing to get hold of, nothing definite, but the more I thought about it— And I told Sergeant Simon, and Lieutenant Slaney too, but I guess the reason it sounded crazy to them is just that—how else could it have happened?"

"What bothers you about it?" asked Mendoza patiently.

"The main thing is the times. Sure, it could have been, but it's tight figuring. Look, here's Cameron and San Dominguez, where it happened. I don't see how I could have been more than thirty seconds getting under way afterward, even call it a minute before I got the car turned and got up speed after that car—and it didn't take me another minute to see it was no go. All right,"—in his urgency Walsh was forgetting some of his nervousness—"there's two minutes, and I'm about half a mile down San Dominguez. Give me another ten seconds to pull in and start to call. I couldn't get through right away, they were busy that night, but it couldn't've been more than another twenty seconds before I was reporting in. Say that's three minutes, even four, after the shots were fired—I don't think it was four, actually, but give it that much leeway—and I was talking maybe another twenty seconds or half minute, and the girl had me wait another ten, twenty seconds while she checked on where that ambulance call was from—Price reported in just before me. So I'm sent to Vineyard and Brook where they got the kids, and that's about half a mile from where I was then, or from where the shots were fired—it makes a kind of triangle, see, with the point at Vineyard and Brook. O.K., now when I got there, which was maybe two and a half minutes later, the first squad car'd already got there, that's Gonzales and Farber, who'd been the first to go after the kids, and they'd been called up *after* Price and Hopper were on the kids' tail. Look, I even made a diagram of it, and this is how it works out in my book. Call it five past nine when the shots were fired at us and Joe was killed. Say it was the kids, they've got to get over to Vineyard—which runs the same way as San Dominguez, it's not a cross street—and be going west there hell-bent for election when Price and Hopper spotted them two-three minutes later. Because Price's call in, saying they were on them, was clocked at seven minutes past nine, and Gonzales and Farber got the word where to join them a minute later. The ambulance call Price put in, same time as he reported arresting the kids, came over at eleven minutes past nine. And at about that time I was calling in about Joe. I can't figure how it could've been more than four minutes between Joe's getting shot and Price and Hopper picking up those kids. And you know, I don't suppose they gave one look at the car and spotted it, bang, right off—they'd take a closer look to be sure it *was* those kids, which cuts down the time a little."

"Mmh, yes. You've really gone into this, haven't you?" Mendoza tilted back his chair, regarding the opposite wall thoughtfully. "That sounds like a very short space of time, but a lot of things can happen in three or four minutes, and you're not absolutely sure of the times on your end, are you? Even if you'd just happened to look at your watch before Bartlett was shot, it could have been off a bit from the clocks in the radio room here."

"Yes, sir, I know. But another thing, as I don't need to tell you, Price and Hopper didn't just slam bracelets on the kids and rush right back to report in, there'd be a couple of minutes there, getting the kids out of their car and so on. . . . Well, I don't know, it just seems to me—"

"Look," said Hackett, rubbing his jaw. "Leave all this thirty seconds, twenty seconds business out, what you're saying is, it seems to you that by the time you got sent to meet that ambulance, the kids had been busy with Price and Hopper a little too long to have been over on San Dominguez when Bartlett was killed. Now I've got just this to say. Time's funny—when a lot's happening, sometimes it seems to go faster and sometimes slower—you've had that experience?" Walsh nodded silently. "I agree with you that it all happened damn fast, but we've got no check on exact times, and nobody can say just on that account it couldn't've been those kids. And the gun checks—as much identification as we'll ever get. I don't need to remind you it was a homemade gun with a smooth bore, so, sure, Ballistics can't say definitely this bullet came out of that gun—but the market cashier and Bartlett both had .38 caliber bullets in them, and the kids had a half a box of 'em left. It looks pretty open and shut."

"I know," said Walsh helplessly. "All I can say is, even making every allowance for the way you do lose track of time in the middle of a thing like that—well, I still feel it's too tight. And, Sergeant, why did they turn off San Dominguez if it was them?"

"Why shouldn't they?"

"It's the main drag," said Walsh, "the best road along there. They were all from that section, they'd know the streets. They must've known that if I was on their tail after they'd fired at us, their best chance of losing me was to stay on San Dominguez, because it's a divided highway and not much traffic that time of night. They could make tracks and still do enough weaving in and out of what traffic there was to throw me off. They'd know I couldn't have got their plate number—it's dark as hell along there, those arc lights are so high—and they'd blacked out their taillight. Look, you get off the main drag along there, most of the cross streets are full of potholes and not all of 'em go through to the next main street, Vineyard. They'd be damn fools to turn off right away, and take a chance on getting to the next boulevard —they couldn't be sure I wasn't on them when they'd turned off, the way they must've if they were going to be spotted where we know Price and Hopper spotted them, on Vineyard just west of Goldenrod going about sixty."

"Well, now," said Hackett. "They weren't exactly thinking very clear, you know, right then."

"They'd just shaken off Gonzales and Farber, Sergeant, after a twenty-minute chase—and Lieutenant Slaney says Farber's the best damn driver out of our precinct."

Mendoza laughed. "That's a point—he's got you there, Art. Of course,"—he sat up abruptly—"they wouldn't have us after them if they weren't damn fools to start with, and damn fools have a habit of acting like what they are. And like the rest of us they have good luck and bad luck." He brushed tobacco crumbs off his desk tidily, straightened the blotter, lined up the desk tray with the calendar as he spoke; but automatically, like a persnickety housewife, thought Walsh. Even in the midst of his earnest effort to get through to them with this, Walsh couldn't help noticing. One of those people who went around straightening pictures, he figured Mendoza was: the orderly mind. He looked it too, very natty and dapper in an ultraconservative way, like an ad in *Esquire*—the faintest of patterns in the tie, and that suit must have cost three hundred bucks if it cost a dime. Of course, all that money Lieutenant Slaney said he had . . .

"And if it wasn't the kids?" asked Mendoza. "What else?"

"It's crazy," said Walsh, "I know. But suppose it was somebody who wanted to kill Joe as—well, who he was. Not just a cop in a squad car. A—a specific cop."

"Now let's not reach for it," said Hackett dryly. "You know anybody who might have wanted Bartlett dead? Who might try it like that?—not just the easiest method, by the hell of a long way. I manage to keep up enough of a score on the board myself so I don't come in for extra practice, but I'd think twice about trying a target shot like that, practically in the dark and at thirty miles an hour."

"I know," said Walsh again, humbly. "It sounds crazy to me too, Sergeant. If it wasn't those kids, I don't know who it could've been, or why. But I just can't figure it as the kids, when I think back over it. The way I told you, I didn't get any kind of look at the car, I had my head down sliding into our car beside Joe. I couldn't say if there was just the driver or three kids or a dozen blue baboons in it. And when I *did* look up, at the shots, it was already almost past, and all I could tell was it was a sedan—but two-door or four-door I couldn't see—and a dark color, and it had fins, so it was a fairly late model. That's all I can honestly say, sir, for sure. I only had it in sight for about two seconds. So I know it doesn't count for much when I say that, thinking back, I get the impression that looking at those tailfins side on, the way I saw the car as it went past, they curved up at the ends."

"The car the kids were driving," said Mendoza, "was a two-year-old four-door Mercury. I don't keep up with all these little changes in design—" He looked at Hackett.

"Straight fins," said Hackett tersely. "When did all this begin to come to you, Walsh—in a dream?"

"Look, sir, I'm just trying to be honest about it. Maybe I was slow on the uptake, but like you say, a lot happened all at once, and it wasn't until I had a chance to sit down and think about the whole thing in—in retrospect, you know, that it added up like this. Or didn't add up. And by then you all had my statement and the inquest was set—and the sergeant said I was crazy, because how *else*—and the coroner wouldn't let—"

"You did quite right coming in to tell us," said Mendoza.

"Second thoughts—" began Hackett, looking a little angry.

"*Tómelo con calma, chico,* if we don't like a little new piece of truth we can't shove it under the rug because we like something else better. Which you know as well as I do. And another thing we all know is that sometimes you get a clearer picture of a thing looking back on it. No, you were quite right to pass this on, Walsh—you needn't be afraid you'll get in any trouble over it."

"Do you think—?"

"I don't think anything right now," said Mendoza. He put out his cigarette carefully in the brass tray. "We haven't got enough to think about. But maybe it wouldn't do any harm to take a little closer look at this thing. *Todos cometomes errores*—we all make mistakes—and peculiar coincidences do occur, no denying."

"Now *look,*" said Hackett, "if you've got one of your hunches, Luis, tell it to go away. Of all the far-fetched—"

"No hunch," said Mendoza. "I'd just like to look at it a little closer. To be sure." He looked at Walsh. "We'll keep this quiet for a while. If it turns out you've been exercising your imagination, I don't want it to get round that you fooled Mendoza for a minute—everybody knows I'm never wrong! But if there seems to be something in it, I'll want to see you again."

"Yes, sir," said Walsh, grinning and then canceling the grin as he remembered Bartlett.

Hackett shut his eyes and said, *"Lo mismo me da*—all the same to me—I'm only the wheel horse that'll do all the work. The games you think up, Luis! Working a case twice, just to be sure."

"Well, this is one we'd like to be very damned sure about, isn't it?"

"That's why," said Walsh. "I mean, I thought I ought to tell somebody, sir, on account of those kids. That cashier's still alive. If he doesn't die, it wouldn't be a homicide charge—except for Joe."

"Oh, that," said Mendoza. He got up, straightening his tie, yanking down his cuffs; his cuff links, Walsh noticed, were heavy gold monogrammed ones. "What the hell, about the kids? They're no good to anybody and the chances are very small they ever would be. They're all under eighteen and wouldn't get the death penalty anyway. This way or that way"—he took down his hat, a rather high-crowned black Homburg, and brushed it—"they'll be around quite a while to make work for us and deviltry for a lot of other people. It's not on that account I'd like to know more about this. I just want to know what really happened. I'm told I've got as much irrational curiosity as a dozen women, which is maybe why I'm a cop in the first place."

TWO

He happened to have a date that night with his redhead, Alison Weir. It was a little different thing, with Alison—he hadn't troubled to figure why—just, maybe, because she was Alison: he could be more himself with her than with any other woman. So over dinner he told her they'd take a little ride out toward Long Beach—something he wanted to look at—and without much prodding added the whole funny little story.

"This boy," said Alison thoughtfully, "he's not just trying to build up something, get into the limelight?"

"I don't read him that way," said Mendoza. "And these days rookies aren't always as young as that—he's twenty-five, twenty-six, old enough to have some judgment. No, I don't know that there's anything in it, and to tell you the truth I've got no idea where to start looking to find out."

"But— Well, say for a minute it's *so*, Luis, though it sounds perfectly fantastic—if it was someone who wanted to kill this Bartlett specifically, surely something would show up in his private life, if you looked?"

Mendoza lit cigarettes for both of them and looked consideringly at his coffee. "Not necessarily. You take a policeman, now—he gets around, and in a lot of places and among a lot of people the ordinary person doesn't. You might say, if you're looking for motives for murder, a cop has a little better chance of creating one than most people. The difficulty is—" He broke off, took a drag on his cigarette, laid it down, drank coffee, and stared at the sugar bowl intently.

"*Siga adelante!*" said Alison encouragingly.

"Well, the difficulty is that if it was anything like that—something he'd heard or seen on his job—big enough to constitute a reason for killing him, he'd have known about it himself and made some report on it. And if it was something that had happened just on that tour of duty —which, if we accept the whole fantasy, I think it may have been— young Walsh would know about it too. Because, although some people still cling to the idea that most cops aren't overburdened with brains, we are trained to notice things, you know. And while I've never met a motive for murder that was what you might call really adequate, still nobody would think it necessary to kill the man because he'd seen or heard something so—apparently—meaningless to him that he hadn't mentioned it to anybody. But this is theorizing without data. . . ."

An hour later he pulled up on the shoulder of that stretch of San Dominguez, just up from Cameron. He switched off the engine and the headlights, switched on the parking lights, and gave her a cigarette, lit one himself.

"And what do you expect to find out here?"

"I don't expect anything. I don't know what there is to find out. You've got to start a cast somewhere."

"Like fox hunting. You just turn the hounds loose where you think there might be a fox? I thought crime detection was a lot more scientific than that these days."

"*Segun y como,* sometimes yes, sometimes no." He was a motionless shadow, only the little red spark of his cigarette end moving there; he stared out at the thinnish passing traffic. "I'll tell you something funny, *chica,* with all the laboratories and the chemical tests and the gadgets we've got to help us—Prints and Ballistics and the rest of it—like everything else in life it always comes back to individual people. To people's feelings and what the feelings make them do or not do. Quite often the gadgets can give you an idea where to look, but once in a while you've got to find out about the people first—then the gadgets can help you prove it." He went on staring out the window.

Alison slid down comfortably against his shoulder and said, "Oh, well, at least there's a heater to keep my feet warm. Pity I don't knit, I could be accomplishing something. . . . I have a theory about policemen. Just like musicians, they come in two types—the ones who learn the hard way, by lessons and practice, and the ones who do it by ear, just naturally. You play it by ear. You do it in jumps, a flash of inspiration here, a lucky guess there. What you're doing now is waiting for your muse to visit you, *no es verdad?*"

He laughed. "You know too much about me. A ranking headquarters officer, he's supposed to work by sober routine and cold scientific fact, not by ear."

"Never mind, I'll keep the dark secret," she said sleepily. "Then when your hunches pay off and everybody says, 'The man's a genius,' you can look modest and say, 'Just routine, just routine.'"

Mendoza went on staring at the boulevard. No place within twenty miles of downtown L.A. was thinly populated, but there were stretches here and there, and this was one of them, where the contractors hadn't got round to planting blocks of new little houses or new big apartments, or rows of shops and office buildings. Half a mile up, half a mile down, half a mile away to each side were close communities, blocks of residence and business, and the port of Los Angeles; here, only an occasional grove of live oaks at the roadside, and empty weed-grown fields beyond. The arc lights on the boulevard were high but adequate; the effect of darkness came from the lack of other lights to supplement them, the neon lights of shop fronts along built-up sections. And from the shadow of the trees, along here.

He wondered if Walsh and Bartlett had been parked under these trees.

Five minutes later a black-and-white squad car came ambling along, hesitated, and drew in ahead of the Facel-Vega. One of the patrolmen got out and came back to Mendoza's window, and he rolled it down all the way.

"Not a very good place to park, sir," said the patrolman tactfully. "Unless you're having trouble with your car, I'll ask you to move on."

"It's O.K.," said Mendoza, "not what your nasty low mind tells you. I can think of at least three better places to make love than the front seat of a car. I'm more or less on legitimate business," and he passed over his credentials.

"Oh—excuse *me*, sir." The man in uniform shoved back his cap and leaned on the window sill. "Anything we can do for you?"

"I don't know. This is about where Bartlett got it, isn't it?"

"Auggh, yes, sir." The voice was grim. "By what Frank Walsh says. That was the hell of a thing, wasn't it? A damn good man, Joe was. I'm Gonzales, sir, Farber and I were in on the arrest, maybe you'll know. There when Walsh come up with Joe. I tell you, it was all we could do, keep our hands off those goddamned smart-aleck kids, when we heard. . . . The hell of a thing."

"Yes, it was. Walsh much shaken up? He hasn't been in uniform long, has he?"

"No, sir, but he's a good kid. Sure, he was shook, but he'd kept his head—he acted O.K. I tell you, Lieutenant, I guess I was the one was shook—and I've been in uniform seven years this month and that wasn't the first time I'd picked up some pretty tough customers who happened to be Mexican—but I tell you, with *those* kids, it was the first time I ever felt ashamed of my name."

"*Vaya, amigo,* we come all shapes and sizes like other people—good, bad, and indifferent."

"Sure," said Gonzales bitterly, "sure we do, Lieutenant, but a lot of people don't remember it when the names get in the paper on a thing like this."

Alison sat up and said that it was a pity, while all this research was going on about a cure for cancer and the common cold, that nobody was looking for a cure for stupidity: it was needed much more. Gonzales grinned and said it sure was, hesitated, and added, "Excuse me, Lieutenant, but—the inquest was yesterday, I mean I was wondering if there was anything—"

"More?" said Mendoza. "Like maybe have I heard a little something from Frank Walsh?"

"Oh, he *did* see you? I didn't want to stick my neck out if he'd got cold feet." At which point Farber up ahead got impatient and came back to see what was going on.

When he heard, he said, "Walsh is O.K., but he's really reaching on this one, Lieutenant. Overconscientious." He was an older man than Gonzales, compact and tough-looking in the brief flare of the match as he lit a cigarette.

"Well, boys," said Mendoza, "they say better safe than sorry. It won't do any harm to take another look. But there's no need to—mmh —worry Bill Slaney about it unless it appears there's something to tell him. I don't want him breathing fire at me for encouraging one of his rookies in a lot of nonsense, and I don't want him coming down on Walsh for going over his head. I'll square him when the time comes, if it's necessary. Meanwhile, could one of you do me a little favor? You're on night tour, I see—Walsh is on days right now. Could one of you get a copy from him of his record book of last Friday night, and bring it to me tomorrow morning? I'll meet you somewhere near the station, or anywhere convenient."

Farber was silent; Gonzales said, "Sure, I'll do that, Lieutenant. If you think there's anything to be looked into. Frank talked to us about it, but it sounds—"

"Crazy, I know. I'm not saying yes or no yet. Just looking. Where and what time?"

"Corner of Avalon and Cole, say about ten-thirty?"

"O.K. Thanks very much. I'll see you then, Gonzales." As the two men walked back to the squad car, Farber was seen to raise his shoulders in an expressive shrug. Mendoza murmured, "Overconscientious . . . I wonder," and switched on the ignition. Then he said, "Better places, yes, but just to be going on with, as long as we're here—" and postponed reaching for the hand brake a minute to kiss her.

At ten forty-five the next morning he sat in his car at one end of that cruise Walsh and Bartlett had been riding on Friday night, and read over the terse history of what jobs they had done between four-thirty and nine. It hadn't been a very exciting tour up to then. On Friday night, he remembered, it had been raining: gray and threatening all day, and the rain starting about three, not a real California storm until later, but one of those dispirited steady thin drizzles. Californians were like cats about rain, and that would have been enough to keep a lot of people home that night.

In the four and a half hours Walsh and Bartlett were on duty, up to the murder of Bartlett, they had responded to four radio calls and handed out seven tickets. At four-fifty they had been sent to an accident on Vineyard; evidently it had been quite a mess, with three cars called in and an ambulance, one D.O.A. and two injured, and they hadn't got away from there until five thirty-five. At six-three they'd been sent to another accident, a minor one, and spent a few minutes getting traffic unsnarled there. At six-forty they'd rescued a drunk who'd strayed onto the freeway, and taken him into the station for transferral to the tank downtown overnight. At seven thirty-five they'd been sent to an apartment on 267th Street, a drunk-and-disorderly. Apparently the drunks hadn't been very disorderly, for they were back on their route again by eight o'clock. At eight-twenty they'd stopped at a coffee shop on Vineyard, and were on their way again at eight thirty-five.

The tickets had all been for speeding, except two for illegal left turns.

Mendoza started out to follow their route. He went to the scene of the first accident, and parked, and looked at it. It said nothing to him at all, of course: just a fairly busy intersection, with nothing to show that four nights ago it had been a shambles of death and destruction.

He went on to the place of the second accident, and that said even less, eloquently. Again, of course . . . What the hell did he think he was doing? Waiting for his muse, Alison said. Waiting for that cold sure tingle between the shoulder blades that told him the man across the table was bluffing hard, or really did hold a full house. Or for that similar, vaguer sensation that for want of a better word was called a hunch.

Nothing said anything to him. An hour later he had got as far as the place where they'd subdued the D.-and-D., and had reached the conclusion that he was wasting time. It wasn't an apartment building, this, but a one-storey court built in U-shape around a big black-topped parking area. There were four semidetached apartments on each side, in two buildings, and across the end a fifth building also with two apartments; at the street side of the first two buildings were double carports, and a single one at each end of the fifth. All the buildings were painted bright pink, with white door-frames and imitation shutters; they looked curiously naked standing there in the open, not a tree anywhere around, or any grass: only the blacktop and in the middle of it a large wooden tub in which was planted some anonymous shrub, which obviously wasn't doing very well—thin and anemic-looking. Six television aerials stretched importunate arms heavenward; presumably the other tenants possessed newer sets of the portable type.

In his exasperation with himself, Mendoza thought he'd never seen a more depressing place to live. Even a slum tenement gave out a warmer sense of life than this sterile, cheap modernity.

There was no parking lane along here, and he turned up onto the blacktop to make a U-turn, start back downtown, and quit wasting time. As he swung around by the twin front doors of the building across the end of the court, the left one opened and a woman bounced out in front of the car; so he had to stop.

"Was it about the apartment? You're lucky to catch me, I was just goin' to market. You're welcome to see over it, won't take a minute to get the key—" She might have been sixty; she was an inch or so short of five feet and very nearly as wide, but every bit of her looked as firm and brisk and bouncy as a brand-new rubber ball. She had pug-dog features under a good deal of wild gray hair, and her cotton housedress was a blinding Prussian blue with a pink-and-white print superimposed.

"Not about the apartment, no," said Mendoza. Oh, well, as long as he was here . . . He got out of the car and introduced himself. "You, or someone here, put in a call to the police last Friday night complaining about a drunk—"

"Mrs. Bragg, that's me, how-do. Mex, hey? Well, I don't mind that, you're mostly awful polite folk, I will say, nor I don't mind the police part either—matter of fact it might be sort of handy sometimes, with them Johnstones. Now there, if I haven't *got* the key, musta picked up the wrong bunch—it's this apartment right here, what'd-you-say-the-name-is, and a bargain if I do say so—"

"I'm not interested in the apartment." But he had to follow her to the door to say it, and she prodded him inside before he got it across. "This call you put in—it was you?—"

"*And* what about it?" said Mrs. Bragg. "Got a right to call the police, I hope, I pay taxes, and not the first time either since them Johnstones've been in Number Three. I don't mind folk taking a drink now and then, and it's none of my business are they really married or not, which I don't think they are, but when it comes to getting roaring drunk three nights a week average, and taking 'em both as it does, him trying to beat her up and her yelling blue murder, well, I've got my other tenants to think of, I hope you can understand that—"

"Yes, of course, why don't you get rid of them?"

"Oh, well, she's a nice woman when she isn't drunk, quite the lady, *and* the rent on the dot first of every month. Funny thing is, it never lasts long, you see—half an hour and they quiet down. Beats me what fun they get out of it, but there it is, it takes all sorts. Thing is, it went on a bit longer Friday night, and I thought it might kind of bring them to their senses if I called the police, *which* it did as it has before—they quieted down soon as they come and the older one, he gave 'em a good talking-to, and never a peep out of them afterwards." She eyed him speculatively. "Might be real handy, have one of you here all the time.

You're sure you don't want to move? It's a real nice apartment—now you're here you might's well see over it, just on the chance. Three and a half rooms, all utilities, *and* furnished real nice if I do say so—just take a look around—and only ninety a month. The gentleman I've just lost out of it, he was a *real* gentleman, if he did have a funny name—Twelvetrees it was, Mr. Brooke Twelvetrees, kind of elegant-sounding at that when you say it, isn't it?—and he took real good care of everything, I was sorry to see him go. You can see he left everything in apple-pie order, to tell the truth I haven't got round to cleaning it up myself since, except for emptying the wastebasket and so on. *Which,* however, would be done before you moved in, even to windows washed. Handy to everything, market two blocks away, and thirty minutes to downtown. Now you can see—"

Submerged in the flood, Mendoza was swept ruthlessly across the tiny living room (pink flowers in the rug, Prussian blue mohair davenport, blond step-table beside a maroon-upholstered chair) into an even tinier bedroom, in which there was just room for a double bed of blond finished pine, a bureau enameled cream, and a straight chair. The bed bore a pink chenille spread with fringe, and there was a small bedside table with a lamp about nine inches high which wore a madly ruffled shade very much askew. The rug here had maroon flowers.

Mrs. Bragg pounded the bed vigorously. "Good mattress, good as new, you can see. Oh, I tell you, I was sorry to see Mr. Twelvetrees go—a real gentleman he was, and finicky as a lady, you can see by the way he left everything so neat. Here's the bathroom, shower *and* tub if they *are* all together so to speak, and real tile, not that plastic stuff." It was mauve, and the shower curtain was embellished with improbably blue fish.

"I'm really not interested—"

"Plenty of closet space, even for a man like Mr. Twelvetrees and he had as many clothes as a woman, you shoulda seen—a real snappy dresser he was. And the kitchen, if I *do* say, is all nice and modern as anybody'd want—" Mendoza was prodded back across the living room to the kitchen, to admire a very small table with chromium-tube legs and a rose-colored plastic top, chairs to match, real blue tile on the drainboard, a practically new refrigerator and stove. Mrs. Bragg pounded the table to illustrate its sturdiness, and it rocked violently.

"There now, he's got it over the trap—you don't need to worry about *that,* it's just what they call access for the plumber, case they have to get at the line underneath, and it don't hardly show a bit, you can see, covered with the same linoleum. You see, it's steady as a rock, you get it in the right place. Everything handy. I don't deny it's small, but arranged very convenient, as you can see—" She made a sudden dart at the narrow kitchen door and snatched up an object from the threshold: a shiny new trowel. "So that's where my trowel got to—he musta been at that Tree of Heaven again. Real helpful he was, and quite the gardener, I often said to him, 'You ought have a place of your own.' He even got me some special plant food for the blamed thing, but it didn't seem to do no good. Well, now, you can see what a bargain the place is at ninety—"

"But really I'm not interested in another apartment—"

"—And I'm not one of those fussy landladies, either. Men will be men, single ones, that is, *and* some of the others, and women I don't mind, none of my business and live and let live I always say, as long as everything's quiet and no rowdy parties. The only thing I *do* draw the line at—just in the interests of my investment here, as you can understand—is pets and children, *that* I can't have—"

Mendoza, between fascination and the feeling that he might willynilly find himself signing a lease on the spot, perceived that Providence was rescuing him. He said in that case the apartment would never do, as he had some cats. *"Cats!"* exclaimed Mrs. Bragg, recoiling a step.

"Three cats," said Mendoza. "That is, a cat and two kittens."

"Cats I will not have. I'm afraid if you want the apartment you'll have to get rid of them." She looked at him disapprovingly, he had disappointed her. Something peculiar about a man who kept cats, and three at that.

"I'm only curious," said Mendoza, recovering his equilibrium, "but do you say that to prospective tenants with children?"

"Tenants with children *or* pets I don't take. I'm sorry, but you should have explained that to start with and I needn't have wasted time showing you over the place. I'm very sorry, but I can't make any exception." She all but pushed him out the door. "I'm sure you can understand that it's *ruination* on a furnished place."

Mendoza got back into his car as she banged her own front door. *"Quiá!"* he said to himself. "And my grandmother asks me why I don't marry a wife! A *ningun precio*—not at any price, take such a chance!"

THREE

He looked, in the places indicated to look, and found nothing. If there was anything funny anywhere, it didn't show in any way. He saw the kids again, the insolent, sullen kids who didn't clearly understand that they'd done anything wrong, just resented the cops for putting them in jail. Who said sullenly, insolently, that the cops were making scapegoats of them (though they didn't use that word) on the Bartlett thing —probably had some reason to put Bartlett away themselves and were covering for the real killer.

He even thought about that, but not for very long, because while all cops in uniform and out, who carried guns at all, carried .38's, they weren't smooth bores and Ballistics would have spotted it right away.

He looked back in the records over Joe Bartlett's career, and at the family, and it was all one big blank.

Hackett went to see everybody again, and it all sounded just the way it had before. Hackett said, "I told you so. Walsh, he hadn't had the experience, that's all, and it shook him—only natural."

Mendoza began to agree. You just didn't run into the kind of thing it would be if it wasn't those juveniles—the fiction-plot thing, the obscure complexity.

Walsh had come to see him on Tuesday, and by Thursday, having taken his closer look at it, Mendoza stopped looking. He saw Walsh again on Friday, and told him it looked like a mare's nest. And after Walsh had thanked him for listening anyway, and gone, he sat there with a couple of days' work in front of him and felt uneasy about it.

He didn't know why. It wasn't a hunch; it wasn't the kids' stubborn denial, although there was a little something there, all right: it had made them feel like big-time pros to have shot that cashier; that one they hadn't tried to deny—of course they couldn't, there were witnesses. And the cashier hadn't died after all: the homicide charge depended entirely on Bartlett.

It wasn't anything he could put a finger on—that made him wonder if he hadn't missed something. . . .

After a while he put it forcibly out of his mind and went back to the several cases on hand when Walsh had first come in.

The day after that he happened to drop in at the same restaurant for lunch that Woods and Goldberg had picked. Federico's, where a good many of the headquarters officers habitually went, was closed for redecoration, and this was a hole-in-the-wall place which opened out unexpectedly into several large dining rooms. It wasn't fancy, but the food was good and not too expensive, and there were no jukeboxes or piped-in-music: you could eat in peace. Consequently it was crowded, and he wandered through the first two rooms into the third looking for a table. There, at the back, he ran into Goldberg and Woods just sitting down, and joined them principally because the only empty chair was at their table. Lieutenant Goldberg of Burglary and Theft he knew, but Sergeant Woods he didn't. Woods was young for a sergeant, not more than twenty-eight; he looked more like an earnest postgraduate student of something like anthropology. He was tall, thin, and gangling, with a pale face under already thinning dark hair, a rich bass voice, and a very quiet manner.

Goldberg asked how life was treating Mendoza these days, and Mendoza said he couldn't complain. The waiter took their orders and went away, cigarettes were lit, and after a little desultory conversation Goldberg asked suddenly, "Say, what should you do for a cat that has fleas? Is the stuff for dogs too strong?"

"Fleas? Cats that are properly cared for don't have fleas. Where does she sleep—or he?"

"She, we've still got a kitten we couldn't find a home for. In the garage, at least I fixed a box with an old blanket, but half the time—"

"*Entendido,* there's your trouble, leaving her outside at night to roam all over. Keep her in—I know people think they're nocturnal animals, but when they live with us they keep our hours, you know."

"Well, I suppose I could bring the box into the service porch."

"You can, not that it'll do much good," said Mendoza. "She'll pick her own bed, and quite likely it'll be yours or one of the kids'. Let her. If you've been feeding her things out of cans, stop it, and get her fresh liver and beef. Wheatgerm oil twice a week, and lots of brushing with a good stiff brush."

"Look," said Goldberg, "I've got a living to earn, I can't spend all the time waiting on a cat, and my wife's got the house and the kids—neither can she. Do you know what beef liver's gone to now? Of course it's an academic question with you. All I asked was about flea powder."

"And I told you what to do. Let a vet de-flea her now. Fresh meat only, horsemeat'll do, and meanwhile brush half a can of talcum into her every day."

"Look," said Goldberg, "she's only a cat."

Mendoza put out his cigarette as the waiter came up and said, "You shouldn't have a cat, Goldberg, you've got the wrong attitude entirely. Cat people say, 'We're only human beings.'"

Woods uttered the deep rumbling laugh that sounded so surprising coming from his weedy-looking frame and said, "Reason I don't like cats around much—like a lot of people, I think—not that I don't like them exactly, but they make me feel so damned inferior."

"Isn't it the truth," agreed Mendoza. "Yes, if they'd only admit it, I'm convinced that's the reason some people say they can't stand cats. Now I'm an egotist myself, I admit it, but it certainly hasn't cured me. Right now I've got a cat that's crazy—in a devilish sort of way—and even he makes me feel inferior."

"Is that so?" said Woods. "A crazy cat?"

"Possessed of the devil. I intended to keep one of the kittens, but I ended up with this El Señor as well because nobody else would put up with him. He's got no sense at all except for planning deliberate mischief, and that he's very damned smart at. I call him El Señor for convenience—sometimes it's Señor Estúpido, and sometimes Señor Malicioso, and other things. I believe he must have been a witch's familiar in another incarnation. But even when he's being stupid, he can look down his nose at me as superior as the other two."

"Madame Cara," said Sergeant Woods, regarding his Beef Stroganov thoughtfully, "says that the highest point of animal reincarnation is represented by cats, and they're all of them superior human souls on the way—er—up the ladder again."

"And who in hell is Madame Cara?" Goldberg wanted to know.

Woods grinned. "This thing I'm on now. That embezzlement. I suppose I should say 'alleged,' like the papers—I've got no proof he did it, and as far as I can see I never will unless I catch up to him—and it looks as if maybe he borrowed one of their spells and made himself invisible."

"Oh, that Temple of Mystic Truth thing," said Goldberg.

"What is mystic about the truth?" asked Mendoza.

"There you've got me, Lieutenant," said Woods. "All I know is what it says on the sign out front. Myself, I thought at first it ought to have been handed over to somebody in Rackets, but of course however the Kingmans came by the money it did belong to them—that is, to the—er —church, which is officially incorporated as a nonprofit organization—"

"Now there's what they call labored humor," said Goldberg.

"—And this Twelvetrees hadn't any title to it just as their treasurer. Yes, I thought," said Woods, looking intellectually amused, "that I'd learned pretty thoroughly what damned fools people can be, but Madame Cara Kingman and her husband've given me another lesson. Twenty-three hundred bucks, if you'll believe me—one month's take."

"Good God," said Goldberg, "I'm in the wrong business. Just for telling fortunes?"

"Well, it's dressed up some. Quite fancy, in fact—fancy enough to attract people with money and—er—more sophistication than the kind who patronize the gypsy fortune teller at the amusement pier. But nine out of ten people are interested in that sort of thing, you know, it's just a matter of degrees of intelligence."

"Twelvetrees," said Mendoza meditatively. "He absconded with the take?"

"That he did, at least he's gone and the money's gone, and at the same time. Where I couldn't say. I've been looking for six days, and not a smell. Mr. Brooke Twelvetrees has pulled the slickest vanishing act since vaudeville died."

Mendoza laid down his fork. "Mr. Brooke Twelvetrees. Elegant-sounding name. Did it really belong to him, I wonder?"

"Your guess is as good as mine. Sounds almost too good to be true, doesn't it? And sort of gratifying in a way—you know, the biter bit and all that—the Kingmans seem to have trusted him absolutely. Yes, he's done a very nice flit, overnight—left a note for his landlady and not so much as a bag of dirty laundry to provide a clue, and disappeared into the blue."

"I suppose you've looked at his recent quarters, then—as well as elsewhere. Out on 267th Street."

Woods stared at him, also laid down his fork, and said, "How d'you come to know that, Lieutenant? I didn't know Homicide was interested in Twelvetrees. What—"

It ran a small finger up between Mendoza's shoulder blades, the feeling he'd waited for before in vain. "Woods—when did he go?" he asked softly.

The sergeant cocked his head at him curiously, and then, as if divining his urgency, answered, terse as an official report. "A week ago last night. Last seen four in the afternoon by the Kingmans. They came in Monday to lay a charge."

Mendoza said, *"Donde menos se piensa solta le liebre*—isn't it the truth, things happen unexpectedly . . . Indulge me a minute, Sergeant —he's just vanished, no sign at all of his leaving for anywhere, even in disguise?"

"Not a smell. We've been working our tails off looking. His car was found abandoned down near the Union Station—nothing in it. None of the personnel there could identify his photograph, and he's a man you'd remember if you'd seen him—especially a woman. Nobody remembered him at an airport or a bus station either. Or any of the places he might have gone to buy a disguise—false whiskers or something. If he dyed his hair, he didn't do it with anything he bought at a drugstore near where he lived or near this—er—Temple. Oh, yes, we've looked in all the indicated places, but maybe he's been too smart for us. And now, why?"

"Aquí está, wait for it—wait. Now what *is* this, what could it—? What kind of a car—did it have long tailfins that curved up at the ends?"

Woods opened his mouth, shut it, and said, "Well, no. It's a two-year-old Porsche, an open roadster."

"You don't tell me," said Mendoza slowly. "You *don't* tell me. Now, I wonder. . . . A two-year-old Porsche. And twenty-three hundred dollars. That cancels out in a way, doesn't it? Not like a battered ten-year-old heap not worth fifty bucks on a turn-in. And he couldn't retire on twenty-three hundred. Not a very big job, was it? —worth all the trouble of a disguise, covering his tracks so thoroughly—leaving the car —? I mean, surely he could have accumulated a bigger take than that if he'd planned to steal any money at all. . . ." What was it in his mind, struggling up to the surface? He sat very still, letting it find its own way out. "Woods—when and how did you take a look at that place Twelvetrees lived?"

The half-untouched food congealed on their plates. Goldberg went on eating, watching and listening interestedly. "Mix-up about that," said Woods. "We couldn't get the address for a while—the one the

Kingmans had was three years old, the place he'd lived when he hooked up with them nearly four years ago. They knew he'd moved, they thought they had the address somewhere but couldn't find it. There'd evidently been no occasion to contact him at home. Thought they had the phone number too, but couldn't find that. That kind of people—or making out they are—unworldly, you know. In the end we got it from one of the—er—members of the sect, phone number that is, and that was Wednesday morning. When I got the address from the phone company, I went out there, of course—Wednesday afternoon—and I looked it over. Well, I didn't take the floors up, but—"

"You didn't take the floors up," said Mendoza. "Maybe you should have done just that, Sergeant. Maybe. That—that perpetual talking machine Mrs. Bragg—she didn't follow you around pointing out all the amenities, I take it."

"I don't," said Woods, "encourage people to watch me work, no. I shut the door on her. And just how do you know about Mrs. Bragg and 267th Street? What's your interest in Twelvetrees?"

"I don't know that I've got any—yet. But I think you and I and my Sergeant Hackett will go out there right away and take a closer look at a couple of things. I'll explain it to you on the way, it's a funny little story—and I may be seeing ghosts, but it just occurs to me that maybe, just maybe, Mr. Twelvetrees is being slandered. . . . All that blacktop, so inconvenient. And a trowel. Of all things, a *trowel . . . Vaya*, I *must* be seeing ghosts—it's even more far-fetched than what Walsh— But no harm to make sure."

They stood in the middle of the little living room, the three of them, at two o'clock that afternoon, and Hackett said, "You haven't got much to make this add up, Luis." They had got rid of Mrs. Bragg by sheer weight of numbers and official supremacy, but she might well be lurking outside, suspicious of their intentions toward her good furniture and rugs. "If you're just relying on a hunch, and the damndest far-fetched one I ever knew you to have, at that—"

"Not at all," said Mendoza. "Sober deduction from sober fact, it's just that I happened to have a couple of facts Woods didn't have. I admit to you I've had a little funny feeling that something's fishy—it's been growing on me—but the facts are there to be looked at, and very suggestive too. Anybody could add them up. I don't say it's impossible Twelvetrees didn't decide to decamp with a month's take when he could have made it the whole bank account, and we all know from experience that people can disappear without trace. But it's odd he should go to so much trouble for a relatively small amount, when it involved abandoning an expensive car and the promise of more opportunity to come— after all, he'd been with this racket for four years, didn't you say, Woods? Evidently it paid off. Why should he walk out on it just for twenty-three hundred he wasn't entitled to? It isn't reasonable—I know crimes get committed for peanuts, but not by people of this kind."

"Which," said Woods, "did occur to me, Lieutenant, but there's a couple of ways it could have happened. Maybe some skirt was making things hot for him and he had to get out. Maybe he was afraid the Kingmans were going to fire him, or somebody was threatening to tell them the tale on him, and he'd be out anyway—and he figured he might as well take a little something along. Maybe it was just impulse. People aren't always reasonable, in fact I'd say very seldom."

"I know, I know," said Mendoza. "But look at a couple of other things to add up. Why a note to tell Mrs. Bragg he was leaving? All he had to do was go six steps from his own front door and tell her in person. She was home that Friday night, we know. He didn't leave in that much of a hurry, not when he took time to pack up all his personal belongings. Why in hell should he thumbtack that note to his front door instead of ringing her doorbell? And if he was in such a hurry, why did he take time out from his packing to do a little desultory gardening on that anemic-looking Tree of Heaven out there? She says she *had* her nice new trowel about noon that day, she knows, because she used it to pry open a can of paint."

"A trowel," said Hackett in exasperation. "A *trowel,* for God's sake."

"All right, all right, it won't take long to look!" Mendoza turned and went out to the kitchen. "I couldn't help remembering it, we get in the habit of noticing things automatically, that's all. Damn it, look—the man had lived here for nearly three years, and if he didn't cook his own meals he made coffee in the morning anyway, he used this table for something sometimes." He laid a hand on it; it was steady, but when he moved it to any other angle it rocked at a touch. "How does a table get shoved around out of its usual place? In the process of cleaning the floor, something like that. I doubt if Twelvetrees was that good a housewife. A bachelor living alone, mostly if he doesn't hire it done it doesn't get done—what the hell? But the table was in the wrong place on Wednesday morning—before you got here, Woods—and Mrs. Bragg said she hadn't got round to cleaning here yet. And that trowel was over there by the kitchen door. Why?" He shoved the table clear away from the trap door in the floor at this end of the kitchen. It was about two feet by two and a half, the trap, and covered with linoleum like the rest of the floor; only a little dark line round it, and the small flat hinges, betrayed its presence. One of the makeshift arrangements to be found in such jerry-built new rental units, in a climate where jerry-building wasn't always detectable at once. Mendoza reached down and pulled up the trap by its dime-store bolt, which slid back and forth easily. "Who's going down?"

"Not you, obviously," said Hackett, "in that suit. I'll go."

"You've been gaining weight, I don't think you could make it. All right, it's my idea, I'll do the dirty work." Mendoza sat down and slid his legs through the opening.

"That's a lie, a hundred and ninety on the nose ever since I left college. Be careful, for God's sake, don't go breaking a leg—hell of a place to haul you out of."

"Hell of a place to get anything into," added Woods to that, gloomily.

"He gets these brainstorms," said Hackett, squatting beside the trap resignedly. "About once in a hundred times he's right, just by the law of averages, you know, and that convinces him all over again to follow his hunches. *Well?*" he bellowed down the hole, where Mendoza had now vanished.

"No me empuje—don't push me! I've just got here." Mendoza's voice was muffled. "I need a flashlight, hand one down. . . . *Válgame Dios y un millón demonios!*" That came out as he straightened too abruptly and hit his head on the floor joists. Like most California houses, this sat only a little above a shallow foundation; the space underneath the floor was scarcely four feet high.

Hackett laughed unfeelingly. "He wants a flashlight—why didn't he think of that before? You got a flashlight, Woods?"

"I seldom carry one in the daytime," said Woods.

"That's funny, neither do I. Use your lighter!" he advised Mendoza heartlessly.

There followed a period of silence but for the muffled sounds of Mendoza moving around cautiously down there; then another curse and a longer silence. Suddenly Mendoza straightened up through the trap and demanded an implement of some kind. "Failing the trowel, a soup ladle or something—look in the drawers. The place is furnished, there ought to be tablespoons, a cake server—"

Hackett rummaged and offered him a tablespoon, a hand can opener, and a long wooden fork. *"Nada más?* A big help you are," and Mendoza vanished again with the spoon and fork.

"Does it come on him often?" asked Woods sympathetically, offering Hackett a cigarette.

"Thanks. Five days out of seven he's as sensible as you please. I've thought tranquilizers might help, but on the other hand, just once in a while he does hit pay dirt. I got it figured that it's because essentially he's a gambler—he's in the wrong line, he ought to have been a cardsharp. He calls himself an agnostic, but that's a lie—he's superstitious as hell about his hunches, whether he'd admit it or not."

"Well, we all have foibles," said Woods. "I knew a fellow once who collected paper bags, had a closet full of them. Card player, is he? I kind of fancy myself at bridge, does he go in for it?"

"I think that's a little genteel for Luis, he likes poker. But he won't play for the kind of stakes you and I could stand."

Mendoza's upper half appeared through the trap; he rested an elbow on the ledge and laid the fork and spoon tidily on the floor. His shoulders had collected a good deal of dust and his tie was crooked, but he looked pleased with himself.

"If you've finished slandering my character, and the phone's still working, *chico,* you can go and call the rest of the boys."

"Hell and damnation," said Hackett incredulously. "You don't mean he *is* down there?"

"Didn't you hear me fall over the suitcases? Give me a hand." Mendoza hauled himself out of the hole up into the kitchen, and began to brush down his clothes fastidiously. "You can stop looking for your embezzler, Woods, and hand over what you've got on him to us."

"Holy angels in heaven," said Woods mildly. "No wonder I couldn't find him. How, when, and where exactly, Lieutenant?"

"Not being a doctor and having only the lighter, I'll pass that one. He's not very deep, only six inches or so on top of him, and I just dug away enough to be sure. The hell of a job it must have been to get him there—and of course I'm premature in saying it *is* Mr. Twelvetrees, but it's somebody, and in male clothing, I think. And, at a guess, he's been there just about the time Mr. Twelvetrees has been missing. About four feet from the trap, say under the door to the living room. And three suitcases alongside him, not buried."

"I *will* be damned," said Hackett. "This one you really got by radar, boy. And I suppose from now on you'll quote it every time anybody laughs at your hunches." He looked at the gaping black hole of the trap— "And how the boys are goin' to love that job." He went to call headquarters for a homicide detail.

FOUR

It was six o'clock before they were finished at the apartment. Mendoza went down again with the surgeon and the men to fix up some kind of light; all of them let out frequent curses, crowded together down there. Woods went down to look at the corpse when its face emerged; he provoked an outburst of profanity on his way up by inadvertently pulling out the wire from the nearest outlet down the trap, and plunging the laborers into darkness. He shoved the plug back in and said to Hackett tersely, "Twelvetrees, all right."

Down below, Mendoza could be heard telling someone to keep his clumsy paws to himself, they'd get to the corpse all in good time, but if there was any little something buried with it by accident, he'd like to see it before it got buried again. "Well, well," said Hackett. "It is, is it? How?"

"Surgeon thinks a bang on the head, or several bangs."

Hackett grunted. They sat smoking, carefully sharing the ashtray out of the Facel-Vega to avoid using anything here, until Marx and Horder climbed out of the hole laboriously with all their equipment and Marx called back down, "What d'you want up here, Lieutenant!"

"Everything, everything! And don't forget the bottoms of window sills and the tops of doors!"

Marx sighed and shrugged at Horder; they went into the bathroom to start. Mendoza came up and hauled out the suitcases, one by one, as they were handed to him. "O.K., boys, now we get busy." He sat down on the davenport and produced a folded envelope. "Treasure-trove from the grave."

They looked at the thing he shook out into his palm—a small round pearl-finished button. "Could've fallen down the trap any time and rolled," said Hackett dubiously.

"Don't think so. It was about an inch under the surface, in the loose dirt shoveled over him. Couldn't have been there very long, either by the look of it, even if it just happened to be there when he was covered up. And I think it tells us what we're going to find out anyway—someone was smart enough to wear gloves."

"Why?"

"It could be off a number of things, this shape and size and color." It was flat on top like a stud, not rounded, it had a shank, it was amber-colored. "A woman's blouse. A man's sport shirt. A dress, even a skirt, though I'd say it was too small for that. But what I think it came from was a glove—a glove with a button, or buttons, at the wrist." He put it away carefully. "Now, the suitcases. They've all been printed outside, and they're clean. Which is very odd indeed, only not in this case, of course." He laid the first one beside him on the couch, brought out a key ring—"From the corpse, I haven't searched him, except for these, when I found the cases were locked"—and opened it. Clothing, neatly packed: six solid-colored sport shirts, in two layers, on top—just back from the laundry, by the way they were folded and pinned: the kind of shirts that sold for fifteen dollars and up. Two of them monogrammed. Another half-dozen less expensive white dress shirts underneath. A leather case with eighteen or twenty ties neatly folded in it. Clean socks rolled up in pairs. Shorts and undershirts, almost all of knit nylon. Three pairs of silk pajamas, all of exotic colors. Two pairs of shoes, on trees and wrapped in paper: one pair tan suede, the other black.

"Thirty bucks at a guess," said Mendoza, setting them down carefully without touching the shoe trees. Under the tied-down flap of the lid was a leather case containing an electric razor, a manicure set, and a number of jars and bottles, all bearing the same green-and-gold label and, in tortured script, the words *Flamme d'Amour*.

"*Qué hombre!*" said Mendoza, removing the top from a bottle of cologne with handkerchief-shielded fingers, and sniffing.

"He wouldn't like himself much right now," commented Woods.

Another fitted case with hairbrushes and comb. Six belts, tidily rolled up. A flat leather jewel case containing half a dozen pairs of links, tie clasps, a monogrammed sterling buckle.

"Don't," said Hackett to Woods earnestly, "ask him for any deductions or we'll be here all night. One of the things he's an expert on is clothes."

"Nobody needs to be an expert to deduce from all this that he was a man of no taste," said Mendoza. "The latest fashion, the expensive, but"—he lifted his lip at the cologne bottle—"Main Street masquerading as Beverly Hills." He opened the second case, which was of the tall and narrow kind designated a fortnighter; it contained four suits, six pair of slacks, and four sport coats, all carefully arranged on the hangers, and four more pairs of shoes.

"However," said Mendoza, "all this has something to say besides that," and he looked at the two cases thoughtfully before opening the third.

This was older than the others, of scuffed brown leather instead of plane-weight aluminum; it looked as if it had seen hard usage. When Mendoza lifted the lid, all of them stared in silence, and then Mendoza called Marx and Horder. *"Pronto,* let's see if there's anything on this."

"Very pretty," said Woods. "Never saw one quite like it—looks kind of antique, would you say? But he wasn't shot, was he?"

"It's an old one," agreed Hackett. "Look at the length of the barrel. A six- or seven-shot of some kind—open cylinder like one of those old colt six-shooters, but not quite the same—" They watched the two men from Prints lift it out carefully and set to work.

Mendoza looked at Hackett pleasedly. *"Cuanto apuestas*—how much do you bet it's a smooth bore?" he asked happily.

Hackett fingered his jaw. "Walsh's business. You want to hook it up to this. I don't know that I'd lay any bets, Luis, but I can't see any connection offhand."

"Can't you? Well, it's all up in the air yet, nothing solid, but I can see a couple of little things to build a plot on, you know—stories to tell ourselves about it."

"You don't suppose that any surgeon's going to be able to say, this man died at eight o'clock P.M. on Friday the thirtieth? After all this time? What are you trying to make out—that Bartlett saw this murder done and just forgot to mention it to Walsh, and the killer followed them and an hour and a half later shot Bartlett? I used to like fairy tales, about thirty years back, but they don't thrill me any more."

"Tengo paciencia, I'm not filling in that plot yet—we'll just file it for reference. But I'll say this about the Bartlett business. Here we've got a homicide that isn't fresh enough so the surgeon can say within a day or a day and a half when it started to be a homicide. Isn't it a little helpful that we've got this other thing nailed down as to time? Coincidences do happen, but this is just the least little bit suggestive, or it could be. We

can't operate on the arbitrary premise that these two things must be hooked up, but let's keep it in mind, because if they are, we've got a much narrower time limit for the corpse than the autopsy could possibly give us. And now let's look at the rest of this." He turned back to the third suitcase.

The top layer here consisted of soiled shirts, handkerchiefs, underwear, and socks, crowded in haphazardly; several ties in need of cleaning, also crumpled together and shoved into a side pocket; clean handkerchiefs, rumpled out of their folds and stuffed into every crevice; two pairs of soiled pajamas and a clean pair crushed in together; a pair of leather slippers. In the bottom was a dressing-gown of scarlet silk moire; it had been neatly folded.

"Yes," said Mendoza, feeling delicately in the pockets of the robe and coming up with another soiled handkerchief and nothing else. "Yes. It all says a little something, doesn't it? What elementary deduction occurs to you, Art?"

"That Woods hasn't been slandering Mr. Twelvetrees," said Hackett absently. "Or at least, if he wasn't planning any embezzlement, he *was* planning to leave. With all his *lares* and *penates*. Because—"

Mendoza said parenthetically to Woods, "Speaking of foibles, you notice he forgets his favorite role now and then—the big dumb cop. You catch him off guard, he can actually pronounce three-syllable words."

"*Estése quieto,* I'm deducing," said Hackett. "He didn't do all that packing in fifteen minutes, and the way he's been so careful to sort and fold everything all neat and tidy, it was him did it. He expected to be using all this stuff for some time to come, it represents quite an investment. It looks as if he'd been packing, he'd got almost everything in, except the stack of clean handkerchiefs and all his dirty laundry, and at that point something happened to put him in the hell of a hurry all of a sudden. He just shoved everything else in, cramming it down any old way—"

"Or somebody did it for him," said Mendoza. "You may get to be a lieutenant someday after all. Yes. You know, I think somebody finished his packing for him. Because from the state of the other cases, he was a finicky customer. Like me. We can't help it, it's an automatic thing, like —like cats washing themselves. I don't, maybe, go quite so far as this one did with his flame-of-love cologne and his nail buffer and his— *vaya por Dios,* are these bath salts?—but I'm enough like that myself to guess at the kind of thing he'd do or not do. And however much of a hurry this one was in, I think he'd have put all that soiled laundry into a bag for packing. I think he'd have had that bag handy, laid out ready for when he wanted it, and so he wouldn't have had to waste time getting it and skipped it for that reason. . . . I wonder what happened to it, that bag. It wasn't in the bedroom on Wednesday morning. . . ."

"Let's look," said Hackett, "for clues that might exist, friend, not ones we dream up ourselves, hah?"

Marx said from the other side of the room, "The gun's clean, Lieutenant. Not a thing on it anywhere."

"Yes, of course," said Mendoza. "I don't know why we bother to take you boys out on a job at all any more. Even those six-year-old shoplifters Juvenile's getting these days know about fingerprints." He got up and wandered into the bedroom. "A large stout paper bag," he murmured to himself, "or a bag made for the purpose—a cotton laundry bag, with a slit in it, or drawstrings. You see them at dime stores, with stamped patterns for embroidering." He lay down prone and looked under the bed. "My grandmother has one, a hideous thing, with a design of hollyhocks on it. Red and orange. And *Laundry* spelled out underneath." He went into the closet.

"I get the general idea," said Hackett patiently. "But there are things called hampers too."

"Not here." Mendoza came out of the closet looking dissatisfied. "The bathroom isn't big enough."

"You were just saying a while ago that bachelors living alone don't pay much attention to these things. Now you want to make out—and it's a piddling little thing anyway, what does it matter?"

"It may not matter a damn, I'd just like to know. You miss the point. It's a personal thing. You take me, I wouldn't notice about the kitchen floor needing waxing or the mirrors needing to be washed, it's only me and my personal things that have to be just so—and he was like that, by his clothes and packing. . . . What do *you* do with soiled laundry?"

"I've got a drawer for it. Easiest thing. Logical thing. Probably he did too."

"No. Not here. Not enough drawers, with all the stuff he had." Mendoza gestured at the one bureau. "And *not* logical, but slipshod, that is. You ought to get married, be taken care of properly."

"Give advice, never take it," said Hackett.

"But that's just it, *I* don't need a wife for that, which is the only reason to acquire one in the long view. I'm much more particular at looking after myself than most women, and I can afford to hire the housekeeping done. *Caray,* dirty clothes in a drawer, I'm surprised at you." He looked in all the drawers; Marx and Horder had left them liberally covered with gray powder, and a number of nice prints had showed up: with very little doubt they would prove to belong to the dead man, or Mrs. Bragg. All the drawers were empty except for sheets of clean newspaper. "I take it," he said to Woods, "that Mrs. Bragg hadn't got round to cleaning in here between my visit and yours, and that you hadn't let her in since?"

"This is all very interesting," said Woods, sitting down on the bed and looking more like an earnest postgraduate than ever. "You've got Twelvetrees down pat, Lieutenant, by what I've got on him. The King-mans and a couple of other people—members of that, er, sect—they all say he was a sharp dresser and finicky about himself. One woman said to me, and it kind of stuck in my mind as an apt description, you know —this Miss Webster it was, the only one I've talked to who didn't like him—she said he was like a big black tomcat preening himself. . . . And that's right as far as I know, about Mrs. Bragg. I told her on Wednesday afternoon not to touch anything here. But it didn't seem important enough to put a seal on the door. Matter of fact, of course, there wasn't anything here really useful to me, I just wanted to keep it open a day or so, maybe have a closer look. But it's her property and she's got a key, I couldn't say whether she's been in or not."

"Yes. A paper bag she might have taken away—we'll ask. But I don't think an ordinary laundry bag."

"What does it matter?"

Mendoza stood in the middle of the room, hands in pockets, and stared vaguely at the maroon flowers in the rug. "Well," he said, "well —it might just be—yes, I can see it happening—that somebody wanted to carry away something—and for some reason wanted something to carry it in. Like that. Because it was, say, a lot of little somethings awk-ward to carry unwrapped—or revealing somehow—or because the somebody didn't have any pockets to carry it in. Or a handbag big enough. And there was the bag ready to hand. . . . A big black tomcat, you said, Woods? Tomcat that way as well as this?"

"Oh, well, I wouldn't say definitely. Myself, I think he'd have liked people to think so, and that's about the extent of it. You've seen his picture?" Woods hauled out the photograph again and handed it to Hackett. It had been blown up from a not-very-good snapshot and was a little fuzzy, but the subject had distinctive enough features that that didn't matter. On the back were noted his vital statistics. Brooke

Twelvetrees, if that was his real name, had been just a little too handsome, with fair skin, blue eyes, wavy black hair, a strongly cleft chin, a consciously winning smile showing even white teeth: five-nine, a hundred and sixty, age estimated as thirty-two or thereabouts. "Quite the ladies' man, *in* that sense only, I'd say."

Mendoza looked over Hackett's shoulder and laughed. "Oh, yes, I see. The arm-patter and door-holder—not necessarily the bed-jumper. These collar ads, usually not much else to them but front. And the same goes, of course, for the female of the species. They get by so easily on their looks, no reason for them to develop in other directions. So let's hear something about the Temple set-up."

"I wouldn't like to say whether it's a planned racket," said Woods. "Maybe the Kingmans are seriously sold on this Mystic Truth business. I didn't pay much notice to the ins and outs of it, but this Madame Cara—er—missionizes at everybody, and I gather it takes in a little bit of everything, from astrology to something called Pyramidology. I went and saw Arnhelm in Rackets, but he's got no record of complaints, they've kept within the law. It's been a going concern for about five years, and it started on capital given to the Kingmans—outright gift— by half a dozen wealthy people, all of whom are still members of the sect. That—" He paused as the preparations for bringing up the body reached a climax. The ambulance men tramped in with their basket: Dr. Bainbridge hoisted his tubby middle-aged self out of the trap with some difficulty. Dwyer and Landers below heaved the body up to reaching hands, head first; it was an awkward thing to handle in that space, but they got it into the basket at last and took it out in a hurry. The burial and the clothes had helped, but it had still been dead a week or so.

As they went out, the men inside heard a long pleasurable sound from the little crowd gathered. A couple of men were questioning the other tenants, those who were home, and a number of the neighbors had drifted over to watch.

Dr. Bainbridge sat down on the other end of the couch, wiped his brow, and lit a large black cigar. "Next time, Luis, let's make it in a more accessible place, shall we?"

"Not my idea. What have you got to give me right now?"

"Not a great deal. Don't know that I can tell you much more after an autopsy, except odds and ends like what he had for his last meal. Though the body's very well preserved. He was killed by a blow on the head, several blows were struck and it may have been just one that did for him or a combination of all of them. Blows were struck from the front and side, the left side—his, that is. Nearest I can say as to time of death is between five and seven days. Say between a week ago yesterday and last Sunday."

"Could he have died round about seven-thirty that Friday night?"

"Certainly. Or the next night. Or ten o'clock Sunday morning. You pays your money and you takes your choice."

Dwyer, who'd gone back down the hole, emerged again with a lidless carton and presented it to Mendoza. "Contents of the pockets. I labeled 'em for you."

"Ah," said Mendoza, but he didn't look at them immediately. "Tell me, Bainbridge, just to reinforce my own opinion—about getting him down there, would it have taken great strength? Could a woman have done it?"

"Oh, well, you *have* presumably heard of the law of gravity," said the surgeon. "Always easier to get a thing down than up. If he was put down there more or less at once after death, when he was still limp, it wouldn't have been much of a chore, no—question of dragging him to the trap and sliding him through. And anybody can dig away enough dirt, even with a trowel, to cover a body as thinly as he was covered. It'd take a little time, and it's an awkward place to work—especially without light—though the kitchen light would have penetrated down the trap some, of course. But it'd just be a matter of patience and care. Certainly, a healthy woman could have done it."

"Mmh, my own idea, Apologies to interrupt you, Woods, just go on talking while I look at this." Mendoza regarded the little collection interestedly.

". . . That," Woods calmly picked up where he'd left off, "hadn't really a thing to do with Twelvetrees and the money, I just had a look because I was curious. But anyway, you can say that this Mystic Truth is a profitable business, because evidently it's attracted people with more money than sense, whether the Kingmans planned it that way or not. Judging from the fact that an average month's gross was twenty-three hundred bucks. Twelvetrees and this old Miss Webster—I say old, but she's sharp as they come—even if she did fall for the Mystic Truth— were the only—er—officers of the Temple aside from the Kingmans. Have some fancy titles for themselves I don't recall offhand."

Left trouser pocket, where the keys had been, forty-eight cents in change, a half-used packet of matches from some place called the Voodoo Club on La Cienega. Right trouser pocket, a slightly soiled handkerchief, a small automatic pencil, and a cigarette case, a handsome affair of rolled gold plate, alternating bands of dull Florentine finish with bright modern: it had a lighter in the top, and on the inner left side was a line of engraving in script: *Brooke, affectionately, Mona.* It was half full of Pall Malls.

". . . Miss Webster, who I gather is fairly well off, doesn't take any salary for whatever she does—she volunteered that herself—but Twelvetrees was getting five hundred per for whatever he did, which seems to have been banking the take every week. Miss Webster wasn't at all surprised that he should run away with money that didn't belong to him. She never trusted him, a young man out for what he could get if you asked her, and not particular how he got it."

Breast pocket: clean handkerchief. Inside coat pocket: used handkerchief, wallet. Mendoza looked at both thoughtfully. And nothing in the other pockets except another handkerchief in the shirt.

"The—er—church property is owned outright—former store building way out on Wilshire. They've fixed it up some, and no makeshift do-it-yourself job either. The Kingmans live on the premises, there's a second storey done up as an apartment—I didn't see that. The whole business is incorporated, as I say, and the Kingmans take a very comfortable living out of the net. They bank at the Security on Western. As of right now there's $14,840 in the term savings account, and a little over $7000 in the checking account. All four officers had access to the accounts, as representatives of the Temple."

Dr. Bainbridge sniffed loudly. "Most successful con game ever put over on the human race, organized religion. Infallible. You'd think we'd have seen through it in a quarter of a million years or so, but most people never seem to."

"*Me lo cuenta a mï*—you're telling me!" said Mendoza. "And essentially as crude a con game as the old pigeon drop, too." But he said it absently; he picked up the wallet and began to go through it.

"Twelvetrees," said Woods, "became a convert to the sect about four years ago, in its early days. He'd then just landed here from some place back East, the Kingmans aren't sure exactly where, and was trying to break into the movies, without much success. Everybody liked him—except old Miss Webster—in fact he ingratiated himself so well that within a couple of months he was appointed treasurer at this comfortable salary, so he quit his job as a clerk in a men's store to devote all his time to the Temple."

"From rags to riches," said Mendoza. "Country boy makes good.

Only he wasn't a country boy. Not when he habitually carried his wallet in his inside breast pocket."

"Did he?" said Hackett, interested. "Yes, that's the smart place—I do myself, so do you—but a lot of men don't, even city livers. He'd been around some, to do that."

"I went," said Woods, "to the place he'd been working, to see if I could get a line on where he was from, references he might have given, and so on. But it's a small shop, not a chain, and they don't keep such records that long. The manager remembered vaguely that Twelvetrees said he was from some place in New England. The studio agency he'd put himself on file with didn't have anything on that at all, all they were interested in was his physique and experience. For what it's worth, Twelvetrees had had a little vocal training and played the piano. He'd stayed on the agency's books, and got a little extra work now and then. And that's just about all I can give you."

"And a few possibly helpful points there, thanks very much." Mendoza had all the contents of the wallet spread out before him. Not too many contents, compared with the usual clutter a man accumulates in this substitute for a woman's bag. Everything had been fingerprinted, and the only prints were the dead man's, at first glance. Two fives, a ten, three single bills. Driver's license; and that lacked the optional thumbprint. Nothing too odd about that, of course: some people still connected fingerprinting solely with criminal records, and refused to give the D.M.V. a print. Social Security card. In the plastic slots, two snapshots, one of himself with a blonde woman, the other of a dark woman alone.

The blonde was very blonde, very Hollywoodish in a strapless gown. Brooke Twelvetrees was conscious of the camera, smiling his white winning smile, head tilted to show off the cleft chin and the wave in his dark hair. That was an interior shot, by flash, and showed the pair of them sitting at a table; Mendoza deduced one of those cheap night-club photographers. The woman in the other picture, a bad snapshot taken on a beach somewhere, was dark, slender, consciously posed.

Mendoza looked at the second picture longer than the other, but finally put them both back into the wallet and everything back into the carton. "Yes. Well, if you think of anything else, hand it on."

"Oh, certainly," said Woods. "I'm only too pleased to be rid of this one, Lieutenant—we were getting nowhere fast, and I've got a couple of other things to get busy on. Not that I won't be interested in what you find out."

Hackett sighed and said gloomily, "We're not exactly casting around for something to keep us occupied either. I don't know why the hell you had to look in your crystal ball and find this one, Luis. There he was, peacefully moldering away, doing no harm to anybody. And now you've dug him up, *I've* got a hunch he's going to be a tough one to untangle."

"Maybe—and maybe not," said Mendoza.

FIVE

It was almost eight o'clock when he ended his block's walk from the nearest parking space and looked up at the sign over the door. Quite a modest sign, and unlighted. This wasn't the most glamorous stretch of Wilshire, but it *was* Wilshire, valuable business property; the building taken over by the Temple of Mystic Truth looked as if it might have started life as a small furniture showroom, or as duplex shops. It had been remodeled, and presented a rough fieldstone front with the entrance at one side, severely modern. A small board beside the front door, discreetly lighted from below, bore the legend:

Sabbath Celebration, Renascence of Atman
Weekly Saturdays 8 P.M.
Novitiates 10–4 Tuesdays and Fridays
Ceremony of the Constellations, 3 P.M. Wednesdays
Ceremony of the Inner Chamber, 8 P.M. Fridays

"Vaya, Vaya" said Mendoza to himself, and went in. There was a very small brick-floored foyer, and double doors standing open at the right let him into a large, darkish place which must comprise nearly the whole ground floor. It was half chapel and half theater—very appropriate, he thought; padded folding chairs in rows like theater seats; a carved wooden fence round what was probably meant for an altar, pulpit, proscenium, or what-have-you; niches in the walls for statuettes—he noticed an Egyptian ibis, the inevitable horned bull, a goddess crescent-crowned in white alabaster.

No usher or attendant: he sat down in the last row. There was a fair crowd already gathered, perhaps sixty or eighty people, and in the next five minutes a dozen more came in. He remained the lone occupant of the last row; everyone else settled as near the altar as possible.

There was just enough light from the lobby and a couple of wall fixtures along each side that he had a fairly good look at the late arrivals; among them he was gratified to spot the Hollywood blonde of the snapshot. She was, in fact, the last comer, and he had the feeling that in better light and a different place it would have been quite an entrance. She glided past him, erect and confident, in something dark that rustled and showed a good deal of white throat, the shining blonde hair, to advantage: and she trailed behind her an invisible cloud of spicy, heavy scent.

Mendoza inhaled thoughtfully and said to himself, *"Flamme d'Amour,* female species?" Something like chypre, anyway. Very interesting, but she would keep. . . . A number of the congregation seemed to know her; she seated herself amid subdued rustlings and whispers of greeting.

Almost immediately the ceremony began. He paid little attention to it beyond remarking that it was handsomely staged. Impossible to gather much about the Kingmans at this distance: thin, ethereal Madame Cara, in a Grecian robe, and Kingman, looking distinctly odd with his naked bald head rising out of a voluminous black cassock. Several other people similarly clad took part. There was an elaborate ritual of procession about the altar; there was a tall gilt chalice, and an invocation pronounced by Madame Cara; there was chanted response from the congregation. There was mention of the great All-Parent, the cycles of the gods, the perfect circle of the four trinocracies, and the lesson of the Great Pyramid.

Mendoza sat back and thought about Brooke Twelvetrees, what they had on him so far, what they had on that Friday night, and about Joe Bartlett.

He couldn't help thinking about Bartlett, at least: he didn't like ragged edges to things, and it would be so much neater if Bartlett and Twelvetrees *were* hooked up somehow. But as he'd said to Hackett, they couldn't proceed on the arbitrary premise that Twelvetrees had been killed that Friday night—it was just something to keep in mind.

Mrs. Bragg indignantly denied that she had removed anything from the apartment, even a paper bag. She had been *in* it, of course: finding the note announcing Twelvetrees' departure, she had checked the supply of linen and dishes, and had placed an ad in the *Times,* first appearing on Monday, which had brought several prospective tenants to look at the place before Woods had showed up. There had been no bag of any kind left—so she said.

The note, of course, had been thrown away with the trash on Monday. She could not recall the exact wording, but remembered that it apologized for his sudden leaving, gave only a vague reason of "important business." As it happened, of course, to be the end of the month, he was paid up to date; having paid the customary two months' deposit when he came in, he was in fact due a rebate, and she had assumed that she would receive an address from him later on to send it to. She hadn't seen his signature or writing before—he always paid the rent in cash—and consequently she could offer no opinion as to whether the note was a forgery.

She had first noticed the note, neatly tacked in its envelope to the outside of Twelvetrees' door, late on Sunday morning as she left for church. It might have just been put there, or it might have been there for two days—she couldn't say: she hadn't set foot out of her own place since Friday night, having been trying to come down with flu and warding it off with rest and various potions. And as her door and Twelvetrees' were in the rear building, and no other tenant had had occasion to call on her those days, there was no evidence on when the note had been tacked to Twelvetrees' door.

The apartments, of course, shared a party wall, and she admitted that loud noises were audible through it now and then, but remembered nothing of that sort on that Friday night. "Of course, with them Johnstones kicking up a row again, and I was over there to Number Three twice before I called the police, well, you can see there might've been something going on in Mr. Twelvetrees' place I just didn't hear." Of course, of course. And Saturday, nothing; Sunday morning, nothing.

His key had been enclosed in the envelope with the note, and she had naturally handled it, not that it was likely to have borne any helpful print. The same could be said of the bolt on the trap, which Mendoza himself had handled.

All the prints in the place belonged to her or to Twelvetrees; but a few places where one might expect to find prints had been polished clean, which was neither very helpful nor interesting—the table in the kitchen, the top of the bureau, the bedroom chair. If that said anything, it said that whoever had cleaned those places probably had not visited the apartment for long (or often), if those had been the only things touched.

The trowel, she said, was kept in a box sitting on the small bench inside her carport, along with a few other tools. She didn't think any of the other tenants were likely to know that: they hadn't any occasion. It was account of Mr. Twelvetrees taking interest the way he had in her Tree of Heaven that *he* knew.

Ballistics would, Mendoza hoped, tell him something about the gun in time.

All those handkerchiefs . . .

The alcoholic Johnstones admitted frankly that they remembered little about that Friday night, and were suffering hangovers all day Saturday. Sober, they were very sorry they'd disturbed everyone. None of the other tenants who'd been home could recall anything helpful at all: nobody remembered whether or not there had been a light showing in Twelvetrees' apartment, or whether his car had been in his carport, either on Friday night or any other. . . .

The congregation gabbled a long response to a cue from the altar, and Mendoza muttered profanely to himself. The car—damn it, he should have thought of that before. Phone in and get an inquiry started right away. Because Twelvetrees' Porsche must have been taken away immediately afterward: whoever had finished arranging his planned departure could not know that Mrs. Bragg wouldn't be out and about, that somebody else wouldn't notice the car unaccountably still there after he had supposedly left. The car had been abandoned near the Union Station, and that was quite a trip from 267th Street. Unless there were two people involved, it must have meant that someone had to take a taxi back to 267th, or thereabouts, to pick up his or her own car. The question of public transportation didn't enter in: he doubted very much that there was any out there, after six or seven o'clock, and in any case it would be infinitely slow. No problem at all if there were two people in the business, of course.

There was also that snapshot. That dark girl, something teasingly familiar about her. Leave it at the back of his mind, it would come to him eventually. . . .

And that seemed to be the last outburst from the congregation; the robed figures had vanished from the altar, and—ah, of course—now came the important part of the whole business, the attendants passing down the aisles with little velvet bags, taking up the collection. Not much audible jingling of hard money; there wouldn't be, by the sum missing from Twelvetrees' keeping.

Missing?

And, *Dios mio,* of course, what had happened to the bankbooks?

The attendants missed him there in the last row; the congregation began to drift out. He let it go past him until the hall was empty, and wandered out after it. What was probably a nucleus of—could one call them?—charter members was gathered in the little lobby around the Kingmans. The blonde; a scrawny old woman in rusty black; a buxom hennaed female with a foolishly loose mouth and a mink stole; a scholarly-looking middle-aged man; others more nondescript.

Mendoza leaned on the wall and lit a cigarette, watching and listening—principally to the Kingmans. He was interested in the Kingmans. He didn't listen long: the lobby was too small for anyone to go unnoticed, and he began to collect curious glances. So he detached himself from the wall, went up to them, introduced himself, and asked for a private word with them.

"Dear *me!*" exclaimed Cara Kingman, opening her eyes very wide on him. "A policeman! What *can* we have done?" He put her down as nearing fifty. She was so thin she looked haggard; her fair hair in its thick coronet of braids had only lost color, not turned gray. She had very pale china-blue eyes, and wore, apparently, no cosmetics: she was a ghost-figure head to foot, colorless, still in her white robe bound with a velvet rope at the waist. Round her neck dangled a long silver chain with a medallion, and her long fingernails were enameled silver.

"About Mr. Twelvetrees . . ." said Mendoza gently.

"*Ah*—poor Brooke," she said deeply, lowering her eyes. "Of course, of course. For a moment I had forgotten—do forgive me. One must put all these worldly matters aside during the Renascence. Martin—" She turned to her husband gracefully.

"We must put ourselves at your service, sir," said Martin Kingman gravely. He had a fine rich baritone, eminently suited to public speaking; Mendoza had noted it during the ritual. He conveyed a kind of ultimate respectability, of upper-middle-class conventionality, which must be worth a great deal in this business. He looked like a reliable family lawyer or doctor: bald, a little paunchy, very neat in a navy blue suit—he had removed his cassock—a white shirt, a sober tie. He had intelligent brown eyes behind rimless glasses. "Anything we can do to help you, of course, Lieutenant. My dear, we'll ask these good people to excuse us—"

A general murmur, curious glances at Mendoza; they began to drift away politely.

"*Dear* Madame Cara,"—the buxom lass—"such a dreadful disappointment for you—we must all *concentrate* on forgetting it—"

"So unworldly, so trusting,"—the scrawny old lady—"There's such a thing as too *much* faith, Martin. Indeed!" Snapping black eyes darted toward Mendoza; she didn't seem to think much of him. Evidently the watchword on Twelvetrees was forgive-and-forget, and also don't-mention; they muttered goodnights as embarrassedly as if he had brought up something obscene.

The blonde touched cheekbones with Madame Cara, delicately. "We must try to remember only the good, isn't that so, dear?"

"The only charitable thing, dear Mona. Now do come and see me for a cozy little private chat, *soon.*"

"Won't you come up to our quarters, Lieutenant?" invited Kingman. "Quite a draft here, and we must think of my wife's health, she takes cold so easily. Now I don't recall meeting you before, do I? There was a very polite young man—er—Wilson, Williams, Woods—that was it—"

"Yes, the case has been handed on to me." Mona. That was nice to know, he thought.

"Oh, I—er—see. If you'll just step this way, the elevator—" Yes, money had been spent here. . . .

"Dead?" exclaimed Kingman. "*Dead*—Brooke?" He sounded incredulous; his rich voice trembled with all the proper emotion. "And in such a way— But then, how we have maligned him!" He sat back in his chair, whisked out a handkerchief, and blew his nose loudly. "This is dreadful news, dreadful."

"My very thought, Martin," said Cara Kingman mournfully. "We found it hard to believe," her pale eyes turned on Mendoza, "that dear Brooke would do anything dishonest—and to steal from the Temple treasury, of all dishonorable things. I said at once—you remember, Martin—there is *some* other explanation, which will be revealed to us in time."

"And you were right, as you so often are. I fear it was my more—um—worldly suspicion, Lieutenant Mendoza, which prompted me to issue the charge. You understand, we had trusted Brooke absolutely, but when he so unaccountably—um, absented himself from the Sabbath service, and a check with the bank on Monday informed us that he had not deposited the collection . . . Really, to my mind it seemed foregone, incredible as it appeared. But now—"

"Ah, the *money*," said his wife. She shut her large, light eyes with the effect of switching off headlights. "The *money*—quite unimportant—we must only *share* the awful responsibility, Martin, that it was because he had the money that he was killed in this terrible way. Some violent, greedy person—a young, *young* soul—knowing he had the money, breaking in, and dear Brooke struggling with him to protect the Temple's property—" She shuddered, delicately.

"Well, you know, we don't think it happened quite like that," said Mendoza. "A casual thief would scarcely take the trouble of burying him."

She gave no sign that she heard, lying back on the couch, robe trailing, graceful. A comfortable living indeed they took out of this: it could almost be called a luxurious apartment, with its wall-to-wall carpeting, furniture not from a bargain basement, everything the latest and best. And entirely impersonal. Mendoza deduced a decorator service from one of the better department stores, and nothing added to the decorators' choice. He did not feel somehow that, left to herself, Cara Kingman would choose to live with beige tweed carpet, champagne-colored curtains, eighteenth-century-reproduction mahogany, and parchment lampshades.

"But how else could it have happened?" wondered Kingman. "Ah, now I think, of course I see the fallacy—you men trained to reason acutely about such things, I daresay the notion of a thief never occurred to you, but I confess I should have accepted that solution at once, myself. How *else?* I assure you, I find it inconceivable that anyone who *knew* the boy—"

"That's what we'll find out. I understand you saw Mr. Twelvetrees for the last time at about four o'clock on the afternoon of Friday the thirtieth?"

"Ah—that's correct," said Kingman. "I—we, my wife and I, had just finished conducting the—um—afternoon class for novitiates. We came out of the sanctuary—ah, that is what you would call the chapel, where our services are held—we have a very modest establishment here, you see, there is only a small robing room besides on the ground floor—together, on our way to the elevator, and met Brooke just leaving. He had been working on the Temple accounts in the robing room, which also serves us as an office."

"I see. What conversation did you have with him?"

"Why, none—none at all, Lieutenant. It was quite casual. I believe I said something like, 'Finished for the day, my boy?' and he replied that he was. He was—um—just going out as my wife and I entered the elevator."

"If I had *known*," she said, opening her eyes again, "that it would be the last time I should see him—on *this* plane, of course! But my mind was still with our dear novitiates, and I daresay that prevented any presentiment I may have had."

"My wife," said Kingman, adjusting his glasses with a precise gesture, "is a gifted psychic, you see."

"But one *cannot* control these things, and I never pretend to do so. That is why I have given up such childish efforts as the *séance*. It is all so false, so forced. One must only *accept,* as it comes. Doubtless it was not intended that I should receive warning, or I should naturally have told Brooke to be on his guard against the forces of evil. Destiny . . ." She lifted a hand, let it fall limply.

"As it was, you exchanged no words with him at all, Mrs. Kingman?"

"None—none. I was tired, I went straight into the elevator. But tell us, Lieutenant, what explanation can there be, if it was not a thief? As my husband says, no one who knew Brooke could have wished to harm him."

"It is," said Mendoza, who was rather enjoying himself, "a little early in the investigation to make any guesses."

"Ah, yes, one would want to be *sure*." She sat up and widened her eyes fully on him. "Now do tell me, Lieutenant Mendoza, what is your birth date?"

"February twenty-eighth."

"Ah, Pisces—of course," she murmured. "I should have guessed it, I feel from you that nuance of understanding. You have great sympathy for people, great insight—but you must always guard against trusting your emotional judgment too much—don't you find that? All you Pisceans, *so* prone to being sadly misunderstood by those less acute of mind. And that fatal pride, so apt only to add to others' misunderstanding of you—a sad handicap—*however,* undoubtedly you find your native Piscean intuition for people most useful in your work."

"My dear, we must not take up the lieutenant's time, when he is—um—occupied on this sad matter so near our hearts. If you would tell us, sir, what else we might do to help you—"

"I would like a list," said Mendoza, "of your members here."

"Oh dear, oh dear," said Kingman, removing his glasses and beginning to polish them vigorously, "surely you cannot be thinking that any of these good people, our little flock—? But it's not my place to question, of course. I can easily supply you with that, if you'll accompany me down to our office— No, no, my dear, you must not stir, all this has tired you, you must rest."

"One must *not* give in," she said bravely. "Anything we can do to help you at any time—please do not *hesitate* to ask. But if you will forgive me now, I do feel quite exhausted—"

"My wife," said Kingman as they stepped into the elevator, "is a very sensitive woman—very sensitive. She is an Aquarian herself, of course."

Mendoza let himself into his apartment at an early hour by his usual routine. Bast, the russet-brown Abyssinian, and her five-month-old daughter Nefertite who had taken after the Abyssinian side of the family and was also russet-colored with black trimmings, came to meet him with shrill welcome. He switched on all the lights and began to look about automatically to see what mischief the unpredictable El Señor had got into in his absence.

The magazine rack was still upright, but quite empty, and all the magazines were spread out on the floor with the morning paper neatly on top of them.

"Now how in the name of all devils does he *do* these things?" Mendoza wondered. He was beyond asking himself why. He looked further, and located El Señor gazing coldly down at him from the top of the kitchen door. El Señor was also five months old, but twice the size of his sister; he had inherited his father's Siamese points in reverse, like the wrong side of a negative, and was nearly black all over except for blond eyebrows, paws, nose, and tail-tip. He had large almond-shaped green eyes. "Señor Misterioso!" said Mendoza. "Do you grow hands when my back is turned?" He began to pick up the magazines.

El Señor leaped gracefully down the narrow mantel from the door, and abruptly became Señor Estúpido; he lost his balance, blundered into the electric clock and knocked it flat, and began trying to climb the wall.

"I put up with you only for your mother's sake," Mendoza told him. He plucked him off the mantel and let all the cats out, went to the kitchen and cut up fresh liver pending their return, and made coffee. He carried a cup with him into the bedroom; with his tie off and shirt half-buttoned he paused to study those snapshots in Twelvetrees' wallet again.

That girl. What *was* it that made her familiar?

Studio agency. Twelvetrees had ambitions toward a screen career. He had done work as an extra, he had met other such people. This girl, maybe. Have I seen her in a film? wondered Mendoza. But he never went to film theaters. He never watched TV.

He shook his head and went on undressing. He had a bath, and all the while that vague familiarity teased at his mind. He got into a robe and went back to the kitchen for more coffee. He let the cats in and fed them.

Damn it. She stood there on an anonymous beach, in a white bathing suit, shoulder-length dark hair tossed in the wind—features too indistinct to identify individually, but something indefinable in the stance, the frozen gesture . . .

He finished the coffee and washed the pot and cup.

It was like a hangnail, he thought, he couldn't leave it alone. He—

Hangnail. Hands. Manicure.

"Por todos angeles negros y demonios de Satanás!" he exclaimed aloud. Of course, of course. He must be getting old.

Marian Marner . . .

SIX

". . . a special kind of model," he said to Hackett the next morning, "it was only her hands they used. You know, for soap advertisements, hand lotion, wedding rings, and so on. But that was nearly twelve years ago, whether she's still in that job is anybody's guess. I'll have a look at the agencies. And the damn funny thing is, I don't even remember where she lived—not that she'd likely still be in the same place, of course. And I didn't, I will say, know her very long. But it's odd how the mind operates sometimes."

"I wouldn't say odd in your case that you mislaid one little wild oat out of the field of them you've sown," said Hackett.

"True. You know the only other thing I remember about her at all is that she had a funny-shaped appendix scar, with a little hook at one end."

"Now that's real helpful," said Hackett. "We'll just camp out on the beach until some day she comes by in a Bikini and we can identify her. I think the agencies are a better idea. I don't suppose she'll be much use when we find her."

"Por que no?"

"Oh, well, I was just thinking of the snapshots—not what you'd call really good portraits, but the best is that one of him with this blonde. If he was really much interested in this Marner girl, he'd have provided himself with a better picture, wouldn't he? This thing"—Hackett looked at it again—"it might be any woman with dark hair."

"Something in that, sure. I'll have a look around for her anyway, and we'll see. I wanted to go after this blonde myself—"

"Como no—naturally, naturally!" said Hackett.

"—But I also want to see Arnheim and get whatever he may have on this Mystic Truth and the Kingmans, as well as following up Marian Marner—and I think I'll let you handle the blonde. You might see this Miss Webster too. The blonde"—Mendoza consulted the list of members Kingman had given him—"is one Mona Ferne, at least I deduce she's the one, the only Mona on the list. Whether Miss or Mrs. it doesn't say. She lives out in West Hollywood, here's the address."

"O.K." Hackett stared at it absently. "Mona Ferne. That rings a faint bell in my mind—"

"Don't tell me this is one of *your* wild oats intruding on the same case. Coincidence has a long arm, but—"

"My past is pure as a virgin's dreams—compared to yours, anyway. No. It's— Mona Ferne, now what does it say to me?—up in lights, sure, there was a star by that name a while back. Quite a while back it'd be, I seem to remember I was just a kid when . . . Wouldn't be the same, I shouldn't think, not young enough for this one."

"Well, go and find out."

"I'm going, I'm going. Enjoy yourself with your old girl friend if you find her."

The address, when Hackett found it on one of the older residential streets out west of La Brea, proved to be a single house. This was a neighborhood of solid money, twenty-thousand-a-year-and-up class: the houses were bigger than most California houses, many of two storeys. This was one of them. It tried to look like the traditional Southern mansion: it was white, it had pillars, but on a city lot there was space only for a strip of lawn, and the enormous blue spruce in the front yard dwarfed it, towering the height of the house again above the roof, and probably darkening all the front rooms. The wrong tree, as it was the wrong house, for a city lot.

But plenty of parking space. He parked and walked up the path indicated by sunken steppingstones to the low brick porch. The woman who opened the door to him was obviously a domestic; her only association with this house would be strictly the dollar-and-a-half-an-hour kind. She was middle-aged, plain, neat, and dowdy, with a mouth like a steel trap.

"Miss—or is it Mrs?—Ferne," said Hackett. "I'd like to—"

"*Miss* Ferne, and she's not here, but she don't buy at the door."

"I'm not selling anything." He produced his credentials. A detective sergeant of police made no more favorable impression on her than a salesman; she looked down her nose at him.

"Miss Ferne ain't got nothing to do with the police. If it's a traffic ticket—"

"Detectives," said Hackett, "don't have anything to do with that part of the business. I happen to be from Homicide, and it's important that I see Miss Ferne. When will she be home?"

The maid retreated a step. "*Murder,* you mean—"

"Well, that's not the legal definition but it'll do in this case."

"Miss Ferne couldn't have nothing to do with a murder—"

"We all have opinions. When will she be home?"

"I couldn't say," snapped the maid. "I guess you better see Miss Carstairs." She retreated farther in tacit invitation and shouted, "Oh, Miss *Angel!*"

Hacket went into the entry hall. He was right: the tree made all these rooms so dark that you'd want the lights on even at noon, to avoid the furniture. The several open doors off the hall looked like entrances to caves. Only the open front door shed any light here, on a polished parquet floor, a couple of fussy little pedestal side tables bearing knick-knacks, a grandfather's clock, a carpeted stairway.

"Well, what is it *now?*"

"The police," said the maid succinctly.

Hackett couldn't place the girl coming down the stair. No house-keeper or secretary or—were there still such things as governesses?—would hold her job a day looking like that. She looked about twenty-five, and she didn't have bad features but she hadn't done anything about herself at all, for a long time. Lank brown hair was pinned back carelessly to straggle, overlong, past her shoulders; she wore no make-up, even lipstick was missing: she had on a drooping black skirt too long for her and an ancient darned gray sweater too large, no stockings, and flat-heeled brown shoes.

"Oh," she said. She stopped at the foot of the stair and looked at him, neither surprised nor much interested, apparently, by her flat tone.

"*Homicide*," said the maid. "He wants to see your—Miss Ferne."

"Has she killed somebody?" asked the girl. "That'd be a little change, and very nice too, if they put her in jail."

"You oughta be *ashamed*," said the maid viciously. "A nicer, kinder, sweeter woman I never—and *you*—"

The girl said detachedly, "You're hired as a maid, Winter, not a nursemaid. I'll talk to the policeman." She jerked her head at him. "You can come in here."

It was, when she switched on the lights, a big, stiffly formal, cold sitting room. She threw herself into a chair and told him ungraciously to sit down. "What do you want to see Mona about?"

"A murder, Miss Carstairs. Someone she knew has been murdered, and we'd just like to hear a few little things, like when Miss Ferne last saw him and so on."

"She's just left, what a pity—she'll enjoy *that* like anything." Evidently she wasn't interested in who had been murdered. "A man hanging on her every word—even a policeman. Heaven knows when she'll be home, she's gone to see her agent. I suppose you could find her there if it's all that urgent—Stanley Horwitz, two doors from the Cha-Cha Club on the Strip. She'd be *delighted* to be chased down."

Hackett watched her curiously. "Thanks very much, I may do that." She was thin enough, even a little too thin: she might have a nice figure under that sloppy outfit. It wasn't the deliberate sloppiness some girls affected, thinking they achieved the casual air: it was just carelessness. Uncaringness. "You haven't asked who's been murdered."

"Well, I know it wasn't Mona, more's the pity, and if it was one of her friends, it's not likely to make any difference to me."

"It was a gentleman by the name of Brooke Twelvetrees."

She sat up from her ungraceful slouch and stared. "Brooke? Who on earth would want to murder *him?* He's not—not *important* enough."

"Somebody evidently thought he was."

"Funny," she said. "And you have to go round asking questions to find out who and why. What a dull job. But I suppose you're used to it. Do they pay you much for sorting through other people's dirty laundry?"

Hackett didn't often get mad, and he was used to overlooking insults from people he questioned, but unaccountably he felt his temper beginning to slide with this girl. "It's a living," he said shortly.

"And gives you that *nice* feeling of power, I suppose, you can b-bully witnesses and beat up gangsters whenever you pl—"

"Oh, for God's sake!" said Hackett angrily, and then stopped. Belatedly it came to him that she hardly knew what she was saying: she was caught up in some violent emotional maelstrom, and he'd just walked into the middle of it. She was trembling convulsively; now she sprang up, crushing both fists against her mouth, turning her back on him.

"Here," he said, anger dropping away from him, "what's the matter?"

She just stood there shaking. He went up and laid a hand on her shoulder. She was taller than he'd thought; unlike most women, she'd reach above his shoulder if she straightened up. But too thin.

"Look, don't do that," he said helplessly. "You'll go working yourself up into hysterics in a minute, and that prune-faced maid'll think I'm murdering you."

She gave an involuntary, half-tearful giggle. "I'm s-sorry. Just a minute. I'll be—all right—in a minute." She groped blindly for a handkerchief, blew her nose; after a minute she turned around and sat down again. "I'm sorry," she said more steadily. "I've been saying horrible things, I didn't mean— Not your fault. . . . You'd better try Mr. Horwitz's office if you want Mona, and if she's not there I think she was going to the Fox and Hounds for lunch."

She sat stiff and upright on the edge of the chair and said it like a child reciting a lesson. A child with nobody to see her hair was combed and her face washed and her nails scrubbed. Hackett was curious and oddly irritated: what was wrong with her? She wouldn't be bad-looking at all if she'd fix herself up a little. She had a small straight nose, nice teeth, a clear pale complexion; her eyes were good hazel-brown with black lashes, and if she was tall for a woman she wasn't all that outsize. And she sat there looking like hell, like some female in one of those funny sects where they thought colored clothes and short hair and lipstick were engines of Satan—worse, because those people did comb their hair and wash their hands. Her nails were like a child's, short and unpainted, and her hands weren't very clean, and that straight limp hair falling stringily down her back . . . And the maid had called her Miss Angel. Angel, my God, what a name, and for this one.

He got up and said, "Thanks very much, I'll see if I can find her there."

She went to the door with him. "I'll give you a little tip," she said, and her flat voice was metallic. "You just start out by telling her you remember all her pictures and think she's the greatest actress since Bernhardt, and she'll fall over herself to oblige you."

"I thought I remembered the name—Mona Ferne—she's the same one who used to be in pictures, then?"

"Oh, goodness, don't say *that* to her. Used to be. She's just taking a little rest between jobs, according to her. A little twenty-year rest." In the merciless light, from the open door, of pewter-gray cold daylight, she looked awful: she looked gray and cold as the sky, and her eyes were too bright, too expressionless on him. "She'll like you, she likes big men. What's your name? . . . Oh, yes, that'll be all right too, a nice American-sounding name. Now I look at you, you look quite nice, because I like big men too. I've got to, haven't I, being so big and clumsy myself, but it's rather an academic question, of course, because it doesn't work the opposite way—nobody ever looks twice at me, no reason. Will you do me a favor, Sergeant Hackett?"

The little fixed smile on her colorless mouth was somehow terrible. He said carefully, "Well, now, that depends on what it is, Miss Carstairs." Something very wrong here.

"Oh, it's nothing difficult. Just, when you *do* locate Mona, and talk to her, or should I say listen to her, I'd like you to remember that she's my mother, and I'm twenty-six years old, and she was thirty-four when I was born—it was fashionable to have a baby that year, you see. Will you do that?"

"Yes, I'll do that."

"Thank you very much," she said. "I'm sorry I said nasty things to you, before. Goodbye." She still wore the fixed smile when she shut the door after him.

Hackett got out a cigarette and lit it, and was surprised to find that his hand was shaking. That one, he said to himself, is just about ready for the men in white coats. But it didn't pass through his mind academically or cynically. And as a cop he'd seen a lot of trouble and grief and evil and lunacy, and he'd learned to shut off much feeling about it because that got you nowhere—you'd just tear yourself to pieces over it and accomplish nothing. But right now he felt something, he couldn't help it, about that girl—he felt so damned sorry for her he could have wept—and that surprised him all over again.

"I just had the feeling," said Mendoza, "that Mr. Martin Kingman is a little too smooth and slippery to be entirely unacquainted with the law. Of course there's a very thin line there, I admit it—that kind is always very smooth. The same essential type, it goes in for politics and the church and show business, as well as legally dishonest jobs, and you've got to separate the sheep from the goats. . . . But it was all very pat, rather like a pair of professional gamblers sitting with a pigeon, you know—I had the distinct feeling there was a cold deck rung in."

"Not surprising," said Lieutenant Arnhelm, and sighed. He looked like someone's jolly and indulgent grandfather, bald, round, and amiable, but in reality was a bachelor and a complete cynic. "They get that way. After all, it's six of one, half dozen of another whether they keep inside the letter of the law or not—it's still a racket. It's still a front they're putting up, and it gets to be like a seasoned vaudeville act, the automatic routine."

"I wish you could give me something else on them."

"I've got just so many men and there are still only twenty-four hours in a day," said Arnhelm. "We can't go looking every place there's a possibility of fraud. Keeps us busy enough investigating complaints. Sure, we keep a little list, just on the chance we'll be looking into this or that some day—another fortune teller takes out a county permit, another funny cult gets set up, we file what information shows up on the applications and so on—but that's as far as it goes, unless somebody comes in with a complaint."

"Yes, and what are the odds on the information being false? It's like income tax returns, you can't check them all. I know those applications for permits, those affidavits—*Have you ever served a prison-term, Have you ever been known by another name,* and so on. Like asking when you stopped beating your wife. Nobody in his right mind is going to put down *Yes,* and give chapter and verse, but so long as he scratches in *No* with a post office pen and signs any name that occurs to him, it gets duly approved."

"I tell you," said Arnhelm, "you go out and recruit the force about five thousand more men, nice bright boys with superior I.Q.'s, and we might begin to do things the really efficient way. Check up on every single application for every kind of permit, among other things."

"All right, all right, I know the problem. And at that, those recruits would do more good walking beats the old-fashioned way—and five thousand just a drop in the bucket for that job, in this town."

Arnhelm agreed gloomily. "And the point is here, what's the difference? It's a way to milk the public, sure. So is any business, in the long view, except that some businesses sell things the public needs. Mostly it's things they just think they need, which is what's called human nature. You're got to gull the public in *some* way to sell anything, but the law draws a line as to how bad you can gull them. As long as people like the Kingmans keep inside the line, we can't go poking our noses into their private racket, any more than we can into the cosmetic business, or the automobile factories, for instance. And if we did it wouldn't do any good, they'd just find more pigeons. People are such damn fools. Why d'you think women go on buying some new brand of face powder? Because the ads say it'll make them look younger. Why do men go on buying hair restorer? Because they're damn fools. We can't cure that situation."

"All true, but it doesn't stop me wishing you had something more on the Kingmans," said Mendoza. "However, thanks very much for the lecture." He started back to his own office thinking about the little he'd got from Arnhelm. The Kingmans, according to the affidavits they'd supplied in the process of incorporating the Temple, hailed from Philadelphia, where Kingman had been in the hardware business. He was fifty-nine, she was fifty-one. References consisted of the people here who had supplied capital for establishing the sect. And that was just about the sum total of usable information.

Sergeant Thoms, who sat at Sergeant Lake's desk on Lake's days off, was still patiently working his way through the phone-book list of model agencies. He shook his head silently at Mendoza.

The autopsy report wasn't in yet. Ballistics was silent on the gun. Mendoza went out for coffee, and at the drugstore counter found Goldberg sneezing violently into Kleenex over a half-eaten sandwich.

"The very man I wanted to see," and he climbed onto the adjoining stool. Goldberg emerged from the Kleenex long enough to say that it was supposed to be his day off but something had come up.

"Whad cad I do for you?"

"Allergies," said Mendoza. "Everybody talks about them but when it comes down to it I don't seem to know much about them, except that they hit you different places. What are the symptoms?"

"Are you kidding?" said Goldberg. The paroxysm over, he put the Kleenex away. "We could sit here until tomorrow while I told you. Almost anything. Me, I've read all the books and spent a lot of money on specialists, and I've come to the conclusion that nobody knows anything about it for sure. They can tell you what you've got—sometimes —and sometimes what to do about it, but by the time you've got one allergy cleared up you've developed another one. What are *your* symptoms?"

"I haven't got any. What I want to know is this. If you find somebody using about three times as many handkerchiefs as the normal person, used handkerchiefs stashed away in every pocket, isn't it likely to be a symptom of an allergy? That's the way it takes most people?"

"That it does," said Goldberg. "Some people have hives too, and some people itch, and various other things, but you can say that practically anybody with allergies is going to have, to start with, the nasal drip and the stuffed-up sinuses, and so he's going to be using a lot of handkerchiefs. Or Kleenex. Why?"

"Yes, I thought so. My latest corpse did, I think. I wonder if he was going to an allergy specialist."

"If he was crazy or a millionaire, he was," said Goldberg.

"Don't they say it's psychosomatic?"

"Listen, damn it, you say it if you want a good punch in the nose— go on, say it's all emotional. That's what they tell you when they mean they don't know and can't do anything else for you. So I'm allergic to about forty things, see, like whiskey and cat hair and the glue on postage stamps; all right, so I get hay-fever when I haven't been near any one of the things I'm allergic to, so what do they say? They say, well, well, Saul my boy, you must have grown another allergy, maybe your wife's nail polish, we'll find out—but if I haven't got the ten or twenty or thirty bucks for more tests, *then* they say, it's psychosomatic, maybe you'd better see a head doctor. Passing the buck. The hell with them."

"I see. I suppose I can get a list of specialists from the Chamber of Commerce or somewhere."

"And I wish you joy of them," said Goldberg, beginning to sneeze again.

When Mendoza got back to his office Sergeant Thoms had finished calling the agencies, without result. "But being it's Sunday, I couldn't get hold of only about half of them, sir, and at most of those places it was an emergency number, not their office, and they couldn't say for sure without checking records. We're to check back tomorrow on those."

"Damn Sunday," said Mendoza. "I suppose none of the doctors' offices would be open either." It would, of course, be easier to check with someone who had known Twelvetrees: always providing they told him the truth. But there couldn't be much in it. . . . "When Frank Walsh comes, shoot him in." He had called Slaney to borrow Walsh for more questioning. He went into his office and called the Temple, got Kingman, and asked him if Twelvetrees had had an allergy problem. Why, yes, so he had. Was he going to a specialist? Yes, Kingman thought so, but couldn't tell him which one definitely—it had been a doctor on Fairfax Avenue, he remembered that, and the name was something like Grass or Glass.

Mendoza thanked him and had recourse to the phone book; and there was a Dr. Graas on Fairfax Avenue. Child's play, and what did it mean? Very likely nothing. Nevertheless, he'd ask. Just on the chance that there was something.

He called Alison. "Would you like to visit a place called the Voodoo Club tonight? I'll pick you up about eight. Preferably in that amber silk thing."

"I can't say the prospect thrills me. Of the Voodoo Club, that is. You know I don't like night clubs—neither do you—why this sudden passion to be conventional?"

"I just want to take a look at it, it may be mixed up in a case."

"That doesn't reassure me," said Alison. "The first time I went out with you it was the same sort of thing, a place you just wanted to look at, and it ended in our getting shot at and my ruining a brand-new pair of stockings."

"*Mi carina bella,* not that sort of thing at all. I hope. I'll take good care of you. Eight o'clock."

"Oh, damn," she said suddenly in his ear. "No, that's not for you, but that devilish kitten you insisted on giving me—Sheba, no!—I've been painting the view out the bedroom window, and she's got into the rose madder—Sheba, get down, *not* on the bed, darling—" The receiver crashed in his ear and Mendoza laughed.

Sergeant Thoms put his head in the door and said Walsh was here. "Fine," said Mendoza, "bring him in and go get some coffee for all of us."

SEVEN

"No you're not lucky to catch me exactly," said Mr. Stanley Horwitz. "I keep legit show business schedule—dark on Mondays—fancy of mine. Usually get a lot done on Sundays too, but it's been slow lately. . . . So you want to know something about Mona Ferne? I could write a book. Homicide—has she killed somebody?"

Hackett said he shouldn't think so but you never knew.

"Pity," said Mr. Horwitz. "Offer you a drink? . . . You boys don't *have* to be so damn moral about rules, you just do it to annoy. No pleasure drinking alone—but I will." He got out a bottle of Scotch, flicked down the lever on his intercom, said, "Milly, I'm busy for the next half hour or so, if that nance who thinks he's America's answer to Sir Laurence Olivier comes in, he can wait. And wait." Mr. Horwitz, who was edging sixty, five-feet-four in his elevator shoes, and possessed a shock of curly gray hair, poured himself a drink and slid down comfortably in his upholstered desk-chair. "I wish you'd have a drink, Sergeant. Nice to see somebody approximately normal in here, for a change."

"Don't you usually?"

"Dear God, these people," said Horwitz. "These *people*. Nobody, Sergeant, nobody at all is mixed up in show business to start with—or wants to be—unless he, she, or it has an exhibitionist complex. Just in the nature of things they're all egotistic as hell, and that's *right* where you can get into the hell of a lot of trouble with them, because they're so very damn smooth in covering that up, you know? You got to keep it in mind every minute, that they're just front. It gets tiresome." He swallowed half of the drink. "And maybe you better keep it in mind about me, because God knows I don't suppose I'd be in this rat race of a business if I wasn't a little bit like them. Just a little bit. Right now, of course, they're all busy overcompensating for the granddaddy of all inferiority complexes, and that makes 'em a little quieter than usual."

"How's that?" asked Hackett.

Horwitz eyed him in faint surprise over the glass. "You grow up in this town?"

"Pasadena," said Hackett.

"Don't you notice what's going on? Time was they *were* this town—this was the capital of honky-tonk, the Mecca for all faithful pilgrims who never missed the change of show at the Bijou. Time was, all the money in this town, the real money, was theirs—show-business money. Everything important that happened here was show-business kind of important. Sure, the legit folk back on Broadway kept their noses in the air, but, brother, when one of 'em got the nod from Goldwyn or De Mille, he came a-runnin'—and for why? The folding stuff, the long green. Oh, this was quite a town in those days, Sergeant. And them days is gone forever. The real money behind this town now, why, all the studios together never used or made money like that—they're just a drop in the bucket of capital now, since the aircraft and missile plants moved in, all kinds of business, and since all this irrigation made us, what is it, second highest in agricultural production of the nation? *They're* just peanuts now, and tell the truth, I figure the people in this town've got fed up with 'em too. It's time. Not surprising. You don't have to know one of 'em personally very long before you find out what they're like—personally—and I guess it just took a little longer for the public to learn, living in proximity as you might say. The gimmick doesn't work any more, not the way it did. The old glamour's dead. They don't get in the headlines—even local—any more, for losing a diamond necklace or marrying a European aristocrat. The gossip columns about the stars are shoved into the second section and a back page at that—there's too much interesting news about Cape Canaveral and the new government contracts at Lockheed and Douglas and what big companies are moving out here with all their personnel, building ten-million-dollar offices and so on. Too many vice-presidents and union officials riding around in Rolls Royces, too many of their wives in sable coats leading French poodles—*and* losing diamond necklaces at the opera—nothing to exclaim about any more, nothing to mark them as royalty, way they used to be. See? Notice how quiet they act these days, trying to pretend they're just like other people, plain down-to-earth folks. That's one of the symptoms. And, brother, how they hate the whole business! How scared and indignant they are, and *how* loud they deny it's happened!" Mr. Horwitz retired into his glass.

"They do, hm? I can see how that'd be. Never thought much about it before."

"You're not in the business—and for that you can thank God. Oh, yes, they're wearing a chip on the shoulder all right—can't do this to *us,* you know?—and at the same time trying to pretend nothing's happened at all, that it's still their town. . . . But you were asking about Mona. Case in point. One of the worst ones. I don't mind gossiping about Mona Ferne, if you're got time to listen—"

"I've got time."

"—And I got the feeling," said Horwitz dreamily, "I might do just that even if you were somebody from TV thinking of hiring her—because she annoyed the hell out of me just before you came in, and that was just once too often she did. To start with, in case you're curious, her real name was Minnie Lundgren, and she came from some place in South Dakota. Won some sort of piddling beauty contest back there, and right away made tracks for Hollywood—read 'Mecca'—to join the royal family. . . . You remember any of her pictures?"

"Hardly. I think I was about three when she was in her heyday as a star. I wasn't noticing females much yet. But I've seen her in bit parts, later on, when I was just a kid. Just vaguely remember the name."

"You didn't miss an awful lot," said Horwitz. "She never could act—she took direction, that's all. They built her up, like they built up a lot of others who didn't really have much on the ball. And you've got to remember that comparatively speaking it's a new medium—anyway it still was thirty-five years back—and fashions in these things, they change like other fashions. She was a star, sure, they made her one. And don't you forget either, Sergeant, that's just the end of one long road, and she nor nobody else gets there, usually, without the cold guts to kick anybody in the teeth who gets in their way. You married? . . . Well, when you come to get married, take my advice and don't pick a beautiful woman *or* an actress. The two don't always coincide. Point is, anybody naturally good-looking, they're awful apt to be—what's the head doctors' word?—narcissistic. Me, me, me, twenty-four hours a day. And some of it's other people's fault, building 'em up all the time, you what am I doing for her, when can she expect a new contract?—good God in heaven, I've given it to her straight enough times, but it just doesn't penetrate. Hear her talk, you'd think she'd had a couple of pictures gross a million in the last six months, and it's just a little legal fuss with the studio leaves her without a contract. Every once in a while she threatens to get another agent, and I wish to God she'd try, but she never will—she knows damn well, if she'd admit it, nobody else would ever put her on the books."

"I suppose she's living on what she used to make—investments?"

"Mostly, I *think,* on Carstairs' money—she spent most of hers as it came in. Maybe he'd begun to see through her at that, he'd tied it up in trust—in two trusts actually, one for the girl. They'd only been married a couple of years, the kid was just a baby, when he crashed. Sure, Mona's got plenty to get along on, but that's not enough for her."

"She is," said Hackett, "a member of a funny cult called the Temple of Mystic Truth. Know anything about that?"

Horwitz shook his head and shrugged. "Can't say I want to. This town used to have a reputation for that kind of thing too, and when you come to think of it, it's natural. You take these people—they're people without roots, you know?—and most of 'em are suckers for that kind of thing. Especially, you might say, as they get older. They feel a lack somewhere, they look around for something solid, for an answer, and because they're the kind of people they are, the orthodox doesn't attract them."

"Yes, I can see that. She'd been going around some with this fellow who got knocked off, Brooke Twelvetrees."

"Oh, *that* one, was it? And that's why you're interested. I remember *him.* She brought him in, pestered me to take him on. Well, you never know where you'll find something good, I looked him over. He had looks, the kind a lot of women go for, but don't get me wrong when I say, like I did about Mona, that's the first and only thing. It's important, but you and I could both name a dozen top stars without much in the way of looks. Mona and some like her, both sexes, got to the top on looks alone, but that doesn't hold you there. It's a thing there's no word for—showmanship, I guess that comes closest to it. Nothing to do with talent. I can name you people"—he did so— "who've been on top for years, without having anything but a lot of gall, *and* showmanship. It was that, even a little bit of it, this Twelvetrees didn't have. The personality didn't project, he couldn't've held an audience with the doors locked and safety belts to fasten 'em down. I said nothing doing, and Mona was mad as hell. . . . No, that was the only time I ever met him, it'd be about two years ago. . . . I heard later Meyer and Hanks took him on, don't know if or where they'd got him anything."

"Well, thanks. Where's that outfit?" Hackett took down the address. "You don't think there'd have been anything serious about their going around together? Just as an opinion."

Horwitz laughed. "Because Twelvetrees was maybe twenty-five years younger? Look, you don't need to be a psychiatrist to read these people. One of the damndest awful things about them is that they never get past a certain stage in life. They're kind of fixed at the mental age where parties and clothes and boy friends and girl friends, and all the—the froth, you know, is all that's important in life. It can have sad results. You take anybody fifty-five, sixty years old, even if he's got good health, nothing chronic, he's glad to let down once in a while, take things easier, stay home Saturday night and read a book. He's got a long way past being interested in kids' things—he's got to other things just as much fun. He's found out he doesn't have to be twenty-five years old and handsome as a movie star to get a kick out of making love to his wife, and she doesn't have to be Marilyn Monroe. He doesn't—you know—have to keep up a front. These people, the front's all they've ever had, and it's the most important thing in the world to them—they can't *let* themselves let down, ever. The front of perpetual youth. In looks and every other way. I tell you, once in a while I find myself in a night club or somewhere like that, not by choice but on business, and I don't know any sadder sight. These people like Mona, hell-bent on having a good time the same way the twenty-five-year-old kids are having a good time. Out of the fronts of things—good looks and clothes and going to parties. . . . Mona and this Twelvetrees? She always has a man in tow, to be seen with. Whatever she can pick up. She's got to. By the only rules she knows, if she didn't have something in pants to be seen with at the good-time places, it'd mean she was dead—as a female. And there are, in this town, enough men like her that she can always find one. But of course she'd always prefer one like Twelvetrees, to the ones her own age working just as hard as she is, with their toupées and expensive false teeth and corsets. Shows she's still an attractive, *vital* female—that's a word they like—to pick up a young man. You want my opinion, well, Twelvetrees was one of these people too, and he probably took up with Mona thinking she could do him some good in the way of contacts. Or just maybe because she paid the bills at the good-time places. I wouldn't say she'd gone down quite as far as that, to pay a fancy man to squire her around, but maybe—and there are nuances in these things, even with people like Mona."

"So there are," agreed Hackett. "Well, thanks very much for your help. Don't know that any of it's much use to us right now, but you never know—and anyway it's interesting to get the inside view on them."

"You find it interesting?" said Mr. Horwitz sadly. "Seems funny to think I ever did. These goddamned awful people . . . like reading the same page in a book over and over. Someday I got to get out of this business. . . ."

Walsh didn't know yet why Mendoza was asking him about that D.-and-D. call; he was doing his best to be helpful, but it had been such a routine thing . . .

"I don't want to prompt you. But just visualize it in your mind—a big blacktopped area with apartments on two sides and across the rear. The one where the drunks were was Number Three, that's in the front of the second building on the right as you drive in. It was about seven-thirty, and it was raining. It was the landlady called in, and she was waiting for you—"

"Funny little fat lady in a man's raincoat," said Walsh suddenly. "Yeah, I got it, Lieutenant. We pulled up where she was, I guess it'd be in front of her place, she was waiting there on the porch, I remember that—and we both got kind of wet going across to the drunks' apartment—left the car where it was, see, it was just a step really but it was coming down pretty steady then."

"Yes, go on."

"Well—I don't know just what you want, sir. There wasn't anything *to* it. It's funny how just the sight of the uniform'll quiet 'em down sometimes. There was this big bruiser of a fellow and a little blonde woman, going at it hammer and tongs—you could hear 'em half a block away, the landlady needn't've come out to tell us where. Soon as Joe knocked and said who we were, they stopped and the man let us in. We talked to 'em a few minutes, you know the sort of thing: hadn't they better quiet down, have some consideration for the neighbors, and that's all it took really." He stuck again there, and was prodded on. "Well, let's see—Joe gave me the nod, I knew what he meant, and I went out to the car to report in. See, Joe figured, and I guess he knew from experience—he was a good cop, Lieutenant, the best for my money—"

"I know he was."

"—He always said, about a deal like that, where they aren't really slum people who just naturally distrust cops, that you don't have to go acting tough, and a lot of times they'll listen to a good stiff talk from a man in uniform where they'd just get mad with somebody like the landlady or the neighbors. That's what he meant, see. We could see they wouldn't make any more disturbance, and so like I say I went back to the car to report in, and Joe stayed to talk to 'em, so maybe they'd think twice the next time."

"Yes. And then?"

"Well—that's all," said Walsh blankly. "I sat in the car and waited for Joe, and pretty soon he came out—with the landlady—she'd stayed in the drunks' apartment with him—and she thanked us and we got back on our route again."

Mendoza made a few marks on paper, shoved the page across the desk. "Look, here's the set-up, let's get it clear. The apartments numbered Five and Six are in the building across the end of this court. The landlady lives in Number Six. Numbers Three and Four are in this second building from the street, at right angles to that. Show me where your squad car was in relation."

Walsh hesitated, finally pointed. "I'd say just about in front of this rear building. I mean not in front of either of the apartment doors there but sort of in between them."

"Damn it, I don't want to force this," said Mendoza softly, "if there *is* anything. . . . When you both got out of the car, you went straight across to Number Three? Bartlett was with you?"

"Why, sure, of course." Walsh stared.

"He was in Number Three how long?"

"I guess about fifteen, twenty minutes—no, say eighteen. Altogether."

"You'd gone back to the car and reported in what it had turned out to be. How long did you sit there waiting for him?"

"About ten minutes, I guess. I remember I smoked a cigarette, it was just about finished when Joe came. I don't get what this is about, Lieutenant, it was just a routine—"

"Yes. Now when Bartlett came out of Number Three, did he come straight across to the car?"

"Yes, sir—at least, I'd think so. Wouldn't have any reason to do anything else, would he? I guess if you pinned me down I couldn't say I *know* he did, because I had my back to that side of the court, you know —he just came up and got in and said, 'O.K., Frank, let's go.' The landlady came up behind him, with that funny raincoat over her head, and hopped up on her front porch and yelled 'Thanks' at us and—well, that was that."

Mendoza sighed. "And if Bartlett didn't come straight from Number Three to the squad car, the landlady would know. . . ." He could ask, but he had the feeling this was a dead end. Call it what, a minute, two minutes, for Bartlett to have seen something, heard something? *"Qué va!"* he muttered to himself vexedly. "Can you think of anything else at all, Walsh, no matter how trivial it struck you at the time, that happened during the whole twenty minutes you were at this place?"

Silence. Walsh was looking nervous and perplexed. "I don't know what you're after," he said. "I just can't think— Well, a couple of the neighbors on each side of the drunks' apartment came out—I think one couple was out when we drove up, I seem to get a picture of them standing there on their front porch under the porch light. That'd be, I guess, Number Four—end apartment. . . . What, sir? I think that was the only porch light on except the landlady's. Then when I came back to the car, I saw the people on the other side—that'd be Number Two, in the first building—had come out on their porch. Wanted to see if we were going to take the drunks in, I guess, but there wasn't any need for that. . . . I don't remember seeing anybody else out. I guess if it hadn't been raining they would have been—you know, the drunks making such a racket—but the way it was, it was just the people from the closest apartments to them who were outside—though probably everybody else was looking out their windows. . . . I don't know what *else* I can . . . Oh, and just before Joe came up, somebody *did* open the door of the apartment next to the landlady's. And that's all I—what, sir? No, they didn't come out on the porch, maybe when they saw it was raining so hard—"

"They," said Mendoza, excluding any excitement from his tone. "Two people, three, or what?"

"Oh—well," said Walsh vaguely, "I don't know. I said 'they' because I couldn't see whether it was a man or woman who opened the door. The porch light wasn't on there. I think there was a light inside but not in the living room, maybe, not right by the door or behind it—I seem to get that impression. I couldn't see—I don't know if anybody else was there besides who opened the door. I just, you know, sort of registered it in my mind, the door opening . . . This what you want, Lieutenant, about *that?* Well, let's see. . . . I remember thinking, they've finally tumbled something's going on, and're looking out to see what—but I didn't *notice* whoever it was—and it was just a minute before the door shut again. Tell you the truth," said Walsh a little shamefacedly, "I was looking at the lightning really, I just kind of saw that door open out of the tail of my eye. I get a kick out of electric storms, and we never used to get them out here much, you know, it's only the last ten or twelve years. . . . I was waiting for the thunder. . . ."

"Yes," said Mendoza. "Now, think about this one carefully. Someone was standing in the open door of Number Five—by the way, wide open?"

Walsh thought, shook his head. "I don't know. I don't think so, but I can't say for sure."

"O.K. Someone's there, and there's lightning in a flash—big stroke?"

"Pretty close. Lit up the whole sky—it was fine."

"Yes. And about that time Bartlett was, maybe, on his way to the car from Number Three? Could it be that whoever was standing there saw Bartlett by that big flash, and thought Bartlett might have seen him—or her?" But that was really reaching for it, surely, he added to himself. A flash of lightning. One little moment—to fix in mind the nondescript features of an ordinary cop—and an hour and a bit later, catch up to him and kill him? And Bartlett would probably have had his head down against the rain; whoever was in that doorway would also see that he couldn't be noticing. . . .

Walsh's expression took on the glazed look of one trying to recapture a past time in photographic reproduction. He said almost at once, "No, sir. I got that piece clear, just remembering it by the lightning, now. This is how it went, see: there's the lightning, just *after* the door opened there—and I looked up, and kind of automatically started to count seconds, the way you do, you know—and it was close, it wasn't quite three seconds until the thunder—and *then* that door closed. And right after that—yes, I've got it now, funny how little things come back to you—I heard the *other* apartment door close, and that was Joe and the landlady coming out of Number Three. And almost right away, Joe opened the car door and got in beside me and said, 'O.K., let's go.'" Walsh looked at Mendoza triumphantly, anxiously. "Is that the kind of thing you want, sir? I don't see what it has to do with—"

"*Oyé, oiga, frene!—Qué se yo?*" Mendoza sat up abruptly. "Wait a minute now, *you* were driving? Bartlett got in beside you, you said—you being behind the wheel."

"Why, yes, sir," said Walsh. "We generally change round like that, you know, if there're two of you on patrol, one drives the first half of the tour, the other the second half. That night, we changed after the coffee break, and Joe took the wheel."

Mendoza looked at him, but he didn't see Frank Walsh's square, honest, amiable face at all. He saw that ugly courtyard, on that dark rainy night—and a murderer opening a door (all right, no evidence, *nada absolutamente,* to back that up, but it made a picture, it filled in an empty space)—and being confronted with that black-and-white squad car, unexpected and so close; and in that moment, one great flash of lightning lighting the whole scene—pinpointing it in time and space. What picture in a murderer's mind of that one moment? A uniformed cop at the wheel of that car, looking up alertly—apparently toward the open apartment door. And Mrs. Bragg's porch light shining full on the front of the squad car *and its L.A. police number*.

That was all. That was enough. Mendoza's patrol days being far behind, that one little fact hadn't occurred to him, that a pair of cops in a squad car changed around at the wheel. The ordinary civilian wouldn't think of it.

So, there was the answer: and say it wasn't backed up by any kind of evidence the D.A. would look at—Mendoza knew surely it must be the right answer. All somebody had known, had been afraid of, was the driver of the squad car number such-and-such. It didn't matter *then*— the idea was that Twelvetrees should vanish, that he'd never be found in his makeshift grave down that kitchen trap—it didn't matter if the driver saw and remembered a face. Not if things went the way somebody planned. But just in case Twelvetrees *was* found, in case questions were asked, and the driver of that car was able to identify a face—

Panic? Impulse? And a very damned lucky shot—or a very damned skillful one . . . into the wrong man.

And, after all, Frank Walsh hadn't seen whoever stood in that open door.

EIGHT

"Every other country in the world," said Alison, clutching Mendoza's arm, "puts decent lights in night clubs and bars. People go to such places to read newspapers and hold philosophical discussions over their drinks. Or at least so I'm given to understand. Why are Americans condemned to these caves of darkness, like moles?"

"It's the Puritan background," said Mendoza, stumbling over a pair of outstretched legs and apologizing. "We still suffer from the influence of all those high-minded, earnest people who had the idea that any-thing a little bit enjoyable, from a glass of wine to a hand of cards—anything that makes life a bit more amusing—is necessarily sinful. It's a holdover—ah, haven," as the waiter's dim figure stopped and hovered in the gloom ahead, indicating a table or booth, impossible to tell which. On cautious investigation it proved to be a booth, and he slid into it beside the vague slender figure that was Alison—at least, it smelled of the spiced-carnation and faintly aphrodisiac scent that said *Alison*. "—A holdover from the days when those righteous old colo-nists felt seven kinds of devil if they let the cider get hard, you know. . . . Straight rye," he added to the waiter, "and I think a glass of sherry for the lady."

"Yes. It's a great pity, all I can say," said Alison. "I expect you're right, and how silly."

"On the contrary," said Mendoza, "very good business. You make people feel there's something a little devilish about a thing, they'll fall over themselves to buy it. Human nature. Prohibition created more drinkers than we'd ever had before. Same principle as banning a novel—everybody reads it to find out why."

"It's still silly. I can't find my cigarettes, have you got one?"

"Only," said Mendoza, groping in his pocket, offering her the pack and lighting one for her, "because you and I were born at par. I got this from Sergeant Farquhar—it's a Scottish proverb, haven't you heard it, and you half Scots? 'Some people are born two drinks under. They need the drinks to get up to normal.'"

"Certainly I've heard it, and my father used to say that redheads—oh, well, never mind, it wasn't very genteel now I come to think."

"If it was about redheads," said Mendoza as the waiter brought their drinks, "I might guess what it was."

"I wouldn't put it past you. Well, in polite language it was to the effect that they're born two drinks over. And he *was*, certainly. Did I ever tell you about the time he challenged the governor of Coahuila to a duel? It was over a dam up in the Sierra Mojadas—the governor kept saying if Providence had intended people to have the water, the dam would have been created in the first six days, you know, but as it was the whole thing was immoral and contrary to God's wishes—I've never seen Dad madder—but in the end the governor backed down and they never did get to the duel. I think myself somebody told the governor the *pedazo rojo norteamericano* was a crack shot."

"These effeminate Latins, all cowards," said Mendoza. *"Salud y pesetas!*" He tasted the rye. "You and I are the unconventional ones, we don't need this to enjoy life. . . . And another thing about these places," he added over a roll of snare drums, "if they can persuade you to drink enough they can save a lot of money on what they call entertainment—anything goes if you're sufficiently high."

A blue spotlight circled a painfully thin girl in silver lamé, on the little low platform at one end of the room, above what was revealed as a five- or six-piece band. On the edges of the light, white blurs of faces, tables crowded close. A tenor sax spoke mournfully, and the girl clasped her hands at her breast and began to moo nasally about missing her naughty baby.

"Oh dear," said Alison. The spotlight, moving with the singer, dimly showed them the Voodoo Club: fake handdrums and shrunken heads for wall-décor, zebra-patterned plastic on chairs and banquettes, and the waiters all Negroes in loincloths. There was also a postage-stamp dance floor.

"Yes," said Mendoza. "Hardly combining business with pleasure. We'll get to the business as soon as the waiter shows up again." Which he did as the girl stopped mooing and the spotlight blinked out. The band went into a soft blues and a few couples groped their way onto the dance floor.

"*Re*-peat, suh?"

"No, thanks. Tell me,"—Mendoza flicked his lighter over the blown-up print of Twelvetrees—"have you ever seen this man in here?"

The waiter bent closer and looked at the print. In the little circle of unsteady light, he was very black, very Negroid; out of the dark his hand came up to finger his jaw, a long, slender hand with oddly intellectual-looking narrow fingers. "Well, I jus' couldn't say offhand, suh. An' we ain' supposed to gossip about customahs, y' know."

"Just take another look, and be sure."

"Don' know nuthin' 'bout him, suh. Anythin' else I can do for you, suh?"

Mendoza shook his head. "So, we'll have to get at it official," he said when the man had gone, leaving the check behind as a gentle hint. "See the manager. I don't suppose there's anything in it, or not much, but you never know—he must have had acquaintances in other circles than the Temple. By the little we've got on him so far, I think he looked on that just the way the Kingmans do, as a soft racket, and he'd hardly find the sect members to his social taste. Except for Mona Ferne—and that was for other reasons. I could wish his landlady had been the prying, suspicious kind who took more notice of his callers. Oh, well. Are you finished with that? Let's go."

They groped their way out to the better-lighted foyer, and Mendoza reclaimed his hat and Alison's coat from the check girl, paid the cashier. As he held out the coat for her, the slab door in the opposite wall opened and there emerged a slender little man who looked exactly like a film gang-boss, from his navy shirt and white tie to his fancy gray punched-pigskin shoes. He had black hair slicked back into a drake's tail, cold black eyes, and a cigarette dangling out of one corner of his mouth. Behind him was a big black Negro wrapped in a white terry robe like a boxer between rounds.

"This them?" snapped the gang-boss.

"Yes, sir," said the Negro.

"O.K.," said the gang-boss, walking up to Mendoza, "what you asking questions for, buddy? Who are you? Got any identification on you? What's this all about?"

"I *told* you, Luis," said Alison, sliding behind him. "Every time I go out with you in new stockings—why you drag me to these dens of iniquity—"

"Hey," said the gang-boss angrily, "what you talking about, lady, den of iniquity? We don't pay a grand a year for a liquor license to go foolin' around with that kind of stuff! Just what the hell—"

"You're the manager—good, just the man I want to see," and Mendoza brought out his credentials.

"Oh, *police*," said the gang-boss, and his toughness fell away from him like a cloak. "Gee, I'm sure sorry, Lieutenant, but I didn't know! Anything at all I can do for you—"

"This man." Mendoza gave him the print. "Regular in here? Or a casual?"

"Yeah, well—" The manager rubbed his ear and exchanged a glance with the Negro. "It's him all right, isn't it?"

"I thought so," said the Negro tranquilly in an accentless, rather amused tone. "I didn't know you were police either, Lieutenant. Sorry, but one way and another I thought Mr. Stuart ought to hear about it."

"You better come into my office," said Stuart abruptly. "You too, Johnny." He led them into a little square room furnished in excellent modern taste. "Sit down. Offer you anything to drink?"

"No, thanks." Mendoza glanced from him to the Negro quizzically.

"I'll apologize," said the latter, "for the—er—costume, sir. In the dark in there, it's one thing, but you feel a little naked out here, you know."

"Customers, they go for the damndest things," said Stuart. "Not that that was my idea—I only manage the place. Excuse me, this is Johnny Laidlaw, your waiter."

"You know how it is," said the big Negro apologetically, "we're sort of expected to stay in character on a job like this—"

"Matter of fact," said Stuart, "unless the bomb falls or something, this time next year it'll be *Dr.* Laidlaw. Right now he's got more schooling than I ever had, which don't necessarily say he's any smarter, but anyway I guess his evidence is as good as mine."

"A medical degree runs into money these days," said Laidlaw amiably, "and you'd be surprised at the size of some of the tips. But this isn't getting to what you want to know. Mr. Stuart, I guess your part of it ought to come first."

"There's your scientific-trained mind," said Stuart. "Well, it's like this, Lieutenant. I just took over here about six months ago, see. The guy who'd been managing the joint, Whalen his name was, Andy Whalen, well, Mr. Goldstein—he's the owner—he found he wasn't leveling, there was rebates to wholesalers and that kind of thing. So Whalen got the heave-ho and I came in. O.K. Well, I hadn't been here very long—some time in September, wasn't it, Johnny?"

"September the twelfth," said Laidlaw.

"Yeah, well, Johnny comes in one night and says a customer's kicking up a row—it was about midnight I remember—and so I go out front to settle it. And here's this guy here," he tapped the print, "raising hell over his check. He's just leaving, see, he's got this blonde dame with him—Johnny says he'd seen them in here before—and when he gets the check he don't like it. I say, what's the beef, and he says can he talk to me private. Now that I don't like so good, because it usually means the guy's caught short on cash and wants to leave his watch or something—but what can you do, I say O.K. and bring him in here. And first thing he says is, 'What's with Whalen?' When he hears Whalen's out, he gets mad all over again. He says Whalen's a pal of his, always made him a cut price, see. I says that's one of the reasons Whalen's out, and I pointed out to him that I'm no pal, and it's a shame he's stuck for more than he expected, but just one of those things, and what about the thirty-four something he owes? Same time, if you get me, I did think it was kind of funny. I didn't know Whalen, but what the boys here've said, he wasn't no goot-time Charlie who'd let his friends in for free."

"That he wasn't," said Laidlaw thoughtfully.

"But that wasn't any of my business. The guy didn't like it, but he paid up. I didn't need a blueprint to figure he'd been a regular here on account of the deal with Whalen, and the blonde didn't have a glimmer of that, thought he was just free with his money, and naturally he didn't want to look cheap in front of her. Anyway, he paid up and out he goes, and that was the only time I ever laid eyes on him. And can't say I'm sorry. But I was kind of curious, and so I got Bob Trimming—that's our regular cashier—in and asked him about it. I didn't get an awful lot out of him, to make sense. You see, the boys, well, they'd got kind of used to the manager acting nasty with them, and catching 'em out for little things all the time, see, and *besides*—well, now you tell the gent what you know, Johnny."

"Now just as it happened," said Laidlaw leisurely—he sat with arms folded across his chest, at magnificent ease, and spoke serenely—"I'd seen that fellow in here, but I'd never waited on him until that night. When he started to kick up the row, Bob called me in on it because I could back up the check, you see. And later on Mr. Stuart asked me to sound Bob out, see if he knew any more about it, as he might talk more openly to me. And I might say I was curious about it too, and I did. Bob's pretty close-mouthed anyway, he doesn't tell all he knows just to be talking, and he'd kept quiet on this, for one reason, because Mr. Whalen isn't a man you'd want to get across. But he knows I don't go talking much either, and he told me the whole thing. I realize, Lieutenant, that all this is hearsay and won't do you any good as evidence, but maybe you'll be interested anyway. What Bob said was this. This fellow came in here quite a bit, once a week at least and sometimes a lot oftener, and he never paid out anything but the tips—and he wasn't a very good tipper. The customer doesn't pay the waiters, as you know, but the cashier out there in the lobby. Bob's on duty, eight to closing time, six nights a week, so he was in a position to see what happened every time this customer came in. The first time he saw the fellow, there was a check for eighteen something, and Mr. Whalen's name signed across it. The customer just tossed it onto the desk and said, 'That's O.K.,' or something like that. Well, Bob wasn't going to take a chance that way, and he called Mr. Whalen. I might add that the fellow had a blonde with him that night too, whether the same one or not I couldn't say, but she'd stepped into the powder room. Mr. Whalen said to Bob,

'Oh, yes, that's O.K. on the house'—but he didn't look as if he liked saying it, so Bob says. And later on that night, after we closed, Bob asked him how to cancel out that check for the accounts, and Mr. Whalen made up the cash out of his own pocket. Well, I don't want to drag this out too long—"

"You're not boring me," Mendoza told him.

"—But the point was, every time this customer came in the same thing happened, and it ran into quite a little money Mr. Whalen was paying out to make up the tabs for the accounts. Now, about six weeks before Mr. Whalen was fired, one night Bob wanted to make a phone call on his break, and he slipped into the phone booth in the lobby, as there wasn't a customer in it at the time. You notice where it is?—well, it's down a little corridor toward the men's room, past the check stand —and as he was standing there in the booth, out of sight, you know, sorting out a dime for the call, he heard Mr. Whalen talking to this cus-tomer. The customer had just come out of the men's room, and maybe Mr. Whalen was waiting for him. Anyway, Mr. Whalen was mad, and told him he'd got to stop coming in here so often, fun was fun but he couldn't afford it. And the customer just laughed and said Mr. Whalen surely didn't mind standing a few drinks to an old pal now and then, it was cheap at the price when it meant Mr. Whalen's job, because he didn't figure Mr. Whalen would like his boss to 'know about that taxi he'd done back in Pennsy."

Mendoza uttered a little exclamation. "Are you quoting this Bob, or were those the actual words?"

"That's what Bob heard, Lieutenant. Neither of us knew exactly what the fellow might have meant, but it sounded like a threat, which is why it stayed in Bob's mind. In fact, several things that were said sounded like double talk to both of us, and thinking it over I came to the con-clusion they must be criminal or professional slang of some sort. The customer told Mr. Whalen not to be such a ringtail, for one thing. And Mr. Whalen said back at him that two could fill in that game, maybe the customer wouldn't like *his* boss to know he'd done a sleep as a cadet—"

"Ah," said Mendoza pleasedly. "Which doesn't surprise me. Yes, go on."

"—And the customer laughed again and said he didn't give a damn, it'd make no difference to him. There was a little more argument, and finally Mr. Whalen got to sounding really desperate, so Bob said, and he said to the customer he'd better not play so deep—meaning, I take it, not to drop in so often for a free ride—if he wasn't looking for a South Gate discharge."

"*Lindo, muy lindo,* oh, very pretty," said Mendoza. "This I like. And?"

"That's about all, Lieutenant. Reason Bob remembered it, you see, was that it sounded a little nasty, threats and so on. Nobody liked Mr. Whalen much, and it didn't come as a surprise when he got fired. And so, as you've heard, the next time the customer dropped in, Bob was going to make him pay, and there was this row. Well, when I'd heard all this, I thought Mr. Stuart ought to know it—"

"*And* as you can see," said Stuart, "what the hell, it was water under the bridge, and I knew damn well the guy'd never come back again—which he didn't. None of my business what he had on Whalen. But just now, when you come in asking questions, Johnny thought I'd better hear about it, because by all this, both Whalen and this other guy, whoever he is, might be mixed up with some funny characters—if you see what I mean. No offense, Lieutenant, I hope—"

"No offense," said Mendoza. He was looking rather amused. "I suppose neither of you would know Whalen's whereabouts now? . . . No, I couldn't expect it. But you've been very helpful, thanks. I may want formal statements from both of you and this Bob."

"Any time, sir," said Laidlaw. "Glad to oblige you."

"Oh, sure," said Stuart, "not that I'd like to have to *testify* or anything, don't look so good in this business, snitching on a customer, whatever kind, but I guess it's up to all of us to help the law when we can. I suppose you can't tell us what this is all about."

"I'm not just a hundred percent sure myself yet," said Mendoza. They left Mr. Stuart brooding over the possibility of occupying the witness stand, and Laidlaw gazing serenely at the office ceiling.

In the car, before he switched on lights or ignition, Mendoza suddenly pulled Alison into his arms and spent several minutes kissing her thoroughly. "Well, and what prompted that?" she asked breathlessly. "You always say a car, of all places—"

"Just general exuberance. I got so much more than I expected, and I think there's more to come yet."

"I see. You seemed to know what those two had been talking about —*was* it criminal slang? And is a translation fit for my ladylike ears?"

Mendoza laughed. "Yes to both questions. Twelvetrees said to this Whalen that he didn't think Whalen's boss would like hearing that Whalen had done a five-to-fifteen stretch—that's a taxi—back in Pennsylvania. To which Whalen retorted that maybe Twelvetrees wouldn't like it known he'd done one year—that's a sleep—for enticing minors to enter houses of prostitution—that's what a cadet does. And later on Twelvetrees told him not to be such an old grouch, that's a ringtail. But one of the interesting things is that last reported remark of Whalen's, when he said Twelvetrees had better take it easy unless he was looking for a South Gate discharge. That's what the cons call it when a man dies, in or out of jail."

"Oh, I see. So maybe this Whalen is the one."

"Maybe, maybe. No, it doesn't surprise me that Twelvetrees had done time—not much, and he wasn't deep in yet—it's on the cards he was smart enough, after one experience, to intend staying inside the law, in one of the rackets that isn't illegal. But a man's past has a way of catching him up sometimes. . . ." He let that trail off, and Alison, knowing his silences, forbore to interrupt his thoughts.

It was two in the morning when he eased the Facel-Vega into the curb just past the entrance to the Voodoo Club's parking lot. The lot was emptying rapidly, the last customer just chased out. He locked the car and walked up through the lot to the narrow space directly behind the buildings which would be reserved for employees' parking.

There were eight cars nosed in there. He peered in the drivers' windows, one by one, with his pencil flash; the fifth one down, a six-year-old Ford two-door, had its registration card wrapped around the steering post, old style, and the name on it was John S. Laidlaw. Mendoza leaned on the fender and lit a cigarette.

He had smoked that and another one—retreating to cover half a dozen times as men came out to their cars—before the rear door, thirty feet away, opened to silhouette briefly a big broad figure he thought was his quarry. The man came down toward the Ford jingling his keys and whistling *The St. Louis Blues* under his breath.

Mendoza had no desire for any violent exercise, and when the man was ten feet off he stepped out of the shadow of the car to show himself. Laidlaw checked for one moment and then laughed very softly.

"You had me scared there a minute, Lieutenant, thinking I'd slipped up on something," he said just above a whisper. "So I didn't put it across you."

"For a few minutes," said Mendoza. "Who belongs to the Buick?" It was the only other car left in the lot.

"Stuart. He won't be out for a while, he's working on the books."

"*Muy bien,* then we can talk here." They got into the car; in the little flare of the match Laidlaw lit for their cigarettes they looked at each other. "Fox knows fox," said Mendoza dryly. "Though you put up a nice front. But aren't you getting on a bit for a medical student?"

"Yes, that one won't do much longer. Just second cover anyway."

"I liked the artistic way this nice honest well-brought-up young fellow puzzled over that talk and finally made it out pro slang. It was about then I pinned you down in my own mind—if we stick to the slang—as a gazer, *no es verdad?* I suppose you figured to do me a good turn—having spotted me—by handing it to me on a platter. Many thanks."

"Tell you the truth, I'd be just as happy not to have you city boys sniffing around here too long or too close, which was the main reason. And I've got no credentials on me, on this job."

"Never mind. I've had enough to do with you Feds that I know lamb from wolf. What is it, dope or illegal liquor?"

"Some of both. I've been sitting on it for a year waiting for the real big boy—this is a drop, and a good safe one. We've left it that way."

"Whalen in it?"

"As a very minor errand boy. He did that stretch for armed robbery with violence—that's his style—a small timer."

"Well, your business doesn't come into mine, I don't think, so I won't ask you any questions about that—"

"Which is just as well," said Laidlaw imperturbably, "because I wouldn't answer them."

"Naturally. The customer who was getting his tabs picked up by Whalen is now dead, and I am, you can appreciate, interested in the fact that Whalen threatened him with a South Gate discharge."

"Is that a fact?" said Laidlaw. "Interesting. I see that. Now I'll open up enough to say this, Lieutenant. Obviously the customer didn't know what was going on here—in the way of *my* business—or that Whalen was in it, or he wouldn't have thought telling the tale about Whalen's past could get him fired. But it could have, indeed. Without giving you details, the owner is innocent as day, and so is Stuart. It's quite possible that Whalen was afraid his real bosses wouldn't like it much that someone knew about him, and also there's this aspect: he had a pretty good job a little higher in the organization than he'd been before, and that was largely due to his ostensible job as manager here. He wanted to protect that. It annoyed the boys operating the drop, just a little, when he got fired. They've sized up Stuart since, and prudently refrained from sounding him out."

"Yes, I saw some of that—if Whalen's nominal boss wouldn't have cared, Whalen would never have picked up those tabs. Nice genteel way to blackmail somebody, wasn't it? No vulgar cash changing hands."

"So it was," agreed Laidlaw. "You understand that we weren't more than casually interested in Whalen as one of the boys, there wasn't any reason to follow up his private troubles with this fellow, as it was pretty clear that one was outside this particular racket. So you probably know more about your corpse than I do."

"Not as much as I'd like. What I came back for principally was to ask if you know where Whalen is."

"Sure I know where he is," said Laidlaw. "I read in the papers the other day, Lieutenant, that you L.A. boys got a pat on the back from some Washington office for being tops among the ten most efficient city forces in the country—but outside that category, we sort of fancy ourselves as pretty hot, you know. We're not much interested in Andy Whalen, but we looked to see where he went. He's driving a truck for Orange State Trucking, on the San Diego–L.A. run, and he lives in room number 312 at the Chester Hotel on Fourth."

"Thanks very much. Would it discommode you at all if I took him in for questioning?"

"I don't think so," said Laidlaw. "His bosses don't rate him any bigger-time than we do."

"What about the trucking outfit? Can I take it he's still on the payroll of the gang in another capacity?"

"Well, now, I don't think we'll go into that, if you don't mind. I'll just say, it's possible."

"You boys with your secrets," said Mendoza. "Well, I may and I may not, right away. All that rigmarole—your quotes from the cashier —gospel truth?"

"And nothing but."

"Mmh. Yes, a couple of little things that occur to me aside from Whalen. But I want to look at him closer, of course. Thanks very much, Laidlaw, and good luck on your business."

"Same to you—happy to oblige, Lieutenant. We like to cooperate with the locals where we can," said Laidlaw blandly.

"I might," said Mendoza, sliding out of the car, "like the polite tone of that better if you didn't somehow sound like a professional race driver assuring his little boy he'll teach him to ride his new bicycle."

"Why, Loo-tenant, suh, I nevah meant no such thing, suh," said Laidlaw. Mendoza laughed, shut the door, and dodged back to the shadow of the wall as the building door opened up there. Laidlaw slid the Ford out to the street; Mendoza waited until Stuart had driven out in the Buick before going back to his own car.

NINE

"You want to make it read," said Hackett, "that this Whalen got so mad at Twelvetrees—six months after he stopped paying this genteel blackmail—that he killed him?"

"I don't want to make it read any way," said Mendoza. "We don't know what dealings they may have had since. All I say is, no harm to look at Whalen."

"I don't believe it," said Hackett. "In the first place, I can't see a rough-and-ready customer like this Whalen taking the trouble to bury him. And there *may* have been a renewed motive, but there's nothing to show they ever laid eyes on each other after last August, when Whalen got fired. I don't—"

"*No seas tan exigente*—don't be so difficult," said Mendoza. "If I want a warrant for Whalen, I've got to be able to give *some* logical reason to authority. And it may be that I will. Like—mmh—looking openly pleased to draw a five-spot when I'm already holding a royal flush."

"Oh!" said Hackett. He laughed. "So that's what's in your mind. It's a thought. Set somebody's mind at rest so maybe he'll do something silly."

"Did you spot, in all these inverted quotes I've been giving you, the one really interesting little thing? You remember that Whalen suggested to Twelvetrees that *his* boss might not like hearing about the little stretch Twelvetrees had done—and Twelvetrees just laughed and said it wouldn't matter a damn."

"Which of course sounds as if these Kingmans knew all about him. Yes. You're laying your blue chips on the Kingmans?"

Mendoza swiveled around in his desk-chair to look out the window at the hazy panorama of the city stretching away to hills invisible this gray morning. "I've sent out queries to Pennsylvania on Twelvetrees and the Kingmans—we'll see what they can give us, if anything. Unfortunately I didn't have the Kingmans' prints to send, but I sent Twelvetrees', of course. I don't know, Art, there's a couple of things that say this and that to me, on that deal. Look at the way Twelvetrees landed here and slid into such a soft spot—five hundred a month, for what? Woods says, he ingratiated himself. Well, somehow I don't think Mr. Dale Carnegie himself would find it very easy to ingratiate that far with Mr. Martin Kingman. What it amounted to was muscling in on Mr. Kingman's own racket and cutting Mr. Kingman's net take by that five hundred."

"Yes, and you know the thought I had about that? Considering the times. It sounds to me as if just maybe those three had made up a crowd before, and for some reason—maybe because he was inside—Twelvetrees was a little late joining them out here."

"Also a thought. But I don't like it nearly so well as I like mine—that he might have pulled exactly the same sort of genteel blackmail on the Kingmans that he did on Whalen. Look. The Temple's been a going concern for over a year when Twelvetrees lands here. You never did catch up to this Mona Ferne yesterday but you will today, and I think what she'll tell you is that her original contact with Twelvetrees wasn't through the Temple, but that she met him somewhere in connection with his movie aspirations. And that she was the one who led him to the Temple. Because he took a job when he got here, remember?—not a very good job, clerking in a store—he was broke, or close to it. I get the picture of this fairly canny young fellow, who's taken one rap and means to find some legal racket—where he doesn't have to work too hard. He'd like to get into pictures—he's got all the requirements, so he thinks, but he finds it isn't so easy. Then, by accident, he discovers the Kingmans and their Temple. And almost immediately he becomes 'secretary-treasurer' or whatever they call it and starts drawing that nice salary for practically no work. Now that looks to me as if he had something on them. That he took one look at Mr. Martin Kingman, maybe, and said, 'Ah, my old friend Giovanni Scipio—or Mike O'Connor—or Harold J. Cholmondeley—from good old Philly.' *Comprende?* And Kingman had to kick in, let him in on the racket, to protect the investment—because, while the people who've fallen for Mystic Truth aren't exactly Einsteins, most of them would think again about dropping folding money into the collection bag if they knew, for instance, that Kingman had done a stretch for fraud or something like that."

"That's so. It makes a picture, all right. And that'd give the Kingmans a dandy reason to put him out of the way. I'll say this too, it makes it look even more natural, maybe, that they stood it nearly four years before getting fed up. Because con men don't use violence, they like everything nice and easy and smooth, it isn't once in a blue moon you find one of 'em committing actual physical assault. It might be that it wasn't until Twelvetrees got a little too greedy and asked too much blackmail that they got worked up to that. The only thing I don't like about it, Luis, is the spot Twelvetrees landed in—treasurer. The Kingmans wouldn't have handed him anything like that, as blackmail payment. Why, he could have taken off with the whole bank account any day."

"So he could. But I think we'd find, Arturo, that it was treasurer in name only—that Kingman was damned careful to keep a check on the account. A kind of gentleman's agreement. You know, let me in on your racket and I won't tell—and on Kingman's side, you level with us on the racket or I'll tell what I know about you. Don't forget, Twelvetrees still had dreams of a future as a big star. His agents wouldn't care about keeping him on their books, he wouldn't have a chance of getting anywhere in big-time show business, if it was known he'd served apprenticeship as a pimp and got tagged for it. He got Kingman to give him a job openly—he wanted an excuse to quit the nine-to-five job he had, which he probably didn't enjoy much. But I'll bet you too that the bank will tell us that one of the Kingmans made some excuse for coming in regularly to check up. It was a fifty-fifty deal, scratch my back and I'll scratch yours."

"Something in that, sure."

"I should hate," said Mendoza, "to have to arrest Madame Cara. She's a very intelligent woman, she says I have great insight and wisdom. But it would have been so much more convenient, you know, if there'd been two of them on the job, on account of Twelvetrees' car. If just one person did it all, how awkward that part of it would be—driving the Porsche clear down to the Union Station, a good ten miles or more, and then having to get back to pick up the car left at the apartment. If, of course, there was one and the murderer hadn't been driven there by Twelvetrees. It's a great pity Mrs. Bragg minded her own business so assiduously. . . . There are a lot of things we don't know yet. But it's very helpful that we can almost pin it down to that Friday night—"

"I don't see that we can," said Hackett. "I don't like it much, Walsh's thing, about Bartlett."

"I do. I think it makes sense." Mendoza sat up and swiveled around to the desk again. "I don't say it's certain, no, but I like it enough that I've told the D.A.'s office to get a continuance on bringing those kids up, until we know a little more. Here's what Ballistics says on the gun. It's one of an experimental lot of smooth-bore revolvers made by Winchester about fifty years ago. Not too many like it will be floating around these days, but it's nothing antique in the sense of being rare or valuable—we're not likely to get an identification of ownership on it that way. Now, as the class will remember from yesterday's lecture, I trust, we all know that a firearm with a smooth-bored barrel is never as accurate over distances as one whose barrel is rifled with spiral grooves. However, at fairly short distances a smoothbore is accurate enough in expert hands. Ballistics had a lot of fun firing different kinds of bullets out of this at different distances, and they tell us that with a cannelured bullet—which, if you will recall, was the type found in Bartlett *and* on the kids—a reasonably good shot can expect quite fair accuracy out of this at up to about twenty-five feet."

"You say it's just coincidence the kids were carrying .38 cannelured bullets and Bartlett got killed with the same kind?"

"If you'd just think about these things, that's all I ask—a little rudimentary logic. The kids had a homemade gun, and quite naturally it also has a smooth-bored barrel. Actually a piece of pipe. Anybody who knows anything at all about guns, and is stuck with a smooth-bore, is going to try to make up for the handicap by using cannelured bullets, which are grooved. Has the class any questions?"

"Yes, please, teacher. How does a slick con man—or in fact anybody we've heard of in this case so far—come to be such a Deadeye Dick with an old cannon like this?"

"Now there you do ask an awkward question," admitted Mendoza. "I don't know. But it's a fifty-fifty chance that it was just wild luck, you know. And I'll say this. We've been thinking that whoever fired those shots at Bartlett and Walsh did it in the dark—a dark rainy night, along a stretch of road lighted only by high arc lights. I went out there last night, before I waylaid Laidlaw, and roped Gonzales and Farber in on a little game. I'd got Walsh to tell me just where the squad car was sitting in relation to the light at the corner of Cameron and San Domin-guez, and I placed Gonzales and Farber there and drove past a couple of times. And you know what? Just the way it had slipped my mind about patrolmen changing round at the wheel, another little thing slipped all our minds when we thought about this before. Go on now, be a detective and tell me what it was."

"My God," said Hackett. "The roof light."

"That's my boy, you get A-plus. Going on and off almost right over the driver's head, whenever the car's standing still. It's a nice straight road along there, and the shoulder where the squad car was sitting is unobstructed for a hundred yards each way. And thirty isn't really very fast, in relation to an object, say, fifteen feet to the side—you've got time to see it, coming up. I think it must have been a double take—that whoever it was spotted the car by its number, maybe when Bartlett and Walsh had stopped that car for speeding. So X speeded up and doubled back, to try his shot without that additional witness—and so, coming up on them, he knew it was the right car, he didn't have to spot the number *and* get in position to fire, all at once. It's just a question—I tried a dry run on it last night—of taking your right hand off the wheel, your eyes off the road, for about three seconds, and firing at right angles out the driver's window."

"That's if there was only the driver—even saying it was whoever killed Twelvetrees, that there's any connection."

"Sure. If there were two, a lot easier. One to drive, one to shoot. But when you come to think, whoever killed Twelvetrees had quite a bit to do that night—"

"I still say there's nothing to show definitely it *was* that night."

"*Pues mira, chico*—look here—all right, but it was *some* night, be-cause if it had been broad daylight Mrs. Bragg, or one of the house-wives in the other apartments, would have seen someone arrive and leave. Going to Twelvetrees' place you'd have to walk or drive past all those other front doors. I refuse to believe that human nature has im-proved so much since I first began to notice it among the five women who're usually at home most of the day in that court, not one was curi-ous enough about a good-looking bachelor to take at least casual note of his movements and visitors. You grant me that's likely? Then I say it's also likely that whatever happened happened that Friday night, when it was raining and overcast and people were staying inside ignor-ing the neighbors. And also because on the Saturday and Sunday nobody seems to recall seeing the Porsche in Twelvetrees' carport.

True, they wouldn't be looking for it, he was probably out a good deal, and nobody would take special note of it one way or the other, there or not there, so that's negative evidence. But we haven't yet found anybody who remembers seeing him after the Kingmans saw him leave the Temple at four o'clock on Friday. The three or four restaurants he habitually used say he didn't come in that night. The garage where he took the Porsche hadn't seen him for three weeks. No gas station he might hit on his way home sold him any gas. His agents don't remember that he'd come in since several days before. The autopsy says he'd had, probably, beef stew, salad, and some kind of pie about two to six hours before he died. Not helpful unless we find the restaurant where he went, and they remember. All right. Nobody remembers either how long the Porsche had been standing where it was left. We've got no evidence, except negative evidence. But why didn't he show up anywhere on Saturday or Sunday?"

"We don't know he didn't," said Hackett. "Maybe somebody just hasn't come forward to say. Maybe this old flame of yours knew where he was those two days. Maybe, for that matter, he never did leave the Temple on Friday and the Kingmans just say he did. Maybe he was killed there and ferried out—"

"*Caray,* let's not make it any more complicated than it is! You're forgetting those suitcases—those carefully packed suitcases. What did we say when we looked at them? He was getting ready to clear out, of his own choice. Now maybe he was just moving to another apartment, maybe he was going to get married, maybe he'd just heard he'd inherited a million dollars and didn't have to stay in the racket any longer—but one of the possibilities is that for some reason his whole private racket was up, here, and he had to get out. Say he was going to clear. Then tell me what he'd have done *too,* just before he left."

"That's an easy one, he'd have taken some of the Kingmans' money along with him. But it depends on a lot of ifs."

"Well, I don't know that it does. There are a lot of fishy things about the Kingmans' behavior, but two things are a little fishier than the rest. In the first place, you'll never get me to believe—no matter whether all this about Twelvetrees' blackmailing them was so or not—that Mr. Martin Kingman is so unworldly and unbusinesslike that he didn't have a home address and a phone number for the treasurer of his Temple. Why didn't he give Woods that information right away, if he was so anxious to catch up with Twelvetrees? And second, he jumped the gun very damned quick, didn't he, on laying a charge? If, as I think we can almost take for granted, the Kingmans and Twelvetrees looked on this Mystic Truth business as nothing *but* a business, there wouldn't be anything very peculiar about dear Brooke missing their Sabbath ceremonies—it must have happened before, his taking a weekend off. He couldn't have gotten into the bank then before ten on Monday morning, either to deposit the month's receipts or close out the accounts. And, *de paso,* that in itself poses a funny little question, you know. If he was planning to run with a big handful of the profit—as much as he could persuade the bank to let him have—why was he packing up and getting ready to leave as early as Friday? It'd be Monday before he could—"

"So there you are, maybe it wasn't Friday."

"Reason it through," said Mendoza. "It wouldn't have been very sensible, if he intended to take off on Monday morning, to start packing on Saturday night. And we *know* it wasn't Sunday night, because Mrs. Bragg found the note on Sunday noon, he'd already gone by then. I wonder if that bank—yes, well, file that for thinking about. . . . Kingman knew what time the bank opened, after all, *and* closed. When he saw Twelvetrees on Friday afternoon, the banks were still open—if he was afraid Twelvetrees was planning larceny, why didn't he contact the bank then? And bright and early Monday morning we find him 'checking with the bank'—evidently because he's leaped to this conclusion over the Saturday when dear Brooke didn't show up—and at a quarter past ten he's up in Theft laying the charge. Which looks—" Mendoza stopped and interrupted himself reflectively, *"Or,* of course—"

"You've argued yourself into a corner there," said Hackett. "If he thought there was any danger Twelvetrees was going to try to clean them out—or already had—then he didn't know Twelvetrees was dead."

"Or it was a double play," said Mendoza. "And also—"

"Oh, the hell with it," said Hackett. "We've wasted half the morning talking about it—let's get busy and collect some more facts to fit into the picture."

"Those we can always use more of," agreed Mendoza. But when Hackett left he was still sitting there motionless, staring out the window. . . . Doubtless still trying to fill in details on his idea about Joe Bartlett, thought Hackett.

And Mendoza knew Hackett didn't go along on that, thought it was a wild one. He also knew it might be, that he must keep an open mind on it himself. His besetting sin was that dislike for ragged edges, wanting everything neat, precisely dovetailed; and criminal cases, like a lot of other things in life, didn't always work out that way. Often there were ragged edges all round the truth—human nature and real life being what it was.

That was a satisfying, dramatic little picture he'd seen, on Walsh's thing—a murderer panicking, killing Bartlett in error. But it might not be the true picture: maybe those kids had killed Bartlett after all, and that had nothing to do with the Twelvetrees case. Maybe it had been Twelvetrees himself who opened the door when the squad car was sitting there and didn't think twice about it when he saw it was the alcoholic Johnstones again.

By the same token, he couldn't let himself get so sold on the Kingmans that he ignored evidence pointing away from them. But he fancied the Kingmans quite highly: if Pennsylvania could offer any suggestions as to what Twelvetrees might have had on them, their stock would go even higher.

He wanted to locate Marian Marner, find out what she'd had to do with Twelvetrees, and he wanted to find out from Twelvetrees' agents anything the man might have said about himself, and possibly contact in that way any friends Twelvetrees might have made among people in that circle, show business hopefuls. The paper had had this since the late extras on Saturday, and probably everyone who had known him had seen the news: if anyone had any information to volunteer, it should turn up today or tomorrow. And just for the record, they'd have a look at Whalen. But on the whole the Kingmans looked like the obvious bet. . . .

He'd see the Kingmans himself.

Before he left his office, however, one of those things happened that a detective had to get used to—some new bit of evidence turning up that made a favored theory more doubtful.

Sergeant Lake, who was going through the amended list of model agencies looking for Marian Marner, came in and said there was a cab driver outside in answer to the official enquiry sent out to all the companies. "Oh?" said Mendoza, rather surprised. "Well, all right, I'd better see him." Because if it had been the Kingmans working together, there'd have been no need for whoever had disposed of the Porsche taking a cab back to the apartment: one would have driven the Porsche, the other their own car.

The cab driver was tall, thin, elderly, a clerkish-looking fellow with rimless glasses and a diffident manner. He had a funny little story to tell, and Mendoza listened to it in growing annoyance that it couldn't be fitted into any theory he had.

"It was just after midnight that Friday night, the thirtieth," the driver said when his slight nervousness had been soothed and he was sitting back more at ease with a cigarette. "I'd just taken a couple to the Union Station, I guess to make the Owl for San Francisco—only passenger I know of leaving about then. Business is always slow that time of night, you know. I hung around waiting for the Lark down from the north, she was late—due in at ten-forty, but she didn't get in until eleven-fifty, some trouble on the line up at Santa Maria, I heard. Well, I guess you aren't interested in all that, it was just—not many came off her and none of 'em wanted a cab—all been met, you see—so I thought I'd go uptown where chances were better for strays. I went up Alameda and through the old Plaza, you see, and it was just as I came by the old Mission Church there, this woman hailed me. I guess maybe you'll know it's dark as hell along there, that time of night—all the shops in Olvera Street was shut then, and those old streets are so narrow, and all the trees in the old Plaza square—well, she had to step right off the curb almost into my headlights to hail me. And that was the only real good look I got at her, rest of the time it was all dark—"

"What did she look like?"

"She looked like the Witch of Endor," said the driver frankly. "And she acted about as queer. I wasn't surprised one bit to see your official query in our office last night—of course it didn't give any description, but the places nailed it for me, I says right off, that's my girl. This one look I got at her, in the head-beam, you see, well, I couldn't give you a real *description,* I mean how tall she was or what color eyes or hair or even what sort of age, naturally. But there she was with this Mexican serape over her head like a shawl, see, and kind of wound around her neck, and what made it look so funny was that she'd put it on top of a hat—I guess maybe to protect her hat from the rain. And the hat had a veil, and she'd pulled that right down over her face. But what I *could* see of her face under the veil, well, she'd just plastered the make-up on —looked like a clown, or something—God knows what her natural face looked like under it."

"Fuera, la drama extravagante," muttered Mendoza. "Can it be? Yes, go on, what about the rest of her clothes?"

"She had on a long coat, that's all I could see. It was a lightish color and it had dark bands, like trimming of some sort, down the front. And when she talked, she had a funny kind of foreign accent. She said 'ze' for 'the,' you know, and 'Please to take me,' and all that, but I couldn't say what kind of accent it was, French or German or what—and she didn't say much. She was just in the light like that a second, and I stopped, and she hopped around and got in the cab before I knew it, hardly, with her suitcase—"

"A suitcase. What kind?"

"I didn't get a look at that, couldn't say. I've got the impression she was carrying it when she stepped out to hail me, that is, she didn't go back to the curb to get it. And once she was out of the lights I could just see she had some kind of bag. Like she'd just come off a train, but I don't see how she could of. She wasn't on the Lark—I'd have spotted her—and anyway if she had been why didn't she take a cab down at the station, instead of wandering up the hill to the Plaza? Anyway, in she gets, and she says in this funny accent to take her to this address out on Polk Street. Well, it was to-hell-and-gone down toward the beach, fifteen miles easy, and I wanted to be sure she wasn't a nut or something without any money on her, so I said that was quite a ways, it'd cost her four-five bucks, as a kind of hint, if you get me. And right away she says, 'That will be all right, my good man,' in this crazy accent, and she hands me a fivespot over the back of the seat. So I drove her. It'd mean an empty run back because it wasn't likely I'd pick up another stray way out there, but if she handed over the five so easy I thought maybe there'd be a good tip. . . . It's a block of tract houses, one of those new subdivisions."

"Let's look at a map." They looked, and Mendoza was more irritated. That block on Polk Street was a short block up and a short block across from Twelvetrees' apartment on 267th.

"—And no streetlights in yet, so I didn't get any better look at her there, and she hadn't done any talking at all on the way. You know, some people want to talk to the driver and some don't, I let them pick. I had a look in the morror now and then, and she was just sitting kind of huddled up in one corner, holding that serape over her face like she was afraid of breathing germs or something. When we got there, quick as anything she hands me over another five, and before I can get out to open the door, give her her change, she's already out, with her suitcase, and says, 'That's all right, my man, I don't want change,' and off she goes. I hadn't even killed the engine yet."

"So, of course, you didn't," said Mendoza. "You made a U-turn and headed back—and you didn't see her go into any of those houses."

"Well, no, I didn't. She was a funny one, but we see plenty of *them* hacking, you know. But that street's too narrow for a U-turn, I had to go up to the next corner. And by the time I got back where she'd got out, no sign of her. But I did notice that the house where she said she wanted to go wasn't lighted at all, as if they were expecting somebody. Only way I knew the right address was, the house next to it had the porch light on and I saw that number."

"Yes. A very funny little story. Thanks very much for coming in. We'll want your name and so on, and a formal statement. . . ." And just how did that little piece of melodrama fit in? Why had Cara Kingman (if it had been) have to taxi back to the apartment? And call such obvious notice to herself in the process? Polk Street. Two blocks to 267th. Which in turn was only about a mile from where Bartlett had been killed three hours earlier. The only thing Mendoza liked at all about this was that it had happened on the Friday night; and that was senseless too, just because he was set on *that* theory.

"*Ca, vaya historia!* I don't believe it, it's a damned ridiculous coincidence," he said to himself. But it had to be followed up, of course. He put on his hat and set out on the six-block walk down to the old Plaza and Olvera Street.

TEN

Once, they'd been going to destroy the narrow alley with its uneven old brick paving and the gutter down its middle, the leaning ramshackle old buildings flanking it. Nothing to do, that was, with a progressive and fast-growing city proud of its modernity. Then a few civic-minded organizations got up indignant petitions and committees, and in the end it stayed, to become a landmark, one of the places tourists came to see: the first, the oldest street of that little village whose name was nearly as long as the street—the town of Our Lady, Queen of the Angels, of the little portion.

At ten-thirty on a gray February morning it wasn't much to see: shabby refaced buildings, haphazard stalls cheek-by-jowl in a row down the middle, over the old gutter, and most of the shops shut, boards up in the stall windows. Night was its time, when the lights softened down the shabbiness and the tourists came, the buyers (tourists or not), and the famous old restaurant was open midway down the street, and the women who'd marketed and cooked and chatted all day in their ready-made cotton housedresses got out their shawls and combs. There'd be a couple of men with guitars stationed somewhere, and the man at the mouth of the street with his little bags of hot roasted piñon nuts, and the music and laughter drifting out of La Golondrina, the restaurant, and the buyers drifting along looking at everything (the women stumbling on the uneven bricks, in their high heels)—at the gimcrack cheap jewelry and the beautiful handcrafted real stuff from the little silver-smithies here and south of the border, at the handmade baskets, and braided-leather and tooled-leather shoes, at the hand-blown glass and the hand-woven cotton (also at the boxed cheap linens from Belgium, and the good stuff and the bad from Japan, from the Philippines, from everywhere in Europe)—and maybe stopping to have their fortunes told by the old woman at the far end of the street.

And even at ten-thirty in the morning, over the whole street there hung the faint scent of glamour—and that was the combined scents from the little cavelike shop, three breakneck steps down from street level, where the candles were made, the incredible rainbow candles scented with pine, with orange, with jasmine and gardenia, and name-less musky saccharine odors.

Most of the shops were shut, but he knew that behind many of them were living quarters. This was a minor little errand, he needn't have come himself, but—he also knew—he might have a better chance of getting whatever there was to get than the most fluent of his Spanish-speaking sergeants.

He could have wished that the article in question had been something other than a serape. That inimitable object of Mexicana, the long strip of rough cactus cloth or cotton, garishly striped and fringed, was to be had at all but a few specialty shops: but maybe that fact was balanced by another, that it had been raining that night.

He started at the mouth of the street and took one side at a time. Not every shop had quarters attached; not everyone was at home. Everyone who was was anxious to be helpful but remembered nothing of any use to him. . . . To be sure, most places had remained open that rainy evening. When one was under shelter, and it was the regular time for business, why not? There was always a chance that the rain would slacken, that a few people who had decided to come to the street would not be put off by the weather. And so it had been: business had been very poor, of course, but a few buyers had come—chiefly people who had reservations at the restaurant and visited the shops afterward. But many places had closed earlier than usual, ten or ten-thirty. Not all, no.

Wine was pressed on him. In one place a very old woman looked on him in contempt and called him a police spy. In the place next door a pretty high-school-age girl asked him please would he talk to her brother and tell him he was crazy: "See, Joe keeps saying he's got nine counts on him to start, being Mexican—what's the use of trying to get educated and so on, he'd never get anywhere, might as well get things however you can. He's in with some real bad fellows, Mama and I get worried—and if you'd just *show* him—" He took the name and address for Taylor in Juvenile; Taylor would see one of the youth counselors contacted Joe and did what he could. . . . By the time he got to the mouth of the street again, having worked his way right up one side and down the other, Mendoza, who was not a wine drinker, was feeling slightly bilious and disgruntled at this waste of time.

But there, in the end shop—scarcely more than an alcove, now, shut off from the street by a large board, with a single room behind it—he found Manuel Perez, improving the out-of-business hour by making up his accounts. Mr. Perez removed his horn-rimmed glasses, listened gravely to Mendoza's questions, and said at once that he remembered the occasion very well indeed.

"At last I arrive," said Mendoza. "Now why didn't I start here? Tell me."

It seemed that Mr. Perez had kept his shop open later than any other that rainy night, not in the hope of customers but because he was waiting for his son, who had borrowed the family car to take his girl to a school dance. *La familia* Perez lived a couple of miles away from the street, and especially on a cold wet night Mr. Perez had not fancied the walk home. The dance was to be over at midnight, and Diego, who was a good reliable boy, would then deliver his girl home and come to pick up his father at the shop: which in fact he had done, somewhere around twelve-thirty.

Meanwhile Mr. Perez had spent a quiet evening sitting in his shop, waiting on the few customers who came. "And you comprehend, later on it's pleasant sitting there alone—a few other shopkeepers who don't live here, they called out goodnight as they left—the Garcias two doors up stayed open late, and Mrs. Sanchez across the way too, it's anything to make a dollar with that one—but the lights go out, one by one, and presently I'm the only one left open, and all is quiet but for the rain, splat-splat-splat, outside. . . . I took the opportunity to write a letter to my brother in Fresno, and later on I read my book—I always keep a book here for the slow times, I'm a great reader and at home with the children it's noisy. . . ." And just about midnight, as Mr. Perez sat reading in his little lonely circle of light, a woman's voice spoke to him from the street.

Startled, he had looked up, and there she was outside the perimeter of light, no more than a dark figure. His glasses were for reading distance and in his surprise he hadn't taken them off, so he could give only a vague description. She spoke hurriedly and with a strange foreign accent on her English; she said she wanted something to protect her hat from the rain; one of his serapes would do, how much were they? The whole queer little transaction happened so quickly that it was not until she was gone that Mr. Perez told himself it was surely odd, when she wanted to save her hat from the rain, that she had not naturally stepped over the threshold into the shop. . . . "But no, she stays outside, she is really only a hand and arm reaching into the light, you understand?" On hearing the price, two dollars, she held out the money, said any one would do, and he took it over to her. But she had forgotten the tax, the eight cents for the state, and when he reminded her she had impatiently handed him another dollar bill, said, "That's all right, don't bother about change," and walked away rapidly. This Mr. Perez had not liked, because he was an honest man and also had his pride, and he did not like to accept tips like a waiter; however, she was gone—"and money is money."

"That is very true. Was she carrying anything?"

Yes, she had had a suitcase; this she had set down a little in front of her to open her purse, and Mr. Perez had seen it a trifle more clearly than the lady. It had been an old brown leather suitcase. And the purse she was carrying, it had glistened as she opened it, catching the reflection of light from the shop—he thought it might have been of that shiny plastic, or perhaps patent leather, a dark color.

"And her hand—you saw her sleeve and hand?" Mendoza thought of Cara Kingman's silver-enameled fingernails.

Yes, so Mr. Perez had. A light-colored sleeve, of a coat he thought, but could not say whether a long or short coat—and it had a dark cuff, like velvet. As for the hand, the lady had been wearing gloves.

"Of what sort?" asked Mendoza.

"One small thing I can tell you about that," said Mr. Perez. "You comprehend, her hand is closer to me, and partly in the light, so I have a better look—for just that one small moment. She handed the money to me between her fingers, and then when I spoke of the tax, she reached into her purse again—impatient, you know—and held the third bill out on her palm, like so. Her gloves were a very light tan color, like raw leather—I don't know if they were leather or cloth—but they had buttons on the inside of the wrist, and when she held her hand out so, I saw that on that glove—her left hand it would be—the little button was missing."

A small amber-colored button in the loose earth raked over the corpse. *"Diez millón demonios negros desde infierno!"* said Mendoza.

"This does not, I fear," said Mr. Perez sympathetically, "please you to hear for some reason."

"On the contrary, it is very helpful indeed. But at the moment I don't know what it means—except that I have been wrong somewhere—or exactly what to do with it. . . ."

Hackett's older sister had a couple of kids, and when they were smaller, a few years ago, once in a while he'd got roped in to sit with them, read to them. There was a thing the little girl had been crazy about, *The Wizard of Oz;* he'd read out of that one a good deal, and right now something in it came back to him. The way one of the wicked witches had just disappeared when she died—nothing left at all, because all there'd been to her was a kind of shell of malice.

He wouldn't, some odd superstitious way, be at all surprised if the same thing happened to Mona Ferne before his eyes. Maybe Mr. Horwitz took a jaundiced general view, but he'd been so right about this one. The front, and that was absolutely all . . .

"Such a terrible thing, I can't bear to think of it," she said in her light, sweet voice. "Poor darling Brooke. He *did* have talent, you know, he'd have done *great* things, I'm convinced—it's a tragedy for *that* reason as well as for all his friends."

"Yes, of course," said Hackett. "When did you see Mr. Twelvetrees last, Miss Ferne?"

She sat in the same chair her daughter had slouched in yesterday, but easily upright, graceful: everything about her was finished to a high gloss, from the lacquered flaxen coiffure to the fragile patent leather sandals with their stilt heels. Ten feet away, she looked an attractive thirty-five; any closer, no. All artificial: the smallest gesture, the tinkling laugh, the expression, the whole woman a planned thing into which God knew what minute calculations had gone. He didn't know much about such things, but he could guess at all the desperate, tedious, grim effort put forth—over the years more and more—on the front: the important thing. The massage, the cosmetics, the diets, the plastic surgery, the money spent and the time used, so much time that she'd had none left over for anything else at all, and so everything else about her had shriveled and died, and she was an empty shell posturing and talking there. All to preserve the illusion that was no illusion, closer than across a room. Any nearer, you saw the lines and the hollows, the little scars at the temples and in front of the ears, the depth of the skillful cosmetic mask, the little loose fold of skin at the throat, and the veins standing up on the backs of the narrow hands with their long enameled nails, their flashing rings, and the expensively capped front teeth, and the faint blistering round the eyelids from strain because she ought to wear glasses.

Those carefully made-up brown eyes widened on him. "Heavens, Sergeant, you can't think *I* had anything to do with—? No, no, I see you must ask *everyone*, mustn't you? Well, now, let me see—I believe it must have been that Thursday, the twenty-ninth it would be. Yes. Brooke dropped by and asked me to go to dinner with him, but I had an engagement already. . . . I never could bring myself to believe it was so, what dear Martin thought—Brooke would never—I've been quite upset about it, but then all of us who *knew* him—and now to have this terrible thing happen! I've hardly taken it in yet, but I'll try to help you however I can—"

"Yes, thank you." This house, Hackett thought—something haunted about this house, with that great tree brooding over it, the rooms like caves until you turned on a light. But this wasn't the ghost who haunted it: the ghost was the other one. . . . She had let him in—looking like hell again, today in an old-womanish gray cotton dress, ugly clumping shoes, her sullen face naked without cosmetics in the daylight from the door. Yet that clear pale skin—looking at her there, he suddenly saw that her eyes were beautiful, her good hazel-brown eyes clear as brook water, framed in heavy lashes. It was an oddly disturbing discovery, and almost immediately he'd made another which disturbed him even more.

And that wasn't his kind of thing, either—the intuitive understanding of emotional secrets. He was a cop, not a psychologist; his business, and one he was pretty good at, was collecting facts and fitting them together to make a picture. Mendoza was the one with the crystal ball. . . .

It was the way she did it, the tone of her flat voice—turning to call up the stairs, "Mother!" All of a sudden he knew about this Angel Carstairs. . . . You'd think she could do *something,* Mr. Horwitz said. *I'm twenty-six years old and,* . . . But she was doing something: the same thing she'd been doing, probably, most of her life. She was punishing Mona—for being her mother, for being what she was. And so anything Mona was or did or said, she had to go the opposite way—just to annoy. It was the negative approach, and also a trap she'd got caught in; because now for such a long while this had been the one reason for Angel Carstairs' existence, she couldn't stop and turn another way and go out to find life away from Mona. Maybe she understood that, maybe she didn't; either way she lived in a little hell she'd made herself, because every way she tormented Mona (reminding her with every mocking *Mother* of their ages, making herself the graceless ugly duckling in mute rebellion against the creed that beauty was the sole importance), she was tormenting herself too.

Yesterday he'd felt sorry for her; today, she made him mad. At the deliberate waste, the senseless negation.

And at the same time, facing this empty shell of a woman, he understood it.

He didn't want to stay in this house any longer than necessary, but he had questions to ask; he went on asking them. Mendoza had guessed right on one thing: it had been Mona Ferne who introduced Twelvetrees to the Kingmans and their Temple. She had met him through a small theatrical group—very careful to emphasize, not amateurs, but studio extras, bit players, that sort—"These *brave* young people, so ambitious and hard-working! I was one myself at one time, you know, and I realize how much it means, any little encouragement and support." Now and then they put on shows, in a community theater they could rent cheap, near Exposition Park; it was at one of those she'd met Twelvetrees. He'd been a new member of the group then; this was four years ago, he'd have been here only a few months. "I saw at once he had talent—oh, he needed training and experience, but the essential thing was there. The work this splendid little group was doing was excellent for him, though the poor boy was impatient at the lack of recognition."

Did she (he didn't expect much on this one) remember any comments Twelvetrees had made about the Temple or the Kingmans, after his first visit there? Well, nothing *specific;* he had, of course, been tremendously impressed, as anyone would be. Such a spiritual atmosphere, and dear Martin so impressive in his robes.

"Yes. Do you happen to know whether Twelvetrees owned a revolver?"

"A *revolver*—heavens, I don't think so, did you *find* one, I mean in his apartment? Oh, I mustn't ask questions, of course, I'm so sorry! I don't think I ever saw him with—But *there,*" she said with a coquettish little *moue,* "I'm telling a lie. I *did.* But I don't think it was his. It was when he was in a play they were doing, oh, all of a year ago it must have been—and he only had it on the stage, of course, it would have been a prop." She angled her new cigarette in its jeweled holder at him, in expectation; perversely he bent over his notebook, pretending not to notice, and let her light it herself.

"And if you don't mind, just for the record, Miss Ferne—were you at home on that Friday and Saturday night?—the thirtieth and thirty-first, that was."

She didn't answer immediately, and then she said, "Oooh, I *will* begin to think you suspect me! Was that when he was—? Do you *know,* I mean? I thought—the papers said—but you police are so clever, I expect you have ways of finding out things." And by now Hackett was unwillingly fascinated, at the apparent extent of the woman's faith in her private illusion. A pretty sixteen-year-old innocent on her first date might get by with such provocative glances and giggles, such arch wriggling girlishness; from this woman it should have been absurd, and instead was somehow horrible. "Well, let me *see.* Of course I know you have to ask, it doesn't mean you think I— As if I'd any reason, my dear Brooke—but I mustn't make a parade of feeling, one has to bear these things. . . . Let me see. That was a week ago last Friday and Saturday? Oh, of course, on the Friday night I went to see Miss Kent. Janet Kent—do you want the address? She's an old servant actually, she was Angel's nurse, such a reliable woman, but she was quite old then and now she can't work anymore, and hasn't much to live on, poor thing. She's very proud, she won't take money, but I *do* give her clothes and things like that, you know, and—not to sound as if I'm praising myself or anything—I do go in as often as I can, if it's just for a minute or two, to cheer her up a little, you see. It's rather tedious sometimes— old people can be *such* bores, can't they?—but I try to do what I can."

"Yes. What time did you get there and when did you leave?"

"Well, it *felt* like eternity, I couldn't get away from her that night, she wanted to talk—she gets lonely, poor thing—and she does so love to play cards, I had to sit down and play with her. I couldn't tell you exactly when I got there, but I think it must have been about seven-thirty, because I left right after dinner here—and when I did get away, I felt so exhausted—*such* a bore—I thought it must be midnight, but it was only a quarter of eleven. I came straight home. . . . And the *next* night, of course, I was at the Temple for the service, as I am every Saturday night."

"Thank you," said Hackett, and stood up.

"Is that all you want to ask me? I do hope I've been of some help, though I don't see how I could tell you anything important."

"One more thing," said Hackett, and made himself smile at her, sound sympathetic, "I hope you don't mind a personal question, Miss Ferne, but—well, you'd been out with Mr. Twelvetrees socially quite a bit, and—er—well, was there anything like a formal engagement, or—er—?" He thought he'd done that quite well, the insensitive cop trying to be delicate.

"*Ah,*" she said, clasping one hand to her cheek, lowering her eyes. "I—I shouldn't like to feel that such a *private* matter would go into your records, to be pawed over by anyone—" An appealing glance. He produced a very obviously admiring smile and murmured something about off-the-record. "I—I can't say what *might* . . . But there were difficulties, you see? Dear Brooke was so proud, and of course I do have more money than he did. And there was a *little* difference in our ages, nothing to matter, but he—I'm sure you understand. But mostly, it was—Angel. I'm afraid the poor girl was quite foolishly in love with him—oh, quite *understandable,* of course, but utterly hopeless, naturally. Brooke *never*— She never *said* anything to show she was jealous, or—but I knew, and so did Brooke, of course. The way she behaved. I've seen her look quite—quite *wild,* sometimes, when we were going out somewhere together. These young girls . . . But it would have made difficulties. Brooke was so understanding, he hadn't said a word to me, yet, but we both knew—you *do* see what I mean?"

Hackett said he did. She added suddenly, a little nervously, "I do hope you won't have to question her, Sergeant—she's so *odd,* she never shows what she feels. Now *I* simply can't help it, a bundle of emotions, but then most women *are,* aren't we? But she hasn't been herself at all the last—well, since we knew, I expect it's been, though she's been very quiet and strange for a week or so. I really wouldn't like her upset further—"

"I don't think it's necessary." Hackett didn't know when he'd been more anxious to get out of a place; it was an unhealthy house, as if a miasma hung over it like that damned tree, darkening the spirit as the tree darkened the rooms. He went out to the entry hall, her high heels clacking sharp and light on the parquet floor there, behind him. And there was the girl again, swinging the door open for him, mocking, metallic. . . .

"What, isn't he arresting you, Mother dear? What a disappointment!"

He felt the hate like an invisible sword poised.

"Darling, you mustn't joke to the police, they might take you seriously. And I hoped you were lying down, you've not been at all yourself lately, you know."

"What d'you mean? I'm all right! What on *earth*—oh, I see, showing how *solicitous* you are of me! How ridiculous, I—" And she caught his glance, that held anger and pity because he couldn't help it, and suddenly, astonishingly, shamed color flooded her face. She flung around furiously and ran away from both of them, up the stairs.

"*So* difficult—young girls," murmured the woman. "So *unpredictable*. Quite wild, sometimes—she has always been— But I mustn't bore you with my troubles. I do hope you'll find whatever wicked person did this dreadful thing, soon. You've been so kind and understanding, Sergeant—"

ELEVEN

There was, of course, one obvious thing to do with this new information, and Mendoza did it; he came back to headquarters and set about getting a search warrant for the Temple and the Kingmans' apartment. As that would take a little time, he deferred his visit there until after lunch and meanwhile did some looking at various other odd bits of news that had come in, and some thinking about them.

They didn't have much on Twelvetrees' close associates aside from the Temple crowd; but barring the emergence of a girl friend with a grudge, or a rival ditto—something like that, maybe from among his theatrical acquaintances—the Kingmans still looked like the best bet, because when it came to motives for murder, money was always high on the list. That Miss Katherine Webster, the old lady, had been about the only one of the crowd who hadn't liked Twelvetrees, but it scarcely looked like anything that would have led to murder. She was one of the Kingmans' prize pigeons, a very wealthy old lady indeed; it was a little confirmation of his idea about Twelvetrees blackmailing the Kingmans, that in the face of old Miss Webster's dislike and openly voiced distrust, they hadn't obliged her by getting rid of him.

Miss Webster employed a chauffeur and had a four-year-old black Cadillac. It had curved-up fins.

The Kingmans had a three-year-old dark gray Buick with curved-up fins.

Mrs. Bragg, urged to remember, said she had at various times seen cars belonging to Twelvetrees' visitors standing in front of his place but, beyond the fact that one she'd noticed once was dark-colored and big, could give no details. He hadn't had many people come to see him; he wasn't there much, and had never given parties, anything like that. She herself had a two-year-old dark red Olds, and (depressingly) it too had curved-up fins.

But there was nothing to guarantee, of course, that Walsh had been right about that, his brief glimpse of that car.

At least, if this rather curious story of the exotic lady who'd bought the serape from Mr. Perez and taken that cab ride out to Polk Street, had come unexpectedly, still it served a useful purpose: it pinned down the night pretty definitely. Again, not exactly solid evidence, but suggestive. Coincidences did occur, but that missing glove button, the scuffed brown leather suitcase, the obvious attempt to evade recognition, and the areas in question—near where the Porsche had been found, near the apartment—all pointed to the fact that she had something to do with this business. Even more eloquently was that indicated by what he'd got from a phone call to that address on Polk Street: people named Fawcett, sounded like a young housewife he'd talked to, baby crying in the background: no, they had not expected any out-of-town visitor that weekend, no one had come to the house all that Friday evening.

And about that time Mendoza remembered Dr. Graas on Fairfax Avenue, and the allergy: not much in it, he'd thought, but you never knew. He called Dr. Graas; and what he learned then sent him calling elsewhere. . . . When Sergeant Lake came in with the search warrant about noon, he was brooding over a half page of notes. He tucked the warrant into his pocket, told the sergeant to have Piggott and Landers meet him at the Temple at one o'clock, and went out for lunch, meeting Hackett in the corridor.

"Let's catch each other up over a sandwich. You're looking gloomy about something, what's gone wrong?"

"Just human nature generally," said Hackett. When they were settled in a booth in the hole-in-the-wall café, he described the Mona Ferne set-up.

Mendoza listened in thoughtful silence, and at the conclusion said irrelevantly, "It'd be a help if we could get that gun identified. I do wonder if it's the same one Twelvetrees used in that play. No, no particular reason it should be, but you know those amateur groups—makeshift arrangements—they need something as a prop, somebody says, 'Oh, I think I know where I can get one.' . . . It might have been his own. Quite a few honest people don't bother about a license, and I doubt if Twelvetrees would have. . . . Bainbridge thinks, by the way, that it may have been the weapon. The wrong end of it, that is. Failing anything else there—we know the man wasn't knocked down against the bedpost or something, the way it's always happening in books—I'm inclined to agree. . . . Yes, nasty—those women—just as you say. And a kind of culmination of everything else between them, if the girl was in love with Twelvetrees too—"

"Not *too*," said Hackett. "That woman's never been in love with anybody but herself."

"*Es claro*. And neither of them, probably, meant anything to dear Brooke. He'd have taken up with La Ferne to begin with thinking she could do him some good in the way of theatrical contacts, but he must have found out by now she doesn't have a pull there any more. It was her money kept him dangling—an ace up his sleeve, *tal vez*. I'll bet you she'd given him other little presents than that fancy cigarette case— maybe those expensive shirts and ties, the flame-of-love bottles. Nuances in these things, sure—nothing crude about it, pay for services rendered—he'd make the graceful protests on the ground of his pride and so on, he'd have been good at that. And in case worst came to worst, and all his other rackets played out on him, and he'd got nothing in prospect better, he might have married her. She'd have jumped at that?"

"Oh, very definitely, I'd say."

"Mmh. But it'd have been a last resort for him. I'll bet you something else, that the services rendered wouldn't, shall we say, call for overtime pay. That kind of woman is always cold as a fish, and Twelvetrees could have picked up something a damn sight more bedworthy. . . . We ought to get something from Pennsylvania some time today. Meanwhile, I'll tell you what I've got. . . ."

Hackett listened, said, "Well, maybe it's a good thing I didn't lay any bets on Walsh's business. Though I still think— But anyway, it begins to look as if it *was* that Friday night. You don't really think you're going to find that light coat with dark trimming, or a glove with a missing button, or the serape, at the Kingmans' apartment, do you? Neither of them is that stupid."

"You never know. One thing to remember here, somebody got one hell of a shock on Saturday night or Sunday when it first came out in the papers that the body had been found. That hadn't been the idea at all, and it's quite possible that until then whoever it was hadn't thought it necessary to get rid of those things. Maybe there hasn't been a chance since. We can hope, can't we? And I've had another idea—to start with, you remember what I said about a laundry bag? Well, I've got some idea of what went into it."

"How?"

"I called this doctor Twelvetrees had been going to. And he said among other things that he'd prescribed this and that, and,"—Mendoza sat back over his coffee and lit a cigarette—"I got to thinking. You know, it's like the roof light on the squad car, and patrolmen changing round—we're so apt to overlook the little, familiar things. I called some pharmacies in the general areas where Twelvetrees might have gone—hit the right one fourth try, place near the doctor's office. And then I thought some more, and what I came up with was this." He handed over a slip of paper.

"Atomizer, bottles, tie—" read Hackett. "What's this?"

"It's a list of things we didn't find anywhere that ought to have been there. *Ya lo creo,* I'm not sure about all of them, but a couple of things we've got for sure. Dr. Graas had prescribed a solution for spraying up his sinuses, and for that he had to have one of those atomizer things. And some antihistamine capsules. *And* the pharmacy says, and the doctor says, that on Friday afternoon, a little after four o'clock, Twelvetrees came into the pharmacy to have both prescriptions refilled, though he had some of each left, and he asked for a double amount because he was leaving on a trip."

"You don't tell me," said Hackett. "More confirmation. That's very nice."

"I thought so. The pharmacist called the doctor to check, and the doctor spoke with Twelvetrees over the phone and gave his O.K. Well, as I say, having my attention called to these little items that hadn't been there—in the apartment, the suitcases, or on Twelvetrees—I began to think of other things we hadn't found. First of all, there's the atomizer bottle, and the spray solution in a bottle about five inches high—holding sixteen fluid ounces, so the pharmacist says—and the little plastic bottle of antihistamine capsules. Both those bottles with his name and the doctor's on them, the name of the pharmacy and the prescription numbers. Those we know were missing. Then, you know, the corpse wasn't wearing a tie. He was all dressed except for that, and all the ties we found had been neatly packed. I think we can say almost for certain he was going to leave for somewhere that night, and he'd have put on a tie before he left. While he was busy packing, he'd have taken it off, or more likely he'd changed his clothes when he came in—hadn't put on jacket or tie while he packed. I can see that, can't you? But he'd leave a tie out, ready to put on. What else? He had on a shirt with button cuffs, so, no cuff links. But he had quite a collection of jewelry, didn't he? I think he'd always wear a tie clasp, or one of those new tie tacks. There'd be that left out ready. And—"

"Well, maybe. He might not have intended to wear a tie."

"Sure, I said some of this is maybe, but keep it in mind. He was a snappy dresser, and it's not hot weather, when a lot of men aren't wearing ties. But here's something that *must* have been there—his watch. You're not going to tell me he didn't have one—how many men you know don't have some kind of watch, if it's only a five-dollar one from the drugstore? The odds are it was a wrist watch, because only older men or very conservative types carry a pocket watch these days."

"That I'll give you. Funny we missed it before—one of us should have spotted that."

"I see him, you know—thinking of what we've got so far—coming home to pack and clear out. Changing his clothes, maybe, and leaving off a few last-minute things that'll hamper him a bit in the process of packing and so on. The tie. The jacket—"

"He had a jacket on. Have you ever seen anybody put a jacket on first and *then* his tie?"

"I'm telling you about this little vision," said Mendoza. "Wait for it. He's packing. He leaves a few little things out, ready, for when he's finished. A tie and tie clasp. His watch. His jacket, probably hung over a chair, with a fair supply of handkerchiefs in it—or maybe a couple of clean ones waiting there on the bureau with these other odds and ends. The atomizer and the prescription bottles—maybe he meant to carry those on him, but I think more likely to put them in last, on top of everything else, to be handy. It's possible he had one of those plastic or leather cases for medicine bottles, to put them in. And possibly a hat. Quite a few young men don't wear hats any more, out here, but he hadn't been in California long, maybe he'd kept his Eastern habits. And another thing we can say for sure about—the bankbooks. He'd have carried those on him, but I think because he'd changed his clothes they were lying there on the bureau with the other things. And the twenty-three hundred bucks, in cash—not a little item to be overlooked, *no es verdad?* And something else that's a maybe—documentary evidence on what he had on the Kingmans. I don't say he'd *need* a document to show the faithful congregation, because—always assuming that he was blackmailing them—it was probably something fairly concrete, like a prison term, that anyone could verify with a little trouble. But the kind of people who go for Mystic Truths are usually pretty hard to unconvince, and Kingman's a very smooth and plausible fellow. I don't think Twelvetrees could have stayed the pace this long without some tangible threat to hold over them, something that would have convinced even Miss Webster."

"Very much maybe."

"O.K., so it is. Then, did you ever know a male from the age of ten up who didn't carry some kind of pocket knife? Whether it was one of those genteel little flat silver things, or a horn-handled sheath knife? *That* was there on the bureau. And while he doesn't seem to have been a heavy drinker, I think almost certainly he'd have kept a bottle at home, for the odd occasion when he wanted a drink before going to bed, or if somebody dropped in. I don't know what it'd be, Scotch or gin or vodka, but I think it was sitting there too. He wouldn't care about leaving the odds and ends of stuff in the kitchen, and there wasn't much—a half bottle of milk, a few strips of bacon, a couple of eggs, a little coffee. But he'd take the bottle along. And I also think there was another package or so of cigarettes, maybe a whole carton—because there were only ten or eleven in his case, and a smoker doesn't let himself get down so low."

"I'll give you that one too."

"So there he is, almost finished packing—we still don't know why he was getting out, or whether he was in a hurry or just leisurely. Anyway, there he is, almost finished, except for a few little things *and* his soiled laundry, for which he has this bag laid out ready—I'm not guessing whether it was a paper bag or an ordinary cotton laundry bag. And at that point he has a visitor. Say two—the Kingmans. Skip the cross-talk, if there was any, and come to the murder. Now, here's my new idea. I see them in a little dither, as we've agreed confidence operators aren't given to violence. They're in a hurry to get away, also to protect themselves, and I see them snatching up this hypothetical documentary evidence, having a last look around to be sure they've left nothing incriminating—wiped off all prints and so on—and starting to leave—only to find that squad car sitting out there. So? They aren't sure they haven't been seen—it doesn't matter then, nobody knows yet there's been a murder, but it will matter, later on. By the time they decide that patrolman, who has apparently seen them there, had better be put out of the way, the car's gone. And they spend a while chasing after it, cruising around looking and getting in more and more of a dither—before they find it. I'm supposing, by the way, that the gun was Twelvetrees', and was lying there on the bureau, all convenient. Well, after they've found the car and had a try at the driver, they've got no way to be sure the man's dead and no danger to them—and so back they come, with another idea, to get rid of the corpse and try to pass his disappearance off as voluntary."

Hackett said, "This is a fine story, I can see Hitchcock making a dandy movie of it. But you're building it without much evidence."

"I know, I know. But go on listening. I think that note to Mrs. Bragg was either already written—by Twelvetrees, just to save time and trouble—and sitting there on the bureau, or he'd mentioned to them that he hadn't yet told her he was leaving, or they'd have had no other way to know that and consequently know the necessity for the note. Anyway, they make the whole plan hastily. Casting around for what to do with the body, they find that trap—and what better place? They can work at leisure, and no need to go trundling the body around in the car. They get the body buried, and they finish his packing for him and dump those suitcases down the trap. By this time they're worked up some more, they've had quite an evening, and there's still his car to dispose of. And then, just as they think they can relax a little, all of a sudden they spot these miscellaneous odds and ends on the bureau. Easy to overlook, you know, the state they were probably in. They'd remembered to put his jacket on him—easier than to cram it into a suitcase already full—but they hadn't bothered to put a tie on—what did it matter?—so they hadn't looked for one. And the idea of going down that trap again to jam all this stuff in a suitcase, or even just dump it—well, can't you see them sticking it all into that bag handy there, and taking it away for disposal later?"

Slowly Hackett nodded. "I can. Yes. But where does this woman down at Olvera Street come in? Why did Mrs. Kingman have to do all that alone? And why was it the woman who drove the Porsche down there instead of him, anyway?"

"That part I don't know," said Mendoza. "Some reason may show up. But so far, I like all that, don't you?"

"It hangs together, after a fashion," agreed Hackett grudgingly. "And one thing, a couple of those items wouldn't be so easy to destroy or get rid of. They could soak the labels off the bottles. But if it's a modern apartment there'll be no open fire, to burn anything. Nothing identifiable about a tie, or the cash—but a watch, even the knife—"

"Especially as dear Brooke was given to having things monogrammed. Me, in that position I'd take the whole collection down to a lonely stretch of beach and consign it to the Pacific, but they haven't had much time, as I say. And speaking of that, I'd better not sit here detailing theories any longer—I'll see them and we'll have a look. What's your program?"

"I'm going out to Eagle Rock," said Hackett rather morosely, "to see this fellow Dave Morris who's some leading light in that theatrical club. See what he can give us on Twelvetrees."

"Then, *pues vamos!*—let's go, and see what turns up."

Hackett hadn't sounded very enthusiastic about all that, but on his way out to Eagle Rock he found himself hoping Mendoza was right, that it was those Kingmans. Because he'd started having a little vision of his own, and he didn't like it. Which was absurd on two counts: the first being, of course, that an efficient police officer should look at a case, and the people in it, objectively. You began feeling sorry for them, or mad at them, or contemptuous of them, and you couldn't look at the evidence fair and square.

And the second count was that the Kingmans were the obvious answer, that a thing like that in his mind was out of a paperback detective thriller; you just didn't run across such things every day.

But they happened, oh, yes. Now and then. Maybe this was one of the times.

And he wasn't happy to think it might be. No reason for it; what the hell were these people to Art Hackett?

Just because she had nice eyes, and he'd felt sorry. . . . The things people did to each other. A lot of talk about active, deliberate evil, and it did harm, no question; but he sometimes thought more mischief was made by the plain stupidity, by the passive, self-centered uncaringness.

A culmination, Mendoza had said. And Hackett could see that happening. The last straw, you might say, for that girl Angel (my God, what a name!). That after Mona had, in a sense, turned her into what she was, the graceless ugly duckling—when she fell in love with a man, knowing he'd never look twice at her, it was Mona who *had* him. Never mind in what way. Making everything boil up in her all at once.

And how the hell any woman—a man like Twelvetrees, another one all front, the too-handsome collar ad— But look at it objectively: people didn't show much common sense about these things. Ever. When it came to feelings. How many men had fallen for a beautiful face and found that's all there was? And he was, wasn't he, just the type a girl like that *would* have fallen for—a girl without experience, younger than her age in some ways.

A girl not in a very sound psychological state to begin with. Whether she knew it or not . . . All right, he told himself almost angrily: build it; how might it have happened?

Mona Ferne would have had his address: the girl would have known where to go. Did she drive, have a car of her own? Find out. What would it be in her mind? Please look at me, *I* could give you more than she ever could! And him laughing at her? Or, If I can't have you, *she* never will!

The gun. His own? Or had she planned it, come prepared?

All that business afterward—no, she couldn't— How could he say for sure? A streak there of deliberate planning, yes; the ways she devised for punishing Mona. She wasn't a mental defective by any means.

"Hell," he said aloud to himself. The law said motive wasn't very important. You needn't go hunting up a plausible motive to match the nice solid tangible facts the law liked—ownership of weapon, presence on the scene, witnesses, fingerprints, and so on and so on. But in practice, that was one of the first things you had to look for. A lot of murders were done for very little reason, a moment's loss of temper, the ten bucks or thirty cents in the victim's pocket, a mere suspicion of wife or husband, things like that; but as a general rule, nobody got worked up to murder without some hell's brew of emotion churning inside them—whether it was what you might call rational emotion or not, lasting a minute or a year.

He didn't like the idea, but he could see it happening, since he knew the girl had been in love with Twelvetrees.

And it was, of course, a really wild one, no evidence there at all—something like one of Mendoza's hunches. He thought he'd keep it to himself for a while, see how things piled up—or didn't—on the Kingmans. If and when there was nowhere else to look, then look.

Meanwhile, he found the address Mona Ferne had given him: Dave Morris was at home and unsurprised to see him.

"I wondered if I ought to come in, when I saw the papers—but I hadn't seen him for a day or so before he supposedly left, I don't know anything really to tell you. Everybody's been calling me up, shall we go to the police or not—you know—" He shrugged. He was a stocky dark young man with an ugly, attractive face, and vitality exhaled from him with every breath; he was a restless talker, gesturing, changing position every ten seconds.

"Well, maybe you can help fill in some of the background, but first, when did you see him last?"

"On Wednesday the twenty-eighth," said Morris promptly. "I've got all this pat in my mind, ready for you, see. Some of us met here to talk over a new show we're thinking of doing, and for what it's worth I'll tell you that it was the first time Twelvetrees didn't jump at a part. He was—oh, what the British call cock-a-hoop that night—kept hinting we might get a surprise soon, that sort of thing. . . . No, nothing definite. He was just—on air, as if he'd just heard he'd inherited a fortune or something. Tell the truth, I wasn't very curious, and when he didn't show at our next meeting, I didn't do any crying over it. . . ."

Morris liked to talk, and Hackett was used to listening. Some more background emerged. Most of the people in this group had got on the lowest rung of the show-business ladder at least; Twelvetrees had been one of only three amateurs, without any experience, among them. "And he was an awful ham, but the girls fell for his looks, you know." It hadn't been for quite a while they'd found out how he'd earned a living —"if you can call it earned"—he'd apparently tried to keep his different lives in separate compartments; and when they did, they'd kidded him about it some. If Hackett wanted Morris's opinion, Twelvetrees didn't take the Mystic Truth very seriously, except of course as an easy living. Which was understandable. Morris himself wouldn't look down his nose at anything like that; eking out subsistence with on-call TV work as an extra was pretty precarious. No, Twelvetrees had never said much about his background, specifically where he came from, except just Pennsylvania. He wouldn't say that Twelvetrees had been bosom pals with anybody in the group, though he was faithful in attendance at their meetings and always eager to take a part in one of their plays.

"Which kind of canceled out, if you get me, because while some of us aren't always able to take on a part—on count of prior commitments we'll get paid for—we do like to have competent actors in our little productions. We get a certain number of producers and so on keeping an eye on what we're doing, you see, which is why we go to the trouble and expense of putting shows on, besides giving ourselves experience. Stop me, by the way, if I get irrelevant, maybe you're not interested in all this. Well, for one thing, he was a bit older than most of us, you know, and the men didn't like him—including yours truly—because, well, we don't usually care much for the too-too-handsome boys who go round preening themselves in mirrors, do we? Yes, he was rather like that. And the girls, a couple of them are faithful devoted wives, and a couple more have enough common sense to see through that kind. And as for the couple left who'd have been thrilled-to-pieces-darling if the divine creature had asked them for a date, he did a lot of arm patting and general showing off, but beyond that, not a tumble."

"You trying to say he was on the nance side?"

"Oh, Lord, no, don't think so. A bit la-de-da, but I put that down to his having deliberately taught himself, you know—not to be snobbish about it—upper-class manners. I think he may have come from somewhere lower down, which is nothing against him, and acquired the polished veneer, and people like that usually overdo it a little. He never acted casual, if you get me. About the girls, I figured myself he had a steady, and for some reason never brought her round or mentioned her. Just conjecture, but maybe when it came to females he preferred the kind he knew in the lower ranks, and didn't care to exhibit one of 'em to us."

"Possible," said Hackett. "Any of these girls in your bunch named Marian Marner?"

"Never heard of her. Not even a Marian in the lot."

"Well," said Hackett. "Of course, he was going around with Miss Mona Ferne—"

Morris let out a bellow of laughter and started to tell him just what *that* amounted to. They'd all got a hell of a kick out of that—not, of course, in front of Twelvetrees. Like all that kind, he didn't have much sense of humor about himself. The first time he'd met her he'd been all over her, putting out the full wattage of boyish charm. Maybe it'd been a dirty trick, but the rest of them hadn't said a word to him—seeing what was going on—about her being a dead one so far as the profession went, *kaput,* washed up long ago, and no use as a patroness. Which was obviously the idea in his mind. And of course she was all too pleased to have him dancing attendance . . . "that *woman,* that damned awful woman." They put up with her because she was a regular at their shows, one admission ticket to count on, and you couldn't offend people who might talk, good or bad, about you in public; one thing you could bet on, they never had got and never would get any cash support from Mona, however much she talked about her sympathy for these brave struggling young people. Had Hackett met her? Wasn't it the damndest thing how she still saw herself as the glamour queen? All the same, not that she needed convincing about it, one reason she'd been a soft mark for Twelvetrees; it wouldn't be every day she picked up a handsome young man so anxious to oblige. And mind you, she wasn't—Morris would say—a fool, when it came to money and so on, either; a shrewd streak there, but by all accounts she never had seen through Twelvetrees, because she was so anxious to believe it was, so to speak, her *beaux yeux* alone that held him.

"Another little reason none of us cared for him—I mean, hell, I'm no moralizing prude, but there are limits. He found out for himself soon enough she couldn't wave the fairy wand and waft him in front of a big producer who'd fall on his neck with the glad cry, 'My boy, you're just what I've been looking for!' But by then he'd also found out she was loaded, and so damn pleased to have him hanging around there was graft to be had—you know, the little present for a good boy."

"We'd figured that one," said Hackett. "Off the record, you think it went any further than taking her around night clubs and so on?"

"Who knows?" said Morris. "All I can say is, I doubt it very strongly. For all I've been saying about him, he was fastidious as a cat—me, I'm not, exactly, but *I* wouldn't have wanted to go any further, in his position, if you take me. Would you? No matter how much you liked the gold cigarette case and the fancy clothes?"

Hackett laughed and said you never knew what you could do until you got really strapped, but it didn't seem Twelvetrees had been down so low. Morris agreed. "Why didn't we get rid of him? Not so easy.

And maybe it's a case of the pot calling the kettle black, because he had more money to spend than most of us, and he was always glad to fork over—props, theater rent, costumes and so on—so long as he was one of the boys and girls all chummy together, *and* got a chance to tread the boards once in a while."

"Speaking of props, about a year ago you people did a show that called for a gun. Where did it come from and where did it go afterward?"

Morris cocked his head. "A gun? He wasn't shot, was he? I know you can't answer any questions, but I'm being a good boy and not asking any because I know that, I'm not disinterested. We're all seething with curiosity—our glamour boy murdered! *Was* he shot? The papers didn't say."

"No, he wasn't. There's no reason you shouldn't know. We found a gun there and just wonder if it was his. This gun you used in the play—"

"Bitter Harvest," said Morris. "I remember. Twelvetrees supplied the gun, all right, but I don't know whether it was his or he'd borrowed it somewhere. He never said. I don't know much about guns, it was a pistol of some sort—" He measured with his hands. "Longish barrel—looked fairly old, but I don't know. When we went over the list of props for that show he said he'd contract to get the gun, and he showed up with it at the first rehearsal—that's about all I know. Don't think any of the others could tell you any more, but you could ask. . . . Loaded? My God, no, at least I don't think so, he wasn't *that* big a fool. Well, actually it doesn't get fired during the play and Twelvetrees had it all the time on stage. We ran that show for seven nights, our usual, and then packed it up, and that's the last I saw of the gun—he took it away again."

"Would you recognize it?"

Morris thought so. Hackett said they'd have him take a look; but when he'd thanked him and started back downtown, it didn't seem Morris had added much useful. Except the cocky mood Twelvetrees had been in on Wednesday night. Not likely to be much in that—or was there? Be nice to know why. Be nice to know a lot more than they did.

Suppose it was the same gun; that didn't say it was Twelvetrees' own, or where he'd borrowed it. . . . Question the whole lot of these people who'd known him, about seeing him with a gun, hearing him mention one. And probably came up with nothing.

A little routine to take care of. Not that it mattered much, but send somebody to check with that Kent woman Mona Ferne had visited on Friday night: (yes, and it might matter, for consequently Mona wouldn't have known if the girl was out). See if anything had come in from Pennsylvania. Also, now they knew that Twelvetrees had been at that pharmacy on Fairfax after four o'clock, it might not be a bad idea to have a look round the places adjacent, see if he'd stopped anywhere else in the vicinity.

He thought again, unwillingly, about that ridiculously unwelcome hunch of his about the girl. . . . He wondered how Mendoza was getting on.

TWELVE

Mendoza was in a very bad mood with himself. It seemed that from the beginning in this thing he had, like some thickheaded ex-patrolman working his first case in plain clothes, been overlooking little niggling details that were, on analysis, of the first importance. The only thing he could figure, and it was a depressing thought, was that he must be getting old.

Mendoza, who had made a little reputation for himself as one of the bright boys at headquarters! Maybe he needed glasses; maybe he needed to take one of those memory courses.

He'd stood outside this damned Temple, on Saturday night, and read the sign, and among other things it had said in black and white, *Ceremony of the Inner Chamber* (whatever in God's name that was), 8 P.M. Fridays. So? So he'd gone along building up this beautiful story about how the Kingmans had committed the murder beginning at about seven-thirty and ending after midnight on a Friday night. When, by their never-enough-to-be-cursed schedule, they were expected to be at the Temple. And it appeared that was just exactly where they had been on Friday the thirtieth. Because Mr. Martin Kingman wasn't the hypnotist to get twelve members of his flock to swear to a lie on his behalf.

". . . *And* Mr. Lester J. Derwent," concluded Kingman, and looked up from the list in his hand. "I hope that's satisfactory, Lieutenant? I cannot help feeling you are wasting time here, on ourselves—but I repeat, of *course* we are willing and eager to help you however we can, we have no secrets, indeed your search warrant was quite unnecessary. I'm sure I speak for my wife too in saying that you would have been welcome to search anywhere without it."

"Oh, of *course*," she agreed immediately, using her eye-widening trick on him. "Anything that will help in this dreadful thing, though I *do* agree that it's a waste of time to suspect *us*. We thought the world of Brooke—"

Of course, of course. One of these twelve people (those who had progressed to some higher Temple rank and were admitted to that particular ritual) was a respected stockbroker—another was a wealthy art patron whose name appeared frequently on the social pages. And there were, in any case, definitely no flies on Kingman, when he sat there so confidently welcoming the cops to pry into his cupboards, the cupboards would be bare.

Mendoza looked at them with a dislike he concealed with difficulty. At paunchy, respectable, plum-voiced Kingman, bald head shining with honesty, as it were; at Madame Cara gracefully arranged on her couch, draperies trailing, silver-nailed hands gesturing, looking rather like an earnest horse. Damned the pair of them.

And he was going senile. Now he was wishing they didn't have all that suggestive evidence to say it had been that Friday night. Not that it would make any difference; the Kingmans couldn't have done it on Saturday night either, on account of their damned Sabbath ritual.

They sat there beaming innocence and integrity at him, this pair of slick fraud artists, and he shut his teeth on some impolite remarks. "Thanks very much," he said. "It's more or less a formality, you know —we have to look everywhere."

"Oh, yes, I see that," said Kingman. "You can't be sure, of course, until you do. Yours must be an interesting job, Lieutenant. Of course you can regard these sad affairs—um—impersonally. I fear we who are involved in them cannot. I still find it quite incredible that the poor boy —ah, well, we must not take up your time with irrelevancies."

"By the way, another little matter, while I'm here. Do both of you have drivers' licenses?"

"Dear *me,* how mysterious," exclaimed Madame Cara. "What can that possibly have to do with—? As a matter of *fact,* no, Lieutenant, we don't. Poor Martin has some visual defect, they never would—"

"Er—technically I believe it is called 'tunnel vision,'" said Kingman seriously, adjusting his glasses. "In our home state, it prevented me from obtaining a license, and I have never, consequently, learned to operate a car."

"I see." That could be checked; but it would without a doubt prove true. And there was the answer, the reason the woman had had to dispose of the Porsche alone. And what the hell good was it to him when they had an alibi for that night?

"I am *afraid* I'm not a very good driver," said Madame Cara with a sudden nervous giggle. "The traffic quite terrifies me. But one must have faith to *accept*—it's a little exercise I practise *every* time I get into the car—whatsoever the great All-Parent *intends,* I say to myself, I must not fear or rebel against. It's really a great pity that Martin can't drive, I'm sure he would be *much* more competent than I am—being an Earth person, you know—he is a Virgoan—of course it's *not* to be wondered at that an Air person like myself isn't good at dealing with these *mechanical* things. I expect you find that true yourself as a Piscean, Lieutenant—a Water sign, of course you are governed by Neptune—"

"My dear," said her husband gently, "we must not—um—proselytize at the lieutenant. I fear he is not much in sympathy with our views."

"Oh, do forgive me," she picked up the cue at once. "Nothing must be forced—understanding must come of *itself,* when the spirit is open to receive."

Mendoza eyed her with exasperation and asked (in the rather vague hope of frightening them a little with how much he knew) whether she had ever possessed a light-colored coat with dark trimming down the front and dark cuffs. He did not, of course, have any hope at all that his men had found such a thing in her wardrobe.

No, she could not remember ever having a coat like that and certainly had none now; it sounded *quite* attractive, very smart.

Mendoza thanked them, listened again to reassurances that they were *eager* to help however possible, and came away. Downstairs, Piggott and Landers were just finishing an expert going-over of the Temple; nothing of any interest had showed up. No weapons, no incriminating documents, nothing unusual among personal possessions or down here: that is, said Piggott disapprovingly, if you didn't count all the funny-looking robes and them heathen statues standing around. Looking downright wicked to him—Piggott was a pillar of the Free Methodist

Church—would it be, he asked (dropping his tone discreetly) one of these *cults*, like, where they had *orgies?*

Mendoza said he doubted it, unfortunately, or they might be able to turn the damned pair over to Vice. He sent the men back to headquarters, and most unusual for him sought out a bar and had a drink before going back downtown himself.

There he met Hackett, and confessed his sins with bad grace. Hackett looked gloomier than ever, and passed on the gist of what Morris had said. He was going to take a couple of men and set out on a hunt for all these show people, in the hope that one of them would remember something more about the gun: Morris had said he had to come into town late this afternoon, he'd stop by and take a look at it.

Nothing had come in from Pennsylvania. "What the hell are they doing back there," said Mendoza irritably, "pawing through all their records by hand? Damn it, and what good will it be if they hand us our motive? You know, I do wonder why Twelvetrees was so set up that Wednesday night?"

"Does it matter?" asked Hackett.

"It might. It might tie in somewhere." He wondered harder about it an hour later. Hackett took off on his hunt, and Mendoza annoyed Sergeant Lake by wandering around the sergeants' office and the anteroom, asking every three minutes whether Pennsylvania had communicated. The patient recheck with all those agencies hadn't turned up a smell of Marian Marner. Then, about four o'clock, a trio of nervous men came in together and said they had something to say about this guy who'd been buried under a house, and who should they say it to?

They were, it appeared, respectively, the owner, cashier, and waiter of a small restaurant on La Brea Avenue, and what they had to say was that Brooke Twelvetrees had been in the place about five o'clock on that Friday afternoon. It wasn't the first time he'd been in; he wasn't a regular, but every now and then he came in early like that, and once when he'd been talking with Charlie here—that was the waiter—he'd happened to mention that it wasn't far from his doctor's office, so maybe it was the days he saw this doctor he stopped in at the restaurant.

And, deduced Mendoza, the times he wasn't going out with anyone later; by these men, the restaurant would be the kind of place without much tone, a cheap place Twelvetrees would go to alone to pick up a casual meal.

Well, early like that, there weren't many other customers, and this guy did a little talking to the waiter and cashier. They'd gathered he was hoping to get in the movies, and he sure had the looks for it, didn't he? That Friday, he'd come in (some confused, anxious calculations of time here) about ten to five, and left about half past. Charlie, specifically asked about his order, came up with nothing more definite than that it *might* have been beef stew and so on. They could try to pin it down by the waiter's checks, but of course the name wouldn't be there, it would be a question of the time the check was filed, and not definite. Anyway, both the waiter and cashier got the impression the guy wasn't feeling so hot—like he'd, oh, just lost his job or got slapped down by his girl or something. He was usually kind of friendly and cheerful, but that time he hadn't much to say. And when the cashier had remarked it sure was good to see all this rain, they needed it bad and he'd bet the farmers were celebrating today, well, the guy had said —with various profane adjectives—that it was nice *somebody* was happy. And he'd paid his check and walked out.

And it was always nice to have additional information, but Mendoza wished he had some idea of what this meant. It might be quite unimportant as far as the murder was concerned. But it looked as if something had happened to spoil some hopeful plan the man had had. On Wednesday night he was on top of the world, hinting mysteriously at surprises; on Friday he was in a bad temper, and packing up to clear out.

Mendoza swore to himself, called the Kingmans, and put the question. After fractional hesitation, he thought, Kingman said, really, the exchange he'd had with Twelvetrees that Friday afternoon had been so casual, he couldn't say what mood the boy had been in. Mendoza was slightly encouraged to detect this as a lie; but what did *that* mean, why should Kingman lie about it?

About then, Dwyer, who'd been out seeing various people, came in and said that if it meant anything, it looked like those Kingmans had been on the hunt for Twelvetrees as early as that Saturday morning. Four people so far, Miss Webster among them, had said that Mr. Kingman had phoned them that morning asking if they'd seen Twelvetrees or knew where he was. Giving as excuse some unspecified business suddenly arisen.

"*Oyé, para qué?*" said Mendoza vexedly. "What's the use—this I don't see head or tail of! I'm getting old, Bert. Old and decrepit."

Dwyer said sympathetically that sometimes a thing got stuck, that was all, until all of a sudden you got hold of something that explained the whole thing. Mendoza said morosely that when and if it came along probably somebody would have to point it out to him, the elementary mistakes he'd been making—premature senility, without a doubt. He told Dwyer about Morris coming in to see the gun, left a note on the sergeant's desk of a few places where he might be between now and midnight, added an injunction to call him *immediatamente* if anything came in from Pennsylvania, took up his hat, and left the office.

He walked into Alison's apartment at seven o'clock and found her contemplating a small canvas propped on an easel in front of the window. She operated a moderately successful charm school through the week, in her spare time was a painter—and a ruthlessly self-critical one. She said now despondently, "I've missed it—it's no good at all, is it? Looks like a postcard."

Mendoza looked briefly at a pleasant, if undistinguished, painted view over the immediate rooftops, and said it looked all right to him. "All *right!*" said Alison crossly. "I don't know what you mean by that! It's hopeless, that's all."

"*Claro qué si,* it's hopeless. *Ambos tu y yo mismo,* you and me both. Stop worrying over that, come and soothe me. I need soothing like the very devil. I need to have my hand held by a sympathetic female and be told what a big strong smart masterful fellow I really am. I might even find it helpful to lie down quiet with my head in your lap, of all ridiculous conventional poses, and listen to the same theme at infinite length."

"*Pobrecito, qué paso?*" asked Alison, sufficiently alarmed by this unprecedented behavior to forget her art. "Come and sit down, tell Mother who's been mean to you."

He pulled her down beside him on the couch. "That's the damned awful thing, *mi vida,* it's nobody else but me—I've been a stupid, thickheaded, imbecilic dunce. I don't know any more of importance about this thing than I did before we found the corpse—and because I *am*—tell me, tell me!—because I *am* a brilliant and gifted detective, quite unused to failure, I'm out of sorts with myself."

"You are," said Alison obediently, "a brilliant and gifted detective, *un macho muy valoroso, un hombre intelligente, y agraciado, y amiable, y de aspecto bravo y bello, y attractivo, y importante, y—y encantador, y concienzudo, y—y elegante, y honorable, y un jefe muy justamente, y—y—y magnánimo, y absolutamente un caballero muy satisfactorio y maravilloso.* Do you feel any better now?"

"A little, a little. This I like to hear. So I am, I know—"

"*Y un egotiste!*" said Alison.

"That I know too." The kitten Sheba, who resembled her mother in being brown, sleek, and affectionate, leaped up beside him, walked onto his stomach, and settled down to purr as he stroked her. "Ah, I do begin to feel better—I am being duly appreciated. . . . Even I think my mind begins to work with its usual acuteness. . . . Damn it, I can still be right! Friday night—Friday night. That ritual or whatever it is, it was over at nine. All right. Say they got away by a quarter or twenty past, they *could* be out at 267th by ten o'clock. I'd give myself an hour at least, that drive, but they could have done it."

"Undoubtedly," said Alison.

"You know nothing about it, *silencio.*"

"I'm only soothing you. Whatever you say is so must be so, *naturalmente.*"

"*Muy bien,* soothe me in silence." He slid down comfortably, cradling the kitten, stretched out and put his head in her lap. "They could have. Now, Bainbridge says two to six hours before death for that beef stew and so on. Seven to eleven. That's all right, that can fit. Say he's raised his demands, and—of course, *claro está!*—because whatever plan he was counting on that Wednesday had fallen through. Yes. They want to see him. They chase right out there after their damned service, and get there about ten, say even ten-thirty. And—and there's an argument. But, a fight? This namby-pamby blackmailer and a smooth con man? Why? Can we say maybe Twelvetrees insulted Mrs. Kingman, and Kingman was protecting her honor?"

"*Oyé, la drama magnífico!*" said Alison. "Next week *East Lynne.*"

"*Chitón,* I'm thinking! Well, anyway, there's a struggle, Kingman snatches up the gun lying there on the bureau—Twelvetrees' gun—and hits him a little too hard. O.K. Then, just as I built it up before—the dither, the inspiration of the trap, etcetera. Only Bartlett had nothing to do with it, it all happened at least an hour after he'd been killed—that was the kids after all. And because Kingman doesn't drive, the woman went off to do that part of it while he buried the body and so on. It'd have taken that long easily, the time it took her to drive in with the Porsche—after they'd made the plan, too—that took some time—to put her on the spot to be the lady in the serape."

The kitten got up, stretched, yawned to show him a pink mouth and needle-sharp white teeth, turned around and settled down again. "*Perfecto!*" said Alison. "*Obvio,* that's how it was."

"You are no help whatever," said Mendoza. "And this is a most uncomfortable position, regardless of all the movies and the award-winning photographs of couples in parks. If it wasn't for disturbing the cat, I'd move. . . . Obviously it is *not* how it was—not exactly, anyway. I can see them finding the trap by accident, or just possibly Twelvetrees had called their attention to it on some former visit. As confidence workers, they're used to making slick plans on the spur of the moment. But how the hell did they know where to find that trowel? They—" He stopped abruptly.

"These are the people from that Temple? Well, she's psychic, isn't she? She divined it."

"*Aguarda, un momento! Si, como no? Yo caigo en ello!*—yes, of course, of course!" He swung his legs off the couch and stood up abruptly, holding the kitten. "Why didn't I see that before? I tell you, I'm going senile!"

"But you get it now, or so you just said. Better late than never. You've solved the whole case—*and* under my helpful feminine soothing."

"Well, not exactly. But look. Is it likely—I ask you—that this brash young fellow with his movie ambitions, his record as a pimp's apprentice—a city man, an apartment liver—is it likely that he was remotely interested in gardening? Not by any stretch of the imagination! Then why did he go to the trouble of convincing Mrs. Bragg he was, buying that plant food for her damned Tree of Heaven and so forth? Why else? —because it gave him an excuse for fooling around it, and probably when he undertook the care of the thing she wouldn't bother with it any more. I'll bet on any odds you name that was his safety deposit box. I'll swear it, he had something concrete on them—and he wouldn't leave it tucked in the toe of a shoe or in a drawer, he wouldn't carry it on him —not that cautious, canny, ladylike boy—to be stolen so easy or maybe involve him in a roughhouse, not that one! He found a safe place to stash it away, where nobody would think of looking—buried with that Tree of Heaven—and he'd just brought the trowel from Mrs. Bragg's carport to dig it up with, to take with him, and that's why the trowel was there in his kitchen. And—"

The phone rang and Alison went to answer it. The kitten scrambled up on his shoulder and began to lick his ear thoughtfully. "For you," said Alison.

Mendoza took the receiver, listened, began to smile, and finally fired rapid orders. "Get hold of Hackett—oh, beautiful, beautiful, just how

I'd figured it!—who's in the office? O.K., I want Boyce, one man'll be enough, and a blank warrant—jump to it! I'll be there in twenty minutes, I want it waiting! I felt all along that was the answer— Tell Hackett to step on it. I'll meet him at the Temple in forty-five minutes. . . . O.K., thanks, get busy!" He slammed the phone down, handed the kitten to Alison, kissed her, and snatched up his hat. "I'm vindicated—not so senile after all! Pennsylvania has come through and I think we'll tie up this case tonight—*se buena, hasta más ver*," and he was gone.

"Well," said Alison, and returned to dissatisfied inspection of the canvas.

What Pennsylvania—specifically, the Chief of Police of Philadelphia —said was that the prints of the corpse identified him in their records as one Robert Trask, particulars as follows—etcetera. Nothing of Trask's antecedents were known beyond the fact that he had come from some place in New England, to the detriment of Philadelphia, some twelve years back. He had been mixed up in various unsavory businesses, but had been charged and convicted only once, seven years ago—contributing to delinquency of minors, a year's sentence.

After he got out, he had been on the scene for a couple of years, and twice private citizens had lodged complaints of attempted extortion on him, but he had managed to wriggle out of the legal net. He had then disappeared, and Philadelphia was interested to learn what had subsequently happened to him.

As for the description appended of a middle-aged couple calling themselves Kingman, it was of course impossible to say definitely without fingerprints to check, but it was likely that they were the same pair known to Philadelphia as Martin and Caroline Sellers. The Sellers had been charged with fraud on a private complaint in the same year that Robert Trask had been put inside, but had got off on some technicality with the aid of a smart lawyer; the case had attracted some local publicity. They had held private séances with all the trappings, Mrs. Sellers being the medium, and been detected in fraud by a local officer of the Society for Psychical Research. Investigation of their background at the time (by the Society, not the police) had turned up the fact that they had at one time been in show business with a mind-reading act, billed as The Telepathic Turners. Turner appeared to be the legal name. Two years previously they had been charged and convicted of fraud—on the same count as the Philadelphia arrest, fake séances—in

Chicago, were fined, and had served a year apiece inside. If Los Angeles could oblige with prints of these Kingmans, Philadelphia could say definitely whether they were the Sellers-Turners; but as the latter had disappeared from the scene so far as the police knew about five years back, it was a matter of small doubt.

"We'll send prints," said Mendoza to Hackett happily, "but it does look like a foregone conclusion. So there's our motive—and I wonder, considering that they were tried the same year Twelvetrees-Trask was, I wonder if that's where he met them. Or saw and remembered them. In a courtroom corridor, somewhere like that. And it's also nice to know that he'd apparently settled on gentlemanly blackmail as an easier racket than what he'd been in—you see how the pattern worked out with Whalen."

"Yes, he couldn't leave it alone." They had just joined forces outside the Temple. "You're going to spring it on them straight?"

"Might just give them enough of a jolt to come out with something damaging, yes."

Boyce asked if there was likely to be a roughhouse about the arrest. "*Nada,* they're con artists, grifters—never any trouble with that kind."

The entrance to the place was dark, only the discreet sign lighted, and the door locked; but there was a bell push. They waited, and presently a light went on and beyond the glass-paneled double doors Kingman could be seen approaching unhurriedly, neat and respectable in his navy suit and immaculate white shirt, the light shining on his rimless glasses. He looked like a verger about to welcome the congregation. He swung back the right-hand door, and there they were, close, crowding in; he took a couple of steps back, but his genial expression didn't alter. "Why, Lieutenant Mendoza—good evening, sir—"

"Good evening, Mr. Turner," said Mendoza, grinning amiably at him. "Let's go upstairs and include Mrs. Turner in this little get-together, shall we? And no fair communicating telepathically on the way! My friends and I think it's about time for you to start telling us the truth—about various things, but mainly about your dealings with the late Mr. Robert Trask, and just how you came to murder the poor fellow."

Kingman took another step back. His round ruddy face lost some of its color. He said dispiritedly, "Oh, hell. Hell *and* damnation."

THIRTEEN

"Oh, *dear*," said Cara Kingman. "Well, I suppose you'd better come in. I was afraid they would find out, Martin, you know I said at the time, let it go and be thankful it was only the twenty-three hundred. You see what's come of it, not that I'd dream of reproaching you, dear, you only did what you thought best." She looked at Mendoza resignedly.

Kingman put an arm around her. "Now don't you be frightened, Cara, but it's a bit more than that, they think we did it, you see. I—"

"*Murdered* him? Oh, Martin! Well—well, we'd just better tell them the *truth*—"

"I'd advise it," said Mendoza, sitting down. "And not the kind of truth you've seen in a crystal ball, Mrs. Turner. Of course there's quite a lot you don't have to tell us. I know that Trask was blackmailing you, and what he had—that last business in Philadelphia. Your present little flock wouldn't like hearing about that, and how well you knew it. A spotless reputation is the chief thing in your business, and it annoyed you considerably when Trask showed up. You had to play ball with him, but that five hundred a month was quite a bite out of your take—"

Kingman said gloomily, "You couldn't speak a truer word."

"It was *wicked*," said his wife. "After all the bad luck we'd had, it's not a very steady living after all—those awful night clubs and so on— horrible places most of them, but I shouldn't be uncharitable, perhaps all this liquor does serve some purpose of *destiny*. But when everything was going so *well,* and we'd quite settled down— We're neither of us getting any younger, you know, Lieutenant, and we must try to save toward our old age, and besides it's been so *nice* here, so peaceful, we'd quite felt we were *settled for good* until that *wicked* young man came. He was, truly. Going to all the trouble of sending back East for that copy of the *Telegraph*—the one where the trial was reported, you know, and our pictures in it too, *quite* good ones, I'm sorry to say— and he had it, what do I mean, Martin, photo—?"

"Photostated," sighed Kingman. They sat side by side on the couch, holding hands, looking at the police solemnly; a little of Kingman's precise manner dropped away, but not much—he'd played his part for so many years, he'd grown into it. "Oh, it was awkward, I can't deny it. In a way, the most annoying thing about it was that, well, it wasn't as if we'd been convicted of any wrongdoing—"

"However, you had been before—in Chicago," said Mendoza, and mentioned the year.

"That *terrible* jail," said Madame Cara, and closed her eyes.

"Now wait just a minute here," said Kingman fussily, adjusting his glasses. *"Wait* a minute. (Don't fret, my dear.) I do *not* think of myself as a—a confidence man, Lieutenant, *nor* do I hold any sort of grudge against the police for doing their duty. That unfortunate affair in Chicago was due to a misunderstanding on my part regarding Illinois law. We have always made an earnest effort to see that we conform to the law—it's only common sense, after all. When you come down to it, Lieutenant, we are only selling a service the public wants and is eager to buy. And I confess I do not see the difference between presenting an —ah—act to amuse an audience, and doing essentially the same thing without the footlights."

"I always *hated* all the traveling about," said his wife. She looked about the room sadly. "This is such a nice place, and I did think we were settled down at last. But—but it doesn't really matter, Martin dear, we'll get along as well somewhere else, I daresay, the main thing is to explain to them that *of course* we didn't *kill* him. Why, I'm sure such an idea never entered our heads, even when he was being *horridest*. Really, Lieutenant Mendoza, we're not that kind of people."

"Boyce, close your mouth," said Mendoza *sotto voce,* "and try to look more dignified. Now to go on a step further—we'll hear your side of it in a moment—the annoying Mr. Trask had recently increased his demands, hadn't he? He was asking too much, and it decided you not to be bullied any longer. You had had a few words with him that Friday afternoon, and far from not being sure what mood he was in, you knew he was feeling ugly. A little side racket he'd been planning had fallen through—" He paused, ostensibly to light a cigarette, watching Kingman: did he know what the side racket had been?—but the other man only nodded glumly. "You had a show to put on here at eight, you couldn't chase after him then, but as soon as you could get away, you drove out to his apartment. You got there about a quarter past ten—"

"I remember noticing," said the woman, "it was *exactly* a quarter past by my watch as we drove into that—that court. Oh, please don't hesitate to use that ashtray, Lieutenant, that's what it's *for*. Really, for the time of night and the traffic—so nerve-wracking—we made excellent time. You see, Martin, how very clever they are to find all this out."

"My dear, you needn't say *I told you so*."

"But I never *would*. I do believe in destiny, so it's no use. Do you know, Lieutenant, we'll have been married thirty-one years on the twentieth of this month, and never *any* serious disagreement between us. I put it down chiefly to the fact that we *do* always remember to be polite to each other, although it is true that Martin is a very even-tempered man."

Mendoza grasped grimly at the tail of his last remark. "There was a quarrel, and you hit Trask—with the butt of a pistol which—"

"Now wait *just* a minute, please, sir," said Kingman. He leaned forward with a kind of desperate earnestness. "I don't know exactly how we're going to prove it to you, because naturally there were no witnesses present. And I must say I do understand how you came to pick on us, though how you found out we were there that night I don't know. But I do assure you that you have—um—leaped to a wrong conclusion when you accuse me of killing that—that *most* unpleasant young man. I hope to *God* I can convince you, sir, that we hadn't any hand in the murder. Never had such a shock in my life as when you turned up and told us—" He whisked out a handkerchief and polished his bald head. "Now suppose I just tell you the whole business straight, so to speak, and if I miss out anything you want to know, you ask, because I don't know all the ins and outs of the—um—circumstances of the murder. You've got it right up to that night, sir. Trask . . . Perhaps I had better explain that that time in Philadelphia he was being held for trial, on a very nasty low charge too, at the same time I was, and that's how he knew me, and knew to send back for that newspaper report. And it wasn't only the money that made the situation awkward and annoying —it was having him around. Any day we'd both have preferred to pay over the money as straight extortion, and never seen him between, but you see, he wanted an open job, as an excuse for not working. I didn't like it, I never liked it, but what could I do? And besides keeping an eye on him, you know, I had what you might call a handle, too. You'll never know how both of us hoped he would make the grade and get into the profession—though he'd nothing to offer but looks, as an old trouper myself I knew *that,* but still, *Hollywood* . . . If he only had, perhaps he'd have gone to looking on us as very small stuff, you see, and left us alone—"

"And also you could then turn the tables and threaten him with his past," said Mendoza. "If he acquired a public reputation to be put in danger."

"Good God, no," said Kingman, genuinely shocked. "God forbid that we should stoop so low as *that*. I tell you, we'd have gone on our knees to give thanks if he'd just left us alone! Well, you're not interested in all this background, I'd better—ah—cut the cackle as our English friends say, and come to that Friday. You said a minute ago that he'd had some plan go wrong, well, I couldn't tell you what that was, but I *did* deduce that for myself, from his manner. Now it's quite true, what I told you, that we exchanged only a few words as I met him leaving. But—um—what actually passed was not exactly casual. He—"

"Demanded that you raise the ante."

"Well, no," said Kingman. "Actually, no. He was simply in a vicious temper. He put on a good front, you know—that charming boyish manner—but only with people who mattered, people he thought could do him some good. He never troubled with us. But that day he—er—lashed out at me, at the Temple—sneeringly, you know—more viciously than he'd ever done before. However, it wasn't until just before the—the ceremony that night that I became seriously disturbed. I must explain that I—oh dear, and possibly I should have mentioned it to you when you searched this afternoon, I do apologize—I have a small wall safe built into the robing room downstairs, where the—um—receipts are kept. Now, Trask did *not* have the combination of this safe, and I can only assume that he must have visited the apartment when we were out, perhaps several times, and hunted until he found the notation in my address book. I should have carried it on me—I have such a bad memory for figures—it was careless—"

"Now you mustn't blame yourself, dear, it might have happened to *anyone*."

"I do not very often have occasion to go to the safe, that is to take *out* cash, over a weekend. Naturally, after the service on Saturday night I put the collection into the safe, but I seldom look at what's there or count it. But *as* it happened, I did have occasion to do so on that Friday night—Cara was going shopping the next morning, and I went to get out some money for her, just before the service. There is no collection for that Friday night service, you see. And I knew there should have been twenty-three hundred dollars in one of the velvet collection bags. You know,"—he took off his glasses, began to polish them slowly with his handkerchief—"on thinking it over since, I can see that he took a gamble on that. In the ordinary way, on Saturday evening I should have simply dropped the collection into that bag and locked it away again—a bag isn't like an envelope, I wouldn't see that it was nearly empty beforehand. He had left some one-dollar bills and a lot of silver, enough to look to the casual glance as if the bag hadn't been touched. You see? If all had gone as he planned, the deficit wouldn't have been discovered, probably, until some time on Monday—when I'd be going to the bank to deposit the month's receipts. But I discovered it then, at seven-thirty that Friday night."

"Yes, I've grasped that," said Mendoza in a bored tone. "So you went out after the service to ask him how come."

"Now I'll tell you," said Kingman, "I may be a fool this way and that way, Lieutenant, but I was not fool enough to think that Trask would walk off with a month's receipts like that if he intended to carry on in the current situation. The moment I made that discovery, I knew he was clearing out for some reason. And I was *thankful*—I tell you!—and if it had been *merely* the twenty-three hundred, I'd have said good riddance, cheap at the price."

"*Which* was what I said, dear, though I *did* follow the thought in your mind. He really had *no* scruples at all."

"But, well, just put yourself in my position, if you can, Lieutenant. Knowing Trask, I thought it very likely indeed that he would not be satisfied with that amount, but would attempt to withdraw more from the bank on Monday morning—before I had discovered what he'd already done, you see. I don't know why he should have stolen that cash on Friday when—if he did intend to withdraw more—he couldn't very well have planned his—his flight until Monday. When I came to reason it out, it occurred to me that *possibly* someone was in a position to blackmail *him,* and he *had* to have that cash on Friday. That he meant to abandon his—ah—racket here, in the face of that blackmail, and stole the cash to satisfy his enemy over the weekend, trusting to luck that I shouldn't discover it—and then on the Monday meant to take what he could from the bank, you see. However, there it was, and the reason I was anxious to contact him was to inform him in no uncertain terms that I knew of the theft, and would take steps immediately to warn the bank not to allow him to make any withdrawals. *That* I didn't want—well, naturally not—but it wasn't only the money—I couldn't very well prosecute him for it, could I? Everything coming out in the open then. I tried at once to telephone him, but got no answer—of course it was early. I tried again after the service, with the same result. So—"

"So you drove out. Very well. And when you got there, you found him packing—"

"It was quite *mysterious*," said the woman plaintively, "and I *hated* it —I felt there was something queer about it then. There was no one there at all, Lieutenant. I do hope," her voice quivered a little, "you will *believe* the truth, I do see as Martin says it's only our *word*. But it *is* the truth. The front door to his apartment was unlocked, after we'd knocked and knocked Martin tried it and the door opened. We knew he was there because there was a light—not in the living room, but the bedroom—you could see it from that silly little front porch. So we went in, and *no one* was there at all. Yes, you're quite right, he had *been* packing—there were two suitcases all packed and locked, and another on the bed half full of things—and things standing on the bureau, all untidy, he'd never have left it like that; he was almost *too* finicky for a man, you know. And the light on. The kitchen light too. We couldn't see that until we'd gone in, of course. And *no one* there."

"That's gospel truth, gentlemen," said Kingman earnestly. "I can't lie to you that I'm a religious man, but I swear by—by everything that's dear to me, that's the *gospel* truth."

Mendoza had been leaning back in a bored way, smoking, impassive; Boyce sitting stolid and foursquare, just waiting; Hackett listening and looking intently. Their noncommittal silence worried Kingman, who had grown progressively more ruddy and earnest. Now suddenly Mendoza sat up and fixed him with a frowning stare.

"The kitchen light was on?" he said. "Was that trap open?"

"*God,* no," said Kingman with a shudder. "And if I didn't have the cold grues about *that,* when I read in the paper how he'd been— disposed of! It occurred to me then that, my God, whoever it was might have—must have—been down there *with him*—when we walked in." Now he lost all of his ruddiness, and mopped his bald head. "He—they —whoever it was, would have had warning—we knocked and waited, you know. If—if there was a way to close that trap from below . . . well, you take me. Must have been down there in the dark—with *him* —waiting for us to leave. God. No, of course we didn't dream, at the time . . . There were all his things, you could see he was getting ready to clear out, and—I don't know—it looked queer, but as if he might have just run out to get something, you know—some errand. I—"

"Did you go into the kitchen? . . . Where was the table?"

"I remember that, dear. It was an impossible kitchen—but of course a man wouldn't care—far too small, and there was only *one* little place for a table, at the very end—but it wasn't there. It was pushed right up against the stove, a very awkward position."

"Did you see a trowel?" asked Mendoza softly. Hackett turned and looked at him. Nothing about the trowel had been released to the press.

They both stared at him. "A *trowel?*" said Kingman; and then he lost what remained of his color. "Oh, my God, is that what he was—what they used—? No—no, I don't remember anything like that. We—well, you know, we didn't know quite what to do. It looked as if he'd be back any minute, and we waited around a little." He mopped his brow.

"You have so much imagination, Martin—not that *I* wasn't a little upset about it too, when we *knew*. But it's all over now, dear, we must simply try to tell them how it was—the *facts.*"

"How long did you wait?"

"Oh, it was quite some time before we decided that he wasn't—and of course then we did think it even *odder,* that he should just walk out like that—and then we thought of looking to see whether his *car* was there. And it was. In the carport. And there was another one too, that is I don't know if it had anything to do with all this, but you see, I opened the back door and looked out—I don't know why, it was the silly sort of thing you *do* when you're looking for someone. And there was a car there. There's quite a wide alley behind that building, you know, and an empty lot behind *that*—and this car was just standing in the alley. There wasn't anyone in it, its lights weren't on or anything. I thought at the time it might be someone visiting the next apartment, maybe there hadn't been parking space in front when—— Well, and *then* Martin said——"

"Now I'll tell you," said Kingman, "I didn't especially want to *see* him. I was *thankful* he was clearing out, I simply wanted to make it clear to him that it was—um—quits between us. And I'll be honest and say too that it seemed a good opportunity to have a look around for that photostat—not that that would exactly take away his hold, because I daresay he could have replaced it, and of course the mere information —that is, anyone could have checked up, once they knew where to check, so to speak. Nevertheless, we should feel much safer—you get me. . . . I hadn't tried to do anything in that line, no sir, not up to then. I won't say I hadn't thought about it, but it didn't seem that it'd

be much use—for all I knew he had a safety deposit box or something—"

"So he did," said Mendoza. "In a manner of speaking. I know where
it was—"

"So do I, now," said Kingman unexpectedly. "I make no apology for
saying that we had a look round. And we didn't have to look far. It was
right there on the bed. I expect you found it with his things, later on.
One of those quilted plastic laundry bags—green—and he'd just
emptied it out on the bed, it looked like, to get at what was in the bottom. I don't want to—ah—sound as if I'm trying to do your job for
you, Lieutenant, but it occurs to me that perhaps when you first saw the
place, things weren't just the way they were then, and it may be you'll
be interested. First of all, there was a big brown manila envelope lying
there with that photostat in it—the newspaper report about us, you
know—and of course I took that. But I think there'd been something
else in that bag—I took it that's where the envelope had been, you see,
there it was among all his dirty clothes, as if he'd just dumped out
everything—because there was another manila envelope, empty, and he
—or someone—had burned something in a big glass ashtray on the bureau. Something fairly bulky, like—well, maybe another photostat.
There was quite a little pile of ashes."

"What was on the bureau besides?"

"Oh, dear," said Kingman, and thought. "I'll try to recall—you understand, I wasn't noticing things to *be* noticing, as it were—I'll do my
best. Let's see, there was a bottle of Scotch, I think it was—I don't
know if it was empty or full—and his wrist watch, and a folded necktie
—and, oh, yes, his hat, a gray felt hat—and a clean handkerchief—and
a couple of little medicine bottles, I think. Well, to go on, as I say I
took that photostat, and we had a look for the money but it wasn't
there, not unless it was in one of the locked suitcases. He must have
had it on him, though you haven't *said*—" He looked at them doubtfully.

Mendoza shook his head. "You find crooks everywhere, true, but we
do pride ourselves on higher standards these days."

"Oh, I *never* meant to imply—! But, odd as it seemed, you know—
the place standing empty that way, as if he'd just dropped everything
and walked out—we weren't much interested in what was behind it.
Not then. There wasn't any reason to wait about. I wrote a note to him,
on a page torn out of my address book—I don't know what happened
to that, perhaps that's how you know about us being there—telling him,

you know, not to try any tricks, and so on—and we came away." He got out his handkerchief again. "I hope to *God* you believe all this, all I can do is tell you everything. I don't know if it means anything, if it'll be a help in clearing us, but we got a traffic ticket on the way home— maybe that would confirm the time, but I don't suppose—"

"Where and what for?" asked Mendoza.

"The officer was *perfectly* right," said Madame Cara. "I do find it one of the most *awkward* things in traffic, changing lanes. But it's like everything else in life—one must seize the opportunity. And while the road was *quite* clear (I *never* take chances, for one must think of other people, you know, if not oneself) it seems it wasn't allowed right there. The officer was really very nice about it, and it was a small fine. I went right down to the traffic court next morning. It was six dollars, five for the ticket and one for education—this new system you know and a *splendid* idea, we can't grudge anything for the children."

"My dear, the place—I don't recall—"

"Oh, of course, it was on Avalon Boulevard, Lieutenant, not very long after we'd left the apartment, I don't know *exactly* where."

"We'll find it," said Mendoza. He looked at them in exasperation, in doubt. "I've got a warrant in my pocket for your arrest on a charge of murder—"

"Oh, *dear* God," said Kingman, "I swear to you—"

"But I'm not going to use it, until we've checked that ticket anyway. I'll be frank to say that it looks to me as if you had the best motive to do away with him, and I thought I had it worked out how you'd done it. But there are just a couple of little things . . . I'll go along with this awhile, and take you at your word. But I'd like to know why you didn't leave matters there. What took you to the bank on Monday morning?"

"Don't think we're not grateful," said Kingman almost tearfully. "Thanks very much, sir, for listening with an open mind. . . . It's a sobering thought that if I hadn't—I should have left the whole thing go, I know that now. But the more I thought about it, the odder it seemed —his being gone, like that—and I thought quite possibly he might not have found my note. Even if he came back. Well, of course I expected he *had* come back, for all his things. But in the event that he didn't see the note—I felt I'd been a coward in a way, I should have seen him and made sure. I tried to locate him that Saturday morning, but nobody had seen him, and there was no answer at his apartment. In one way that relieved my mind, I thought he'd come back, finished packing and left

—but we didn't *know,* you see. I was still worrying that he might try to get something out of the bank—"

"He had absolutely *no* scruples," said the woman. Her large plaintive eyes swerved unblinking to Mendoza. "We *are* grateful, Lieutenant, for your kindness. . . . After *so* much trouble and upset and worry, it didn't seem fair. Such an unpleasant young man. But, you know, it really is very strange, they say there is *some* good in everyone, and there was, I daresay, a *very* little, in him. . . . I was so surprised—do you know, he liked flowers. He liked to grow things. Perhaps he came of a long line of farmers, or something. He was quite enthusiastic over the landscaping around the Temple, just that little bit of fern or whatever it is, in built-up boxes, I expect you noticed it—he even brought a little garden fork one day and poked around at them because the earth was too dry, he said. Really very odd. But then people *are.*"

"—*And,*" said Kingman, "more especially I worried about it, because he'd have discovered by then that I had been at his place and taken the photostat—he might try to clear out the bank account in revenge, you see. Well, we worried around it all that weekend, and on Monday morning when I knew there'd be someone at the bank—before opening time, that is—I called. All I meant to do was to ask them not to let him make any withdrawals, because he had—um—severed connections with us. I was very stupid about the whole thing, Heaven knows I should have known better, but what with worrying and not being able to sleep—you see, I got hold of the assistant manager, and I had to give *some* reason for calling to warn them—after all, just because a man resigns or is fired from his job, it isn't any reason to suspect him of larceny—and before I knew it, he'd got out of me that Trask had gone off with that cash. And as soon as he heard that—Mr. Rowell, I mean—he got excited and said of course I'd be seeing the police to lay an official charge, and perhaps he'd better go with me because it would save time if he could give the police the man's official signature and the recent records and so on—"

"I see," Mendoza said amusedly. "You couldn't get out of it?"

"It was like a nightmare from start to finish. I never intended to do such a thing, but of course it would have looked queer after that if I hadn't. What I was afraid of, you know, was that Trask *would* be caught up with—or even if he'd seen it in the papers, that I'd accused him—why, he might have told all he knew about us just to get even. It was a terrible position. I had to seem as if I was giving the police all the help I could, and at the same time I held back what I felt was *possible* to, because, my God, I wasn't anxious for them to find him, wherever he'd gone and why. I said I wasn't sure where he lived because, you know, he might have mentioned to someone there where he was going —and no one could prove we did know, I tore that page out of my address-book—and I was sure no one had seen us there on Friday night. And then, as soon as we'd—er—got that on record, so to speak, I wondered if the police would somehow find out anyway, and look for fingerprints there—and whether we'd left any—"

"I was wearing gloves. I always do when I drive and it was cold that night, I didn't take them off at all. And as I told you at the time, Martin, I don't believe you would have left any either, because we just *looked* mostly, didn't we?—not touching anything. You see, there wasn't any need to open drawers and so on, Lieutenant, there *was* this photo-thing right on the bed—we burned that as soon as we got home —and when it came to looking for the money, well, all the drawers were wide open and empty, because he'd been taking things out to pack, you know. We just felt all through the things in the open suitcase, and they were clothes, they wouldn't take prints, would they? Martin *did* try the other cases to see if they were locked, and they were. So—"

"And then," said Kingman with a strong shudder, "when you came and told us he'd been *murdered*—! And in such a way . . . I did some more worrying about it then, I can tell you—"

Mendoza got up, looking at them thoughtfully. "Yes, well, we'll leave it this way for the time being. I needn't caution you not to leave town and so on—you'll be familiar with the—mmh—ritual, shall I say?"

"Believe me, Lieutenant, we're grateful—that you believe, I mean—"

"Oh, I never said I believed you," said Mendoza gently, smiling at them. "Just that I'm not quite ready to use that warrant—yet. We'll see. We like to be sure about these things—I'll do a little more thinking on it."

FOURTEEN

"I have not been brilliant in this thing," he said. He lit a cigarette and in the cold clear night air the little column of smoke was frost-white.

"They're not cleared," said Hackett. They stood there on the curb in front of the Temple, between the tail of the Facel-Vega and the bumper of Hackett's humbler black sedan. Hackett had his hands in his pockets, shoulders hunched, staring down at the sidewalk.

"By implication you might say they are," said Mendoza. "That traffic ticket. I can't see a third person unknown mixed up in this with them, and we can't get away from the fact that that woman who bought the serape and took that cab ride had something to do with the murder. If she didn't kill him, she disposed of the car. And if Mrs. Kingman-Sellers-Turner *and* her husband were on Avalon Boulevard about eleven o'clock or a bit after, getting a traffic ticket, then she wasn't that woman. Without using a siren, would you guarantee to get from 267th to the old Plaza or thereabouts inside an hour—even at that time of night? Most of the signals would still be working."

Hackett didn't look up, but rocked meditatively back and forth a little. "I might. She came down kind of heavy on playing the scatter-brained woman driver, I thought."

Boyce said, "I can't say I'd like to ride very far with her, Sergeant—I mean, after just listening to her dither."

"*De veras,*" said Mendoza. "Nor me. Babes in the woods. No way to prove they'd known where Trask lived because Kingman tore that page out of his address book." He laughed. "*Ca!* No, I haven't been bright here. . . . Do I believe them? It's a story, you might say, too full of double takes and dither not to be true. This gentlemanly old trouper and his amiable scatterbrained wife . . ."

"Would you think I was crazy, Lieutenant," asked Boyce diffidently, "if I said I felt kind of sorry for them? It must be an awful hard way to earn a living."

"Yes, but look at the living!" said Hackett sardonically.

Another frosty little cloud rose around Mendoza's head. "Well, this is probably the first really big money they've made. . . . There are points in that story. Oh, yes."

"What the *hell*," said Hackett savagely, "they're slick actors, they pick up cues from each other and build a scene out of thin air, and you swallow it whole! You swallow this—this concoction as meek as be damned—like any new ranker on his first case—"

Mendoza smoked in impassive silence for a full half minute, looking at him; Hackett moved restlessly, got out his keys to play with. *"Que paso, chico?"* asked Mendoza softly.

"Damn it, nothing's the matter except that I'm fed up with this whole slippery business. We haven't got anywhere at it, and we ought to have *some* idea by this time! I—"

"Tómelo con calma, early days—we found him on Saturday, this is only Monday. We'll get there. Something on your mind?"

"Yes," said Hackett, "yes, there's something on my mind, but I'll turn it over once or twice and tell you about it in the morning. Nothing we can do tonight anyway. I'll see you at eight." He turned away abruptly and got into his car.

"What d'you suppose is eating the sergeant?" wondered Boyce.

Mendoza dropped his cigarette, put a foot on it, and pushed it carefully into the gutter. "That I couldn't say. . . . I'll drive you back to headquarters. You might get on to Traffic and locate that ticket."

He did a little wondering about the usually even-tempered Hackett on his way home, but more about the case. There were indeed a few interesting points in that story—which he was inclined to believe. Irritating, of course; but some new piece of truth—or what looked very much like it—came up and you had to change your mind, look at things another way. . . . Something else in Trask's safety deposit box. (And didn't it point up one of the elementary pitfalls for detectives, that! Rudimentary deduction according to types of people—the man couldn't have been a gardener. You couldn't know. People, they just didn't come in standardized patterns. And not a bad hiding place, either: shades of *The Purloined Letter*.) Something else of the same species as the document held over the Kingmans? Something burned in an ashtray.

He slid the car gently into the garage, let himself into the apartment, switched on all the lights. All three cats came to welcome him, and because El Señor was usually standoffish, Mendoza made a little fuss over him, encouragingly. . . . A note from Mrs. Carter, the cats last fed at four o'clock. Another note from Mrs. Bryson, which announced simply, *He's learned to open cupboards.*

"Now have you?" he said to El Señor, who had both paws round his neck and was sampling his necktie. *"Basta, ya!*—not good for cats, leave it alone! Sometimes you act like a very smart boy indeed, too smart for your own good." It was apparently true: the low cupboard doors of the record cabinet stood open, and so—uncannily—did one of the cupboards over the kitchen drainboard.

"This," said Mendoza, "is too much of a good thing altogether. Must I put locks on all the cupboard doors? Or keep all the things not intended for curious cats on the very top shelves?" He put El Señor down on a kitchen chair, went to get their evening meal from the refrigerator.

Somebody else in the same position *in re* Trask as the Kingmans. Not surprising. Somebody refusing to pay—did that account for his ugly temper that day?—but surely not a reason for him to clear out. Somebody a good deal more determined than Kingman, walking in on him and killing him. . . .

As he put down the three dishes, the phone rang. "Oh, Lieutenant Mendoza, I thought I heard you come in," said Mrs. Bryson in his ear from the other end of the building. "Did you find my note? . . . Yes, the *oddest* thing—really, you know, it sounds silly but sometimes I'm almost afraid of that absurd kitten!" Mrs. Bryson was large, buxom, fiftyish, and blonde; she had no children, and perhaps consequently a deplorable habit of cooing baby talk to her beloved cats—but one must overlook these faults in otherwise nice people. "When I came to let them out for a little run, about two o'clock, he had your record cabinet open and an L.P. record out on the floor—Bach's *Suite No. 2 in B Minor,* it was—and was sitting *looking* at it. Really quite uncanny."

"Well, at least he has good taste," said Mendoza.

"What I called about, I forgot to put down that your grandmother phoned, and you're to be reminded that her goddaughter, I think it is, is getting married on Saturday, and you're expected to come and—"

"And bring a gift," he supplied as she hesitated. "This autocratic old wretch, I know how she put it! Thanks very much, Mrs. Bryson. . . ." He had no intention of doing either. In the first place, he had not set foot inside a church for twenty-two years and had no desire to break the record; in the second, the goddaughter was an unpleasantly smug and pudding-faced girl whom he disliked.

He let the cats out and got undressed.

Somebody—somebody—from that theater crowd? Senseless to blackmail someone who hadn't any money. . . . But there were other things of value than money: someone, perhaps, who could do him a favor—introduce him to a producer, cast him in TV?

Mendoza took a bath. He let the cats in. He sat up in bed smoking, and El Señor sat on his lap and tried to catch the smoke wisps, batting at them with his large blond paws. "Señor Rídiculo," said Mendoza.

Someone—

He put out his cigarette and switched off the light. A few more facts, and maybe it would suddenly come unraveled.

One small fact came in the next morning, from the routine gathering of miscellany. About that bank: that it kept old-fashioned banking hours. And that helped quite a lot in reconstructing Trask's plans. And then Hackett came in, and abruptly handed Mendoza a wholly new idea. . . .

"And where did that idea come from?" asked Mendoza. "It's definitely a thought, but a little offbeat . . . that girl Angel. Mmh, yes. Motives, motives . . ." He looked at Hackett's back in mild curiosity. Hackett, terse and noncommittal, had put forward this theory walking around the office as he talked, and stood now looking out the window.

"I know it's one of those things that doesn't happen often—"

"It's not as odd as all that—kind of thing that has happened. But what's reached you about it? You're acting as if you were telling the tale on your sister."

"Sister be damned," said Hackett. "I know it's senseless, Luis, but I'm sorry for the girl. She hasn't had much of a break from life. That damned woman . . ." He shrugged and turned around.

Mendoza was leaning back looking cynically amused; he shot Hackett a glance from half-shut eyes. "What heresy is this, Arturo—my big dumb sergeant smitten? *Cuidado, amigo!* That's one of the beaten paths to the trap, feeling sorry for them."

"Don't be a fool—and you can keep your opinions to yourself. Just because *you* make a hobby of collecting the free samples without any intention of buying—"

"*Ay qué risa!* Where've you been hibernating, friend—since when is it free? This one I don't believe, *de veras absolutamente*—Hackett the impervious, and old enough to look after himself, God knows—Hackett the stolid—Hackett who never so far as I know, the ten years I know him, takes out the same girl three times running—and not because he's looking for free samples but because he's got a wide streak of caution, having some common sense if not quite as much as me! You don't tell me—"

"No, I don't tell you, damn it! I said I felt sorry for her and that's exactly what I meant, no more and no less. For which reason I'd also be sorry to prove that she killed a man. I'm well aware that you keep your emotions all carefully locked away in a secret compartment somewhere to take out and look at once in a long while—but if you think real hard, you may remember one or two occasions, maybe when you were a tender young rookie answering traffic calls and manhandling drunks, when you had a kind of feeling of sympathy for somebody who'd got knocked around a little through no fault of their own. I don't," said Hackett, "say you ever *did,* because about you I wouldn't be sure, but maybe there was just once you felt a little something along that line for a second, hah?"

"*Esto queda entre los dos,* only for your ear—because I wouldn't want it to get around that this thinking machine Mendoza is a real live human being—if I sat here quiet and concentrated a while I might remember a couple of those times. But I won't tell you about them, to set a bad example. I've got a reputation to maintain, you know. Everybody thinks Mendoza's always been what he is now, you drop a little problem in one slot and his month's pay in another, and click-click-click, out comes the right answer—*no es verdad?*"

"*Es verdad. Lo siento muchísimo*—sorry, boy," said Hackett tiredly. "I just—I can *see* it happening, that's all. The way she is, that girl—all tied up in knots, poor little devil, and that woman hardly knowing she's alive. I don't know, but I'd bet you she's got nobody on the face of the earth to talk it out to, to give her any little sympathy, and you know as well as I do that's damned important. If you can blow off steam to somebody, even a stranger on a bus, it's a safety valve. You talk enough, you don't do anything about it. A hate, a grievance, a—desire. And she's not the kind who'd ever have made friends, at school or later on—ever had *anybody.* All this eating at her inside, keeping her—all to herself. If you get me. She'd put people off, she'd never have reached for it. . . . She's just a—a mess, to look at. And prickly, because she's been hurt. Another thing I thought of, it's on the cards she got started acting standoffish because when she was just a youngster and that woman was still in the big-time, more or less, a lot of the kids she knew'd have pretended to like her because of who her mother was. And kids know these things. Just stiffened her up all the more, suspicious, you know, so she couldn't *trust* anybody enough to be friends. So it's all got magnified inside her, because it's stayed inside—and nobody to sympathize a little—"

"That's all very true," said Mendoza. He swiveled his desk-chair around and looked out the window himself, and for about five seconds he thought about the time when he was graduating from the sixth grade into junior high. Nobody down there that side of Main Street had much money, but every other boy in the class had some sort of new suit for that occasion, even the Los Reyes kid and Johnny Li-Chong; and his grandmother had tried to get a few dollars out of the old man; she'd gone on asking a long time after he had, himself. The old man, with all those bankbooks tucked away then (if they'd only known it), sitting on a fortune out of canny investments of his gambling takes, and grudging her the five bucks a week for groceries, the twenty a month for rent of the cold-water flat. . . . He'd been ashamed, getting up there with the rest of them in the same shabby old pants and mended shirt he'd been wearing all year. But she'd said to him afterward, how proud she'd been that he was the tallest boy there, and how Mr. Jackson the principal had told her he was a good smart boy and a credit to her. . . . And somehow the clothes hadn't mattered quite so much. Little things like that, they weren't always so little in the long run. Somebody to listen to you, somebody to share a feeling. Even if there was nothing to do about it.

He swiveled around again, absently straightening his tie, brushing a small fluff of cat hair from his sleeve. He was still of two minds about this suit—he should have looked at the bolt by daylight first, he reflected: you couldn't exactly call it loud, but the faint pattern was a good deal less discreet than he had thought. A nuisance; he'd call Harrington down for it too, the fellow ought to know better with a good customer. He said, "Well, we can kick this around a little, and I'd like to see those two, you've aroused my curiosity. But I'm wondering if and how that might fit in with a couple of suggestive little things in that story of Kingman's. Something burned in an ashtray. That laundry bag. Something else there besides the stuff on the Kingmans, and it looks as if whoever killed him was interested in it. Maybe . . . Sure, sure, *if* you take the Kingmans' story as gospel. *But*—"

"There wouldn't be anything like that with her," said Hackett doubtfully. "I don't know if I do take that story or not—it hangs together, sure. And on the face of it, it's more likely that it was somebody with that kind of motive."

Mendoza agreed. "Let's see what we've got on these people." They looked, and besides Hackett's character analysis as gleaned from Mr. Horwitz and his own observation, there wasn't much and it didn't look remotely interesting. Higgins, sent out routinely to see the old Miss Kent that Mona Ferne had visited that evening, reported everything in order: the old lady confirmed that Miss Ferne had been with her that night from about a quarter to eight until half past ten or so. Where the girl Angel had been, that they'd find out.

"It's just—bits and pieces, and it could be I'm crazy. But that first time I met her, she didn't seem interested at first in who'd been murdered, and when she heard it was Twelvetrees, she was very casual about it, who'd want to kill him and so on. And then two minutes later she was ready to go into hysterics. Keeping up a front, it could be, and not quite managing it. And then yesterday the Ferne says to me—*and* not realizing what she said, because she couldn't be less interested in the girl, you know—that 'Angel's been odd' for a week or so. It just added up in my mind, the way I say—"

Mendoza said, "Yes? Yes. . . . Girl have a car?"

"I don't know. Probably."

"She'd have money of her own. There was something said about a trust fund from the father. Not really big money, maybe, but substantial."

"I'd think so," said Hackett heavily.

"I don't know that you sell me on this, quite. But we'll have a look. No harm. Suppose we go and see them if they're home." Mendoza got up and reached for his hat.

They were home. When the sour-faced maid opened the door to Hackett and Mendoza, letting a little light into the dingy entrance hall, the first thing they heard was the girl's shaking voice, loud, from the living room: "That's a *lie*—you know it's a lie!"

Mendoza handed his hat to the maid and walked past her, ignoring her protesting query, to the doorway of that room. He looked at the pair of them interestedly, and added a few mental comments of his own to Hacketts.

Mona Ferne was elegantly slim in honey-beige and dark brown today. Evidently she'd been about to leave the house: her alligator bag, gloves, a chic little brown felt hat with a veil waited on the arm of the couch. He paid academic tribute to the finished article, while guessing far more accurately than Hackett how much time and effort had gone into it. The gleaming perfect flaxen coiffure, the figure, the face—a very expert piece of work, all of it; and from fifteen feet away, before he heard her speak or saw her move, he knew it was all just about as emotionally affective as a combustion engine. . . . The girl. Could be pretty. Alison would say, and be right, built to wear clothes—the height and the figure. Not one of the types he admired himself.

"*Darling*," said the woman, "I'm only saying—" And she saw them then in the doorway, and for the fraction of a second her eyes held an expression which surprised Mendoza very much indeed.

Vaya, qué demonio—? he said to himself.

And the girl turned to follow her glance, and looked startled—looked confused, and took a step back to bring up against the white brick hearth, and leaned there.

"Why, it's the nice police sergeant back again—*do* tell me, Sergeant Hackett, have you found whoever it was did this awful thing? Is there something else I can do for you now?—I'm only *too* anxious—" But her eyes were busy on Mendoza, recognizing him as worthier quarry. She came forward gracefully.

Mendoza glanced at Hackett, who was looking at the girl. Incredulities came at him from two directions, he thought. That girl. And—

"You may indeed help us, if you will, Miss Ferne—it *is* Miss Ferne, I take it?" He knew instinctively just the sort of thing this one would like, would respond to: essentially it was the small-town Main Street mind—a veneer of sophistication very thin; and he smoothed his moustache thoughtfully in the approved man-about-town manner, gave her a faintly sardonic smile nicely blended of veiled admiration and cynicism. "Lieutenant Mendoza, madam. I apologize for intruding at such an early hour."

"But not at *all,* Lieutenant! Anything I can do, of *course*—" She gushed at him a little, and he let his eyelids drop and put more cynicism in his expression, to conform to type. He knew exactly the kind of girl she had been, all giggles, curls, and inconsequence; the tiresome kind, not a thought beyond the conventionalities; and the kind too who wouldn't grow out of it to any extent. "Do sit down."

"Thanks very much. You can oblige me first of all by telling me something I'd very much like to know. Who owns this coat here?" He nodded at it, getting out a cigarette.

It was the first thing he'd noticed in the room. It was flung carelessly over the back of the couch, a woman's long wool coat, full-cut and voluminous: it was creamy beige and its sleeves had wide dark brown velvet cuffs.

Before the woman could answer the girl spoke. "It's *not* mine," she said. "I never saw it before. I f-found it in my— I thought *she*—it's not mine!"

"Darling, I don't understand you lately. How absurd, you're not forgetful so young, are you?—of course it's your coat, Angel, I've seen you in it a dozen times. One of the few halfway *smart* things you have. But why should you be interested, Lieutenant?" She wasn't much concerned with the coat or the girl; she sank into a chair, carefully arranging the display just right, and preened herself under his gaze.

"That's your coat, Miss Carstairs? Well, well." He went over and picked it up. It was a costume coat, with a narrow rolled shawl collar, no buttons: its only decoration the dark velvet cuffs and a dark panel of velvet down each side of its front. "That's very interesting," and he divided a smile between them.

"I never saw it before! I—I—I— What's it got to do with *you?*"

Hackett came into the room, stood looking at the coat as Mendoza turned it in his hands, examining it. "We're asking the questions here, Miss Carstairs," he said harshly.

"Oh, now I don't see any reason to be mysterious about it," said Mendoza gently. The coat bore a label inside the collar with the name *Jay-X, Fine Fashions*. Not a name he was familiar with, but any department store buyer could supply information, and he had an idea what the information would be. Hardly a brand name you'd find at Magnin's or Saks': third-rate-quality wool, inferior cut. About thirty-nine-fifty retail, he judged. "We have reliable evidence that a woman wearing a very similar coat to this one is intimately concerned in the murder of Mr. Twelvetrees. Naturally I'm interested in knowing"—he cocked his head at them—"whether it was, in fact, this coat."

"In the *murder!*" exclaimed Mona Ferne. She sat bolt upright, graceful, horrified. "What *are* you saying? That *Angel*—? But that's ridiculous! Why, I expect there are hundreds of coats like that—"

"Oh, I don't know," said Mendoza. He sat down, with the coat over his lap, in the chair nearest hers, where he could direct leers as broad as he could manage with more effect; he noticed that she'd automatically chosen a seat which put her back to the light. "It's not a fashionable line this year, is it, the very full cut, and the velvet—more of a spring coat, too, by the weight."

"I think she got it last spring," said Mona Ferne vaguely. "I can see *you're* one to watch, Lieutenant Mendoza!"—and she actually giggled at him, looking up under her lashes coyly. "You know too much about feminine styles to sound quite respectable!"

Caray, but with this one you could lay it on with a trowel, he thought. With a trowel. Appropriate . . . What was this, what the hell was this? Motives. He remembered saying to Alison, sometimes you have to find out about the people first. "You're flattering me, lady," he said, and let a little more interested admiration show in his eyes. She giggled again and smoothed her hair, to show off long garnet-colored nails.

"I never—" said the girl Angel. She came to the middle of the room, looking from him to Hackett; she twisted her hands together, tight and nervous. "You mean—whoever killed him had—? I don't underst— I never saw that coat before in my life! It's not—it's not—it's not—"

"Do control yourself, Angel, you sound quite hysterical, dear. I'm sure the lieutenant doesn't mean he thinks an innocent young girl like you had anything to do with such a horrible thing." It was a vague murmur: most of her attention was on Mendoza, a new man to gauge, to angle for, to play to.

The girl Angel stared at her; suddenly she raised her clenched fists to her mouth. "No," she said against them. "No, I didn't—why would I—I didn't—*him!* I never—"

"No one's accused you of anything, Miss Carstairs," said Hackett in a colorless tone. "We'd just like to ask a few questions, if you don't mind. Do you have a car of your own and what make is it?"

She nodded mutely at him; she whispered, "The s-same as—hers— it's a '58 two-d-door Cad— I don't like it m-much, I don't—I don't drive much, *she* made me— Listen to me, please listen, I know by the way you look you think—but why, *why, why?* No reason—*him*—He wasn't *anything*—and I tell you I never saw—"

"Do you mind telling us where you were on the evening of Friday the thirtieth?"

"I—was—here," she said dully. She was looking at her mother again, not Hackett. "All that evening. Like every night. Like always and forever and eternity. I was here—and nobody else was."

"Really, Sergeant," said Mona Ferne, absent and sweet, "you can't think *Angel*—" And now her eyes were busy gauging Mendoza's suit, the Sulka tie, the custom-made shoes. Gauging his prestige value as something in pants to be seen with. He read them (fascinated, curious, passionately interested in this woman, now) as he would read a page of print. *Money,* they said—*more than presentable, if not exactly handsome—charming—knows the score.*

"The maid—?" said Hackett.

"She isn't here—at night," said the girl. "Nobody—I went to bed, I think, about—about midnight—I—" But that was absently said too; she was still looking at her mother. "The coat," and that came out in a whisper. "Somebody with a coat like that—? D'you mean—the one did it, k-killed—" Slowly she turned back to Hackett. *Could be* and *was,* different things: she looked plain, dowdy, in a shapeless gray dress, flat brown shoes; hair pinned back carelessly to fall lank and lifeless, and no make-up. "Please," she said, "how can you think—you *do* think so, I see you do, but I don't understand! I didn't—he was *nothing!* The coat. The—I never saw it before, why d'you think it's *here,* because I f-found it there in my wardr—just a while ago, I thought— It's a hideous coat, I'd never have—I brought it down to ask— *It's not mine!* I—"

"When did you buy it, Miss Carstairs, how long have you had it?" asked Hackett woodenly.

"Oh, my God," she muttered. "No. I don't—not—*oh, my God!*" And she moved from her rigid stance; her eyes went blank and she ran, as a child or an animal ran from inexplicable wrath. They heard her on the stairs, stumbling.

"So clumsy, poor child," murmured Mona Ferne, and crossed her legs the opposite way, with nice attention to arranging the skirt at just the proper place to show off the ankle and not the ugly swell of the calf with its blue-mottled veins.

Mendoza nodded at Hackett to go after the girl. And he knew: now he knew: and it was a psychic knowledge, the D.A.'s office would laugh at it—so, look for solid tangible evidence to back it up, sure. But the thing inside him, that was worried by ragged edges, by the picture hanging crooked, by the answer to the problem that he didn't know (and that offending his essential egotism, too), settled back with a satisfied sigh and said, *So, that's the answer.* He felt better; he felt good.

Much of the reason Mendoza had this little reputation as one of the bright boys (maybe a head doctor would say) was that he had to prove it, over and over again: anything he didn't know, it was a kind of insult to the essential Mendoza; he had to find out. So finding out the answer, the truth—it affected him like a good stiff drink, and he felt fine.

Now he knew. But he didn't know why, or exactly how.

He gave Hackett a glance and nod, to go after the girl: and he gave Mona Ferne a look that was almost a leer and hitched his chair a little closer to hers. . . .

FIFTEEN

Hackett caught up with the girl at the top of the stairs. She was leaning on the bannister there, crouched and shaking, silent. The maid stood in an open bedroom door nearby, staring curiously.

"What's the matter with her *now?*"

The girl straightened abruptly. "Oh, go away!" she said wildly to both of them. And then, "No—wait—Winter, please, *you* can say, you can tell them! That coat I brought down, just now—you've never seen me in it, have you?"

The maid sniffed. "I dunno, couldn't say. I don't take no notice what *you* wear much. It ain't Miss Ferne's, that I do know."

Angel shut her eyes, leaned on the bannister again. "You wouldn't say—if you could. I know. People never—like me, want to help—and no wonder. No wonder . . ."

Hackett said angrily to the maid, "Go away, for God's sake! Go downstairs or somewhere. I'm—questioning Miss Carstairs officially and that means privately."

A spark of interest showed in the maid's eyes. "Questioning? About the murder? Did she do it? For the Lord's *sake*—all right, all right, I'm going . . ." But she lingered on the way, looking back avidly.

"I didn't," said Angel. "Really I didn't."

Hackett surprised himself by saying, "I know you didn't. And damn it, it *isn't* any wonder you haven't any friends and stay around alone, when you look like this, when you don't go to meet people halfway! Why the hell don't you cut your hair and comb it once in a while?—put on some make-up—get some decent clothes—my God, you've got the money! Make a little *effort* at it, for God's sake. It doesn't mean you're acting like her, going to turn into one like that, you know. There's a—a middle course to these things, after all! You can't expect anything out of life if you don't put something in—hanging around here feeling sorry for yourself like a spoiled kid—"

She looked up at him through a straggling lock of hair that had come unpinned, fallen across her cheek; she brushed it back, and her mountain-pool eyes were blurred by tears. "Oh, God, I know," she said. "I know. How did *you* know? I—I got off on the wrong track, it was *her,* but I—but it's too late, I don't know *how,* I don't know *anything,* how to do—how to—be nice, make people—I want to, I *want* to, but I don't know where to start, or *how.* She—"

"You listen, you just listen," said Hackett. He was mad; he didn't know exactly what he was going to say or how they'd got onto this, but at the same time he thought this was about the oddest examining of a witness he'd ever done. He made her sit down on the top step and sat down beside her—like a pair of kids, he thought. "Listen, you've got to get out of this house, this damned haunted house. That tree—my God, it's like living in a cave. Don't be silly, it's never too late to *do* something. Only you've got to put a little effort into it."

She blew her nose and looked at him solemnly over the wadded handkerchief. "I j-just hate my name," she said. "It's such a *silly* name. She—thought it was cute. A baby named Angel. Only I g-grew up, and it's *silly.* A great big lummox like me—she said that. D'you think I could change it?"

"You can do anything you want to, damn it. It doesn't matter what your name is, it's what you are yourself! Listen, you know what you ought to do? You ought to go to one of these charm schools. Sure it sounds silly but they'd teach you all those things, see? You could be a pretty girl, Angel, just take a little trouble."

"C-could I?"

"Well, sure. I know someone runs one of those places too, she'd help you a lot—Miss Alison Weir, she's in the phone book. You remember that, now, and do something about it."

She mopped at her eyes again. "Is she your g-girl friend or something?"

"No," said Hackett. "Not mine, she doesn't—belong to me." Suddenly (this was the strangest little interval he ever remembered experiencing) he was filled with inexpressible sadness for all the lonely, cheated, needing people. Because, once or twice, he'd seen Alison Weir looking at Mendoza when she didn't know anyone was watching her. At cynical, marriage-shy, self-sufficient Mendoza, who ranked women

along with poker as off-hours recreation and that was all. . . . "Listen,
stop crying, can't you?"

"I'm n-not really. I'm—it was just—yes," she said with a little gasp,
"I've got to get out of this house. *Her* house. I knew she hated me—
I've always known that—ever since I stopped being a baby and began
to grow. To let people know she was getting older *too*. And to be a—a
person, not just like a—pet she had, other people taking care of it. But
I didn't think—it was so much that she wouldn't mind if I was arrested
—for—"

"Nobody's going to arrest you," said Hackett. He thought, damn it,
it's got to be the Kingmans—logical thing; that story was a slick bunch
of lies, that's all. They were on the spot at the right time, they had a
motive; what the hell else did you need? Look around and the solid evidence would show up. But, he thought, *but* . . . That coat. Oh, hell,
coincidence. And she was easily rattled, of course she'd deny it in
panic. He took a breath to begin talking calm and sensible to her, persuade her to tell him all about the coat; and Mendoza came out to the
entry hall down there, shot a glance up the stairs, and beckoned him
down.

"Now don't you be scared," and he got up reluctantly. So Mendoza
wanted to question her himself. "You just—"

But Mendoza was taking up his hat, thanking the Ferne suavely for
her help. He looked at the girl with narrowed eyes, a little grim, and
Hackett cursed himself for ever saying anything about . . . And what
the *hell* had got into him, anyway, feeling like that?

When the door was shut and they started down the sunken steppingstones to the street, he said irritably, "And what the hell got into
you? You looked like the villain in an 1890 melodrama, twirling your
moustache and ogling that—that—"

Mendoza grinned, getting out his keys. *"Vaya,* I always like to oblige
a lady. She expected it of me." He looked at Hackett curiously. "Very
odd," he murmured to himself. "You, of all people, too. I won't say
you have quite as good a brain as me, but I've always found you
reasonably quick on the uptake, and you've worried through more complicated cases than this on your own." He shook his head and slid
under the wheel.

"What are you talking about? Look, Luis, that coat—it looks funny,
but she'd naturally deny it when she knew why we were interested. She
got rattled—"

"Oh, the coat," said Mendoza. He had brought it with him, presumably with the Ferne's gracious permission. "It's not the one that figured in that little adventure, so don't worry about it. . . . Every once in a while I'm surprised to find all over again that some cliché is true. But it does astonish me to find this one operating on you. At least I hope it's just that—the one about love causing temporary derangement—and not that you're losing your grip on the job."

"I'm *not*—will you lay off that? What d'you mean, you've got an idea—"

"*Nada de eso,* nothing doing," said Mendoza. "I shouldn't have to explain anything to you, so I'm not going to. But when I think how close I came to— An idea? I have a very good idea, now, of what happened, but there are still a lot of little things to fill in. Work it out for yourself if you can—meanwhile, be quiet, I've got serious thinking to do."

They were greeted in the anteroom of Mendoza's office by an unusually excited Sergeant Lake. "Lieutenant, I've found that Marner woman for you—"

"Oh, good," said Mendoza. He didn't sound very interested. "One of the agencies?"

"No, it was the damndest thing, it looked hopeless, you know—not a smell anywhere—and then I go out for coffee and buy a paper and there she is on the front page! Look."

They looked, and Mendoza laughed. "Well, I will be damned! And I wonder now if maybe that ties into this. . . ." It was a good-sized cut, of a pretty brunette and a middle-aged man; and the story took up two short columns. *Pickering to Wed Second Wife* was the head. "*Revealed yesterday was the forthcoming marriage of Thomas ('Toby') Pickering, the famous producer and vice-president of Capital Films, Inc. A widower for eleven years, Pickering, 47, confirmed that he is shortly to wed Miss Marian Marner, 38, model. Miss Marner—*"

"Producer," said Hackett. "I don't see quite how, but it might— Anyway she knew Twelvetrees-Trask, we'd better see her—"

"*Pronto,*" agreed Mendoza. "You get hold of this Pickering on the phone, Art, and find out where she is. I've got some routine jobs for, let's see, about three men, Jimmy—who's available? I'll brief them . . ."

After a good deal of trouble with a succession of receptionists and secretaries, Hackett got hold of Pickering in his *sanctum sanctorum.* (Easier to get on the direct wire to the President than to any Hollywood film official.) Pickering, curiously enough, seemed to know more about it than Hackett did. His voice on the phone was incisive, crisp. He said, "Hell. We were hoping it wouldn't be necessary. And I hope to God we can keep the whole damned mess away from the press. But if you've got hold of it, of course, that's that. Yes, well, look, Sergeant —sorry, what did you say the name was?—Sergeant Hackett, suppose I call Miss Marner and we arrange to meet in your office. O.K.? Say eleven-thirty. . . . Right. I don't know if you have any control over that part of it, the press, but I hope— Oh, you do. Yes, but there'll be the legal end, if there's a trial and so on. Well, we can say the hell with it, if people want to gossip let them—it's one of the hazards in my business—but that isn't to say we wouldn't prefer the whole damned thing was kept under cover. If you see what I mean. At the same time, I'm aware that you'd like to know what we have to contribute, and while I'm not at all happy you've connected us with it,"—a short laugh —"maybe I shouldn't be surprised, I understand from that recent magazine article we've got a police force to be proud of. . . . O.K., I'll contact Miss Marner and we'll be in your office at eleven-thirty."

Hackett relayed this information to Mendoza when he came in with Higgins, Dwyer, and Landers. "Good, good. I have a fair idea what they're going to tell us, but it'll be nice to know the details."

"I'd like to know what's in your mind. You act like it's about all over, barring an arrest. I tell you, that girl . . . I still think you swallowed that tale of the Kingmans' too easy. We know they had a motive, we know they were there at the right time, or thereabouts— what more—"

"*Atrás, atrás,* out of the way!" said Mendoza briskly. "Before we get to the arrest, there are all these niggling little details I have to find out, to satisfy the D.A., and no time like the present to start. You're getting paid to be a detective too, I'm not going to explain it in one-syllable words—you go off somewhere and think, maybe it'll come to you."

Hackett said a rude word and went away. Mendoza sat down at his desk and called the Temple. He asked Madame Cara a couple of questions, and the answers were just what he expected to hear. Then he went through the phone book, made a list of the clothing wholesalers and divided it up with the three men, and they started on that tiresome routine.

By the time Sergeant Lake looked in and said Miss Marner and Mr. Pickering had arrived, among the four of them they had accumulated a dismaying list of retail stores. Mendoza shooed the others out to go on checking, and Hackett came in, still looking disgruntled, behind the two new witnesses.

Mendoza looked at Marian with interest. Twelve years hadn't changed her a great deal; she didn't look much younger than she was, but she was still pretty, her figure was still very good, she was smartly dressed. She checked a little when she saw him standing there at his desk, and then said, "Oh—well, hello, Luis. I didn't know we were coming to see you. And I don't suppose it's Sergeant Mendoza now, is it?"

"Lieutenant."

"Yes, you were always one to get on. I used to know this one, Toby." She sat down in the chair Hackett held.

"Really, well, that makes things a little easier maybe," said Pickering, looking slightly amused. He was handsomer than the newspaper cut had suggested: a biggish man with thick graying hair, erect carriage, and his voice and eyes said he was aggressively capable. He took the chair Hackett indicated and planted it firmly closer to hers, sat down, and looked at Mendoza consideringly.

"We can trust him," she said, "that I'll say." She smiled a little tautly. "He's sharp enough to cut himself, but he'll be honest."

"I don't know that reassures me," said Pickering. "We've been compounding felonies and maybe acting as accessories before the fact all over the place. This is going to make the hell of a stink if it has to come out."

"Well, suppose you tell us about it, and we'll see if it has to come out," said Mendoza. "Things don't, always. You'd be surprised how many little things—and sometimes big—come into a case that don't get aired in court. I've got some idea of what you're going to tell me, I think, and it's possible that it needn't come into the legal end. I'd say even probable, barring one or two little bits that may serve to confirm times and so on. I can't say for sure, and of course I can't guarantee that a smart lawyer wouldn't get hold of it and bring it up to confuse the issue—but if it's what I deduce, to do with the late Mr. Twelvetrees' blackmailing operations, well, that's got nothing to do with the murder —I don't think, anyway."

They all looked at him. "I see," said Pickering interestedly. "You know who it was, and you think it was—another reason? I see. . . . But all the same, I suppose you want the loose ends tied up." He got out cigarettes, gave her one, lit both with an angry little snap of the lighter. "I can't say I feel vindictive toward whoever killed the bastard."

"Vindictive, possibly, no," said Mendoza, "but it's a funny one, an offbeat one, Mr. Pickering—if it's what I'm beginning to think. Let's save a little time. I think Miss Marner was being blackmailed by our late friend?"

"Attempted," said Pickering. "Just attempted, Lieutenant. I saw to that. I don't think there's any necessity to go into details—"

"I think maybe we'd better," she said quietly. "Maybe not in a formal statement, if we've got to make one, but you'll want to know enough to—add it up, won't you, Luis? I don't mind. I mean, it was—in a way—the sort of thing that might happen to anybody, though I don't excuse myself. It was—oh, well." She shrugged; her tone was even but her hand shook as she raised the cigarette to her mouth. "And a legal charge too—I wouldn't like to go to jail for it now—I don't know how that kind of thing works, if you could—"

"I think it would be a question of a fine, that's all," said Pickering, "but if the press get hold of it there'd be a little mess, and while it wouldn't make any difference to my position, anything like that—and the hell with it if it would—we'd just as soon that didn't happen. But if you think we'd better come out with the whole thing, hon, O.K., we're in this together."

"I do, Toby. Well, I don't want to bore you, Luis, but I guess you'd better have a little background—not that I'm trying to excuse myself, as I say. I got married a while after we knew each other, and it didn't turn out so well. To make a long story short, he was a drinker and I got to drinking too, and by the time I'd got the divorce, well, I wasn't much good for anything. I'd lost a lot of jobs, and the agencies got to know I wasn't—very reliable, and finally I couldn't get *any* jobs. It's all right, I don't mind talking about it now—I pulled myself up and used some common sense, got back on an even keel. But it was while I was— down—that way, and pretty desperate—I hadn't any money and I had to do *something*—I ran into this Shorter. He had a photography shop, a little hole in the wall, but it seemed he did a nice side business in—in feelthy peectures, if you see what I mean. Well, he offered me good money and I took it. I did two series for him—six shots apiece—and maybe you can say the whole business was what—pulled me up, because I loathed it, and I got to thinking, how low can you get? I used that money to live on while I got myself back in some kind of physical shape, and after a while I got a decent job, in a department store. As a clerk really, but when they found I'd had modeling experience they used me for that too, sometimes, at the fashion shows. I just quit there last week, because Toby and I are going to be married.

"Well, every once in a while I'd think about those pictures, and I didn't like the idea of them floating around. Shorter had the negatives, of course. A-about two years later, when I'd saved some money, I went and saw him and asked if he'd sell the negs to me, and he just laughed and said for five hundred apiece. I didn't have that kind of money. Well, about a year ago I was introduced to this Brooke Twelvetrees at a party. A couple of girls I know do extra work, bits in TV mostly, and it was in that crowd I met him, he was a hanger-on, I gathered. I didn't think much of him one way or another, you know—I saw him maybe three or four times in this crowd, at parties, that's all—it just came out of the blue when he—approached me." She took a breath, leaned forward to put out her cigarette.

"You take it easy now," said Pickering, and she smiled at him.

"It's O.K., Toby, I don't mind really. . . . You see, I—I got to know Toby, and we'd been going around some together, and of course there'd been a little smart talk—you know—gossip. And when I read in the paper one morning, about three weeks back it was, that Shorter had been arrested and all his—stuff—confiscated, I nearly died of fright. I mean, there'd have been those things I posed for in with the others, and identifiable as me, if the c—the police—"

"I thought the name Shorter rang a bell," nodded Mendoza. "I remember."

"I figured out," Pickering broke in, "from a couple of things that bastard, Twelvetrees I mean, said, that he was responsible for that. D'you know whether that was a—so to speak—routine investigation, or if they had anonymous information? Do the police act on that kind of thing?"

"Not my department, but I can find out about the arrest from Vice. Yes, certainly, Vice and Narcotics especially, the anonymous tip often sets the ball rolling. Sometimes it turns out a dud, sometimes not."

"Well, what I think happened was this," she went on. "Twelvetrees knew Shorter, that came out when he approached me with these negs. He said—because naturally I asked how he got them—he *said,* in a jeering sort of way, not as if he expected to be believed, you know, that Shorter'd had a premonition about being arrested and had handed over some stuff for safekeeping. But later on he started to say something else, about how he and Shorter had been together inside—and caught himself up. I think he might have been in prison, and met Shorter there. And it's just a guess, but I think Shorter showed him some of his—

things—and Twelvetrees recognized me in those pictures, either then or later. He didn't do anything about it because *I* couldn't do anything for him then, you see? I mean, he wasn't interested in me any other way but—for money. It's a funny thing to say, but when it came to girls to —go around with, well, I gathered from what Netta said—she's in the crowd that knew him best—he was a little nervous of anything from the right side of the tracks. You know? He didn't feel at home with the kind who—oh, likes ballet and cocktails instead of the amusement arcade and beer."

"Very much in character."

"That I believe," agreed Pickering. "You let me carry on, hon. The way I figure it, Lieutenant, when he heard on the grapevine that it was a serious thing with Marian and me, then he saw how he could do himself some good. Maybe you know he had—time out to laugh—movie ambitions. That—! Well, I think he stole those negs from Shorter and then 'shopped' him, as our British friends say, before he could find out or retaliate."

"Quite possible."

"Anyway, he showed up at Marian's place—"

"On that Tuesday evening, maybe?" said Mendoza. "Evening, because you'd be at work all day, he couldn't have a private talk with you. And it wasn't Wednesday because he was elsewhere that night. Or was it Thursday? On Wednesday night he was hinting joyously that some good fortune was coming his way."

"He *told* someone? My God, he—? Is that how you—?"

"No, he was too canny for that. And while we're clearing up details, how we got onto you was that he had a snapshot of you in his wallet. Why?"

"So that's what happened to it," she said slowly. She sat back, looking angry. "May I have another cigarette, Toby, please. . . . Netta told me he'd asked her for one. She was looking through some she'd just had finished, and he was there and asked if he could have the one of me. She refused, but he must have taken it anyway when her back was turned, she said. I think—maybe he wanted it to check against—those others, to be sure. She said it wasn't a very good one, but it was full-length, and you know people photograph differently sometimes from the way they really—though with *those*—well, I don't know. And maybe he just stuck it away and forgot it—or more likely kept it as window dressing, he was the kind who liked to have you think he had a raft of girl friends. . . . It was Tuesday he came, Tuesday the twenty-seventh. He had one of the negatives with him, and—and prints of the rest. He—" She broke off, trying to control her shaking voice.

"You take it easy, hon, I'll tell the rest." Pickering lit a fresh cigarette; he looked very angry. "The bastard. I'll tell you how the lyrics went, Lieutenant, if you haven't already guessed. He didn't know quite how it was with us, if you get me. He had it figured that Marian was the hell of a lot more interested in my bank account than in me, *and* that I could be scared off if I heard all this. As a matter of fact, I knew— she'd told me. He didn't want money—"

"He wanted the nice send-off with a big producer," said Mendoza. "That figures. A heaven-sent opportunity for him, our stage-struck glamour boy! No wonder he went to all the trouble—which, I agree, is likely—of stealing those negatives and getting Shorter put away. And he was thinking ahead too, probably. If you weren't impressed enough to whisk out a contract right away, after you were married he could always do it the hard way, bring pressure to bear on the grounds that you couldn't stand the publicity."

"*Ah,* that damned little—! Yes, I suppose. Well, anyway, Marian had sense enough to call me, after putting him off on a plea of making up her mind, and I took over from there. He thought he had her scared, had us just where he wanted us." Pickering laughed, short and ugly. "Money isn't everything, but it sure as hell helps. I hired a couple of the best private detectives in town"—he named the agency—"and we wired Marian's place but good. We really set up the trap—me and two other witnesses in the bedroom, *and* the tape recorder. He came over swell." He grinned. "One qualification he had for the business, nice clear-cut voice and good diction. We'd coached Marian, of course, and she slipped him enough leading questions that we got the whole layout, his whole plan, in detail. Beautiful. And then she did a little acting and gave in, said she'd do whatever he wanted—only of course we didn't tape that. My God, I'm giving myself away—but you can see the spot we were in, only way to handle it—and besides he'd made me damn mad. I wanted to cuff him down good, so he'd stay that way."

"Very nice, very nice," purred Mendoza. "It's deplorable of me, Mr. Pickering, but I don't think I'll be vindictive enough—or honest enough —to turn you in for all these little legal misdemeanors. I'd probably have done much the same thing myself. I suppose you saw him on Friday, the next day. It was, I assume, on Thursday when you sprung the trap."

"That's right. I saw him Friday morning, as soon as we had legal statements drawn up by the witnesses and so on. We'd set it up—she'd told him to come by about eleven and she'd introduce us, give him a good send-off. And, brother, we did. Marian wasn't there. I told him what we had on him and just how I felt about it, and that, by God, I enjoyed. I told him first, as far as his damn fool ambition for the movies was concerned, he was dead before he started, right now, because in the inconceivable case that anybody ever hired him to sweep a stage I could and would see he got fired—I could blacklist him in this town, in that line, and he knew it. I told him I wouldn't lose one damn thing but a little of my upright reputation if he gave those negs to the *Examiner* tomorrow, and that sacrifice I wouldn't mind, it was just on Marian's account I'd prefer the whole thing kept private. I always had a kind of admiration for that old bird—was it the Duke of Wellington?—who said *Publish and be damned.* And I told him I'd take great pleasure in charging him publicly with attempted extortion, and putting in all this nice clear evidence to prove it. And, let's face it, money talks—even to the law. I could have arranged for a trial like that to be held *in camera,* and protected ourselves that way while he got it in the neck. At that point he began to back down fast, said he'd never dream of doing anything with those negs to embarrass Marian. O.K., fine, says I, and just to guarantee that, we're going with you right now to get them and if you get out of town within twenty-four hours, I'll keep still, I won't lay the charge. But I'll check, and if you're still here, brother, you get everything the law can hand you—and if some damn fool jury lets you off, I've got the money to put you behind a dozen eightballs, other ways. I don't need to tell you he didn't like it—that's an understatement, when he saw I wasn't going to back up a sixteenth of an inch from that stand, he called me every name in the book. But he had to go along, he couldn't do anything else—unless he wanted to get slapped in jail besides losing out everywhere else."

She gave a little half-tearful laugh. "He didn't know much about Toby, you see, or he'd never have started all this."

"That I believe," grinned Mendoza. "So you all took a ride out to 267th Street."

"We did. I went with him in his Porsche, and the detectives trailed us. And the hell of a squalid little hole it was, wasn't it? We didn't waste any time—he got the negs and gave them to me, and I identified them as the ones we were after *and* the whole dozen of them, and burned them right there—"

"In a big glass ashtray. Mmh. He had them in a brown manila envelope in the bottom of his laundry bag, and he emptied the whole bag out on the bed to get them for you."

"He did," said Pickering. "What's more, there was—"

"Yes, I know, a second envelope. I know all about that one. But not a third?"

"Not that I saw, no."

Mendoza leaned back, looking thoughtful. "Motives. Yes, I wonder. Well, and so now we know why Mr. Twelvetrees was clearing out in a hurry."

"That was bluff," admitted Pickering. "I'd got no way of checking to see if he really left town. But I would—and he knew it—have come back to see if he'd left that place, and I knew where he worked, this damn fool cult, that Temple—and I'd have gone there to check. Hounded him a little, anyway."

"Sure, sure. That he knew too, and I see how his mind worked on it. He had to cut his losses. What time was this?"

"We got out there about a quarter of one, and it couldn't have been much after one when we left, we didn't linger at it, as I say. No, I didn't give a damn where he went or what he did, once those negs were burned. Matter of fact, I didn't try to do any checking, but he might have thought I would—like all that kind he was a coward when you backed him against a wall. He was so mad at me he'd've liked to kill me, but he didn't have the guts, even with a gun there to his hand. And what the hell he wanted with that—I mean, that wasn't his line, the direct action. Maybe it made him feel big and dangerous. . . . I couldn't tell you the make and model, a pistol of some kind, it was in one of the drawers of the bureau. I saw it when he yanked the drawer open to get a handkerchief—he had a sneezing-spell. . . . Yes, I think I'd know it again." Pickering laughed contemptuously. "Oh, he'd've liked to see me drawn and quartered, and he had about fifteen years on me too, if I had a better reach—but he never lifted a hand. You know what he did? It was the damndest thing. He came out of that apartment with us when we left, and went over to the carport on the other side of the building. And just as we were pulling out of that court, he came out with a trowel or a fork or something and started to dig around that funny-looking shrub planted in a tub there. Going at it in a kind of blind fury—as if he had to dig at *something,* if it was only a shrub."

Mendoza laughed. "Yes—and so that answers another little question. I've heard it said that gardening's a very relaxing occupation in cases of nervous tension. Maybe his doctor recommended it."

SIXTEEN

"Answers," he went on to Hackett dreamily, after they had gone. "We're getting them in, finally. *Va aclarando*—it's clearing up. And very nice too. So now we know almost all that happened to dear Brooke that Friday. His unlucky day, all right. He was finished here, after that business with Pickering. . . . It looks as if Marian's got herself a man, *absolutamente*. . . . He'd have no chance at all to get anywhere in show business, and he was also finished taking an easy living out of the Kingmans, because Pickering knew his connection with the Temple: he'd promised to hound him and he would. Everything had turned sour on Brooke Twelvetrees. First of all, he had to get away from 267th Street, in case Pickering did come back to check after the twenty-four hours' grace. . . . There he is, hacking away at the Tree of Heaven in his blind fury at the way everything's turned out. I can see him, when that thought takes shape in his mind, stalking back into the apartment, throwing down that trowel anywhere—he's forgotten he had it—and starting to pack. He—yes. Yes." Mendoza was sitting on the end of his spine, eyes shut, looking peaceful, hands clasped across his lean middle. *"Eso es,* of course. He got here with just that old brown leather suitcase, he's had no occasion for luggage since, and he's accumulated too much to go into it. So he leaves his packing, he gets out the Porsche and goes off to buy a couple of new suitcases."

"I follow you," said Hackett. "That's nice deducing, but is it very important?"

"It might be. I think on the way he started thinking a little more clear and shrewd, and his first idea would be, What can I salvage out of this? He *could* try to go on blackmailing the Kingmans from a distance, but that's always a little more difficult. And I think he must have been very tired of the Kingmans and their Temple. Also, I think he needed some cash right then—he was the kind who spent everything as it came in, maybe he hadn't even enough for those suitcases on him. So he thought of the Kingmans' safe—and then he thought of the Temple bank accounts. . . . Cut his losses, sure, and take everything along he could lay hands on. Now we don't know how long he worked at his gardening, how long he spent starting to pack. But we've got a kind of *terminus ad quem,* because the bank shuts at three. This just came in this morning. If it hadn't been that particular bank, this would be a different story, because a lot of banks now stay open later on Fridays and don't open on Saturday at all. But that one sticks to the old rule. So we deduce that by the time it came to him how he could salvage something out of the wreck, it'd be too late to get into the bank when he got there —it'd be quite a drive, you know. *De paso,* it's maybe a little confirmation of how our friend Kingman could get into the dither he did, you know, apparently he didn't know that, wasn't familiar with the banking hours. Because if he'd known the bank was open from nine to twelve on Saturdays, he'd have been down there to lay his warning then, and all this would have started two days before it did. Are you with me?"

"*Yo seguir,* right behind. Twelvetrees figured to take the cash and let the credit go, clear out the bank account and vanish into the wild blue yonder, probably under the name of Eustace J. Humperdink. O.K. He took a little chance clearing out the safe in the Temple—being too greedy. That he should have left alone."

"I think it was more economy than pure greed. He'd gone to a little trouble to get hold of the combination, silly not to use it now. And it wasn't a long chance at all. Not when it was a matter of hours. He knew Kingman probably wouldn't open that safe until Saturday night. And he fully expected to be at the bank when its doors opened Saturday morning, primed with a glib story for the manager of sudden unexpected expenses that had to be paid in cash—I wonder what he'd have said. I wouldn't put it past him to have intended forging some notes of instructions from the other officers. Yes. Clear out of 267th, he'd think, and get settled for the night in some quiet hotel, and maybe he meant to sit up over those forged notes, to have them ready. He wouldn't have closed out the bank accounts, that'd call for more red tape—just stripped them down to a hundred or so. No, it wasn't too much of a chance. . . . Well, he went to the Temple and took the month's receipts. He went and got his prescriptions refilled, and he bought those suitcases somewhere—probably a big cheap department store where the clerks are always in a rush, don't notice individual customers usually. And he had an early dinner, and he drove back to 267th Street—he'd get there about six-thirty, a quarter of seven, if he left that restaurant at five-thirty. It had started to rain, you remember, it was coming down steadily, that would slow him on the drive. And he started to finish his packing."

"Yes. And?"

Mendoza's long nose twitched. "I'm doing all the work. Can't you fill in a bit? Come on, think hard."

"Well—I think he wrote that note to Mrs. Bragg, to have it ready. He didn't want any backchat, or delay in getting away either. *And* it's nice to know he had the gun—it was his. . . . Can we say he had a visitor, then? Before he got away, when he was nearly finished packing. . . ." Hackett fingered his jaw, looking troubled. "I don't know—"

"There are a lot of little things I don't know, but I know who the visitor was. Thanks to you."

"Now look—she—"

"*Eso basta,* you stop right there. I'm tired of listening. I think, though there are jobs you could do, you'd better take the rest of the day off. I'm worried about you—you're going to pieces. I could take time and explain, but I think it'll be salutary for you not to be told—force you to do a little thinking of your own."

"Are you ordering me?—" began Hackett stiffly.

"*Es mas listo de lo que parece,*" said Mendoza to himself with a sigh. "Smarter than he looks—I hope. You go and have a nice quiet drink somewhere, Arturo, and maybe take in a movie. And don't worry, trust your uncle Luis, everything will be O.K. with a little luck."

"Oh," said Hackett, staring at him. "You *don't* think— And what are you going to be doing, if I'm allowed to ask?"

"I have dispatched minions—that's a nice word, no question but English has certain advantages—to discover, if possible, where the coat was purchased, by whom, and when. I think we'll get it, because it was only yesterday, you see, it'll be fresh in the salesclerk's mind. And for other reasons too. *De veras,* this love of melodrama. . . . I am presently going to call on a new witness, or at least one we haven't thought very important, and meanwhile I am going to sit here and do some serious thinking, along the same line the famous idiot boy took with the lost horse. Goodbye, Arturo. Shut the door when you leave."

Hackett looked at him, opened his mouth, thought better of that and shut it, and stalked out.

Oddly enough, he did more or less what Mendoza had told him to do, though without conscious plan. He went and had a drink, and then he walked up Main Street for a little way, thinking—not to much purpose—and dropped into a newsreel theater.

He didn't take in much of the news; when he came out he went back for his car and drove up to Fairfax Avenue in Hollywood. He located the doctor's office and the pharmacy, and drove slowly on from there, watching the right side of the street. He stopped and parked twice, to go into large shops where luggage was sold, and drew blank. It was at the third place he got somewhere, a big department store branch; one of the clerks thought he remembered a man who looked like Twelvetrees' picture coming in to buy some luggage: he couldn't say exactly when, a couple of weeks back he thought, and he couldn't remember exactly what the man had bought.

Still, it all helped a little. Though the suitcases didn't matter, weren't important. But at least it gave him an illusion of working at it.

It was nearly four o'clock, and he remembered he hadn't had any lunch. He had a sandwich in a drugstore, and started back downtown, aimlessly.

He was on North Broadway, stopped at a light and looking around idly, when he saw the sign. It was an old movie house, newly refurbished in the desperate hope of better business, and for the same reason running a new gimmick to compete with TV. Like the fad for foreign films, there was a little boom these days in silent movies; maybe it made the middle-aged feel young again, and the kids superior; a lot of people seemed to get a kick out of saying, *Did we ever think that was good?* This house featured them once a week, so the sign said, and the one running now was called *The Girlhood of Laura Kent*—the name leaped at him from below the title—*with Mona Ferne*.

He turned into the next parking lot and walked back. On the way he suddenly found himself thinking about that gun. It had been lying on top of the bureau, Kingman said; so Twelvetrees had taken it out of the drawer, where Pickering had seen it, to pack. His visitor presumably had not (was that a fair deduction?) come with the idea of killing him, or he or she would have been prepared with a weapon. It was surprising how tough the human body was: you couldn't be sure of killing someone with a bang on the head—when it happened like that it was usually the sudden violent impulse and the blow landing just right at random. But if a suddenly enraged visitor snatched up that gun, why in hell hadn't he or she used the other end of it? A much surer way. The noise, yes: but that was the last thing anyone in a sudden violent rage would remember. . . . So, the gun hadn't been loaded.

Yes, it was, he thought the next second. Or the cartridges for it were there. Because a while later it was used on Bartlett.

He stopped under the theater marquee, and in absent surprise he thought, Well, well: so he had come round to Mendoza's viewpoint on that, Walsh's thing.

He went up to the ticket window, past the resurrected poster where Mona Ferne's young, insipidly pretty face smiled. "This *Laura Kent* thing, when does it go on?"

"You're lucky, just starting now."

Hackett gave up his ticket stub to the door attendant and groped his way down the aisle. Even in the dark there was an empty feel to the house, and when his eyes were adjusted and he looked around, he saw that there were only about twenty people in the place. Wouldn't think it'd pay them to stay open. . . .

As he watched the opening scenes of what could never have been a good picture (even allowing for changes in style) he thought of what Stanley Horwitz had said. *Couldn't act—just took direction.* Too true. And the kind of thing she had done: this was probably a fair sample.

It must have been one of the earliest pictures she'd starred in, by the date: it was thirty-four years old. A year older than he was: but when his memory started, a few years later—well, it was hard to say, you remembered childhood backgrounds distorted, sometimes, but he'd have said that even then audiences would have been a trifle too sophisticated to go for this. But they must have: she'd done this kind of thing another nine or ten years and it had gone over pretty well.

It was supposed to be funny and what the posters still called *heart-warming* at the same time. The tired old plot of the tomboy who hates being a girl and goes swaggering about in jeans playing baseball (or riding broncs or driving racing cars or flying airplanes) until Love Enters Her Life and overnight she becomes a demure clinging vine. . . . Of course the photography wasn't so good, but it was interesting to see what she had been: he had an idea, now, of the goal she was aiming for with all the effort put out. This vapidly pretty girl with blond curls and spontaneous adolescent giggles.

The dramatic action was jerky, everything drearily spelled out. She waded in a stream, casting a line with what even Hackett could see was inept awkwardness. She rode in a horse show, smart and boyish in jodhpurs. She went skeet-shooting with her distinguished sportsman father, in—

Suddenly he heard his own voice, loud and shocking in that place,

"My God!"—and found he was standing up. It couldn't be—but it was, he'd swear it was!

He sidestepped out to the aisle and ran up it. And as he ran, a few pieces fitted themselves together in his mind, and he thought, So that was it. The coat, the damned coat—but—

"Telephone?" he gasped to the doorman, who gaped at him and pointed out the public booth in the lobby. Hackett fumbled for a dime, slammed it into the slot. . . . "Jimmy," he said when he got Sergeant Lake, "let me talk to him—I don't care if he's in conference with the Chief, I've got—"

"He isn't here, Art, you just missed him."

Hackett said a few things about that. "Know where he's gone?"

"If you'll let me get a word in edgewise. He was just back from somewhere, looking like the dealer'd handed him a royal flush first time round, when that Miss Weir called and out he goes again in a hurry."

"Oh, O.K., thanks." Hackett hung up. It was twenty past five. He seemed to remember that that school of hers closed at three-thirty, four, around there: she was probably at home. Try, anyway. He found another dime, looked up the number.

"Miss Weir? Art Hackett. Is Luis there? . . . Luis, listen, I've got something, something so—"

"Well, well," said Mendoza, "have you limped up to the finish post, *chico*? Congratulations. You'd better come round, we've got something here too."

At about the same time that Hackett was brooding over his drugstore sandwich, Alison was saying helplessly, "Now drink your tea while it's hot," and wondering why it was that in the American mind, apparently, tea was connected with trouble. Could it be still reverberations from the Stamp Tax? When someone was in trouble, a little under the weather, or having a crying spell, automatically you made them a nice hot cup of tea.

She had found the girl outside her apartment door when she came home, a forlorn stranger who told her numbly, like a child repeating a lesson, "Sergeant Hackett said to come and see you. I'm sorry, I didn't know where else to come. I didn't know what to do. But I had to get out of that house. I had to. I'm Angel C-Carstairs."

She was shaking and cold, and she'd had some kind of bad shock, Alison saw. Having heard a little about this case from Mendoza, she recognized the girl's name; she made her come in and sit down, she made the tea and gave her soothing talk, and then all this began to come out. Incoherent at first.

"I didn't know—I thought I'd never seen it before, but it must be hers, because—because she kept saying— Like, you know, if you keep on telling a person he's stupid, he *will* be. She *did* that with me, I know it, I know it in my mind but I c-can't seem to do anything about it— telling me I'm too big and clumsy. You know. It was like that, about this—as if she thought, if she said it to me enough I'd begin to believe it—the way everybody else would. And it's not *true,* it's silly. That I could ever—be in love—with somebody like that! Like Brooke! I didn't even think he was handsome, I mean he was *too* good-looking— you know—"

"Yes."

"Oh, I don't *know* what I'm doing here—perfect stranger to you. I'm sorry, I'm sorry, but I didn't know—I just had to get out of *her* house — You see, it was so funny, the way she kept insisting it *was* my coat, as if after a while I wouldn't be sure about that either, and say it was— and then after they'd g-gone, she got onto this, kept saying she *understood* how I'd loved him, felt jealous—and then I thought *why* it could be. I didn't believe it—I don't know if I believe it—but if she did—! Oh, I've hated her, I've hated her so—you can't understand that, how anybody could—my own mother, but you don't know, *you* probably have a n-nice mother—"

"Drink your tea," said Alison. She was beginning to understand what this was all about, and automatically made quiet responses while she thought, I'd better call Luis. Persuade her to talk to him, if she will. "Actually I don't remember my mother at all, she died when I was two, and my father brought me up. Not much of a bringing-up, I expect, either, because he was an engineer and we lived in Mexico mostly, traveling around from one godforsaken spot to another—construction camps, you know. But people are just people, no better or worse for being mothers or fathers. And hating doesn't do any harm except to you—"

"I know, I don't *want* to, I—I don't think I do, any more. It's all *over,* all of a sudden, and I don't know what to do—but I shouldn't be here, I'm sorry. I've g-got money, and in the bank too, I mean I'm all *right.* I expect I'd better go to a hotel. It just *hit* me all of a sudden, the reason. And I don't know—now—how I *do* feel about her. Doing that. Not him—but trying to—wanting to—"

"Yes. I think the only way to feel is sorry for her, don't you? Not resentful. It's just a thing you have to face up to."

"I—I guess I'm not very good at that."

"Then now's the time to start," said Alison firmly.

Angel had calmed down a little; perhaps the kitten had helped, curled up beside her purring. "I always wanted a c-cat. She never— But I *could* be different, couldn't I? I could learn better. To cope, sort of, you know. You know what I always wanted to do? It's silly, I guess, *she* said . . . But I liked it better than anything else at school, even than poetry. I l-like to *cook*. . . . She kept *on* at it, until I suddenly saw, that was all. And they think it was me, that's what she wanted them to— Not Sergeant Hackett, he's nice, but the other one. That I *was* in love with Brooke. But does she think I'm c-crazy, not to *know* how I felt—and didn't feel? Oh, I don't understand—and—"

"You'd better tell Lieutenant Mendoza about this." And then Alison spent ten minutes persuading her.

"I *couldn't!* Don't you see—even if—even if I don't feel anything—like that—for her, she *is*—! I couldn't—like t-telling tales—"

"Don't be childish," said Alison. "This is serious, you know it is. And I doubt very much if it'll come as a surprise to Luis, when—" even you know about it, she finished in her mind, but Angel was rushing on.

"And besides *he's* the one thinks I—! He *looked* at me when he left —I knew what he was thinking—"

"That I doubt too," said Alison. "If he looked at you one way, it probably meant the opposite. I'm told that's the secret of his success— experience at the poker table. Now you go and wash your face—you've been crying and it'll make you feel better—and you'd better take an aspirin too, and lie down on the bed and rest quiet until he gets here. You can trust Luis not to jump to any wrong conclusions, and it's much better in his hands."

Angel went meekly to do as she was bidden, and five minutes later Alison, looking in, found her sound asleep, curled up on the bed like the kitten.

She left her thoughtfully, shutting the door, and was sorry Mendoza arrived so soon. He listened to her rather incoherent account and said, "Awkward. I'm not quite ready to break this yet, I want a bit more information, and I hope her—mmh—precipitate flight doesn't scare Mona. No odds if it does, though, she'd only do something else damn silly. No finesse at all."

"But what an awful thing, Luis—her own mother—"

"Physical sense only. She's never had a thought in her head besides herself. In this case, anything expedient to get out from under. Now I wonder if that was why she took that laundry bag away? Just in case."

"Will Angel have to testify against her? She's just about at the end of her tether now—"

"*Es poco probable,* I don't think so. Not if we get a nice tight legal confession, which I'd like. She'll have a rough time for a little while, the publicity, but these things die down—something else'll come along to make gossip."

"There's good stuff in her, I think—she'll take it, and maybe be the better for it. My Lord, how I long to get *at* her and fix her up—she could be a good-looking girl, you know. And what a time to think of that. . . ."

"Any time's the time to think of a good-looking woman, *chica*. You do just that, and earn Art Hackett's gratitude. I'd heard the one about beauty being in the eye of the beholder, but I never believed it before. Another good man gone wrong. . . . Yes, I'm afraid so, *lo siento en al almo,* to my deep regret. Many a man ruined for life by marriage, I only hope he'll have better luck."

Alison said, "Yes?" She watched him relax on the couch, stroking the kitten.

"Well, where is this girl? I've got other irons in the fire—"

"Count five and start pretending to be a human being," said Alison dryly. "I'll get her."

And he gave her his one-sided smile, caught her hand as she passed and kissed it. "Sorry, *querida,* it's routine to me, sometimes I forget it isn't to everybody. I'll be nice to her."

But she hadn't taken another step before the phone rang, and it was Hackett. . . .

Angel looked a little better for the rest, with her face scrubbed, her hair combed. She sat erect on the edge of the couch like a child in school, with Alison beside her, and only gradually relaxed under their quiet voices, their reassuring phrases.

"It was," said Hackett, "a picture made before you were born, so you wouldn't know anything about it. But what startled me was that there's a scene of her shooting—target-shooting—and the way it was taken, I don't see how it could have been faked. She was doing it, not someone doubling for her—and she wasn't missing a shot. Quite a little exhibition."

"I don't know anything about the picture. But I can tell you a little about that, I guess—" She stopped, looked stricken again, and again Mendoza was patient.

"Miss Carstairs, I'm not lying when I say we'd get all this elsewhere if not from you. There's only a few little things I want to ask you right now. I knew about your mother this morning, when I looked at that coat and saw it was brand-new, and heard her trying to convince us all that it was yours, and that you'd had it for some time. You're not betraying her in any sense, believe me—you're only filling in a little for us that we could learn from others."

"I see that," she whispered. "I—I don't like it, but you'd only—find out anyway, and I don't suppose—this'll be as bad as—if there's a trial and so on." She stiffened her shoulders, took a deep breath. "Mr. Horwitz could probably tell you more about it. I know I was awfully surprised when he mentioned it once—it was the first I'd ever heard of it —it must have been that picture he meant. He said everybody had been surprised to—to find she was a second Annie Oakley. You see, she was brought up on a farm, or anyway a very small town, I'm not sure which, in South Dakota, and she used to go out hunting with her father. She got to be quite a good shot. Later on she—I think she felt it was unwomanly, you know—she never mentioned it or *did* it any more. My father—I've heard Mr. Horwitz say—was a sportsman, he liked to hunt, and I don't know but maybe she used to go with him then. But that'd be twenty-five years ago, and so far as I know since then she's never— But Brooke wasn't *shot*, was he?"

"Not Brooke," said Mendoza. He took the old Winchester revolver out of his pocket and laid it on the coffee table. "Have you ever seen this before, Miss Carstairs?"

She looked at it for a long moment. "I—why, yes, I think—I think that's the gun Brooke stole . . . She wasn't really angry about it, just a little put out. She never could have refused him anything, you know," and faint contempt was in her tone. "She was terribly silly about him. I knew—even I knew—he just fawned on her, flattered her, because she —gave him presents, and I think she used to pay too, when they went to some awfully expensive place. I—it was *shameful*. I wouldn't have liked him anyway but when he did that—"

"Yes. He stole this gun?"

"He called it borrowed. He was going to be in some play where they had to have a gun," she said dully. "I said my f-father liked to hunt, he had some guns, and two or three of them she never sold. This was one of them. It's not the kind you hunt with, of course—the others are rifles—but she kept this on account of burglars. She said. He saw it one day, it was in the den with the others in a case, and he took it. She said he should have asked, of course she'd have lent it to him. He never gave it back—I don't know if she asked, or maybe gave it to him to keep. I do know it was loaded when he took it, she always kept it loaded. In case she needed it in a hurry, she said, if someone broke in."

"Twenty-five years," said Hackett to Mendoza, meditatively.

"I don't know, it's a thing you don't lose entirely. If you've had a lot of practice. You'd get rusty, sure, but—in an emergency—you'd instinctively do what old experience told you."

"Probably. A great help, anyway—the old experience—in that particular target shot."

"Claro está. Miss Carstairs, I've got just two more questions to ask, and then we're going to see that you're settled in a hotel. Miss Weir'll go along and I expect lend you whatever you need, and we'll stop bothering you for a while. Can you tell me anything about Miss Janet Kent?"

Angel's eyes hardened a little. "Yes, I can," she said steadily. "She was a—a sort of nurse-supervisor for me for about ten years, from the time I was five. I don't think she meant to be—unkind, but she was awfully—oh, strict and old-fashioned, and crotchety. She was old then, and looking back now, I can see she used to—to fawn on *her* and pretend to admire her so much, because she was afraid of losing her job, not being able to get another. But—*she*—swallowed it all whole, you never can give her too much flattery, she never sees through it. And when I got too old for Miss Kent, *she* gave her a sort of pension, just because it makes her feel magnanimous to have someone dependent on her that way. I—I feel sorry for Miss Kent now—once in a while *she'd* get me to go with her there, you know, and it's just sickening—to me anyway—the way Miss Kent kowtows to her, you almost expect her to say 'my lady' and curtsey—oh, you know what I mean—like a whipped dog—because she's old, nearly eighty, and she hasn't got anyone or any money, and if *she* ever stopped giving her this little bit to live on, Miss Kent'd have to go on the county. *She* just revels in it, of course, the funny thing is she thinks Miss Kent really means it—"

"Yes. Now I want you to take your time and think about this one," said Mendoza. "You know, of course, that your mother has made a very inept effort to cast suspicion on you. She didn't choose you deliberately, but when we found the body, you see—which hadn't been intended—and began finding out a few things close to home, she got nervous. She had a few things she hadn't got rid of, to link her with it, and now she was afraid to try to dispose of them, that we might see her doing that. So it had to be someone in the same house, in case of a search warrant. And that meant you. You know about the coat. There's something else. Something about two feet long or a bit more. Fairly heavy, but partly flexible. Is there anywhere in that house where she could put such a thing, where it would be definitely connected with you and still you wouldn't come across it right away?"

She didn't think twenty seconds; she said simply, instantly, "Why, of course. My old trunk. That is, it's—it was my father's, there were some old family pictures in it and odds and ends. She was going to throw it away once when I was about seven, and I begged to have it. I—I never knew anybody in either of their families, you see, my grandparents or aunts and uncles—and it made it seem I had more of a family somehow, those old pictures. I used to t-tell myself stories about them. . . . I keep it way at the back of my closet, it's locked, and there are things in it I expect it's silly to keep, but the kind of things you don't throw away. My high school graduation dress, and the school yearbooks— and a c-couple of letters—things like that. I don't open it once in six months, now."

"Locked," said Mendoza. "Where do you keep the key?"

"In the top drawer of my dresser."

"And where were you from six o'clock on last evening? At home?"

"Why, no—for once I wasn't," she said without bitterness. "I felt I had to get out—away—I went to a movie by myself. . . . No, of course I haven't looked in the trunk since."

"Thank you very much," said Mendoza smiling. "That's all for now."

And as they waited for Alison to pack an overnight bag for the girl, over Angel's protests, Mendoza suddenly asked, "You didn't pick up a traffic ticket on your perambulations today, by any chance?"

"A— No, why?"

"Neither did I. Oh, I don't know—round out the case," said Mendoza vaguely. "Traffic tickets, they've had quite a lot to do with this case, one way and another. If Frank Walsh hadn't given me that ticket and subsequently found I'm a tolerably reasonable individual to talk to, he'd probably have done nothing about his doubts on Bartlett. Let Slaney convince him he was just being overconscientious. And if Madame Cara hadn't got a ticket that night at—as we now know—the corner of Avalon and DuPont at seven minutes past eleven, I might easily have decided to use that warrant and charge them with the murder. And in the first instance, if Walsh and Bartlett hadn't stopped to hand out a traffic ticket right there, she wouldn't have had such a good chance to spot the squad-car number she was looking for, and take those shots at the driver—the wrong man. Funny how things work out sometimes. If she hadn't done that extra kill, nobody might ever have known a thing about it. Twelvetrees-Trask quietly moldering away there with his suitcases. Woods would have gone on looking, and finally filed it under Pending, and that would have been that. . . . It was the extra kill—and the traffic tickets—that tripped her up in the end."

And Hackett asked, "But why? What possible motive—"

"Eso tiene gracia," said Mendoza, "that's the funny thing. I don't know. I've got a little idea, but I don't *know*. Maybe she'll tell us."

SEVENTEEN

And it was a curious ending to a curious case, how readily she told them, eventually.

When they brought her in the next morning and confronted her with the green plastic laundry bag and its contents, which had been locked away in Angel's old trunk, she went on talking for a while about her poor misguided child, so frantic with unrequited love.

She sat in the chair beside Mendoza's desk, which she had unobtrusively moved to put her back to the light from the window, and smiled at him, and at Hackett, at the silent policewoman and the stolid police stenographer, in perfect confidence. She was in black today, as glossily turned out as ever—and the little loose fold of skin at her throat shaking a little as she turned her head from one to the other, the little strain lines about the eyes (because she should wear glasses) showing deep, and the raised blue veins on her hands; the thick, skillful cosmetic mask could not hide the lines and hollows and shadows.

"Miss Ferne," said Mendoza finally, "it's really no use, your going on like this. Sooner or later you'll have to listen to me and believe it. We know Miss Carstairs had nothing to do with the murders. We know who did, and we have evidence on it. The salesclerk where you bought that coat on Monday remembers the incident very clearly—do you know why? Because, as Mr. Horwitz told us, you never were much of an actress and you can't do character parts. You overplayed it quite a bit, with that black hairpiece fastened to a turban, and the fake accent that puzzled everybody because it was partly French and partly German and partly just your own idea of how any foreigners talk English. You didn't fool anyone—the cab driver that night, or the man in the shop where you bought the serape, or the clerk on Monday—they all knew you were putting on a very crude act—"

"That's a *lie!*" she exclaimed. "I can! I'm a great actress, everyone always said so—it's only jealousy, I'd be showing these snippy young things today if—"

"We have the whole story from Miss Janet Kent, too. You make a mistake there in believing she really was devoted to you. All she was interested in was the money you gave her. Just as Brooke Twelvetrees was—wasn't he? That's why she fawns on you and flatters you—that's why she was afraid not to oblige you, when you came to her last Sunday and asked her—told her—to be ready to back up an alibi for you for the night of Friday the thirtieth. You hadn't thought you'd need one up to then, but after we'd found the body you thought you'd better have one. Miss Kent didn't like it, though I'm afraid she thought it was an illicit love affair—"

She smiled and smoothed her hair. "Of course. And that's a lie too, she *is* devoted to me—simply devoted. Servants always like me. You probably forced her to tell."

"It's always a mistake to count on other people in a business like this. They just haven't the incentive, you know, to go on telling lies. And when she heard that it was a murder case, she told us all about it. You made quite a few mistakes that night, and not the least of them was in overlooking all those odds and ends on the bureau. His hat, and the medicine bottles, and his watch and pocket-knife, both monogrammed, and the half bottle of Scotch and so on. It was convenient that you'd also overlooked that laundry bag on the chair. Into that it all went. But you couldn't face going down that trap again, so you took it with you.

"You thought you'd covered your tracks so cleverly, with the act you put on for the cab driver, for the salesclerk—" Mendoza laughed and shrugged. "You have a most unfortunate love of wild Gothic melodrama, Miss Ferne—no appreciation of dramatic subtleties at all! As I daresay directors have told you—many years ago." He let some contempt show in his eyes.

"A lie," she said in automatic reaction, "it's all lies."

"But things went on going wrong, we found the body, and that brought you into it—when we'd identified him—if only on the outskirts of the case. And when you talked to your dear friend Cara Kingman on Monday, she told you that the police had connected with the murder a woman wearing a light-colored coat with dark bands of trimming on the cuffs and front panels. That really frightened you, because you still had the coat—"

"*Angel* had it. You found it."

"I mean the real coat," said Mendoza patiently, "the one you were wearing that night."

"You don't know," she said almost slyly. "I never owned a coat like that in my life. You *don't* know."

"But I do," and he smiled gently at her. "I had to do a little serious thinking on it, but it came to me. It was your fur coat you were wearing that night, wasn't it? That specially made brown mink with the white satin lining. It was the one halfway clever idea you had—to turn it inside out and wear it that way when you needed a quick disguise. People could see what you'd done in good light, of course, but in the dark like that, it was quite effective. Only the fur on the inside borders still showed, to look like trimming in the dark. And the rain ruined the lining, didn't it? You were afraid to send it to the cleaners, they'd be bound to ask questions and remember. When we searched your house last night, one of my men examined it, and we've gone back just since you've been here, to impound it as evidence."

"You can't do that—"

"I'm afraid it's quite legal. As I say, you were frightened when we got that close to home, and you went on making mistakes by most unnecessarily trying to cast suspicion on your daughter. And most ineptly! The rawest new rookie in uniform could have followed the trail you left. You had a long hunt for a coat made just like that, you spent most of the day at it, in your crude disguise, and we've found several clerks who remember you and your specific request. You finally found what you wanted at a small shop called Betty Jo's, on Beverly Boulevard, at about four-thirty. You paid thirty-seven-fifty for it. You hid that damning laundry bag in your daughter's trunk that evening, put the coat in her wardrobe. Had you kept the bag in case you needed a scapegoat? I think so. You didn't have a chance to plant them in Miss Carstairs' room until she decided to go out to a movie. You knew where she kept the key to her trunk—but you'd decided to be bold about the coat, which was a very stupid mistake too. . . . Once you'd gone to all this trouble, you were really hoping we'd come with a search warrant: I saw how pleased you were, yesterday morning, when we walked in and saw that coat lying there. But your daughter's an intelligent grown-up woman, Miss Ferne, however much you hate to acknowledge it, and you couldn't have forced her to admit owning that coat and forgetting it, or to believe she'd been in love with Brooke Twelvetrees." Suddenly he got up and stood over her. "You were the one in love with Twelve-trees—weren't you?"

She looked up at him for a long minute, wide-eyed, a little smile still on her painted mouth. Then she said, "You're much cleverer than I thought the police were. You *do* know, don't you?"

"We know. We know all about it, Miss Ferne. But maybe you'd like to give us your version."

She fitted a new cigarette into the jeweled holder and he leaned to light it for her. "I wonder—it might be good publicity." She laughed. "You know what they say about publicity?—it doesn't matter what you get in the papers *for,* just get there! I daresay,"—and her tone was complacent—"I'd have a number of contract offers, afterward. . . . I don't believe Stanley's been *trying* to do anything, just spite, and besides he's getting old, losing his grip. I'll get a new agent. . . . Because of course I'll get *off,* nobody would say I was guilty—when they know why. Not if there are any women on the jury," and she giggled, and then looked thoughtful. "Or perhaps men would be better. Yes. I must remember to tell my lawyer. I'll have someone really good, to put on a good production. . . . It might be interesting."

"I'm looking forward to it. You were going to give us your version."

She smoothed her hair, looking up at him sideways, coyly. "He insulted me, that was why, really. And a *lie.* Yes, I did love him—dear Brooke—and I'd been kind to him, awfully kind. I felt sorry for him, you know, the poor boy hadn't any money but the *pittance* Martin could afford to pay him. And he was proud, really he was, I thought—he didn't like to take presents from me, but he always gave in so charmingly! And he spent too much money on me, at quite nice, expensive places—"

"Like the Voodoo Club."

"Oh, yes, we went there a lot. It was only fair I should try to make some return. But he was shy too—I thought—" she gave a little gasp.

"I was sure he loved me too, only he was too shy and proud to say—because I had more money, and then there was just the *tiniest* difference in our ages—"

"Just twenty-eight years' difference," said Mendoza crudely.

For one moment her face was convulsed with rage. "You—! It doesn't matter, it doesn't matter—it was a lie, a lie, a lie! He was going away, he was packing—when I came—he let me in, we were in the living room but I could see into the—I'd made up my mind to smooth matters out *for* him—you know—and tell the dear boy I *returned* his love—I'd be proud and happy to marry him—I knew he'd been hesitating to—you know—try his fortune with me. And he—and he—it was a lie, of course, he was drunk or he'd gone mad or something! I told him —and he *swore* at me, he called me—"

"An old hag," said Mendoza softly. (And this was it, the offbeat little idea in his mind.) "He said you're an old desiccated bag of bones, a wrinkled mummy, he'd as soon go to bed with his grandmother—a silly old painted bitch pretending to be sixteen—" And he stepped back quickly from her clawing fingers, and Hackett and the policewoman took her by the shoulders and forced her down to the chair again.

She sat rigid for a minute, and the mask of rage smoothed out to her usual vapidity. "You see, I nearly killed *you* then. Any woman— And he was mad, it's a wicked, *wicked* lie, all anyone has to do is *look* at me," and up went the manicured hand, gracefully, to the perfect coiffure. *"Real* beauty doesn't fade, of course. And I *do* have enough self-respect to keep myself *up,* retain the youthful *outlook*—that's the great secret. You remember that, dear," she said condescendingly to the policewoman. "But even though I knew *it was a lie*—as anyone can see —I, well, I suppose I lost my temper. Just for a minute. I slapped him, I know, and he must have been frightened—of me, imagine!—because he stepped back and picked up that gun. I'd given it to him, you know —silly boy, it made him feel like an adventurer or something, I think— it was an old one of Bill's. He couldn't ever have *shot* anyone with it, he didn't have the courage for that. I reached for it and got it away from him—really you could say it was self-defense!—and I must have hit him with it, because he fell down and when I *felt* him, well, he was dead. It was his own fault, he shouldn't have *lied* to me like that! You can see how it was."

"I can see. So you started to leave."

"Well, there wasn't anything else to do, was there? He was dead, and while it *was* his own fault, I didn't want to be connected . . . It was raining quite hard then, and when I opened the door—I'd left my car on the street that time, very foolishly—there was this sudden great flash of lightning, it lit up everything—"

"Including the police car sitting right outside. And the driver. And its number. Yes, I know all about that too. And several people have identified the gun. It was that extra kill that was your biggest mistake, Miss Ferne. . . . You thought the driver had seen you, and you decided—shall we say—you might as well be hung for a sheep as a lamb? So you thought it over, and went back to get the gun, and then you found the car had gone. You spent quite a while hunting it."

She looked down and then up through her lashes, demurely. "I know that whole thing was foolish, I realized it almost as soon as it was over. But I *was* frightened, and not thinking very clearly—and of course women haven't logical minds, have they? There wasn't any way to be *sure* I'd really killed him, that was the trouble. It was awful, driving all over looking for that car—I passed several police cars, but I couldn't always read the number, and I was frantic—and then, it was like a miracle, I saw it just ahead, stopped, and the roof light showed up its number, the right one. Seven-four-seven it was. So I went around the block —of course I'd made sure the gun was loaded. . . . You know, I hadn't fired a gun in years, and I was always better with a rifle too, but it *came back,* if you know what I mean. But I couldn't be *sure.* So then —I was thinking *much* more clearly by that time, of course—I thought, well, Brooke was leaving anyway, why not just make it look as if he'd gone away? And then it wouldn't matter about the policeman, no one would know Brooke was dead. So I went back, and that time I parked behind the building. I hadn't any trouble getting in, you see, he'd already put that note for the landlady, with the key in it, on the front door. And at first I thought of putting everything, Brooke and the suitcases, into the car, and going down to the beach—but it would have been awfully difficult, being a woman I'm *not* very strong, of course. And then I thought of that funny trap door. I'd only been to his place once before, you know—he was ashamed of it, I think—but he'd shown it to me then, because I noticed the hinges on the floor, such a funny place, and asked. I think it was clever of me to remember and take the time to *bury* him. Dead things begin to—to—you know, have an *odor,* after a while. I didn't think it needed to be very deep, just *enough.* And it was the oddest thing, very lucky, there was a trowel, just lying there on the couch in the living room—I can't imagine why. Very lucky, because of course you couldn't use a spade down there, there wasn't room. It took *ages,* after I'd pushed him down there, and I was terribly frightened once when some people came in—I don't know who. They knocked, and I knew the door was unlatched—they might come in—so I just closed the trap and waited. I'd left my purse in the car. I knew there wasn't anything damaging for them to see. They stayed an awfully long time, I could just barely hear the voices, you know. I thought they'd never go—"

"Weren't you," he asked of private curiosity, "at all nervous down there in the dark with a dead man?"

She stared up at him. "I was waiting for them to go, so I could get on with burying him. No, why? You said, about later on, I couldn't face going down again—how silly—it wasn't that, it was my shoes—I'd almost ruined them, quite expensive shoes, and I didn't want to get them dirty again after I'd . . . And I *did* think, those things—to *plant* on someone else, if . . . I remembered to wear my gloves all the time, except just at first, and I wiped off things I remembered touching then. Only I lost a button from one of them, somewhere—"

"Yes, we have both the button and the glove."

"Oh—have you? You *are* clever. . . . And, you know, when I slid him down the trap—I *have* been a little worried about this—there was a lot of money, all in a great roll, fell out of his trouser pocket, *and* the bankbooks—for the Temple accounts, I mean. I've been worried about those, I didn't know what to do—Martin should have them back, but— Oh, and I kept the money, of course— You needn't say I stole it, the way Brooke did, because you know, I'd spent that much and *more* on him, it was only fair! . . . And I cleaned everything up tidily, the last thing—that was *after* I came back in the cab, of course. I emptied the ashtray and put some scraps of waste paper into the wastepaper basket, an empty pack of cigarettes and torn paper, there on the bureau—" (Yes, of course, Kingman's note, and Mrs. Bragg emptying the basket.) "The car was an awful nuisance. Of course it had to go too, and I thought if it was found near the station people would think he'd gone away on a train. *That* was stupid—I didn't think until I was almost there—I should have left it at the airport, much closer to the apartment, so much easier. I took along the smallest suitcase because I thought that would look to a cab driver as if *I'd* just got off a train— but then I realized I couldn't take a cab right at the station, in the light. You know," she simpered at him, "people always do look at me, and they'd be bound to remember. So I thought, something to put over my hair, and I put on a lot more make-up too, heavy eyebrows and so on, like that, as a disguise. And, oh, that suitcase was so heavy! I walked and walked, looking for some place I could get a scarf, something like that—but everything was going right for me that night, I found a place open—and you're lying when you say that man, and the driver too, knew I was acting a part! I always said I could do character work, though it's not *necessary,* of course—I *am* better, I admit that, at ingenue types. And when I did get back, such a time it took too, I put the note back on the door where it had been, and the key, and—I never thought anyone would find out, and what did it *matter?* But you were cleverer than I thought—I can't imagine how you came to find him. . . . All the same, I don't think I mind, because I really believe this might be the great turning point for me, you know? Some really *useful* publicity—and of course a good new agent, someone *young*—"

"Maybe so, Miss Ferne," said Mendoza. "Thank you very much, I think that's all we'll ask of you right now. You can sign a typed statement later."

"Come on, dear," said the policewoman.

"Oh, may I go now? I must see about a lawyer, I suppose. Goodbye, Lieutenant." As she was led out the door she was saying again, to herself, "Someone *young*—with the *youthful outlook*—that's the main thing, the important thing—"

Hackett said angrily, wonderingly, "She never asked about Angel at all. Where she is, how she feels. And, my God, this is going to be tough on Angel. . . . Even without a trial, if the lawyer persuades the Ferne not to try denying that confession—"

"She'll probably try," said Mendoza. "Claim the brutal police forced her to sign it. Rather odd business altogether, but then—as Madame Cara said to me—people *are.* And, speaking of clichés, that's one we always come back to in our business, don't we?—you look far enough, there's a woman at the bottom of every piece of mischief. For me, *nada de eso,* thanks. Too dangerous."

Hackett looked at him there, leaning back in his swiveled-around chair, looking out the window. Hackett said, "There's another one says the most accomplished and wary Casanova meets his downfall sooner or later and gets led to the slaughter. I'm just waiting for the day it happens to you—I'll be there to cheer on true love."

Mendoza swung around and laughed up at him. "A lot of people are waiting for that day, boy. You'll all wait a long, long time. Maybe forever."

"Cuanto apuestas, how much do you bet?" asked Hackett.

Mendoza looked interested at once. "At what odds, friend? If they're long enough— But what'd we make the *terminus ad quem?* Retiring age, maybe?"

"I was just talking," said Hackett hastily, "no bets. Not with you. Retiring age? My God, you'd get up out of your coffin to chase a pretty woman—"

"Probably," said Mendoza, "probably. But not so headlong that I'd run into the trap."

Hackett laughed a little shortly and went out. Mendoza looked after him and shook his head: a pity about Hackett, if he was really serious over this girl. However, these things happened. *"Eso allá el,"* said Mendoza to himself, "his own business." But very probably he'd be of little use for a while until he recovered from temporary lunacy. . . .

At which point Sergeant Lake came in with a sheaf of new reports, and Mendoza sat up, demanded coffee, lit a cigarette, and began to go through them with interest. Always another job coming up, in this business.

This accidental poisoning, for instance, had it really been accidental? Sergeant Galeano thought not. Better hear what he had to say, and begin to think about it. . . .

THE
KNAVE
OF
HEARTS

ONE

"So that's all, enough! The same old story—*¡siempre la trampa,* sure! I'll be damned if—"

"Oh, damn you and whatever you want to think—the trap, always the same susp— And what makes you think I'd have you? *¡A ningun precio,* thanks very much. Get out, go away, I can't—"

"*¡Un millón de gracias, le deseo lo propio*—the same to you!" He lost his temper about once in five years, Mendoza, and when he did it wasn't a business of loud violence; he had gone dead white and his voice was soft and shaking, and his eyes and his voice were cold as death and as hard. "You—"

"Get out for God's sake—*¡largo de aquí!*—you can go to hell for all I—" And she didn't lose her temper often either, but it didn't take her that way when she did; she was all but screaming at him now, taut with rage, and if she'd had a weapon to hand she'd have killed him.

"*¡Rapidamente,* anywhere away from you! *¡Y para todo, muchas gracias!*" That was sardonic, and pure ice; he snatched up his hat and marched out, closing the door with no slam, only a viciously soft little click.

Alison stood motionless there for a long moment, her whole body still shaking with the anger, the impulse to violence; she breathed deep, feeling her heart gradually slow its pounding. And now, of course, she could think of all she should have said, longed to say to him. This cheap cynical egotist, only the one thing in his mind—every obscene word she knew in two tongues, she'd like to—she should have—

And then, a while after that, she drew a long shuddering breath and moved, to sit down in the nearest chair. The fury was dead in her now, and that was another difference between them; it never lasted long with her. She sat there quite still; her head was aching slightly, then intolerably—aftermath of all that primitive physical reaction.

The little brown cat Sheba leaped up beside her, asking attention, purring; Alison stroked her mechanically. The kitten he had given her, the only thing she had ever let him give her.

And wasn't he a judge of women indeed, that way, all ways! It was even a little funny: one of the first things he'd said to her after they'd met—"A respectable woman like you, she's so busy convincing me she's not after my money, *vaya*, she's never on guard against my charm."

Ought to take something for this headache.

She got up, went slowly through the bedroom to the bathroom, swallowed some aspirin. In the garish overhead light there she looked at herself in the glass impersonally. Alison Weir, and not bad for thirty-one either; her best point, of course, was the thick curling red hair, and the fine white skin and green-hazel eyes complemented it. You might think Alison Weir could do pretty well for herself, even with that foolish too-young marriage thirteen years in her past, and no money now, to count. The women you saw—plain, dowdy, careless, and bitchy too—selfish and mean women—who somehow managed to find men for themselves . . .

"Oh, God," she whispered, and bent over, clutching the slippery bowl against the pain. The aspirin hadn't taken hold yet, but this was a worse pain than the headache.

It was true, of course. She had forgotten now exactly what thoughtless little phrase had started the ugly sudden quarrel—his sarcastic answer and her quick, angry protest fanning the flame. But in essence, his cynical suspicion was true, how true. Setting the trap, to have him all hers.

She could not face the woman in the mirror, the pale woman with the pain in her eyes. She went into the bedroom and sat down on the bed.

But from the beginning she had known him for what he was. Not for any one woman: not ever, apart from his womanizing, all of Luis Mendoza for any human person. He was just made that way. Like one of his well-loved cats, at least half of him always secret to himself, aloof. And maybe all because of the hurts he'd taken (for she knew him very thoroughly, perhaps better than he suspected, and she knew his terrible sensitivity). The hurts he'd taken as a dirty little Mex kid running the slum streets—long before he came into all that money. So that he'd never give anyone the chance to hurt him again, ever, in any way. Never let anyone close enough to hurt him. She had known: but knowing was no armor for the heart.

There was an old song her father used to sing: one of the favorites, it was, around the cook-fires in the evening, in every makeshift little construction camp she remembered—always one of the locally hired laborers with a guitar. The easy desultory talk after the day's work, sporadic laughter, and the guitar talking too, as accompaniment, in the blue southern night. *Ya me voy . . . mi bien,* I must go, my love . . . *te vengo a decir adios*—I have come to tell you goodbye . . . *te mando decir, mi bien, como se mancuernan dos*—to tell you how disastrously two people can be yoked . . .

What use had it been to know? It was all her own fault. Maybe she deserved whatever pain there would be, was—she had known how it would end. Quarrel or no, he would have gone eventually. When he'd had enough of her, when he'd found a new quarry—when instinct told him she was coming too close, wanting too much of him. And she did not need telling that all this while she alone hadn't held him—there'd been others, for variety.

Toma esa llavita de oro, mi bien . . . take this gold key, open my breast and you'll see how much I love you . . . *y el mal pago que me das*—and how badly you repay me . . .

And the time had come, and he had gone; she would not see him again; the interlude was over. It was for Alison Weir to pick up the pieces the best way she could, and go on from here.

Toma esa cajita de oro, mi bien . . . take this gold box, look to see what it contains . . . *lleva amores, lleva celos*—*y un poco de sentimiento*—love and jealousy, and a little regret . . .

Shameful, shameless, that she could not feel any resentment, any righteous hatred, that—for what he was—he had left her to this pain. No self-respect as half-armor against it: despicable, that she could summon no shred of pride to keep anger alive.

It was going to be very bad indeed, somehow finding out how to go on—somewhere—without him. That was no one's fault, hers or his. No one deliberately created feelings; they just came. No one could be rid of them deliberately, either.

It was going to be very bad. All the ways it could be, not just the one way. Because there had been also (would it help, this objective terminology for emotions?) a companionship: their minds operating on the same wave length, as it were.

"But I should be ashamed," and she was startled to hear her own voice. "I should be *ashamed*—" not to hate. She put her hands to her face; she sat very still, bracing herself against the pain.

"Post-mortems!" said Mendoza violently. "Religion! 'Saved from Satan and thus confessing my sins!'" He slapped Rose Foster's signed statement down on his desk. "What the hell are we supposed to do with this?"

"Don't look at me," said Hackett, "I didn't handle the Haines case, and neither did you—by the grace of God. All for the best in this best of all worlds, isn't it?—damn shame Thompson had to drop dead of a heart attack at fifty, but at least it's saved him from some rough handling by the press. What'd the Chief say?"

"You don't need the answer to that one," said Mendoza. *"Tomemos del mal el menos*—the lesser of two evils. Nothing definite to the press —no statements for the time being. Get to work on it and find out, find out everything, top to bottom! But no washing dirty linen in public." He lit a cigarette with an angry snap of his lighter and swiveled round in his desk-chair to face out the window, over the hazy panorama of the city spread below. He didn't like this business; nobody in the department who knew anything about it liked it; but he might not be taking it so violently except for that damned fight with Alison last night.

He smoked the cigarette in little quick angry drags, nervous. Women! There was a saying. *Sin mujeres y sin vientos, tendriamos menos tormentos*—without women and without wind, we'd have less torment. *Absolutamente,* he thought grimly. Scenes like that upset him; he liked it kept nice and easy, the smooth exit when an exit was indicated and that was that. Usually he managed it that way, but once in a while— women being women—a scene was unavoidable. He might have known it would be, with Alison: not the ordinary woman. He was sorry about it, that it had ended that way. Apart from anything else, he had liked Alison—as a person to be with, not just a woman—they'd understood each other: minds that marched together. But women—! Always wanting to go too deep, put it on the permanent basis. Sooner or later the exit had to be made. He was only sorry, hellishly sorry, that this one had had to be made that way.

But it was water under the bridge now, and the sooner he stopped brooding on it the better.

God knew he had enough to occupy his mind besides.

Abruptly he swiveled back and met Hackett's speculative stare. Art Hackett knew him too damned well, probably guessed something was on his mind besides this business. . . . Hackett didn't matter. Hackett nice and cozy in his little trap, not knowing yet it was one: Hackett two weeks married to his Angel, still the maudlin lover.

He picked up the Foster woman's statement again and looked at it with distaste. *I know I done awful wrong and now I been saved into the true religion I want to clear my conscience once for all . . .*

"If that," said Hackett, "is so, it's damned dirty linen, Luis. And it can't be kept a secret forever. There was the hell of a lot of publicity over Haines, not too long ago. It'd be news with a capital N—and when it comes to that, would it be such a hot idea to hide it up, for the honor of the force so to speak?" He shrugged and shook his head.

"That," said Mendoza, "is just one unfortunate aspect. As you say, at least Thompson's dead and whatever they say about him he won't hear. Also, he makes a very convenient scapegoat, doesn't he, tucked away underground? We can always give it out the poor fellow was failing—all very sad, but such things will happen, obviously he was prematurely se-nile and didn't know what he was doing. Which is one damned lie. And what the hell is this worth?" He flicked the statement contemptuously. "Sure, a lot of publicity—before the trial, after the trial. A lot of people sympathetic to Haines and his family, believing in him. Here's a damn-fool female turned religious fanatic—who's to say she didn't make the whole thing up, just to get her name in the papers?"

"She had his pipe," said Hackett. "The wife's identified it."

"All *right—¡vaya por Dios!*—the wife was panting to identify it," said Mendoza irritably. "Did she really look at it so close?"

Hackett got out a cigarette and turned it round in his fingers, looking at it. "You taking the stand we can't be wrong? It happens, Luis. Not often, but it happens."

"No lo niego, I don't deny it. It happens. If it happened here, sure, the press boys'll get hold of it, and you know what they'll say, what the outcome will be, as well as I do. Stupid blundering cops—prejudiced evidence—and the muddleheaded editorials about the death penalty and circumstantial evidence! *¡Es lo de siempre,* the same old story—*¡por Dios y Satanás!"* He laughed without humor.

"And bringing it up again," agreed Hackett, "every time somebody we get for homicide looks wide-eyed at a press camera and says, 'I swear I'm not guilty.' You needn't tell me. But there it is."

They both looked at the couple of stapled sheets on the desk with re-sentment.

The Haines case had been officially closed on the police books, for over a year. Haines had appealed the verdict, of course; there had been delays, the desperate little seeking of legal loopholes, but in the end he'd gone to the gas chamber for the murder of Mary Ellen Wood. And all that time, during and after the trial, no police officer who'd worked on the case had had any smallest doubt of his guilt. That wasn't prejudice, or carelessness, or stupidity: it was the way all the facts pointed. There was a lot of nonsense talked about circumstantial evidence; people very seldom committed serious crimes before witnesses, so circumstantial evidence was usually the only evidence there was, and quite valid evidence too. In fact, as Mendoza remembered hearing a judge remark once, witnesses being as prone to error as they were, circumstantial evidence was frequently worth more than eyewitness testimony.

This was an efficient, modern police force, noted for its integrity and competence, its high standards for recruits. Detective-Sergeant Thompson had happened to get the Haines case, but it might have fallen to Mendoza or any of his sergeants, and if it had, none of them would have come up with a different answer—not on all the evidence that showed.

Mary Ellen Wood, nineteen months ago, had just turned twenty. She was a pretty girl, brown-haired and brown-eyed, and she was popular on the L.A.C.C. campus; but by all accounts she was a shy, serious girl who didn't spend much time fooling around with the boys in study hour or afterward. She was majoring in English literature and history, and she was a good student. She lived with her parents and two younger sisters in a nice middle-class house in a nice middle-class neighborhood in Hollywood. She had worked at temporary office jobs a couple of summers, to earn her tuition and buy clothes, but during the school year she held no regular job, did occasional baby-sitting for a little extra money. The Haineses—Allan Haines and his wife Sally—had hired her for that a number of times. They lived only a few blocks away from the Woods, and they'd met Mary Ellen through Sally Haines' twenty-year-old brother Jim Fairless, who went to L.A.C.C. too. The Haineses had two small children, a boy six and a girl four, and were expecting another.

Most people seemed to have liked Mary Ellen, and those who knew her best (outside her family: you couldn't always go by what the family said) said she was "a nice girl"—not the kind of girl to, well, do anything she shouldn't—and a steady girl too: usually dated only on weekends, and helped her mother around the house. So the family had been somewhat alarmed almost right away when she didn't come home at her regular time that Wednesday afternoon. By six o'clock her father was calling the hospitals, and by seven the police.

So eventually there were quite a few trained men looking for Mary Ellen and asking questions about her. For nearly a week they looked and asked. They learned, among other things, that Mary Ellen had confided to one of her girl friends that she'd had a little trouble with the husband at a place she'd been baby-sitting: no names mentioned. When it appeared that she hadn't vanished voluntarily, they began to look at the people she'd worked for. But before they got round to the Haineses, Sally Haines happened to go into a little garden shed in the Haineses' back yard looking for a rake, and she found Mary Ellen's brown hand-bag on the shelf there. The girl's belongings were all in it, including iden-tification. Mrs. Haines realized at once what it was, and like an honest citizen she called the police.

Probably Sally Haines had done some bitter thinking about her be-havior as an honest citizen. Because then, of course, the police had taken a good look at the Haineses and their property; and without much difficulty they had found Mary Ellen, hastily buried in the carth floor of the garden shed. Sergeant Thompson had taken over then, and within thirty-six hours he had arrested Allan Haines on a charge of murder.

The autopsy showed that the girl had been raped and shortly after-ward beaten and strangled: two of many blows or the strangulation could have been the actual cause of death—the surgeon thought it had been the blows.

She had last been seen, by anyone who knew her, at a little past three o'clock on the campus that Wednesday. She'd been offered a ride home, but declined, saying she already had one—she was meeting someone. However, no one of her acquaintances on campus had been her date, as far as could be ascertained—and Thompson had looked very thor-oughly. Especially, of course, he had looked at young Jim Fairless, who would have had knowledge of and access to the Haineses' garden shed. But Fairless had never gone around with Mary Ellen, he had a girl of his own; and he also had an excellent alibi—you couldn't ask for a bet-ter. The surgeon had pinned down the time of death to between that Wednesday afternoon and the following afternoon or evening. It was midterm, and Jim Fairless had cut the last two days of classes that week for a vacation. He'd left Wednesday noon with his girl, a young married couple as chaperones, and an engaged couple, both of whom were classmates of his at college, for Lake Arrowhead and a few days of winter sports. All five of them said he'd been with them continuously over that weekend.

So then Thompson looked at Haines, and it appeared that Haines had left his office at around one-thirty that Wednesday and couldn't prove where he'd been and what he'd done afterward. He was a salesman for a wholesale garden-supply firm and didn't keep regular office hours; nobody thought anything of his being out that afternoon. Questioned, he'd told a lie about where he'd been; and when that fell through—by then he understood that he was the number-one suspect—he said all right, he'd tell the truth, God forgive him but he'd gone to see this woman, this Rose Pringle. He said he'd met the woman at one of the companies he sold to: she wasn't an employee, she'd been applying for a job there. He didn't know much about her except her name—he'd only met her twice. Just one of those things—he must have been crazy, but there it was. He gave an address, where he said he'd been with her that afternoon; it was a shabby run-down apartment off Vermont Avenue and the tenants had just moved, but the name had been Foster, not Pringle. A couple of neighbors who'd known them casually said they didn't think it likely that Mrs. Foster'd be up to nothing like that, she was a real quiet modest little thing and not very pretty anyways. Press appeals were made, and radio appeals, for the Fosters to come forward, but they never did. They might not have liked the idea of publicity, or they might have gone out of the state and never heard they were wanted.

And then Edith Wood, Mary Ellen's seventeen-year-old sister, admitted that Allan Haines had been the husband who'd—well, call it made advances—to Mary Ellen once, when she was baby-sitting for them. He usually brought her home afterwards, of course, like the fathers always did, and it had been one of those times, in his car. But Mary Ellen had told Edith he let her go right away when she struggled, and seemed ashamed of himself, apologized: he'd been a little tight, hadn't known what he was doing—Mr. Haines was really a nice man, he'd never do anything like that in his right mind, so to speak. And she told Edith for goodness sake not to tell their parents about it, or they'd never let her take another job at the Haineses', which was silly because he'd been terribly ashamed and nothing like that would ever happen again, she knew.

Haines admitted all that; he said he'd lost his head, he'd had a few drinks too many that night, but he'd been horrified at himself afterward

—a nice girl like Mary Ellen. Certainly he'd never thought of her that way before or since; he hadn't, before God he hadn't, met her that afternoon and assaulted her and then—scared of inevitable retribution when she accused him—killed and buried her.

"My God," he said, "if I *had,* wouldn't I have had better sense than to bury her in my own back yard—leave her bag right out in plain sight?"

But murderers did that kind of thing, time and again. There was a school of thought which held it was the unconscious seeking of punishment; in Mendoza's opinion it was just vanity (the earmark of all criminals, that was)—the conviction that they were invincible.

Then a couple of L.A.C.C. students came in to say that they thought they'd seen Haines that afternoon, sitting in a car near the campus. It would have been about two-thirty. They'd cut the last half of a study hour to go out for coffee at a place on Vermont, and half a block or so this side they'd passed this fellow sitting in a car. Why had they noticed him particularly? Well— That wasn't hard to figure if you looked at his photograph. Haines was a good-looking man, and he ran a classy open Thunderbird; both the students were female. They identified Haines positively as the man they'd seen.

Yes, he was there, said Haines; it was the first time he'd visited Rose Pringle, he'd been looking for the address. All those narrow little side streets off Vermont there, he'd finally had to look at a map, and that's what he'd been doing when those girls walked past—just pulled up to the curb a minute, locating the street on a city map. He hadn't noticed the girls, hadn't given a thought to the fact that he was near the L.A.C.C. campus—why should he?

Both the Haineses said that anyone could have walked into their back yard and disposed of the body there. It was a lot two hundred feet deep; there was a hedge between the shed and the house, and an unpaved alley at the end which was used freely for foot traffic. After dark—

But it seemed peculiar that Haines hadn't noticed anything. There were a neighbor and his wife who'd seen him entering the shed around eight that evening and again on Thursday; he had to admit he'd been in the shed perhaps three or four times that week. And hadn't seen the strange handbag right in plain sight on the shelf?—there was an unshaded hanging bulb that lit up the whole place bright as day. No, he hadn't or maybe he had and just thought it was his wife's. Did Mrs. Haines usually keep her handbags in the garden shed? Well, of course not; and he couldn't say why, if he had noticed it and thought she'd left it there, he hadn't taken it into the house to her. He hadn't noticed the very obviously disturbed earth in the shed? No. The photographs taken at the time showed the grave open, but everyone present at the opening had testified that there had been fresh-turned earth heaped there, earth left on the spade hanging in its place on the wall rack—evidence of the digging was plain to see, and the grave right in the center of the floor. It was a small but significant point: if somebody from outside had done it, how had he known, first, that the shed didn't have a wooden floor, and second, that he'd find a spade convenient to hand?

Haines said that it was obviously a shelter for garden tools: anyone who'd ever passed down that alley might have known. But there were no footprints in that fresh earth except his, no prints on the spade—and there was a pair of cotton work gloves handy there on the shelf.

What more did an investigating officer want? It was open and shut. Haines had been attracted to the girl, had made advances once at least: that was sure. She'd been buried in his shed with his spade, and if he hadn't done it, it didn't look as though he could have entered the place without noticing the evidence of that. ("I was worried that week," said Haines desperately, "I had a couple of business problems on my mind, I was kind of absent-minded—I just didn't *notice*—I only went in there a minute, a couple of times, to get a trowel, the rake.") He'd been seen near the campus at a significant time, as if he were waiting for someone. Mary Ellen had expected to be met and given a ride home, she'd said. And Haines couldn't produce his witness to say what he'd been doing instead.

It looked run-of-the-mill. Contrary to all the detective stories—any experienced cop knew—murderers weren't often very clever. Most of them in fact were damn fools. Thompson built it up this way. Haines had been on his way to a business call in that area, say about two or a bit past, and he'd run into Mary Ellen (she'd gone to that coffee shop on Vermont before her last class). There'd been a little casual talk; he'd seen another chance to get her and offered to meet her and take her home, in an hour. Mary Ellen—believing herself safe with him, seeing him as only a friendly neighbor—had accepted. He waited, and met her there at three o'clock. Drove somewhere, maybe up in the hills in Griffith Park, where any screams wouldn't be heard. She hadn't fought her assailant; her nails weren't broken or her clothes torn. Maybe she'd been taken so completely by surprise she hadn't had time, or maybe he'd knocked her unconscious right away. In his notes

Thompson had also outlined a tentative idea that the girl might have been genuinely in love with Haines, been led on to a voluntary assignation. That was just an idea, and it wasn't the case stated by the prosecution at the trial, because there was no proof. If it had been like that, Haines would have had no reason to kill the girl, unless he was a lunatic. More likely, after he'd raped her it came to him what a spot he'd be in when she accused him, and he took the easiest way out. There was no blood in his car, no evidence of the assault—of course, he might have taken her out, into the bushes somewhere—but they did find a little blood on the old blanket folded on the floor of the trunk, and it was type O, Mary Ellen's type. (Also Haines' type, and he said Yes, he'd skinned his hand on a wrench one day when he was working on the car, that must have been how the blood . . .) He'd probably stashed her in the trunk, with her own coat bundled round her so no blood would get on the floor, and either late that Wednesday night or the following night made the grave. (It was surprising how often a killer who disposed of the body liked to have the spot under his eye, close to home. Plenty of precedent there, and for the other mistakes he'd made.) The garage was at the back of the lot, close to the shed. Mrs. Haines wasn't the gardener—Haines did most of that—and she seldom entered the shed, so he hadn't bothered to do a perfect job. Maybe forgot about the purse or intended to dispose of it later. He hadn't (with that inevitable conviction of safety, that he was too clever to be caught) expected to be linked to it; when he was, he was taken by surprise. And in the same impulsive way the murder had been done, he produced a spur-of-the-moment alibi. He made up this Rose Pringle out of his head, gave an address at random (remembering a street name he'd noticed as he waited for Mary Ellen). Yes, senseless, but people did these things—he might even have been cocky enough to figure that when he confessed cheating on his wife like that, everybody would believe it was the truth because surely, otherwise he'd never have admitted it. He might even have gambled that whatever woman lived at that address could be bribed to back him up. Bribed, of course, by Mrs. Haines (Haines was sitting in a cell downtown then)—for Mrs. Haines, faced with the choice of keeping a cheating husband or losing a murderous one to the gas chamber, had stayed by him; protested her belief in him; bought TV time to appeal to the Pringle woman to come forward.

Several good attorneys had fought hard for him too, but there was just too much suggestive evidence. And after that, the appeal, the bitter accusations from Mrs. Haines of prejudice and stupidity on the part of the police, the denial of a new trial, the sentimental news stories when Mrs. Haines' baby was born, the date of execution (twice postponed) finally settled.

Haines had died in the gas chamber thirty days ago, for a murder nineteen months old.

And yesterday morning a diffident young woman had walked into a precinct station in Santa Monica and said she wanted to get something off her conscience.

TWO

Mendoza had seen Rose Foster this morning; the job had been thrown at him because Thompson was four months dead. So he didn't have to reread her statement; it had come out more directly, more convincingly, in her thin little voice than in the steno's dead prose.

She was thirty-two, she said, and she looked that in one way, but in another way much younger. She might have been pretty had she paid more attention to herself—a slender, frail-looking woman with a lot of untidy brown hair and timid blue eyes; shabby in a cheap housedress, mended stockings, no make-up or jewelry.

"Pringle was my maiden name, see, I—I was giving it out places I looked for work, account some places, they don't like to hire married women—give single ones first chance. And I had enough trouble findin' work anyways, I ain't—haven't had much education, got to take what I can. . . . Jack, he'd 've just killed *me*, sir, if he knew—that was why. Jack, no use not facin' it, he wasn't no good noways, he liked the drink too much. An' ever he got drunk, knockin' me around—that was the way of it, see. . . . This business, really how I come to leave him—get up enough grit, leave him—I was too scared before—he'd 've come after, give me what-for to run off. I felt awful bad about it—but I just *dassn't* do anything about it, while Jack—he'd 've *killed* me. . . . Mr. Haines was nice to me. Not many been like that, and with Jack the way he was—I guess that's how I come to *do* such a sinful thing. . . . I got to say it, I got to clear my conscience—Reverend White says I got to, to be truly saved in the Lord—I got to tell you, it was all just like Mr. Haines said. He was—with me—that day, just like he told you. *Sinning*. Maybe you think that's awful queer—he'd look at me—but, see, he was sorry for me to start—first time we met, I'd got turned down for a job that place, I couldn't help crying, right out in the street too—it was hard to get along, get enough to eat and all, with Jack all the time gettin' fired for bein' drunk—and Mr. Haines, he was kind, he bought me a cup of coffee and talked nice, and he got me a job cleaning offices, another place. . . .

"And you know—that time—his wife was havin' a baby, I guess she was kind of crotchety to him, know what I mean, and he—I guess any woman who was nice to him, he'd 've—oh, I was *awful* scared that time, for fear Jack'd walk in and— And after, when it come out in the papers, I about died o' fright. . . . No, sir, Jack, he never read no papers, he didn't see about it. We was behind in the rent, I just wanted get away, and I told him the landlord says we got to get out. Wasn't nothin' strange about that, it was always happening. And he had the offer of this job up in Banning. We went there, and he never heard nothing, I guess, about—that murder. But it laid on my conscience day 'n' night—like the black sin it was—I got so I couldn't stand it no longer—even if Jack *did* kill me. . . . And the Reverend, he come to a 'vivalist meeting up there, last week it was, and seemed like he was preaching right at *me,* he knowed all about it—a strong preacher he is —and after, I went up an' talked with him. He said—and it do seem funny, I never thought about it just so before—there wasn't no law I had to stay by such a bad husband, and anyways, Jack or no Jack, do I want my soul saved alive from Satan, I got to get my conscience clear —no matter what you do to me for the awful thing I done—"

Yes, convincing. If for no other reason than its appalling human wrongheadedness. He said to Hackett, "What's it worth?" but he'd known, listening to Rose Foster, that it was the truth. The well-used pipe she'd kept, the pipe that Haines said he must have left there, maybe that wasn't such good evidence—but whether it was his or not, it wasn't very important.

He said, "Very damned dirty linen to wash, even in private. But it happens." Because, with the most intelligent and honest police force, the fairest trial, the cleverest lawyers, with all these, chance—and the human element—sat in the game too, and sometimes stacked the deck. For every once that this happened, it happened ninety-nine times the other way round: somebody who was guilty got off, because of the finicky rules about evidence, the little legal loopholes, the design of the law to give the innocent every chance.

"What do we do about it?" asked Hackett. As Mendoza didn't say anything at once, he took a last drag on his cigarette, put it out in the ashtray, and stabbed a finger at the second sheaf of papers on Mendoza's desk. "Don't drag your heels so hard, *amigo*. I got an idea what those are. While you were in with the Chief I met Farley downstairs and had a little chat with him. He says you requisitioned all those letters Sally Haines has been sending us for quite a while, and he told me something about 'em. Very interesting."

Mendoza said softly, violently, *"¡Diez millon es de demonios negros desde el infierno! Hay que poner en claro este lío*—this mess we've got to clear up, *pronto*. Interesting! If there's an ounce of truth in these, I can think of better words." He pushed the second sheaf across the desk. "Take a look and suffer some more—for the honor of the force!"

Sally Haines had fought harder for her husband than his lawyers; she'd never given up fighting, and it looked as if she'd never forget her bitter grudge against the police. There were a dozen letters in the pile, all addressed to the Chief. Mendoza said, "The top three. The rest are just random accusations."

Hackett read, grunted, grimaced, reached for another cigarette. "Oh, brother. Piper's close to home, I had that one." He started to read the letters again.

The first was dated a week after Haines' trial. *It should be evident to the stupidest policeman that the murderer of Mary Ellen Wood is still free—and still murdering. Three days ago another girl was found dead in very similar circumstances. I refer to Celestine Teitel. If and when you arrest the criminal in that case, I beg you to question him, investigate him, in re Mary Ellen Wood—he may have been her killer too. I pray my husband will be cleared of guilt when the real killer is found.*

The second was dated nearly six months later. *You did not find Celestine Teitel's murderer—now he has killed Jane Piper. Can you protest there is not a strong probability that these murders were done by the same man?—as was the murder of Mary Ellen Wood! If you ever arrest him, I pray you get to the truth about that at last!*

The third was dated fifteen days ago. *Now the real murderer of Mary Ellen Wood has another death to his account—Pauline McCandless. Surely the most casual investigation shows the similarity of these crimes —are you still so sure that my husband murdered Mary Ellen? Celes-*

*tine Teitel—Jane Piper—Pauline McCandless—they died the same way
as Mary Ellen, and I swear by the same hand! You have not caught
him yet—if you ever do, ask him about Mary Elllen Wood! It is too
late to save my husband's life, but his name may yet be cleared.*

Hackett said, "I'm not up on Teitel and McCandless, but I've got to
say she could be right about Piper. Just on the bare facts. And what's
that worth?"

"Not the hell of a lot, at first glance." All those killings had been the
same kind; but it was an ordinary kind in any big metropolitan place
with its inevitable share of the violent ones, the mentally unstable ones,
the professional muggers prowling dark streets.

Celestine Teitel. (Mendoza had looked back over those cases only
superficially as yet; he'd look deeper.) Age thirty, unmarried. Elementary school teacher. Taught at a public school in Hawthorne, shared an
apartment with another teacher. Regular, quiet habits, not many
friends. An amateur painter: often went out on weekends, to the beach,
the mountains, to paint. One Sunday she didn't come home again, so
her roommate called the police. She was found two days later, by a
couple of surf-fishers, in a lonely cove up the coast toward Ventura,
where apparently she'd been sketching—all her equipment there, un-
touched. She'd been raped, beaten, and strangled.

Jane Piper. Age twenty-eight, unmarried. Also a very respectable
young woman—and successful, a legal secretary to an old and staid
firm of corporation lawyers. Lived alone in a three-room apartment
near Silver Lake. Drove a good car. But the best cars now and then
needed expert attention; so there she was, her car temporarily at a garage, leaving her office one day at five o'clock to go home by bus. No
one who knew her saw her alive after that. She was found up in
Topanga Canyon, a little way off the road, next day. She had been
raped, beaten, and choked to death. There was some indication that the
intention had been to bury her—someone had started to dig a hole,
anyway, about twenty feet down the hillside.

Pauline McCandless. Age twenty-four, a librarian, just graduated and
working at the Culver City main library. Unmarried. Not very pretty: a
serious intellectual girl. Lived with her widowed mother in Hollywood.
Regular habits, no known male friends. She failed to return home one
night, so the police went hunting her; they didn't have to hunt long. She
was found in an empty lot in Walnut Park; she'd been raped, beaten,
and strangled.

Looked at like that, anyone might make the hasty judgment—obviously the same murderer. It wasn't so simple, so neat; that kind of crime happened too often, committed by too many types of men. Sometimes women almost asked for it, walking dark streets late and alone, picking up with any stranger who bought them a drink; but it happened to respectable women too. Over this period of eighteen months perhaps a dozen women had met similar deaths within Los Angeles County. Offhand Mendoza remembered a few details on those. A woman assaulted, strangled: the killer, a near-moronic eighteen-year-old with a record of petty theft—"I just had to stop her yelling, I only squeezed her throat a little bit, didn't go to kill her." A girl raped, beaten: the killers, a gang of juveniles riding high on cheap whiskey. Another one, another one—all the same pattern, the assault, the blows, the choking: this killer a respectable middle-aged family man who'd lost his head just once; that one, an equally respectable-looking mama's boy who'd suddenly gone berserk. When a woman was killed in the course of an assault, it was almost bound to happen that way: the man tried to stop her noise and, lacking any weapon, used his hands. Men who went in for rape were predisposed to violence to start with, and without intending murder frequently committed it.

The only difference about those three, Teitel, Piper, and McCandless, was that they'd never got anyone for them. Those cases were still marked *Pending*.

"Well?" said Hackett. "Do we work them all over again?"

"On a civilian's random hunch?" said Mendoza sharply. Absently he lined things up on the desk in more precise order, calendar, desk box, blotter, ashtray; brushed ash off the polished wood. He looked tired and all of his forty years for once, if as natty and dapper as always: a slender dark man with a black hairline of moustache and widow's peak of thick black hair, the sharp arch of heavy brows accenting unremarkable regular features. He sat back, twisting the heavy gold seal-ring round his finger in aimless gesture. "The Haines business we'll work over again, but hard. These others—we'll see. Who's still on McCandless?—Galeano. You've been on that Braxton thing—turn it over to Galeano, and get what he's got on McCandless. I want you in this with me. . . . And, *de paso,* you'd better tell your loving bride to expect you when she sees you while we're busy on this—we'll all be working overtime."

"That you needn't tell me," said Hackett equably.

"Look at McCandless. I'm going back over Wood. And in the meantime, let's both look for any common denominator. Before we—mmh

—jump to the unflattering conclusion that Mrs. Haines is brighter than we are, I want something a lot more definite to say there's a hookup in these cases. I'm going to brood over them tonight—I'll see Mrs. Haines tomorrow. I want any inspiration that comes to you on McCandless by tomorrow afternoon."

"O.K., I'll get on it." Without further wasted words, Hackett heaved his bulk up and went out in search of Sergeant Galeano.

Mendoza sat staring at the Foster statement for a minute, vaguely; roused himself, summoned Sergeant Lake, and sent him to rummage in the back files for all those records.

While he waited for them, he did some thinking about common denominators.

Hackett got home finally about eight o'clock. The indefinable new warmth flooded him—there inside the door with Angel in his arms, the smell and look of this their own place not yet quite familiar, but home. She nuzzled his collar and said she'd kept something hot for him.

"I see you're going to make a fine wife for a cop. No complaints about irregular hours, bein' neglected for some nasty corpse—"

"A casserole," said Angel. "Very French and exotic. I did think maybe strawberry mousse afterward, but when you called— So I made a trifle instead. A *very* good one, first time I'd tried the recipe. I never came across oregano in a sweet sauce before, but there's something about it—odd but rather nice—"

"I might've known," said Hackett. "You never missed me at all, with a new recipe to try."

"I did too." She raised her mountain-pool eyes to his. "Art."

"Mmh?"

"Did you see much of your boss today? . . . I just wondered. Alison's had a fight with him, I think. We were going downtown together this afternoon, I went to pick her up, and she begged off. She looked—oh, I don't know, all washed out, way down. . . . No, she wouldn't exactly *say*, but you know, she didn't need to—I—"

"You don't tell me," said Hackett slowly. A little something different about Mendoza, he'd thought: Mendoza a bit more nervous, irritable, than usual. So maybe this was it. He kissed the top of Angel's brown head absently; he said, "Damn Luis. You think they've split up? No, she wouldn't go looking for a shoulder to cry on—not that kind—but she'd take it hard. . . . Sooner or later he always walks out, sure."

"Just like that, goodbye and good luck! Doesn't he have any feelings at all?" she asked bitterly. "As if she was a— Oh, I was so *damned* sorry for her, darling! Of course she didn't need to tell me, I know her well enough to—"

"You weren't by any chance, my Angel, thinkin' of getting me to play go-between, maybe try to persuade him back to her? Because I'm not exactly a coward, but I got better sense than to fool around with high explosive, and when it comes to interfering with Luis' private life—"

"Heaven help us, you big lummox," said Angel crossly, "that's the *last* thing I'd wish her! The sooner she gets over that man the better—I can't *imagine* what women see in him—or you either, for that matter! Oh, he may be a wonderful detective and so on, but—!" She pounded a chair cushion into shape as angrily as if it had been Mendoza himself.

"Oh, well," said Hackett, "'passing the love of women—'" Which was all too true: even his Angel took funny ideas sometimes, or didn't quite understand. You had to expect it. And he guessed a lot of women would feel that way about a man like Mendoza. The one that always got away: the one you couldn't trust (the way it looked to them)—whether or not they felt the charm. A lot of guff talked about equality and friendship between the sexes: people weren't made that way; men still knew men better, and women women—for any real emotional understanding.

Mendoza—the only way you stayed a close friend to Luis was not trying to go too deep with him, intrude on privacies. And of course, men weren't given to that in friendship anyway, which was maybe the reason they could always stay better friends longer than women: they left each others' emotions alone. It wasn't any of Art Hackett's business, and it didn't make any difference to the friendship, what Mendoza did or didn't do in his private life.

At the same time, in this instance there was Alison Weir, whom he liked, and owed something, and felt sorry for. . . . She'd been a good friend to Angel. Maybe if it hadn't been for Alison his Angel wouldn't be the sane and pretty girl she was, nor his either.

"It's *senseless,*" she said. "Tearing herself to pieces over a man like that—"

But Luis, and it was a damn funny way to put it (even in thought)—it wasn't really selfishness or irresponsibility in him, that he was like that. It was more something like shyness. As if he was ashamed to show any real emotion, to show himself uncamouflaged to anybody—so he was afraid to get in too deep.

Well . . . people. "Darling love, there's nothing anybody can do about it. People—just made the way they're made." He was suddenly, immensely sorry for both of them—for anybody who didn't have what he and his Angel had.

"I know. . . . I wish she'd meet someone really nice, and—and solid, and good for her—"

"A real satisfactory husband just like me," he said, trying for a smile.

"Oh, you—I'll make up my mind if you're satisfactory or not in about thirty years. Nobody can be sure in less. But really, I *do* wish she'd find someone *right* for her. If—"

"You can't pick for somebody else. Best bargain in the world come along and want her, she'd probably have no use for him." He didn't add, while Luis was still above ground: he didn't have to.

"No," she agreed morosely.

"You say something about keeping something hot?"

Angel's eyes took on the absent dreaminess which meant she was thinking about recipes. "Mmh. Something new and nice. I'll get it. . . . And the trifle. I thought maybe I'd do the strawberry mousse tomorrow—"

"Is that one of those things won't keep? Better not count on it. We're going to be havin' some heavy homework, so to speak."

"Oh. A new case?"

"Yes and no," said Hackett. "A nasty one—I've got a feeling, a bad one."

"I thought the great Mendoza was the one who had hunches," said Angel, making a face.

THREE

Mendoza sat opposite Sally Haines in her slightly-too-neat living room and looked at her, and at her brother Jim Fairless. He hadn't troubled to do much listening to her yet: no use until she'd got it all said, just what she thought about the blundering cops.

She had a reason to say it, and a right. It would be no use either to argue with her, to point out that policemen and the law in general had to go on factual evidence, that it was only about once in a thousand cases that factual evidence pointed the wrong way or, conversely, that careful police investigation didn't turn up all the factual evidence there was. No use to point out the fact that—you might say, looking for first causes—if her husband hadn't had some reason to be cheating on her, to be with Rose Foster that day, he'd probably have been easily cleared by a straightforward alibi.

There were excuses for the law's mistake; that didn't make it any easier to acknowledge—either for Mendoza or Sally Haines.

He sighed and got out a new cigarette. "—won't admit it even now!" she was saying fiercely. "Now that this woman—but you'll have to, in the end! You—"

Yes: there'd be some nasty publicity, the governor would issue a posthumous pardon, everybody would make excuses and apologies, passing the buck, a lot of the ordinary public would lose faith in their police force, and none of it would be any use to Allan Haines. Whose life had been a stiff price to pay for one illicit roll in the hay: and probably (considering Rose Foster) not a very good one at that.

"Mrs. Haines," he said at last, his eyes on his cigarette, "we all appreciate how you feel about this. You may not believe me, but we're not exactly feeling indifferent about it either. But I haven't come here to listen to recriminations for what's past help now. I'd like to ask you a question. Those letters you wrote to us—"

"Don't tell me someone read them!" She laughed sharply. He had seen Thompson's private notes, and he thought Thompson had sized her up pretty well. Quite a pretty woman, blonde, slender, tall; probably an excellent wife and mother: but Thompson's scribbled terse notes summed her up—*bossy, in a nice way*—*likes family under her thumb*. He had added, *Reason? H. fed up—but not enough guts break real clear?* Maybe, thought Mendoza; it didn't matter much now. Yes, she'd be smooth about it, but she'd been the man in that family. Haines hadn't been his pigeon and he'd never met him, but it wasn't hard to figure him, the easy-going salesman type, agreeable, friendly—the type who often went for a woman he could lean on a little. (And at the same time often picked one, for the extracurricular exercise, who'd lean on him, flatter him.) All of which was quite irrelevant now.

"You made some accusations, Mrs. Haines, concerning three other homicides. I'd like to know just what led you to link them up."

"Better late than never!" exclaimed Fairless with a sarcastic smile.

He shared this apartment with his sister; and that was another item on the account. Someone had to help support a widow with three kids, and he'd come in for part of that responsibility, Mendoza deduced. "Red-letter day, Sally—the cops are asking for help from somebody with at least an average I.Q.! My God, having to ask *that,* an obvious thing like *that!* But I suppose when they make ranking cops of your kind—"

Mendoza returned the smile. "It's quite as obvious to the police as it is to you, Mr. Fairless, that there are certain points in common among these cases. But they're only three out of a dozen very similar cases, you know. Why did you single them out, Mrs. Haines?"

"I should have thought that would be obvious too," she said in a hard tone. "I knew it would happen again—that kind of man—I watched the papers, I followed everything printed about any murder like that, that was how— Do you really need an outsider to point out such a simple fact?"

Mendoza's smile tightened a little. Generally he had himself well in control, and he had come here expecting nothing else than this; he had intended merely to verify his deductions, say as little as possible. But he disliked this bad business almost as emotionally as these people did, and the tone of Fairless' voice, making *your kind* a thin euphemism for *a dirty stupid Mex,* raised unaccustomed anger in him, suddenly. He said softly, "To save time—and perhaps our tempers—was all you had to go on the fact that these three were women of similarly respectable backgrounds?"

She did not condescend to show him disappointment, to miss the satisfaction of stating the obvious. "*All?* I should think it was enough! That kind of thing doesn't often happen to such women—the opportunity—men like that—"

Mendoza stood up. "It happens. You picked them for that reason—I thought so. I've only one other question, Mrs. Haines—one you were asked before, but you may have thought of an answer by now. In those letters and others, you put forward the theory—I might deduce, suggested by wide reading of detective novels—" and he let his smile turn sardonic, "that Mary Ellen Wood's body was buried on your property in a deliberate attempt to make your husband the scapegoat. Have you any—mmh—candidate to name who might have had reason for that? Anyone with a grievance? Who might also have been the kind of man to commit that murder?"

"No, of course I—but it *could* have been! Oh, I don't know, about that! But the other—it's so obvious!" He had put her a little on the defensive now. "Girls, women like that—not the kind to let themselves be picked up by any stranger—just as Mary Ellen wasn't. Not as if they'd —been alone down on Skid Row at midnight, anywhere like— It can't have been just the usual thing with them, the way it usually happens, just as it wasn't with Mary Ellen—whoever—"

"I assure you, the implications are plain—even to a policeman," said Mendoza. These people had suffered a wrong, but there was no law that said he had to like them for it. As he walked down from the door to the street and the long elegance of the Facel-Vega there, he was aware of their hot eyes on his back. Aware that Fairless was wondering how a cop could afford to run a car like that—and making the obvious deduction.

He wanted to turn and go back, say to Fairless, Oddly enough, friend, it's honest money: if maybe the old miser rang in a cold deck now and then to win his capital, by the time it came to me it was on the level and it's stayed that way.

He was surprised at himself for the sudden temper, over such a small thing. This damned business . . . And he wasn't so juvenile as to harbor any honor-of-the-regiment chauvinism for the Los Angeles Police Department as sacrosanct; but for some nineteen years a large part of his life had been bound up with it. It wasn't very often that the L.A.P.D.—or any other efficient police force—got itself into a position like this, and it wasn't a happy position for any representative.

The hell of it was, he was beginning to think it might be a bigger, cruder blunder than anybody had suspected . . . not just on the Wood case. And that he didn't like: very much he didn't like that.

It was a quarter to one of this hot, still September Sunday. Mrs. Haines' apartment was in Bellflower; he drove up to Hollywood, to where the Woods still lived. The house was a sprawling frame bungalow, neatly maintained, on a quiet street. The girl who answered the door was relief and promise after Fairless and Mrs. Haines: about nineteen, luscious young rounded figure innocently displayed in shorts and halter top, and a boyishly friendly grin. Edith Wood, the sister.

"Oh," she said to his explanations. "Well, I'm the only one home, but I guess you can come in, Lieutenant. Off the record, I'm always getting warned about strange men, but after all if you're not safe with a policeman, when *are* you? The rest of the family's gone to the beach, but I had an essay to do for English Lit. . . . About Mary Ellen?" —and she sobered. "Unless it's something awfully important, maybe it's just as well you ask me—Mother and Dad, well, they've never really gotten over it, you know—"

"Understandable," said Mendoza, sitting down.

"Can I get you a drink or something?—I was just going to have some lemonade, it's all chilled in the refrigerator—no trouble. . . . But what's this all about, after all this time?" She had nice topaz-colored eyes, intelligent, and she cocked her cropped brown head at him shrewdly.

"Unfortunately," he said, "I'm afraid you'll be getting the answer to that in the papers soon. If I told you all about it now, you might be a little prejudiced against me as a representative detective. All I—"

"Oh, I don't know," she murmured.

"All I want to ask you, it's something you may not be able to tell me." Maybe it was the contrast of his reception here, but he felt oddly at home in this big, cool living room with its comfortable shabby furniture. The girl looked sideways at him (frankly interested, curious, a little *gauche* as yet and yet knowing that: her awareness of herself and him somehow endearing); and suddenly he knew it wasn't the room, or the friendly welcome, made him feel that way. Something more personal. She reminded him of Alison . . . not in any physical way: in herself. The kind of girl Alison would have been, eleven or twelve years back. This direct look, this promise of something more subtle than beauty. Alison . . .

"*¡Caray, soy on loco completo*—going senile!" he thought to himself irritably. Let it go, for God's sake, forget it, no post-mortems! (And a whisper at the back of his mind saying, but you know why, don't you? Just think a minute: you will have to face it, admit it, sooner or later, you know.) "What I want to ask you, Miss Wood,"—he flicked his lighter quickly—"is about your sister's friends. If you'll indulge me a moment without knowing why. She wasn't going steady with anyone? Were there many young men she dated?—how many?—who were they?" Thompson had covered all that, but you had to start somewhere.

She studied one scuffed toe of her old flat sandals. "It's funny, isn't it," she said irrelevantly, "after a while you get to a place where you can be—objective—about it. You know? Where you can look back without feeling an awful lot." She shot him a quick glance. "If you know what I mean, you can see that somebody dead—somebody you really loved—that there were good and bad things about them. . . . Have you found out Mr. Haines didn't do it after all?"

"Why should you think that?"

"Oh, well, I never thought he did, you know. He hadn't—that kind of violence in him. If you know what I mean. I mean, well, you get *feelings* from people—ideas of what they're like. You know? I don't know, maybe it's a funny thing to say—Mr. Haines, well, if Mary Ellen had been the kind of girl who didn't care, the casual kind, you know, he'd 've—made love to her, and neither of them would have thought much about it. But he wasn't the kind to use any force about it." She was still looking at her sandal, the visible scarlet-nailed toes. "I never said all this to Mother and Dad, they never thought but what— And the police were so sure, too, and after all they ought to know more about it than me. I just wondered if you'd found out anything more. Maybe I'm only imagining things, and I won't ask any"—with a shy half-defiant grin—"awkward questions. But I don't know why you'd be around again now, unless—Oh, well. Maybe we've just got to think, something like destiny. . . . I—Lieutenant, I guess I wouldn't like to have Mother and Dad have to hear this—you know, sometimes older people think a little different about these things—"

"Off the record," he said. "I promise." He put out his half-smoked cigarette in sudden distaste.

A sidelong smile. "Well, I—you know, it was almost a year and a half ago, I was only seventeen. . . . You said you wanted to know about boys she— Naturally, you sort of forget all the things you— didn't really like in somebody, when they're dead—"

"Sisters," he said, reading between the lines, making it easy for her, "don't always get along. Sure. Off the record." That was one of the little difficulties he'd often faced: anybody recently dead—hard to get at the truth about them from conventional relatives and friends.

"Mary Ellen and I always got along O.K.," she said absently. "Nothing like that. No, I never said so, nobody'd have listened anyway, but I never could *see* Mr. Haines doing it. I did wonder if it might have been the new one, the one she'd just met."

Mendoza ripped open a fresh pack of cigarettes with less than his usual care, offered her one, lit both. Talk about stacked decks! The kind of thing that turned detectives gray. With all the scientific gadgets they had to help, what the job came down to was coping with people. You could ask all the indicated questions, look in all the indicated places, file it all in black and white for careful study, and still you could never be sure you had it all. Some quirk of human nature, some irrelevancy, innocently, by chance, screening the one important piece in the jigsaw puzzle. And coming out—if it ever did—by chance too. . . . Thompson had been a good man. But because a shy seventeen-year-old had hesitated to speak up, a little something never coming out.

"The new one," he said noncommitally. "Who was that, and what about him made you think—?"

"I never said anything to anybody about it, there wasn't anything *to* say—just a crazy idea, maybe. I never met him," said Edith. "Mary Ellen didn't talk much to me about that kind of thing, not as much as she would have to friends her own age. Like Judy Gold or Wanda Adams. The reason I just sort of wondered, you know—well, it must have been someone she knew, mustn't it? That was one of the reasons the police thought of Mr. Haines. It was afternoon, broad daylight. Ordinarily, Mary Ellen'd have come right home after her last class, or if she had a little shopping to do, she'd have been home by five or half past. So it must have been right then, and—just as they said about Mr. Haines—whoever it was offered her a ride home, something like that. Because she'd never have let herself be picked up, and nobody could be kidnaped off a city street in broad daylight. . . . That Sergeant Thompson was very nice and sympathetic, but"—she cocked her head, wrinkled her small nose charmingly—"it's not quite the same, getting a—a background in questions and answers, as knowing at first hand. Is it?"

"No. This new boy?"

"Not a boy. Mary Ellen—that's what I was getting to—she was awfully particular, too much so. Old for her age, people said—you know, serious—I guess she was, you know, mature. She'd never go out with a lot of boys who asked her, because of some silly little thing about them, the way they dressed or used slang or drove a car. She thought most boys her age were uninteresting, didn't know how to act to a girl. That was why, I guess, she'd never gone steady with anyone. There were some nice boys she could have gone with, but—it always seemed to me —she thought she was too good for them. She *expected* too much, if you know what I mean. And that was why she was all excited about this one. She'd only met him a couple of days before, I think, the way she talked. She hadn't been out on a date with him yet, or we'd have met him and I could tell you more about him. But she thought he was going to ask her, she said. I don't think I ever saw her so—you know— *set up* over a b—a man. She was really a little silly about it. She said he was *smooth,* had awfully nice manners, and he wasn't smart-aleck or kiddish like the boys at college—she thought he was twenty-nine or thirty. His name was Edward Anthony. I remember, I said he sounded like a gigolo—somehow I got the impression of those, you know, courtly manners, a little *too* smooth—and she got mad and wouldn't say any more about him."

Yes; human nature. See those other girls. . . . "Where did she meet him, do you know?"

"She got mad before she told me that. This was the day before she was—was killed, Lieutenant, I ought to have said. She was really sold on him. . . . Well, I don't know that anybody *would* have mentioned him to the police—I don't think Mother and Dad ever heard about him. Mary Ellen kept things to herself a lot, that sort of thing anyway —she never said much to me. And it all went—sort of fast, after they —found her, you know, and everything seemed to point to Mr. Haines, and—with Mother and Dad carrying on so, and of course I was— I don't suppose anyone'd have listened to me if I'd had anything definite to tell. But since then—thinking about it without feeling so much—I've just wondered. Maybe it doesn't mean anything at all, of course. She knew a lot of people she'd have taken a ride from if they offered it. But —most of those, she'd known quite a while and ridden alone with before, and why just *then* should one of them—?"

"Edward Anthony," said Mendoza. "Yes. Maybe it means something, maybe not." He looked at her, getting up: at her direct eyes and the something in the cock of her brown head that reminded him of Alison. "I'm sorry, it's going to be hashed over again, Miss Wood. Not nice for any of you. Just one of those things."

"He wasn't the one, you've found out. How awful," she said. "How *awful*—for everybody. Poor Mrs. Haines—and you too."

"That's probably the first and last sympathy we'll be offered in this mess," he said bitterly. "Thanks very much for the kind thought."

And he was already, that early in the case, beginning to have a nightmare vision. . . . They cracked jokes, in Homicide, about Mendoza's hunches: Luis and his crystal ball. Hunches didn't come out of nowhere; he knew himself well enough to acknowledge that it was an almost feminine sensitivity for people, so that the nuances got through to him by something like radar, which produced most of his hunches. And they would be very damned helpful sometimes, pointing a direction to make a cast. But right now he didn't welcome the hunch he had, and he hoped to God he was wrong.

FOUR

He got addresses from Edith Wood; he looked up those two girls she'd mentioned, friends of Mary Ellen's. Neither was home, this summer Sunday. He made appointments to see them later, with a curious Mr. Gold and an alarmed Mrs. Adams. He sat in the car and looked at some other names and addresses he'd taken down. The law offices would be closed, of course. Finally he turned back east and drove down to Hawthorne, to the apartment house where, sixteen months ago, Celestine Teitel and Evelyn Reeder had shared quarters.

Miss Reeder had moved, the manageress told him crossly (he'd disturbed her afternoon nap, by her *déshabillé*). No, not *then:* about two months ago. She'd got transferred to another school, and wanted to be closer. Well, she'd left the new address, on account of letters and so on. . . . Yes, the manageress *could* look it up, she supposed, if it was urgent. Mendoza exerted himself to put out a little charm; she thawed, and retreated to rummage through her desk.

Three o'clock found him back in Hollywood, out west this time. He ran his quarry down in the upper apartment of an old duplex: a dreary, neatly sterile place of drab color and content. Miss Reeder resembled her apartment. She sat bolt upright on a sagging sofa and regarded Mendoza uneasily; he deduced with no difficulty that in Miss Reeder's philosophy all males were slightly suspect to start with, and one with a moustache, smooth address, and elegant tailoring was admitted to a *tête-à-tête* at obvious peril to any virtuous female. She was about forty, sandy-haired and spectacled.

"Celestine—" she said with a little gasp when he'd explained, asked his question. "Such a *terrible* thing—an awful warning of what *can* happen. I'd been nervous about it, I begged her to use more caution, you know—going off to such lonely places to do her sketching—one never knows what dangerous characters—"

He listened to her, murmured agreement, asked his question again.

She stared at him a little fuzzily, her pale eyes enlarged by thick lenses, seen full on.

"Oh, Celestine was a very quiet person, never one for—for much social life. I—neither of us went out a great deal—only her sketching that took her out to such places. . . . *Gentlemen?* Well, I don't think—no, I don't recall that she ever— But surely, Lieutenant, I'm afraid I don't quite understand, it wouldn't have been anyone she *knew!* Some criminal—some mental defective—lurking—"

He asked the question again, patiently. Miss Reeder adjusted her pink plastic glasses and looked thoughtful, looked startled. She said slowly, "Well, it *is* a peculiar coincidence—now you ask about it specifically—naturally it never entered my head to *mention* at the time, because, my goodness, the kind of person people like ourselves would know—it just didn't seem at all *relevant*—but now you recall it to my mind . . ."

He dropped in at his office downtown an hour later. Hackett had been and gone; he had left a page of notes on McCandless centered on Mendoza's desk. Mendoza glanced over them without sitting down. Hackett didn't know about this little idea, but Hackett wasn't lacking in brains or imagination; if something had suggested it to him too, it would be just more confirmation.

Not a great deal to say about Pauline McCandless. You got the impression, a colorless nonentity of a girl, not many friends, not many interests outside her home and her work at the library. She was on duty there, that particular week, from nine to six; she'd just finished a tour of night duty. And she didn't come home after six o'clock, that day. So—

September the fifth. Daylight saving still on, but even without it not dark then. "*¡Caramba y todos los diablos del infierno!*" he muttered. "Chance—chance! But we've been stupid here, damn it."

Hackett hadn't been able to contact the mother yet; he'd talked with a couple of the girls who had worked with Pauline. They said among other things they'd felt sorry for her, because the mother was a tiresome hypochondriac who'd never let the girl call her soul her own—awfully old-fashioned and puritanical.

This isn't much to go on, sorry. Not much to get, I'd say. But see times on Piper and Wood. Can't count in Teitel on that angle, or can we?—daylight, but not town, lonely spot. ¿Y pues qué, what of it? I don't buy the idea yet but, Galeano wonders too, somebody she knew? Maybe?

Mendoza exclaimed violently, "God damn it to hell and back!" Sergeant Thoms, who at Sergeant Lake's desk on Lake's days off, put his head in the door and asked if Mendoza had called. "I did not—there's nothing, *nada absolutamente,* you or me or the Chief or the newest rookie in uniform can do about this! Only one indicated move occurs to me—the city should instantly requisition enough money to give every member of the force a course in elementary logic. I'm going home, Bill. I may take myself straight up to Camarillo as a voluntary mental patient. Better yet, I may take several precinct lieutenants and a few of the sheriff's boys along with me."

"You sound like you need a drink," said Sergeant Thoms.

"And that is also one excellent idea," said Mendoza. He tucked Hackett's notes into his pocket and left and, unusually, he did stop for a drink on the way home.

After the drive across town in traffic, in hundred-degree temperature, the air-conditioned apartment was haven. Two of the cats came to greet him pleasedly, the ruddy brown Abyssinian Bast and her adolescent daughter Nefertite, who was convalescent from surgery to insure that the number of cats in the household remained static. She talked to him loudly all the way across the room, in the piercing voice she had inherited from her Siamese father; and Mendoza had a good idea what she was talking about. "What has he been up to today, this witch's familiar? And where is he? No *se preocupe,* I don't blame you two well-mannered ladies!"

The record-cabinet door was open; the electric clock lay on its face on the mantel; several books had been pulled out of the bookcase, and the leather case for cuff links, from the dresser in the bedroom, lay open on the kitchen floor, quite empty. "*¡Qué exasperación!*" said Mendoza, not amused. "*¡Señor ladrón malicioso e ingrato, ven acá!*"

El Señor regarded him interestedly from the top of the refrigerator, but made no move to obey this peremptory command. Twice the size of his mother and sister, he looked rather like a small lion in color transposition—his black coat, blond paws, eyebrows, stomach, and tail tip shining clean, his sea-green eyes cold for this lack of respect due any member of his race. "What have I ever done to deserve you?" Mendoza asked him. He plucked El Señor off the refrigerator, put all the cats out, and spent half an hour crawling about the floor searching under the furniture, before recovering all three pairs of his extra links.

That cat was getting just too damned smart at opening things; for once he was disinclined to be indulgent.

He poured himself a large drink straight from the bottle of rye in the kitchen and took it into the living room. It wasn't once in six months he had more than one drink a day, but what with this and that he needed more now. The hell of a state this force was in, to slip up on one like this, right under their noses! To have a muddle-minded female civilian spot it first for what it was. All right, for the wrong reason—or not all the right ones, just on a wild guess really, but—! And, *claro que sí,* good excuses why it hadn't been spotted before. Sure. This was a big town, the biggest city in the world in area if not quite in population; its police force was perennially shorthanded, and also—more to the point —different police forces held tenure within its borders. The county boys, outside city limits: suburban forces. All cooperating together, but it added to the difficulty of keeping things straight.

Teitel: she'd been found just within the county border, along the beach, so the sheriff's boys had looked at her first, and then when she was identified the Hawthorne police came in because she'd lived there.

Piper: also found in the county, and later handed over to the Wilcox Street precinct on account of her Hollywood residence: later turned over to Headquarters.

McCandless: headquarters got her right away, because Walnut Park wasn't an incorporated suburb, was within the regular L.A.P.D. jurisdiction.

Not as if one investigating officer had been in on all those cases from the start. Not as if they were offbeat homicides, to get a lot of publicity, so that all the details were common property. Hawthorne had one, the L.A.P.D. had two, and those two nearly nine months apart.

Teitel, a year ago last July: nearly fifteen months ago, two and a half months after Mary Ellen Wood. Piper, last January, six months after Teitel. McCandless, two weeks and a day ago—September fifth—nine months after Piper.

And what in between, in this sprawling metropolitan place with its fifty or sixty surburbs, its six and a half million people? Other assaults, rape and attempted rape, and a few ending in murder.

He finished the rye, all but a mouthful. All right, for God's sake! he said to himself. Wasting time tabulating the excuses. Too much time wasted already. Get busy doing some constructive thinking about it.

He swallowed the last mouthful, sat there laxly, empty glass in hand. After a while he noticed that there were a couple of notes propped on the desk: notes from Mrs. Bryson or Mrs. Carter, his neighbors who ran in and out waiting on the cats, or from the maid-of-all-work, Bertha. Presently he'd read them; right now he was too tired, suddenly.

No more little black-scrawled notes from his grandmother. Never any more, since six weeks ago. No more of her fondly automatic orders about regular meals, late nights, this pernicious habit of gambling: the transparently cunning little traps to get her Luis safely married to some decent, modest wife who could coax him back to the priests.

He got up, went to the kitchen to pour another drink. He could hear her saying disapprovingly, Better you get yourself a good solid meal, you are tired and irritable because your stomach is empty, boy—men, they never know how to take care of themselves, like children they are.

"Damn," he said to his drink softly. Things tied up. True enough, he hadn't eaten since morning—in a while he'd get something, or go out—but that wasn't altogether the reason he was so violently out of sorts with himself. And his new bad business wasn't, either. He'd been this way before that, and sooner or later he'd have to look at it square, straighten it out with himself. As that small voice kept telling him.

Alison . . . Because you got into trouble lying to yourself, rationalizing. Let yourself get by with it once, after a while you couldn't tell lie from truth, about anything.

All *right*. He swallowed half the new drink. He was beginning to feel it now; he eyed the rest of it dubiously. *In vino veritas?*—maybe. If so, not very flattering to think the real Luis Rodolfo Vicente Mendoza was the one that showed in liquor. Spoiling for a fight with anybody who crossed his path: which was the reason he didn't drink much.

All *right*. He'd been sorry to break with Alison that way, but it had been boiling up for five weeks. Admit it: not for the usual reason, the one he'd told himself it was. For a reason a lot of people would think was lunatic. But then, they weren't Luis Mendoza.

Alison, always a little different thing with her, from the start: not the ordinary woman. He could talk with Alison. A *rapport* there, sympathy aside from sex. So that in the end, he had betrayed himself to her. . . . As long as he could remember anything, it had been the two of them together, the old lady and himself: his parents dead in an accident before he was a month born—there'd never been anyone else. His grandfather didn't count, the old miser, an ogre-on-the-hearth, and the two of them contriving little schemes to bypass his wrath, to get enough out of him for the luxury of a pound of sugar on the grocery bill, new two-dollar shoes instead of new soles on the old ones. (The old man sitting on all that money then, nobody knowing.) The only person, she was, who had ever known Luis Mendoza inwardly, seen him without all his defenses. And she'd been eighty-seven, she'd gone quick and peaceful, and it was just in the nature of things: but loss of someone like that was still a loss.

And so there he'd been that night, the urbane, suave Mendoza, stripped of his camouflage, betrayed by that sympathy between. He could feel now the comforting circle of Alison's arms, the softness of her breasts, hear her soothing murmur; and suddenly he downed the other half of the rye and swore aloud. The galled bitterness of humiliation, for unavoidable memory—of having nakedly revealed himself in weakness. . . . And ever since, awaiting the excuse to break with her . . . because she knew too much of him, she had got too close.

Running, not for the usual reason: not bored with her, not really wanting to be done with Alison, not taking alarm at the trap set.

So now he'd got it straight with himself, what he'd been dodging in his own mind, and it wasn't as important as it had seemed, unexamined. Just the way he was made. He was still sorry for the quarrel, but this way or that way, probably just as well: better stay away from the path to the trap, these respectable women with standards—*¡pues sí!*

All of a sudden, for getting that uneasily postponed self-examination off his mind, he felt much better; he felt fine, no longer tired. Maybe it was the rye. For the first time in six weeks he felt wholly himself, the old Mendoza.

Because another rather peculiar thing had happened to him when she died. He'd never given much thought to time: the year, it was four figures on a letterhead, no more. He wasn't conscious of feeling any different this year than last, and the man he faced in the shaving mirror didn't look any different—the hair just as thick and as black, the stomach just as flat, and in spite of all the paper work, the eyes just as sharp. But quite suddenly, when she was gone, it came to him that half his life had gone with her. Maybe more: you couldn't know. That he'd turned forty years old last February.

He'd been having some odd and unaccustomed thoughts about it, at intervals, since.

Now he forgot all about it, and he was back to where and what he'd always been. He felt fine. Which was a very good thing, because he had some intensive work and thinking ahead of him: come to think, this would probably be the last evening he had to himself for some time. Might as well enjoy it.

A meal of some kind—it was still early—and then, who was he likely to find unspoken for at short notice? That blonde, Florence Something, look up the number—she'd do. Nine o'clock. Meanwhile, do a little ruminating on this case . . .

He began to cut up fresh liver for the cats, and his mind switched off the blonde temporarily to dwell on four dead women.

FIVE

"Four of them," he said to Hackett next morning. "I don't say yes and I don't say no to all four, but there are points in common that might say a very loud yes. And I wonder if we've missed others."

"Now that's something," said Hackett. "A mass murderer in business for nineteen months, and nobody noticing it?"

"Caray, you call four a mass? Well, I don't like it much either, and the Chief is going to like it less, but there *are* excuses for us, Art—we had some good solid evidence on Mary Ellen Wood, and of the other three we only handled two, nearly a year apart. . . . Spilled milk. Point is, no one man ever looked at all four. And it doesn't mean much, the common denominator Mrs. Haines spotted—that all four were quiet, respectable females. Put any kind of woman in the right place at the right time, that kind of thing might happen to her."

"Claro está," said Hackett. "Admitted. It's the times, which I don't suppose Mrs. Haines knew about from the papers."

"¡Ay de periódicos todos!" said Mendoza. "To hell with all scandal-mongering pressmen—don't mention them to me!" The story had broken this morning; both the conservative and radical press had devoted some space to it, and it would be featured in their sister afternoon papers too. "Yes, that's the whole point. When it happens to a respectable female—one who doesn't pick up strangers, go roaming around alone at midnight, that kind of thing, to ask for trouble—it's because accident put her in the way of it. Like that Jonas thing—I've been looking over this year's crop—or the DeValle girl. The car stalls in an unsavory district on her way home from the swing shift, something like

that. There've been thirty-odd cases of rape and attempted rape through headquarters this eighteen months, and in all but seven or eight of them the woman was at least partly to blame, for voluntarily putting herself in danger. And I'm not counting the statutory cases, where it's legally rape because the girl's under age—I mean the real thing, sex by force. Thirteen of those cases ended in homicide. Of those thirteen women, six can be called—mmh—respectable. The others had asked for it, just like those where it didn't end in murder—hanging around bars alone, picking up strangers, or they lived or worked or visited in the back alleys of bad districts. And two of the first six, it was chance putting them in a dangerous place late at night, in the way of dangerous men. But here we've got four women who got in the way of a rapist-killer at very odd times of day indeed, and odd places. That is, I think four, depending on what you can tell me about Piper. Mary Ellen Wood, between three and five in the afternoon—because if she hadn't been prevented, she'd have been home by five. Celestine Teitel left home that Sunday about nine in the morning, probably got to that stretch of beach by ten or so, and she'd planned to be home by six, so it was between those times. Pauline McCandless left the library at six and so far as anyone knew was going straight home—it wouldn't be dark until eight or so, and she'd be in the middle of a crowd on the bus. How does Piper line up on this? She lived alone—is there any evidence of her plans that evening?"

"As a matter of fact," said Hackett, "there is. Reason we started to look for her as early as we did. She was expected at a bridge party in the apartment manager's place that evening. They said it wasn't like her not to call if she couldn't make it. And being good friends—she'd lived there five years or so—the manager and his wife went up and let themselves into her apartment, to see if she'd been taken sick or something, you know—called her office to see if she was working late—finally called us, thinking, maybe, a street accident."

"So there we are. Four. Not late at night, not in the dark, and not in slum districts. Sure, all right, put a question mark on Teitel, on that angle—it was a lonely stretch of beach, anybody might have turned up there. But here's the Wood girl in the middle of Hollywood, Piper down on Spring Street surrounded by members of the Stock Exchange, and McCandless waiting at a busy intersection for a crowded crosstown bus. I ask you!" Mendoza shrugged and laughed. "Sure, excuses for us not spotting it. Like the way you figured it with Jane Piper. That for some reason, innocent or not, she'd put herself in the way of violence—maybe walked down to some bar on Main for a drink before going home, something like that— was coaxed or forced into a car, and driven to a lonelier spot. The likeliest way it could have happened, that hour, that place—about the only way it could have happened. And ditto for the others. We came nearer the truth on Mary Ellen, though we got the wrong man. It must have been somebody who knew her, that was seventy percent sure to start. Somebody should have seen the same thing on these others."

"Barring Teitel, I'll go along," said Hackett. He didn't look very happy about it. "It looks that way."

Mendoza was leaning back with his eyes shut. "Unsuccessful women," he said somnolently. "Damn their minds, their salaries— women without men attached, this reason or that. Teitel wasn't bad-looking, neither was Piper, but that hasn't much to do with it some-times. Am I jumping to conclusions to say, on those two anyway, fe-males just a little too intellectual, too—mmh—superior and objective, to attract the average male? And McCandless saddled with a difficult mama who'd discouraged her from All That."

"And if that's not just the famous Mendoza imagination," asked Hackett, "what does it say?"

"It says I'll give you ten-to-one odds that if we can get the evidence, if anybody remembers, Jane Piper and Pauline McCandless had re-cently met an answer to a maiden's prayer. Just the way we know now Mary Ellen and Celestine Teitel had. A young or youngish man, who seemed attracted, who looked like—to put it crudely—a good bet. A man of the type to appeal to these women, which means he put up a good appearance, he was—for want of a better word—a gentleman. A man who seemed trustworthy. A man," said Mendoza, suddenly sitting up, opening his eyes, getting out a cigarette, "those women would not only be attracted to, because that in itself says nothing—the most re-spectable high-minded women, nine times out of ten they'll feel the ani-mal attraction to the big male brute, never mind if he's the plumber or the garage mechanic or whatever—but a man of some, what do I want to say, address, prestige. A man who used correct grammar, dressed well, had nice manners. Yes, I see it going like that—"

"Slow down, *chico*," said Hackett dryly. "This is what the text-books call theorizing without data."

"Sure, sure!" Mendoza knocked ash into the brass ashtray angrily. "That's for sure. But those women, what man but one like that could take them so easy, those places and times? I'm telling you, Art, that's the way it was, the way it must have been—*¡no cabe duda!*—I can see it. When they vanished from crowded places like that, in broad daylight, and the times so tight. Mary Ellen, here's this fellow she's just met—older than the college boys she knows, more sophisticated, more exciting—meeting her that day, making a date for after her last class. Teitel, that's the one we can't say definitely about, but I think she belongs on the list—and how might it have gone there? Did she happen to meet him casually on her way to the beach that morning, or suddenly decide to invite him along? Or maybe they had a date, unknown to Miss Reeder—who'd probably cautioned Celestine about strange men, so Celestine didn't mention it to her, to encourage more moralizing. This fellow with the looks, the manner, to attract Piper—another mature woman, an intelligent woman—but lonely women are too often fools—meeting her, calling her, that day—saying, maybe, I'll drive you home, or let's have an early dinner together, I'll get you home in time for your bridge party. And, God help us, Pauline McCandless!—from what you got, a walkover for any male who paid her a little attention! And she wouldn't have mentioned him to Mama, but she might have to a girl friend her own age—"

"None of those at the library had anything to say about that."

"Did you ask specifically? We will, but she hadn't been there long, probably didn't know any of those women intimately. What we want is a girl she'd known longer, maybe a college classmate—and of course, even if there was somebody like that she'd confide in, she might not have had the chance since she'd met our Romeo. But I think she'd met him, Art. And that when she left the library that day, she had a date with him, if just to have a cup of coffee at a counter—because Mama expected her home at the usual time."

"This same smooth-talking collar ad who already had those other three to his account. I don't know, you're building an awful lot on awful little, Luis." Hackett passed a hand over his jaw thoughtfully. "It could be, I agree with you it looks like a man they knew—or men—"

"Figure the odds on that!" said Mendoza. "Three different men, even in a town this size, with the same qualifications? *¡No hay tal!* Be like drawing a royal flush in the first deal—theoretically it could happen, but does it ever? What tripped us up here, it's the fact that almost without exception when a woman gets raped, and occasionally murdered as an outcome of that, it's the outside thing—the random thing. The way Miss Evelyn Reeder put it—anyone people like *us* know, not that kind! It'd be very damned convenient, in all sorts of ways, if we could generalize like that—say for sure what kind of intelligence, personality, capability, occurs in this class, this race, this nationality, place, age, city area, economic level, educational level—*¡ay qué ris!*— people aren't made that way. Miss Reeder says to me, *a mental defective.* Maybe it's a sad commentary on the state of human culture, but how many convicted rapists you know of have been either lunatics or morons?"

"About one in ten, I'd say, show pretty low I.Q.'s, but not always moron level—and the other nine, generalizing, are just given to violence, smart or dumb."

"*Eso es* . . . Random violence, that's the pattern. You don't go looking among the family and friends. But that's where he was in these cases, and just by the law of averages, it's one man, not three or four. No, we've got very little evidence yet, but I'll give you odds that as we get more it'll show the pattern I can already see here. Mary Ellen had just met this maiden's dream, was hoping he'd ask for a date. Edward Anthony—and I hope to God these girl friends can give us a little more on him, what he looked like, where she met him, what job he was in— All the sister knows is that he was about thirty, a smooth talker. Damn, eighteen, nineteen months ago—casual little things like that, people forget. We'll see. . . . Celestine Teitel, as we now know, had recently met a fellow she described to Evelyn Reeder as *charming.* His name was Mark Hamilton, and she met him at the music-and-art-supply shop where she bought sketching materials—he was a customer too, they got talking casually. Miss Reeder couldn't say whether they'd ever been out together, except for once when he bought Celestine a cup of coffee at the drugstore next to the shop. Now we'll go looking on Piper and McCandless, and I think we'll find that they'd just met somebody like that—with another euphonious, respectable-sounding Anglo-Saxon name—and that if we get descriptions, they'll match up."

"Maybe—maybe. You sound damn happy about it," said Hackett. "My God, what the press boys'll say about this one!"

Mendoza sat back and shut his eyes again. "Crossing bridges. Let's wait and see." The press stories this morning had been all Haines and Rose Foster; they hadn't got hold of the mass-killer idea yet. "Wishful thinking, that Mrs. Haines won't come out with it to the first reporter who interviews her. I'd like to shut her up, if for no other reason than that it might not be such a good idea to let him know these cases have been linked up. But, on the other hand, it might be a very smart idea indeed. Let him know we're looking. You never know with these characters. I'd rather like to keep these others in the background—get him for Mary Ellen, and just quietly mark off the other three as incidentally solved. No *lèse-majesté* from the press, or not as much—not as much public viewing-with-alarm. But Mrs. Haines feeling the way she does, understandably, *that* we can't hope for. . . . We'll be using every man we've got, there are a lot of places to look—"

"And damn all to go on," said Hackett gloomily.

"Oh, I don't know. On Mary Ellen, there's Haines—I don't buy Mrs. Haines' detective-story plot, somebody who wanted to get him in trouble, but our Romeo must have known a little something about that yard, that garden shed—he didn't just stumble on it as a convenient place to stash a body. He lived around there, or he knew somebody around there. He had some reason to frequent the neighborhood, to walk down that alley—once or twice anyway. Then there's the shop where Teitel met him. I think. We'll get other starting points, with luck, from people who knew Piper and McCandless. Really too many places to look, too many directions to put out a cast. We'll get him—we'll get him in the end—it may be a long hunt, but by God we'll get him. . . . Happy? *¡No seas tonto!*—don't be funny! But before I start figuring out the answer to a problem, it's a help to know just what the problem is."

"How do you build him?" asked Hackett after a pause. "A nut? One of those where it doesn't show?"

"Let's not go all psychological," said Mendoza almost amusedly. "Your guess is as good as mine, on that. . . . They knock themselves out, the head doctors, trying to tabulate what's normal, what isn't, when it comes to that old devil sex. Can't be done. Comes right back to the individual. It's a damn funny thing, you know, and I suppose I'd get sued for slander to say it in public, but the psychiatrists have a lot in common with the Communists—such a desperate effort to classify people, make rules applying to the general type. Talk about waste of time. . . . This one? Sure, there's something wrong with him, obviously. God knows there are always enough willing women, nobody needs to get it by force, *¿como no?*" He put out his cigarette, immediately groped for another. And his tone on that was rueful, cynical. He hadn't enjoyed the blonde much, last night. A silly female. Just, in effect, a female—compliant—and obtuse. Nobody to talk to, to enjoy being with, just for herself. You might say, on a par with the waitress who fetched you a meal when you were hungry. That kind of thing.

Not like—

He went on sharply, hastily, "Something offbeat, sure, but not lunatic in the legal sense. He likes it by force, maybe—he's got a grudge against females, maybe—not what we call normal. But in any other— mmh—area of life, quite possibly he looks sane as you or me, and one thing we can say about him, Art, just as I pointed out, he's not legally insane, by the McNaughton rule. *Pues no.* He knows what he's doing, he knows he can go to the gas chamber for it. Because he gives them different names, you notice. Edward Anthony—Mark Hamilton. A family resemblance there, and if, as, and when we get the names he gave to Piper and McCandless, they'll be the same kind, names out of the popular circulating-library stories. I'll bet you—I'll bet you. . . . Who can say exactly what's wrong with him, and why?" Mendoza opened his eyes and smiled at Hackett. "Cross out the head doctors' pompous talk, *chico,*" he said softly, "and off the record—can any man say there hasn't been a time he didn't have the impulse to violence with a woman—to let her know he's a male creature? Or with some men, to repay her for being female? Tell the truth to yourself if not to me."

And after a moment Hackett said as softly, "Like they say, *touché.* It's a thing in us, if we're men at all."

"Two sides to every coin, *entendido.* . . . Given any choice, would you rather be finally judged by a psychiatrist or a priest? What's the difference?—the one blames your grandparents, the other blames you. *¡Ni qué niño muerto!*—me, I'm done, *finalmente,* with the priests and all their works, but if you pin me down, I think they're a little closer than the head doctors—it's the individual who decides what the individual does, or thinks, or feels, or wants."

"There I'm with you. *De veras.* Sure we do, sure!" said Hackett rather violently, and stabbed out his cigarette as if it was a personal enemy. "Is it because we're—the male animal, so to speak—or just because we're human?"

"I'll pass on that one, boy."

"That's a kind of answer from authority, God knows," said Hackett, and his tone was angry, hard. "You've had enough experience to say— and walked out on enough women."

Mendoza looked up at him, silent for a moment, his eyes turned cold and remote. So, he thought, of course—Art had heard about it now, from his Angel, probably. Words unsaid between them here, now, about a woman they both knew: personal words, irrelevant to this case they would work together. *"Mi amigo bueno,"* said Mendoza, amiable, soft, friendly, "let's keep it the professional discussion—*¿conforme, compañero?*"

Hackett met his eyes. "O.K., agreed. *Excusas muchas, por favor* . . . So how and where do we start to look? You're the one gives the orders." And if that was just very subtly sardonic, he didn't emphasize it.

Mendoza smiled. "I'll tell you what occurs to me . . ."

SIX

The man who had once called himself Edward Anthony, and at another time Mark Hamilton, and other names, was dressing to go out. He'd thought for a while he would have to call and make an excuse; the idea of going out, anywhere away from the safe haven of his own apartment, started him shaking—after he'd read all the papers today. But he felt better now; there wasn't really any reason to get the jitters, not yet anyway, he'd realized that when he reread everything in the *Times* story— that one had more details.

They had come so much closer than he'd ever thought they could, that he'd been terribly frightened at first—all the past two weeks and a half, since the story about Haines had come out in the papers. Every day he'd bought all the editions of all the papers, to see what more they'd found out, and it was like the hand of God starting to reach for him, what they *knew*. The worst of it was, of course, that they might know a lot more than they let the papers print—you couldn't be sure. You read about these smart young reporters who ferreted out police secrets, but did they exist?—and he had an idea that these days the responsible newspapers cooperated with the police, withheld things if they were asked. They might know more—but when he thought about it straight, they didn't know anything important, they just couldn't: his real name or where to find him. He didn't see how they could ever find out, so there wasn't any danger really. He mustn't get nervous for no reason.

The things they'd found out were all dead ends, couldn't lead them anywhere. All the same, it was frightening to see it all printed like that, little things nobody but him had known. On that Monday there'd been the Haines story, about that woman confirming his alibi after all, and the question printed in big black type, to startle—*Who Murdered Mary Ellen Wood?* Then on Tuesday, the interview with Mrs. Haines, and how she thought those other three cases were connected. And for a while the police just kept saying, No comment, on that. But then on Thursday and Friday there'd been rerun stories on those three, and with a lot more detail than had got into the papers before, and the police—maybe pressed by those reporters—had admitted that they were working over those cases again. A lot of deductions and speculations—that was all the reporters. The police wouldn't tell *them* what they were thinking, but policemen read newspapers too, and one or two little things might give them ideas if they hadn't had them before. But of course, even on those things, they could only find out so much—nothing would lead them anywhere. Would it? About how whoever killed Mary Ellen maybe had lived in that neighborhood where the Haineses lived—and that, by what had come out about the other girls, the murderer had planned his crimes, because of giving different names—and what the proprietor of that record-and-art-supply shop had said—and the names—and what those other women said. You wouldn't think people would remember little niggling bits of casual conversation so long . . . but of course women were all gossips, and especially when it came to what they called boy friends and so on. . . .

Lascivious, lewd-minded, setting the trap for men always, all of them. Whether they realized it or not—and some of them, of course, were entirely innocent, poor things. The way Mary Ellen had been.

He remembered that little man in the record shop. The little man, his pictures in the papers on Friday and Saturday, who said he remembered the fellow Miss Teitel got talking to a couple times there. But he didn't really, because the description he gave was vague, would apply to lots of men.

He looked at himself anxiously in the mirror as he knotted his tie. Surely it would? Nothing at all definite, as if he had a scar to remember, something like that. The proprietor had said, "He was kind of tall, maybe five-eleven, and thin, and he had brown hair, and he was clean-shaved"—all true, but true of thousands of men—"and blue eyes," and that was wrong, his eyes were brown. People didn't really observe closely, remember accurately. No danger there.

No danger really from what the women said, those friends of Jane Piper, and Pauline McCandless, and Celestine Teitel. The names, sure. Christopher Hawke for Pauline, Stephen Laird for Jane. But the names didn't mean anything, and none of the women had known much about

him to tell their friends, even the little while they'd known him before
. . . Anything like what he really did, where he worked, where he
lived. It didn't add up to anything, to a useful description or a definite
fact.

Unless the papers hadn't printed all they'd said; but how could any of
them know anything, just from the little those women could have told
about him?

There wasn't any way the police could connect who he really was
with any of those names and women, was there? All the time, he'd been
himself *too,* with a permanent, different name and background, and
none of them had known anything about that. And these others, friends
they'd mentioned him to, had never laid eyes on him. Had they?

The papers had said some bad things about the police, because of
their getting Allan Haines for Mary Ellen, and not suspecting about
these other girls—but other times, in other articles, he'd read how most
modern police forces were efficient and honest, with all sorts of
scientific experts to help them, and particularly this one here. It was a
handicap, not having firsthand knowledge of all this—were they fools
or not? In today's papers and some of yesterday's, there'd been pictures
of some of them. The one in charge of the investigation, it had been a
little surprise—he was Mexican, a lieutenant, it said. The fellow with
him in that picture, Sergeant Hackett his name was, was quite ordinary-
looking except that he looked awfully big—unless this Lieutenant Mendoza was awfully small, and there were standards about that for police,
weren't there? They had to be over a certain height. You couldn't really
tell much from a picture. This Mendoza, that was one thing, of course
—he'd be a Roman Catholic and consequently not very smart or
knowledgeable. *They* weren't allowed to think independently, and any
of them that *were* very smart were sent into the priesthood, they
wouldn't be in the police. That was easy to figure, and encouraging.

What were they thinking, where were they looking? They'd have to
make a big pretense of hunting, with all the papers said about their stupidity.

But he just couldn't see any way they'd ever get to him, who he really
was. He didn't like it—he was uneasy—that people had remembered
the names he'd given, and even a little about him, or what he'd told
those women. He hadn't thought even that much would ever be found
out. But it couldn't be dangerous; he'd been too careful.

He was finished dressing, and it was too early to leave; he sat down to reread the *Times* article again. Just to be sure there wasn't anything really dangerous.

No; since he knew how it was with him, he'd been careful. Just luck that he hadn't been found out the first couple of times—the one back home, and then the second one. After that, he knew he had to be terribly careful, just in case he couldn't stop himself, and oh, God, he had tried, he had tried not to. Because when he hadn't been found out—the police *there* said it might have been anybody who killed Rhoda, a woman like that—and again with that Anderson girl—it had seemed to him that God meant to give him another chance. And he'd tried.

Because it wasn't right, it was terrible when he thought about it calmly, afterward. Some of the time—right *then*—it seemed the only possible, righteous thing. These women who had tempted him just being women, who knew the awful weakness in him, who had seen him stripped of all camouflage, all spiritual dignity and control—impossible to let them live. That first time it had happened, he hadn't had a thought for his own safety. Just a thing he had to do and he'd done it, that was Rhoda, and nobody had connected him with it at all. But terrible, terrible, how the devil was so insidious, tempting. . . . It hadn't been quite as hard, somehow, when Father was alive. There under the same roof, a living presence reminding him and, of course, keeping him busy, occupied—idle hands opportunity for the devil—there'd been the shop to tend, always things to do, talk about. The times this awful fleshly hunger came over him, he'd made himself sit down quietly and read the Scriptures or something improving and calming like that. Mostly. But once he was alone, there was the opportunity, nobody to ask where he was going, what he was doing, thinking, feeling. And so, eventually, there he was seeking out the wanton woman—

And once he'd gratified the lust, the temptation worse, worse, and oftener too—useless to fight, though he fought it, he tried, but always it was eventually too strong for him. . . . And *then* he'd have to destroy the source of temptation. It was like riding a toboggan out of control down a steep hill, everything faster and faster once he *was* out of control, and the inevitable crash at the bottom. The way it was, he knew now—almost surely—never any different, whenever he got to the place with one of them where he *had* to let go, give in to the lust, then it took him all the way down, helpless, and it always ended in the crash, the holier kind of lust, the savagely beautiful time of total destruction.

You could really say, all their fault for being what they were—the whole source of sin—but he knew all the same that something was a little wrong in him too, because other men didn't go out of control this way. Of course, a lot of men hadn't had the advantage of a really religious upbringing, but— *Better to marry than to burn,* that was St. Paul, and he'd thought that was the solution—after the Anderson girl, he'd thought that. It wasn't the best way, the ultimately right way, but if it was your wife it wasn't sin. He'd been trying to arrange it that way, with Mary Ellen. But it was difficult, there were preliminaries to getting married. The girl expected to be taken around a little, to get to know you, and so on, and it was just too long and nerve-racking. He'd been so upset after the Anderson thing, he'd held himself in desperately for a long while, nearly a year, and then he'd decided he must get married, it would be all right then. Didn't much matter who, but Mary Ellen was a nice girl, he'd liked her—not like Rhoda or Julie Anderson. But that was the trouble, you couldn't meet a girl one day and marry her the next, and he couldn't wait, he couldn't stop himself—

But *hadn't* he known how it would go, even before? Because, the way the papers said, he'd given a wrong name. . . . Muddling to reason out, but he didn't think so, not that time. He'd been frightened over Julie Anderson, because it was so close to home. Of course, later he'd decided it was safer—down there—his real home, his own place, nobody knew about that, and he could use it in safety, in leisure. . . . But nobody knew Julie was dead, and in the end it had all blown over with no trouble. But it had set him thinking, just in *case*—mightn't it be a good idea to start all over again, the way he had when he came here first, with a new name and background? That had been in his mind that day—a different name and all—he hadn't consciously planned to do it, but when she'd said her name and he had to introduce himself, the *Edward Anthony* had come out quite naturally. Queer, how things happened. . . . He'd felt all buoyed up right then, as if everything was going to be different from then on, it was a new beginning, he would *be* Edward Anthony and no one else, he'd marry this nice girl so it wouldn't be sinning, and get all straightened out. It would mean—this had crossed his mind regretfully—quitting his job, starting in fresh somewhere else, and what he'd do about papers, certificates, that would be a problem—but worth any sacrifice.

Just chance, meeting her like that there in the college cafeteria. He'd been thinking, then, if he just had enough to keep him busy all the while, outside work hours—and he'd gone there to ask about the evening classes— And there was Mary Ellen, at the table where he took his coffee. Friendly, but of course innocently so. A nice girl.

And he'd tried to do it right, meant to take her out, the ordinary thing, work up to marrying her in the conventional way. But it all went wrong, too fast, the first time he found himself alone with her in the car that day, only two days later. . . .

It just showed how people could get the wrong idea, too, from plain facts. Sally Haines had been quite right in saying he had a reason to put Mary Ellen there, but it wasn't anything to do with her husband. It was *her*. All of a sudden, he'd thought of where to hide Mary Ellen, and if they did find her, it would be a terrible shock to that woman, and serve her right. He hadn't, at the time, known her name or anything about her, just what he'd seen and heard, passing the place as he did almost every day. (He moved away afterward, of course.) A most unwomanly woman, who wore trousers, and several times he'd heard her speaking very sharply to her husband, really ordering him around. One of those women who thought herself superior to men, you'd think common sense would tell them how false a notion—it said quite plainly in the Scriptures that—

It had been too bad about Allan Haines. He was sorry about it, it hadn't crossed his mind that anything like that would happen, but when it all came out he hadn't felt quite as bad, because of Haines confessing his sin. A married man, too.

And it was lucky he hadn't given Mary Ellen his right name. As if it was meant he should be saved. But that was the end of any new start as Edward Anthony, of course. And of any real hopefulness that even if he did manage to get married— But that would be the best solution, if he could ever control himself and be patient enough to get there with a woman. It was what he'd tried for every time since, with Celestine and Jane and Pauline: what had been in his mind.

Only then, those times, knowing what might happen, he'd been very careful to give them another name, tell them wrong things about where he worked and lived, and so on. If it had ever worked out, well, he'd just have forgotten this permanent name and place, started over again (the way he'd hoped with Mary Ellen), but it never had. . . . It all happened just like before—he couldn't stop himself.

Another thing about that, he'd been careful—after Julie—not to *try* with any woman who knew him in his own background, by his own name. A few times it had been hard. He'd meet some woman like that, in the way of business or introduced by someone who knew him, and want her—and knowing what might happen, he didn't dare . . . He never planned it out, cold. Just, suddenly the day or so after that, he'd find himself in conversation with a strange woman somewhere, the way it had been with Celestine . . . and meeting Jane Piper in the bank elevator that day, talking—and afterward, waiting for her to come out, so he could pretend to meet her by chance in the street, invite her to have a cup of coffee with him. . . . And Pauline sitting there alone on the beach, looking lonely. Everybody talked to strangers, casually, on the beach. Of course, he knew honestly that his instinctive good manners, his quiet behavior, were reassuring to respectable women: he wasn't the ordinary kind who tried to pick them up. Well, a man in his line of work, a job with some prestige, educational requirements—he acquired that manner.

Oh, he'd been careful, but sometimes it was hard. Right now, for instance, there was this woman he felt powerfully attracted to, and God, God, he must be careful, because she knew him as who he really was—properly introduced—and if anything like that happened to her— Well, it mustn't, that was all. When they'd connected those other three with Mary Ellen—guessed that it had been a man known personally to all of them—if another one happened—!

He got up and walked around the room uneasily, loosening his collar, feeling hot and excited, trying to get himself in hand. Hard. Times like that, before, when the immediate lust was focused on a woman who knew him, he'd just found another who didn't. A strange one . . . That was how the Scriptures said it, *the strange woman.*

Thou hast ravished my heart, my sister, my spouse; thou hast ravished my heart . . . How fair is thy love . . . Turn away thine eyes from me, for they have overcome me . . .

Very strange indeed that that kind of thing should be part of the Scriptures: Father never would allow that book to be read aloud, or read at all for that matter, and true, true, it was dangerous reading. Whatever it meant, whyever it was included.

Thy lips, O my spouse, drop as the honeycomb . . . Thy two breasts are like two young roes . . . This thy stature is like to a palm tree, and thy breasts to clusters of grapes. . . . I said, I will go up to the palm tree, I will take hold of the boughs thereof; now also thy breasts shall be as clusters of the vine . . .

No, no, that was not the page to find the truth. Where was it, what was it? *A strange woman is a narrow pit*—it was Proverbs, of course— *she also lieth in wait for prey. Thine eyes shall behold strange women, and thine heart shall utter perverse things*—

But hopeless, even by what the Scriptures said, because that went on

—how did it go on?—*they have stricken me, shalt thou say . . . they have beaten me. . . . When shall I awake? I will seek it yet again.*

Oh, but he must take care, take care and be strong to keep himself from it! This one, she excited him, she disturbed him. And suddenly, thinking about her, he wondered if it was the red hair, if she reminded him of Rhoda. The mind made odd connections: even when they were so different, a dirty slattern like Rhoda and this one—this one with the unusual, rather nice name: Alison.

Take *care*. Because she knew him as himself. And he must not, he could not, this time, go looking for a substitute—when *they* were hunting, alerted. It must not happen again for a long time. Better, never: but perhaps that was too much to hope for.

And it was time now he left. Get hold of himself, to put up his usual quiet, gentlemanly appearance.

He had dropped the *Times* on the floor a while ago, and now he picked it up, tidily folding it together, to leave the room neat. As he did so, a small line of print took his eye, there on an inside page where the front-page story on the murders had been concluded—right in the next column this was.

Regrading of Beach Street, it said. And below, the name jumping out at him with the effect of being in blacker print.

Colibrí Avenue.

He started to shake again; the paper rattled in his hand.

Oh, no, he thought. Not just now. This bad time. When they— Yes, of course it had always been far too steep a grade. Even for an unimportant narrow lane leading off the coast highway there, toward a few scattered houses back in the little canyon. But just *now,* why in heaven's name must there come the big bulldozers, the men with spades and picks, just to make it an easier road for a few cars?

Not a long street, not a wide one. The men with the spades—

They'd find her now, they'd find Julie Anderson.

Oh, God, he thought.

But, twenty-seven months, nearly twenty-eight. A long time, there might not be much—

I must be careful, he thought distractedly. Take good care to look and act just as usual.

And not, *not,* however hard it was, not let himself get so excited, interested, in this new woman. Or any one. There must *not* be another one now, soon.

He took an anxious look in the mirror, was reassured. Must go, they'd be expecting him. It was all right, he could carry it off. The main thing to remember was that there was no possible way for anyone to connect him, the man he really was, with all these women. There mustn't ever be a way.

He was afraid this new one, who excited him so, would be there tonight—no help for that, though the less he saw of her the better. But so hard, when it all came boiling up in him, hot and demanding—to keep himself from—

Must be very careful, and *try*.

"Oh, all right, all right!" said Alison resignedly. "I'll be there, Pat."

"Well, you needn't sound as if I'd applied the Chinese water-torture to persuade you," said Patricia Moore. "I only thought you might enjoy—"

"You needn't waste time on the pretty fiction," Alison told her. "I'm not a fool, and you're not the only one who's scheming to cheer up poor Alison. Really, it's insulting—I should be allowed some private life, and why everybody's leaped to the unflattering conclusion that I've suffered some tragedy and *need* cheering up—"

"You think too much about yourself," said Miss Moore with dignity. "Why *you* should leap to any such conclusion I don't know. I know nothing about your private life, or very little, and I've always been under the impression that it's perfectly ordinary behavior to invite a few friends in for the evening now and then."

"I said all right—sorry to sound cross, Pat, it's been one of those days when everything went wrong, and I've got a headache, that's all. I'll see you on Sunday, then." Alison put up the receiver before Pat could say anything more.

It was true, of course: a horrible day. And what other sort did she expect, an old-maid teacher? Teacher: what it came down to, though it sounded so glamorous and exciting, a charm school, where doubtless all sorts of romantic secrets were dispensed. . . . *So* romantic, she thought viciously, teaching these shallow little dunces to wash their faces occasionally, not to wear four-inch heels and dangly earrings to work, or shave off all their eyebrows! Damned little morons. Gum-chewing fat fools like that Green girl, no self-discipline to go on a diet, expecting she'd turn into Cleopatra by a sort of osmosis if she sat through a six-week course. And the Bernstein girl— *But I don't get it, Miss Weir, I mean about not using too much make-up. Listen, my cousin Rose, she just plasters it on, what I mean, and she caught a real nice fella, makes good money too, he don't seem to care—*

She leaned on the table there a minute, resting her forehead on the cool impersonality of the telephone. Be-all and end-all: *a real nice fella.* Well, so it was, so it was inevitably—women being women. *¿Qué mas,* what else?

Never mind the girls, they weren't so bad really. Not the girls: her own friends, so damned irritating . . .

She laughed, and sat up, and found suddenly, shamingly, that she was crying; she blew her nose, took herself in hand firmly. She never cried, Alison the competent and cheerful, who'd stood on her own feet and weathered enough trouble so far to stand up to this—this disgustingly conventional kind of trouble, losing a man!

Of course when it came to one's private life, no one needed to go around telling. Friends talked, guessed—*how* they talked and guessed! None of them knew anything definite, naturally; but somehow these things got round. And quite suddenly, she was being besieged on all sides by all these well-meaning people. As if they'd got together and—

Well, no. Because several different sets of them, as it were, had different candidates to trot out before poor Alison (or the other way round). And come to think, that must represent some hard undercover work, some cunning social traps, because unattached men weren't so easy to find.

It was really very funny, looked at objectively. She could imagine the anxious debates about poor Alison: Well, *I* never met him, did you?— and I wonder what sort of *thing* it was, none of our business of course, but I *gathered* from what Pat said once—oh, not gossip, because she doesn't, but anyway . . . Such a pity Alison was still single, such a nice girl, if she'd only meet some really nice man— And inevitably, Who do we know who might *do?*

Funny, and completely exasperating. How could people be so obtuse?—to think, apparently, that it was like a mathematical problem, one canceling out one—of anything.

Even Angel, she thought helplessly. Angel, of all people, who ought to know better. After the time she'd had with Art Hackett, knowing he was the only one she wanted as soon as she'd laid eyes on him, and Art so maddeningly gentle and careful and friendly, not saying a word, not even holding her hand at the movies—all because he'd got the idea it wasn't fair not to let her look around a little—she'd never known many young men, been around much. Angel complaining she could kill him, he made her so mad, and what more could she do or say to the big dumb ox?

Oh, Angel ought to know how useless it was, trying to substitute one man for another. But even Angel had a candidate to exhibit. . . . It *was* funny: a very respectable, rather shy young man, he was, Bruce Norwood, with such punctilious manners: a wholesale candy salesman, for heaven's sake, and he shook hands coming and going, and never said *damn* or *hell*. Suddenly it was so hilarious that Alison laughed aloud.

After Luis. *Luis*.

But all of them, any of them . . . Pat Moore's offering (and what could these people think of her, to choose such men?) was almost as ridiculous; that one she'd only met the other night—a cadaverous, solemn young man named Markham who worked in a bank. And the Corders across the hall insisting that she come over for dinner, just a few friends, nothing formal—and pairing her off just as insistently with an earnest, oddly courtly young bond salesman named Richard Brooke.

People. Meaning so well. So incredibly stupid. After *Luis*.

And the pain like a cancer there again, forever, so that she couldn't bear it. God, it must get less after a while, after a long while? The telephone rang under her hand, and her heart jumped at the sudden clamor: force of habit: always the quick fierce thought, it *might* be—he might— But it never was, it never would be.

Some one of these well-meaning silly people. Or one of their impossible choices of a man for poor Alison.

She let it ring three times before deciding to answer.

SEVEN

"Oh, my God," said Hackett resignedly. "No rest for the wicked. But do *I* have to go and look at it? Farnsworth can—"

"Well, I don't know, Art," said Sergeant Lake. "Maybe bein' around our Luis so much, it's rubbed off on me—getting hunches. Or maybe everybody's just jittery, with the papers building it up. But only reason the sheriff's boy called in is, he spotted it for maybe the same one—and he sounds damn convincing."

"Good God, *another?* I'd better talk to him. Switch the call through, will you, Jimmy?" Hackett was sitting at Mendoza's desk, at the end— or so he'd thought—of another grueling day on this business. (Why the hell did the tough ones always come in hot weather?) The county-patrol sergeant was hanging on the phone patiently. Hackett got the details from him, swore, asked the exact location; told Lake to assemble a homicide crew for him from the night men just coming on, and called his own number. As he listened to the phone ring his expression was grim (another field day for the press tomorrow, another dead woman), but it softened when Angel answered.

"Did I catch you in the middle of something that's got to be stirred, or measured in millimeters?"

"I *don't,*" she said indignantly. "Inspired cooks use guesswork, mostly. And you're going to tell me you won't be home. I think the police ought to have a union, you weren't in until eleven last night—"

"That's a dandy idea, only first we'd have to unionize all the crooks, pro and amateur—they don't keep regular hours either. Just one of those things, my Angel. . . . I don't know when, darling. I'm just leaving for some place down near Malibu."

"For heaven's *sake* . . . You needn't ask, I always miss you. Shall I keep something hot? . . . Well, maybe you'd better stop somewhere, if it's all hours. I don't know why more detectives don't have chronic indigestion, the irregular hours they— All right, but try to come home *some* time, just to let me know I *am* married."

On his feet, hat in hand, Hackett hesitated. Spoil Luis' evening with this?—he grinned to himself briefly. Mendoza had called in ten minutes ago; he'd had a busy and irritating day, and had announced that he was taking the evening off to soothe himself at the poker table with any pigeons he could pick up at his very respectable club. Just three things Mendoza was good at—in fact, brilliant—his job, women, and poker; Hackett's heart had bled momentarily for the unlucky pigeons who got inveigled into a game with him.

He dialed quickly. Probably catch him in the middle of that necessary (if he was going out) second shave, or a bath—fussy as one of his cats, Luis was. Come to think, Hackett would feel sorry for any woman who succeeded in marrying him. One of those people who couldn't sit in a room with a picture crooked on the wall or a wrinkle in the rug, and a damn sight more persnickety about his person than most society ladies. Tomcat, thought Hackett, listening to the phone ring at the other end: both affectionately and ruefully he thought it: a lean, sleek black tomcat, that way and this way.

Mendoza answered and he broke the news. "*¡Fuera!*" said Mendoza. "*¿Qué mono,* isn't this pretty? Where? . . . *¡Santa María!*—I trust you realize you have robbed me of approximately five hundred bucks, friend—I was counting on sufficient luck tonight to win back a pittance of my income tax. . . . All right, *¡allá voy,* I'm coming, I'm coming! I am also dripping bath water all over the carpet, and El Señor is using my left leg to sharpen his claws. *¡A tú, mil maldiciones!* I'll meet you there, damn it."

It was, of course, the worst hour of the day for getting somewhere in a hurry. Mendoza cursed steadily all the way down Sunset Boulevard from La Brea to Beverly Glen, before he took himself in hand. One very damned good way to get ulcers or a heart attack: getting mad at traffic. He made fairly good time at that, down to Pacific Palisades— not much choice of routes; all of them were jammed at this time of day, and like most residents he'd learned to stay off the freeways at crowded hours. Then, where Chautauqua took that sharp left turn and dropped suddenly down a steep little hill, just before its end, of course he got balked—you always did, there—it was the hell of a place to get by. Narrowing to about a third of the usual width. And down there was the Malibu road, the main drag, the coast highway, with another secondary street running up diagonally, Chautauqua jutting down at another: one of those three-way signals timed to outlast eternity, whichever of the three you waited for. But he got the green at last, and swung the Facel-Vega onto the coast road and made tracks up toward Malibu.

Just before the entrance to Topanga Canyon, Hackett had said. The traffic department played a little game with L.A. County residents, finding the best places to hide street signs, behind light poles and bushes and traffic signals; but he spotted the street easily, not by its sign but by the two big bulldozers parked there for the night. Two hundred feet up the narrow winding road he came on the scene of activity. An ambulance; Hackett's car; two county patrol cars; a battered sedan probably belonging to the foreman on the job. Men standing around talking and smoking, not doing much, Hackett looming in the midst of the little crowd talking to a diminutive wiry fellow. The county sergeant introduced himself, shook hands.

"I was just telling Sergeant Hackett, Lieutenant, I took one look and says to myself, this one belongs to the downtown boys—it's just maybe another of your current Mr. X's jobs, same kind of thing anyway, way she looks."

"I don't know that it's worth missing your five hundred for, Luis," contributed Hackett. "Though I kind of think it might be our boy, too. Held it for you to look at—not much the doctors can do here—maybe not anywhere else. At a guess, the corpse got to be a corpse somewhere around two years ago, a bit less."

"Ah," said Mendoza. "Like that? Well, well. I said I wondered if we'd missed any."

". . . and, my God, Joe thinks a dead dog or something at first, you know, when he hits it, and then he sees the hair and yells—and, my God, it's—" The little fellow was still excited and shaken.

Mendoza walked on to where the interns from the ambulance stood smoking. No, not a very savory corpse, though quite well preserved by burial: this was sandy soil up here—that had helped; and she was dressed too, which helped some more. Hard to figure the time, maybe: the autopsy-surgeon would want soil samples. She'd been blonde. What looked like a cotton skirt and blouse, black with a red print—traceable?—the remnants of black sandals, but yes, everything surprisingly well preserved.

Hackett said beside him, "And treasure trove, a handbag buried with her." Dwyer had it laid out carefully a few feet away, on a tarpaulin; he and Higgins squatted over it looking doubtful.

"Don't think we can expect any prints after all this time, on this rough plastic stuff, Lieutenant. You want to take a chance handling it a little?"

"With tenderness, Bert. Just in case . . . don't touch that metal clasp, I beg you—or anything smooth and stiff—"

"All right, all right, I've been to kindergarten." And there came out on the tarp, in the still-blazing late afternoon sunlight, a collection of humble objects. They all squatted close around; no move to touch anything yet. The little everyday things any woman's bag might contain, unimportant while she lived—maybe a man's life (and other women's lives) depending on them when she was dead. A crumpled handkerchief. A cheap, much-tarnished dime-store compact. Three half-used packets of matches. A dilapidated pack of Luckies, a few cigarettes left in it. A purse-sized bottle which had held cologne. A blackly tarnished once-silverplated lighter. Two lipsticks, brass-gold cases decayed black. A dirty powder puff. Four or five little papers, probably sales receipts—

"*¡Por el amor de Dios,* get them!"—as the hill breeze swirled them
off the ground; Dwyer made a grab for them and Mendoza received
them tenderly. A scarlet leather wallet, bulging-fat. What had been a
piece of Kleenex, lipstick-stained. A quarter-size bottle of aspirin. Nine
brass bobby pins. A small black address book.

"*¡Una donación de la Providencia!*" said Mendoza happily and, for
once careless of his clothes, knelt close over the address book, unfolded
the clean handkerchief from his breast pocket, with utmost care in-
serted the tip of a shrouded forefinger under the cover of the book and
lifted it. Hackett delicately held down the first page there as the breeze
swept over them again.

One of those I. D. inserts with lines indicated for name, address,
phone. Carefully filled out in a round childish scrawl. *Julie Anne Anderson, General Delivery, Topanga*—

"Christ!" said the little wiry man loudly. He had come up behind
them there, curious, in time to hear Hackett read that aloud. They
looked up at him. He'd been lighting a cigarette, dropped the match
and then automatically bent and ground it into the dirt—native west-
erner, fire precaution on his mind six months a year. "Christ! *Julie*—
that's *Julie?*—we dug up—"

"I will be damned," said the county sergeant interestedly. "So she
was dead after all. Well, there's a date for you, anyway, and she's kept
damn well, I will say—wouldn't have said the stiff was that old myself."

"Tell, tell!" begged Mendoza. "What, when, and how?"

The sergeant cupped both hands, half turned, expertly snatching a
light from the breeze, took a long drag on the cigarette. "It got transferred downtown to Missing Persons—your boys can give you the details. Let's see, it was June two years ago, call it twenty-seven months.
Not a big thing, you know—this chippy walks off somewhere, and the
girl friend she lived with keeps saying something's happened to Julie.
We looked around, asked questions, but what the hell? It looked a little
funny that she hadn't taken most of her belongings with her, but a girl
like that, they come and go, and she might've taken off with some guy
who'd just hit the jackpot at Vegas, or for some other reason expected
to start out fresh somewhere. She didn't have much to leave, that's for
sure. We figured it like that. It hapens. Don't know what headquarters
figured, what else they got."

"It happens. A girl like what?"

"Waitress at a joint up the road, along Zuma Beach. Part-time," said
the sergeant, and spat aside. "Lived with another girl in a rented shack

up in Topanga. Had quite a lot of company. Funny thing, though, never any other girls."

"Either of them ever been tagged officially on it?"

"Uh-uh. No complaints, no loud parties, and outside city limits. We're all for morality down here, Lieutenant, but we'd need about twenty times the number of men we've got to keep the citizenry in order on that count, and what the hell?—live and let live—they didn't run a pro house, they both held regular jobs. Like Prohibition. You can't enforce laws against human nature. You got a whole roomful of files listing every easy dame, amateur *and* pro, up in the big city?"

Mendoza laughed. *"¡A ver, otro chiste*—tell another joke! Sure, I know, impossible. And so nobody was really much concerned. As you say, these women drift. But also, they're apt to come in for this sort of thing,"—he nodded at the corpse. "What made you think of our Mr. X?"

"I've seen a lot of stiffs, Lieutenant, and a few this long gone. And like we can see, she's kept damn well. I took a good long look, and I didn't need a doctor to tell me what happened to her. She was raped and beaten, and I think choked too—"

"You can still see some of the marks," agreed Hackett. "Far as the rape goes, maybe it's just inference, but her clothes are torn—that's what it looks like. Surgeon'll say for sure, let's hope he can. But the main thing is, along with that, she was buried. Like Mary Ellen."

"Y-e-s," said Mendoza. He got up, brushed down his trousers mechanically, looked at the little book balanced on his handkerchief-shielded palm. "And it rather looked as if our Romeo meant to bury Jane Piper too, didn't it? I see what you mean, Art, but it's a little thin. Natural thing to do with a corpse. A lot of murderers do it. Of course, it isn't very usual with rape cases, that I grant you. Our Romeo's only done it once that we know of, and maybe meant to once more. Of course—" He was staring down the hillside, to the glittering stream of traffic sailing by, beyond to the smooth white beach and the summer-tranquil blue-green glass of the Pacific coming in in low lazy breakers—"of course there's something else. A part-time whore, sure, she meets all sorts, she's more apt to meet violence maybe, but on the other hand, who needs to rape her? . . . Yes. Maybe he didn't know she was a whore? And when a rapist assaults a respectable woman, and ends by killing her, sometimes it's in the course of stopping her noise but sometimes too it's deliberate, with the idea that she might be able to identify him. Why would it matter here? Even if she knew him, she wouldn't be likely to bring a charge, if her reputation was commonly known—to invite trouble on herself—"

"Yeah," said the sergeant. "Don't want to butt in, Lieutenant—I just ride herd on speed demons and like that—but I read the papers, and I've had a couple ideas about your Mr. X. You got a real job on your hands with this one, any cop knows—the citizenry, damndest thing, they seem to figure a guy like Mr. X goes around wild-eyed and acting queer all the time, ought to be a cinch to spot him. We know better, hah?"

"Don't we, indeed. Me, I'm a very democratic fellow, I listen to any-body's ideas."

"Well, you take women," said the sergeant. "Sure to God they can drive a man nuts without half trying—but whatever the head shrinkers say, a man don't have to be legally nuts to turn into a rapist. What oc-curred to me about Mr. X., I just got to thinking about two guys I picked up. Different times, I mean. One of 'em, his wife yelled for help and we kept him overnight—she wouldn't lay a charge and we had to let him go. Seems he couldn't get a kick out of it unless he hurt her. I don't know why, about that one—if there was any reason except that it takes all sorts. The other one was kind of interesting. We picked him up —it was nearly five years back, around there—on the complaint of a girl who'd dated him. Said he assaulted her, in his car. There was quite a legal hassle over it, because she didn't have too good a reputation— point is, what came out about him, in his defense. Don't ask *me* if the head shrinkers are right, saying the way Mama housebroke us accounts for whether we turn out ballet dancers or hoods. But this guy, his mother had been a lush, and he had the hell of a grudge on her for, you know, neglecting him, embarrassing him in front of kids he knew, and bringing men home for a roll in the hay with the door open, that kind of thing, so he got what he called a 'distorted view of sex'—you know. Seemed he had a kind of puritanical complex about it, he had all the normal instincts but he couldn't get worked up to really laying a female unless he made it like rape. I don't know, it just struck me your boy might be made that way. So he can't get there at all unless he gets it by force."

"You find them," said Mendoza. "So you do. And that's for the law-yers, afterward—what the hell good does it do us looking for him?" He dropped his cigarette, ground it under his heel. "What was that one's name?"

"Brooke Edwards."

"It rings a bell. We've been back through the files on every sex case the last fifteen years—"

"Broth*er*," said the sergeant respectfully. "And following 'em all up? When've you and all the rest of the L.A.P.D. been eating and sleeping?"

Hackett groaned. "Well may you ask! You ask me too sudden, I'd have to stop and think if my wife's blonde or brunette."

"And they turn down the last proposal for a pay raise," said the sergeant philosophically. "Ridin' around in nice late-model cars all day, in natty uniforms, not a thing to do but hand out traffic tickets to V.I.P.'s who hadn't ought to be expected to obey the ordinary laws. And have the gall to ask more money for such a soft job! I read the letters-to-the-editor, don't I know."

"Where did Anderson work?" asked Mendoza abruptly.

"Joint called Tony's, about four-five miles up the road. . . . Yeah, same owner far as I know. Couldn't tell you about the girl friend, that's quite a while for a dame like that to stay one place."

"Missing Persons may have something to offer," said Hackett.

"Yes—I'd like to talk to the girl friend. Well, this may be a mare's nest—maybe one of her customers thought she'd overcharged him and got mad—but we'll follow her up as far as we can to be sure. The press will be a lot surer right away than I am—"

"They always know," agreed the sergeant.

"Have you had dinner, Art? Suppose we take a ride up to this Tony's and see what we can get. The ambulance can take her away now, downtown—I'll send a note along to rout out Bainbridge *immediatamente,* I want all he can give me right away. Statements and so on, tomorrow will do. Thanks very much, Sergeant—come on, Arturo."

EIGHT

That, of course, had been one place to start a cast—one of many places, so big and vague an area that a lot of men had spent a lot of time looking, not sure just what they were looking for. They'd weeded out about fifty of the known rapists, men involved in other kinds of sex offenses, from the past twelve or fifteen years—men who in age, physical description, educational background, might possibly be their boy, by what had been learned from the girl friends. And damned little that was.

It added up to confirmation, the same man; but beyond that, all too vague in detail.

They knew now from Pauline McCandless's bosom confidante (a girl who'd shared her room in college) that Pauline had met this Christopher Hawke at the beach—not that she was the kind who picked up boys like that—but he'd been really nice, you could tell, Pauline had said (a little defensively, it could be deduced). Awfully polite, not forward or anything like that—and good-looking, tallish and thin with brown hair, about thirty. He was a bookkeeper or something, some office job, worked for Western Oil, and he had a new car, sort of racy and bright blue, a hardtop roadster.

They knew from the apartment manager's wife and a girl in Jane Piper's office a little of how it had gone there; Jane hadn't said quite as much as Pauline, and also that was longer ago, people forgot. Jane had met a Stephen Lord or maybe it was Laird, some name like that, casually in the bank; they'd got to talking, and he'd seemed nice and polite, nothing brash, so probably if he'd asked for a date she'd have said yes, though they couldn't say if he had. He had, they seemed to remember, been very generally described as tall and thin and brown-haired and about thirty.

Which was more or less what they had from the proprietor of the shop where Celestine Teitel had met him, and from Miss Evelyn Reeder. One of Mary Ellen Wood's closest girl friends had been out of town that relevant week, hadn't heard anything from Mary Ellen, but the other one, Wanda Adams, gave them a little confirmation. Mary Ellen had confided the story of her casual meeting with him—in the college cafeteria—and her hopes that he'd follow it up; she was, said Wanda, but really smitten with this Edward Anthony. Who was described as tallish and brown-haired and about thirty.

It added; but that was just defining the problem. They started to work on it the best way they could, by routine. They looked at the sex offenders; they looked at other files. They drew an arbitrary circle on the map, its center the Haineses' former house (because you couldn't take the whole damned town—it was a nightmare of a job even for twenty square blocks) and looked to see who had lived there at the time and moved since. No guarantee that their circle took in the right block—or if he'd lived within ten miles, then—or that he had moved, of course. No guarantee that, if he hadn't lived around there long, a landlady would remember him, give any kind of description. And he might, even if he'd been there, have been then and now a family man, or living with relatives, in a private house. But just to give the boys another little job, out there tramping the streets in this heat, Mendoza was having them conduct as detailed a canvas as possible on all single men renting apartments or rooms in the district.

That was odds or evens: pure luck if anything turned up there. They drew a blank, expectably, at the L.A.C.C. registrar's office. Mary Ellen had said he'd told her he was thinking of registering for an adult evening class in woodworking. But the registrar didn't have his name, that one at least: so they took a long hard look at every male then and presently registered in any of those courses. None of them who answered the physical description even vaguely corresponded otherwise; they all looked like upright citizens.

There was a lot of routine that had to be done even though it was thin hope; you just never knew where you'd hit pay dirt. They looked at all the men listed in the phone books and city directories who were surnamed Anthony, Hamilton, Hawke, Lord, Laird. They annoyed the local offices of Western Oil and got a list of all their male office help to look at. They looked at all the male employees of that bank building where Piper had met him, and at all the shops and offices around that music shop where Teitel had met him.

Inevitably they'd got repercussions from the press stories. Sometimes publicity helped; it jogged the public memory; and they couldn't pass up any bet, however absurd it looked. So they wasted time investigating about a dozen men suggested by nervous and imaginative people phoning in to say excitedly they were *sure* he was the one, he acted so *queer*. Among those, they did pick up an escaped mental patient from Camarillo, a gentle, bewildered middle-aged man who assured them that his only motive in talking to strangers in public was to spread the news that any day a superior race of Venusians was due to invade the earth and destroy all life, and he wanted to urge as many souls as possible to seek out salvation in time. "It matters not the *church,* you know, if they are received into *some* faith—so many scoffers and sinners, all doomed to perdition unless they take immediate steps—"

And Hackett said, "Welcome the Venusians! At least we wouldn't have to worry about Romeo any more."

The rest of those were all innocent as day—at least of any connection with this case: two amateur poets, three amateur inventors, a medical student in the throes of studying for finals, and assorted ordinary
citizens.

They hammered at Sally Haines grimly, and at Fairless, ignoring the
jibes and insults: they got a list of the Haineses' acquaintances, of men
who might have had some kind of imagined grievance against Haines—
or her. They looked at everybody who'd worked in Haines' office.
Maybe ten or fifteen years back that vague description of Romeo's car
as racy would have helped a little: but you could use the word for a lot
of standard models this year, and bright blue wasn't so unusual a color.
That was something to check against any suspect when they isolated a
few with something definite on them.

From all the places they had made casts, they'd drawn fish; and that
was one of the worst headaches they had to cope with now—keeping
tabs on all the might-be's. They knew now of approximately a hundred
men, one of whom might be their boy. Men whose general physical descriptions tallied, out of the list of sex offenders; residents near the
Haineses; employees in that building (and of Western Oil, and Haines'
old office, and places around that shop); even a few men from the
phone list of those names, and—just groping in the dark—from their
files of men with any sort of record. As time went on, they'd doubtless
collect more. And an eye had to be kept on them; they had to be investigated in the hope of narrowing it down more, eliminating, and pinpointing.

Of the names thus singled out they hadn't found all of them in person, not yet. Some had changed addresses, drifted away—who could
say where?—and they had to be located, looked at, just to be sure.
Some of them would be honest citizens—a press appeal would bring
them in to report and clear themselves; some of them would have
reasons for staying clear of the cops, and would have to be found the
hard way if at all; and the one they wanted would be lying very low indeed.

They had just so many men to work the routine; in this ten days they
had accomplished a quiet miracle in checking all the places they had,
all the people. But that was the kind of thing that didn't show—the
press boys couldn't make a good story out of patient clerks poring over
file cards, tired street men plodding from house to house in the pitiless
October heat, asking the same questions. . . . The radical papers
jabbed fretfully at the police, accusing, challenging, deploring. The

others ran cautious editorials pointing out the excuses for delay, the difficulties of the hunt. The public wrote letters to the editors agreeing or carping: people who disapproved of the press printing anything about such sordid affairs ("simply encouraging our youth to dwell on filth"); people who had theories; people who advocated a vigilante committee to aid the police. ("¡No faltaba más que eso—that's all we need!" said Mendoza.)

The Chief was wisely avoiding all but noncommittal comment. He knew Mendoza, but no officer was much different there: the hourly demands for progress reports, the exhortations, merely irritating.

And now, this one.

"Discard and draw," said Mendoza, edging the Facel-Vega out into highway traffic. "Another one—just maybe in the series—another chance of more evidence, another trail to follow. But also the chance of another dead end. You're looking thoughtful—has inspiration visited you?"

"Favour que me hace, you flatter me," said Hackett. "I was just thinkin', Luis," and he sighed. "I can remember eating breakfast because it was eggs a new kind of exotic way—with cream and green pepper and melted cheese and little bits of ham mixed in—"

"Scrambled eggs Creole."

"I guess. But I didn't have time for lunch. And what we hear about this joint of Tony's, I don't suppose we can expect much of a meal."

"You think too much about your stomach," said Mendoza. "And if you're not careful, that girl will have you grossly overweight. I swear you've gained five pounds just in the month or so she's been feeding you. You'll get high blood pressure and have a heart attack and have to retire at forty if it doesn't kill you—"

"But it's such a nice way to die," said Hackett wistfully.

Mendoza didn't think much of Julie Anderson. The fellows in the detective novels, everything was so nice and neat for them: the interest in clues was their obscurity. In real life, the first problem usually was to decide whether it was a clue at all and, next, if it belonged to this particular problem. What had happened to Julie Anderson had happened to a lot of women in the last twenty-seven months, and their boy hadn't accounted for them all, that they knew. Among the small list of things his known crimes had in common was the fact that the women had all come from a very different background than Julie Anderson's.

But it had to be looked into, of course.

The proprietor of Tony's just laughed when they asked him about her. If he tried to keep track of all the chippies he had in and out of here, he wouldn't have time to run his business. Sure, he remembered Julie—and was interested to hear about the murder, *that* was something, and probably (he added thoughtfully to himself) would bring in some trade. . . . Yes, he remembered her going off, it had been a damn nuisance, but these girls, no responsibility, she wasn't the first *or* the last had just walked out without warning. And what the hell were they getting at, asking if he knew anything about her private life?—he was a respectable married man. So what if she hadn't had a very clean reputation?—he had some like that working for him sometimes, and sometimes the other kind, he didn't ask for a letter from their ministers before he hired them, and it wasn't any of his business what they did in their off time. And about the girl friend he didn't remember anything if he'd ever known anything.

The Missing Persons files told them her name, Madge Parrott; she'd made a statement at the time, as had various other people including Tony. Nothing had indicated that Julie hadn't just drifted off voluntarily. Madge had admitted that Julie had recently got acquainted with a free spender, some kind of oil worker on vacation, who'd taken her around. Men like that were more or less transient workers—he'd moved on, too, and they couldn't locate him; it looked probable that Julie had gone with him. Neither of the girls apparently was a very orderly housekeeper, and Madge was forced to say that she couldn't be a hundred percent sure Julie hadn't taken a *few* things, but if so she hadn't taken much, and not her only suitcase. But oil workers made money, and maybe she expected him to get her everything new and better.

So, *de veras,* it was a democratic country and theoretically its agencies didn't favor one class over another, but things didn't always work out that way in practice. Here there hadn't been an anxious family of respectable citizens to demand more extensive police action: the girl was a loner, not important to anybody, and the police thought they'd figured out pretty accurately what had happened, and why go on wasting time making sure, for a girl like Julie? So there it had been left, understandably from the professional view—not so easy to forgive for the ordinary civilian who saw things in black and white.

Especially, thought Mendoza bitterly, when a paper like the *Telegraph* finished doing a job on it, blowing it up.

Madge Parrott had drifted on, no one seemed to know or care where, about a year ago. It was on the cards that publicity, a radio appeal, wouldn't turn her up: she might not care for the idea of being mixed up with cops again, whether or not she had a concrete reason for staying clear. She might be in New York, she might have forgotten all about Julie Anderson. But they'd try to find her.

Dr. Bainbridge, mildly surprised at the body's state of preservation, said he thought she'd been raped. He couldn't as an honest man swear to it on the witness stand, after all this time, but he rather thought so, from a couple of secondary indications. At any rate, she had probably died of head blows, possibly of choking; the throat was lacerated, and the skull cracked in two vulnerable spots.

The story broke in the papers before the final results of the autopsy were in, but those boys didn't need definite facts. She'd been youngish, she'd been choked and beaten, and buried: that was enough to connect her with Mary Ellen, and by inference with the others. A couple of papers reported the find in fairly noncommittal language, but the *Telegraph* blew it up under a byline every man on the force was coming to hate, Brad Fitzpatrick.

The chances were Fitzpatrick hadn't ever possessed much love for authority, but a couple of other circumstances entered in. His paper had a policy of taking the most bombastic stand on any newsworthy subject, which the editors fondly claimed as crusading. More important, all this had come along at the psychological moment for Fitzpatrick, who had a personal grudge against the police uniform. He'd been picked up four times for speeding and twice for drunken driving; when Traffic picked him up the third time on that, two months ago, the judge threw the book at him and revoked his license. Consequently Fitzpatrick (who like everybody in that category had been unjustly treated— according to them) took great pleasure in needling the force on this business; and though he wielded a very blunt pen, he knew to a hairline where to stop short of personal libel.

He had some very nasty things to say about Anderson. . . .

NINE

Along with seven or eight other press boys, Fitzpatrick was waiting on the steps to catch Mendoza that next Saturday when he came back after lunch. "You got anything new for us, Sherlock, like maybe you just found out she bleached her hair?" Fitzpatrick was a big fellow in the forties, running to paunch, and a sloppy dresser; he grinned insolently at Mendoza over the shoulders of scholarly-looking Edmunds of the *Herald,* little Rodriguez of the *Daily News,* Wolfe of the *Citizen.*

"Nothing to make a story of, boys. You know routine doesn't get us there overnight."

"Anything welcome, Lieutenant," said Edmunds mildly. "Any little scrap of stuff—"

"Sorry, nothing you haven't got. You know about the radio appeal for the Parrott girl." Mendoza edged past; the group re-formed and barred his way again.

"My God, two and a half years they take to find out there's a mass killer—now they've got nothing to say about how they're hunting him! You have any idea how to detect anything, Sherlock—or d'you just sit around up there playin' Deuces Wild with your sergeants?"

Mendoza gave Fitzpatrick a tight, polite smile. "Once in a while we get a little exercise cruising around handing out tickets to honest upright citizens."

"What the hell!" said Fitzpatrick, scowling. "Don't you try to hide out any more facts on us, *amigo,* to cover up your bungling! I got a hunch that's just what you—"

"*¡Hombrate!*" said little Rodriguez softly.

Mendoza's grin tightened; Fitzpatrick was indeed a clumsy fellow, but it didn't make him less annoying. "Out of the way, boys, you bother me, I've got work to do." They let him by reluctantly; and his expression was still grim when he came into his office. Sergeant Lake eyed him and said he supposed he'd had to run the gauntlet again. "You are," said Mendoza, "too young and innocent to hear my unexpurgated opinion of Mr. Bradley Fitzpatrick."

"Oh, I don't know, might broaden my experience like they say," said Lake. "Art's got a little something for you."

Mendoza went on into the inner office and demanded Hackett's news. "I don't know that it means much," said Hackett, gloomily. "We've turned up a couple more of our suspects-in-embryo, that's all. Just creating more work—now we'll have to look *at* them hard instead of for them." He flipped over a little stack of file cards on the desk. "John Tewke, sex record, indecent exposure—two years back. He'd moved, and we've spotted him working at a gas station in Sunland. George Canfield, nothing to say he's anything but an honest citizen, he's one of those worked in Haines' office at the time—you remember he was fired, so he never asked for a reference and we didn't know where he'd gone. Now we do, he's working for some outfit in Compton as a clerk. And here's that one the sheriff's boy was mentioning the other day, Brooke Edwards. I didn't remember it myself, but it seems there was quite a little publicity on that case—he got off, the girl's word wasn't good enough—and he changed his name all legal by deed poll afterward, so people wouldn't connect him. He's now Richard Brooke, working as a bond salesman for a respectable brokerage down on Spring. And Adam Pfeiffer, who lived two blocks down from the Haineses house then and moved about a month later—nothing on him except that he fits the description and we couldn't find him. Now we have. He got married, which is why he moved, and he's living in Glendale and driving a milk route. He doesn't sound very dangerous."

"I am forced to agree," said Mendoza. He sat down at his desk and flicked the cards away contemptuously. "I am the biggest damned fool walking the face of the earth, Art. Will you explain to me why, why in the name of heaven I went on driving eight-hour tours in that squad car?"

"What? When?"

"Sixteen years and four months ago," said Mendoza bitterly. "Out of a precinct house in east Hollywood. When the old man finally died and we found all those bankbooks and the safe-deposit boxes stuffed with land deeds and gilt-edged stock. Will you *tell* me? The hell of an inheritance tax they slapped on it, but there was still quite a lot left. In the neighborhood of three million apiece for the old one and me. I could have bought a yacht. I could have gone round the world. I could have opened an exclusive night club. I could have retired to study Yoga or sleight of hand—"

Hackett grinned. "Coals to Newcastle, that last idea—just judging from the couple of times I've sat in a card game with you."

"But no, me, I'm a nice idealistic earnest young fellow, I'd got interested in being a cop and a cop I stayed. Everybody ought to have some regular occupation in life, I said. And so what do I end up with? Mr. Bradley Fitzpatrick and our elusive Romeo. And I have the premonition I'll have them for the next ten years, if I last that long."

"*¡Animo!*" said Hackett with forced cheerfulness. "You never know when something's going to break."

"If you're going to play Pollyanna, you can go and do so somewhere else." Mendoza passed a hand over his face tiredly. He made jokes about it, but he wasn't feeling humorous in this situation. Like all the men working the case, he was tired; he'd been putting in sixteen hours a day since it broke—more than any of them, because he was the man in charge and he couldn't give himself time off. He was the one who had to keep all the threads separated, untangle the knots, and decide which ends to follow into the skein.

Tired . . . But he'd worked such hours before, cases as tough as this one, and never felt this deadly mental exhaustion—perilously near to losing interest in the whole damn thing, let somebody else worry about it . . .

He put his elbows on the desk, rested his head in his hands a minute. He had a little reputation at headquarters, Luis Mendoza, as one of the stars. Not because Luis Mendoza was any brainier than the next man—egotist though he might be, he knew that—but because he had come equipped with that tidy mind. Maybe from some crafty old Castilian military expert four hundred years back, or maybe from one of those Aztec engineers who'd so precisely designed those sacrificial pyramids the archaeologists kept finding. He liked things orderly, squared off. Give him something all in a tangle, he had to keep working at it until it was all straightened out. You might say it was just single-minded stubbornness, and it was helped along a little by that sensitivity for people giving him the nuances.

And usually he hit every new problem thrown his way hard and fast, feeling enthusiastic, feeling just naturally capable of solving it—because he was Mendoza, this bright fellow with a deserved reputation.

He hadn't hit this one like that, even the first day. He hadn't felt all that usual enthusiasm for proving himself all over again. He'd fumbled at it a bit, too, worrying about decisions, unsure right away where to look, how to tackle it. And right now he wasn't that headquarters star at all: he was a tired, irritated, even uncertain man—remembering again, vague and irrelevant, that he'd turned forty-years old last February.

And remembering (in the sympathetic silence there, Hackett letting him take a moment to himself) that aberration of last night . . . A little sluggishly his mind rose to tell him in defense, Not used yet to the old lady's being gone, missing that sense of family. *Eso era todo,* that was all, that was all.

Sergeant Lake came in and laid a slip on the desk before him. "Teletype, Lieutenant."

Mendoza raised his head slowly. "All right, thanks, Jimmy."

He had come in late and gone through all the usual motions: made a little fuss over the cats, cut up fresh liver for them, undressed, and had a bath. He sat up in the big bed smoking, for a while, and they came up around him, his only family now, his dear creatures so graceful and amusing to watch. The two small ones washing, settling down for the night, and the miniature lion El Señor trying to catch the smoke wisps in his big blond paws. And quite suddenly the grave silence of the big, solid-built apartment late at night had struck him to the heart with loneliness—Mendoza, always as self-sufficient as one of his cats!

He was a man content in the life he had: so it was a strange and even frightening thought, sliding into his mind unbidden: what did he have? He had upwards of six million dollars, and three cats to welcome him home.

But, a momentary mood: to the outside world Mendoza looked pretty much the same all the time, equable of temperament—but inside, he was up or down from mood to mood between two seconds. The way he was made: keep up the mask, the camouflage.

So he got up, and went and poured himself a drink. He brought it back to the bedroom with him, and as he sat down on the bed he knew what he wanted more than the rye. He wanted most violently to be with Alison. There was oddly, no desire in him to make love to her, he was too tired: only to be with her, for the desultory talk they'd so often shared, or no talk at all, just the sense of her presence in the room. Alison of the quick unsentimental mind, the humor that matched his own, the personality tuned to the same wave length.

And he looked at himself in the mirror and told himself he was the kind of fool he'd never thought to be. The trap, the trap—however pretty it was hidden. This sentimental Anglo-Saxon notion, true love everlasting. A fable for the children. It was the tangible plane only that mattered: in a wider sense, hadn't he found it out long ago?—all the other pretty fables too, the ones the priests told.

And he laughed, and told himself wryly he was an egotist: he wanted somebody to talk to, somebody sympathetic. Come down to it, it was probably one reason Luis Mendoza liked women, who by all convention learned to be such sympathetic listeners to men. And he drank the rye and put out the light, and after a long while he slept. . . .

The teletype was from a place called Murrietta. Madge Parrott had come into the police station there in response to the radio appeal. She was employed in a local restaurant; and Murrietta wanted to know whether they should take a statement and if so what about, or if L.A. would underwrite the cost of importing her.

"Hell!" said Mendoza. "I want to talk to her myself, I can't tell any-body else what questions to ask—"

"Tell them to send her up, no expense spared."

"No. No. Ten to one she's got nothing to give us at all, but if she has, I won't have the press at her—just in case it's something that shouldn't come out. Bring her up, we'd have to let them interview her. And if Anderson turns out to be irrelevant to this case, I'll be damned if I give the press any more reason to blow it up. They'd make headlines—New Witness Discovered. Let's keep it all nice and quiet until we know. Where the hell is Murrietta, somewhere south of Elsinore, isn't it?— give me a map. . . . Yes, there you are, call it ninety miles or a hun-dred. *Pues bien, iré*—I'll go down myself, probably overnight. O.K.? What time is it?—twenty of two. I'd better get going then, you can carry on here, I'll be back tomorrow morning."

"I don't envy you the drive in this weather."

"Might as well be doing something as nothing."

"Nothing," said Hackett. "Are you kidding?"

Mendoza laughed and went out. All the reporters had gone, down-stairs, except Fitzpatrick, who'd buttonholed Edmunds and was laying down the law about something to him, gesturing emphatically. Both of them stopped talking and got on Mendoza's heels like a pair of well-trained hounds; they'd thought he was placed for the afternoon. "Some-thing new come up, Lieutenant?" "Where're you off to, Sherlock?"

"It's too hot to work, boys," said Mendoza, "I'm taking the afternoon off to visit a blonde."

"And I could believe that damn easy!" Fitzpatrick shot at him as he went past. Mendoza took the Facel-Vega out onto Main openly; he couldn't very well do anything else. He grinned to himself, thinking of Fitzpatrick, licenseless, fuming at the driver they allotted him. No sign of them, though they'd be coming, but an old sedan with a "Press" sign and Edmunds at the wheel right behind him when he caught the signal at First. He'd have to go a little off his direction to lose them; he didn't mind. He was ordinarily a scrupulously cautious driver, but what was the use of running something like a Facel-Vega if you didn't let it out occasionally? He drove sedately up to the Hollywood freeway and took off like a scalded cat in the fast lane; this time of day it wasn't crowded, and within five miles he'd lost the press.

They wouldn't figure he was going home at this hour; he turned off at at Hyperion and went on up northeast, no further attempt at conceal-ment. Home, he folded pajamas, put them with his razor into a brief-case, called on the one of his four helpfully cat-venerating neighbors at home, Mrs. Bryson, and asked her to see that his darlings were let in and out and fed for the next eighteen hours. Thoughtfully he put away the cuff-link case in a drawer (El Señor had yet to master drawers), set out fresh meals for them, and left.

It was just before seven when he got to Murrietta. He could have made it earlier; once he was out of the metropolitan traffic, somewhere the other side of Whittier, he made good time southeast. But from the look of Murrietta on the map, he wouldn't find much effete accommo-dation there, and he stopped at Corona for an early dinner.

At the police station in Murrietta, which was about what he'd ex-pected from the map, he announced himself to a big indolent-looking sheriff with remarkably shrewd eyes, who surveyed his tailoring, his moustache, his I. D. card, and the Facel-Vega parked outside the little building and obviously didn't think much of any of them. "You must be real anxious to talk to Madge, Lieutenant, run down on purpose like this. Don't strike me as very likely she'd know much about a nut like the one you're after, but that's your business."

"Well, you never know," said Mendoza amiably. A young fellow even bigger than the sheriff came in, was introduced as a deputy, and adopted a similar expression of politely veiled scorn for this city fop who called himself a police officer. "Where'll I find her?"

The sheriff said kindly, "You go down this road 'bout a mile and a half and take the west cutoff toward Fallbrook, and half a mile or so on you'll come to the Apache Inn. That's where she works, see. Randolph Newbolt runs the place, you just ask somebody for Mr. Newbolt and he'll likely let her take time off to talk to you."

"Thanks very much."

"You can't miss it, I guess." The deputy added his bit to this fraternization with the foreigner. "Big brick place—there's a sign. Randolph gets quite a play—fanciest place we've ever had around here, liquor license and all. People come in from Temecula and even Elsinore."

"Well, well, how gratifying," said Mendoza. "I'll find it, thanks." Their combined, benevolently amused gaze followed him back to the car.

He found it. And why, he wondered, the Apache Inn: a somewhat sketchy memory of native history failed to place any Apaches within five hundred miles. Also, why Murrietta? Perhaps there was something as peculiar about Americans as the rest of the world seemed to think, when they deliberately commemorated the names of their public enemies. (Mendoza regarded the famous Robin Hood of El Dorado from the policeman's viewpoint, not the romanticist's: merely another outlaw.) Then, as he got out of the car, he looked thoughtfully at the Apache Inn from another angle, and reflected that maybe the nation was safe as long as Americans went on admiring the outlaws, who in one essential aspect at least were the nonconformists.

It was new, only slightly garish, and well filled this weekend evening with local ranchers and their families, a few tourists and city vacationers from the Elsinore resort. He found Newbolt, who was annoyed.

"You would turn up on a Saturday night, to take one of the girls out of service! Oh, well, can't be helped, we got to cooperate with the law, I guess. I'll get her for you."

TEN

"Brother," said Madge Parrott, "don't go thinking I'm trying to corrupt the cops, but you're a sight for sore eyes! Somebody from town, that knows the score. Gee, that's a real nice suit you got on, nice goods. It's been so long since I seen anybody in coat and pants that match—well, around here you might as well put on a full-dress suit, know what I mean. Brother!" She heaved a sigh at him across the marred narrow table of the little booth, in this nondescript restaurant-bar serveral cuts below the Apache Inn, where they'd settled at her suggestion.

Mendoza grinned at her. He'd placed Madge at one look: essentially a nice honest girl, just a little too democratic. He was reminded of the sheriff's sergeant at Julie's grave the other day—what the hell?—that was Madge. She was in the late twenties, round-faced, brown-haired, not bad-looking. The waiter came up and leaned on the table. "Got a night off or did Randolph fire you, Madge?"

"Night off, Jimmy—real important business, this is a big cop from L.A.—you know that thing I was telling you about."

"Yeah?" Mendoza received a curious stare.

"I want a Daiquiri if the city's going to pay for it, Lieutenant, it's kind of expensive—"

"The city can stand it. You can bring me rye, straight. Now, Miss Parrott, first of all I want to ask you—"

"Oh, gee, don't call me Miss Parrott, I won't know who you mean! Honest, this one-horse burg! I sure hope I'll have to come up, testify at the trial or something—you know. Get out of here a while, anyhow." She leaned an elbow on the table, heaved another sigh. "I'd never've come back—I was born here, you know, worse luck—if it hadn't been for Ma getting sick. But there you are, it wasn't fair to expect Betty to take her, she's got a husband and kids to look after and I don't. The doctor says maybe only a year or so," and her face saddened momentarily. "That won't kill me, and it's a kind of a duty. But you know how it is—country gives me the jim-jams. . . . But you didn't come down to listen to all this. I read in the papers about Julie," and now her expression hardened. "I was—tell the truth, I'd been already doing some thinking, one reason and another—come to that in a minute—and even before I heard you wanted to see me, I was goin' to call you, because I don't know but I guess maybe you ought to hear what I got to say."

"I'd rather expected you might feel the way Mrs. Haines does. Stupid cops."

She glanced up, quick and surprisingly shrewd. *"You* think it's—the same one did that? The papers I saw said maybe."

He shrugged. "I don't know. I hope you can tell me something to point one way or the other. Between us, I'd be just as well pleased if something says no. We've got enough on our hands right now."

"I guess you have," said Madge. The waiter brought their drinks. "But maybe I can tell you something, at that. I don't know—you're the one to, you know, kind of put it together. You want to ask questions, I suppose, but can I just go on and—and tell you what I been thinking and all, a while?—you stop me and ask, if there's anything you want to know special."

"Go ahead."

She took a reflective sip. He thought irrelevantly that it was probably a middling-respectable family, and nobody down here knew the somewhat lesser reputation she'd had up around the big city. It figured. And he sympathized with the way she felt: he was a paving-neon-lights-and-crowds man himself. A lot of pretty scenery in the country, and no smog, but essentially the country was things instead of people, and people were always so much more interesting.

"I didn't feel exactly that way about the cops," she said. "I guess I could see how it looked to them. After a while I figured it that way myself. You know how you do—you really know inside it's a different way, but everybody so sure opposite and telling you good reasons it *is* —and besides, wasn't nothing I could do about it. See, it was all little things I guess a man just wouldn't see was important."

"Try me, Madge."

"Oh, you," she said with a sidelong smile. "I wasn't born yesterday, don't need more 'n one look at you to know—you know all the answers, it comes to us girls."

"Don't flatter me, no man ever does."

"And maybe you got something there too," she said abstractedly, moving her glass around in a little circle. "Maybe none of us ever really know all the answers, even about our own selves. . . . See, it was that new dress she'd just got, real bargain it was, one of those places up in Hollywood sells secondhand stuff but not really secondhand, know what I mean—clothes the movie stars, people like that, turn in—kind of people they can't be seen in the same thing three times, you know. Things not worn a bit, and specially designed. Julie being a blonde, if she did help it along a little, she could wear black real good, and it was a swell dress, must've cost a hundred or so first place. She was crazy about it, she'd only worn it once yet. And there was all her make-up— you know, foundation stuff and powder in big boxes and rouge and cologne and talcum and eye stuff, kind of thing nobody carries in their purse. And her best shoes, transparent vinyl plastic with rhinestone heels, eight dollars she'd paid for those on sale. I said to the cop, sure,

O.K., she just *might've* gone off, her own self, without saying anything to me—though I *know* she'd have left a note—if it came up in a hurry, but she wouldn't 've gone off without her new dress, her best shoes, all her make-up. She liked Coty's, and gee, that's not dime-store stuff, it'd cost something to get all new. . . . And that's one thing about vinyl plastic—it goes with any color, see—and they was good shoes. Even if she'd gone off with Al Bruno, way they said, or somebody else she expected 'd buy her all new stuff, she wouldn't have just left things like that. Sure, maybe work clothes, old stuff, odds and ends not worth much, but not those things—or a couple pieces nice costume jewelry and so on. I mean, why should she?" Madge sighed again. "All the same, way they put it, I couldn't say for absolutely sure. You know?"

"Sure. Logical. You think she'd have let you know? You two, you didn't just come and go, independent of each other?" He was letting her take her time.

"Just between you 'n' me 'n' the gatepost, Lieutenant, I *know* she'd have told me. I kind of see how the law's got to figure, but most ways it don't make much sense. I mean, they say, you got nothing in black and white to prove it, you can't be sure. But you know 's well as me, you know for damned certain in *yourself*—gee, there I go swearing again, sorry—you know what a person'll do or not do when it comes to little ordinary things like that. All right, maybe you don't about big things— people do a lot of funny things that aren't what you'd expect of them, about big things like falling in love and so on—but about things like *that*"—she gestured vaguely—"you know, they don't change. Julie, she was brought up nice, she was a nice girl."

Mendoza didn't smile; that didn't strike him as a funny remark; being a realist, he knew that the quality Madge would call Niceness hadn't much to do with sexual morality. He said, "That's very interesting. No, I don't suppose you got that across to anybody at the time. You mean she wouldn't have run out on you without explaining."

"That's it. She was always right on time with her share of the rent and all, and it was nearly the end of the month. Julie and I always got on good together—well, of course I'm not the fussy suspicious kind always picking little fights over what brand of coffee to buy and all like that—you know—and neither was she. You got to have some consideration for anybody you live with, and we both did. I mean, well, I was working in Santa Monica, and supposing I found I had to work late, see, I'd call up Julie at the restaurant and say—so's she wouldn't expect me home same time, make enough supper for me. And, like if she was getting dressed for a date when I wasn't home, and got a run in her ny-lons last minute, say, she'd leave a little note, saying she took a pair of mine and 'd pay me back. And like that. So, O.K., say all of a sudden she decides to go off with Al, and even say it *was* in such a big hurry she couldn't phone me where I worked, why, I know she'd have left a note. Just a little scribble some kind to *say,* and if she was leaving most of her stuff, probably she'd put down something like I could have it all."

"That figures," he agreed.

"But that's water under the bridge like they say, and I guess too"— another sideways look—"they didn't pay an awful lot of attention to me on account of they didn't think a girl like Julie was much loss—or one like me anybody to waste time listening to. I suppose you know what I mean."

Mendoza finished his rye. "I'm not interested in your bed manners, Madge—"

"More's the pity," and she grinned at him. "No, a cut above my kind, aren't you? Could I have another drink? Just one—I don't usually—too expensive and Ma's death on it, I can't even have beer in the house. No, but at least you got enough good sense to know just because I've slept around a little it don't say I'm a fool *or* a liar. . . . Thanks ever so much," as he signaled the waiter. "Look, here's the way it was, see, and stop me if I talk too much. They looked for Al some, to see if she *was* with him, but they never found him and I guess after a while they stopped looking. What the hell—you know?" She shrugged. "Julie didn't have no people, she was raised in a Catholic orphanage back East somewheres. Look, Lieutenant, what I'm goin' to tell you, it'll maybe sound like—like those people who say *I always knew there was something funny*—after a thing's happened, when they never at all. But, gee, at the *time* I didn't have no reason at all to connect it!

"Here's how it was. It was June when Julie went away like that— twenty-fourth of June—and like I say, I didn't like what the cops said but I finally thought maybe it was so. Time goes on like it does, and about a year ago—just a year ago this month—I have to come home, look after Ma. Well, I been buried alive in this hole ever since, and you get so's any little thing out of the ordinary, it makes a change—you gawk out the window at somebody from the next township. So a couple months back when some oil company sends out a crew to do test holes up on old man York's ranch, I happened drive up there one Sunday afternoon with Betty and Joe—little ride, see. And one of the fellows in the crew turned out to be Al Bruno."

"Ah," said Mendoza. "Chance succeeding where hard work failed. You got together with him, of course—"

"I did," said Madge. "When he was off for the day."

"—And where was he when we wanted him before?"

"In Alaska. He got sent up there, some godforsaken place, right after he left L.A. that time. He didn't know nothing about Julie, I mean, he didn't even know she was—gone. We talked it over some, but we both thought, kind of silly to go to the police now—and even if they were interested, if they started looking again, it was all so long ago they wouldn't be likely— Well, the thing was, it just put the whole business in my mind again, know what I mean. I—I liked Julie, you know. We got along real good. . . ." She stared at her new drink in silence for a minute. "It *wasn't* like her, do nothing like that. I sort of got to wondering about it all over again. And then it started to come out in the papers about—this crazy guy you're chasing, killed all those girls. I don't see the papers regular—busy and all, and we just got a weekly here, I see that mostly—but last week, I did see a couple *Times,* and there was a lot in them about these murders—what those other girls said and all. Like I say, I'd been remembering back on account of Julie, and all of a sudden it connected up in my mind, like, and I thought, Hey, *could* it be—? But it was pretty far-fetched. Until you— found her. Like that. And then I really did some thinking."

"About what?"

"About this guy, this funny guy. Now if you're goin' to ask how many times she saw him, or what his name was, or anything like that, I couldn't tell you. Looking back, it seems quite a while both of us had seen him hanging around. Different places. You know, I guess, we had a shack up Topanga Canyon. Well, places we saw this fellow, it was like in at Tony's where Julie worked, and another restaurant further up, and six-seven times on the beach along there, and once I do remember at the general store in Topanga, you know that little kind of shopping center halfway up. We had him spotted for a weekender."

"A weekender—?"

"You know, somebody comes to the beach just weekends, regular. The boating crowd does that, but they hang around Santa Monica mostly on account of the harbor and boat docks. Some people have beach cottages, or know people who do—and sometimes the family'll be there all week, on vacation, and the man just comes weekends—but a lot of young fellows, ones that like swimming and surf-fishing and so on, they'll make a beeline for the beach after work Fridays, stay at a cheap motel or rent a cheap cabin, you know. Sometimes a bunch of them go in together for a cabin. Especially in the summer."

"I get it. He looked like one of those?"

"Well, I guess the reason we thought so must've been we only saw him around on weekends, or mostly. But I don't think he'd be in with a bunch of fellows, for a couple reasons I'll say in a minute. If you're goin' to ask why we noticed him at all, well, it was a kind of joke really. It was because he acted like he'd fallen hard for Julie, and he was"— she made a helpless gesture—"he wasn't dry behind the ears, you could tell. Like a yokel getting his first eyeful of burleycue. You know? A regular Snerd. I mean, there he'd be, gawking at Julie as if he was trying get up his nerve, ask her for a date. Like I say, it got to be a little joke between us. She'd spot him somewhere and nudge me and say, Don't look now but here's my biggest fan. You know?"

"Mmh. For how long?"

"I've done some thinking on that too, and the nearest I can say is, just that spring and summer. I mean, if you get me, it wasn't anything either of us was keeping tabs on. I'd say probably from around end of April, beginning of May, to—to when Julie left. Got—killed, the way we know now." She looked up at him suddenly. "Can I ask you something? I guess, nobody to—*claim* her, like—the city'll bury her, won't they? It don't seem exactly right. I haven't got much, but I'd like to do something—one thing, I guess you could say I owe it to her, taking all her stuff like I did. I don't know how Catholics do—Julie didn't go to church, but from a couple things I heard her say, I guess she'd want a Catholic funeral, and maybe I could pay the priest or whatever they—?"

"We can see there's a service read and so on, sure. Go on, tell me about this fellow."

"Well—he acted like that. Real gone on her. When I said a Snerd, I didn't mean he was homely. I mean, far's I remember, you wouldn't turn to look at him for any reason. He—"

"*Dios mio,*" said Mendoza softly, "could you identify him?"

Madge lifted her shoulders hopelessly, spread her hands. "Mister, I saw him maybe a dozen times, sure, but across a restaurant, just for a minute in the store or maybe thirty feet away on the beach—and not to *notice* him, I mean to really see what he looked like, were his eyes blue or his nose straight or his teeth crooked—just seeing he was *there*. We weren't interested in him as a fellow, just his being *there* again. No reason to memorize what he looked like as a fellow—it was just the joke!"

"Yes, I see, damn it. I know what you mean. Hell," said Mendoza. "And it's a very long chance he's the same one."

"I don't know, I just wondered," said Madge miserably. "I been over and over it, trying to remember better. But all I come up with, he *could*'ve been, from what these other girls said. He was a little bit taller than average, I seem to remember, not an awful lot but some—maybe an inch taller'n you are—and built just ordinary, and I think he had browny kind of hair. Awfully ordinary, really. That's all I can say. And *I* never got any closer to him, never heard him talk. Now don't go asking me what day it was, because I just plain don't remember, but I've sort of got the feeling it wasn't very long before Julie left. She came home one night and told me—she laughed a lot about it—this country boy'd finally got up nerve enough to talk to her. I don't know where, Tony's or some place else—I don't remember if she was out on a date that night or working, see. She said he come up and, you know, tried to start a conversation with her, and just like you'd expect he kind of stammered and didn't know what to say. It was really funny, because—well—"

Mendoza laughed. "Dot the *i*'s, because all he'd have had to do was show up with a couple of the other boys some night. Sure."

"Listen," she said defensively, "neither of us ever welcomed just *anybody* with open arms. It wasn't that kind of thing. But I guess you see what I mean, it was account of him being that way made me think—when I been thinking it over just lately—he was a kind of loner. Didn't know any fellows around there, let alone share a cabin with any, or mix much with any crowd. You see?"

"Mmh. Logical. Tell on."

"That's about it. If he told Julie his name that night, she didn't remember it or tell me. She wasn't interested—neither was I, then. But when I read about what happened to these others, I thought about him. It *could* be. I don't know what you think about it, and what I've said— all I knew about it, and her—doesn't look as if she'd ever have gone out on a date with him, nothing like that. But if he offered her a ride home from Tony's some night—we didn't have a car—or from the store, why, she'd have said yes quick, anyone would, a little thing like that."

"Yes," he agreed. And all this was—like most of everything else they had to go on in this business—a very small scrap of what was only might-be evidence; but there was another little list of just possibly suggestive facts which was leading him on to wonder if it did connect. He stared at his empty glass, and he thought, Not Mary Ellen. *But that was in the middle of the week.* Topanga Canyon—the beach up toward Ventura, the other side of Malibu (and that was on a Sunday)—the beach street where Julie had been buried. Yes—no? Coincidence? Meaning anything at all?

He looked up at Madge without seeing her very clearly. "Yes," he said, "yes. *Tal vez*—just maybe . . ." Balance the credits and debits. Another one to add to the list. The press had already done that, but on the other hand, maybe on this one some much more useful pointers where to look? He said, "I want a statement from you on this."

"Sure, anything I can do to help, Lieutenant."

"Let's see if the sheriff can supply us a steno at this time of night."

And he wondered doubtfully if they closed up the police station at nine o'clock, maybe, and all went home; but when they came past there was a light in a rear window, so he parked and took Madge in. The front office was empty, but there was talk and laughter from the rear and he went down a little duty hall. There in a back room sat the sheriff, the deputy Mendoza had met, and three others round a table under an unshaded electric bulb, over what looked to be a lively hand of poker. There was a good deal of smoke, a half-empty bottle, and a general air of camaraderie.

The sheriff laid down his hand, innocently turned his back on the table, and came up to ask what he wanted. Mendoza explained. "Oh, sure, I guess we can take care of that for you. Andy here's a pretty fair steno if you give him time." He wasn't too pleased at having the game interrupted, but he knew his duty. "Madge really had something for you, eh?"

"Very gratifying, in a way," said Mendoza, absently. He and Madge and Andy foregathered in the front office and Madge made her statement. They watched Andy copy it, Madge signed it neatly, and Mendoza said, "I'll take you home, Miss Parrott—or back to work?"

"I guess not much point in that now, they'll be through the rush, and Mr. Newbolt's nice, he won't grudge me the pay anyways."

Mendoza took her home through a labyrinth of dark lanes, and on his way back wished he had blazed the trail to the main street. He found the police station again, went in, and thanked the sheriff cordially for his invaluable aid. "I see you're—mmh—whiling away the evening with a little friendly game." He gave them all a vague general smile. "I've been so busy lately, no time to relax—but they do say a change of occupation's sometimes more restful, don't they?"

At this broad hint the sheriff looked doubtful, looked resigned, and then slowly another idea (Mendoza saw it germinate) occurred to him; his eyes rested a little thoughtfully on Mendoza's gold cuff links, custom-made shoes, and Sulka tie. He said genially, "Like to sit in a few hands, Lieutenant? Glad to have you, hah, boys?"

"That's very hospitable of you," said Mendoza; he coughed gently. "I don't often get the chance of playing, I'm afraid—they keep me busy, you know." He beamed around at introductions, advancing to the table. "Very nice of you indeed, I'll enjoy a few friendly hands. Oh, nothing to drink, thanks, I never drink when I'm handling cards. . . ."

ELEVEN

Hackett sat looking at those file cards for a few minutes after Mendoza had gone, and then got up and stood staring out the window. There wasn't really a great deal for him to do right now. A lot of hard work on this business, but it wasn't as if there were a dozen witnesses to be questioned and requestioned by the top officers: most of the work at this stage was collecting facts—the men on the street did most of that— and thinking hard about them, arranging them in different patterns. And he didn't know that any amount of thinking was going to get them anywhere.

Maybe a hundred men (he hadn't counted) who could be Romeo, just because of a very arbitrary connection somewhere. A connection to the Haineses' former neighborhood in general. To Haines' office. To sex-offense records. To the neighborhoods around where Piper and Teitel had met him. Things like that. And all of these possibles had to be looked at closely to be sure; the L.A.P.D. simply didn't have the manpower to do that all at once, and would have to take them in batches, hoping to eliminate as they went along. You had to start looking somewhere, but on an offbeat one like this that sort of routine wasn't always very useful. Chance played such a large part, sometimes: the random coincidence.

He might never have lived within ten miles of the Haineses; he might have known about that big back yard and the garden shed from having visited someone around there once, on business or socially. He might never have been in trouble with the police: millions of citizens never had. He might have been in those other districts, where he'd picked up Piper and Teitel, just on one occasion.

Hackett sighed. Routine. Sure, it put together a lot of cases. There had to be routine. But from experience he knew Mendoza was right in saying that routine, hard work, wasn't always the whole reason you got somewhere or didn't. Mendoza the gambler seemed to feel it was as if Providence—or Something—sat up there dealing hands around, and this deal you got a couple of nice fat aces, next deal nothing but low cards. And on discard-and-draw, sometimes you got just what you were after to fill out your hand, and sometimes the fellow across the table, the one you had to beat, got all the court cards instead.

Mendoza, of course, didn't think there was anything to it but blind chance, the way the deck got shuffled. Hackett, who wouldn't call himself a religious man, persisted in feeling vaguely that always, when it came to the last deal—when all the chips were down—the deck was stacked against the Opponent.

And of course—he'd seen that kind of thing work out more than once—the random chance could favor you as well as the fellow across the table.

He came back to the desk and without sitting down he looked at the city map he'd been studying when Mendoza came in. There was a little thought, he couldn't call it an idea, in his mind about that. Something he couldn't very well explain to Dwyer or Higgins or Landers, any man out on the street collecting facts: something he couldn't formulate except vaguely to himself.

Take a map, any map, but maybe especially one of this place, the whole city. It told you directions and distances and the names of streets; it couldn't show you all the little things, or the intangible things. What kinds of neighborhoods; where one kind turned into another kind. Relationships of buildings and houses and empty lots. What a given place really looked like. Or, of course, what kind of people lived there.

And it was people who were important. Inevitably.

This place. The biggest city in the world in area, four hundred and fifty-seven square miles of it. There were jokes about that; there was an L.A. City Limits sign at Boulder Dam over in Nevada, another somewhere up in Alaska. Well, it had just grown—one reason and another —and in all directions. And as far as people went, they were from all over: take any crowd at random, only about one in eighteen would be California-born. And all kinds of people.

Very convenient indeed if you could generalize with confidence, if people fitted nice and neat into the general-type slots—figuring it economically or any other way. Sure.

And you couldn't throw in your hand and demand a new deal, but you could always draw, hoping you'd get something useful.

Hackett got his hat and went out, to chase a will-o'-the-wisp he wasn't at all sure was there.

The Haineses had lived a little way up from Franklin Avenue in Hollywood. Franklin was a minor dividing line of neighborhoods, right along there, running more or less across the top of Hollywood east to west. Not very far above it was the line of foothills, with the San Fernando Valley on the other side, no natural passes here; there wasn't much level ground above Franklin. Twenty or thirty years ago Franklin had been an exclusive street to live on, as had the few little winding streets north of it then developed and built on. Down below, there had been and were side streets crossing Western, Van Ness, Gower, Vine, Cahuenga—the main drags—which were residential, but not as exclusive: respectable middle-class, some better than others, some rental-zoned. But business had grown inexorably all around and between Western and Van Ness, here, and while there were still quiet residential side streets—the Woods' house was on one of them—a lot of it to this and that side was beginning to look a little down-at-heel. As for Franklin—who had the money to keep up city estates like those now? Mostly they were two-storey stucco, bastard Spanish or Mediterranean, at the top of immense sweeps of terraced lawn: looking down their noses, like a row of elderly dowagers at a modern miss in a bikini. And not so well kept up these days as they had been. Hackett reflected, driving past, that falling heir to one of them when old Aunt Mary died—as a lot of poor devils had—would be acquiring a white elephant. . . . And here was the street the Haineses had lived on, Birch Avenue. He turned up it.

After the trial and the denial of the appeal—probably when all the money was gone to the lawyers—Sally Haines had sold the house. Hackett didn't know who owned it now, but he wasn't interested in the house. He drove past it; like some of its neighbors it was vaguely colonial-style, white stucco and frame, with a low wall; like most of them, pretty well kept up. This wasn't a brashly fashionable area by any means; these houses were just a little newer than the big places along Franklin, built when it was beginning to be prohibitive to maintain a twelve-room house. It was conservative upper-middle-class here; the houses were all twenty or thirty years old, but the taxes would run higher than Hackett would care to pay.

He turned left at the next narrow street and two city frontages up saw the mouth of the little alley to the left. It didn't continue across; probably its existence was due to some divergence in the original subdividing of this area. He remembered that it wasn't very long—a block or so—and seeing the place in three dimensions, rather than on a map, he could see why it attracted traffic. These streets ran diagonally up here, and anyone on foot who was going or coming from nearby on Birch Avenue, or Archer a block up, or View Terrace, which he was on now, would find the alley a little short cut, closer to Franklin.

They had drawn a circle on the map, twenty square blocks or thereabouts, and men had canvassed the whole area collecting statistics. And maybe none of it meant a damned thing. Also, of course, they had looked at this particular small center of the circle a little closer (and so they had before, at the time of the Wood case). If there was anything out of the ordinary, anything here, somebody should have spotted it by now.

Hackett told himself he was a damn fool clutching at straws, wasting time like this. He parked, walked across the little street, and started slowly down the alley.

It was wide enough for a car, and up ahead he could see that some people had put rear double doors on their garages so they could come in and out by the alley. The first three houses from the corner, to his left, had achieved privacy by a high brick wall, a reed fence, and a wire fence overgrown with ivy. The next house apparently didn't care who looked into its back yard; there was just a low stucco wall about two feet high, and he could see the rear and side of the frame garage, lawn, flower beds, rattan and aluminum patio furniture, the whole of the house, and a clothesline with a dozen diapers hung on it. The house next to that was the one the Haineses had owned.

There wasn't even a wall here, just a low picket fence a man could easily step over. Privacy had been arranged by the hedge—he didn't know what kind—planted about twenty feet up the yard, right across except for a gap where there was a wooden gate. Midway between that and where he stood was the famous garden shed, a little corrugated-iron affair, utilitarian rather than beautiful, where tools would obviously be kept. Grass grew listlessly brown in patches this side of the hedge, but this part of the yard wasn't landscaped: there was the big cement slab where an incinerator had stood before the city outlawed them, and off to the side a clothesline.

Quite handy for disposing of Mary Ellen, especially after dark, as it had undoubtedly been. Provided you had a flashlight; because you couldn't switch on the light in the shed even if you knew it was there. He walked on, to the boundary of the property that side, where the next garage cut off the view of that yard, and discovered that you could see into the shed: the door was half open and he could make out part of a shelf and the earth floor.

He wondered who lived in that house now and whether they boasted about living there, showed visitors the shed, or kept quiet about it.

He walked on up the alley, and there was nothing at all out of the way to see. Back yards, patio furniture, fences, wall. Four garages this side with alley entrances; most of the garages on the right side, toward the rising hill above, had alley entrances. On that upper side, you couldn't see into the back yards as well because the hill rose quite steeply there, and probably only patches of those yards nearer the houses were leveled to make patios and drying areas.

He turned around and came back, stopping to look over at the little shed again. The inspired hunch did not visit him; nothing said anything to him. He walked on moodily, head down, and about a dozen steps on collided violently with something.

"Oh, excuse *me!*"

"My fault, not looking where I was going," said Hackett. The young man had emerged, apparently, from a fancy iron gate in a tall hedge on the upper side of the alley. He'd left it open behind him, and Hackett could see a flight of worn stone steps leading up toward the house level. The young man was about twenty-five, blonde and nice-looking, with a friendly grin.

He looked at Hackett, and he said, "You must be the new roomer. Mrs. Andrews said you'd be coming in today. Looking at the garage?—it's a damned narrow spot to turn in or out, but it can be done, unless you run something brand-new. I don't have any trouble, but I've got an old Plymouth, which you probably noticed—I'm your stablemate."

"Well," said Hackett cautiously, "as a matter of fact—"

"Somebody *did* tell you which garage? Ma Andrews isn't always very definite—nice woman, but she doesn't have any more to do with us than she can help, *which* is a welcome change from most landladies, isn't it? It's the one next— Look here," said the young man suddenly, "let's not shout. Come up here—there's that Smithers woman out in her yard, and I don't want to get Ma Andrews in trouble. Not that we *know* the Smithers would, but better safe than sorry." He drew Hackett inside the gate. "It's the next garage down, belongs to Mrs. Markstein next door. She lets Mrs. Andrews—they're old friends, you see."

"I see," said Hackett. In a dim way, he thought he did.

"I suppose she told you to be careful. Er—going and coming and so on. I mean, you never know—just takes one of these letter-of-the-law people, and Ma Andrews'd be out of luck."

"I see," said Hackett again. A doubtful small excitement rose in him. Did he? The young fellow had evidently assumed he was turning in this gate. "Er—" he said, "supicious neighbors?"

"Oh, well, no, or she couldn't have kept it up this long, but you know how people are—I understand there's a couple of new families around, who don't know her, and let just one whisper get out about devaluing the property—"

Hackett shoved his hat back a little and remarked conversationally, "That's right, hit them in the pocketbook and they really feel it."

"Too true. And while there are a few drawbacks—she doesn't like you to keep a bottle around, but she'd never dream of poking her nose inside your room to see, you know—very welcome change from most landladies—and they're all much more comfortable rooms than you'd find anywhere else, as you know or you wouldn't be here. Well, I won't keep you, I'm late for a date now—my name's Robbins, by the way— let's see, you're Garner, aren't you?—nice to have met you, I'll see you around." And with another friendly grin he swung off down the alley.

Hackett waited where he was, head cocked, and heard garage doors pulled back, the coughing protest of an old engine warming up; it died away down the alley.

And here was something they had missed.

Zoning, he thought. I'll bet that's it.

He came out to the alley again, and counted houses down to its mouth. The sixth one in. He walked up the hill to Archer Street, turned left, and counted down. A big, dignified old Mediterranean stucco, ten to twelve rooms, probably: grass a little too long in the strip of front yard, a couple of loose tiles on the roof.

He went up and rang the doorbell, and in a minute took off his hat to a pleasant-faced gray-haired woman in a printed cotton housedress.

"Yes?"

"I'm Sergeant Hackett from headquarters—police," and he showed her his I. D. card. "I'd like to talk to you for a minute if I may, Mrs. Andrews—isn't it?"

Her expression tightened a little. "There was another man—just the other day. I don't—oh, well—"

"Yes," said Hackett, and came in as she stepped back with a reluctant gesture. Old, good furniture, nothing fancy, but the living room looked lived-in, comfortable. Some sewing piled on one chair; she picked it up, the needle still stuck in it, held it on her lap as if to remind him he'd interrupted her.

Hackett sat down opposite and gave her his big, warm, reassuring smile. She looked like a nice woman, and a fairly sensible one: he thought the best way to get at her was direct. He had a straightforward mind, compared to Mendoza's more devious one. On the rare occasions when they were annoyed with each other, Mendoza was inclined to call Hackett's a simple mind, and Hackett to believe that Mendoza really preferred to go the long way round (like a cat stalking a bird).

"Yes?" she said again a trifle impatiently.

So he told her why they were asking questions, what they were working on up here and why. This fellow, who might be anybody—so little evidence on him—and such a dangerous one. She'd have been reading about it in the papers? (She nodded, eyes down.) She'd understand they had to grasp at any straws in this hunt. And the odds seemed to be that he was a single man, fairly young, of good address: a man probably living in a rented room or a small apartment.

"Yes. I told the other man—I don't know why *I* should be expected—"

"Well, Mrs. Andrews, you didn't tell the other man quite all the truth, did you?" asked Hackett gently. The random chance: this was it. You couldn't blame whatever man had covered this street. They couldn't—either from the standpoint of legality or manpower—search every house: no reason—impossible. They hadn't the time or the men. They asked questions and wrote down the answers they got, that was all.

"What do you mean?" she exclaimed sharply. "Of course I—"

"You don't live here alone, do you? You have several young men renting rooms. Now don't start to protest and evade, please—I'm not from the assessors' office or the zoning commission, and I couldn't care less. I'm not goin' to run down and turn you right in for it. But you look like a sensible woman to me, and I don't think I need to point out to you that you might be hindering us a lot in this investigation. You wouldn't want this fellow to keep on killing innocent women and getting away with it, would you? I'm sorry, but I've got to ask you questions and I've got to have the right answers."

She looked at him in silence for a moment and then, unexpectedly, she begun to cry. In the midst of her tears she was embarrassed and angry at herself, it was obvious; and Hackett was embarrassed too. He said vague soothing things; he found the kitchen and brought her a glass of water. It was a big house, just as he'd thought; and he supposed —guessing at the situation—that there had to be laws about these things, but it did seem a little unfair that you shouldn't be allowed to do what you wanted with your own property.

He never did tell her how he'd found it out: and it turned out to be —when she was finally prodded to tell him the story—about how he'd figured. She and her husband had retired, come to California, and bought the house in 1946, just after the war, when prices were way up; they'd paid thirty thousand for it, and even then it was too big a house, of course, but she used to entertain a lot, and it didn't seem extravagance by what they had. A substantial private pension from his old firm, and savings. But when he died a few years later the pension stopped, and prices kept going up, and the income from savings investments didn't go up, of course, and she was at her wits' end. There were no children, no relatives. She tried to sell the house, but they told her she couldn't ask more than eighteen thousand, nobody wanted old houses now, and she probably wouldn't get that if she sold it. She found out why when it had been on the market for a year. The people who wanted that big a house and in this kind of neighborhood wanted something new, more convenient, in a more newly fashionable area: the young people wouldn't look at it, they wanted a modern ranch-style in the suburbs. The taxes were higher than in most newer districts because it was so close in to town, but of course it would never be potentially valuable business property. And by now a lot needed to be done to it— paint, the roof, electrical connections, a new faucet in the main bath—

It was property, it was value, but it wasn't paying any dividend; it was eating up the pittance she had, and she couldn't get rid of it, turn it into cash. It might seem to the casual glance that she was well enough off: widow of a white-collar man, with a little capital invested in stock:

certainly not indigent, all that implied. People didn't stop to *think*. There'd been times she'd really gone hungry, until . . .

But this was all residential-zoned up here, it was illegal to rent out rooms; if it hadn't been for a few old neighbors being sympathetic, she'd never have managed it as long as this. She usually had four or five young men, and Minnie Markstein next door rented her garage to two of them; so a garage went with those rooms, you could say. She'd never dared advertise, but one told another, and they were nice big clean quiet rooms in a good neighborhood—better than average. And besides—

"I've been far more careful, I've had to be, than most—" She didn't like the word *landladies:* her mouth was wry, saying it. The sense of this belated thought calmed her agitation, and she blew her nose, sat up straighter. "Really, if you're thinking that this criminal you're looking for could ever have— Why, it would be quite impossible! I'm very careful to have only the most respectable, quiet, irreproachable men— no drinking on the premises at any time, and I—"

"Mrs. Andrews," said Hackett patiently, "a man like this may be all of that and more. Men like this don't go roistering around the way a lot of people seem to think, and they can just as easily be well-educated and—er—gentlemanly as not." Her eyes disbelieved him; he sighed. Even people who weren't—as Mrs. Andrews was—elderly, nice-minded (as they'd call it), and conventional, had difficulty grasping the fact that a rapist-murderer didn't necessarily have to be a lunatic, and if he was, it wouldn't necessarily show and he might not be a lunatic all the time, in every area of life. "Do you ask references?"

Her mouth worked a little; she dabbed at it with her handkerchief. "I —sometimes, sometimes not. I've had several young men—at various times—who'd just come to California, and besides—well, people don't expect to be asked for references these days, before renting a room. D-do they? I do go a great deal by personal impressions. Only twice in ten years have I been forced to ask someone to—find other accommodation. . . . Well, most of them have stayed quite a little time, seldom less than six months—I have two young men with me now who have lived here for almost two years. One way I do judge is by what sort of work they do, you see. I don't ever take ordinary workmen, tradesmen —if a man works in an office, or a bank, or somewhere like that, I know he's of better class, and—"

Very convenient, thought Hackett, the little general-type slots. "Yes. Do you keep any records, Mrs. Andrews?"

"I've had two medical students, and a young lawyer just getting started— Records? Well, I—" She dabbed at her mouth again. "They —I always have them pay me—in cash," she muttered unwillingly. Yes, of course: no records for the tax people. Like Prohibition, he thought fleetingly: inviting normally honest people to subterfuge. And probably the late Andrews had taken all the business responsibility, and she'd be rather vague about that kind of thing. He went on asking questions. . . . Well, no, she didn't keep any books, it wasn't necessary, the money came in and she paid the bills in cash. She gave the roomers receipts, and she kept the kind of receipts that were for legitimate deductions, personal medical expenses, and so on, but . . . The names. She didn't know (miserably, defiantly, she didn't know) that she could recall to mind the whole list—every young man she'd had in her rooms in ten years. There had been some who stayed only a few months, and there were usually five of them all the time.

God, thought Hackett. Call it thirty, forty men altogether. More? Try to pry the names out of her; try to chase them down and have a look. (On top of those they were still looking for and at.) And if she couldn't remember all the names, and if this was the place Romeo had been, she might so easily not remember just the one vital name. Also, he guessed shrewdly, the whole business had always been so distasteful to her that she'd stayed as clear as possible of her roomers (she did not, for instance, assume any cleaning duties—that was strictly their responsibility), and who could say, if she was now confronted with a man, whether she could say for certain that he'd once rented one of her rooms—and when?

God, he thought. Another teaser. A little gossamer thread-end leading into the skein, that might so easily break off, or just lead nowhere at all.

He got out his notebook. He said, "Now, Mrs. Andrews, I'd like you to try hard to remember the names of the men living here twenty months ago. And if possible, what they looked like. . . ."

TWELVE

When he got home, he found his mind was still busy on it, refused to be switched off. And that was bad, that was the way to get to that exhausted state where you couldn't think straight about anything. He had to make a deliberate effort to shove it aside; and then over dinner Angel reminded him of it, indirectly.

"Art—does he seem any, oh, different, or anything, *since?* . . . The great Mendoza, of course. . . . Oh, well, I just wondered. If he has any conscience at all, if he thought enough of her—as a person—to miss her a little. You know. . . . Well, we went shopping together today and she's still taking it awfully hard, I think—you know how she is, she'd die before she let anyone— I don't know what she *sees* in— But that's a silly thing to say, of course. You can't pick and choose about who you love."

"I suppose a lot of people have said the same thing about you," agreed Hackett, and she laughed.

"Don't fish for compliments—I'm not ready to give you any testimonials yet! Only spoil you. . . . I don't know. I *had* rather thought of having a little party, and inviting them both—he's really quite nice, you know, there's no reason she shouldn't— But she didn't seem to think much of him."

"Who's this, what are you talking about?"

"Oh, goodness, Art, don't be so slow! Somebody else for Alison, of course—somebody really nice and dependable. . . . Well, it isn't so easy to find a single man, I'll admit to you he isn't exactly the average maiden's dream, but he's presentable, and not at all bad-looking, and— and he means so well, and I should think he'd be awfully kind—"

"To dogs and children and his old mother? You ever know one that kind that stirred a single heartbeat? Who is this Romeo?" And, damn, there it was in his mind again.

"Bruce Norwood, you must have met him—that thing at Janet's, wasn't it? He's a wholesale candy salesman—"

Hackett reflected, vaguely remembered Norwood, and let out a sudden bellow of laughter. "My Angel! If he's the one I remember, good God, you expect her to take any interest in him? A damp codfish. With," he added, remembering more, "such ladylike manners."

"I suppose you couldn't be expected to appreciate really cultivated people, associating with all these low types—" But her mouth trembled a little and she began to giggle. "Oh, dear, I guess he *is* a bit like that, but—but if she could find someone . . ."

"Darling, maybe she doesn't want to. You can't manage people's lives for them."

"I know, I suppose not," she sighed. "But I *am* so sorry for her."

"What I know of Alison Weir, she'd feel awful annoyed at you if you said so right out."

"I know that too," said Angel, brooding with her chin in her hands.

And Hackett, thoughtfully stirring sugar into his coffee, reflected that there was a little something different about Mendoza these days. He was more irritable, more nervous. Put it down to all the worry and work on this case, the needling from the press—but they'd had as troublesome cases before, they'd withstood other press onslaughts, and come through, and Mendoza hadn't . . .

"Well, none of our business," he said. "You women. Of course I understand what it is—you've got such a paragon of a husband yourself you want every other woman to get married too, just to compare and envy you."

"You're getting as egotistical as your boss," said Angel, making a very attractive grimace at him. "The worst of it is, this Norwood man seems to have been quite impressed with Alison—the once he's met her —and wouldn't need much encouragement. Oh, well, I suppose it isn't any good. Just one of those things. . . . Did you like the salad dressing? You didn't say, and it's something different—"

"Very nice," he said, a little somnolently, sliding a couple of fingers under his belt. And Mendoza was sometimes wrong, but he hadn't been about that extra five pounds. Hackett ruminated on them somewhat uneasily, and wondered if he could learn to do without sugar in his coffee . . .

When he came into the office, a little late because it was Sunday morning, Mendoza was sitting at his desk studying yesterday's reports. He had shaved, but his collar looked slightly wilted and his suit was the same one he'd had on yesterday. For the average citizen he looked well dressed; for Mendoza, rather raffish.

"¿Well, *amigo, qué hay de nuevo,* what's new?" asked Hackett.

"The odds are down—about even—that we can count in Anderson. I think." Mendoza handed over Madge Parrott's statement, and Hackett read it.

"Isn't that nice," he commented thoughtfully. "Just like all the others, nothing to say he's the one killed her, nothing to say who he is, and nothing to point which direction to look for him. I've got a little more of the same," and he told Mendoza about Mrs. Andrews' roomers.

Mendoza cast his eyes to heaven and said, "*¿Por mi vida!* People. Dear me, Sergeant, nobody here could be your killer—they've all been to college and wear neckties at work. And yes, of course, another batch of maybes to locate and look over. . . . Yes, indeed. . . . On second thought, I rather like your Mrs. Andrews."

"You have any bright ideas about short cuts?"

"I'm full of bright ideas," said Mendoza. He leaned back and shut his eyes. "I'll take half an hour to tell you about them, and then I'm going home to have a bath and a couple of hours' sleep. I didn't get any last night—"

"These motels, sometimes pretty bad."

"I believe there were some motels roundabout—I didn't investigate. I sat up until three this morning playing draw with the sheriff and some of his boys, and then headed for home. I did stop for a cat nap in the car somewhere around Riverside, but—"

"Look, friend," said Hackett. "Peace officers are supposed to be all buddies together, and cooperate, and so on. You want Riverside County startin' a feud with us? How much did you take those innocent country boys for? Of all the dirty tricks—*and* on a legitimate errand you'll claim mileage for, too!"

Mendoza opened his eyes and smiled. "But they were so contemptuous of the city fop, Arturo—and so transparently hopeful of taking him for a ride! Not to be resisted, I swear. The stakes were the hell of a lot lower than I usually stoop to. And none of them were smart gamblers, to quit when losing high—they *would* go on, to get the best of me in the next deal, you know. Disastrous logic. Only ninety-three dollars . . . And I said I left at once and didn't stop until I got to Riverside. And I don't suppose I'll ever have occasion to visit Murrietta again."

"Let's hope to God you don't," said Hackett piously, "or you might get lynched. Let's hear the bright ideas."

"I would like to know," said Mendoza, "what day of the week Jane Piper was killed. Also Pauline McCandless. I'm offering modest odds that Piper was killed on a weekend and McCandless in the middle of the week."

"Why?"

"You see what Madge Parott says, they had this fellow figured for a weekender. It just suddenly occurred to me that a few facts do point vaguely to the beach. Jane Piper was found in Topanga Canyon. Celestine Teitel—who was last seen on a Sunday, remember—was both killed and found on the beach. Julie Anderson lived at the beach, was probably killed there, and was buried there."

"So what?" Hackett shrugged. "I see what you mean, but the latest of those in time is Piper, and that's nine months, ten now, back. If he ever lived or week-ended there, he might not have for most of that time."

"*De veras.* But I don't know, a number of little things occur to me—just nothing over what Madge said, and also—yes—the dates. The dates. Let's think about them consecutively a minute. We've just found Julie Anderson, but she's the earliest to be killed we know of. Yet. Nearly twenty-eight months ago, now. Then we get Mary Ellen, nine and a half months later—and, *de paso,* inland, while a later one was again at the coast. Just keep that in mind. Then a gap of only two and a half months, and Celestine Teitel. Six months later, Piper. And another nine months later, McCandless. Think about those women, and think about what Madge said. You know what I come up with, Art? He's changed a little." Mendoza lit a cigarette and smoked it dreamily, eyes shut. "Bear with my romantic imagination for a few minutes—let's build him up from the few scattered bones we have. . . . You know, a lot of people who come here from somewhere inland, they like the beach—one of the first places they go to look at, and quite often they settle down there, or go back as often as possible. *¿De veras?*"

"This is woolgathering," said Hackett. "Sure, but that's a very general observation."

"So it is. Anyway, somewhere around thrity months ago, here's this fellow hanging around that particular beach—a few times, at least, whether his normal beach spot was Malibu or Zuma or anywhere down to Playa del Rey. This fellow who was so smitten with the pseudo-blonde Julie. Gawking at her, as Madge says, like a yokel getting his first eyeful of burleycue. Expressive phrase. Not dry behind the ears.

No—mmh—address with a girl, not knowing what to say to one. Awkward. And he didn't need to have known other men around there to have known Julie's reputation, what kind of girl she was—any man with any sophistication at all, he'd know or guess that pretty accurately after meeting and talking with her."

"Well, maybe. It isn't always so obvious. To everybody—I don't count you and your invisible radar."

"O.K. Just file that to remember. Julie wasn't intererested in him because of that, he doesn't seem to have got very far with her—until, of course, he picked her up in his car—if he did—and assaulted and killed her—if he did. But nine months later or so, he'd acquired a little more sophistication. Just a little more—because I don't think he'd have had to be an accomplished gigolo to strike Mary Ellen Wood as 'smooth.' She was comparing him to boys her own age, boys who use a lot of slang, make it a point of honor never to dress up much, boys who are used to informal manners and a little uncertain about any other kind. A somewhat older man who, maybe, had been raised with rather old-fashioned standards of manners—and don't you find that in small towns, Art?—a man who, shades of Mrs. Andrews, had the kind of job where he wore a suit, a white shirt, a tie—he'd impress Mary Ellen, as a contrast to the boys she knew in slacks and sport shirts, their loutish humor. Don't you think? I can see that. And then look at Celestine Teitel, so soon after. She was thirty, and she was an educated woman but —don't we gather?—not a very sophisticated one. A teacher, and she was enough like Miss Evelyn Reeder that they were friends and shared an apartment. I mark Celestine as one of those shy, serious women, much younger than her age when it came to anything to do with that old devil sex—you know the kind. Maybe raised strictly. She wouldn't be much of a judge of male sophistication, and what she'd notice and admire in a man would be lack of brashness, crudeness as she'd have called it—somebody with quiet manners, polite to a lady—what was it Edith Wood said?—courtly. Somebody like the charming Mark Hamilton she met that day at that record shop. You hear the word 'charming,' it conjures up visions of sophistication, but it wouldn't necessarily have meant that to Celestine."

Hackett lit another cigarette. "You're always so good at this kind of thing, I admit. And it *is* Sunday morning—we can't be expected to work at full speed all the time."

No interrumpir, I'm deducing, which is hard work. . . . Six months later, Piper. And there was a woman who must have been out and about a little anyway, had a moderate degree of—sorry to overwork it, but it's really the only word—sophistication. True, I think some of the attraction she may have felt for him, the reason she might have unhesitatingly gone with him somewhere, just might have been—mmh—maternal. A university graduate, a trained legal secretary—twenty-eight—and without a man. Permanent. Not at all bad-looking, but she had one of those determined-looking noses, you know, and a chin. Like Sally Haines. A little bossy in a nice way? Nevertheless, between the time Romeo acted so inept with Julie and seventeen or eighteen months later when he met Jane Piper, he'd taken on a little polish. Can we say, *city* polish? Inevitably, from rubbing elbows with sophisticated city people at his job, in the course of ordinary life. A little more polish than he'd had when he came here—about three years ago—from some inland country place."

"All of which is very nice deducing," nodded Hackett. "And you know as well as me that not one word of it might be true. Say it's our boy all the way through, count Anderson in. O.K. Julie had knocked around some—she wasn't used to really nice boys with genteel manners. Maybe that one was a little less self-confident than he'd show normally because he *did* know Julie's reputation and he'd never had anything to do with a bad girl like that—"

"Look, boy, he was at least twenty-nine, not sixteen."

"Kinsey to the contrary, you still find them. And the rest of your pipe dream is just based on the different way he impressed these girls, so they each said something different about him. The little they did say. I mean, it isn't as if you had Julie saying he was a country boy with straws in his hair, and McCandless saying you couldn't tell him from the latest Parisian movie actor."

"Quite true. But I don't know, Art, there are little nuances that build him that way to me. Coming here—from a smallish place inland—thirty to thirty-six months ago. Liking the beach. Renting a cabin, even buying one, for weekends there—but holding a job in the city. That we can say, because if he'd lived in Santa Monica—anywhere west of Beverly Hills—he wouldn't have been at L.A.C.C. inquiring about evening classes, he'd have thought first of U.C.L.A., nearer him. If, of course, he was really there for that reason that day. He has some kind of white-collar job—take your choice, banker, merchant, clerk, salesman—"

"Doctor, lawyer, bookkeeper, pharmacist—"

"*¿Basta, ya!* The hell of a wide field, sure. He doesn't mix very well, he's a loner. For this reason or that. He is—or was, or said he was, interested in woodworking, in doing something with his hands as a hobby. Leads? If we had a crew of five hundred men to check *¿ya lo creo!* The list of every male between twenty-five and thirty-five who crossed the California border—at a border station, and how many of the eight thousand per day coming in do?—inside three years. *Vaya,* laugh. Of everybody who rents boat space in Santa Monica Bay. Go and knock on all the doors of the seven thousand beach cottages—"

"Between Balboa and Ventura? You want to hand on this case to whoever succeeds you when you retire? And if he was once in one of them, it might not have been within a year."

"I said if," said Mendoza irritably. "But damn it, we'll do some work on this angle, nevertheless. Find out the days of the week for Piper and McCandless—all of them. Do I remember McCandless was on the fifth of last month?—let's see, that was a Tuesday. There you are, and she was found inland, in Walnut Park. Just like Mary Ellen, who was killed on a Wednesday. All right, negative confirmation if nothing else. So in checking our list of possibles, let's also find out whether they rent, own, or borrow beach places or ever have. When they came to L.A. and from where. If they have any hobbies like woodcarving—why didn't I get on that one before?—I should have seen that—damn, I'm too tired to think straight." He massaged his temples wearily. "What kind of a list did Mrs. Andrews give you?"

Hackett groaned. "Twenty names. There must have been more—that she admits. I've got them here, complete with jobs where she remembered, and a few very vague descriptions. What priority does the list get?—wait its turn at the bottom of the lists we've got already?"

Mendoza stood up, yanked down his cuffs, brushed his gray Homburg absently; he looked down at the little stack of file cards, Madge Parrott's statement; and then he said softly, "Top A, boy. Get busy on it right now—haul some men off something else."

"And why does it strike you as that important?"

Mendoza went to the door, hat in hand. "People," he said. "It always comes back to people, doesn't it? I'll tell you—you ought to see it for yourself. We've got several lists culled from several categories. But of all the categories we've created to collect examples of, the Andrews list is the only one which was, you might say, prejudged for us on the basis of character. She looked at all those men, at some time, with an eagle eye, Art—and what was she looking for? For ultimate quiet respectability, sobriety, gentlemanliness, the white-collar job, the good manners. And I think—just from the few bones of him we have—our boy is one like that. So let's track these twenty down, *presto, pronto,* and then prod Mrs. Andrews for some more names. Because I think there's just a little better chance that he was once in her house than there is that he was once in Haines' office, or in our records, or anywhere else we're looking for him."

"I get you," said Hackett slowly. "That might be."

"We'll see. I'm going home. I'll be back about two."

"Make it later, catch up on your sleep—you look tired."

"I'm O.K.," said Mendoza almost angrily, pulling the door open. "I'll see you then."

He went home; he had a bath and lay down in the darkened bedroom, but he didn't sleep. A cat nap in the car, in the dawn this morning, and not much sleep on Friday night either. Something he'd never had to think about, his physical well-being: it annoyed him to have such a thing intrude on life now, especially now. His mind prying away obstinately at this business, refusing to be switched off, that was it; he'd lain awake on Friday night working it all over again, worrying at every angle to see if he'd missed some detail to suggest a lead, wasting futile anger on it—building up things Fitzpatrick's paper and others had printed, until they looked like deliberate personal attacks on himself. And that wasn't all: unbidden, the unruly mind (what had the mind to do with it?—tangible plane only, only) turning again, taking him, telling him— Until he forced it back to this in self-defense. This safer— this quieter—this bloody-handed killer less dangerous . . .

Not only senseless but unsafe: you stopped thinking objectively about something—right then you stopped thinking effectively. But lying sleepless in the dark like that, the body tired and the mind refusing it rest, this was what happened. The magnification, the circular subjective pseudo-thinking.

Right now he should be able to sleep, God knew. About two hours Friday night and two hours this morning added up to four hours, out of thirty-six, of rest. . . . The cats, pleased to have him home in the middle of the day, coming up around him, purring, a restful sound—restful feel of warm sleek bodies under his hand. He did not sleep.

There wouldn't be anything in the medicine cabinet; he never kept drugs because he never needed them. Aspirin? About three years ago he'd had a wisdom tooth that needed filling—second time in his life he'd been to a dentist, the first being when he had the physical, when he joined the force, nineteen years back; the dentist then had said cheerfully, Never make much money on you. . . . He seemed to remember getting some aspirin for that wisdom tooth.

He got up, rummaged and found it, and cautiously swallowed one tablet. It didn't seem to do much. He was tired, God, he was tired, but he couldn't sleep. A vague kaleidoscope whirled before his closed-eyes vision, red and black spots on the cards, stylized profiles, King-Queen-Jack, Queen-Jack-King, Jack—ace, the bad one, *Serpiente,* the ace of clubs, bad luck, bad luck—*aces and eights, the dead man's hand*—all superstition, senseless, sure, but— Could have kept that ace as a kicker; there were the low ones, eight of diamonds, eight of spades, to fall back— But, get rid of the dead man's hand, the bad luck. . . . A man who liked, or thought he might like, to make things with his hands: wood carving—Beach, the beach: north along from Balboa, the exclusive places, the expensive places there, Newport, Emerald Bay, Balboa Island, Playa del Rey, and on up—God, such a stretch of prodigal coast gold in the sun—seventy miles along the Pacific, the beaches of this metropolis, the beaches in reach of residents, who might mean any one of those seventy miles when they said *beach.* On up—Huntington, the harbor beaches, Sunset, Rocky Point, Palos Verdes, Redondo, Hermosa—*hermosa, hermosita,* my darling, my beautiful . . . El Segundo, Venice, Santa Monica, Topanga, Point Dume . . . any place, any place. Take one thing at a time, the job doesn't look so big: he was seen along Malibu, Topanga: start there. . . . Get him in the trap, by God, if it took till a year from Christmas. . . . The trap, the trap . . . *Mi hermosa, mi vida, querida,* leave me alone, leave me alone, I've got work to do, let me sleep. . . . Nice quiet polite young fellow, and the devil sleeping inside him to be raised easy. Why? What did it matter?— for the lawyers. . . . Sure to God drive a man nuts without trying, *absolutamente.* . . . An offbeat one: not the usual thing . . . never the usual thing with her, with her. . . . The red and black spots dancing, the devil with horns and tail mocking, spreading the hand before him— discard and draw, you'll never get together any other hand, boy—aces and eights for the dead man. . . . Go away from me, my darling, let me sleep.

At two o'clock he got up and dressed—the silver-gray Italian silk, the austere charcoal tie with the discreet scarlet fleck, the narrow-brimmed Homburg at just the correct angle—and drove back downtown to headquarters.

THIRTEEN

The man who had been Edward Anthony was lying on the sway-backed studio couch which had come with the little cabin; he lay very still, staring up at the ceiling, but inside he was a maelstrom of emotion, because he had just had a very exciting new idea.

He could hear the breakers coming in out there, just now and then, because there was also the highway traffic going past; but when the glittering-garish rows of cars thinned out for a little, then there was the sound of the low lazy surf coming in, breaking gently on the smooth beach. He liked—almost best of all the things he liked about the beach—watching the surf on a day like this. When it was gentle and slow, and beyond the white crests the sea like glass. He didn't like it when it was rough—a gray winter day or a windy day—with the breakers like white-maned lions showing their teeth. But a day like this, he'd often sit on the sand for hours, just watching the sea come and go. It was restful. He'd never seen the sea until three years ago, and it fascinated him.

Which was, of course, why he had bought the little beach house, with the money Father had left. It was, the man had said, a bargain, and he supposed it was: much more solidly built, of good stout oak timber, than any other he'd seen, these little three- and four-room places built for temporary rentals mostly, ramshackle—but this one built by someone, some old man (the agent said) to live in all year. The disadvantage to it, which the agent had talked fast to avoid mentioning, was its isolation from any other habitation, from the nearest little shopping center. That had been funny—the agent that day—because that was what he liked about the house, the way it sat alone here, away from everything. What a house looked like—his surroundings in general—meant little to him; but he liked being away from the garish beach business places, the beach cabins clustered like frightened children all together, close-crowded. When he came down on Friday nights, after work, he'd bring the few perishable items of food, just what he'd need for the weekend, and it didn't matter about the nearest grocery being five miles off.

He never went into the sea: he couldn't swim and didn't particularly want to. He simply liked to watch it, and smell it, and listen to it. It was very restful to have this place to come to, away from the city and people crowding in on him all the while.

Because that was one of the things which annoyed and distressed him, since he'd come here. He realized quite well that it wasn't just because he'd been brought up in a small town and that he found so many of the people he met here almost frighteningly sophisticated, holding what seemed to him immoral opinions, and—once or twice, when he'd unthinkingly expressed disapproval—laughing at his. It hadn't been all that different back home; even among regular churchgoing people, people you'd think were righteous-minded, there had been many who had taken on too-free ways and thoughts, and laughed at Father. The thing was, here he was alone, with no solid background behind him, so to speak, and inevitably he'd learned to keep quiet, to look and sound as much as possible like anyone else here. Lip service, you might say. For one thing, the job: he wouldn't have it long if he didn't know how to seem ordinary, correct by their standards—or if he came out with something which most people would think odd. Back home, he hadn't mixed much with anyone; he hadn't needed to—there was Father, and the shop; but here he'd had to, a little at least.

So it was nice to have this place all to himself, to come to and rest.

Julie had liked it, he remembered, all but where it was. "It could be fixed up a lot nicer than our place," she'd said, "it's a swell cabin, but gee, stuck away off like this! You'd have to have a car—and you oughta put up curtains over the back window too, but I guess a man wouldn't notice that—" That had been just before he got hold of her, before the awful craving that he'd held down got too much for him and he—

She hadn't wanted to come, he remembered. She'd been a little short with him, not interested in him, but she *had* wanted a ride home from Tony's. Not interested in seeing his place, but he'd stopped all the same and persuaded her to come inside. . . . One like Rhoda, she'd been, not a nice girl, and he'd thought—

But there it was.

And the house was, he realized then, a safe place, because she had screamed quite loud at first, but nobody had heard—nobody around to hear. Nobody hearing Celestine either. . . . He'd liked Celestine, a nice quiet modest girl, and he wanted her to see his house—he hadn't meant anything wrong when he asked her to stop by on her way that morning. Why, how could he have, when he told her just how to get here and all, openly? But once they were alone here together, all of a sudden— And of course, he couldn't leave her any place nearby. Though you couldn't be sure, perhaps, that the papers printed everything the police knew, still there hadn't been any suggestion that anyone thought it hadn't happened where they'd found her, up in that cove. Most of the blood had been on her clothes. . . . Realized then what a safe place the house was, and he'd planned it here with Jane, he'd thought perhaps here he might ask her to marry him, even so soon— But she'd got frightened; he'd said he'd drive her home and then came this way and she was alarmed—those foolish women—and it had been awkward, difficult, he'd had to stop her noise, and then when he touched her . . . Known then it had to *be,* and she wasn't moving or screaming—she'd fainted—and he could drive where he wanted, somewhere quiet, and— And a Friday night, it seemed quite natural to come the rest of the way—home—afterward; only not until he was on the coast road remembering her still there in the back of the car, another awkwardness. . . .

Nevertheless—the house, home—it was a violation of his secret place; he'd never let anyone inside it since.

Julie. They had found Julie, just as he'd been afraid they would, and yet it was good that they had—for it had put this strange and exciting idea in his mind.

He tried to think about it calmly, to examine it from every angle. For it might only be his fear for his personal safety which made him think— But every detail he could list pointed the same way. It was very strange; he could almost call it awesome.

Could it be—that was the idea—that God did not intend him to be punished? That his crimes were not sin at all, but intended retribution, and he the instrument? He knew that many mad people conceived such an idea out of their madness. But he was quite sane, and he wasn't ready to accept it as the truth yet, he was only balancing all the reasons that seemed to point that way.

It was surely, surely more than random coincidence, to begin with, that the man who lived in that place where he'd buried Mary Ellen had known her, that there should have *appeared* some reason for his having killed her. Well, perhaps by itself it was all perfectly natural, looked at in separate segments, as it were: her meeting this boy, this Jim Fairless, at the college, and then the Haineses, and because she lived within eight or ten blocks of them, the Haineses hiring her that way. And it had been quite by chance—or had it?—that he happened to live in that place, where he walked past the Haineses yard every day. But he remembered how surprised he had been, afterward, when it came out in the papers where she had lived, in the same district—roughly—as he did; that was something more than coincidence, when he'd actually met her at the college, a good three or four miles away, maybe more. People from much farther off, hundreds of them, going to that college: and the one girl he spoke to, Mary Ellen.

Of course, say it hadn't been: say it had been a girl from—from Huntington Park or somewhere: not knowing, he'd still have put her in Allan Haines' yard, probably, and then They would have looked at Haines just the same, wouldn't They?—and maybe Haines would have been accused just as it had happened.

Nevertheless, it was odd. When he thought about the others it seemed more than coincidence, too. The way he had met them casually (but as if it was arranged) in places where people round about didn't know him, so he could say whatever he pleased.

Of course he *had* been careful, there: the fact that They hadn't found him was mostly his own planning. And yet, when he thought, why had he happened to meet just *those* women? All coincidence—the random chance—and yet, could God have arranged it particularly, was it conceivable that they were all due punishment? Rhoda and Julie, obviously —bad women—and could it be that the others had possessed some taint, some potential evil which—?

Beyond what they all had, of course: the whole source of temptation.

It was a queerly exciting thought, for—in the first place—if it was not intended that he should be brought to punishment by men, then all his carefulness had never been necessary and it was not necessary to feel any anxiety now or again. However cunning They might be (and he had been much encouraged to read what the papers said of Them, for responsible newspapers would not print falsehoods) nothing They could do would bring Them any closer to him. And—secondly—as a corollary to that, nothing *he* could do would put him in any danger.

There was nothing to say if it was true, about those others; but he'd known about the evil in Rhoda and Julie, of course, and now (as if it was intended he *should* know, and be reassured?) he knew about this other one too. That woman, the one who had introduced him to her first, mentioning it quite casually (as so many people did, such things, here and now). A divorce, she said. Something about—*One of those impulsive teenage marriages, quite short I believe, but a pity all the same*. A pity. A woman, then—this one who excited him, interested him, this *Alison*—who had deserted her lawful husband, and that was not only evil of itself but led to other—

And so perhaps, if the idea was true, it was indeed meant— But he must be very sure.

They didn't seem to know very much, certainly, all this while: as stupid as the papers said? *Something* in what the papers said: there must be. Of course. Two weeks since They'd found Julie, and nearly seven weeks, eight, since They'd known Allan Haines hadn't killed Mary Ellen. Still, nothing bringing Them any nearer. Was there? He didn't think so, he didn't see how there could be, but he'd like to *know*.

He went on staring up at the ceiling, lying motionless there, listening to the surf outside across the highway—and thinking about the idea.

On Tuesday the *Telegraph* came out with a front-page head, *Key Witness Held Incommunicado?* Somehow, God knew how, a rumor had got out—garbled, of course—about Madge Parrott. They didn't know who, or why, or in connection with which murder, but Brad Fitzpatrick made quite a story of it regardless. That little word *alleged* had saved many a newspaper from a libel action. The story was all secondhand report and speculation, but it was surprising how few ordinary readers discriminated—it was in print, it must be so. The impression a hasty reading left was that the police had had presumably sensational information from a new witness, whom they were holding secretly, refusing all cooperation with the press. There was a subhead, *The Public Should Be Told,* and references to the Gestapo.

Mendoza saw it on the way downtown, stopped and bought a copy, and arrived at his office white-hot with anger. The office men took one look at him and examined their consciences uneasily, as did every other man he hauled up before him in the next hour. But what it came down to was—no one in particular to blame: reporters always hanging around, and a thoughtless word muttered within twenty feet of one like Fitzpatrick was enough.

Nevertheless, they all got a tongue-lashing about careless talk; and all but a couple of them retired shaken. It was rare for Mendoza to vent his temper on juniors, and it was somehow more devastating to be reviled for a fool in three-syllable words, packed in ice and tied up with cutting sarcasm, than if he had used a horsewhip. Hackett remained imperturbable in a corner; and Sergeants Curraccio and Lake, who long ago had learned to bow to the storm on occasion and let nature take its course, said, "Yes, sir," and waited stolidly for dismissal. When it came, Lake was even brave enough to say, "Excuse me, Lieutenant, but there's someone waiting to see you."

"Unless it's the Chief, let him wait!" said Mendoza. "I've wasted enough time on this damned business. Get out, get out!" Lake sighed and did so. Mendoza swung round in his swivel chair to face the window, lit a cigarette with an angry snap of his lighter. "The public should be told! *¡Qué va!* Show hands round the table, boys, all friends here!"

"Oh, well," said Hackett mildly, "a little something there, Luis. They've got a right to know whether their tax money is going to fools or not. And you've got to admit the other papers have been pretty fair on the whole. After all, they had something on us to start—Allan Haines."

"*¡Estúpido!*" said Mendoza violently. "That's it, that's it! Enough to make any citizen uneasy—he might find himself in Haines' shoes any day! Which would not be enjoyable, but if it's an honest error at least he knows the odds against it—and that, when it does happen, it's usually rectified before they lock the door to the gas chamber. Fitzpatrick and his ilk slant it to read that we're either morons or a new Gestapo—a little of both—damn the public! And that's bad, that couldn't be worse, because in the last analysis it's the public we look to for help and cooperation."

"Don't lecture me," said Hackett. "I can read too."

"Then you're a damn sight smarter than seven of ten ordinary citizens! *It is alleged,* sure—they spell it out, but what does it mean to them? It says in the paper, the paper said! *Obvio,* it's true, it's in print! And so—and *so,*"—he swung back and pointed his cigarette at Hackett—"how many people the boys are out talking to, questioning, have been a lot harder to get at, have thought what the hell, why waste time, tell them anything—the cops can't see through a pane of glass anyway! How many have been scared of getting in trouble with these arrogant, brutal cops, and told them the easy lie—don't know nothing about it!—when one of them might have given us just one valuable little pointer—! *¡Válgame Dios!* Sure, let Fitzpatrick say anything he pleases short of libel about us, but if I say he's delayed the hunt, put a spoke in our wheel, how he'd yell foul!"

"*Tómelo con calma,* take it easy. Just one of those things. Here's the latest news. Myself, I think we've done pretty well for ten days on the Andrews list. Twelve out of the twenty."

"What do they look like?" Mendoza took the reports, glanced over the names.

"Offhand, I'd say three out of the bunch are worth looking at a little closer. I've checked them—the top ones. Item, all three correspond roughly to the description. Item—"

"Yes. George Hopper, William Bell, Michael— Yes, I see. Resident at the house twenty to thirty months ago—approximate dates, of course, damn the woman. Clerk, salesman, clerk."

"Not very elusive," said Hackett. "A couple of them, she remembered where they worked, and they were still there. Some more big as life in the phone book. The rest were tougher—So Bert and Tom and I divided 'em up and went to look at them, and these three come closest to the description. Three or four more we can definitely mark off on that count—bald, or fat, or something. Four or five of 'em left the Andrews house when they got married, but of course that doesn't really say much. He *might* be. I don't think so, you don't think so, but it happens. But for what they're worth, I think these three look at least as promising as a few others we've got."

"Yes, we'll look at them. But from a little distance, Art. Through men who can smell a reporter when one's hanging around, and whose tongues aren't hung in the middle. Bert and Farnsworth, maybe."

"Why the long way round? This isn't a pro deal, where we might warn off the big boy sniffing around open. Everybody who's innocent here—and there's only one guilty man—will cooperate, answer questions. In spite of what you say about the ordinary citizen, most of 'em have a kind of touching blind faith in us, you know."

"Even if that's so, we won't give Fitzpatrick or anybody else any small excuse to yell Gestapo. We can't afford to. *Claro está,* a lot of those on some other lists of possibles we've got, men with records—nobody cares what we do there. But let us openly approach one man who holds a fairly good job, substantial-looking citizen, respectable background, and what'll be the next thing?—pray make it public why, Lieutenant! What's your ground for casting public suspicion? This case has attracted too much publicity as it is. Things the press usually expects us to keep to ourselves—the cry goes up here, let the public know! And what grounds, Art, what the hell could we say there? You know and I know, on a thing like this, you look everywhere you can, it's just logical routine to look the places we're looking, in Haines' office, in that neighborhood, and so on—but it doesn't look that way to a civilian with no experience of hunting. So we have an open session with, say, this George Hopper," he flicked the top name on the list, "and the press boys print it, *Suspect Questioned,* you think Hopper as an honest fellow—if he is—likes it? How come *suspect,* he says—and so do the press boys. And we say, Why, he once lived in Mrs. Andrews' house. That's all, boys. Just that. You think it makes sense to anybody who hears it? There's the moronic cops for you, grasping at straws, trampling roughshod over a man's reputation!"

"O.K., O.K., I got your idea in the first sentence, I agree with you. I've been a cop a while too, I know how these things go. Calm down, Luis, or you'll be the one to get high blood pressure. All I will say is that it's goin' to make it a harder job, posing as poll takers and insurance investigators and contacting acquaintances and neighbors instead. . . . This is getting you down, boy, you're letting it ride you."

Mendoza didn't answer that for a minute, lighting a new cigarette; then he said in a more restrained tone, "I know, I know. Sorry. But you know one of the things I keep thinking about, Art? Today's the thirteenth day of November. It's seventy-eight days since Pauline McCandless was killed. And between some of them there was quite a gap, six months, nine months, but he only waited two months and a little between Mary Ellen and Celestine Teitel. We don't want another one."

Hackett said, "God, no. . . . I'll contact Bert, get started on these. You know what's in my mind? You better tune up your private radar and come through with a hunch, because I think on this one it's a long chance routine's going to get us there."

FOURTEEN

But Mendoza had no hunches. He sat there doing nothing for a while, after Hackett had gone; the letdown from the outburst of anger had drained him of energy. He had slept three hours last night, finally, and all the force left in him was nervous mental force. Sometime today he must get something to make him sleep tonight.

He roused himself at last and began to look over the reports. No, it didn't show, to make an exciting story—the plodding hard work, the collecting of statistics. They had a lot of information now, on a lot of their possibles. (And Romeo might not be on any list they had.) They had, of course—praise heaven for small mercies—been able to eliminate some, for good reasons: this man had been in jail for two years; that one was vouched for in San Francisco at the time of one of the murders; that one had been in the hospital. But because of the little they had on their man, they hadn't too many reasons to eliminate. There might, as Hackett said, be a wife and family: he might not look the way they thought at all.

Presently Sergeant Lake came in and reminded him of the man waiting. A Mr. John Lockhart. No, he wouldn't say what he wanted, just to talk to the man in charge. No, he wouldn't be fobbed off with anything lower.

"I know what he wants," said Mendoza. "He wants to tell me all about his theory of this case, which he's sure I'll find interesting because for so many years he's been an amateur student of crime—or possibly, worse yet, of the psychopathic criminal. He may even be a professor of psychology or something. He may be a nut who wants to confess to the murders, and so we'll waste time checking and find he hadn't been released from Camarillo when McCandless was killed. Tell him to go away, Jimmy. But tell him politely. Offer him somebody else again."

"That might be," said Lake. "They do come in. Though he doesn't look like a nut, Lieutenant."

"Does he match our description for Romeo?"

"Well, you couldn't hardly say so. About sixty-five, five-seven, upwards of two hundred pounds, and bald."

"I don't want him. Shuffle him back in the pack."

Lake grinned and went out. Mendoza brooded over the reports some more, and at twelve-fifteen left, to run the gauntlet again and get some lunch. He had quite a time getting past the press downstairs. The *Telegraph* story had caught the rest of them off balance; they all wanted to know about it. Mendoza told them, without naming the witness. They had questioned approximately fifty people with just as important information, he told them, and there was no reason to hold any of them in or out of jail as material witnesses; the police were not doing so.

"Yah, tell that to the marines!" Fitzpatrick heckled from the back row. "We've got definite information—"

"From the ex-patrolman, retired, who changes the targets on the practice range?" inquired Mendoza icily. "You shouldn't waste your talents with the *Telegraph*, Mr. Fitzpatrick—you'd make better money writing pulp fiction." He pushed past them and they let him go, muttering, breaking up into little cliques behind him.

But when he was settled in a rear booth in the quiet dimness of Federico's, where a lot of headquarters men habitually lunched, he found he wasn't hungry. He had not wanted breakfast either; he had a dull headache from the sleeplessness and, probably, hunger, and he knew he should eat. He ordered a meal, and had two fingers of rye, then black coffee, beforehand; when the plate was set before him, he could not eat more than a few mouthfuls. After a while, when he'd had a second cup of coffee, he beckoned the waiter and asked for more rye.

It was Adam, the tall, grave Jamaican Negro; and he leaned on the table and said, "You didn't eat hardly any of your luncheon, Lieutenant Mendoza. I never knew you had a drink middle of the day, except once or twice. It's in my mind, you're worrying over this bad fellow you're looking for."

"I suppose I am, Adam."

"Liquor and no food, it won't help you find him any sooner, Lieutenant. Better you let me bring you something else—if you don't fancy the beef, I make up a real nice ham sandwich. Tide you over, like. And a little brandy in your coffee, sir, but that rough hundred-proof stuff, it's only fit for Irishmen. They like to make whiskey so, let 'em—civilized folk got no call to drink it."

Mendoza laughed and said, "No, it's O.K., I'm not hungry. Bring me the rye. You know when I do want a drink, I want the most kick for my money."

"Now, Lieutenant—"

"Hell and damnation," said Mendoza softly, "are you trying to wet-nurse me, boy? If I don't get served here, there's a bar three doors down."

Adam bowed his head and said mournfully, "I serve you, sir."

At one-fifteen Mendoza came back to the big new police building, and he was walking carefully and watching himself. The liquor he'd had, Hackett or another man would be feeling just a pleasant glow, but he wasn't used to more than two at once, and it never took much to set him feeling it anyway. He knew logically he'd have been better off to force himself to eat, but the alcohol had set his brain working at normal speed, and that was what he'd expected and reached for. Just to take him over the afternoon, put some spurious energy in him, and tonight he'd take a couple of the little non-barbiturate sleeping tablets he'd got at the drugstore, and get a decent night's sleep. And tomorrow he'd be himself again, operating on all cylinders.

He didn't know what the hell had got into him, letting a thing take him down physically like this. Getting old maybe. Maybe just that he was an egotist, couldn't take criticism, couldn't stand failure—even temporary. But the liquor had picked him up beautifully, if *that* was only temporary; he had stimulated a few vague ideas to buzzing round the back of his mind.

Which was excellent, but no legwork himself today—better not drive. And if the one bright idea came to him, the inspired hunch—stirred up from the subconscious (if there was such a thing)—it'd be worth any little hangover afterward.

He walked into the lobby and they were still there, waiting around in their little cliques. They formed the gauntlet again.

"I just dare you, Sherlock, tell us *anything* definite you know about the killer yet! Don't give us that one about warning him before you're ready to close in—you admit it, you're not in fifty miles of—"

"I've given you all you're going to get," said Mendoza, smiling at Fitzpatrick. "And the rest of you might give some thought to the old saying about birds of a feather. Quite frankly, after Mr. Fitzpatrick's exhibition today, I don't feel inclined to tell any of you anything ever again. Very damn nervous I'd feel, telling you that my cat had kittens —the next edition would headline the front page with the news that I keep seven lions in separate cages in my living room."

Edmunds grinned mirthlessly and said, "Don't generalize, Lieutenant."

"Doubletalk!" jeered Fitzpatrick. "The whole Christdamn bunch of you trying to cover up—and cover up what?—that the taxpayers might as well throw their cash down the sewer for all the good they get—you free-riders sitting around on your fat asses all day! Tell you what *I'd* like to know, Sherlock—"

"What would you like to know, Mr. Fitzpatrick?" asked Mendoza dreamily. He was rocking very slightly, heel to toe, and he was still smiling steadily.

And little Rodriguez, who had once most fortunately been at the scene of arrest of a certain gunsel who had previously accounted for one of Mendoza's sergeants, looked twice at him, stepped smartly back and murmured to Edmunds, "*¡Cuidado!*—give him room!"

"I'd like to know just how many innocent men like Allan Haines have been railroaded to the pen or the gas chamber by your bunch of—"

"I just told you a lie, Mr. Fitzpatrick," said Mendoza gently, and he took three steps past the rest of them, to face the big man scowling and shouting at him. "I told you I'd given you all you'd get. A black lie, Mr. Fitzpatrick—" and his fist connected sudden and solid, three times, and the big man went down without a sound and stayed there.

"Oh, very nice," said Edmunds. "I've often wanted to do that myself."

"And not a cameraman in the crowd, oh, Jesus," moaned Wolfe, "what a break, what a—"

"Go and write up the new headlines, boys!" said Mendoza, swinging on them savagely. "Tell the public all about its cops—half of them cretins and the other half gangsters! Blow it up, make it a good story, you'll all get gold medals from your editors for increasing circulation! And if we never catch up to Romeo, what the hell, it's only five women —we kill thousands per year on the freeways! Has anyone else any questions, friends?"

They scattered before him, making for the nearest phones, Wolfe still moaning *No cameraman*. The elevator operator peering excitedly out of his cage withdrew hurriedly as Mendoza came stalking toward him.

"If I were you," said Mrs. Lockhart, cold-creaming her face briskly, "I'd just forget the whole business. I don't care who or what anybody is, there's such a thing as decent manners. Treating you as if you were just some no-account know-nothing coming in to waste their time! Well, of course it said in the paper the one running the investigation is a Mexican—I suppose you couldn't expect anything else. For certain, the few of those brace-air-ohs as they call them, I've seen, they bring in for harvest, I wouldn't say they were very smart."

"Now, Mother," said John Lockhart mildly, "let's not jump to conclusions and go off half-cocked. There's people *and* people, and funny enough it is, you find smart and dumb everywhere. Policemen aren't so very damn different, I guess, Tokyo to London, as you might say—or small town or big. And these boys got an awful big headache here, they got no time—I can see that—to waste on damn-fool civilians coming in with crackpot ideas. I guess where I wasted *my* time was not getting that sergeant to take in a little message, say who I am."

"*Three* days wasted," she said resignedly. "We've only got three weeks. Marian was going to take us to Palm Springs, and we figured to stop at Las Vegas on the way back, just to see—I don't hold with gambling, but interesting to *see*."

Lockhart took off his shirt and draped it across the back of the straight hotel-room chair. "Now, Mother," he said, "you want, I'll put you on the train back to San Diego, you and Marian go on, have a good time. It isn't fair, make you miss your whole vacation on account of this. I never meant to. But way it is, well, you're either one kind or the other. There's a lot of people, they can leave a jigsaw puzzle in the middle, and a lot too who can figure, Hell, it's none o' my business, and turn their backs, and sleep sound. And then there's people, you might say, born to be cops—in or out of uniform. Nothing to do with good or bad, just the way you're made. Like you find good dogs in any litter, but some of 'em, they just come built to run a trail or work cows. Nothing you teach 'em, they just got it installed as you might say. I often thought, you take a cop—if he's a good one, Martha, he didn't start being a cop day he got into uniform. He always was, and he always will be. And he isn't the cop just eight hours out o' the twenty-four. Way I figure, this one these boys are after, whoever he is—whether it's Gideon or not—he's a bad one, and if I've got any help to offer 'em, it's my duty as an ordinary citizen, cop or no cop."

"Oh, I'm to go back to San Diego, am I! While you racket round Hollywood on your own! I may think you're a fool, John Lockhart, but that's all the more reason to stay and see you behave yourself."

Lockhart grinned at her, hanging up his pants. "Now, that's a compliment—afraid some o' these here starlets'd find me so interesting, maybe corrupt my morals if I hadn't a wife along, keep me in line! I'm sorry, hon, I know it kind of spoils the vacation, but there it is. . . . These fellows really got trouble." He came to the bed, looked down at the afternoon edition of the *Daily News* spread out there. "Can't say I blame this Mendoza for taking a poke at that reporter. Beats all how they seem to figure. I guess," and he sighed, for he was something of an amateur philosopher, "it's just human nature. Not liking any kind of authority. . . . What I seen of this place, must be hell with the lid off, try to police it. Seems to go on forever, city limits. Way down to the ocean—why, that must be thirty miles. Makes you think. Quite a job. Must be they got four, five thousand men. Makes you wonder how the hell-an'-to-gone they *start*."

"We're on a *vacation*," said his wife, tying a hairnet over her neat gray sausage curls.

"Sure, honey. I'm damn sorry it turned out this way. But I couldn't do nothing else. I mean, you got to figure, it's not just that I want to know for sure about Rhoda—what the hell, one like that. It's just—I can't say, what's the odds, none o' my business. If I got any help to give, I got to give it. I mean, it's—like it might be Marian. Anybody . . . The fellows call themselves psychiatrists—way I read 'em they make out everybody's a little nuts. Well, I don't know . . ."

"Downright rudeness!" she said. "Not as if you were just *anybody!*"

Lockhart took up his pajama coat and stared at it earnestly. "I got to get in and tell them, Martha. Just in *case*. It's my duty. The oath, it don't specify Illinois or Maine or California—not the sense of it. These fellows, they got trouble on their hands. Don't blame 'em for maybe bein' short-tempered. I would be. . . . *The* very hell of a place to police, this must be. And I read somewhere, a while ago, it's supposed to be a crack city force, the best in the country, it said. Wonder how they operate on a thing like this—start to look—place this size." He put on the pajama coat absently, began to button it—thinking, speculating.

"A *vacation,*" she said. "And then this has to come up." And there was in her tone, besides exasperation, pride in his sense of responsibility, his strength as a man of honor.

"I got to try," he said soberly. "Just in *case*. You go and have a good time on your own, Mother, wherever you fancy. . . . Thing is, man's made a certain way, he's got to do certain things. Funny way to figure, too, I can't help thinking—we put off this vacation twice, and so I land here just this time, to see the stories in the papers. Not to make out I'm all that important, but it makes you wonder if it was *meant*. Maybe all *for* something, make something happen or stop it happening. You don't know. Coincidence—maybe so. And maybe *meant*."

"You go along again in the morning, if you feel you've got to," she said gently. "I'll make out all right."

FIFTEEN

"Oh, damn," said Alison to herself. She hung up the receiver, resisting the impulse to bang it back in place. Lame ducks! she thought. Why do I have this fatal attraction for them?

Funny—or, of course, if you looked at it deeper, maybe only natural —all these *substitutes* foisted on her, lame ducks. Natural, perhaps, because a man who hadn't acquired a wife before he was thirty or so was apt to be either a little, well, backward in some way—irresponsible, something like that—or the habitual wolf, nothing permanent. Unless he was just unlucky—some people were, both sexes. Hard to figure a reason, maybe. And about nine of the first kind to one wolf, out of my random ten.

"Damn," she said again. She wasn't interested, by any remote stretch of the imagination, in this one—or any of them these well-meaning people had urged (so subtly) on her. But there was that thing called empathy, making her uneasily aware of other people's feelings. She supposed it was odd, when she set herself up as an authority (in a way) on social behavior, that she should be so inept at that kind of thing, the easy excuses of prior obligations and so on. But, inevitably, the empathy told her of the other person's feeling, and almost without thought she softened the phrase, flavored it with the friendliness, the warm apology, that invited insistence . . . and so there she was, *stuck*.

And if she *had* to go out with the man, if she had to saddle herself with him for an evening on that account, why hadn't she said, all right, tonight, get it over! Now, four days to have it hanging over her. Saturday night.

Damn. He'd been so very persistent.

She wandered back into the living room. Ought to do her nails tonight. Sheba had had a catnip orgy in the middle of a sheet of newspaper spread on the floor; she was asleep on her back, four black-gloved paws in the air, still wearing an ecstatic expression.

Probably not an awful lot of money, thought Alison vaguely; no need to dress up. The amber silk: it was old, but good.

Luis had always liked it.

Funny. This particular lame duck—funny about people. Not bad-looking, enough intelligence and, oh, manner, to hold that kind of job, but—nothing there, somehow. A window dummy animated, very correct, very courteous, and very empty. She didn't *want* to go out with him, Saturday night or any other: why on earth hadn't she said so? All very well to be polite, but you got yourself into things, unavoidably, if you couldn't be just a little rude sometimes.

Of course, some people, you had to make it more than a little to get through to them.

Empathy.

She reached down for the paper, folding it over, and Mendoza looked up at her from the top of the second page there. It wasn't a good picture, a candid shot snatched last year—she remembered when they'd first run it—taken when there was all that fuss during the Ackerson trial. He was coming out of some building, hat in hand, glancing up sharp and annoyed at the photographer. Reprinted here to illustrate this multiple-murder business there was such a clamor about. . . . She hadn't been following, it, she wasn't much interested; but it seemed—now she thought—quite a while they'd been featuring it. A tough one, maybe. He must be worrying at it—that terrific single-mindedness, that drive she knew so well—if he'd lost his temper far enough to have a fight with this reporter, so the headline said. . . .

She folded the paper and took it out to the kitchen. She poured herself a cup of coffee and sat at the table drinking it slowly, warming her hands on the cup. A hot, humid night, but her hands cold. Cold hands, warm heart. Didn't they say too—lucky at cards, unlucky in love. Unlucky! Well, it depended which way you looked at it.

(*Toma esa llavita de oro, mi bien.* . . . Open my breast and see how much I love you. . . . *Y el mal pago que me das* . . . and how badly you repay me. . . .)

Live and learn, she thought a little numbly. Trying to make it the cynical, the sardonic reflection. At least, live and learn.

Long ago, that anonymous woman who'd insisted on talking to her on a train somewhere—funny, couldn't remember where—"It just don't *matter,* how he is or what he is, or how he is to *me,* if he's just *there,* that's all. They keep saying better leave him—they don't know, that's all. It just don't *matter*—"

A lot of women like that. Silly women, muddle-headed women. Men drunkards, thieves, bullies, leading them unspeakable lives. She'd always wondered at it, felt a little scornful. How could they, how did they? No pride, no self-respect as a human person. No—no human entity of their own, was that it? Not Alison, the high-headed, the self-sufficient, with standards and ambitions! Never proud Alison, to let a man degrade her so.

(*Toma es cajita de oro, mi bien.* . . . Take this gold box, my love, look to see what it holds . . . *lleva amores, lleva celos*—love and jealousy. . . .)

She knew now what women like that were talking about. Shameful, shameless, but it was so: it didn't *matter*. Nothing else mattered at all, if he was just *there*.

Not that you could ever imagine Luis being unkind, cruel, any way. All that sleek cynical surface, veneer; he worked so hard to cover up that awful softness in him, that he was a little ashamed of, somehow. Empathy again . . . Luis, smiling one-sided and cynical on some sardonic little remark—and his hand so gentle on the kitten in his lap.

But this way or that way, it just didn't matter. And she wasn't—that was how far she'd come—even ashamed at any loss of pride; she was just trying to get through this painful time as best she could, because surely to God after a while it would stop being so bad—it had to.

And intellectually she knew it was as well she couldn't shut herself up brooding here, had a living to get—must let people crowd in on her, day by day—but that didn't make it easier to take.

She finished the coffee. Ought to do her nails tonight. It didn't seem very important, worthwhile: fussing over herself, for—other people.

For this—this ridiculous and suddenly persistent store-window dummy. It wasn't funny any more, it was almost tragic. What you asked of life, what you got.

And that was perilously near to maudlin self-pity, which was a dangerous thing. She forced herself up, emulating briskness; she went into the bathroom, got out the nail-polish remover. That coppery color, if she was going to wear the amber silk on Saturday . . .

"Oh, well, after all he was in a rather awkward position, the Chief," said Mendoza with a one-sided mirthless grin. "Officially—even to me —he can't approve that kind of thing, but at the same time he's a cop too, and he sympathized with my feelings. He said so—off the record."

"Justifiable, but don't do it again?" said Hackett.

"That's about it."

"It wasn't just an awful smart thing to do, Luis. Makes it look, in a sort of way, as if there was something behind Fitzpatrick's charges."

"All right, so it wasn't. These things happen."

"They do say," remarked Hackett, "that the fellows like you, couple of drinks set them spoiling for a fight, are overcompensating for an inferiority complex."

"I'm," said Mendoza, "being subjected to sufficient irritation by this case *and* the press, and I can do without the reported maunderings of the head doctors."

"It was a joke," said Hackett hastily, "—the idea of you feeling inferior to anybody, from the Archangel Gabriel down." He eyed Mendoza covertly, wondering. About a couple of things. Because, while this thing was enough to get anybody down, he'd known Mendoza a long time and he didn't remember ever seeing him quite like this. He just wondered.

It took people a little different, but in most ways the same. Kept his private life very damn private, Luis, but circumstance had put Hackett in the way of knowing Alison Weir; and Hackett looked, maybe, like the big dumb cop of fiction, but he saw more than he showed or talked about. It wasn't hard to figure Alison; Mendoza was a different story. The camouflage, the front to the world. Didn't matter why. . . . Sharp enough to cut himself, Luis, except just here and there. They said the wolves, woman after woman, were proving themselves: that figured. Other ways too, with most of them. Not that you could generalize. Go back to beginnings—maybe because his name was Luis Rodolfo Vicente Mendoza, this place and this time, and he'd got the *dirty stupid Mex* routine so often. Reason he'd make himself a little reputation as one of the bright boys. Had to show better than anybody else. Not that the head doctors had all the answers, but—

Same time, reflected Hackett (looking at the page of Tom Landers' notes in his hand without seeing it very clearly), same time, there was something else—individual, and yet in a way another generalization. The wolves. Part that natural charm: part too, damn what the head doctors said about inferiority complexes, part the extra-strong sex drive. They contradicted themselves there: admitted that was the engine power, that old devil sex—direct drive, or rechanneled in other directions—that was the power plant for the whole works. The ones who lived the longest, lived the hardest, lived the highest—the producers, the creators, the leaders, always the ones with the stronger-than-average sex drive. And also the bad ones, the violent ones, too: naturally. Equal to aggression: just depended which direction the aggression took, right or left. Dexter or sinister . . .

So, sure, say the Freudians had a little something: that was what it went back to, essentially. Trouble with the wolves, a lot of them never found out there might be, there could be something more important to a woman than just the one thing. That there was always one woman more important than all the rest put together.

The head doctors, Freudian or Adlerian or whatever, had a little something too when they said *Areas*—The water-tight mental compartments for different subjects. The ultimate civilized man, Luis Mendoza, a lot of ways; just, maybe, one way still the ultimate Neanderthal (as God knows aren't we all, this way or that).

Hackett just wondered, looking at him. Such the hell of a smart boy, any other way.

And himself. *Passing the love of women* . . . Oh, sure to God there was something to it—sex loyalty, give it the fancy name. . . . Angel asking, wondering too, his darling Angel, sharing that certain empathy, that essential thing between: putting it in words, *"Could* he, Art, I mean the way you say he's so irritable lately, so—really—unlike himself, I mean, I just wondered . . ." And himself being noncommittal, jocular, changing the subject—easy and affectionate. A different thing. Not to give Luis away, if . . .

He just wondered if maybe, in that one area, Luis Mendoza was growing up a little bit, finding out the truth.

And he had a very odd thought just then, staring down unseeingly at Landers' report. He thought that, looked at one way, Luis Mendoza and this bloody-handed killer of women they were hunting had something in common. *Woman*—to them it meant the one same thing.

Only Luis Mendoza—and that was a very damned peculiar thought too—he was a man on the right side, across the table from the Opponent, and a sane man; and so when all the chips were down he might see that he'd been drawing to the wrong hand—there were higher cards to find in the deck.

Hackett was annoyed with himself for unaccustomed sentimentality. It was just—he wondered. And maybe hoped. Because, come down to it, *passing the love of women* . . .

"You'd started to tell me about a bright idea," he said, "before the summons came to appear before authority. What was it?" Mendoza was swiveled around, brooding out the window. "The beach," he said, "the beach. Could we do something there? I just—"

Sergeant Lake said from the door, "Excuse me, Lieutenant, but that fellow's back again, that Lockhart that came in yesterday. He asked me to give you this." He advanced and laid a card on the desk.

"Persistent," said Mendoza. He swiveled round and picked up the card; and then he sat motionless, head cocked, studying it. After a moment he said softly "¿Y qué es esto, what's this? *Mr. John Lockhart*—and in a vile scrawl, *Chief of Police, Mount Selah, Illinois—in re the Wood case, etc.* ¡No me diga, don't tell me! Something definite, something helpful, a little break at last? I've got a feeling—cross your fingers, Arturo! By God, I wonder. I'll see him, Jimmy, bring him in *pronto!*"

"Needn't apologize," said Lockhart. "Should have said who I was yesterday, what I come about. The truth is, a place this size, well, it don't seem like a police station to me somehow, know what I mean. I guess I was figuring, at that, way it'd be back home—not all that much to do, Sergeant Wills says, Somebody to see you, I say, Shove him in. Should have had better sense—place like this, must be hell to keep in order—even in the ordinary way, you'd be busy."

"That you can say twice," agreed Mendoza.

"I'd sure be interested, see through this place, how you go to work. If it wouldn't discommode you any, after I say what I come for. My place looks pretty damn piddling compared."

"Cops are cops," said Hackett, who had liked Mr. Lockhart on sight. They came all shapes and sizes: you found some small-town ones the inept free-riders, and in big towns too; and then you found the ones like Lockhart, who'd have been good anywhere. Looked small-town, farmerish—but shrewd as they were made. And a cop, first and foremost, that you could see.

"I was just saying to my wife last night—you know, it makes you wonder if it was *meant,* some way. Put off this vacation twice, we did, on account of this and that—meant to come two years ago when Marian had the baby, see. That's our youngest daughter, she lives down in San Diego now, husband's a regular Air Force officer. So that's where we landed a week ago. I generally keep up with the news, but you know how it is on a vacation, I didn't do more'n glance at the headlines, until three-four days ago. And then I saw about this business up here, and I made it my business, get hold of some o' your local papers to see *all* about it, what was said about this joker. And I just got to wondering. Now I don't want to stick my neck out, butt in where I'm not wanted, gentlemen, but I figured I'd better come in and tell you about it. Just in case. Because, you don't need to tell me, on a thing like this you aren't fussing about gettin' together the lawyers' evidence for later on, you just want to spot this boy for sure. In your own minds, whatever the evidence is or isn't."

"And isn't that the truth," said Hackett.

"What have you got to tell us, Mr. Lockhart?" asked Mendoza.

Lockhart wasn't to be rushed. "Might be we can make this short 'n' sweet—maybe I'm just seeing ghosts. See," he grinned slowly, "for all Mount Selah can't claim more than eighteen hundred population, we got a newspaper, and I've had a little experience, how reporters build up a story. Point is, the papers are all I've seen, and might be they got the evidence twisted some. Any case, they haven't had it all to print, I don't guess—and might be if and when you tell me what you've got on this joker, I'll have to say, Sorry, boys, I thought I had a little something, but seems I was wrong. And on the other hand I might not. I just wondered from what *was* in the papers, figured I better find out. I'll admit, be a pretty damn big coincidence when you figure the odds—this is a big country, and there's a hell of a lot of people in it—and this is the first time I been out o' the state of Illinois. Fine thing to think, maybe Providence sendin' me here just now, to give you a little help. And *at* that, come down to it,"—he brought out a short fat cigar and began to unwind the cellophane slowly—"even if there's any evidence of connection at all, don't know that it'd give you much. Except another victim—and a kind of fishy smell. Which, mind you, was all in my own mind."

Mendoza half rose, holding out his lighter; he looked a little excited. "You think you know him? Are you telling me you know him? *Dios mío,* coincidence, Providence—out of a hundred and eighty million people—I don't care what the hell you call it, give us what you've got, friend!"

"Like that, hah?" said Lockhart. "Thanks,"—he bent to the lighter. "Me, I don't usually get stuff like this, o' course—place like Mount Selah, a Chief of Police isn't so much expected to be a detective as, you might say, an M.P. Keep order. The rambunctious teen-agers, and now 'n' then a burglar, and the drunks on Saturday night. You know. But kind of reading between the lines in the papers, I figured this might be a tough one, even for you boys. . . . Where to hell-an'-gone can you start to *look?* Sure. . . . I don't know, Lieutenant Mendoza, I just don't know. And I don't want to waste your time. I guess best way to get at it, if you could tell me right off, did the papers print pretty accurate what you got on this boy, and did they print most of it? The description and all?"

Mendoza pulled open the top drawer of the desk and handed over a sheaf of documents. "You're welcome to read the statements. To save time, I'll say roughly yes. Add up the secondhand reports we've got on him, it comes out—a fellow between twenty-nine and thirty, around there, five-ten to six feet, brown hair, take your choice about eye color, thinnish, dresses pretty well, white-collar worker, nice manners, no noticeable regional accent, drives—or did drive—a bright blue car, recent model. And that's about it."

"That's all the official evidence," said Hackett. "The boss here, he can work up the prettiest dreams, and without eatin' hashish either, and he's had one about our Romeo. How much it's worth, who knows?"

"O.K., so it's a pipe dream—I keep Sergeant Hackett around to pour cold water, Mr. Lockhart—he pours enough on a hunch to drown it, I know it wasn't much good, but if it keeps bobbing up, I tell him to go to hell. Like a Geiger counter in reverse, if you take me. So O.K., I build this one up—from this and that in the statements, the nuance, the tone of voice, and the kind of women they were, you know, and so on —I make him coming here from a smallish inland place about three years ago, liking the beach, buying or renting a place there to spend his weekends in—raised with rather old-fashioned manners, quite possibly even a little diffident in his manner, not aggressive anyway, the kind a nice modest shy young lady feels safe with, you know? I think this last three years, approximately, is the first time he's lived in a city—I think he's had a high school education but not college—I think—"

"I guess you can stop right there," said Lockhart, "because it sounds mighty close. Nothing like evidence, I know. The hell of a long chance it's the same, the size of this country." He looked at his cigar with a troubled expression. "If it *is* so, gentlemen, it's some my fault these other women got killed, which isn't the kind of thought I like to take to bed with me. But what could I do? The law isn't interested in your feelings about a thing, even if you happen to be Chief of Police. You got to have it in black and white before they let you charge anybody, and that's just what I didn't have."

SIXTEEN

"So, what's the story?" demanded Mendoza. He lit a new cigarette, nervous and excited. Maybe the break in the case? "Go on!"

"Well, I don't need to waste a lot of time describing Mount Selah to you—maybe a kind of typical small town. Most of us know each other, know each others' business—you've heard all the jokes about small towns. But a place like that, it's a bad place to commit a crime, because of that very fact. Now it might surprise you some,"—and Lockhart grinned—"to know we usually got four-five professional chippies around town—not a very good town for their business, not because we're any more moral than other folks but because, like I say, you're a lot more apt to get found out in a town like that. We don't as a rule do much about 'em—if it wasn't the couple we know about, it'd be some we didn't, and hell, there that kind is, you can't legislate altogether against human nature."

"Live and let live," said Hackett.

"About that. Rhoda Vann was one of 'em. Been around town for years, on and off—woman about forty, liked her drink a little too well, but I will say she usually stayed home to get drunk, didn't go round creating disturbances. Not much of a looker, big red-haired woman, seen her best days. She lived in the Crosley Hotel, which is a fancy name for a twelve-room fleatrap down by the river. Couple of other women, much the same sort, had rooms to each side of hers. You'll gather, place like that, nobody pays an awful lot of notice to funny noises in the next room.

"Well, it was three years ago last month Rhoda got killed. Girl who lived across the hall went in to borrow something one morning and found her. She'd been killed about ten P.M. the night before, so the doctor said. It was a damn funny setup to start with, because nobody as far as we knew or could find out had any reason to kill her—and like I say, your private business isn't so awful private in Mount Selah. She was a good-natured soul, generous to her friends, never held a grudge,

and so on, and as for what you might call underworld connections—
you know, gangster stuff, like if she maybe had something on somebody
—hell, I don't think Rhoda'd ever been farther than forty miles from
Mount Selah in her life, there just wasn't anything possible in that line.
She hadn't anything a thief'd be after—only a lunatic'd go to burglarize
anybody at the Crosley—and it looked like something personal, because of the way she'd got it. Beaten and choked to death—"

"And raped first?"

"Well, not exactly," said Lockhart, "but nobody needed to go raping
Rhoda, and everybody in town'd know that. But the coroner—Dr.
Williams—he did say she'd had relations with somebody just before.
Maybe that don't say much. Point is, there wasn't any motive we could
turn up, on anybody who knew her. And she hadn't been as you might
say receiving callers that day and night. She'd been feeling poorly, coming down with a cold, she said to a couple of other girls, and she'd
stayed in alone with a couple of bottles for company.

"I'll make this as short as I can. Among her stuff there was a brand-
new bottle of aspirin, unopened, and it came from Wise's drugstore.
Everybody knew the Wises too. Damn funny pair. The old man, old
Abraham Wise, had just died, couple o' months before, and Gideon—
his boy—was running the store alone. Nobody ever had much to do
with the Wises. Old man wouldn't let 'em, what it came to. He was a
religious crank, puritanical as they come and a little bit more, and the
list of things he didn't like—called sinful—I guess it'd reach from here
to Kingdom Come. That kind. Quite a character—and a strong character, not to say a tyrant. My wife and some other womenfolk always said
he browbeat his wife to death—and all I know, maybe he didn't always
use his tongue either. She died when the boy was about three, and the
old man brought him up.

"Gideon never mixed hardly at all with other kids—one thing, the
old man kept him too busy, he had to come right home from school, get
to work on his chores and so on. Had him helping in the store before
he was ten—which is all right, I'm all for giving kids responsibility, but
Gideon, seemed like, was expected to do a man's work. Old man was
too stingy to buy anything new, make life a little more comfortable—
they still cooked on an old wood stove, for instance, and most days
you'd see Gideon out behind the house chopping wood. Old-fashioned
—damn foolishness, I call it. People used to feel sorry for Gideon, but
the old man kept him so much under his thumb, he hadn't no chance to
get out and mix much, even if he'd wanted. The old man's religion was

old-fashioned too, he didn't think there was a church in town really holy enough, and they didn't go to any. Once in a while they'd go over to Pisgah to a revivalist meeting—they had an old broken-down Model A Ford—but ask me, main reason the old man didn't go to church regular was the collection."

"And one very damn good reason it is," said Mendoza, "among others." He was leaning back, eyes shut, smoking lazily. "Just as we go along, I expect old Abraham's brand of religion listed Woman pretty far down on the tabulation of important things—"

"And pretty high up on the list o' sinfulnesses. I never paid all that much attention to what he believed, but that I can say. He was always quoting John Milton—he'd had a good education, you know—"

"That passage about what a pity it is God didn't find a purer way for people to produce offspring." Mendoza laughed. "Very curious idea—illogical thinking. If there was, it'd take on all the same connotations the present method gives rise to. Me, I'm old-fashioned myself, quite satisfied with the *status quo*. Yes. Young Gideon didn't mix, he was a loner. So he didn't get much ordinary human background to compare with his home life."

"I don't suppose. Time he got to the age when he could have got out, tried to break away from the old man—high school, along there, the rest of the kids dating and so on—he didn't seem to want to, didn't know how to go about it, and by then I guess he'd been so filled up with these ideas, he thought that kind of thing was sinful anyway. You take some kids brought up too religious that way, they can't wait to get away, turn against it soon as they can. But some like Gideon, they swallow it all serious and just carry on where their folks left off.

"Well, there's Gideon Wise. He was twenty-six when the old man died, looked some older, maybe because he was so serious. Not a bad-looking young fellow, nothing extraordinary either way—you wouldn't turn to look at him twice. Round about five-foot-ten or a bit more, brown hair and eyes, kind of sallow complected and built thin—usually dressed sort of formal, way the old man had, a suit and white shirt. I said both of 'em had a decent education—Gideon graduated from high school at seventeen—average bright and maybe then some. The old man had raised him strict about manners, and he was always a lot more polite, in a kind of funny old-fashioned way, than most young fellows these days."

"Arturo," said Mendoza dreamily, "do you feel a little tingling sensation up your spine? Don't keep us in suspense, Mr. Lockhart—what evidence did you have?"

"Gentlemen, damn all—except for a bottle of aspirin. What the hell did that mean? I didn't think much about it to start with. Why should I? Gideon Wise—last man to think of in a thing like that! I went and asked him about the aspirin, because I was kind of surprised to find it there. They had their own label for stuff like that, is how I knew where it came from. I didn't see Rhoda going into Wise's for anything. The old man wouldn't have served her, probably chased her out, and anyway he never would stock liquor the way the other drugstore—Bill Green's place—does. Green's was where most people went, because he carries everything you expect to find in a drugstore. Old man Wise never stocked any women's cosmetic stuff, or wine and liquor, or magazines—a lot of stuff he thought was foolish and sinful, you see."

"*¡Uno queda aturdido*—you overwhelm me!" said Mendoza. "At least the courage of his convictions, but why didn't he starve to death?"

Lockhart grinned. "I often wondered. Funnily enough, though—well, I'll come to that in a minute. Like I say, I went and saw Gideon, and he said—looking me in the eye honest as you please—Rhoda called the store a couple of nights before she was killed, asked him to bring her the aspirin. He said he didn't realize right off who it was calling, or maybe he'd have said no, but as it was, he'd said he'd bring it—he was just closing up—and though he knew Father'd have disapproved, well, a customer was a customer. And he took it over to her and she paid him and that was that. He said it was Tuesday night—she was killed on Thursday—and Green's was closed, which was why she called him. And he just couldn't say why she hadn't opened the bottle and taken a couple. *That* kind, he said, who knew what they'd do? He'd never had anything to do with that sinful woman before or after, and that was all he knew.

"And right there, gentlemen, *I* had a kind of little tingle up the spine, and I knew. I couldn't tell you why—something about the way his eyes looked when he said her name—something about the way he looked at me—I don't know. I just knew, all of a sudden, he's the one did it. I couldn't figure why—I still can't. But I went away and thought about it, and I asked the other girls on that floor in the Crosley, and one of 'em remembered Gideon coming, knocking on Rhoda's door. She—this girl—she was just coming out, see, and saw him there. She got quite a kick out of it, because of course she knew who he was—the holy Gideon Wise—and was kind of disappointed, she said, when she saw he had a little parcel with him, so he was probably just delivering something, not calling on Rhoda for the usual reason. But she couldn't remember which night it was, hadn't been that interested. She wasn't the girl who found Rhoda, or maybe she would have. It was just a little thing she remembered, hadn't noticed much at the time—it passed right out of her mind after, until I asked. It might have been Tuesday night.

"Well, I don't need to tell you there's nothing there. Rhoda being the kind she was, maybe she got to hitting the bottle and forgot all about the aspirin, sure. But—" Lockhart spread his hands. "I didn't think so then and I don't think so now. I didn't see Gideon again, no reason to ask any more—it was all in my mind, just a *feeling*. Nothing at all to build a charge on. I just knew, somehow, sure as death. I couldn't tell you why. I can see him going to visit Rhoda, you know—or maybe just, you might put it, decidin' to stay once he was there, with that bottle of aspirin. Not even old Abraham could outlaw human nature entirely, and for all Gideon was a backward sort I don't guess there was anything wrong about him that way. Don't suppose he'd ever been in ten feet of anything female, that way, and we know what they say about the pot with the lid on too tight. I can see, with the old man gone and nobody to keep tabs on him any more, Gideon might have found out he still had a little of the old Adam in him. And maybe when he got there that night, knowing what Rhoda was and all, he just all of a sudden let go. But I don't know why he should have killed her—and if I wasn't just woolgathering, it wasn't anything very sane, because it was a pretty bloody business. Unless, maybe, he just felt so damn guilty afterward and took it out on her."

"It could be, it could be. I like this very much—it could be a big piece of our jigsaw puzzle. The first one—setting the pattern . . . I don't suppose you'd be here telling us all this if Gideon Wise was still behind the counter of his drugstore in Mount Selah."

"That's so. I don't know where he is, gentlemen. This was three years back last month, like I say. Old Abraham two months dead. How he'd managed to save that much I don't know, but it came out he'd had nearly five thousand in the bank. It came to Gideon, of course. We'd wondered if he might maybe kick over the traces some—you know—but he never showed a sign of it, that couple of months. Before Rhoda. Then,"—Lockhart leaned to deposit the stub of his cigar in the ashtray—"day after I'd talked to him about that, he shut the store and left town. They rented the building—matter o' fact it belongs to my brother-in-law—there wasn't a lease. Gideon just went over to Bill

Green, it came out later, and offered him the stock at his own price. They'd rented the old place they lived in too, and he never took any of the furniture—nothing but his clothes, and the money out of the bank, and got a ride up to the county seat with Jim Hotchkiss, where he could get a train. To somewhere. And that's all I know. What was in my mind, what brought me here today—I saw that woman, and she wasn't killed by a sane man. Especially if I'm right and it was Gideon. I'm no doctor, but they say anything improves with practice. When I read about this joker you're after here, and what you think he looks like, and the way he's killed these women—I just wondered. It connected up in my mind. Because in a kind of way, I never felt very easy about Rhoda and Gideon. Nothing I could do about it. I don't know how much this means to you, of course. Don't know if you'll think it worth even mentioning, that a couple of people—after Gideon'd left and people were talking about it, you know—remembered him saying once or twice he'd always wanted to see California."

"This story I like better and better," said Mendoza. "Are you offering odds against it, Art?"

"I don't think so," said Hackett slowly. "It sounds an awful lot like our boy, Luis. The pattern. Coincidence is a funny thing, but most coincidences, you look at them twice and it's not so random as it looks— good solid reason behind it. But evidence, my God—"

"The hell with that," said Mendoza, sitting up with a jerk. "Since when have we had any good legal evidence on this at all? Mr. Lockhart summed up the situation for us on that—the dismal truth is, if we picked him up in the next hour, tell me what we'd hold him on, even for a day! ¡Ay qué risa! Over two and a half months since Pauline McCandless, the latest one—up to twenty-eight months ago on Anderson. None of them so conveniently clutching a strand of the murderer's hair or a button off his coat, to identify him—no nice footprints or fingerprints—nothing, nothing to say the man who killed them is this man or that man, nothing to match up to any man we bring in. Not a soul alive who ever met these charming newly acquired boy friends— just secondhand reports of what the women said he looked like. Don't we know how many men conform to that vague description! The pattern in more ways than one—we're stuck for evidence just the way you were, Mr. Lockhart. For once, I'm not thinking about the D.A.'s office —we can't. We've got to spot him, and then look for the evidence to bring him in on."

"That makes sense, Lieutenant, but you may never get any."

"And if we don't, maybe there's another card up our sleeve. Whether our boy is your Gideon or not, he's not a sane man—if he once was, not after four, five, six. Patterns—patterns, sure—you can go by them some. A lot of woman-killers, mass killers in general, have the notion they're specially appointed executioners, under God's protection. Sometimes when they're caught up with, it sends them all the way over the edge. We might just get a confession. We might just get a suicide. But I'll worry about that when we've spotted him, for ninety percent sure, anyway. And I'm hoping to God, friend, your boy is our boy too, because if he is, you're the only witness this side of the Mississippi who can recognize him. In fact," said Mendoza, gazing at Mr. Lockhart fondly, "you are worth your weight in gold here and now, and I'm tempted to give you a bodyguard to see you don't get killed in traffic or fall off any ten-storey buildings until you've had a good look at all our possibles—"

Lockhart grinned. "I'll take good care o' myself, always have."

"Because just in case you can tell us that one of our maybes is Gideon Wise, this background rings up a lot more preponderance of suspicion on him—evidence or no. Especially if he's changed his name, which we seem to be taking it for granted he has. Why? Did you make him a little nervous, possibly? I wonder. Or maybe he just wanted to make a fresh start. . . . But I'd like to know if he's here, I would indeed."

"How many possibles you got and where are they?"

Mendoza closed his eyes. "I haven't counted lately. In round figures, about fifty. With special check marks on a dozen or so."

"I pried three more names out of Mrs. Andrews yesterday afternoon," remarked Hackett. "Haven't located two of them yet."

"You boys must have been busy," said Lockhart. "When and where do I look at them?"

"Art, you can act as a special escort. Take the Andrews list first, I think. They're all scattered, Mr. Lockhart, miles apart all over the damn town, and we've been dodging reporters and—mmh—looking at them from a distance, no direct questioning yet, because there's just no solid reason whatever to connect any of them with any of the murders. So you'll look at them one by one, please, in their daily habitats—it'll make a nice guided tour of L.A. for you. It may take two days, it may take three. Because we haven't been able to tie strings to all of them, of course—in any way. I'm banking heavily on the Andrews list, which Hackett'll explain to you—we've got four possibles there who just might be a little more possible than any of the rest, and so there are men keeping an eye on them, sniffing around a little closer. And of course, our Romeo may have no connection with your Gideon, and whether he has or not we may not have him anywhere on our lists of maybes. And just in the event that it *is* Gideon, and he isn't in our lists, it wouldn't be a bad idea to look in the phone book and so on—he might not have changed his name. We may find him living somewhere, innocent as day, as Gideon Wise. And even if he did come to California, there's a lot of it outside L.A. But I have a feeling about this—just as I do about Mrs. Andrews' clandestine roomers. That we're coming a little closer."

"And suppose I look at all of them and say no."

"Way the cards fall. Like shooting craps blindfolded, damn it. Sure. We don't *know*. If you don't spot him among these, that doesn't say one of them isn't still our boy—no link with Gideon. Doesn't say yes or no —we might not have him listed at all, as I say. All we can do is look."

"So we go and look," said Hackett with a sigh, for summer had absent-mindedly overstayed itself into this month, "and you'll be sitting here in a nice air-conditioned seventy-seven-degree temperature, waiting for the green light. Some day, Mr. Lockhart, I'm going to get to be a lieutenant too."

"You malign me," said Mendoza. "I'm going to be out chasing a little hare of my own. No, wrong metaphor—hoping to find one to chase. We'll see—we'll see. . . ."

SEVENTEEN

Say it was or say it wasn't, thought Mendoza, sitting behind the wheel of the Facel-Vega waiting for that three-way signal where Chautauqua ran into the coast highway. If Lockhart looked at this George Hopper, this John Tewke, this William Bell—at any one of the fifty, sixty men they had listed in this long, patient, dull hunt for the maybes—and said, that's Gideon Wise, it was (call it) seventy-five percent sure that was their boy. No more, because there was nothing to say for sure

Gideon Wise had killed Rhoda Vann: just that little tingle up Chief Lockhart's spine (and how well Mendoza knew the feeling!) But something more, nice and definite, to point out Romeo: and then they could go to work on him, look for the kind of evidence the law demanded.

But! The odds might not be quite astronomical that Gideon and Romeo were the same man; they were the hell of a lot longer that there'd be any tangible evidence to be got, even when they'd spotted him.

The light changed at last and Mendoza slid down the hill behind an old Ford and turned into the slow lane of the Malibu road. Like roulette, he thought. Cover yourself with the side bets. Most of your stake on the one chosen number—*por las malas or por las buenas,* all or nothing—but the side bet on red or black.

They could use all the little pointers of evidence there to be found. Maybe to be found.

Himself, he was operating on all cylinders again, the thinking-machine Mendoza. With the little advertised tablets, he'd slept: he got up feeling dull, slow, but a couple of cups of coffee spiked with a finger or two of rye, he was O.K., he was himself. If he'd admit it, if he ever thought about it that specifically, this was always his chief stimulant, the one thing in life he got the big kick out of: the challenge. Running a trail, when it began to warm up a little.

A feeling for people, sure, he had: what produced his hunches. But essentially, he told himself, he was the thinking machine. He didn't give one damn, admit it honestly, for the corpses: what the hell, people lived and died, liked to think there was an ordered destiny to it, a benevolent God or a stern paternal one arranging it all: damn nonsense, wishful thinking; people lived and died, blind chance. Quite a lot of them not worth mourning. Never missed, important only to themselves. He was sworn to uphold the law of the land but, admit it, that wasn't why Mendoza had built a little reputation as one of the bright boys: he didn't give one damn for the law *per se,* or people in the abstract. *Lo que no se puede remediar, se ha de aguantar*—what can't be cured must be endured. He was a realist and a cynic; he wasn't a police officer because he had any earnest high ideals about people or the law. Oh, admit it, it was the hunt he'd enjoyed always—the purely intellectual brain stimulation of getting all the pieces tidily put together.

He'd fumbled around at this thing for a while, got off to a bad start, and maybe all the press hullabaloo had thrown him off stride, maybe that was it. That had, praise heaven, settled down somewhat now: he had an idea there'd been a quiet word between the Chief and a couple of editors, but whatever reason, the *Telegraph* had eased off on its campaign against the uniform.

And he felt all right in himself again; he was really getting *to* this now, the old Mendoza.

Right now, with the fattest part of his stake riding with Chief Lockhart, he was about to place a side bet.

They had a lot of scientific gadgets to help them these days, but to a great extent those were most useful after the hard work was all done, to produce legal proofs for the D.A., to confirm the little hunch. In the last analysis, any definition of detection came right back to the formula stated by the idiot boy who found the lost horse.

Mendoza liked the Gideon Wise thing, and one reason was that it gave him a little more character to build on, for Romeo. If. But Gideon or not, Romeo was apt to be that general type.

So now Mendoza idled down the right lane of the coast highway thinking and looking—for a place which might have struck that one's fancy.

A loner (Gideon or not): one who tended to shy away from crowds and people in general—shy, lacking self-confidence, just not liking people, or preferring his own company. So he would like a place more or less isolated, not crowded cheek-by-jowl with a dozen and one other little cabins. People like that tended to get set in their ways, to dislike change of any kind, and so if he was financially able at all, ten to one he'd buy or rent a place—which would also be cheaper in the long run than staying at a different motel every weekend. (Gideon had five thousand dollars, or nearly: not much to buy much of a place, but he might have found one for that—especially a very isolated, maybe a dilapidated place.) A man, and one like this, probably wouldn't care a great deal about what a place looked like: he'd just want something reasonably weatherproof, isolated, and within his financial reach. (Gideon had probably an ingrained distrust of time payments, from his miserly father; and there was the car—he must have bought a car when he landed here, to be going back and forth from beach to city. Yes, but he'd recently bought a new, or fairly new, car—so maybe the old one had been a piece of used tin he'd picked up cheap.) And, *de paso,* of course his financial state depended on other things: when he had bought or rented or leased a place down here, whether it was just after he'd got to California, whether he had a job then, what kind of job it was. He wouldn't, probably, have much preference to the exact location: unless he'd fallen in love with a particular stretch of beach, and that you couldn't reckon with. He had been seen, at any rate, along here somewhere, and beach dwellers tended to be curiously insular; they stuck mostly to their own little length of coast, the familiar stores and restaurants and bars. (Probably not bars, with Gideon.)

Coming down off Chautauqua here, Mendoza was a little way out of Santa Monica proper and its beach; he didn't think Romeo would have been attracted there, for a couple of reasons. Inside city limits, prices and rents would be higher, and also, that whole stretch of coast behind him, until you got a good way below Venice, was solidly built up—jerry-built cabins literally leaning on each other all the way along, except for the fishing piers and boat docks. Below Venice was Playa del Rey, a little too exclusive and expensive.

And it was from here on up he'd been seen. A long while back: but Pauline McCandless had met him at the beach two and a half months ago, or thereabouts. She'd worked regular hours; so it had probably been on a weekend. So he still liked the beach; he might still own or rent a place here.

Mendoza looked thoroughly as he idled along, scanning the right side of the road. Along here not a great deal to see. Except for occasional abrupt little cutbacks, the palisades went up steep and sheer, and there were houses at their tops, but dignified family houses, view houses that sold in the thirty-thousand bracket. Down here, an occasional restaurant built on several levels against the hillside; gas stations; entrances to little canyons. Here was Colibrí Avenue, where they'd found Julie; he turned up it, but the half-dozen houses up there, on the winding little street, were all too big and expensive to be called beach cottages. He came back and went on up the highway.

He was working hard, the purely intellectual exercise he had set himself so many times before—getting into the skin of the man he was hunting, trying to feel as he would feel, see as he would see . . .

Here was the broad, curving entrance to Topanga Canyon. He wasn't bothering about Topanga, though Romeo had been seen there once. It was too big, and there were too many people living in it, scattered thickly around, a lot of shacks, a few nice expensive houses. Within five or six miles of the coast, at this end of the canyon, he didn't think there'd be any cottage isolated enough to appeal to Romeo: that was a friendly, fairly crowded community. It might be that Romeo had a place there, but it was too big to cover this way.

On up, it was all emptier: and the hill dropped away so that there were stretches of flattish, sometimes rolling land to his right, inland. Once in a while a house, a street. He stopped and marked his first possibility a mile up from Topanga—a small cottage standing alone about forty feet off the highway, nothing around it: he had to come up on the shoulder to read the house number, and it looked empty. (But this was a weekday.)

In the next ten miles he collected fourteen possibles: cabins in isolated situations, eight of them on side streets off the highway—or rather dirt lanes which might some day be called streets—the rest on the highway. He put check marks beside those; he had an idea that Romeo might like to be as near the sea as possible.

He drove five miles past Zuma Beach West and with some trouble made a U-turn and headed back, keeping an eye on the ocean side now. Less to be seen on that side: mostly public beach, some government-owned and sternly fenced off. Restaurants. He didn't bother to turn off where the highway swerved inland around Malibu village: that was all movie-star class in there, nothing for him.

Just where the highway began to swerve back toward the coast, he saw another possible. On a narrow dirt track leading toward the beach a few hundred yards off—the main road here curled round in a semicircle, and the track bisected it. He braked, turned in; stopped and looked at the place.

A frame cottage, old, unpainted, weathered: about three rooms. Railed porch around four sides, and a carport, empty. It wasn't attractive, but it looked solidly built for a beach cabin. There wasn't another building within half a mile or more: the nearest houses would be the big places up in Malibu village. The track went on, about thirty yards, to the highway, and across the highway there was a good public beach.

Mendoza thought Romeo might have fancied a place like this. There didn't seem to be a street name for the track, or a number on the cabin, but he sketched out a little map of its location. That made fifteen.

He found four more on his way back to where he'd started. He'd spent the entire afternoon on this, and it might all be a mare's nest; but you never knew. He turned around again and drove a mile up the highway to a little, gaily painted real estate office.

The man who had been Edward Anthony was in his shabby Hollywood apartment, making the hours pass. He was feeling very excited and eager and impatient—also very confident—and it seemed that time had stopped, that this day (and tomorrow, and the next day) would go on forever.

That it would never get to be Saturday night.

He had not gone to work today and he wouldn't tomorrow, because he was afraid it would show somehow, that he couldn't seem his usual self. He had called up and said he wasn't feeling well, he was coming down with a bad cold, maybe the flu, and thought he'd better stay home the next few days—and besides, he didn't want to infect anyone else. Mr. Rasmussen hadn't liked it too well, but he'd said all right.

He just didn't feel he could go through the same sober routine of everyday; and it was, in a way, a red-letter day (as they called it), when the truth was at last revealed to him, and he felt it deserved to be marked as a holiday. Red-letter day. Red for blood, red for—

He walked up and down the little sitting room excitedly, thinking about it. Yes, yes, of course many foolish people, mad—deluding themselves—and he'd been slow to accept it for that reason. But now he was quite sure.

He had not recognized it at the time, but there had been some of that evil taint in all of them, not only Julie and Rhoda; and so that was the reason, and the little worried guilt he had felt had not been necessary. It was quite all right. Everything was quite all right: he would never be punished by God or man. And so Saturday night would be all right too.

It was odd to think how nervous he had been a while ago, when there was that headline about a new witness. Who, how could there be, and did they really— And then it all came out, only a desperate kind of lie, the newspaper or the police, it didn't matter which—nothing in it—and that police officer having a fight with a reporter . . . It just showed all the more clearly that they hadn't anything really—losing his temper because it was true, what the paper said— If they had anything, they'd be only too pleased to tell about it, with all that was being said. All true. Very stupid. Although of course he *had* been clever . . .

But that was irrelevant. They didn't matter, his cleverness didn't matter, because it was *intended,* all arranged—no danger, no danger. Quite safe.

Things you thought coincidence, just random chance—afterward you saw how they were meant. His safe, secret place, the little house standing alone: he'd only just realized what a very ideal place it was. Partly on account of Julie. He'd felt it was a kind of violation, then, but that was while he'd still been feeling the guilt—afterward—and now he knew there was no reason for that. Of course, of course.

An ideal place—for the future. A lot of excited, rather incoherent plans were drifting round his mind, but mainly he was thinking about Saturday night.

Take care, of course. Reasonable care. Only sensible. But nothing would interfere, it would all go as he planned it out.

He was only sorry it was Saturday—a whole day wasted, for he usually drove right down there after work on Fridays. But this was more important, naturally. She had been reluctant, hadn't wanted to go out with him at all, which was a little unflattering, but he didn't think for a moment that she had any idea— Probably that evil in her sensing the holiness in him, and—

It was extremely uplifting, this wonderful knowledge of *justification*.

Saturday night. Other Saturday nights. Others. As many as he liked, any time at all.

He would tell her they were going to a restaurant along the beach. A lot of fashionable places down here, she'd think nothing of it; people thought nothing, here, of driving thirty miles for dinner. And once he stopped, at *his* place, no one to hear if she—

Saturday night. Other Saturday nights.

If he could just calm down a little, if he could go to sleep maybe and not wake up until it was time—if he could— Must put up his usual appearance, but he'd manage that all right *then*— Only, all the other times, he hadn't planned it out at all, it had just happened; and this was so much more exciting . . .

He made a little ceremony of getting out the knife, unwrapping it. It was a good knife, good and sharp, but he was still of two minds about it, whether he'd been right in buying it. He wasn't at all sure it would be as—as satisfying, as uplifting, somehow, with the knife. And of course a great deal more blood—which *might* be better in a way, and yet—

He liked the feel of the knife in his hand. There was a nice stiff leather sheath had come with it, to fasten on your belt—it was a hunting knife really, of course—and he decided to carry it anyway. If he buttoned his coat over it it wouldn't show—and then, if he decided to use it, it would be *there*.

He ran his finger delicately down the blade and shivered a little, pleasurably. Good and sharp . . .

He was walking fast up and down, again. Looking at the clock every few minutes.

Queer, very queer, but God's ways were mysterious. This one, she didn't look like Rhoda—this Alison—except for the hair—but there was a link between them, of course, the same kind, the same kind. Killing *what was in Rhoda* time and time again. Of course. All of them, the essential evil, the devil mocking. Bringing out the awful weakness in men.

Such a long time to Saturday night . . .

Mendoza was feeling pleased with himself and with Mr. Ralph Stebbins. Sometimes you reached in blind, not expecting much, and drew an ace the first time round. He'd had a nice little story planned for the real estate fellow—how he was looking for a particular kind of place, he'd been driving round and seen these he liked, and could he be put in touch with the owners? But Mr. Stebbins wasn't the usual brash real estate salesman. He was a weathered-looking old Yankee New Englander with a mouth like a steel trap, a pair of very sharp blue eyes, and a rustily unused-sounding voice. One look and two words, and Mendoza had shut the office door behind him, sat down, and laid all his cards face up on the desk between them.

"This is all very much maybe, as you can appreciate. These places, it's just a random list of possibles from a first hasty look—"

Mr. Stebbins said, "Dunno. Ain't s' many places with just these qualifications. Alone 'n' all."

"No. But it might be up in one of the big canyons—I might be wrong from the word go about the kind of place it is, the kind he'd like. This is just a first cast. I could set some men looking all through the property descriptions at the Hall of Records, sure, and track down the owners' names in time. A lot of time. But frankly, I haven't got a man to spare at the moment, and then, too, this is home territory for you, and you've got an excuse to ask questions—you'd find out with less trouble, quicker. I realize I'm asking you to waste a couple of days, cooperating with us for no profit—"

"Dunno," said Mr. Stebbins. "Reckon it's profit to the hull community, if you catch up to a murderer. Business ain't so good as all that lately. I just run this place to give me suthin' to do anyways. Retired eleven years ago and come out here and dang near went crazy sittin' around. Be kind of interesting, help you fellows out a little."

"I'd be very grateful. As I say, it may all be a mare's nest, but—off the record—I think we're coming a little closer to an idea who he is, and this is for legal evidence—just in case—to locate him." The chances were, as in many of these multiple cases, if and when he was brought to trial, it would be on a charge of only one or two of the murders; and the way it looked now, though Julie Anderson was the oldest one, they might be able to collect more legal evidence on that one than the others. Maybe Madge Parrott *would* recognize him—a little step further on, that would be. . . . "I don't need to tell you that all this is off the record, not to be gossiped about."

Mr. Stebbins sniffed. "Never was much of a talker. Wife's dead these four years, I live alone—nobody but the cat to talk to and she looks a-plenty answer-back but she don't speak English. You leave it to me, Lieutenant. I'll find out for you 'n' let you know, soon *as*."

EIGHTEEN

Hackett had the uneasy feeling that he was taking an undeserved holiday from work. He and Chief Lockhart got on fine together, and he liked Mrs. Lockhart too, meeting her when he delivered Lockhart back to his hotel. After all the hard routine day after day on this thing, it made a little break to be driving Lockhart around, pointing out all the suspects-in-embryo. It was, he figured, a long chance that any of them was Gideon Wise—or was it? But they had to look, though it seemed a time-wasting process.

They'd started out on the Andrews list, but had missed a few of them —men off sick, one on a late vacation and not expected back until Monday—so they'd have to come back to those; and two of them were on Mendoza's list of those under more careful scrutiny, too, but it couldn't be helped. They'd covered a dozen that first afternoon, started in again next morning and got to twenty that day—what with driving back and forth, though Hackett had tried to group them in batches to be found in roughly the same areas.

They'd covered quite a lot of territory, and they'd got on fine, enjoying each other. There was still a long list to look at, and this Saturday morning they were setting out again bright and early, as so many business places closed at noon.

"What's the program today?" asked Lockhart, getting in beside him.

"Three down in Compton, a couple in west Hollywood—we'll be chalking up mileage. Talk about a guided tour."

"You sure are showing me the country, all right. Not that you seem to have any what I call country round here—one town runs right into another, seems like, and it beats me how anybody ever finds their way around."

"Even natives get lost sometimes. I thought first we'd recheck on this one we haven't seen yet, in Hollywood—it's more or less on the way and he's on the Andrews list. Try where he lives."

"O.K. That the one works at a bank, or the shoe clerk? Oh, I remember, sure. Hell of a job," said Lockhart cheerfully, "keep 'em all straight. Funny to think too, all the scientific things we got nowadays, still comes back to awful simple first principles. Looking at a man. Having a feeling about him. The way you say the lieutenant does pretty often. About the only experience of *that* I ever had, with Gideon—and a damn funny feeling it is. . . . That's a pretty long cast the lieutenant's making, on checking those beach places."

Hackett grunted agreement. "A real wild one—but knowing Luis, I wouldn't be too surprised if it came off. Sometimes he seems to have a kind of sixth sense about these things, way I say. Doesn't come off every time, or every tenth time, but once in a while . . ."

"Pretty smart boy," said Lockhart.

"Sharp enough to cut himself—except just here and there," said Hackett absently. He caught the light at that corner, and as he waited, unfolded the list from his pocket to check the address again. Gates Avenue, that was— And at that moment something rang a faint bell in his mind about that address. He couldn't place it at all, and he didn't have the feeling that it was connected with the case, with anything professional. . . . They were, naturally, checking these men at the places they worked, but this was a home address for one who was off sick; they hadn't been here before. It was a steep side street off Glendale Avenue, and when he saw it, saw the shabby old four-family flat, it said a little something more to him.

Not much. He'd been past here before, that was all. No, stopped here, about where he was now, sliding into the curb. He had the vague impression—somebody Angel knew, was it—? Halfway it came to him, himself and Angel in the front seat, and somebody in the back saying, "I'll just run in and leave this for—" and a name. Somebody they knew knew someone who lived here, or had lived here then. He didn't remember any more about it, and it wasn't very important, was it?

". . . That fellow down at the beach, you said he's found out about who owns most of those places or rents 'em."

"And not a name on any of our lists coresponds. I said it was a wild one—but there's three or four left to go. Hello, Bert," added Hackett, putting his head out the window. "What's the word?"

Dwyer came over and got in the back seat. "Morning, Mr. Lockhart. You and Art still out chasing your wild goose? You know something, on a thing like this I get awful damn envious of the detectives in books. Those fellows that only spend about a week to every case, and twelve hours out of every day they're consortin' with beautiful girls and important millionaires and I don't know what all—something exciting goin' on every minute, whether it's bedding down with a blonde or having a gunfight with a gangster. Not that I'm complaining, you understand, about not running up against a couple of hoods shootin' around corners at me."

Hackett laughed. "How often I've had the same thought."

"This one—I've got half a dozen I'm collecting statistics on—I've got nowhere on yet. Wasted two days already. He doesn't seem to know many people. The only one I talked to who knew anything about him is a woman who lives across the hall—and I don't know that I got half of what she said down right, she's got an English accent you could cut with a cleaver—and she don't know much, except she thinks he's a very nice young man. Now I want to talk to the landlady, and nobody answered the door yesterday afternoon so I came back after supper last night, and her daughter tells me she's gone on a visit to her sister in Laguna Beach. Daughter doesn't know anything about the tenants, she's just there temporary, but Mama's expected back very late last night or this morning. So I start out here this morning, and *now* the daughter tells me Mama's decided to stay another day—she called last night—but she'll be home for sure by six tonight. So I'll have to come back again."

"It all comes of female emancipation," said Hackett, "letting them gad around all over alone. Is he still in?"

"Far as I know. I'm not allowed to look at him close, but this woman across the hall said yesterday she thinks he's home sick all right, she didn't hear him go out for a couple of mornings. Cold or something."

"Yes. Well, no harm looking." Hackett got out of the car. "That wouldn't make him too sick to answer the door. Now, Chief, you stay out of sight, we'll reconnoiter the terrain inside and hide you where you can get a glimpse and hear him, and I'll be the fellow with the wrong address looking for Mr. Smith."

Which program was carried out, but to no avail; the door stayed shut and silence came from beyond it. "Either he's shamming and told his boss a lie to play hookey, or he's died of pneumonia maybe. Hell," said Hackett, "that means another trip back later on. Oh, well, all in the day's work . . ."

"Alison," said Mendoza aloud, and woke with a start. He lay for a moment orienting himself to a new day (a moment ago, she'd been there close, smiling at him). He swore in a whisper and sat up.

The cats were awaiting his waking in their own ways: Bast curled philosophically on his feet, her daughter diligently washing her stomach, El Señor sitting on the bureau by the window making chattering noises at the birds in the yard.

Mendoza got up; he felt like death. On Thursday night he had looked at the little tablets and told himself it was absurd and dangerous to be dependent on such things, what had got into him? He hadn't taken any, and had lain awake until three o'clock, and taken one, and then had to drag himself out at eight still half asleep. So last night he had taken two, and now as usual he felt only half here mentally. He groped out to the kitchen, fed the cats and let them out, started the coffee, and with no strength to shave or dress until afterward, sat there waiting for it.

Just as it was arriving at the pouring stage, there was an excited flurry outside: El Señor and a bird. Mendoza went out and took it away from him; it wasn't much hurt, and it lay there in his hand, warm, shamming dead instinctively in this moment of terror, a small gray sparrow with bright shoe-button eyes. He laid it in the crotch of the big oak tree down the yard, and brought El Señor in to give it a chance to recover its breath. "No! ¿Comprende? Bad cat! Yes, I know it's your nature, hijito, and you are annoyed at my obtuseness, but I can't help it. No birds!" And very likely El Señor, brooding on this piece of injustice, would think up some diabolical revenge while Mendoza was absent.

He poured the coffee, and added a little rye to it, and drank it too hot; shuddered, and began to come back to life a little. He took a second cup, also spiked with rye, back to the bedroom with him; he didn't want any breakfast.

And as he faced the man in the mirror, shaving, the old lady whispered to him over his shoulder, A bad place you come to, boy—men never know how to look after themselves—that is what we are for, Luis, that and a few other things maybe, *hijito.* You laugh at the old ways and ideas, Luis, but live a little longer, *mi nieto,* you come to see they would not be there at all if they were not forged out of the genera-tions' sorrow and joy. Listen to me, *hijito,* use the little sense the good God gave you . . .

Damn, old one, old enough to know my own mind, he said to her. Turned forty this year, and damn the head doctors who said it was all what you took in before you walked alone or learned the alphabet! You grew up, got your eyes open, came to be a man standing alone, an intel-ligent, rational man. God knew he had loved her, he had grieved for her, though she was old and it came quick and easy; but what a mixture there (look at it steady and whole!) of superstition, sentimentality—and the dry shrewdness which was maybe the part of her he had kept. . . . Running back and forth to the priests . . . The old fairy sto-ries to amuse a child, the legends heard from a thousand mothers down the generations—and not until he was grown and away had he recog-nized them for what they were: the garbled tamed stories, once pagan religion, of a people of older and darker blood than the haughty fair-skinned Spaniards with their guns and their pride. . . . Of smiling Tlazoltcotl, mother of the gods: Tonacatecutli, the god of gods; Tona-tiuh of the sun; Xiucoatl and Ometecutli and Mictlantecutli who held the sword of death; and Cihuacoatl the beautiful goddess, Chac who sent the rain or drought, and Kolotl of the dog face, and the great Quetzalcoatl, the feathered-serpent god. *A long time past and just sto-ries for children,* she said, half believing, half fearing. . . . Did any man ever escape entirely from the blood in him?

He laughed at her and at himself; he laid down his efficient modern electric razor and he laughed. Conventions—traditions! The old lady insistently boasting about her pure Castilian ancestry, once she had all the money—the elegant Wilshire Boulevard apartment—and all the di-amonds. He laughed at her very tenderly, remembering.

You god of my race, great Quetzalcoatl, help me now, be with me now, thou supreme being of the thunder and the fire—and our smiling lady Cihuacoatl of the lovers, watch over me, be near!

Well, boy, I loved you, she said to him; perhaps a foolish old woman, and if you think I told you lies—*¡oyé vaya!*—lies I told you—but I loved you. . . . You were yourself, you went your own way, not mine: you turned your arrogant back on the Church and you sought out the strange women and the modern ways and thoughts: but you were yet mine, *hijito*—I loved you and I marked you.

He put the razor away; he turned from the man in the mirror and came into the bedroom, and he thought absently he would have to decide what to do about the diamonds. All the jewels. The old lady, cautious and shrewd, any sum over five dollars wealth to her; he'd tried to educate her a little, but she had never seen the investment on paper, essentially the promise to pay—she liked the tangible value. The portable value. Just in case. So, all those diamonds in the safe-deposit vault. All those rubies. The emerald rings, the emerald necklace and bracelets . . .

(Not the rubies, for Alison. The emeralds, yes, the emeralds fine for Alison of the red hair.)

He knotted his tie nice and neat, and he went out to the kitchen and had another finger of rye without chiding himself at all, and he told himself at the same time it was the rye, turning him maudlin and sentimental, what the hell, it was just to carry him through—

Get the best price he could for the jewelry she'd thought was safe investment: no hurry about it, except of course to pay the goddamned inheritance tax.

(The emeralds for Alison.)

Cihuacoatl, our lady of lovers, be with me now, son of the race which sacrificed to you, need I have, need I have.

He drank half of a third cup of coffee. His stomach felt a little queasy. He let the cats in. He checked his pockets for wallet, silver, keys; he went out to the garage. Another day. The continued hunt. By God they'd get him—if it was a year from next Christmas. Give Mendoza the thinking machine a clear field, half a chance—

Today, for the very first time, there was just a hint of rational autumn in the air. The kind of thing even Californians, unthinkingly gearing their feelings about seasons to their Anglo-Saxon ancestors' ideas, expected of November. The gray sky, the little cool wind—even if the temperature didn't drop below sixty-eight and Chief Lockhart's middle-western-weight suit felt just a little heavy.

They'd almost cleaned them up today—only six or eight left he hadn't seen; and if the truth were told Chief Lockhart was feeling a little guilty and worried. None of these fellows he'd seen was anything like Gideon Wise, and when you came to think about it, it was pretty damn far-fetched to figure one of them would be. Out of a hundred and eighty million people—the distance between Mount Selah and Los Angeles—kind of thing that just didn't happen.

Wasting his own time and the time of these big-city fellows who'd been so nice to him, and spoiling Martha's vacation, all for nothing. He'd been woolgathering; it just wasn't *reasonable*.

Which was mostly the reason he said to Hackett, at five-forty that afternoon, "What say we just go by that place we were this morning, try to get that one off our minds? If we're anywhere near. He might be back now, if he *was* out—or answering the door."

"O.K.," said Hackett dispiritedly. He was feeling somewhat the same way about it himself; he'd be just as pleased to get this cleaned up, know Yes or No for sure.

He bucked the traffic up Glendale Avenue, turned off at Gates. The curbside was crowded at this hour, a lot of old apartments around here without garage space for tenants, and he had to park nearly half a block away. And it was just as he slid into the space there, reached a hand to the parking brake, that (the funny, irrelevant way these mental processes worked) he remembered about it fully, it came to him. It was Alison Weir, the one who knew someone in that place. "I'll just run in and give this to Pat," she'd said, and he'd let her out, driven round the block and picked her up again— "Thanks, Art, as long as we were passing—"

They walked back, and a voice hailed them cautiously from the curb. Dwyer sat there in the open door of his car. It was beginning to get dark, the halfway hour—in the Spanish they called it between dog and wolf—and he was an anonymous shape, a little red moving spark of cigarette-end there.

"Well," said Hackett, veering over to him. "You here yet or again?"

"We're earning our salaries these days," agreed Dwyer. "On a job like this I take against females. Mostly who I've got to talk to, you know, and I'm lucky to find one in five home the first time I ring the bell. Don't they have anything to do at home any more? My wife isn't gadding around all day, six days a week—at least I don't think so—"

"Frozen foods," said Hackett, "and vacuum cleaners with all those attachments to clean everything from curtains to the baby."

"That's a big town for you," said Lockhart. "Place like Mount Selah, there's no place much to go and they can't go very far. You still waiting for this landlady?"

"Not very long. Daughter said six. Five of now. I'll give her till six-thirty and call it a day. I suppose this is your last stop too."

"I hope so," said Hackett. He and Lockhart went in, climbed up to the second floor. Lockhart lurked around the corner of the landing and Hackett rapped on the door; after an interval he rapped again, louder.

There was a furtive slither of sound in there at each knocking, but no one came to answer the summons. He rejoined Lockhart. "But he's in there. I think. Or maybe he keeps a cat or something. Funny."

They started down the stairs. "Maybe he's just not feeling like company," said Lockhart. "Heard something in there, hah?" In the street he stopped and looked back at the door. "Might hang around a while, maybe he'll show."

"Oh, let it go," said Hackett. "Long chance. Maybe he hasn't got a decent bathrobe and was shy about facing anybody in his pajamas." He was getting hungry and he wanted to go home.

"Well, I don't know," said Lockhart slowly, "just occurred to me, you know—"

Dwyer came over. "No go? Wonder if he's playing hooky, off with a blonde somewhere, and his boss paying his sick leave."

"It's Saturday night," said Lockhart. "Let's see, he's been off work sick about three days, didn't you say? Round about the time a cold keeps you down. Might be he's feeling better by now, reckons to go out somewhere—it being Saturday night. Even in a big town, they tell me, Saturday night's the night to go places. I don't know but what I'll hang around a spell, just to see."

"Well—" said Hackett.

"You go 'long, Sergeant, don't bother about me. You'll be wanting to get home to that Angel girl o' yours, and dinner. I kind of got my teeth into this thing now, and it's been a washout so far—feel I been wasting all our time—but we don't want to miss any chances."

"I'll be glad to drive you back to your hotel, Chief," volunteered Dwyer. "Probably hang around another half hour or so like I say."

"Yeah, let's give it that much time," said Lockhart. "No harm. If that's O.K. with you, Sergeant. Martha, she's got friendly with a woman in the hotel—nice woman, widow traveling alone—they were goin' out to some fancy place for tea and do a show, I don't suppose she'll be back much before seven. You go along, I'll just wait around a while."

"Well, all right," said Hackett, "if you feel like it."

"Got nothing much else to do," said Lockhart.

Hackett left him there, sitting in Dwyer's car. He figured it was a waste of time in a way, but of course you never knew. They'd been using a headquarters car on this, so now he had to go all the way back downtown to exchange it for his own, and the traffic at this hour was murder. When he got there, he went up to the office from force of habit, to see if anything new had come in.

Nothing had. Mendoza had gone out for a meal, and Sergeant Lake was just leaving, about to switch over this number to the night man in the communal sergeant's office.

"Feels like fall today, thank God," he said to Hackett. "Hottest summer in forty-seven years, they say. You should hear Caroline at me—you'd think it was a personal insult for me to be sitting here in air conditioning all day."

"Well, it must be aggravating," said Hackett.

"Sure. But she's the one wanted that house in the valley. Good ten degrees hotter out there. But I guess I'd better figure on some kind of air conditioner at that."

"Wait for off-season, you'll get it cheaper."

"I suppose. Well, I'll be off. Scarne called in, I left the message on the book."

"O.K., I'll see you." But as Lake reached to the switchboard, the phone rang there on his desk and he picked it up automatically.

"Headquarters, Homicide. . . . Sorry, he's not in. A message—"

"Who is it?"

"Stebbins."

"I'll talk to him. Go on, Jimmy." Lake went on out and Hackett took the phone. Mr. Stebbins, cautious, was reluctant to impart a message, but Hackett convinced him that he knew all about it; it would be safe with him and he'd pass it on to Lieutenant Mendoza.

"Well," said Mr. Stebbins, "if you say. I've got another 'un for him. Had quite a time on it, too—funny piece o' proputty, mostly gov'ment land round it, and no number or street. You tell the lieutenant—he'll remember the place—it's that little cabin just this side o' Malibu village, all by itself off the highway, little bit in from the beach."

"O.K., I've got that, what's the name?" Hackett jotted down brief notes on the pad, added the name as Mr. Stebbins read it out to him. "I will be damned," he said, looking at it. "I will be— Listen, Mr. Stebbins?—you still there?"

"I'm here."

"Does he rent or own it?"

"Owns it. I found the feller sold it to him, 'bout three years back. Hanley and Sellers handled it—'twas an estate sale, old feller who built it died roundabout then. Awful hard place to sell, account of being way off by itself, you know, and nothing fancy. Old feller's daughter said, get what you can. They finally sold it for forty-two fifty."

"I see. Thanks very much, Mr. Stebbins, we appreciate this—"

"No credit to me. Got to think of the community, ain't we? Feller runnin' around killing women. Hope I've helped. Got a couple more to look out—you tell the lieutenant I'll let him know soon's I do."

"Yes, thanks very much." Hackett hung up and looked at the scribbled name.

Well, a lot of people owned beach property, of course. It didn't say much of anything. Not really. Except that this was a name they had. A name from the Andrews' list, and the name of the fellow who lived in that apartment he'd just left—where, presumably, Dwyer and Lockhart were still hanging around. Or just leaving: it was twenty to seven.

Didn't say much. Except that Luis' private radar had operated again, maybe. Or maybe just coincidence.

But Luis was going to be interested; and it would be interesting to know, when Lockhart did get a look—

The phone rang and he picked it up. "Dwyer," said a rather breathless voice in his ear. "No time to talk—tell the Lieutenant—it's this one, Lockhart's boy—he spotted him ten minutes ago when he came out. We're tailing him, he stopped for gas at the corner, I got to get back—I'll call in when we know."

"Hackett said, "O.K.," to the dead air.

NINETEEN

It was a curiously noncommittal way for it all to come to an end—the long time of plodding, patient hard work, the endless routine, the false casts and the empty coverts drawn. At this end of a day, here in the empty office all alone, knowing for—almost—sure. Just a couple of telephone calls, a name. Simple first principles.

And of course it wasn't ended, not by the hell of a long way. Not yet. They hadn't anything on him at all, of tangible evidence, the kind the D.A. and the grand jury would listen to. A lot of hard work still to come, to get him in the net. But, for almost sure, now they knew. Now he wasn't anonymous any more, they had a name and a face and an address.

He got through to the central board and said, "I've got to keep our line open, Al—call my wife and tell her I'll be late, will you? Thanks." He wondered why Lockhart and Dwyer had taken off after the fellow— no reason at this stage—Lockhart with his teeth in it, born cop sticking to the trail, an automatic thing. He hoped to God Lockhart would have better sense than to confront him, charge— On the other hand, of course, in the moment's startlement he might come out with some damning admission, and Dwyer was there as a witness.

Brisk steps along the corridor outside, and Mendoza came in. Hackett raised a circled thumb and forefinger at him. "The winner and still the champ—both your long gambles have come rolling home, *chico*. We've got him, I think."

"Don't tell me! Who, what, and when?"

"It's Michael Markham—bank teller—moved from the Andrew house eighteen months ago. He's also Gideon Wise. Lockhart spotted him just now—" he gave Mendoza a quick breakdown on that. "I'm waiting for Bert to call back. Don't know why they got on his tail, but—"

Mendoza leaned on Sergeant Lake's desk. He looked rather drawn and excited. "Stop thinking about your wife's cooking. You're at least as smart a small-town chief and one of your own men. It's Saturday night—maybe Romeo has a date."

Hackett looked up at him. "God, yes, sure. Sure. What a fool I—"

"Evidence, evidence! Not a hundred percent sure, no, of course not! But, by God, how I'd like, for once in my career, to frame a charge— on this one, right now! Bring him in on *something,* keep him all nice and cozy in a cell while we look for the legal evidence! One thing, we'll have eyes on him twenty-four hours a day from now on."

"I had a sort of underhanded idea just now about Lockhart—if he confronted him—"

"*Pues sí,* sure—an idea. We'll think about it. You said both gambles?"

"You spotted his beach place. Stebbins called just before Bert." Hackett shoved over his note.

Mendoza smiled slowly, reading the scrawl. "That place. I thought when I saw it, ideal for our boy. I'll have no snide remarks, Arturo, after this, about my crystal ball. Pure intellectual reasoning and logic

. . . Michael Markham. Nice respectable-sounding name. Nice respect-able-looking fellow. His bank will throw seven fits, won't they?"

"Crossing bridges," said Hackett wryly.

"Not very long odds now, is it? Sure, no evidence, nothing certain—but off the record, not for the D.A.'s ear—*or* Mr. Brad Fitzpatrick's!—now we know. And, hell and damnation," said Mendoza, "I don't see—barring a full confession—that we can charge him with Mary Ellen Wood, more likely one of the others—and what will you bet the *Tele-graph* takes him under its wing and plays him up as another innocent being railroaded? *Claro que sí,* crossing bridges, but . . . And I wish Bert would call in, damn it. . . . I'd like to know—if our boy has a date tonight."

"Here he is now," and Hackett picked up the phone as it rang.

". . . at this apartment house," said Dwyer. "He's driving a royal blue two-door Chevvy, last year's model, by the way. There's a booth in the lobby here, that's where I am. We've spotted the apartment, we think, at least the floor, and Lockhart's about ready to have kittens on the landing—seems like he's havin' visions of the guy murdering some woman in there while we wait around—"

"And it could be that's not as far-fetched as it sounds," said Hackett. "Don't swear, Bert, I'm hungry and tired too. Hold on a minute." He relayed the news to Mendoza. "What about it? Send somebody to take over the tail, sure. It might be a date, he may be taking some girl out, or it might just be a party there, half a dozen people. And if he does go on somewhere—Lockhart's got the jitters, but there's no reason—"

"No reason," said Mendoza. "Famous last words, maybe? O.K., yes, sure, relieve Bert, tell him to try to leave word there—leave Lockhart behind—if our pigeon flies on. But—no harm going over to take a little look ourselves, or—you go on home, I'll chase up there myself, you've had a full day—"

"Not on your life. I'd like to have a look at what we've been chasing too, and Angel already knows I'm held up. . . . Bert? I'm sending somebody over to relieve you—if you have to go after him somewhere, leave Lockhart there. Not that you'll likely have any idea where, but you might just overhear some indication—try for it anyway—Give me his plate number. O.K. The boss and I are coming over too, take a look. What's the address?" He wrote it down as Dwyer gave it, and then (his mind catching up with pencil as it were) he recognized it, and for half a second there he had a very funny feeling.

That was the apartment house where Alison Weir lived. Of course, a lot of other people lived there too. There must be thirty-eight or forty apartments in that house.

"I'll get the car, meet you downstairs," and Mendoza was gone. Hackett went into the sergeants' office, picked Landers at random, gave him his orders to meet Dwyer, and went downstairs. The Facel-Vega was idling at the curb; he got in.

"Where are we going?"

Hackett looked straight ahead through the windshield and repeated the address. There was silence beside him for a second and then the Facel-Vega took off with unaccustomed violence into traffic, and when Mendoza swore it might have been just at the traffic.

It was a big apartment house. A lot of people lived there.

A bad hour to go anywhere in a hurry, and Mendoza seemed to be in a little more of a hurry than usual. He drove in silence, except for the automatic curse when he caught a light, and Hackett didn't speak because he was still having that rather funny feeling about the address. About two addresses.

Gates Avenue. She knew someone who lived in that place. Or had. People moved around; that had been five or six months ago.

And Mendoza had them on the Hollywood freeway, at a steady fifty in the fast lane.

There had been only two and a half months between Mary Ellen Wood and Celestine Teitel.

But, thought Hackett, this is as bad as Lockhart—no reason, getting the jitters. It's only about seventy-five percent sure; circumstances— look at Allan Haines— No evidence that *is* evidence at all, and we can't— Besides—

"*Christ!*" said Mendoza, and jammed on the brakes. They skidded and screeched to a stop. A line of cars—traffic piled up a mile ahead, it looked like—

"Accident." Hackett put his head out the window, peering ahead. "Nothing moving. Ambulance up there, couple of squad cars—not a hope, Luis. You know what one little pile-up does on a freeway."

Mendoza cursed steadily and fluently in both English and Spanish for three minutes; and then he sat back and lit a ciagrette. "I'll give myself ulcers. Damn fool. Like kicking the chair you fall over. Can't be helped." But when a motorcycle patrolman came by five minutes later he beckoned him over, produced his I. D. card, and asked, "Can you get me out of this, one direction or another? I'm in a hurry."

"Sorry, sir, it's piled up both ways for three miles. Big produce truck turned over, and two killed. They're cleaning it up as fast as they can, I think there'll be a westbound lane open inside thirty minutes."

"O.K., thanks. Can't be helped." Mendoza leaned back and smoked calmly, waiting. "Fifty-fifty, he's gone to a party there or he'll take a girl on somewhere else. Not such a good chance Dwyer'll be able to get any idea where, and leave word."

"Lockhart seems to be jittery for some reason."

"Mmh. Not surprising. Yes, I'm remembering the gap between Mary Ellen and Celestine too. Don't blame the dealer for a bad hand—way the shuffle came out. Be thankful we know who he is."

"Sure, that's right," said Hackett. He wondered if he ought to tell Mendoza about this other thing—how she'd known someone at that other address—he thought of Dwyer saying, woman across the hall, who thought he was a very nice young man. Maybe someone who had introduced— This was jitters with a vengeance. Irrelevant.

There had been long intervals between the others. A lot of people lived at that address.

It was thirty-five minutes before there was a lane clear. Mendoza got them off the freeway at the first turnoff and went on up into Hollywood by side streets, choosing direction automatically, making rolling stops at stationary signals. When they came to the apartment house, on its tree-bordered narrow street, the curb was packed solid with cars, not a space left; Mendoza double-parked and was out and around the car before Hackett had his door open.

Small lobby, dimly lighted: public phone booth to the left—elevator —stairs. No sign of Lockhart or Dwyer.

"He said they thought they'd spotted the apartment, but didn't say which floor—"

"¡No tiene importancia!" said Mendoza, and started up the stairs fast. Second floor, nothing: all quiet. Third floor, nothing. Hackett was breathless, pounding up the stairs without a break: out of condition; he thought, that extra five pounds, damn it—he must— And there were only four floors, and he heard the woman's excited, alarmed voice up there and thought, No—

Narrow, dim, dark apartment corridor. Dwyer was there, sprawled up against the wall, blood on his shirt, blood on his face and hands— people in an open apartment door there, exclaiming—a man kneeling beside Dwyer, saying something about calling the police—

"Bert—" Hackett shoved the man away, going on his knees too, reaching, ripping the shirt open. A knife slash, not too deep but damn bloody—bruise on his face too—

"Art—" Dwyer tried to pull himself up, urgent, straining— "Lockhart's after him—it was Lockhart—here when he came out with the girl—saw him—he—"

Footsteps up the stairs behind, and it was Landers, gasping from the climb. "What the *hell*," he said, "I got tied up in that freeway jam, I just—Bert, what's—"

And the apartment people exclaiming, asking questions. "Shut *up!*" said Hackett savagely, pressing his handkerchief on the knife slash. "When and what, boy? Quick—"

"Came out with this woman," gasped Dwyer, "God, I been out—he hit me against the wall, my head—don't know how long—just looked at my watch before, it was ten past seven, I'd just come up after calling you—Lockhart—the guy saw him, Lockhart said *Gideon*—and he went wild all of a sudden—the guy I mean, he said—crazy—he said, *Rhoda, you knew about Rhoda,* and then he said, *But this is Rhoda, still alive, still alive, she won't die, I keep having to kill her*—and he hit the woman—and we— He had a knife, Art, he come at me with the knife—and ran—Lockhart grabbed my car keys, he's after him—"

"Oh, my God, must have sent him right off—" Hackett shot an automatic glance at his watch: God, three minutes past eight, that had been fifty-three minutes ago! "Take it easy, Bert, you're not bad, just lost some blood. Luis—"

But Mendoza was turning, listening with head cocked: again, footsteps on the stairs, and here came Lockhart. He looked very unlike the neat, elderly, paunchy grandfather they knew: he was hatless, wildeyed, almost crying.

"Sergeant, thank God—I lost him, damn it to hell, I don't know the damn town, the streets—I was *on* him a couple blocks, but I lost him—"

"All right, take it easy," drawled Mendoza, quite calm himself in the midst of this uproar. "Tell us what happened."

"My fault, shouldn't've spoke to him—didn't know how it'd set him off. My God, my God, right over the edge—this woman with him, they come out and— He kept saying, *But why aren't you dead, Rhoda, I killed you so many times, have to kill you again*— He hit her and I went after him, but he knocked me down—got Dwyer too—I—the woman, he hadn't knocked her right out, she was still on her feet but dazed like, you know, and he dragged her after—good-looking woman, red hair— Damn it to *hell,* if I'd known the damn town! I—"

Hackett stood up. He thought, God, God. Where? How could they—? And Mendoza said, "No. No. *The apartment—which apartment?*"

Dwyer made two tries before he got it out: "It was apartment 406, Lieutenant—I think—"

"No," said Mendoza. He said it very calmly. Hackett looked at him, turning; it seemed that time had suddenly, just this one moment, slowed down, and he had all the leisure in eternity to turn his head and look at Mendoza.

"No," said Mendoza. Quite suddenly every vestige of color drained from his face; he looked gray. He dropped the elegant gray Homburg in his hand. He said, "No." And then he said on a great gasping breath, *"Alison—Alison—Alison—"* and he turned and plunged down the stairs.

Hackett snapped to Landers, "Get an ambulance," and ran after. "Luis, wait—" He didn't catch up to Mendoza until they were in the lobby. He only just flung himself into the car before Mendoza revved the engine.

The manufacturers claimed that a Facel-Vega could be gunned from a stand to a hundred m.p.h. in eighteen seconds. Hackett had never believed it before. He couldn't hear Mendoza over the engine, but he saw his lips moving, *Alison, Alison*—and a kaleidoscope of light and dark flashing past, and then the long screech of brakes, the long skid, and the violent stop, and Mendoza left him—he was out of the car, the car slewed around in the street. He was fling himself at the black-and-white squad car in the opposite lane.

Hackett got out and went after him, pounding across this anonymous dark street. "What the *hell*—here, you get off—" The patrolman was trying to manhandle Mendoza, and Mendoza, sprawled half into the squad car, was reaching desperately for the hand radio. Hackett hauled the patrolman off him.

"All *right,* we're headquarters, let him go—here's identification—" He clawed for his wallet.

"Code nine! Code nine! Request assistance!—Mendoza, headquarters! I'm taking this car out of action—what's your number for God's sake?—car nine-four-three, out of action—I want another car *immediatamente, pronto*—along Sunset, heading west from Edgemont —repeat, heading west from Edgemont—a car to join me—Code three, full siren—repeat, Code nine, Mendoza, Homicide, request—immediate priority—a car to join me—"

"What the *hell!*" said the driver of the squad car. "Sergeant—well, O.K., but I don't—" And Mendoza had him by the shoulders, a big fellow six inches over Mendoza, shaking him ruthless and hard.

"Clear the way for me, clear the way—full siren— Christ damn you, if you lose me I'll cut your heart out—"

Hackett just made the righthand bucket seat as the Facel-Vega took off like a rocket. The siren started behind them. Dark flashing past, and then the tortured screech of brakes, the skid around a turn, and Sunset Boulevard—kaleidoscope of neon lights, the siren howling behind, and the lines of traffic ahead skittering over to the curb, out of the way.

And Mendoza said over the snarl of the engine, quite calm and certain, "The beach place. The beach place. Nice and lonely. *María madre, María madre,* the beach place. Please God. Yes. Alison. *Dios te salve, María, llena eres—*"

Sunset Boulevard, but he'd never seen it like this before, a long joined line of pink-green-scarlet-green-blue light, sliding past. Speed of light. Speed of— *Look out!* Desperate screeching swerve, no crash, safe —time being—

"For God's sake, Luis," he said numbly. "For God's sake."

The faithful siren screaming behind. Two sirens. The second squad car. Thank God—for what? Pick up the pieces afterward. They said a Facel-Vega could do—

"Alison," said Mendoza, "Alison."

Hackett didn't know where they were now, lost track. Sunset, wherever. Lights and no lights and lights again, the sirens behind—Luis, for God's sake—

He saw there ahead (time slowed down again, they seemed to approach it with infinite leisure) a lighted side street and a yellow-and-black taxi nosing out into the intersection. Nosing out too far, not hearing the sirens in time. Too far—going to hit it, going to—

Hackett shut his eyes and thought, *Angel darling.* He felt a slight blow in his right side, heard a rending crash. They were still traveling, and apparently in one piece. He opened his eyes. There was peculiar noise: it was, he saw (taking it in slowly) the fender of the taxi, part of the bumper too, suspended on the right fender of the Facel-Vega, crashing and banging there, a great extraneous length of metal, incongruous— His hand explored, found a deep dent in the door at his side where the swerve hadn't quite saved them a collision, at this speed. This car was built like a tank and tonight that was a damned good thing.

The wind force dislodged the fender, it fell off awkward and sudden, another crash. Spare a thought for the squad-car drivers behind, faithful, sirens screaming like lost souls— Luis, Luis, easy, don't kill me just when I've got Angel, my darling— The long sloping lazy curves, around what had been the big polo field, now was a big tract of jerrybuilt new houses—and no car could take these curves at such a speed—

"Santa María, madre de Dios," said Mendoza very distinctly, "I pray you, I pray you."

Hackett looked at the speedometer and looked away, trying to forget the three figures it registered. The siren was a little way behind now, the first siren. The driver of that squad car, no wonder, didn't want to commit suicide.

"I am a very great fool," said Mendoza. "I am the greatest fool in the world." If Hackett had had breath he'd have agreed.

Luis, for God's sake— But he had not said it aloud, he hadn't breath or strength to say it aloud.

The siren, both the sirens, had caught up a little. A thought, a prayer, for the blindly obedient squad-car drivers. And damn good drivers. Yes.

And another curve. And Mendoza uttered a sound of purely animal rage; the tortured brakes screamed—they slewed around in a half circle: the speedometer needle arched away left toward zero. The Facel-Vega skidded around halfway, brakes shrieking, caromed off the rear of the T-bird last in the line of traffic, hitting it side on, and stopped facing the curb. The leading squad car, braking frantically, sideslipped to a tire-screeching stop against the curb a foot away. The second one, at five-m.p.h. less speed, managed to skid to a violent stop facing the opposite direction.

That place it was, end of Chautauqua, where the road narrowed down to the Malibu road— God, didn't seem like ten minutes from Hollywood, thirty miles, thirty miles—and the three-way signal at the bottom of the hill— The traffic, thick there, had heard the sirens, but it hadn't anywhere to go, out of the way. It huddled there helpless, trapped in the narrow roads and the one wide road, nowhere to go— here, crowded close in to the curb, bumper to bumper both lanes—stationary, frightened, impotent.

The sirens behind moaning on a low note now. God—

Mendoza swung the wheel, sobbing in fury and desperation. Hackett crouched away instinctively—there was the long rending screech of metal on metal, as the Facel-Vega was jammed through where no car could go, scraping between the cars there to the left, climbing the curb, smashing past the light pole, knocking it half over drunkenly—ramming down the sidewalk past the shabby store-fronts— And a crash and another crash and they were somehow through, past, swerving around right in a great sweeping turn— The sirens, no, only one behind —other driver not so crazy, take that incredible chance after them— and straightened to the new road, the coast road. New sound, not just the wind of their passing—

He looked out and saw. The collision with the T-bird, or the desperate scraping past that solid post there—the whole side of the car was stove in, and now that right fender was jammed solid against the tire, screeching loud—wear it through in five miles, and a blowout at this pace—

Angel, my darling.

But the siren clearing the way again now, and now the brakes screaming again, the further long skidding turn, don't look at the speedometer—

The Malibu road curving inland now, along where that cabin was, if— *And over there to the left, in lonely dark, the tail lights of a car.* God, could it be—were they in time? He'd had fifty minutes' start—but no sirens clearing the way.

A violent swerve left, to a rougher road. No tail lights now.

"Mary, Mother of God," whispered Mendoza, "be kind—"

Stationary. Stopped.

Hackett sat for ten seconds, realizing it. The simple fact. Stationary, and alive. He thought he was still alive.

Siren moaning to the lowest note behind: more brakes squealing. He got out of the car—painfully, entangling himself in the gearshift. He blundered after a slim, dark figure that must be Mendoza, far up ahead, silhouetted just a minute against sky—

Night, dark, sea smell. *The beach place.* Sure, of course. He ran through hampering sand; he heard Mendoza running ahead, the patrolmen, heavy, behind. Heard his own hard breath. He raised a groping hand, feeling for his gun.

Wooden steps: he nearly fell, caught himself. And Mendoza was there, snarling at him, seizing his hand—"*¡No fuego, imbécil!*" God, God, of course couldn't use the gun: who was on the other side of the door, the window? Small place—

A door. He ran at it heavily, hard as he could, one shoulder forward. Mendoza was gone. Car-door slam: the second squad car. A man, two men, joining him. He heard loud running on wooden flooring, round the other side of the house—he heard Mendoza shouting, a distance away, somewhere at the back—"Michael Markham! Gideon Wise! We're coming in—surrender yourself!—we're coming—"

He shoved and struggled at the door—too solid, too thick—panting, listening to his labored breath and that of the men beside him. He heard glass smash in, back there. Heard an animal howl inside the house, beyond this door. And a little gleam beside him as one of the men— Hackett caught the wrist quickly. "Don't fire! God knows who—" Sounds inside there now. God, God. He heard himself sob furiously at the door. Luis—He jerked out his gun again, jammed it below the doorknob at an acute downward angle, the sharpest he could manage, and shot out the lock.

He fell through the door, from dark to dark, the other two men behind him.

Noises, animal noises of men fighting, somewhere near. "Luis—" Damn fool Mendoza, never would carry a gun— He fell against a wall, feeling frantically for a light switch, clutching the gun ready for when he could see—

No reckoning time. Five seconds, five minutes since Mendoza had left him, got in? He felt frantically along the wall—noises quite near now, men struggling there— And there was the little lever under his hand, and suddenly there was light.

And God said, Let there be light.

TWENTY

Hackett stood there in the sudden blazing light, leaning on the wall, because there wasn't anything for him to do. The three patrolmen, one over there in another doorway, two beside him, just stood too. Looking.

But after a minute Hackett moved. It was a reflex action, and curiously enough at least some of what made him move was the thought of what Brad Fitzpatrick might say in the *Telegraph*.

"Luis, stop it—get off him. You can't bring him in like that—" No telling how long Markham-Wise had been out: Mendoza didn't care, hadn't noticed. He had him down on the floor, there was blood all over him—the knife dropped a little way off, Mendoza hadn't needed a knife, but blood on it— "Luis!" said Hackett, and he reached down and hauled Mendoza up, off the long limp body under him. The other men moving now, going through the house. "He's out, let him be, you don't want to kill him—" And he thought what a foolish thing that was to say.

Mendoza swung on him, blind, berserk, struggling away; and then one of the men called, "Sergeant—there's a woman here, I just—" and Mendoza left him. Just as blindly he stumbled past Hackett into the little bare-furnished bedroom there, and knocked the uniformed man aside.

Hackett looked down at their Romeo. His last mistake had been king-size all right: interfering with something that belonged to Luis Mendoza. That arm looked broken, way it—and his face would never look the same again, and there was a surprising amount of blood, when no weapon had—

He said to the other man in the room, "Keep an eye on him," which was foolish too, because that one wasn't going to wake up in a hurry or be going anywhere when he did; and he went into the bedroom. He said to the man there, "Go and put in a call for an ambulance."

"Alison, Alison, *mi novia, mi hermosita, amada, querida— Madre María, te suplico*—Alison— *Dios te salve, María, llena ores de gracia, el Señor es contigo—es con—* God, I can't remember the words— Mary—salute you—of grace, of—help me remember—*Santa María, madre de Dios, ruega, Señora, por nosotros ahora y en la*—no, no, not hour of death—"

Hackett pulled him upright away from her there—she lay crumpled, sprawled half on bed, half on floor, bruise visible on one cheek, unconscious, but no blood, thank God no blood. But blood on him—a long deep gash down one cheek, maybe getting in the window—and on his shirt, and a sleeve ripped half out of his coat—blood on that arm. "There's an ambulance on the way. Stand still, damn it, let me— Don't move her, Luis, if it's a head injury she—"

"*Padre nuestro*, God, help me remember the right words, I can't— *que estás en el cielo, santifacado—santifacado—venga a nos tu reino*— will be done, Thy will—I can't—Alison my darling, *querida, mi vida*—"

Hackett heard the ambulance coming. Time had ceased to mean anything tonight. He went out to meet it. But he wouldn't let the interns take Markham-Wise; dead or unconscious or whatever, Markham-Wise they'd hang onto close. He helped one of the men load him into the back of a squad car. "Take him downtown, fast. For the moment, booked for common assault—tell them I'll call in, give them chapter and verse. No, I know they won't keep him, he'll end up in the hospital, but it won't be the Santa Monica emergency, it'll be the guarded wing at the General, and a uniformed sergeant right beside him when he wakes up. Get going, report all this to the headquarters desk, and don't let him out of your sight until he's between two Homicide officers."

The interns were having trouble with Mendoza. Hackett went in and held him off. He searched Mendoza's pockets for the keys, dragged him out to the car. God only knew if it had another ten miles to go before that tire went, but the hell with it. He manhandled the strange shift, got the car turned and took off after the ambulance.

*"Te suplico, María madre—*pray you, I pray you—*y perdónanos nuestras deudas, así como nosotros—*can't remember, forgive me—Alison—"

He didn't know the town, the streets: he followed the ambulance siren blindly. The engine was pulling faithful—built like a tank—but the teeth-on-edge screech of the fender jammed on the tire was bad . . .

Back toward Santa Monica, chasing the siren this time. Up the hill into town, down unknown dark streets and bright streets, and then the ambulance suddenly disappeared down a lighted ramp off to the side. He went straight on, braked in front of the building. Mendoza was gone before he got the hand brake on. Hackett got out and went after him, tiredly. There were steps, a big plate-glass door. A dimly-lighted lobby narrowing to a long darkish corridor, room doors either side. A white-uniformed woman clerk behind a long counter to the left, and benches, a public phone, and a man—intern or a house man on night duty—white-smocked, fending off Mendoza, looking surprised and indignant.

"Por favor—me diga, por favor—por el amor de Dios—"

"What's all this? Here, you're hurt, man—"

"Doctor," said Hackett, "—sit *down,* Luis, take it easy!—police business, Doctor—the accident case just brought in, please go and find out—tell us how she is. For God's sake, Luis, sit down and be quiet—"

"Oh," said the doctor. He gave them a curious hard stare, but he recognized authority when he heard it; with no wasted word he turned and hurried off.

Mendoza walked a little way up the corridor after him and sat down on the leather-padded bench along the wall there. Hackett sat down beside him.

He wondered if—the law had some funny quirks, of course—those reported words (two witnesses) constituted a legal confession. Might be a smart lawyer could claim duress, something like that. He wondered if maybe the fellow was permanently right over the edge, in which case it was an academic question; or if maybe they might get a more complete confession. Always better to tie up a thing neatly, if possible.

He thought somebody ought to look at Mendoza, see how bad those cuts were, didn't think very bad, but— He didn't have the energy himself. He just sat there waiting. Mendoza had fallen absolutely silent; he bent his head between his torn, bleeding hands and sat there motionless.

After a while the doctor came back down the corridor, and stood looking at them, curious, perplexed, interested. Hackett got up. "Well, the young lady isn't much hurt," said the doctor. "I think a slight concussion—bruises, but all superficial—mild state of shock. Otherwise nothing wrong. We'll keep her overnight, but there's no reason—"

"You're telling me lies," whispered Mendoza. "Lies—all my own fault, damned stupid—you're telling me—"

"I'm telling you she'll be quite all right," said the doctor irritably. "What's all this about? Police— Here, you, you can't—" Mendoza had seen behind him, down there, the orderlies with a stretcher going into the last room on the other side of the hall, and he broke past the doctor's outflung arm and ran toward the closing door. The doctor ran after him. "The patient's had sedation, she can't— Damn it, come back here—"

Hackett sat down on the bench again. He thought a little numbly, Thank God. He wanted a cigarette, but when he got one out he found his hands were shaking too much to light the damned thing, so he just sat there holding it. Ought to call in, report. Ought to try to contact Lockhart, let him know it was all O.K. Find out how bad Bert was.

In a minute he'd go and do that. . . . And he thought, God, if Lockhart hadn't hung on just that extra half hour—! What they owed Lockhart, the born cop. . . .

The door opened down there and the doctor came out holding Mendoza by the arm. Hackett went a few steps to meet them.

"Now for the love of heaven, Luis, light somewhere and let the doctor take a look at you. You—"

Mendoza put a hand to his temple, and Hackett saw that the big gold seal-ring was missing from his finger; he knew where it would be, on another, slenderer finger. "I'm O.K., Art," and with that he collapsed on Hackett in a dead faint. The doctor took his shoulders and Hackett took his knees and they laid him out on the bench. While the doctor propped his legs up Hackett untied Mendoza's tie, opened coat and shirt. A couple of ugly knife cuts along the ribs, nothing bad, a little blood lost.

"Luis, boy—"

"What *is* all this?" asked the doctor, a hand on Mendoza's wrist.

Hackett sat down on the edge of the bench alongside Mendoza's knees. "That rapist-killer you've been reading about. We just got him. Just now."

"Be damned. You don't tell me. That's his latest—?" He jerked his head down the hall. "She was damned lucky. You *don't* tell me. . . . Not, of course, this impetuous Latin here? Shouldn't think he'd have to go in for rape—must say it surprised *me,* I've never seen anybody come back even that far after a shot of codeine—just because somebody's babbling Spanish at her a mile a minute. Live and learn."

"Our Romeo's in Central Jail. Correction, hospital wing of same—or the General. This is Lieutenant Mendoza of Homicide."

"His pulse is damn slow," said the doctor. "You *don't* tell me. The one I've been reading about too—ruthless hunter of men—little reputation as a Sherlock?" He looked down at Mendoza.

"He's not just exactly himself, tonight," said Hackett. "He's been learning a little something too. They do say, never too old to learn."

Mendoza opened his eyes and apologized for being a damned fool. "Move over, *chico,*" said Hackett. "My heart's still going pitty-pat from that wild ride you gave us. You've smashed up that twenty-thousand-buck wagon of yours pretty thorough."

"The hell with the car," said Mendoza. "Have you called in to report?"

"Ah, Richard's himself again. No, I haven't. I've been, if you must know, sitting here decidin' what to spend a lieutenant's pay on. Because it looked like I'd get your desk after they'd committed you to Camarillo. The rest of the time I was just reflecting what a shame it is, brilliant mind decayed so sudden. What with," said Hackett, "you trying to remember your superstitious Romish prayers and calling on the saints, like—"

"That's a lie," said Mendoza instantly. "'S a damned lie. I'm a rational man—agnostic—" He tried to sit up, and the doctor pushed him down again.

"Better take it easy a while."

Hackett stood up. "Maybe so," he said almost gently, "maybe so, boy. Until all the chips are down on the board. . . . I'll go call in. You better let the doctor patch you up."

He sat at Mendoza's desk that next morning, and Sergeant Lake dodged in through a crack in the doorway and said he couldn't ho.d them out there much longer. "They want a detailed story, and the Chief—"

"Well," said Hackett, and sighed. "Sure. And we've got something to boast about now, haven't we? Give it another five minutes. I'll see. . . ." The latest report from the jail hospital was, from their point of view, encouraging. Markham-Wise was over the edge all right, but talking: talking a lot, about all the women. Disconnected, but that you had to expect, and it could be put together, interested listeners said, pretty consecutively. Very nice.

But the reporters probably didn't want to listen to harness-horse Hackett, the faithful sergeant. No.

He called the other hospital. The patient had been discharged. He rang Alison's apartment and got no answer. He dialed Mendoza's number, and after four rings, just as he was about to hang up, Mendoza answered him.

"Reporters . . . the Chief. . . . Yes, sure. All right," he said vaguely. "All right, Art." And Hackett heard her say something in the background, and Mendoza laughed, and then in a minute came back on the line. "I'll be in, " he said. "Sometime. I'll be in, Arturo—" The receiver was fumbled back on its hook and the line went dead.

Hackett sat holding the phone a while, feeling a little peculiar inside for a big tough sergeant of cops. He'd known Luis Mendoza a long time, but he didn't ever remember hearing him sound quite like that.

At peace. With himself, and with life.

Anchored in safe harbor after a stormy voyage.

Absurdly, he found his eyes were a little wet. And for once he didn't care that a call went through the central board; he dialed again, and Angel answered on the first ring.

"Nothing particular," he said. "Darling. I just wanted all of a sudden to talk to you. . . . Yes. . . . She's—O.K., she's with him. . . . Yes, darling. . . . I do too."

He put down the phone and buzzed Sergeant Lake. Stood up and shoved the desk chair in nice and tidy; the desk was nice and neat the way Luis liked it. "O.K., Jimmy," he said. "Shove 'em in. They'll have to put up with me—I'll give them the story now."

But not quite the whole story.